Precious Gifts

Debbie
Enjoy the dream!
All the best!
Veronica Stone
2004

Precious Gifts

Veronica Stone

PRECIOUS GIFTS is an original publication.
This work has never before appeared in book form. This work is a novel.
Any similarity to actual persons or events is purely coincidental.

Front cover by Jason Mathews

Published by arrangement with author

Printed in the U.S.

ISBN # 0-9745316-1-8

First printing

10 9 8 7 6 5 4 3 2 1 06 05 04 03

For my Father who never got to
see his precious gifts grow.

Chapter 1

BRAND HAYWORTH, Earl of Brentwood, swallowed the last sip of his drink and slowly turned to look at the doctor. "All right. How bad is it, George?"

The doctor ran a hand through his hair. He hated giving bad news. "If you continue as you are, you won't reach sixty," he said flatly.

Brand scowled. He wanted to see his grandchildren. Swallowing, the doctor leaned forward.

"I will repeat what I told you last week. You aren't a young man. You spend far too much time in a stressful business that your son is more than capable of running. Your heart can't take it. I suggest you turn your estates over to your sons and take a holiday."

Brand smiled. "George, if only it were that simple."

"But it is. You could start by giving Christopher more control of the business transactions. Let Stephan and Jessica run the shipping side. I do believe Stephan does most of it now. Jonathan has developed a superb horse line. I'm sure your consultation isn't even necessary."

Brand nodded. His older sons were exceptional business men. They needed very little from him as far as business advice.

George shifted slightly, "If you marry the girls off and ask Christopher to handle Nathan, your stress will lighten considerably." Leaning forward, he gave Brand an intense look. "Brand, if you don't do something, you won't be around to see grandchildren."

Brand broke into laughter. "I may never see any grandchildren anyway. None of my children want to settle down long enough to start a family," he said, running a hand through his hair. "I'll think about this. My brother has been after me for years to go with him to America. I believe he might need your services when I inform him I'm actually thinking about taking that trip."

George grinned. "You won't regret your decision. You'll see how much better you feel once you transfer the power. As far as Colan is concerned, your brother has been beyond my help for years."

Brand rubbed his hand over his face. "I still worry about my children. I need to make sure they are taken care of after I'm gone. Elizabeth would be proud of the boys. Each has made a place for himself, except Nathan of course, but the boy is still young. It's the girls that have me worried. She would have properly seen to them. I'm just too soft where they're concerned. Jessica and Allison aren't as affected by my indulgence as is Melissa. I've created a monster in that one."

"Now see. That's just what I'm talking about, Brand. You can't get yourself all worried over such things. Your girls are beautiful and should have been married off long ago." Holding up his hand, he cut Brand off. "I think it is best if you leave the matter to Christopher. The men those beauties will attract will definitely put you in the grave. Especially after it becomes known that you're marrying them off. All that aside, and a word from your physician, you must relax. Try to keep things calm around you. The pains you're feeling now are a warning that your heart isn't going to put up to the strain."

Brand frowned and looked out the window. He was the head of the Hayworth Estates and had been for nearly thirty-five years. His father died when he was eighteen, leaving him a financial ruin that had taken years to restore. And restore he did. Now his doctor was telling him to give it all away. Scowling, he sighed. I guess if things didn't work out after a year, he could always return and take it all back.

"I'll do it," Brand said leaning forward with both hands on the desk. "I don't know what I'll do with all my time, but I'll do it," he stood to move near the window.

George grinned. "Knowing Colan, I'm sure he'll have plenty for you to do. But remember, even in America you have to rest." Brand nodded as George got up. "It's really the best course of action, Brand. It's really the only way." He finished picking up his bag and patting Brand on the shoulder. "Send a runner if you need anything."

Brand frowned as he returned his gaze to the lawn outside the window. Jonathan was out near the stables grooming a horse. The sight made Brand smile. The boy had several servants on hand, but Jonathan insisted on rubbing the horses down himself. He barely trusted Brand to help him with his horse line. Just like a Hayworth, Brand thought proudly. Turning, he went to the door and yanked it open.

"Hobkins, get in here," he bellowed moving back to his seat behind the desk. The desk was piled high with invoices, transactions, and other matters requiring his attention. It would take him almost a year just to get things changed over. A small sharp pain shot up his neck and Brand sucked in his breath at its intensity. Leaning back, it took several deep breaths before the pain began to subside. Frowning, he tipped his head back and stared at the ceiling. He might not make it a year. He must get out sooner rather than later. Grandchildren? Would he ever get to see any?

"You called, my lord?" Hobkins asked coming through the door and closing it behind him. Brand smiled. Hobkins, at seventy-five, had manners that were meticulous and precise. He was a short man, about five-foot eight, with hair as white as snow. If Brand didn't know better, he would think he was lord of the realm based on the way he dressed and held himself.

"Yes, Hobkins. I need you to round up all my children for a meeting with me. Here. Tonight."

"My lord, Lady Jessica just docked. I do believe she will be unable to attend," he answered. Brand scowled. Hobkins could tell you at any given moment what any one of his seven children were doing. It was uncanny.

"Hobkins, tonight. You tell my wayward daughter anything you have to, but make sure she's here. I'll expect everyone around eight o'clock and dinner will follow. That should get Stephan here without complaint. Inform Miriam we'll need to prepare a great deal of food if were going to feed those boys."

"Yes, my lord."

"Also, I need Andrew here by five. We have things to discuss." Rubbing his hand across his face, he slowly leaned forward on the desk. "I think you should send a note to my brother, too. I need to see him sometime today, or at the latest, tomorrow morning. Perhaps he'll come for the dinner tonight."

"Yes, my lord. Is there anything special you wish for dinner?"

"Tell Miriam she can decide. Don't leave it up to Allison or Melissa. We'll end up with something exotic just to goad the boys."

"Very good, my lord." Hobkins said backing out of the room.

Brand shook his head as he began to shuffle through the stack of papers closest to him. Three invitations. He sighed. People continued to send him invitations, though he had not attended any social functions for more than ten years. It seemed silly to respond, when everyone knew he would not make an appearance. Leaning back in his chair he casually tapped the envelope on the edge of the desk, as an idea began to form in his head.

HOBKINS MOVED ALONG THE HALL, stopping long enough to retrieve his coat and gloves. It would take him all afternoon to find his lordship's unruly brood of children. He also had to convince them to appear promptly at eight. Pursing his lips he combed his white hair back before placing a hat on his head. No doubt he would probably get killed trying to locate the youngest lad. Nathan kept company with some of London's most disreputable lads. Shaking his head he gave his coat a final pat before moving off toward the kitchen looking for the plump Mrs. Lang.

The Brentwood housekeeper was an efficient director. She ran the house by humiliating its people and making them feel guilty. Her subjects, knowing they didn't live up to her standards, would double their efforts to please the woman. Hobkins pursed his lips. He recalled several instances when he changed his own behavior to please Mrs. Lang.

He found the short, gray-haired woman talking intently with the maid responsible for cleaning the fireplaces. Mrs. Lang's tone of voice told him clearly she was lecturing, and he surmised that the maid was not cleaning them up to snuff.

Mrs. Lang looked briefly at him then nodded to Molly who reddened further before slipping off to disappear out the side door.

"Poor mite. She just hasn't got the task set in her head," she said as she moved to the stove to pour Hobkins a cup of tea. "I do believe she'll come around though. She's a very hard worker."

Setting the cup on the table, she nodded for him to be seated before she moved to get her own cup. Hobkins fidgeted a moment before taking his assigned seat. Mrs. Lang insisted on tea no matter who you were. Hobkins drank three swallows before she sat down. He cleared his throat. "Well, now," she said moving to her own chair, "What can I help you with, Stanley?"

Hobkins turned scarlet. Mrs. Lang insisted on calling him by his Christian name, though he didn't dare use hers. "I have just come from his lordship and have been sent to inform you that his children are expected promptly at eight to dine." Giving her a minute for the shock and panic to sweep her, Hobkins quickly lifted his cup and drained it completely before adding, "All seven of them."

"At eight, you say?"

"Yes. Eight it is. His lordship's brother will also be present." Rising to his feet, Hobkins pulled on his gloves. "I will leave you then to tend to your chores."

He quickly left the kitchen hoping it didn't look like he was running. He knew if he didn't hurry, Mrs. Lang would give him a list of things to which he was to attend besides rounding up his lordship's brood. Reaching the fresh air, he took several breaths before settling on Master Jonathan as his first task. The lad would be one of the easiest to convince to attend his father's meeting. Perhaps the lad would help locate a few of the others as well. Straightening his coat, he headed to the stables to locate a horse.

Chapter 2

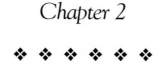

"WHAT DO YOU MEAN by eight tonight or else? Whom did what and when, Hobkins?" Jonathan asked rubbing the black Arabian's forelegs.

"I have orders from your father you are to be in his study by eight. He didn't specify why, he just told me to get you there."

"And if I refuse?" he asked lifting a brow.

"I will most likely have to drag you in there myself," Hobkins said stretching to his full height of five foor eight inches.

Jonathan laughed. Being six-two, they both knew Hobkins would never be able to lift his leg, let alone drag him clear to Brentwood. "All right Hobkins," he said, resting his arm on the blacks back while he gave Hobkins a measuring look, "I'll go if you give me a little hint as to what this is all about."

Hobkins stiffened slightly as he compressed his lips into a thin line. Jonathan laughed, "All right, all right, I'll be there. I wouldn't want to send you into a stupor by being difficult. I'll leave that up to Nathan or Jessica."

"Very good, Sir. I'm sure they won't let you down."

Jonathan paused his rubbing to look at Hobkins. The man looked pained. "You are getting everyone there, aren't you Hobkins? He doesn't want just me, does he?"

"No, my lord. All seven of you will be there promptly at eight."

Jonathan lost his humor. "There isn't anything wrong, is there, Hobkins? Nobody's sick or anything, are they?"

Hobkins shrugged. "You'll have to wait till eight, Master Jonathan," he said turning to walk away. Jonathan's frown deepened at Hobkins retreating back. A meeting, huh? A meeting that required the entire family could only mean one thing. Jessica, Melissa or Allison had finally caught a groom he thought smiling.

"Hobkins, is father marrying off one of the girls?" he shouted. So his father had finally done it. He had found one of his reckless sisters a groom. His smile broadened as he envisioned Jessica throwing a fit when she was told she had to marry. Or funnier yet, Melissa fainting once she learned she was being given away to a lucky groom. Laughing to himself, he began to whistle looking forward to going home for once. More often than not he was called home to stand as a buffer between a pair of his siblings while they tried to settle their differences. Why it fell to him to be the buffer, he didn't know? But ever since they were children, his brothers and sisters had come to him when one of the others was irritating them. He briefly wondered if this was another such meeting. He grinned. The image of Jessica's outrage at being given away in marriage made him laugh. He shook his head, a silly smile lifting his lips as he slowly resumed his work on the black's coat. Jessica a bride! The thought set him off laughing.

"ALL RIGHT HOBKINS, what's happened now? Is Nathan at it again?" Stephan asked as he loaded the last box onto the back of the wagon headed for the ship at the end of the docks. "Father wouldn't want all of us there without a pretty damn good reason. Now out with it." He said as he wiped the sweat from his brow.

"Sorry, My lord, but I don't know the reason."

Stephan laughed at the comical expression on Hobkins face, "You can't be serious! You always know what's going on. Most of the time even before the person in trouble does." Seeing Hobkins wasn't saying a word, Stephan decided to guess. "Maybe Jonathan sold a valuable horse for practically nothing? Or Christopher gave away some land he wasn't supposed to?" Hobkin's blank stare made him straighten from the crate he'd just loaded, "I'm not in trouble, am I?"

Hobkins shrugged. "You'll have to ask your father when you arrive tonight at eight Master Stephan. I really don't know." Hobkins turned to head back toward his horse.

"I better not be the one in trouble. Everyone else better be there, Hobkins." When there was no response from Hobkins, Stephan added, "I'll visit Father for a month if your lying to me Hobkins."

The stiffening of the already stiff back was the only indication Stephan had that Hobkins had heard him. Frowning, Stephan cursed. A meeting! Bloody hell! That's all he needed was to have his father breathing down his neck. He shook his head as he lifted the crate. What mess had he been in that would warrant a trip to Father's study? He cursed again as he pushed one of his crew off the dock. His temper was rising. Nothing came to mind. What was he walking into now?

"SORRY, HOBKINS, got another shipment going to Southbend in the morning. I need to load that wine in the hold or it will never get there by noon," Jessica said from behind the desk. The sound of the crew moving above kept Hobkins glancing at the ceiling as he searched his brain for a logical argument that would convince this unruly young lady. A knock at the door made Hobkins sag in relief. He needed a good reason and nothing seemed to be coming to mind.

"Enter," she bellowed, as a tall scruffy looking man opened the door. He gave Hobkins a brief once over before directing his attention to Jessica. Arty was her first mate as well as a personal friend. "What is it Arty?"

"Didn't mean to interrupt Captain? The men want to go ashore and . . . "

"Not bloody likely. That wine needs to be in the hold and accounted for," she said sternly, "Besides, I need an able crew tomorrow."

"Aye, Captain. They were sort of figuring that a smaller crew would be needed since it was a day trip and all."

"Oh, they were, were they?" she snapped striding out of the cabin. "Stay put Hobkins. I'll be right back."

Hobkins gapped at the door for several seconds before straightening his jacket. His eyes traveled around the cabin as he admired the trinkets Lady Jessica had acquired in ports all over the area: Hand crafted wooden things, porcelain figures, and what looked to be dishes made of pewter. Hearing her voice drift down from above Hobkins felt his nerves tense. Soon he found himself straining to hear what was being said. He jumped as Jessica marched back into the room her face alive with excitement. Her appearance made him swallow. She was looking every inch a pirate.

"Sorry Hobkins. The crew's a little tired after that last trip. A small Northerner caught us unaware. We're lucky we survived. Still, no one tells me when he or she needs a leave. They'll be getting that tomorrow. I don't have another trip till the end of next week. Tell Father I'll see him sometime then," she finished, dismissing him with the silence that followed. Hobkins swallowed again knowing he was just seconds away from a tantrum from this lovely lady.

"I dislike being the one to tell you this, Miss," Hobkins said moving toward the door, "But you must come. Your father received the physician again today." Jessica's head snapped up at the mention of the physician.

"Is it bad?"

"I'm not sure. Your father doesn't tell me. I only do as I'm told. The meeting is at eight," he finished as he pulled the door closed behind him. He made a mad dash off the ship.

HOBKINS, almost ready to call in the elder sons to help locate the youngest one, finally tracked him down in the eighth pub he entered. Relief flooded him when he saw the lad drinking and playing cards. Hobkins briefly straightened his coat before moving to stand next to Nathan's table. The four young men seated around the table turned, in unison, to stare at Hobkins. Two were completely foxed.

"Hobkins, old man, what can I do for you? Ale?" said young Nathan, as he pushed Hobkins into a chair while Percy Anderson slapped a mug of ale in his hand.

Hobkins coughed and set the mug on the table. Glancing quickly at the other gents, he cleared his throat, "Your father requires your presence at eight in his study. Dinner will follow." He stated as he rose to leave.

Nathan laughed. "I think you wasted your time, Hobkins. These fine gents and I have things to attend to. Don't we lads?" The other three nodded and grinned. "Just tell Father I can't make it. I have prior engagements."

Hobkins frowned and resumed his seat, "Everyone is required to be there."

Nathan paused, as he lowered his drink to the table, "Is this another 'gang up on Nathan' bout? Did Christopher start again?"

"My lord, I really couldn't say. Your father gave me orders that everyone was to be in attendance. If I got any resistance, I was to do what was needed." He glanced at the other gents then back to Nathan.

"Which is?"

Hobkins shrugged, "I would rather not have to say. Just join your family at eight in your father's study," he said rising again. Nathan frowned and grabbed his arm.

"Wait a minute, old man. I need more information than that before I come to the sharks."

"Jessica, Melissa, and Allison will be there," he said, lifting his chin a notch.

"Will they now?" Nathan stated, both brows arching. Lifting his mug, he casually leaned back in his chair to study Hobkins. "Could Father have found one of the lucky girls a groom?"

Hobkins shrugged and put on what he hoped was a knowing look. Nathan hooted. "I'll be there, Hobkins. I wouldn't miss that for the world. I do hope it's Jessica," he said to the table at large. Hobkins made his exit then, leaving the four to joke and laugh at the girl's expense. Sending a prayer heavenward for the lad's quick intuition, he headed to finish up with the final three. All still lived at Brentwood, it was just a matter of getting them curious enough to be home at eight for dinner as requested.

"Allison, must you keep this infernal cat with you all the time? He isn't at all friendly. How do you expect anyone to sit out here with you?" Melissa huffed as she flounced down on a bench next to where Allison worked pulling weeds from around a rose bush.

"Nero likes the outdoors as much as I do and since I can't manage well without his sight to guide me, he goes with me. You could always stay out of the garden," she stated pulling a clump of weeds and tossing them to her left.

"Father has six gardeners to keep these gardens groomed. Why do you insist on doing it yourself? You're filthy, and that gown is ruined."

Allison smiled. Melissa was a spoiled brat and material things meant everything to her, as did social standing. She hated to be talked about, or worse yet, miss out on gossip about another lady of the ton.

"Since *I* can't see the ruined gown, I don't think it should bother *you*."

"Well, of all the stupid things I've ever heard you say. Just because you are blind doesn't mean you have to walk around looking like some urchin. I'd be willing to help you. I could tell you whenever you have something out of place. Like the ribbon in your hair, it's lopsided and your slippers are covered with dirt. You're . . . "

"Melissa, I like fixing my own hair. Furthermore, my slippers will rot off my feet and the gown, as well, if you give me one more piece of your unasked for and unwanted advice. My appearance is fine with me."

Hobkins cleared his throat which made both girls flush. "Your father wishes to see you in his study at eight."

"What for? Did I do something wrong?" Melissa asked jumping to her feet.

"He asked for everyone, Lady Melissa. All seven of you."

"Then it couldn't be something I've done," Melissa said, resuming her seat. "Jessica or Nathan must be the one in trouble," she stated looking at Allison. "I think we just get to listen in on the entire affair for a change. Won't that be wonderful, Allison?" she asked leaning forward on the bench.

"You're despicable, Melissa. If we got excited when you were in trouble, I don't think you would appreciate it."

"You're always such a kind heart, Allison," she pouted, patting Allison on the shoulder as she walked toward the house. "I'll be there just the same. Though I have to say, I won't let the others know I'm gloating if it turns out to be Nathan in trouble. But if Jessica's finally got caught at something, I can't be responsible for my behavior," she said disappearing into the house.

Allison shook her head. "I worry about her. She can be so cruel. Tell Netty when the meeting is Hobkins," she said, "I'm sure she can get me there on time and properly dressed," she added as she wiped hair out of her face while leaving behind a huge smudge of dirt.

"Very good, Miss," Hobkins said disappearing into the house. Allison resumed her weeding as the silence settled around her. What could possibly have happened now? She thought, a frown marring her lovely features.

"MASTER CHRISTOPHER. Your father requests your presence at eight o'clock in his study."

Christopher nodded. "Is there anything I should prepare for?" he asked glancing up from the books in front of him before returning his attention to the ledgers.

Hobkins shrugged, "He didn't say."

"No matter. I'm sure whatever it is, Father will speak to me about it. I'll just go a little early."

Hobkins nodded as he backed out of the study. The children of this household were the oddest bunch. They each wanted the others to be the ones under scrutiny by their father, when in truth Brand dealt with all their problems in a fair and just manner. Tipping his head slightly Hobkins wondered what the meeting was about. The lord had asked for his brother to be present as well. Perhaps he was dying. The physician had been called again after visiting only two weeks ago. Shaking his head, he hurried to send a messenger to the adventurer. Colan was one person who wouldn't question the summons. He would show up directly.

Chapter 3

THE STUDY was deserted when Christopher entered ten minutes before eight o'clock. The liquor was replenished and Miriam had already sent in pastries. Moving back to the door, he yelled for Hobkins.

"Yes, my lord?"

"Where is my father? I thought he'd be here."

"He'll be here promptly at eight," Hobkins stated backing out of the room, leaving Christopher to stare after him.

"Trying to find out what's going on before the rest of us, big brother?" Jonathan asked moving into the room and going directly to the brandy. He poured two drinks and handed one to Christopher, then took a seat on the sofa closest to the fire.

Christopher smiled, taking a sip of the drink. "You know I hate secrets. I don't like anything dropped in my lap."

"I think Father has a marriage up his sleeve. Hobkins didn't say as much, but it was implied."

"Why that wily old dog! Hobkins didn't let a thing slip to me," Christopher said taking a seat in one of the four high-backed chairs. "Which girl is it to be then?" he asked leaning forward.

"Your guess is as good as mine. All three of them are of age. Hobkins may have indicated a marriage but he was tight lipped about the details."

Both men came to their feet as Allison and Netty entered. Jonathan walked forward to take Allison's arm. "How is my favorite lady today?" he asked planting a kiss on her cheek.

"You're getting more silver tongued as the years go by," she said smiling. "And how are you, Christopher?"

Christopher smiled. "I'm fine now that you are here to brighten up the room."

Allison laughed. "You're a devil."

"His flattery is way out of practice, Allison. He probably could woo a piece of paper or a book better than a woman," Jonathan said, leading her to the sofa to sit next to him. Christopher was cut off in his reply by Jessica's entrance.

"Well, what the hell did Nathan do this time?" Jessica said in a loud booming voice as she moved to pour herself a brandy. Taking the glass, she plopped herself down on the edge of the big desk her leg swinging back and forth as she drank. "Does anyone know?"

"Jessica nice of you to join us. Please remember where you are and watch the language," Christopher stated, scowling at her unladylike behavior.

"I'm glad to see you too, Christopher," Allison said, sipping the brandy before giving him a grin.

"You could have worn a damn dress."

Allison laughed. "Christopher, if she can't swear, neither can you. How did the last trip go, Jess?"

"It was a complete success. I sold Stephan's cargo and mine for a much higher price than we anticipated. The firm wants six more shipments of equal size from each of us." All three offered their congratulations as Jessica held up her glass for a toast. "As for the dress, Christopher, I almost sailed to Southbend instead of coming here. It was a last minute decision and I didn't have time to put myself into one of those uncomfortable corsets."

"I think you look outstanding," Allison said, laughing.

Christopher and Jonathan chuckled.

"What's so funny?" Melissa asked suspiciously as she slowly walked into the room.

"We were just talking about the man Father has chosen for you to marry." Jessica said, drinking a long draft from her glass. Melissa's face paled briefly, then her eyes narrowed as she realized Jessica was teasing her.

"Always a great sense of humor, Jessica. Too bad Father will never have a man who wants you," Melissa stated. Jessica tipped her glass at Melissa and gave her a slanted smile. Melissa decided to ignore her as she took a seat next to Christopher.

"Does anyone know if Nathan is coming?" Jonathan asked, taking a chocolate pastry and handing it to Allison. Allison accepted it with a smile. Jonathan always hovered over her making sure she was comfortable.

"He'll be here," Allison said, taking a bite of the sweet.

"At least one of you has faith in me," Nathan said leaning against the doorframe. "I wouldn't miss the opportunity to see one of my sisters served up on a silver platter to some arrogant pup."

Allison laughed. "You definitely could use some lessons on being suave with the ladies."

"Ah, dear sister," Nathan said, dropping a kiss on her cheek on the way to the liquor. "If you only knew how the ladies hang on my every word."

"Those aren't ladies, lad," Stephan said flopping into the chair closest to the door and swinging one leg over the arm. "I think you would faint, if a real lady hung around you."

The room erupted in laughter getting a smile out of Nathan. Allison tilted her head hearing the familiar thump of her tiger's tail. The animal loved sweets and could make himself into a terrible nuisance if ignored. A low mew came from the door's direction. Frowning she leaned forward and threw her remaining pastry toward the sound. The large tiger snapped it out of the air before retreating down the hall.

"Allison!" Melissa exclaimed.

"Would you rather have him in here? You know how Nero loves sweets. That will be the only time he bothers us."

"You should really teach him manners, love," Nathan said from his position leaning against the mantel.

"I've tried, but the sweets make him crazy and he forgets." Soft chuckles followed that statement, getting a snort from Melissa.

"That was definitely ladylike," Nathan stated.

"Oh, shut up!" Melissa snapped.

"I'm glad to see everyone could make it tonight. Sorry for the short notice," Brand said, moving to stand behind the desk. "But I haven't the time to cater to all of you." As seven pairs of eyes locked with his, he smiled. "I suppose I should get right to the point. It's rare to have you all in one room at the same time," he said, chuckling to himself, "I'm taking a holiday with Colan."

Silence followed that statement, before Christopher cleared his throat, "How long a holiday?" he asked leaning forward in his chair.

"One year." At the flood of questions, Brand held up his hands. Immediate silence followed. "If all goes well after a year, I plan on retiring permanently."

The room was completely silent. Everyone looked at one another. "Are you ill, Father?" Allison asked in a small voice, bringing everyone's eyes back to Brand.

"It seems George thinks my heart needs a bit of a rest. A holiday will let me live to see my grandchildren since none of you seem in a hurry to have any."

"Why the hell didn't you tell us you were ill? We would have helped you." Jessica yelled in her father's face.

"Jessica, my hearing is fine. I don't think you, as a lady, should be speaking like that to your father."

Jessica blushed and apologized. "I just can't believe it. You were as healthy as a horse for as long as I can remember."

"Well, you aren't here very often. The physician has been here six times in the last year. Two visits in the last month," Melissa stated giving Jessica a smug look.

"Is this true, Father?" Stephan and Jonathan asked at the same time.

"Yes." Up went his hands again. The protests and questions stopped. "I didn't want to worry anyone needlessly and I planned on cutting back. Christopher has already been running a lot of the business, while Stephan runs the market, Jessica has the shipping under control, and Jonathan hasn't had my input with those horses in almost a year."

"But you're still ill?" Allison asked.

"George says I need to get away completely. I can't bother my heart with anything. Not even the fuss over which meal to have at dinner."

"So what does this mean?" Jessica asked finally taking a seat in the chair next to Stephan's.

"It means that I've decided to pass the estates to Christopher now, instead of when I die. That way if anything drastic happens in the next year, I will still be around to help repair the damage." After the stunned looks and murmurs died down, he continued. "That means, anything that goes wrong will be brought to Christopher. I've also been advised to let the shipping part of the estates go. I will allow Stephan and Jessica to keep possession of that area. The stable will go to Jonathan."

"Forgive me for interrupting, but this sounds remarkably like a will," Nathan drawled.

"Actually, Nathan, I had planned my will to be something like this. I wanted each of you to follow your interests and I would then give you that part of the estates as your inheritance. Of course, the main body is entailed to Christopher, being my heir. He will receive the title when I do eventually pass on." Everyone sat stunned.

"Father, this is hard to digest. Are you sure there is no other way?" Jonathan asked.

"Actually, I've been doing a lot of thinking since George left today. I haven't spent any time to myself in more than thirty-two years. After your mother died, I threw myself deeper into the estate. I think Colan is right. I need to get away and relax and enjoy the things I've been missing all these years. George just made me understand my body can't take it anymore. Besides, it isn't as if you aren't doing almost everything now anyway."

"I feel like you're deserting us," Melissa stated from her chair.

"Now, it isn't like that. I will be in contact. I don't plan on leaving for America for at least a month. Your brother can write to me for help."

"Write to you? But where will you be?" Melissa whined.

"I will be staying with Colan."

"Father, I believe we have a couple of matters to clear up," Christopher said, still unsure about this situation.

"Yes, yes, of course. I'll need to pack and get things ready for you. I only have a few transactions going."

"But what about Allison and me?" said Melissa, "you haven't said what we're supposed to do. I was supposed to go to London for the season this year. You promised to take me to Aunt Gingers."

"Didn't you hear a word Father said? He's ill. You're only thinking of yourself," Jessica said, giving Melissa a disgusted look.

"Jessica," Brand said, giving her a stern look. Returning his gaze to Melissa, he nodded, "I've already thought about your season. I've decided to still send you to Ginger's, but Nathan will have to escort you instead of me. Christopher will help, of course. He has business in London anyway. Of course, there is one slight alteration. Jessica and Allison are going also." Brand said leaning back in his chair to prepare for the verbal lashing from Jessica.

Jessica laughed, "Father, I would be an embarrassment to good Aunt Ginger's name. She would probably disclaim me within a week."

"Father, she's right," Melissa said scooting forward in her chair, "Allison and I don't need her ruining our chances." Hesitating, she added, "Perhaps Jonathan would make a better escort. He is connected with the social elite."

Brand held up his hands. "I have made my decision and it's final. Jessica you will be going with Melissa and Allison. Nathan will be your escort."

Jessica's face darkened. "I don't know what you think it will accomplish."

"I'll tell you young lady. I want all three of you married in three months time." Melissa fell back in her chair, pale, Allison gasped, and Jessica shot to her feet.

"Married?" she bellowed. "I will not marry! And definitely not some arrogant peacock from London," she hollered.

"Then, I suggest you choose someone without those qualities." At her defiant look he added, "if in three months you haven't chosen a suitable gentleman, then I will pick a mate for you," Brand said taking a sip from his tea cup. Wrinkling his nose, he looked into the cup. Tea! What a sorry state indeed. Looking up he saw all three of his daughters sitting with their mouths open. Holding up a hand he shook his head.

"Now before you all start shrieking at me, let me finish. I believe the usual marrying age is sixteen?" he said with a pointed look at Jessica. "I want grandchildren and I need to know you're going to be taken care of before I can truly relax. Your mother would be disappointed at the way things are right now."

"I have my own ship. I can take care of myself. I don't need some conceited pig running my life," Jessica shouted barely controlling herself.

"I am giving you the chance to find your own man. He doesn't have to be arrogant or conceited. But, if I have to choose for you, I will try not to pick a man like that." Nathan couldn't stand it anymore, he burst out laughing.

"Jessica, I'll be willing to help," he hooted nudging Stephan, who was likewise grinning. Jessica's eyes darkened to almost jade.

"Don't do this Father," she said barely above a whisper.

Brand frowned. He knew she was going to be furious, but this was just too much. "Young Lady, you realize most girls at twenty-three, have no choice in the matter. Your groom would most likely be twice your age. You would be marrying for the wealth and standing he would bring to my estates. I am being fair in letting you choose a man for yourself. Don't argue with me or I will pick him out tomorrow!" he finished in a roar.

"Father, remember your heart," Allison said looking pale from her position on the couch. "I'm sure Jessica just needs time to adjust." Brand wiped his hand across his eyes and resumed his seat. Jessica, tight-lipped, moved to stare out the window.

"Father, don't you think this is a bit rash?" Jonathan asked patting Allison's hand.

"No, I do not. I have been indulgent far too long. The girls aren't the only ones that must get married. Christopher will as well."

"What!" Christopher shouted coming to his feet. "The girls I can understand, but why must I marry?"

"You will produce the heir," Brand said simply.

Christopher's jaw muscles worked. "How long do I have?" he stated, sarcastically, while trying to remain in control.

Brand looked at him and hesitated. How long would it take to find a lady with excellent qualities to pass on to his grandchildren? "I think six months is sufficient."

Christopher's jaw tightened, but he only nodded and resumed his seat. Brand let out the breath he had been holding expecting Christopher to argue further. But, of course, Christopher wouldn't say anything. He was, after all, the most loyal child he had. The lad always did as asked, rarely asking any questions.

"Do the rest of us have to wed?" Nathan drawled from his corner.

"It isn't required at this time," he said, nearly laughing as the three men physically relaxed. Brand glanced at the other four, all stiff and pale. "This isn't exactly what I had planned. Please understand my position. I promised your mother I would look after you all and I feel this is the only way I can do it under the circumstances."

At the reluctant nods from his children, Brand smiled. "Let's worry about all this tomorrow. Miriam has prepared a delightful dinner. I think full stomachs and a good night's rest will help you come to terms with the things we discussed. Tomorrow is soon enough for questions." Standing, he took Melissa's arm to escort her to dinner. "Aunt Ginger is looking forward to your visit. Are you excited to go?" Stephan heard his father say as he grabbed Jessica's arm to lead her into the dinning room not wanting to miss anything. Things were beginning to get interesting.

BRAND AWOKE THE NEXT DAY feeling refreshed and alert. The day was going to be wonderful, though all seven of his children weren't particularly pleased with him. Christopher had asked to see him at seven this morning. Never one to wait patiently, Christopher most likely had been up half the night sorting through estate business trying to figure out exactly what Brand needed to do before he left. Brand smiled. At least it would be easier to pass it to Christopher. If Nathan had been first born, this wouldn't have worked out.

Brand entered his study to find Christopher already there. Piles of papers surrounded him where he sat.

"Good morning, Son. How are you today?"

"Fine. I have arranged everything according to its importance and made a list of the things you have to wrap up before you go. There isn't much, since you have slowly been letting things slip in my direction. Also, I thought Nathan should take care of the invitations, since he's to go to London on social business."

"Nothing like getting right to it," Brand said pouring himself a cup of coffee. The American drink was far better than tea. "Coffee? Tea?" Christopher held up his cup shaking his head. "I knew you would have everything organized. Yes, I believe it would do Nathan good to have the social calendar planned. Of course, Ginger will have most of that taken care of," he said, taking a seat behind his desk. The piles of paper seemed higher than those around Christopher. Brand sighed as he scooted forward in his chair. It was going to be good to go and leave all this behind.

ALLISON WAS STARTLED AWAKE BY MELISSA as she came bounding into her room full of excitement. "I can't believe we're going to London. Finally! Too bad Jessica has to go. She'll probably ruin everything. But I'll wager she stays at home. Socializing just isn't her thing."

Allison sat up and wiped the sleep from her eyes. "I think Jessica will go to London," she murmured moving her legs over the side of the bed where she rose and moved to the sink.

Melissa frowned. "You do? But why would she go? She never does what Father says."

"Do you want Father to pick your husband for you?"

Melissa's frown deepened. "You're right. Jessica is going to Longon."

"I think it will be fun. We have never done anything together and I think we'll have a grand time," Allison said, picking up the dress Netty laid out. Slipping it over her head she felt Melissa automatically come to fasten the buttons down the back.

"Jessica doesn't know the first thing about being a lady," Melissa said pushing Allison's hair over her shoulder so she could fasten the top buttons.

"Melissa, I would be more worried about the commotion I'm going to cause bumping into people and knocking things over, than the small slips Jessica might make in her social manners."

Melissa hands froze on the second to the last button. Allison laughed, reaching over her shoulder to do up the last two buttons herself before moving to sit at her table. "Just now thinking of that?"

"I'm sure you'll be fine. Netty will be going and once you get the area memorized, you'll be fine."

"I'm to memorize all of London?" Allison asked turning around to face Melissa. Melissa frowned. Allison's hair ribbon was lopsided and the dress wasn't lying correctly. Allison was tall for a woman and had a figure that would definitely catch a man's eye, but without her sight, Melissa wondered how she was ever going to manage.

"I'm sorry, Allison. I'm such a selfish person. I was only thinking how Jessica would hinder my finding the perfect man, when you probably will have it the hardest of us all."

Allison smiled. "I will pray that it all works out."

Chapter 4

A FORTNIGHT later the three women started out for London with every intention of following their father's instructions. Yet, somehow, things didn't work out quite like they'd planned. Nathan grumbled at the two extra carriages containing the many gowns needed for a season. For the five occupants the trip seemed endless. Jessica cursed Stephan for sailing her ships and ruining the business, while she had to parade herself around in uncomfortable attire while men ogled her like a cow at market. Allison's mood soured as everything Melissa had said earlier made her worry she'd make a spectacle of herself. Christopher, with the added responsibility of the estates and the slow progress they were making, prodded and poked at Nathan until he moved to ride in one of the baggage coaches just to get away from him. Melissa complained endlessly about how wrinkled she was getting finally forcing Jessica to sit on her just to give her something real to complain about. For revenge, Melissa put dust in Jessica's hair, adding that to the bags forming under her eyes and the sweaty conditions, about which she was already complaining.

Allison felt instant relief at hearing her cats low mew when they stopped to reload one of Melissa's trunks that had fallen off the coach. She had been forced to leave Nero behind when they'd left for London but now that he obviously escaped and followed them she felt instantly secure. Nero had always been her eyes and had kept her from harms way. With Nero beside her London didn't seem so bad.

Nathan rejoined them by the time they reached London and all five craned their necks to see the town house in which Aunt Ginger lived.

Once inside, Aunt Ginger made them feel welcome and at home. They soon forgot the uncomfortable three days it took to get to London. Of course, Nero didn't go over well. Neither did the fact that Jessica had arrived wearing breeches, but Aunt Ginger had pursed her lips and directed them all to their rooms for rest.

The next day they were all hustled out of their beds at an ungodly hour and their social season began. Christopher left on business, leaving them in Aunt Ginger's hands.

"First," she stated, over the breakfast they were eating, "there is to be the season opener on Friday. This is the ball that starts everyone out. It's at the Hawthorn's and anyone who's anybody will be there," she said taking several bites from her plate before speaking again. Melissa was grinning and fidgeting with excitement. "We have our work cut out for us. It will be quite the accomplishment to have you presentable by then but I'm sure we can manage."

Nathan burst into laughter at the looks that crossed his sister's faces. But instantly lowered his gaze and began shoveling food into his mouth when Aunt Ginger's stern gaze landed on him.

"As I was saying, Jessica we will start with you. The breeches must go. You will wear a dress at all times and start acting like the young lady you are."

Jessica's mouth dropped open, but before she could say anything, Ginger was speaking again. "Melissa, your constant complaining must cease. Ladies do not act that way. They are demur and proper at all times." At the outraged look on Melissa's face, Nathan quickly shoved more food into his mouth to prevent himself from laughing. "Allison the cat must go! I don't know what Colan was thinking giving that thing to you."

"But I can't manage without him."

Ginger sat up straight. "Had you really planned on bringing him to the balls?" she asked sternly. "Gentlemen will not come within ten feet of you. The cat must go." Allison frowned but didn't say anything.

"Nathan, you will need to learn how to behave in a dignified manner when escorting these three beautiful young ladies. We don't want to attract rakes or the like." Nathan's face flushed at the veiled reference causing Jessica to laugh. Aunt Ginger's lips thinned. "You are a family. As such, you will refrain from maliciously harming one another. I want nothing but compliments about each other. If you have nothing good to say then say nothing at all," she said looking sternly at them before wiping her mouth with a napkin, "it will take hard work and constant instruction from me, but I'm sure we'll be fine by Friday."

The next three days were grueling. Ginger was constantly correcting and nagging at them. All four of them felt they were completely inadequate to enter society. The whole process was tiring. Each night the four dropped into bed from exhaustion only to be hauled out of bed at dawn to begin the process all over again.

Jessica, in a foul temper, never once said anything the least bit offensive, though twice Nathan had grabbed her to prevent her from doing bodily harm to Aunt Ginger. But all and all, they were presentable. Thursday morning dawned and Allison awoke to the familiar licking of Nero. She slowly sat up, wondering why she was still in bed. She could feel the sun on her face and knew it was later than Ginger usually let her sleep. Her answer came two minutes later, when a cheerful Netty came into the room to help her dress.

"Your Aunt has a practice day planned today. You'll have to be on your best behavior."

Allison groaned, falling back on the bed. Melissa bounded into the room chatting nervously about the ball. "You're not putting that green on her, are you Netty? With that blond hair, she should wear the blue," Melissa said pursing her lips.

"What difference does it make? If Netty has the green gown ready, I'll wear the green. It will match my eyes that way."

"But the blue brings out the stunning color of your hair."

"All the more reason to save it for when I need to look my best," Allison said rolling her sightless eyes.

Melissa frowned. "Jessica has red on. It really makes her black hair look gorgeous, but don't tell her I said that."

"She won't," Jessica said smiling from the door. Melissa scowled at having been caught giving a compliment.

Three sisters so different, Netty thought. All beautiful in their own way. Jessica, the oldest, was raven-haired with a firm hardened body from commanding her own ship. She had eyes the color of wet grass and a temper that made the devil look like a saint. At twenty-three, it would be hard to find someone who could match her commanding air without stifling her.

Melissa was all woman. She had a voluptuous body men drooled over. Her golden hair had just enough red in it to make it look like waves of molten fire. She was healthy and vibrant. Her green eyes were framed in a heart-shaped face adding the final touch. This one would be easy to find a husband for. The question was, which one would best be able to handle the swarm of men that would plague him the rest of his life. Being the youngest, at eighteen, didn't help matters any.

Last was her Allison. A gentle woman with a big heart and a soul as pure as the day she was born. Even with the loss of eyesight at twelve, the girl wasn't bitter. She could always see the good in someone. She had a fine figure and a pretty face that helped hide her flawed sight. With silver-blond hair and striking green eyes she was very exotic looking. Even so, Allison, at twenty-two, would be the hardest for which to find a worthy man. But Netty had no doubt Ginger would choose well for each of the ladies chatting before her. If nothing else, it would be fun to watch.

The day progressed with a slowness that was almost unnerving, but Friday finally dawned sending Melissa into instant panic.

"We have to at least discuss what we're wearing. The same man is escorting us all. Our attire must flow, not clash," she said holding up a deep blue gown.

"Fine. Just tell me what color you want me to wear and Netty will lay it out for me. I refuse to wear pink," Allison said brushing Nero's hide with a horse comb.

"Jessica, choose a color so I can decide what the rest of us should wear."

"Why?" Jessica asked from her position in the only chair in the room.

"You're the oldest. Christopher will most likely have you on his arm, leaving Allison and I to follow behind on Nathan's," she added giving Jessica a look that clearly indicated she was stupid.

"I still don't see the point in this, but I'm wearing blue. Ginger picked it out."

"Blue!"

"Is there a problem with blue? Remember, you're lucky I'll be in a dress."

"No, there isn't a problem," Melissa said quickly. Jessica had actually been trying to be a lady. Melissa didn't want to rock the boat and start out the first ball in shambles. This would present them to society and mark them for the entire season. "Blue is fine. I'll wear yellow and Allison can wear teal."

"Teal! But yesterday you said green made me look washed out," Allison said pausing in her brushing.

"It does, but teal will look stunning."

Allison shook her head "Your logic is beyond me," she said getting to her feet while Nero moved under her hand. "Whatever you think is best. I'm going to see Nathan." Grabbing Nero's collar she cleared her throat. "Find Nathan Nero," she said as the cat perked up its ears and started out the door.

Ten minutes later, after a few false turns and wrong rooms, Allison found herself in Nathan's room.

"Nathan, are you awake?" she asked moving in the direction of the snoring. Silence followed her question. Holding out her hands in front of her, she located the bed, only to have Nero ruin her intrusion by jumping up on the bed and licking the face protruding from under the quilts.

"Bloody hell," Nathan moaned from under the cat's weight, as he tried to keep his face away from the wet tongue.

"Nero, get down! You'll kill him!" Allison shouted trying to tug the tiger off.

"I'm going to kill Uncle Colan next time I see him for bringing this cat to you," Nathan said pulling the quilts over his head. "Now go away."

"Nathan, I need to talk to you about tonight."

"Wait till I get up," Nathan said pulling the quilts tighter.

"Nero," Allison said, waiting as Nero obediently grabbed the quilts in his mouth and headed for the door. Flopping down on his side he rolled over and was completely rolled up in Nathan's blankets.

"Bloody hell, Allison. I've had a late night," Nathan complained, turning on his side to stare at the cat. "My blankets will be full of bugs," he added flopping back on the bed.

"Nero doesn't have bugs," Allison stated sitting on the edge of the bed, "I really need to talk to you. I'm scared about tonight."

Nathan opened one eye to look at her. She looked lovely. The ribbon in her hair was slightly lopsided, but other than that, she looked fine. "I think you look lovely, and I wouldn't worry about tonight," he said closing his eyes again.

"That's easy for you to say. I'm the one that has to go someplace I've never been before without being able to see. I'm going to make a fool of myself. I just know it. Are you planning on staying right next to me the entire evening?"

Nathan frowned. He hadn't thought about what she would do with herself. He'd planned on playing cards and keeping a distant eye on the three of them. "Christopher's going. I'm sure between the two of us we'll be able to stay with you."

"Do you mean it?" she asked hopeful. Seconds later she was scowling with concern. "But what if I'm asked to dance, will you meet me between partners?"

Nathan frowned again. This was going to be harder than he realized. Sitting up he looked at her. "Maybe we should let people know you're blind. I know we've practiced with the height and eye contact, on which I commend you, but I think it would be easier on everyone, including yourself, if people knew." Allison had been shaking her head before he even finished. "Why the hell not?" he asked in frustration, "it's not like they won't find out."

"I don't want to be stared at or treated like an invalid. Just promise not to leave me stranded."

Nathan frowned, but nodded his head. "Fine. We'll do it your way this time but if it doesn't work out, everyone is to be told." Allison hesitated, but finally nodded.

"Will you ask Christopher about tonight?"

"Why can't you?"

"He'll be more willing to help, if you explain it to him in your male way. Or better yet, tell him I'll bring Nero, if he doesn't help me."

"All right," Nathan said chuckling, "can I go back to sleep now?"

"Of course. Nero has had sufficient time to plant all his bugs in your quilts," she said walking to the door. Kicking the quilts in the direction of the bed, she smiled and left the room.

Nathan lay back on his pillow frowning. How the hell did she plan on keeping her blindness a secret? Granted, she did walk without hesitation, and they had practiced for months at home on how to greet a person of a certain height by Nathan mentioning it to her, while she said hello and smiled to the imaginary person. He'd taught her how to accept a glass from him without spilling it. But even with all the practice, things popped up and happened that they couldn't predict. Now faced with a ball of this magnitude Nathan wondered if they were all insane for trying to pass her off as normal. Like she said, was he supposed to hover over her the entire evening? Wouldn't that look just the least bit odd? Maybe Christopher had some ideas. Flipping his legs over the side of the bed, he quickly dressed and headed to find his brother.

Christopher was in the library. His blond hair was messed up from having ran his fingers through it so many times. By the looks of him, he hadn't been to sleep yet, either.

"Hello brother. How do things fare so far?" Nathan drawled, leaning his back against the bookcase.

"It's a mess. The entire estate is in the middle of one transaction or another. Father had fifteen things going at once."

"No wonder his heart was complaining."

Taking a deep breath Christopher ran a hand through his hair before leaning back in his chair. "Can I do something for you, Nathan?" he stated sounding irritated.

"As a matter of fact, I need some advice." Christopher's eyebrows shot up and a lopsided smile formed on his lips. "Not in that area, believe me, it's Allison," Nathan said pacing.

Christopher's grin vanished, "What now?"

"She wants to take Nero with her to the ball."

"Bloody hell. She can't do that."

"I know but she's worried about the way she'll look to other people. You know she doesn't want anyone to know she's blind. I've been practicing with her on social skills but she broached some really important issues that I hadn't even thought of. When she's dancing, who's going to meet her when her partner is through?"

"That's easy. She's always returned to either you or I just like the other two will be."

Nathan smiled, "I forgot that."

"That's because you don't associate with ladies," he stated giving him a pointed look.

"I don't think you need to keep throwing that in my face. I can behave anyway I damn well please," he said coming away from the wall. "Are you planning to stay with her the entire evening?"

Christopher stared at him a full minute, his brows arched high in disbelief. "That's why you're here. This isn't a social evening for you, Nathan. You're supposed to introduce your sisters into society. Didn't Father explain all this to you?"

Nathan began to scowl, "Not exactly. He said I was to weed out the undesirables and encourage the ones I thought respectable. I assumed that meant really get to know the gentlemen. Which in short means, play cards and drink with them whenever possible."

Christopher snorted in disgust. "That is what you would think. Father meant you are to act like a concerned older brother, making it seem that our sisters are untouchable. You encourage those worthy gentlemen and make it seem like you'll kill the ones that aren't."

"This whole affair is starting to get on my nerves. I planned on having fun, not being someone's baby-sitter."

"You'll do as you're told. Father is really ill. He would never hand over his estates if he weren't. The least you can do is watch out for your sisters. The way they look, I don't think it will take long for the gents to start pounding on the doors."

Nathan scowled at his brother, "Are you at least going to help me? I'm just supposed to be a partial observer, while you're the mean older brother."

"Wrong. You're the brother that has to deal with the whole affair. I'm only going tonight to let everyone know Father has retired from his business life and I'm stepping into his shoes."

"But I don't want that responsibility. It will drive me mad to see men drooling after our sisters. I'll more than likely break someone's face."

"You will conduct yourself as a gentleman or pay the consequences."

"Which are?"

"I will have Stephan send you out on one of his ships as a cabin boy."

Nathan grinned. "It just might be worth the punishment, if you promise to put me on Jessica's ship. She has a few lady mates, I'm told."

"I'm not joking, Nathan. For once in your life, do something right. Everyone is sick of carrying you along. You're twenty-five years old, become a man, for gods sake."

Nathan's face darkened and Christopher saw his jaw muscle work. "If it's the last thing I do, I will get even with you for that crack. You probably suggested this to Father."

Christopher watched him storm from the library and smiled. Nathan was ruled by his temper. It had always worked when they were kids and just a little shove still seemed to do the job.

Chapter 5

JONATHAN sat quietly across the chessboard from the Baron of Essex. The Baron was a man of sturdy build, six three in height, black hair, blue eyes, and of impeccable character. Jonathan smiled to himself at that thought. The Baron had been involved in a number of things scandalous. Of course, Jonathan wasn't going to say anything since his own reputation would get blotched as well.

"What has you grinning like a fool, my friend?" Morgan Sinclair asked leaning his large frame back in the chair, "do you have a move up your sleeve that will put my king in jeopardy?"

Jonathan's smile widened. "Not at the moment but it's just a matter of time." Moving his rook he took Morgan's bishop putting Morgan's queen in danger.

Morgan smiled at the move but didn't seem affected by it. "Perhaps the reason you are smiling has nothing to do with the game. Maybe you know of my mishap?" he asked his voice taking on a hard edge.

Jonathan's grin vanished as his instincts told him something was wrong. "Are you accusing me of something?" he asked drawing his brows down in concern.

Morgan shook his head. "No. I was merely testing to see what your reaction would be. If you'd known anything about the wine I think your response would have been different."

"What's happened now? More smugglers?"

"Not exactly. But it is the reason I came for a visit." Morgan said as his eyes locked on Jonathan's. "My leads seem to keep bringing me in this direction."

Jonathan frowned at that. What the hell had happened? "I wondered at your visit after all this time. It must be at least six months since I've laid eyes on you."

"Actually it's been eight. I've been dealing heavily with some vineyards in France. The ships run slow this time of year so I tried to get as much of my wine to my client before this awful weather moved in. But as I've mentioned, I've run into a couple of problems and they all seem to come from here."

"You already said that," Jonathan stated getting irritated with the hedging Morgan was doing.

"It seems this client of mine is a large exporter of wine all over the world. He had a few bad years with his own grape fields and has bought wine to sell as his own. Of course, it isn't exactly his wine but the people who buy from him, buy wine for his name. So naturally, I make a fair profit. But of late, my client has been bitter toward my wine and me. In fact, he has sent back two whole shipments. Do you want to know why?"

Jonathan felt the hair on the back of his neck rise. Morgan's face was now a barely controlled mask of rage and his voice had taken on a hard edge. "I'm afraid to ask."

"Someone has been tampering with my wine!" he exploded, rising from his chair to pace. "I have twenty-three barrels of wine that are completely ruined. My client refused to except any more wine from me, stating that he could produce that swill himself. He also stated he would be getting his wine from someone else. Can you guess who that might be?" Morgan asked stopping behind the chair he had been sitting in to look at Jonathan.

"Are you implying Stephan had something to do with this?"

"Funny you should mention him. My client wouldn't tell me the merchant supplying him wine but I did some checking. Stephan is now supplying my client," he bellowed.

"But there has to be a mistake," Jonathan said, "Stephan has never done business this way, and even if he were strapped for funds he would never resort to stealing. It's just not in his nature."

"No? Then how do you explain this situation?"

"Please, Morgan, sit down. I think the best thing we could do at this point is to get a hold of Stephan and ask him about this. I'm sure there's an explanation for this entire situation."

Morgan resumed his seat. "I've known you for a long time and I respect you. But if your brother is responsible for this situation I won't be held responsible for my actions."

Jonathan had little doubt that Morgan would meet out a punishment if necessary. He'd seen Morgan in several fights over the years and having him on your side was in your best interest. "Morgan, since you've never met Stephan, I have to ask that you give me the courtesy of doing some investigating before you cause trouble where it might not be warranted," he said shaking his head. "I can honestly say, there has to be a logical explanation for why Stephan is supplying your man. He's too honorable to steal."

Morgan stared at Jonathan for a good two minutes before he ran a hand through his hair. "All right, Jonathan. Since you're a man of your word I'll trust you on this. But if your brother is involved I demand the right to take it out of his hide myself."

Jonathan nodded his head slowly. He suddenly felt like he'd just made the biggest mistake of his life.

Chapter 6

BRAND RECLINED IN THE CHAIR before the fire listening to his brother go on and on about America. It was a place of opportunity and the land of the free. Brand didn't really care what the country was like as long as he could find relaxation.

"Brand, are you listening?"

Brand gave him a sheepish look. "I was, but got distracted." Looking back at the fire he scowled, "do you think I will live to see my grandchildren?"

Colan snorted. "You're too ornery to die just because your heart is complaining a little."

"But do you think the children will come out of this all right?"

Colan laughed at that. "You put Christopher in charge. The man can organize chaos itself. Your girls will marry, and well. I'd bet my life on it."

Brand smiled. "You're right, of course. Christopher will see them wed in three months time. I just hope they find nice gentleman that will take care of them. Maybe I should have given them more time."

Colan frowned. "Jessica will take every second you give her to fool around with that ship of hers. It's better that they are limited. Quit fretting about it. Your children are adults and can handle things on their own. What could possibly happen?"

Brand frowned into his teacup. That was exactly what had him worried.

IT WAS JUST HOURS BEFORE THE BALL and already Ginger had been in Allison's room twelve times to tell her this and to make sure she didn't do that. Allison was beginning to get a headache and they hadn't even left the house yet.

"You look lovely dear. Your Aunt just likes to fret. The teal does make your hair stunning. Lady Melissa does have a fashion sense."

"Thank you, Netty. If Aunt Ginger comes in here one more time to tell me my hair is crooked or my dress needs pressing I'm staying home."

Netty laughed. "Now child, your Aunt has a lot on her mind. She just wants the best for you and your sisters."

"I know. But let her bother Jessica and Melissa. I have enough to worry about without being concerned about my attire."

"You'll be fine. Just remember what you've practiced with Master Nathan and remember Master Christopher will be there to help should anything go wrong."

"But what if I make a fool of myself?" she said then paled, "I'm not ready for this. I'll just tell Ginger I'm ill," Allison said holding her hand to her head to see if it felt hot. "Not even a flush. Netty get me something warm to heat up my head. If I'm going to be ill, it better be convincing."

"You will do no such thing, young lady," Aunt Ginger said from the doorway, "you will go to this ball and that's final. I can't believe you would resort to something so childish."

Allison flushed at being caught trying such an underhanded thing. "I feel terribly uncomfortable. Maybe Melissa and Jessica can tell everyone they have another sister at home and I'll go to the next one."

Aunt Ginger pursed her lips. "Allison, you will be fine tonight. I will stay close to you and Nathan will, as well. You needn't worry about being left alone. Between the three of us, I'm sure we can handle anything."

"But I'm starting to get extremely nervous," she answered fidgeting in her seat. Nero came over and laid his head in her lap as she absently rubbed behind his ears.

"Netty, do get that cat off her. He's getting hair all over her. Look what he's doing to the gown."

Allison frowned at that. "He's all right," she said even as she felt him being pulled off her lap. "I don't know why all the fuss. I don't see any hair."

Netty laughed and Allison thought she heard Ginger giggle. "In any case, the cat stays off your gown."

"Allison, you look beautiful," Melissa bubbled, bursting into the room. "I told you the teal would look wonderful on you. You should see my gown. I think I look stunning."

"Always a braggart," Jessica stated walking into the room and flopping down on the bed. "This is the most uncomfortable contraption I have suffered in almost a year. I think I'm going to suffocate," she said pulling on the corset.

Melissa grinned. "That would be wonderful. Then you wouldn't have a chance to embarrass us at the ball."

"Now children, no squabbling. Everyone is going to the ball and everyone is going to behave themselves. It's quarter past so we better get moving. I do hope Nathan is ready. I haven't checked on him in half an hour," Ginger said rushing out of the room. "Hurry girls," she called as she disappeared down the hall.

"I hope Nathan makes us late," Jessica said pulling the corset down in place again. "This stupid thing doesn't even fit right. I can't bend over either. Netty help me get it off," Jessica stated undoing the buttons on her gown.

"But your Aunt wants you to wear it," Netty fidgeted not wanting this one's dragon temper directed at her.

"She'll never even know until it's too late. Just undo the laces." Five minutes later Jessica stood buttoned back in her gown leaning from side to side. "Whew, that feels wonderful. I can actually breath," she said bending over to touch her toes before straightening. "See?" Melissa pursed her lips and glared, before flouncing out of the room, the door slamming behind her.

Jessica looked at Allison, who was absently rubbing her hair to make sure if seemed in order. "If she says one word to anyone, I'm going to tell every man that comes within ten feet of her that she's simple."

Allison laughed. "She won't say anything. It would make us late for the ball."

Jessica lifted Allison to her feet. "You look radiant," she said though she noticed immediately that Allison was looking pale and frightened. "Try to relax and remember we're all there for you," she said guiding her toward the door. "If it makes you feel better, I'll let you know immediately if you do anything out of the ordinary." Allison nodded and missed a step as she heard the whistle Nathan let out as they descended the stairs.

"You look lovely. Both of you," Christopher said smiling.

Nathan groaned, while Christopher slipped each girl's cloak around their shoulders. "This is terrible," Nathan said, "all three of you look so stunning, I'll never be able to keep the men away." Christopher grinned at him as he watched each girl flush at the compliment. Taking Allison's arm, Christopher led her out the door.

"Remember, you're supposed to be the fierce brother."

Nathan scowled at Christopher's retreating back. "I suppose you're going to spend the evening playing cards and having fun.

Christopher just smiled, "I'm sure you'll manage just fine no matter what I'm doing."

"If I see you playing cards, I'm joining the tables."

"Nathan, just get us there. I'm sure I can take care of myself. That will leave only two ladies for you to worry about," Jessica stated walking out the front door to the awaiting coach.

"See! She's already bossing and we haven't even left the house. What are you going to do with her?" Melissa snapped moving after her brother who had stopped to explain the layout of the coach to Allison. Turning to face Melissa, Christopher scowled.

"I'm not going to do anything. I think having to go to the ball, will be punishment enough." Taking Allison's arm he helped her into the coach then climbed in behind her. Jessica followed. Nathan practically threw Melissa into the coach to staunch her complaints.

"If that's all the better you can escort a lady, no wonder you haven't brought any home," Melissa snapped, trying to keep her gown from getting wrinkled.

"Quit fussing Melissa or I will give you to the first man that asks for you." Christopher stated as Melissa's mouth snapped shut. Her eyes shot daggers at Nathan.

"Aunt Ginger already left for the ball. We are probably going to arrive just a few minutes after her. Try to act with grace and decorum. We are representing Father and Mother," Christopher said giving each a steady look. "Jessica control your temper, Nathan try to act the gentleman, Melissa refrain from complaining, and Allison, relax. I'm sure everything will be just fine."

"Christopher, if I'm having trouble, will you promise to take me straight home?" Allison asked ringing her hands.

"If you have any trouble? Like what kind of trouble?"

"I don't know. Maybe I'll knock over the host or spill a drink on our hostess. Maybe I'll walk into a wall and stand there talking to a bush half the night while everyone is laughing at me."

"Stop!" Melissa hooted, "I can't breath when I'm laughing," she gasped while everyone laughed even harder. That's how they arrived at the Hawthorn estates.

Christopher jumped to the ground and helped the ladies out of the coach. "Remember. Be on your best behavior."

"If you two treat me like an invalid, everyone will know I'm blind," she whispered climbing to the ground as both men took an elbow.

Nathan grinned at Christopher who returned the smile. "If you start talking to a bush I will take you home," Christopher said taking Jessica's arm.

"Do you promise?" Allison asked from Nathan's left arm.

"I promise," Christopher called over his shoulder.

"Don't worry, Allison. Jessica and I both agree to help you," Melissa said from Nathan's right. Ginger said Christopher being the family figureheads should walk with the oldest girl. Nathan would then bring in the other two. Melissa had hated to be second but no amount of arguing could change Ginger's mind.

"I can't do this. I'm going to ruin everything," Allison blurted halting in her tracks.

"Allison, just think of this as a test to your independence. You said you would never leave the house, but you managed to tend the gardens without any help from anyone. I will stay by your side the entire evening," Nathan said, rubbing her arms. Color slowly returned to her face.

"Are you sure I don't look stupid?" she asked just above a whisper.

Nathan smiled. "You look beautiful." Taking Melissa's arm he hurried them up the steps before Allison could change her mind.

They entered the foyer and Melissa gasped. "Have you ever seen such a thing?" she asked to no one in particular.

"No, I haven't," Allison said dryly.

"Oh, Allison, it's beautiful! We're in a large room full of plants and windows that reach the ceiling. Long red velvet curtains hang to the floor. There's a railing at the end of the room and beyond that is the ballroom. A chandelier, with at least a hundred lights is hanging in the center," she said pulling on Allison's arm. "Along the wall, at the back, are more windows with the curtains. It's really spectacular," she said handing her cloak to Nathan as she pulled Allison toward the ballroom.

"Melissa, wait. I need Nathan with me!" Allison screeched in a panic.

"Oh, I'm sorry. I forgot in the excitement. We have to be announced, too." Nathan caught up to them glaring at Melissa.

"Don't be in such a bloody hurry."

"Nathan watch the language," Allison said clutching his arm.

Jessica and Christopher joined them. "They said we are to stop at the top of the stairs and wait for our names to be announced, then descend into the ballroom." The small group moved in the direction of the stairs. Walking past couples and single men.

"Allison," Melissa whispered, "all the people look like kings and queens. And the gowns..." she said in awe. Allison smiled at that comment. She could picture people in brightly colored gowns of silver and gold with crowns on their heads. She covered her mouth as a giggle tried to escape. Nathan mistook it as panic and asked her if she was all right.

"Fine. I was just picturing everyone as kings and queens."

Nathan smiled, but worry started to mark his face, such an innocent woman stood beside him. Her family had always protected her. What if she ran into some vindictive woman who verbally attacked her? Nathan frowned at the thought, but immediately another thought came to mind: Jessica giving the lady a black eye for attacking Allison which got them kicked out of the ball and all future balls. Thus would effectively end their season and get him off the hook and back to the life he loved. Smiling at the pleasant thought, he wondered if he should suggest it to Jessica just to plant the seed.

"Lord Christopher Hayworth and his sister Lady Jessica." A short pudgy man in a tailored black waistcoat announced. His hair was covered with a powdered wig and he had white gloves on his hands. Nathan wanted to laugh at the man, but then noticed practically all the gents in the room had on the silly wigs.

Christopher and Jessica started descending the steps into the throng of people.

"Lord Nathan Hayworth and his sisters Lady Allison and Lady Melissa." All eyes were trained on them as they descended into the ballroom. Melissa was slightly flushed with the excitement and the stares of so many men, but Allison was pale and had a claw like grip on his arm.

"Relax," he said through his smile, "we're coming upon the host and his lady. He's about six foot five on your left and she's about five foot three on his right." Allison smiled and nodded her head.

"I had wondered if any Hayworths were still alive," Daniel Hawthorn asked smiling. He shook Christopher's hand and kissed Jessica's. "I see now why you have been hiding such splendor away. I think I would hide them, too."

Christopher laughed. "I don't think it will be easy, but it's time we came back into society." Jessica smiled and nodded to the hostess.

"This lovely creature next to me is my wife, Luana." Christopher kissed her hand, as did Nathan. Allison felt her hand being kissed and smiled then nodded to the height of five foot three. Melissa came next and Allison heard a giggle from her. Nathan ushered them along as another group was announced. They would visit with the host later in the evening. Christopher guided them far into the room making for a section along the wall that wasn't occupied.

Stopping he turned to let the others catch up. "I think it best if we stay to the edge until Allison gets used to the room. So many people will be confusing enough for her." Allison smiled her thanks and Jessica and Melissa nodded their approval. "Now, if you will excuse me, I have people to see and talk with before dinner. If you have any trouble, Nathan, just hunt me down."

"How do you like that? We're not even here five minutes and already he's deserted us," Jessica stated crossing her arms as Christopher walked away. Melissa quickly slapped Jessica's arms down.

"Don't do that, you ninny. You look like a brawler," she snapped looking around to see if anyone saw.

Jessica's jaw clenched. "If you know what's good for you, you will refrain from correcting me this evening or I will embarrass you so bad you won't step foot in another ball." Melissa tensed.

"Behave yourselves. Remember we're on our best behavior," Nathan remarked leaning casually against a wall. The girls were wondering how they should act, when a grinning Aunt Ginger glided up.

"You were simply marvelous. All of you look so beautiful and charming," she added for Nathan's benefit. Nathan gave her a lopsided smile watching her clasp her hands together in delight. "All the bachelors in my area murmured among themselves at your beauty. I'll wager your dance cards will be full in no time."

As Aunt Ginger rattled on, Nathan stared at his sisters from a bachelor's point of view. Allison was the prettiest. Her teal gown made her hair look almost silver. Melissa was too desirable for her own good. That thought made Nathan scowl. Jessica stood with her back straight while she gracefully sipped a glass of champagne. She was probably the one most like a lady, though she would fast deny it. Black, blond, and silver. Three very beautiful women. How did he end up keeping an eye on them at their first ball? This should be Christopher's job.

"Hopefully that won't happen."

"What?" he asked coming away from the wall.

"Oh, nothing to worry about. Come girls I would like you to meet a few friends of mine." Aunt Ginger said moving off.

"If you don't mind, Aunt Ginger, I think we should stay here longer. Allison needs time to adjust," Melissa said giving Allison a quick peek before waiting for Ginger's reply.

Allison raised her chin wondering if Ginger would say 'Oh pooh, she's fine' and drag them off into the masses.

"You're right, Dear. I would never have thought of that. Just relax and I'll bring the ladies around to you," Aunt Ginger said, turning to disappear into the crowd.

"Allison, this room is beyond words. Every ten feet on the wall is a light to match the chandelier. It's breathtaking. To our left are the doors leading into what looks like the banquet hall. I can see tables anyway. The rug on the floor looks Persian and expensive. To our right is another room. I have no idea what is in there. It has the same curtains on the windows, but there are too many people in the way to see what's inside. Directly in front of us are two sets of doors with about fifty feet separating them. They lead out into the gardens, I think. I can see lights and wooden benches. It has to be the gardens. There are people everywhere," she finished in a rush.

"It sounds lovely."

"For once Melissa isn't exaggerating. This is a very beautiful home," Jessica stated glancing around the room.

"It sounds too large to actually live in," Allison said, tipping her head to the side.

"It is large, but I bet they live in another part of the house and use this only for entertaining," Melissa said looking again at the room to the right. "They must be very rich."

AS THE THREE GIRLS CHATTED and Nathan leaned nonchalantly against the wall bored with the entire affair, Jared McMaster was observing them with interest. Hayworth? Drawing his brows together he wondered briefly if they were offspring of Brand Hayworth, the Earl that had haggled his brother, Royce, out of a sizeable amount of money. Brand had done business with Royce two years ago, buying a ship worth almost twice what he paid for it. Royce had acted upset at the final price but Jared knew he'd respected Brand's head for business and dedication to shipping. They had settled on the price out of respect and admiration.

These must be his children. How many did he have? Jared's brows lifted as the black haired girl slapped the red head in the back of the head before walking to stand beside the brother. The red head was throwing a proper tantrum to the silver haired one who only nodded and sipped from her glass. Too bad he was married, these three already claimed his interest. The fact that all three were over the normal age of a season, made it worth a man's time to find out why.

"Watching the display?" A petite raven haired lady asked as she slid up against his side while slipping her hand around his arm.

Jared smiled down at her before returning his gaze to the three women. "Not watching, just curious."

The petite woman scowled up at him. "For not watching, your eyes seem to be permanently frozen on them."

Jared laughed at her giving her arm a squeeze. "I was truly just curious. They are a striking group though, aren't they?"

"Especially the brother. He looks simply charming."

"Watching are you?"

The lady gave him a seductive smile, "Just curious."

Jared laughed. "You vixen," he added giving her a look in return. The lady flushed at his attention. "I was wondering, if by any chance, they were related to the man that finagled Royce out of his ship," he said looking back at the four.

"Does that matter?"

Jared rolled his eyes. "No, but it makes for an easy introduction," he said pulling her along toward the group. "Royce may be interested in one of them."

"Oh, Jared. You're not planning on being a match maker again, are you? He almost killed you the last time."

Jared scowled down at her before continuing on. "He was simply in a bad mood that day. What could he possibly dislike about these three?"

Ruth McMaster shook her head. "It's your head. I would hate to see you loose any part of this magnificent body."

Jared squeezed her arm. "I'll let you examine me later to make sure it's still in proper form. Besides Royce won't even suspect me. I've gotten better at this."

Ruth snorted but quickly looked around to make sure no one had heard her. It wasn't ladylike to snort but Jared could lie like the best of them especially when his hide was on the line.

NATHAN WATCHED THE DARK HAIRED MAN across the way stare at his sisters and immediately was on guard. The man looked familiar yet he couldn't place him. The only people he associated with, of late, were gamblers and womanizers. Obviously, the man could be either one. Seeing the lady join him made him frown. Womanizer. Moving closer to his sisters he frowned. The man was coming their way.

"To our left, about six-two with a woman on his right about five-four," he whispered putting on what he hoped was an unsavory smile. Christopher had said he was supposed to look unapproachable.

"Forgive me for intruding, but I couldn't help wonder if by chance you were related to the Earl of Brentwood? He has done business with my family a few times," he explained tucking his wife against his side.

Nathan immediately relaxed giving them a genuine smile. "The Earl is our father. These are my sister's Jessica, Melissa, and Allison," he stated waiting while Jared kissed each of their hands, "and I'm Nathan."

"Jared McMaster, at your service. And this stunning woman is my wife, Ruth."

Ruth blushed but excepted the kiss Nathan gave her hand. "Don't let him fool you with his manners. He's just good at pretending."

Jared mocked injury at her words before turning to smile at the girls. "Are you enjoying the ball?"

"Oh yes. It's lovely," Melissa said blushing at having blurted that out like a simpleton.

Jessica grinned, making Melissa's face redden further. Nathan ignored them by asking if he was the McMaster that dealt in ships.

"We build the best in the area."

Jessica stepped forward. "I, for one, am glad to have met you. I sail one of your ships and I must say they are quite sound."

Both eyebrows went up on Jared's face and Ruth looked like she was about to faint.

Melissa laughed looking suddenly distraught, "she's teasing you."

"I am not. I named her the Titan," Jessica said giving Melissa a glare, "quite a fast ship, too."

Jared glanced at Nathan to confirm her words. Seeing him grin, Jared suddenly felt his face flush.

"You sail, like a passenger?" Ruth asked trying to understand exactly what the tall woman was saying.

"She's a captain of her own ship with a crew that seldom, if ever, complains," Allison supplied, feeling the need to defend Jessica all of a sudden. Getting a nudge from Nathan she turned her head slightly trying to look like she was looking at either of the two people in front of her.

"I don't doubt that she does," Jared finally said easing the tension that had suddenly sprung up. "I believe I recall Brand mentioning such a thing once."

Nathan chuckled at the look Melissa had on her face. She looked like they were going to burn her at the stake. "Jessica has been sailing for almost all her life. She just bought her own ship about four years ago."

Jessica smiled seeing Jared struggle to accept all he was hearing while Ruth looked absolutely shocked.

"I must say, Lady Jessica, you have knocked me speechless."

Ruth regained her composure enough to comment. "Believe me, that's not an easy task with him."

Jessica smiled at the pair, truly liking the situation. "It happens all the time. I'm used to it now."

Melissa was openly scowling at her now. "You could have refrained from mentioning that fact tonight. Once word gets out, no man will come within ten feet of you. More than likely they'll wonder if your going to make them walk the plank," she snapped crossing her arms in anger only to turn scarlet as she realized she'd just made a spectacle of herself.

"It won't bother me any," Jessica added giving her a devilish grin.

Nathan seeing a storm brewing stepped between them before looking again at Jared. "How is your business doing?"

"It's going quite well, though my brother handles everything now. I just deal in investments." Ruth pursed her lips at that, getting a pat on the arm from Jared.

Nathan smiled. "Just my kind of gent."

"You deal in investments?"

"Here and there," he answered slowly grinning as Jared's smile widened. Jared was a gambler.

"I believe I've done some business with you."

Nathan nodded his head. "I believe so. Your horse is doing well, or so my brother says."

Jared shook his head. "That was just pure luck on your part." At the nudge from Ruth and the look on her face Jared instantly lost his smile and began to stammer. "Of course, that was years ago."

Nathan grinned, "Years."

"And how, pray tell, did he get a horse from you?"

Jared stiffened and tilted his head. "I believe that's our song playing. If you'll excuse us," he added before grabbing his wife by the hand and pulling her toward the dance floor. The dancing had indeed begun.

"They're a nice couple," Nathan stated, smiling as they twirled away.

"Do they live close to us?" Allison asked.

Jessica shrugged. "Not exactly neighbors or anything, but father has bought at least six ships from the brother over the years. They make a fine vessel."

Melissa gave her a pinch. "Do you have to keep talking about such manly pursuits? If you go off spouting all that ship drivel I'll never find a husband."

"You could always go and mingle with Aunt Ginger." Nathan suggested pulling her away from Jessica, who looked ready to push her into the champagne fountain.

Melissa's face brightened. "That sounds wonderful. Do you mind Allison?"

Allison shook her head. "No, I'm sure Jessica and Nathan can stay with me." Melissa patted her hand before heading directly to Aunt Ginger's side. Nathan had to smile at the instant chatter that sounded from that area.

"Why didn't you send her off earlier?" Jessica said looking at the spot Melissa had pinched.

"If I had known you two would be at each other's throats all night, I would have."

Allison smiled. "I think it best she goes with Ginger. We embarrass her."

Jessica snorted. "She needs a little embarrassment. I had no idea she had such a superior attitude. Someone should knock her down a peg or two."

Allison frowned. "That isn't very nice."

"No, but it's true," Nathan added thoroughly irritated with Melissa for thinking she was better than her sisters.

"I'll volunteer to set her straight," Jessica said, her smile indicating she had a few ideas already.

Nathan laughed, "Maybe later."

ROYCE HAD BEEN WATCHING HIS BROTHER with the three women and felt has temper rise. Jared was always trying to set him up with a woman. Which lady was it to be? Ah, the raven haired one. Royce snorted. Jared was partial to black hair and always chose women for Royce that were dark haired. Royce much preferred the silver-haired one. The dark lady was beautiful he had to admit. Her black hair was pinned up and cascading down around her face in ringlets. She moved with natural grace and was very confident. The red head was furious and prissy looking. Royce frowned. How he wished he could listen to their conversation without being noticed. Jared was up to something, he was sure. The silver haired female caught his eye though and he couldn't understand why. She was beautiful, all right, but so were half the women here. The red head had a better body he decided as he watched her march over to stand by an older lady, who was surrounded by a group of the social gossips. Resuming his look at the other two he frowned. It must be the combination of the gown and the hair. Her hair was pinned up to one side and shimmered like moonlight. Royce snorted at himself. Some female just out of the cradle, by the looks of her, and he was ogling her hair. Still, it wouldn't hurt to dance with her. Just one dance and the opportunity to set Jared straight for once. Royce was willing to let Jared think he was actually going to court someone again. He smiled. It would get Jared off his back for a while too. At least this time, he would choose a lady he preferred rather than getting stuck with Jared's choice.

"TO YOUR LEFT, a man about six-four and alone," Nathan whispered grabbing another glass of champagne from a passing servant and putting it in Allison's hand.

"I am Lord McMaster and I couldn't help but notice my brother talking with you. Are you a client of ours?" Royce questioned nodding to each lady.

"Yes, we are. In fact, I captain one of your ships," Jessica said smiling. The man was surprised, but got over it quicker than his brother had.

"I'd heard the Earl had a daughter who sailed, but I thought it to be rumor." Jessica's brows went up at that. The man was actually challenging her.

"So you know who we are?"

"No. I wasn't sure until you said you sailed."

Nathan frowned. This man was being very vague. "I'm Nathan Hayworth and these are my sisters, Jessica and Allison." Royce nodded to each woman but frowned when Allison didn't even acknowledge his presence. She was scanning the crowd. Nathan watched the big man in front of him. He had brown hair, blue eyes and looked a lot like his brother. Nathan sensed a hardness about the man and didn't like the way he was looking at Allison. Nathan sucked in his breath when the man turned and asked Allison a question. The whole right side of his face from middle cheek back was scarred like it had been burned. Nathan quickly glanced at Jessica who was also staring at the scars. Nathan looked back at Royce only to be met with a cold blue gaze. Nathan flushed. It wasn't the first time he'd seen maimed or scarred men. Most of the men he gambled with were pock marked, and such, but to have someone approach him here was a bit unnerving. Nathan looked away and cleared his throat.

"I do hope we will be doing business with you in the future," Nathan stated looking back at Royce.

Royce clenched his teeth together. The same old reaction to his scars, yet it still bothered him. Everyone looked at him with sympathy or disgust. It had been six years since the accident, but Royce still wasn't used to his face. Nodding his head, Royce made to depart then remembered why he had come over in the first place.

"If you don't mind, and the lady wouldn't mind, I would like to dance with her," Nathan arched his brows, then quickly looked at Allison. She had no idea Royce was asking to dance with her.

"I'm sure Allison would be pleased to dance with you," Jessica said quickly watching Allison stiffen and pale slightly. Royce noticed the reaction and felt his temper near exploding. So she didn't want to have anything to do with a scarred freak. He couldn't exactly read disgust in her eyes, but her body language told wonders.

"That would be lovely," Allison heard herself saying. Suddenly feeling extremely nervous, she began to panic but Nathan's voice calmed her.

"Enjoy yourself," Nathan said taking Allison's glass from her.

Allison held out her left arm and felt Royce take it. He led her thirty-two steps out into the room then she felt him turn to face her. Trying to stay calm and remember all the practicing she'd done with Nathan, she reached out her left hand to place it on his shoulder and felt nothing. Paling some she moved her hand slightly to the right and still felt nothing. Starting to panic she felt tears form in her eyes.

"I don't think this is a good idea," she stammered while she lowered her hand back to her side. "Would you please return me to my brother?" she asked her voice noticeably quivering.

Nathan watched from his place next to Jessica as Royce led Allison out on the floor. She looked like any other female being led out for a dance. But as soon as they reached the dancing area he had backed away from her and Nathan watched in horror as Allison raised her hand and encountered air. The big oaf was too far away. Starting out on the floor, Nathan halted as the man grabbed Allison in his arms and began dancing with her. Looking around he slowly moved back to Jessica's side.

"She will want to go home now," Nathan said as Jessica grabbed his arm.

"Poor Allison. Ginger was wrong in making her come here. We'll never get Allison out of the house again."

Allison felt an arm come around her waist and her other hand was firmly grasped. She concentrated on controlling her tears but felt like everyone was staring at her. This was such a mistake. She should have just let her father choose a man for her instead of being humiliated in front of the entire social world. Royce watched the emotions cross the lovely face in front of him. Blind! Why hadn't her brother said anything? Royce had felt his anger evaporate the instant she held out her hand. She looked scared to death when her hand hadn't come in contact with his body, and Royce, being shocked, hadn't reacted fast enough. Feeling a little guilty, Royce tried to think of something to say, but she was trying very hard not to cry. Finally the tension was too much for her.

"Are they looking at me?" she whispered.

Royce glanced down at her bent head. "Who?"

"The other dancing couples?"

Royce looked around them then back at her "No, but if you keep your head down like that, I'm sure they will be." Her head instantly snapped up. He almost laughed at that, but seeing her lovely features up close, he felt something inside him stir. "Why do you hide your blindness?"

Allison frowned but didn't say anything. Trying to figure out what she was thinking, Royce studied her face. She had beautiful aqua-green eyes that reminded him of the sea on a sunny day and her features were soft.

"You haven't answered my question."

Allison faltered in her steps but Royce didn't seem to notice. "I don't know what to say."

"Perhaps you could start with why you didn't let me know you couldn't see before we came out here?"

"Would you still have danced with me?"

"Of course, but I don't understand why you hide what you are?"

"And what is that? A freak? I don't want to be handled like a fragile doll or have people leading me around like a child. I don't want people feeling sorry for me!" she finished through clenched teeth.

Royce knew exactly those feelings himself. After the accident, he'd stayed in his house and responded to all the estate business by letters. He excepted no visitors except family. Jared had been a big help but slowly bitterness had taken over Royce's life. He began to get sick of being treated like an invalid. His anger took over causing him to retreat farther away from everything and everyone. Finally, three years after the fire, Jared had brought home a woman. The lady had been told she was to dine with the Earl of Salisbury. Royce could still remember the look on the ladies face when Jared had introduced her to Royce in Royce's study. She lasted a full minute before fainting at his feet. Royce had flown into a rage and ordered Jared to remove the woman and never to come to his home again. Jared, of course, returned each week with a different female. Royce moved from rage into indifference as each woman fainted at his feet. Then one day, the years of anger and self-pity dawned on him and he started returning to his life. At first, it had been hard. People had been cruel. The stares and whispers had been the hardest to endure. But he hardened himself against that and now two years later he was back in high standing with the ton. He was an Earl after all and mothers all over London wanted a good match for their daughters. Though he rarely courted anyone, due largely to the fact that the ladies were disgusted with him, he still wished for a normal life with a wife and children. He had a large estate to pass onto a family of his own and someday he hoped to find a woman who could get past the scars.

"I think you should return me to my brother."

"We will finish the dance."

Allison didn't like the tone of his voice. The man was obviously displeased with her. She just wanted to go back with Nathan so they could return home. She would let her father choose a man to marry her to. She really didn't care, now. The person marrying her wasn't getting much anyway. In fact, her future husband was going to need someone to run his home, since Allison had very little experience in that area. She could sew, but again, it was nothing fancy. Writing wasn't a problem, as long as someone read the letters to her, then checked hers for neatness. If they were willing to accept her like she was, how could they ever accept Nero? Who in their right mind would marry a woman with a tiger?

The music seemed endless. Though Royce danced much better than Nathan did. Royce also made her ten times more nervous than her brother did. Royce was solid and stood well over six four. Allison wondered what he looked like.

"How is your first dance, Allison?"

"Melissa?" Allison asked over her shoulder.

"Who else, silly? And who might this be?" Melissa said pausing in her own dance to stare at Royce.

"Lord McMaster," turning slightly back to Royce she said, "this is my sister, Melissa."

Melissa held out her hand as the gentleman beside her scowled at Royce.

"Charmed," Royce murmured kissing her hand. When his eyes meet Melissa's, he saw the reaction so common to his scars and felt himself smile stiffly. Melissa looked ready to faint.

"And who might your gentleman be?" Allison asked, unaware of the tension between the three other people.

"Oh," Melissa stated blushing at her manners.

"Joshua Leaders, my lady," the gentleman said kissing Allison's hand. Allison smiled and dropped her hand back to her side.

"Finish your dance. I'll speak to you when we're through," Melissa stated pulling Joshua away.

Allison cocked her head to one side. "That's odd. She seemed in a hurry to get away from us." Then Allison giggled. "I think she might be worried I'll embarrass her. She's quite vain, you know."

Royce's features darkened. "Why do you let her treat you that way? A family should be loyal to its members."

"Oh, she's loyal. It's just that she needs a husband..." Allison's voice trailed off as she realized she almost told him too much about their situation.

"She needs a husband for what?"

"Like any lady, she expects to have a husband. She doesn't want me scaring off any possibilities." Allison said as Royce once again took her in his arms to finish the dance set.

"Like a lady such as yourself?" Royce asked not really expecting an answer and sure enough he didn't get one.

Chapter 7

"JONATHAN, there better be a good reason for pulling me away from the docks. I have shipments and reports stacked up from months ago. To top it off, I'm supposed to sail tomorrow morning on Jessica's ship," Stephan said striding into their father's study.

"It's a pretty good reason, I think," Morgan stated from his chair behind Stephan.

Stephan whipped around in surprise. "Who are you?" he demanded trying not to be rude but his temper was already up for being summoned like some common lackey.

"Stephan sit down," Jonathan said, "this is Morgan Sinclair, the Baron of Essex. He's come here with a complaint and I need you to clear it up."

"Sorry, Baron. I just have a lot of things on my mind. What can I do for you?" he asked sitting in the chair next to Morgan.

Again Jonathan answered before Morgan could. "It seems there has been some trouble over a client. Jacque Beaudaniere?"

"Jacque Beaudaniere? I've heard of him. In fact, he's a new client of mine." Stephan said looking at Jonathan then back at Morgan who was obviously simmering with anger. Alarmed, Stephan moved on to his next question. "Is there something wrong with Beaudaniere?"

"No. It's just the way you acquired his business," Morgan seethed, determined to hold his temper and give Jonathan a chance to ask his questions.

"What are you implying?" Stephan said, to Morgan's aggressive tone.

"I'm not implying anything. I'm saying you stole that client from me," Morgan shouted coming to his feet.

"Morgan!" Jonathan warned coming to his feet as well. "Stephan, have you been shipping wine to Beaudaniere for very long?"

"No. Jessica just put in an order for me to fill this month. I've only sent wine to him one other time. It was about a month ago."

"Who is Jessica?" Morgan snapped.

"She's our sister," Jonathan stated, a sick feeling forming in his gut. This had Jessica written all over it.

"What exactly happened between you and this client?" Stephan asked, not understanding the situation.

"My client, Jacques Beaudaniere, ordered seven shipments consisting of a considerable amount of wine. I sent two, both of excellent quality. It was my third shipment that Beaudaniere refused. In fact, he sent it back. He said the wine was watered down. I opened the wine myself and he was right. It was watered wine. Someone had filled half the kegs with water. Beaudaniere refused the other three shipments and is now getting his wine from you," Morgan said pacing behind the chairs.

"But that isn't our fault. He came to us since we are the only other shipper with a good reputation."

"So you would have me believe. But someone tampered with my wine? I investigated within by business but if I had to guess, I would say it was someone who needs a healthy profit for a struggling company," he stated giving Stephan a pointed look.

Stephan flushed. "My company is not struggling. I admit it isn't doing as well as it could be, but I've no need to steal."

"Now hold on you two. The key here is to find out who is responsible before going off half crazed."

"Ask this Jessica of yours. If she's the one who brought in the new client, then she will probably know about the wine."

Stephan swung at Morgan barely missing him. Jonathan grabbed Stephan from behind pulling him out of Morgan's reach. Jonathan felt uncertain at this point. Morgan was probably all too correct about Jessica.

Chapter 8

"I HAVE TO GO WHERE?" Jessica asked Christopher, who was barely visible behind the stack of papers on the desk in Ginger's study.

"I have a message here from Jonathan requesting your presence at home. It seems there is a problem with the shipping."

"I knew Stephan would mess things up. Well, I'll be on my way. Tell Father I'll need an extension on finding a groom," she said smugly.

"Wrong," Christopher's voice stopped her before she even made it to the door.

"What? I can't possibly find a husband, if I'm going up and down the coast, straightening out the mess Stephan made of my business."

"You'll just have to figure something out. Besides, Father isn't the one you should talk to about this. I am."

"You?"

"Father gave the responsibility over to me, remember? I, of course, will tell Father of your choice in husband, but the decision is completely up to me. Do you wish me to choose your husband for you?"

"Why you bastard! You've known this from the start," she said. "I can't believe Father didn't tell us. Did you know about this before we left?"

Christopher hesitated then gave a nod. Jessica exploded.

"Bloody Hell! Then you need to allow me more time. Say, a week. I need to see what Stephan has done to my business. No, better make it two weeks with travel time and all." Christopher was shaking his head before she even finished. "Why not?" At his stubborn look Jessica lost her temper. "You keep pushing me and I'll sail for another country and never come back!"

Christopher stood at this statement. "Don't you threaten me. I will take away the whole shipping business, until after you wed, if you continue to behave like a child. Father wants you married in three months time and I'm going to see that you are!" he finished in a shout.

"Then give me the two weeks I'm asking for," she gritted out.

"No."

"Christopher, you're forcing me to react badly," she stated, trying to regain control.

"I have enough to worry about without you threatening me. You will head home and return as fast as you can. You have until September before you need to be married."

"You can't do this," she said, eyes narrowed. When he didn't budge, she straightened and left the room.

Christopher grimly heard her slam out of the house. She was going to be a problem, whether he wanted to admit it or not. She was far too strong-willed to just go along. Sighing he sat down at his desk and pulled the closest mound of papers to him. Father had a lot of unfinished business and his sisters were only part of it.

"YOU HAVE TO GO BACK HOME?" Allison asked absently stroking Nero's fur.

"Yes. I'm leaving in the morning. Arty was the messenger Jonathan sent. I'll travel back by horse with him. We should be there in couple days."

"Would there be anyway for me to come along?"

Jessica stopped what she was doing to look at her sister. "You're not planning on hiding out at home are you?"

"No. I'm going to let Father choose my husband for me."

Jessica's mouth dropped open at that. "I think you better reconsider that idea. Christopher is the one choosing our husbands if we can't."

"Christopher? But Father said he was going to..."

"I know what he said, but Christopher just told me he was put in charge of that area. Father told him about it before we left."

Allison frowned. "It doesn't matter either way. I'm sure Christopher will pick a good husband for me. Really, I don't think I would know what to look for in a man, anyway. I only danced with one of them and he knew I was blind instantly. It's too hard to pick a man, when you can't see their face."

"I understand, Allison, but I think you should choose your own husband. In fact, I will personally investigate any man you think would suit you. How does that sound?"

"But you're not going to be here."

"As to that," she said dryly, "Christopher has practically guaranteed my return. I will only be gone for two weeks. In that time, you should have a list of men for me to investigate."

Allison felt a little hope slipping into her heart. "Do you really think you will have the time to deal with me and my problems? You're looking for a husband, too."

"Of course. Now go tell Melissa she's got a grace period of two weeks before I return. She should be happy about that."

"She's already had two men show up today to take her on outings. Ginger had to assign a permanent maid as chaperone."

Jessica rolled her eyes and laughed, "At least one of us will be married by the end of the month."

Chapter 9

MELISSA SAT NERVOUSLY beside the blond man who had danced with her the previous night. He hadn't said much to her while they were at the ball so when the butler announced that the Earl of Cantenbury was there to see her she had nearly fainted. He was a huge man towering over her by nearly a foot. He was broad shouldered, blue eyed, and very handsome. The Earl didn't talk much or look in her direction but Melissa figured he was shy. So to help along the situation Melissa tried several times to engage him in conversation but he had curtly answered her giving her the impression she wasn't suppose to talk. As the ride moved along, they reached London's main square and her spirit's rose. The city was alive with activity and people milled around all the little shops. He informed her they would lunch at a small place on the north side of town and then walk through the shops where she could look at the things the shopkeepers had to offer. She was so excited she almost forgot about the silent giant beside her. The constant frown on the Earl's face had her feeling she was making all kinds of mistakes. As they traveled through town, a tangle of three carriages blocked their path forcing them to reroute.

"We'll have to go back and cross by the docks," the Earl said.

Melissa nodded, though she needn't have bothered. The Earl wasn't asking her a question, he was telling her what they were going to do. Melissa pursed her lips. This man was gorgeous, but would never do for a husband. Too bossy! Shrugging she decided to look forward to the sights of London and the shops instead.

As they circled around and started down toward the docks, a horrific smell started to get overwhelming. The Earl handed her a handkerchief and held one of his own over his nose. She felt like laughing at how ridiculous they looked, but the burly men wandering around without any shirts stunned her. They were half naked! Eyes bulging she watched as they moved goods around on the docks. Their straining muscles hauling crates easily.

"I'm sorry you had to witness the dregs. I had forgotten how awful the docks are this time of day. The Three Kings is just up ahead. We will be away from the stench shortly."

Melissa flushed at his words. Her brother worked in a place like this. She never thought much about it, but apparently it wasn't part of the social ton to work on the docks. She would have to remember that in the future. Looking back over her shoulder she saw a giant of a man lifting a crate onto his shoulder as he balanced his way up into a ship. He sure was a fine figure of a man. Even if he was a dreg, as the Earl had called him.

Chapter 10

ALLISON LAID HER HEAD ON HER ARMS and listened to the sounds around her. She had only seen Jessica today and she hadn't had time to chat. Nathan wasn't home and Christopher never came out of the study. Ginger informed them she was setting up luncheons for them to meet with the other ladies of society. Figuring on having time alone, Allison had walked to the edge of the garden and laid down on her stomach to listen to the sounds of London. Being so close to the park, she could pick out sounds of people talking. They were too far away to understand, but some children were playing a game somewhere off to the north of her. Large flocks of ducks were voicing their hunger to some laughing women. A dog barked off to the right making Nero growled. She heard him disappear into a hedge along the garden fence as birds chirped over her head. But the most frequent sound she heard was the rumble of carriages and the clip clop of the horses pulling them. London, it seemed, was a very busy place.

Drifting on the current of city sounds, Allison didn't hear Royce approach. He watched the lovely girl in front of him and could tell she was listening to the sounds around her. Moving forward he stopped instantly hearing the low growl coming from the hedge.

"What is it, Nero?"

"Excuse me?" Royce asked. Then arched his brows as the relaxed girl in front of him sprang to her feet as if she'd been burned.

"I didn't hear you come up," she blurted wiping her hands down her gown as she got to her feet.

"Do you have a dog in the hedge?" Royce asked eyeing the growling bush.

"Ah, not exactly. Nero, stay! It's all right," she said hoping the big cat stayed hidden.

Royce, still eyeing the hedge, moved closer to Allison. "I was wondering if you would care for an evening of dinner and the opera?" Royce immediately felt his face flush. The opera! She wouldn't be able to see that.

"That sounds lovely, " she said, disbelief clearly on her face. The Earl of Salisbury was asking her to an opera. Imagine that. "I will have to ask my brother, of course." Wouldn't Melissa be surprised, she thought, excitement making her fidget. Smiling she asked, "Would you like to go ask him now? He should be in his study."

"All right," Royce said watching the girl try to contain her excitement. Royce wrapped her arm around his, purely fascinated with her as she tried not to grin over the idea of the opera. Her face was aglow with excitement.

Allison felt nervous. She couldn't believe the Earl had come to see her. They hadn't exactly been on the friendliest of terms and she was blind, for God's sake!

"By the way, if Christopher lets me go with you, this will be my first visit to the opera."

Royce frowned. People were going to stare. She would probably feel the tension and think it was due to her blindness. "Of course," he answered beginning to doubt his actions. Maybe he shouldn't have come here?

They walked into the house and Allison verbally gave directions to the study. "Is the door closed?"

"Yes."

"Good." Christopher was home. Lifting her hand she knocked. 'Come in' came the muffled reply. "I hope he's in a good mood," she whispered pushing the door open and pulling Royce inside. Royce frowned. Was her brother an ogre?

Christopher looked up from his papers and stared at the two people in his office. One, in particular, made him scowl. "Thank you, Allison. Could you have Netty bring us more brandy, please?"

Allison laughed. "He's not here to see you, silly. Lord McMaster's is here to see me," she said giggling. "He's asked me to the opera and dinner."

Christopher stiffened. "He did, did he? And do you want to go?" Something in Christopher's voice made her slowly loose her smile. Did he know the Earl?

Royce was frowning too. Not only did Christopher know him, but he didn't like him. The same brown haired bitch had taken them both for a ride.

"Of course I want to go. I wouldn't be in here, if I didn't," Allison answered still puzzled with Christopher's tone of voice.

"I see," Christopher said. Allison frowned when she heard him shuffling papers. Hearing the ink well being dipped into made her purse her lips. He was ignoring them.

"Christopher! What is the matter with you?" More paper shuffled. Turning toward Royce she apologized. "I'm sorry, my lord. I don't understand why he's being so rude. I think it best if you go and I'll speak with him. I'll send word about later."

"You will not be going anywhere with him and that's final."

Allison whirled around to face her brother. "And why not?"

"I think you should ask him." Christopher stated, staring at Royce. Royce felt the muscles in his jaw tick. How could he have been so stupid? Of course, it had been nearly seven years ago when Helen Montgomery had pitted Christopher and Royce against each other. Both had been heirs to Earldoms and she was after the one with the largest fortune. Naturally, both men were oblivious to the true intentions of the greedy bitch, but each had pursued her knowing of the other until she'd finally chosen Royce. Christopher, having six siblings to hand out portions of the estates to, had lost. Shortly after her choice was made, Royce had his accident. Helen's true self had came forth and she left him, without a backward glance. She'd married a rich young Earl three weeks later. Royce had been angry, at the time, but now looking back he was thankful Helen had left him. It was believed the lady still maintained several lovers while spending the young Earl's money lavishly. Christopher was obviously still bitter at the humiliation he'd suffered even though the woman was a complete waste of a human being.

"Lord Royce, do you know Christopher?"

"We know of each other. Though, this is the first time I have spoken to him."

"Then Christopher? I don't understand your attitude."

"My attitude isn't the issue. Father said I was in full charge of you and your sisters. I say you can't see this man and you won't."

Allison felt herself flush. "I am twenty-two years old and I believe Father made it clear I was to choose myself a husband. In short, I am to go on outings to figure that out." Turning to Royce she completely ignored Christopher "If you will pick me up at seven, I'll be ready!" she stated slamming out of the study.

Christopher stared at the closed door for a second, then turned his cool gaze on Royce. "You will not show up at seven."

"And if I do?"

"Do you honestly think I would let you date my sister? Look at you." The disgust in his voice was Royce's breaking point. He grabbed Christopher by the shirtfront and yanked him across the desk.

"I would watch what I said, if I were you."

"A little touchy about your disgusting appearance?"

Royce pulled back and swung. Christopher ducked and landed a punch to Royce's ribs. Royce grunted lifting Christopher over the desk as papers went everywhere. The two man circled each other looking for a clear shot.

"I see I have it right. That ugly face of yours is a sore subject." Royce's fist landed hard against his jaw sending Christopher back over the desk.

"I'm taking your sister to the opera and you should get used to this ugly face. I plan to be around after your sister," Royce stated heading for the door. Christopher's words made him pause.

"Need a blind woman to stomach that face?" The words hung in the air, as Royce clenched and unclenched his fists several times. Taking a deep steadying breath, he walked from the study. If he had stayed, he would have killed him.

Chapter 11

JESSICA WALKED THROUGH THE FRONT DOOR and heard utter silence. "Is anybody home?" she yelled tipping her head to listen.

"In the study," came a faint reply.

Jessica handed her gloves and hat to the now present Hobkins and headed for the study.

"Okay, Jonathan. What the hell did Stephan do to my business?" she asked walking up and putting both hands flat on the desk.

"Your business is fine. It's Jacque Beaudaniere that worries me."

Jessica flushed. "I don't know what you mean."

Jonathan scowled. She was guilty. "It seems the Baron of Essex has run into a bit of trouble and Stephan ended up gaining an excellent client with a healthy appetite for wine."

"I don't know anything about any trouble," Jessica said straightening to move to a chair. She halted in her tracks when she saw Stephan lounging in one.

"Me, mess up your business? I think you messed things up quite well on your own."

"What's that suppose to mean?"

"Don't play stupid. I've been friends with the Baron long enough to know he does his research before he accuses someone of treachery. What happened?" Jonathan demanded.

"Nothing."

"Jessica!"

"Fine. What do you want to know? Yes, I am supplying Jacque wine, what of it?"

"The Baron claims his wine was tampered with. Do you know anything about that?" Stephan asked sitting forward in his chair.

"Well, of course not. Why would I need to water someone's wine?"

"Ha! I never said anything about watered wine." Stephan stated smiling like a cat with a mouse. Jessica turned scarlet and quickly glanced at Jonathan.

"Tell me it wasn't you." Jonathan murmured.

"It wasn't me."

"Don't lie!" Jonathan exploded. "You watered down his wine and stole his client? That's beyond the code. My God, Jessica, you're a thief."

"I am not a thief. He's the thief. He stole six of my clients when I first started out. I vowed to get revenge and Jacque's account was the only one worth the six he took," she shouted pacing in front of the desk.

"What six clients?" Stephan asked standing.

"He's the one who took Marcus and Antonio."

"Those weren't ours yet."

"He told them we were amateurs and only had one ship."

"That was the truth."

"He took New Guinea and Gibralter as well."

"And how did he manage that?" Stephan asked sternly.

Jessica frowned. "Arty said he overheard the Baron stating seven ships could deliver more goods than two."

"The truth again."

"But those would have allowed us to purchase more ships. We wouldn't have been forced to run up and down the coast," Jessica argued.

"It doesn't matter. Any businessman will tell you, it's fair business to tell the truth about the competition. You've done an underhanded thing and ruined our reputation as shippers." Stephan yelled pointing his finger straight at her nose.

Jessica felt the tears form in her eyes. It had been years since she had wanted to cry, but to have her brothers yelling at her for something even she thought was stupid, made the tears fall without her consent. Bowing her head she nodded.

Stephan ran his fingers through his hair. Taking a deep breath to control his temper, he asked, "you mentioned six. Who are the other two?"

"Curtis and McNally," she said quietly.

"Those two left after finding out you sailed our ships," Stephan bellowed with renewed anger.

"He probably told them I was sailing," she said not looking up as she sank into a chair.

"Of all the dumb things you've done Jessica, this one takes the cake. Jonathan, what the hell are we going to do now?"

"I don't know," he said rubbing his hands across his eyes. "How much money do you have? Could you pay the Baron back?"

"I could just give him the money I get for each run, but that still doesn't restore his reputation."

Jessica was openly crying now. "I didn't think this far ahead," she whispered.

"That's obvious," Stephan stated frowning. "What could have possessed you to do such a thing? You must have known the Baron wouldn't let a thing like this go. Especially at the prices Jacque is paying."

Jessica just shook her head.

"Well, it's done," Stephan said as Jonathan awkwardly patted Jessica's shoulder. All we have to do now is figure out what to do about the Baron. Wiping the tears from her eyes she sat straighter in the chair, realizing that she could fix this.

"I have a solution. I will give him my ship. I have to marry, anyway, I don't think my new husband is going to let me sail," she said sniffing.

Jonathan frowned at the sadness he heard in her voice.

"How much of the business is hers, Stephan?"

"She owns the Titan and has a third in my market."

Silence followed. "There's still the reputation she ruined."

"That's simple. The captain of my ship is not widely known to be a woman. You could start a rumor of the Captain's treachery, using a different name of course. Explain to him how the captain lied about the Baron and watered his wine. That should restore the Baron's name. My ship could be given to him as restitution. I only ask that you give my crew a place on one of your ships, Stephan."

Jonathan didn't like her suggestion, but he admired Jessica for owning up to the trouble she caused.

"Perhaps that won't be necessary. I will talk to the Baron and maybe we can work this out as gentlemen. But in the future, I hope you will think about what you're doing. And above all, obey the laws."

Jessica nodded as she left the room. Tears flowed down her cheeks as she made her way to her room. In the future! Ha! She was going to be married in a little over two months to some arrogant bastard who wouldn't let her be herself. She might as well become a nun. She was never going to fit the role she was being forced into.

"WELL, WHAT DO YOU THINK?" Stephan said drinking his entire glass of brandy before filling it again.

"I think we are in serious trouble. Morgan is a reasonable man, but I happen to know he doesn't like to be cheated. I also know, he doesn't deal well with the culprit once he catches him either"

. "But Jessica is a woman and our sister. Surely he will be understanding about this?"

"I think that Jessica being a woman will make it more difficult. No one likes being bested by a woman."

Stephan nodded and drained another glass. "I suppose you have some sort of plan?"

"No. I was hoping you might have one."

"Damn, what a mess. I was hoping she wasn't involved.

"What am I going to say?" he asked running a hand through his hair. "I actually told Morgan it was beyond us to steal."

"When will you see him?"

"Tonight. I had planned on telling him smugly we were not involved and that I was more than happy to help find the thief. Now I haven't a clue what to say. Bloody hell, there must be a way for everyone to come out of this all right?"

"Jessica's idea does have merit. We could invent someone to take the blame and then pay Morgan off. Jessica could purchase another ship from me. The Barons name would be restored and we would still have our business."

Jonathan nodded. "We still have to tell the Baron the truth. If he agrees to the plan then we'll proceed from there. If he doesn't, I think the Hayworth name may be mud to a great many people. Christopher should be informed of this."

"Oh, no," Stephan said holding up his hands, "you tell him. Last time he gave me a black eye."

Jonathan frowned. "I hope Morgan will agree. This could ruin everything."

"This should never have happened. Jessica wouldn't have done this, if mother were here to keep her in line."

"There's nothing we can do about it now. Lets just hope Morgan is understanding." Both men looked at each other then downed another glass of brandy.

Chapter 12

MELISSA GLANCED FOR THE THIRD TIME at the clock above the mantle at the end of the dining room. The Earl had been talking for fifteen minutes and Melissa was bored to tears. This man was the most boring fellow ever born. He talked of nothing but himself and she was not to say a word! He answered his own questions with remarks of his own. She sat there adjusting and smoothing her napkin until she thought she would go mad. The man ate like a snail too. Chewing each bit six times. In her boredom, she had actually counted.

"Shall we shop?" he asked, nearly getting knocked over as Melissa hastily got to her feet.

"That would be wonderful."

Leaving the restaurant, he led her into the square of shops. It didn't take long before Melissa felt depression replace her excitement. The Earl selected things he thought she would like and then gave his approval of each item. Melissa was becoming quite furious. He was a complete bore! After the fifth stifled yawn, Melissa was about to ask to be taken home when she located a small portly gentlemen selling ribbons, silk, and other cloths. Detaching herself from the bore, she hurried over to the booth.

"Excuse me?"

The man smiled a broad smile. "What can I do for such a lovely rose? The man asked, pulling out some cloth that would look stunning on her.

"Do you have ribbons in the color of teal?" she asked giving him her broadest smile.

"Of course, but I think yellow or red would set off the color in your hair better," he stated holding out the two colors.

"It's not for me. But you are correct, red is one of my favorites." The man grinned at her and handed her the teal.

"This is perfect. How much are they?"

"For you, one shilling." Melissa smiled. She had that with her. Paying the man she received her package and turned to leave only to run smack into the bore. Looking up she could see he was angry.

"You should have said you wanted ribbons. I would have bought them for you." The tone in his voice told her she had made a mistake.

"It's all right I..."

"Next time just let me know."

Melissa had to bite holes in her tongue to keep from giving him a good tongue lashing. When she saw they were going in the direction of the knife booth, she rolled her eyes. Hunting stories, her favorite.

Chapter 13

ALLISON TRIED TO SIT STILL as Netty worked on her hair but she was too excited and nervous. "Why do you suppose Christopher doesn't want me to see Lord McMaster?"

"I haven't a clue, love."

"Well, if he doesn't come for me tonight, Christopher is going to regret interfering. I will have Nero bite him."

Netty laughed. The big cat was all talk. She had never seen it do more than growl at anyone.

"It isn't funny, Netty. Christopher was very rude to Lord McMaster. I doubt he will come back. I haven't exactly been very friendly to him myself. If Christopher doesn't let up, I will never get to know him."

"What do you mean you weren't friendly? I don't think Lord McMaster would have come around, if you had been rude and unpleasant."

"That's just it. At the ball the other night, I danced with him once and bungled the whole situation. He knew I was blind instantly. Furthermore, I got a little short with him when he implied Melissa wasn't loyal to her family. I haven't exactly shown my social graces."

"Well, you must have done something right. He wouldn't have come to see you today, otherwise."

Allison frowned. She wondered exactly why he had come?

Royce at that exact moment was wondering that himself. He had never pursued a woman after a ball like this. Yet, Allison intrigued him. Perhaps the fact that she was living a little like he was, made him think they could relate. But Allison hadn't seen the stares and odd looks they had received last night. Royce ran his fingers through his hair angrily. He probably shouldn't see her tonight. Christopher didn't like the idea. Why it hadn't occurred to him that Christopher and Allison were related was beyond him. A different son had always been with Brand Hayworth when they had made the ship deals. Royce's brows drew together. How many Hayworth children were there? Three girls and three sons? That was a very large family. Did they all know about his involvement with Christopher? Obviously not, since none of them present at the ball had said anything. His frown deepened as Jared entered the study.

"What's on your mind, brother?" the younger man asked grabbing a glass and filling it with brandy.

"Nothing."

Jared laughed. "A frown like that doesn't come from thinking about nothing. Could it have anything to do with the beautiful silver haired Lady Hayworth?" Royce's frown deepened as his eyes narrowed. "So it does. Has she fainted at your feet yet?"

Royce gave a heavy sigh. "Jared, you're always poking your nose into my business and I don't like it. The only reason I danced with the girl is because I saw you scanning the three. I knew the raven haired one would end up in my company and I was trying to beat you to the quick."

Jared hooted. "So you did know? Ruth said you would."

Royce scowled. "Did you want something?" he said clearly annoyed now.

"Actually, I do. I was wondering if you were going out tonight?"

"I don't think that is any of your business."

"Probably not. But as your brother, I feel it's my duty to warn you of danger. Nathan Hayworth says you are planning to take his sister to the opera. He advises against that."

"How the bloody hell did you learn of this already?"

Jared smiled. "I had a friendly game of cards with the lad. Lost too! Why is he warning you off?"

"None of your business." Royce stated walking to look out the window.

"Nathan wouldn't tell me either. You know I'll just tag along tonight and find out."

"You're a rotten brother."

Jared plopped down into a chair by the hearth. "I know. Mother says I was born to irritate you. Of course, I'm one not to shirk my duty, so here I am."

Royce shook his head. "Allison is something to look at, isn't she?"

"Definitely," Jared said, and then laughed when Royce gave him a stern look. "Well, she's not to my taste. A bit too exotic for me."

"I probably won't see her tonight. I shouldn't subject her to the stares and taunts I always receive."

"I thought you were past all that. Your scars are hardly noticeable anymore."

Royce snorted. "People are uncomfortable around me."

"She mustn't mind, or she wouldn't have danced with you last night and she wouldn't have agreed to the outing tonight. Besides you already asked her. You can't stand her up now."

Royce frowned. She didn't know he had scars. The stares were oblivious to her, too, but what if someone said something to her? She wouldn't have the slightest idea what they were talking about. Perhaps he should tell her about the scars. If she still wanted to go with him, then he would take her. Shaking his head he knew he wouldn't tell her for fear of losing her. She was the first breath of fresh air he'd had in years.

"I think I will take her someplace else tonight. Perhaps a carriage ride around the park or something like that."

"You'll get mugged."

"Then I'll bring her back here for dinner and cards."

"She'll be marked as your whore."

Royce frowned. That was true. "How about if you join us for dinner? It would be a social evening then."

Jared tapped his fingers on the rim of his glass. Royce was acting odd about this. Perhaps this woman meant something to him? After just one dance at a ball? Jared slapped his thigh. "All right, Royce, you have yourself a chaperone. I expect to bring my wife along so that means putting Apollo and Zeus away," he stated knowing the two large wolfhounds set his wives nerves on edge. "It also won't be as fun as the opera. Will your lady still accept your invitation?"

"I don't know. I'll send someone over now."

Jared watched in amazement as his recluse of a brother wrote a message to a lady he hardly knew. And he was inviting her to his home, no less. Jared's brows drew together. Perhaps there was something here he was missing.

"I'M READY, NETTY. How do I look?" Allison asked standing in the middle of the room, twirling.

Netty smiled. The ribbon in her hair was crooked and the dress was caught up in the back. "You need a few minor adjustments, love."

Allison stood patiently while Netty fixed the dress. "I always seem to get it caught up back there. What does it catch on?"

"It folds under the petticoats and I guess you can't feel the difference in material. You always manage with the front."

Allison frowned, feeling the lumpy back of her dress, "it feels all wrinkly."

"That's the petticoats. Now touch this."

"I still feel the wrinkles but there's material over it," Allison smiled, "I think I will be able to do it next time. How is my hair?"

"Still crooked. You hold your left elbow too low when you tie it up."

"Oh. Would you fix it for me, please?"

Netty smiled, adjusting the ribbon. "You look beautiful."

"Thank you. I hope I can manage in his lordship's home. I wonder what it will be like?"

"I'm sure it's grand. Miss Melissa could give you every detail in a minute. Unfortunately she isn't going with you."

"Perhaps his lordship will talk about his home and give me all the details. I don't know how he expects me to play cards, though. I didn't have the heart to point that out."

"I'm sure you'll work something out, dear. His brother is going to be there. Does he know about your blindness?"

Allison frowned. Royce had promised not to tell anyone. Jared was his brother and if they were anything like her brother they didn't keep secrets from each other. "I expect he will know, but I'm glad I won't have to suffer seeing the sympathy in his eyes. I will be completely defeated if any of them treat me like a child."

Netty smiled at the stubborn lift of Allison's chin. "There you go, love. You are absolutely breathtaking. Neither of the men will treat you like a child because you look too much like a full grown woman."

Allison smiled. "You flatter me, Netty."

CHRISTOPHER swiped a stack of papers off the desk and got to his feet. Of all the people to come calling on Allison, why the Earl of Salisbury? The bloody bastard. What was the Earl thinking? Christopher wasn't going to forget the whole incident and act like they were the best of friends? Moving to the window, he stared out over the beautiful gardens Ginger had around her house. He could still remember Helen Montgomery as if it were yesterday. She had beautiful brown hair with striking hazel eyes. She was the sweetest woman he had ever met, and she had treated Christopher like a god until that bastard had come along. Helen had been seeing them both, but at the time Christopher hadn't known it. It wasn't even eight months later that she was married to someone else. Though Helen had told Christopher she was marrying Royce, God saw to it that Royce was treated with what he deserved. The fire had left him horribly scarred, forcing Helen to marry another. Christopher frowned at his own thoughts, he never wished for another human being to suffer from something so terrible as that, but deep down he was glad the two had never married.

It was starting to get dark outside and Christopher leaned a shoulder against the window frame. He wondered how life would have been if he'd married Helen. Would they have had children? He also wouldn't be worrying about finding someone to marry in the next six months, either. He was pulled from his thoughts by a knock on the study door. Turning, he frowned as Nathan strolled in looking remarkably content.

"What brings you here looking so smug?"

"Oh, nothing really. I just happened to have bested your old enemy's brother, today. I took him for nearly three hundred pounds."

Christopher smiled. "McMaster?" At Jared's nod, he grinned, "he happens to be close to my age and I think old enemy is a bit strong."

"Perhaps," he remarked sitting in the chair with his feet up on the desk, "but I don't think you'll have to worry about Royce seeing Allison tonight. I told his brother to give him a message about seeing her. Jared wanted to know the reason, but I didn't enlighten him, and he seemed to take me seriously."

Christopher frowned. What was he supposed to do if Royce showed up this evening. Allison would never forgive him if he didn't come. She might retreat into herself after that kind of rejection.

"What's wrong?"

"I was just thinking about what this will do to Allison."

"Don't worry about her. Once you explain the situation to her, I'm sure she will understand."

"You didn't see her today. She was trying to prove a point to me today. She made sure I knew she was old enough to make her own choices and I didn't need to interfere."

Nathan laughed. "Father gave you the right to interfere. Besides, she'll feel compassion for you Christopher. Allison has a gentle heart."

"Maybe so, but she has a temper, too."

"A little steam never hurt anybody, especially coming from a woman."

Christopher looked at his brother and shook his head. Nathan would some day meet a woman that would throttle him good before he would ever believe that women were dangerous when their tempers were raised.

Chapter 14

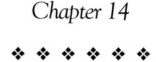

JESSICA ROLLED OVER ONTO HER BACK and stared at the ceiling. Her eyes were swollen from crying for the past hour. She was such a fool. Her brothers thought bad of her now. How could she have possibly thought she could best the Baron? He was thought to be one of the most disreputable men around. But as usual, her ideas weren't thought through entirely and she ended up in trouble. Thank goodness she hadn't been caught in the act. Arty and Dane would have hung. Scrambling off the bed, Jessica ripped off her traveling clothes, put on tight fitting breeches with knee high boots, a billowy white blouse and a bandana she wrapped around her neck. Tying her hair up in back, she slammed a hat on her head then left the room. It didn't take her long to find Arty. He was waiting for her just outside the kitchen door.

"It took you long enough, Captain. I was beginning to think your brothers meant to keep you all night."

"I think that was the plan, but I've changed them," she said heading for the stables. "We're leaving up the coast tonight."

"But the crew's in the village. It will take me half the night to find them."

"I'm sure you're able. Get Dane to help."

Arty stopped in his tracks, "but captain, Dane never comes ashore."

"He will. It's dark out."

Arty frowned. Something was terribly wrong. "Captain? Is there a problem?"

"Arty you talk too much," Jessica snapped lengthening her stride into the barn. Grabbing a saddle, she quickly saddled a brown mare then turned to saddle another. "We are sailing before anything changes. My brothers want to sell my ship," she stated frowning at the lie. It was her fault her ship was being sold. The Baron would never agree anyway. She would be completely ruined when he was through with her. She wasn't going to allow that to happen. Arty nudged her out of the way his face set with determination.

"Don't worry, Captain. We'll round the men up tonight."

Jessica patted his shoulder a small twinge of guilt nagging at her.

Chapter 15

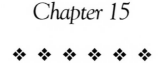

"IF YOU CAN'T HAVE SOMETHING IN BLUE ready for tomorrow, then I will take my business elsewhere," Melissa said firmly glaring at the woman who stood an inch or two shorter than she. Nathan rolled his eyes and crossed his arms. Melissa acted like she knew everything there was to know about fashion. The shorter woman pursed her lips and laid the material on the couch.

"If Mademoiselle would hold still long enough for me to get proper measurements, then perhaps I could accomplish the tasks she has set for me. Of course it will cost more, Cherie."

Nathan burst out laughing at the expression on Melissa's face. She didn't know what to do. The woman was being accommodating yet bumped up the price.

"But of course, Madame Boudoir. I was only getting impatient. I have a ball tomorrow night that I don't dare miss. I just can't seem to find a thing to wear."

Madame Boudoir smiled at Melissa. "You are a beautiful flower. No matter what you wear, you will be the belle of the ball, wee?"

Nathan wanted to retch though Melissa was smiling brilliantly at that drivel. Walking around the backside of Melissa, Miss Boudoir gave Nathan an outrageous wink. Nathan smiled and nodded his head. She knew her business. Melissa would have thrown her out if the gown wasn't supplied by the next evening. Turning back to the window he frowned as a coach moved up the drive and an elegantly dressed man descended from the coach. McMaster! What nerve!

Moving into the dining room, Nathan paused seeing Nero. The big cat was sitting in the entrance. Nathan moved to go around him only to have the cat growl at him.

"Nero, I will cut off all your food if you don't get out of the way."

The cat crouched and continued to growl. Moving toward the door deciding to ignore Nero, Nathan found himself flat on his back with Nero casually licking his neck. The great cat had come at him so fast and unexpectedly that fighting wasn't even a thought. Nero had him pinned to the floor, his great weight holding him down so that he could barely manage to breath. Knowing the cat had never done anything like this before Nathan wasn't really worried. A slight shifting of his body to get a better breath of air brought Nero's head up and those green eyes staring into his. Swallowing Nathan realized Nero meant business.

"I will get even with you, Nero." The cat blinked at him, growled, before moving one of his big paws farther up his chest. The weight was making it difficult to breath. Damn this was all he needed. Christopher was going to be furious. Closing his eye's he tried to relax. Was life worth risking a permanent maiming? Taking shallow breaths he relaxed deciding a fit from Christopher was the better than missing parts.

ALLISON JUMPED when Hobkins announced she had a visitor. Allison smiled. If Nero was doing his job, Nathan would be occupied and Christopher was busy in the study. That gave her enough time to grab her cloak and reticule and be gone before anyone noticed. Allison quickly made her way down the stairs toward the foyer.

Royce watched her descend the stairs with a smile. She was a lovely woman. Her hair was cascading down the side of her head falling in ringlets around her shoulders. She wore a pale blue gown that made her eyes look a stunning green. She was tall for a woman he noticed when she came to stand in front of him.

"You look lovely," he said smiling. She blushed then laughed as she held out her hand.

"Thank you, my lord. I will have to take your word for it."

His smiled deepened. She was comfortable with her sight and suddenly he wished he could be as comfortable with his own flaws.

"I think we better go, my lord. My brothers are not pleased."

"They don't want you to go?"

"No. In fact, Christopher forbid it. But I'm old enough to make my own decisions My Father is the one tell me yes or no. And he would approve of you."

Glancing around the foyer, Royce frowned. The Butler stood there ready to open the door. He wore a look of impatience but other than that he wasn't letting anything else show.

"Shouldn't you at least tell them where you've gone?"

"I did. I left a note on my brother's desk. It will probably take him hours to find it, but I did leave him one."

Royce's frown deepened. "I don't like this."

"I won't be able to go otherwise."

Royce glanced at the butler, Hobkins shrugged and opened the door. Royce frowned at that. "Perhaps I should speak to Christopher?"

"No!" Allison said grabbing his arm, "he will only cause a trouble. My maid knows where I've gone so all he'll have to do is ask her." Allison said knowing she had told Netty to stay hidden for at least three hours before she made herself available to questions. Allison smiled, "it will be fine. Trust me," she said sweetly heading for the door.

"I don't like this," Royce mumbled.

"Where is the owner of the house?" Royce asked as they approached the carriage.

"My Aunt Ginger lives here. She was going to the opera with some important ladies. She's trying to throw all three of us girls into the social set. Isn't that sweet of her? Unfortunately, I don't feel I will be going to many balls in the future. I think one was all I can stomach."

Royce smiled as he handed her into the carriage. "I think you did fine at your first ball."

"You would," she said sitting and pulling her gown around her legs. "I made a fool of myself in front of you. I was like a shy goose the rest of the night. I only danced a few times and two of them were with Nathan."

"I noticed."

Allison frowned. Was that approval in his voice? "Are you teasing me?"

"On the contrary. I'm glad you didn't dance with many others. I wouldn't want to fight to many for your attention," Royce frowned at himself. He hadn't meant to say anything like that at all. The woman was making him into a besotted sod. Glancing at her he saw she liked what he'd said. The smile on her face was telling.

"Did you tell your brother of my sight?"

Royce's eyebrows went up at that, "I told you I wouldn't and I didn't."

Allison frowned. "I wish you had. I could have relaxed then."

"We could tell him when we arrive?"

"No. I don't want him to treat me like a child."

"Jared wouldn't do that," Royce said remembering how his brother had treated him when the accident had first happened, "in fact, I think my brother will like you very much."

Allison smiled relaxing against the seat. This was going to be an interesting evening.

Chapter 16

"WE LEAVE IN THE MORNING on the first tide. I want all the crew located and brought on board," she told her men as she threw her belt on the table and reached down to pull out her black boots and knife. Shutting the closet doors she sat behind her desk in the cabin and faced the two men.

"Won't your brothers come looking for you, Captain?" This came from Arty who was already worried.

"I'm sure they will but I'm hoping the water will be high enough to get us adrift."

"They'll follow in the Gallant or the Lisa. Both are unloaded and waiting to go on their next trips."

"Is the Titan empty?"

"Yes, ma'am. Except for the silk from Gallaway."

"Excellent. We'll take that to Meroco and sell it. That was payment for the shipment of wine, correct?"

Arty nodded.

"That will take us at least two weeks. I'll purchase some goods in Meroco to sell further up the coast taking about a month at sea."

"What about London?" Dane asked using his sign language.

Jessica frowned up at the man. He was six foot six inches and at least three feet wide. A giant among men with dark bronzed skin, white hair, and red eyes. People gawked at him no matter where he went but as a sailor he was indispensable. No one messed with a woman captain when Dane was aboard.

"I'm not returning to London."

Arty shifted feet and glanced at Dane, "I thought your father wanted you to marry."

"He does. I will just pick someone out on one of our runs and hire him on as a member of our crew. I'll still get to sail and Father will be happy to know I'm married."

Arty and Dane both frowned. "They're not going to like this."

"I don't care. My brothers will sell my ship," Jessica exploded

"But whose going to respect a husband that works under his wives command?" Dane signed scratching his head. Jessica frowned. No one. This was becoming harder than she thought.

"I'll figure something out. Get the crew back aboard and get this ship adrift." Both men gave her a look that said they clearly didn't agree with her. But Jessica ignored them and began shuffling through the papers on her desk. What a mess I've gotten myself into now, she thought. Putting her head in her hands, she struggled for an idea that would get her out of this mess. A soft knock at her door made her jump a good foot. "Yes?" she bellowed.

A small scrawny boy of twelve came scurrying into her room. He had black curly hair with hazel eyes and was already taller than she was.

"Um, my lady. There's a big burly man on the docks that wants to board the Titan. He claims he has permission to see you but Sampson and Johnson won't let him on without your approval."

Jessica tensed. It was probably Jonathan. The crew already knew who Stephan was. Rising to her feet she put on her hat and strapped on her knife, "thanks Michael. You keep watch and if the man makes one wrong move..." she left it hanging knowing Michael had no idea what to do. It always left him shaking in his boots.

Jessica turned down the hall and headed topside. The man standing with Sampson and Johnson was Stephan. Jessica's brows went up. Why didn't the crew let him aboard? Spying Arty it became clear. He must have warned them no one was to board least of all her brothers. As she walked closer she could make out her brothers raised voice.

Glancing at her Stephan turned his ranting on her. "Just what the hell do you think you're doing, young lady? I was under the impression you were willing to correct your mistake," he bellowed and Jessica felt her anger rising. He had just announced to the entire dock that she was female.

"You idiot. Keep your trap shut until we reach my cabin or I will have Arty here permanently fix it that way," she snapped pivoting in place and walking back toward the stairs. Arty and the other crewmen surrounded Stephan and led him after their captain.

As he entered the cabin, Jessica didn't give him much of a chance to vent his anger. With a signal to Arty, Stephan found himself bound and gagged before he could even shout a word. His eyes blazed with anger. Jessica frowned at him.

"You've ruined everything. I don't know what to do with you. I can't take you with me and you'd never let me hear the end of it," she stated pacing back and forth in front of him. "I could leave you in a port along the coast but you might get hurt and I couldn't live with that." Glancing at him, she said, "if I let you go, I don't suppose you'll keep this from Jonathan?" Stephan jerked and pulled on his bonds, shouting words against the gag. Jessica winced, "I didn't think so. Damn it Stephan." she said frowning as she knelt in front of him. "What am I going to do?" The cold look in his blue eyes made her want to cry. "Out. All of you," she bellowed waiting for the crew to leave. Running her fingers over her eyes she resumed her kneeling position. "Stephan, I don't want to marry a man I don't even know. I'm too strong willed and a husband can beat his wife. Knowing me, I will not take kindly to that." Stephan's eyes didn't waver. Jessica tried again. "I know I was wrong in watering the Baron's wine but our business was in trouble and he was the cause." She stood and resumed pacing, "I can't give up my ship. The crew wouldn't work well for you. They are little more than bandits. You'd probably throw the lot overboard for their speech alone. You idiot! You always seem to get in the way." Stephan struggled again and Jessica panicked. The longer Stephan was tied up the worse it would be for her. She could give him to the crew on either of the other ships in port and tell them to release him once she was gone. Shaking her head she discarded that idea. Arty and Dane were the only two she really trusted and besides that crew was loyal to her brother.

Slumping her shoulders in defeat she pulled out her knife and slit the bonds at his wrists. Stephan surged to his feet and pulled her across his lap and began spanking her. Jessica screamed and tried to get away. After four whacks she started to scream for Arty and Dane. Five! Six! Tears stung her eyes and began leaking out of the corners of her eyes as she realized that neither mate was going to show up. Seven! Eight! She was now openly crying as the stinging blows fell on her bottom. Nine! Ten! Suddenly, she was dumped in a heap at his feet. Jessica was sure her backside was permanently damaged as she shifted to keep the weight off her backside. Climbing slowly to her feet she pushed her hair out of her eyes and seriously considered punching Stephan in the stomach. Sniffing she wiped her sleeve across her nose.

"If you ever," he snarled, "ever make me do that again, I'll make it twice as hard and twice as many," he shouted clenching his fists. "I can't believe you tied me up!" he snapped, taking several deep breaths to keep from spanking her again. Jessica sniffed again. He was madder than she'd ever seen him. "I never thought you were such a fool. What possesses you to do the things you do?" he stated trying to gain control.

"I...I..." Jessica just lowered her head. She didn't have a reason. Father was giving her no choice in her future and she had never been good at handling a situation when the odds were so unfavorable. "I feel trapped. I don't do well with that kind of situation," she stated sniffling.

Stephan ran a hand through his hair, "Jessica, nobody does. But you have to face the trouble you cause and if it means losing your ship, so be it. Your crew can work on one of mine. I was even thinking I might sell you one of my ships if yours is given to the Baron." Jessica's head snapped up. "It might never happen, Jess. You were right about your new husband. He might not let you sail. Men don't like women who do that sort of thing."

Her eyes saddened immediately. "I don't understand why Father is doing this. I've managed to take care of myself this long. Why can't I continue as before?"

"You have not!" Stephan shouted with renewed anger, "you just lost everything in one stupid move," he bellowed.

Jessica's eyes flared, "I haven't lost everything. The Baron might not even want my ship. I make a good profit on each run and if I were to sail longer trips I could make even more."

Stephan frowned. She was a dreamer. Father was right to want to marry her off. She was too unstable for her own good. Nathan was exactly the same. "I think you better get used to the idea of marriage," he stated giving her a pointed look.

Her eyes changed to jade and the tears began to fall. Stephan pulled her into his arms as she clung to him, "I should have been born a man."

"The Baron would have called you out, for your little trick, if you were."

"I would have won and still had my ship. I wouldn't be forced to marry some arrogant bastard, either."

Stephan frowned at her. "Jessica, Father did give you the chance to pick yourself a man. If it were me, I would start seriously looking for one before I was forced with one I didn't even know. Make the best of the situation. Maybe there's a man out there who wouldn't mind a female sailor. I would start looking for him."

"In three months? I would have to carve him out of the air myself."

Stephan smiled. "At least you're joking again. Remember my lessen if you feel yourself being cornered again," he snapped slapping her rump. She hissed and jumped back three feet. Stephan grinned. "I'll see you back at the house," he added giving her a look that said if he had to hunt her down she would be getting worse than he just gave her.

"I should have never cut you loose," she said but whispered it in case he actually might have heard her. Then a thought hit her. "Arty, Dane, get your sorry asses in here," she bellowed. The two peeked in the door and she started yelling.

Chapter 17

MELISSA CAME TO A HALT at the sight of Nero perched on Nathan's chest. "Nathan, whatever are you doing?"

Nero growled deep in his throat but didn't move a muscle. "Get him off," Nathan said in a neutral voice.

"And how do you expect me to do that? He's growling."

"Sweets," Nathan practically screamed. The cat had been on him an eternity. His patience was wearing thin. Soft slippers came into view as Nathan watched Melissa set the tray of pastries on the floor and pushed it toward Nero with a broom. Groaning as the cat shifted his weight to reach the food, Nathan sucked in a full breath of air as the cat moved all the way off.

"Are you all right? What did you do to him?" she asked crouching down to peer into Nathan's face.

"I didn't do anything. Allison's caller showed up at the door and Nero pounced on me." Melissa laughed, nearly falling over backwards in the effort to take a full breath with the tight corset on. "It isn't funny. I think my ribs are broke," he stated sitting up and running his hands gingerly over his chest.

"What the hell is going on?" Christopher said taking in the scene, "where's Allison?"

"She went on an outing," Melissa stated rising to smile at her brother, "isn't that wonderful? And she was worried. Who was it Nathan?" The look on Nathan's face made her brows shoot into the air. Turning back to Christopher she took a step back, he looked ready to kill. "Is there something going on that I should know about?"

"No," Christopher snapped turning to head for the door. Hobkins had his cloak, hat, and gloves ready for him. Nathan frowned.

"I better go with him. He might get himself killed."

"What's going on?" Melissa said, scrambling after them.

"Just stay here and stop fussing?" he said catching the stuff Hobkins threw at him.

Melissa humphed as her brothers stormed out of the house slamming the door on the way. Hobkins looked at her and shrugged his shoulders.

"Of all the...they act like it's a crime to date. Father only gave us three months, you know." Hobkins nodded and strolled off in the opposite direction. A low growl came from behind her. Melissa whirled to stare at the cat.

"Allison won't be happy with you if you harm one hair on my head and besides I just gave you so many sweets you should be kissing my shoes in appreciation," she stated flouncing around to head up the stairs.

ALLISON STARTED FEELING NERVOUS as they drew closer to their destination. Royce said it was a short trip to his home. Allison felt awkward asking so many questions about his house, but without Melissa to guide her, she felt like a fish out of water. Hopefully, she wouldn't trip over something or break something of value. Christopher would really have a fit if he had to pay for damages she caused on a date she wasn't even suppose to be on.

"My house is just up the road. It isn't very grand."

Allison smiled. "I'm glad to hear it. I was just fretting that if I break something Christopher would have to pay for it. He wouldn't be happy about that"

Royce chuckled but didn't say anything else. Allison began to worry again.

"Are you sure Jared won't treat me like a child? If we tell him about my sight, that is?"

"No. Jared won't say anything to even imply you are blind. He will spend the evening pulling things out of your way all the while trying to carry on a conversation with you as if he wasn't doing anything of the sort. He will try to keep you comfortable."

Allison laughed. The thought of a big man jumping and pushing things out of her way seemed extremely funny. But then she remembered his wife, "what about his wife?"

"Ruth? She's a bit of a puzzle. She keeps Jared under tight wraps but she's one of the sweetest women I've ever met. I think you'll like her."

Allison relaxed. Even if they didn't treat her like she wanted to be treated, it didn't really matter as long as they kept the secret from the social world, "will they keep my secret?"

"I'll make them promise before I tell them," Royce stated leaning forward and opening the door as the coach came to a stop, "we're here." He hopped out and turned to lift her out. She was placed on the ground and instantly smoothed her skirts. The nervous feeling was getting stronger by the minute. She hadn't been anywhere without one of her family members in seven years. She felt instantly out of place.

Royce took her arm and noticed the pale look on her face, "You look fine. If you'd rather we didn't tell them I'll help you out as best I can."

Allison frowned. "I don't know. Usually I'm with family and they tell me where everything is and what everyone looks like. I feel really blind," she said wondering if she was making a mistake, "I think we should keep the secret."

"All right, then. I'll describe the house for you. My house is directly in front of you. There are seven steps up to the door, where Miles my butler is holding the door open. He's about five foot five with gray hair and glasses. He's a nosy busybody but we just ignore him," he said guiding her up the steps and through the door. Taking her cloak and reticule he handed them to Miles along with his own things, then took her arm again. "You're facing the foyer. There's a wooden bench to your left and a long table next to that. If you walk straight you will be in the great hall that has a set of stairs running up to the upper levels. But we're going to the right which leads into what we call the family room," he said leading her along the hall to the room. "This room is somewhat on the masculine side. There's a sofa to the left with three chairs directly opposite them. A fire is burning in the hearth, which is located directly in front of you. The room has two tables in it. One to your right and another to your left. There is a smaller table that is between the furniture. We have pictures on almost every wall. Mabel, my housekeeper, insists on having plants in the house so there are," he paused counting the plants, "six of them in this room." Allison smiled. He described the room perfectly.

"Do we get to stay in here? I think I can keep from making a fool of myself in a room this size."

Royce chuckled directing her to the sofa. "Sorry, Mabel doesn't allow us to dine with guest anywhere but in the dining room. But you'll be fine. Is that description clear enough for you or do you want colors too?"

Allison smiled. "No, that's fine. Melissa is the only one who tells me the colors, price, style, and worth of each item in a room. It takes her all of ten minutes too."

Royce smiled. She was truly lovely. Her eyes were glowing with excitement and Royce felt his shields slipping a little. She was such an innocent woman. Could she possible come to like him? He frowned as Jared and Ruth arrived.

"Brother mine, how nice it is of you to invite us to dine," Jared said coming forward with Ruth on his arm.

Royce rose to his feet pulling Allison up with him. Leaning forward, he kissed Ruth's cheek and shook Jared's hand. Then introduced them to Allison.

"We've already met. How lovely you look, Lady Allison. You have to be one of the most beautiful women I've had the honor of meeting. Of course, my wife is the most beautiful." Allison blushed and heard Ruth hit her husband.

"Quit teasing the girl, Jared. You'll scare her off."

"Me!" Jared said moving to the table to the left to pour some refreshments for the four. "Port? Brandy?"

"Yes, thank you," Ruth answered and Royce nodded his agreement.

"That would be fine," Allison added resuming her seat on the sofa. Royce moved to stand next to the arm of the sofa. Ruth seated herself in the chair opposite Allison.

"Jared tells me you and your family buy ships from us. Have you sailed on any?"

Allison smiled. "Yes. In fact, my brother has four of your ships and my sister has one. They have both taken me up and down the coast a number of times."

"Oh yes. I had forgotten your sister sails."

Allison hesitated. Did she approve or not? She couldn't quite tell by her tone of voice. "She's quite good, actually. She says she should have been born a man," Allison said, and then blushed. Silence followed her statement making her palms sweat.

"Here's your Port," Royce stated placing the glass in her hand as she reached to take it. It was so smoothly done he felt himself smile. Jared and Ruth would never know she was blind. Neither suspects a thing, Royce thought as he listened to the two ladies chat. Jared was putting in a remark or two making Royce smile. Allison was really good at her charade. She never directly looked at either person but it wasn't done in a way that the other would take that as rude. They probably thought she was extremely shy. She must have practiced for years.

"Royce?" he blinked his eyes at his brother then smiled, "are we playing cards after dinner then?" Jared said looking at his brother with amusement. Royce stiffened. Cards! She couldn't play cards. Trying to think quickly he moved to the table to refill his glass.

"More refreshments?" he asked stalling for time. At the negative shakes of the head he replaced the decanter and turned to face the three, "I thought maybe Ruth would play something on the piano and we could just chat."

Jared stared at his brother like he'd gone deaf. Looking quickly at the ladies he read boredom on Ruth's face and nothing on Allison's. "That sounds lovely but for the whole evening?"

"Are you implying I can't play well?" Ruth teased.

"Not at all," Jared quickly said making Allison laugh, "I just thought that since Royce and Allison didn't get to go to the opera maybe they had a little more excitement in mind."

Royce frowned. Jared was up to something.

"Like what did you have in mind?" Allison asked.

"Oh, I don't know. I thought a good game of whisk would be fun."

Allison frowned and lowered her head, "I'm not very good at cards," she said truthfully.

"That's all right. Perhaps kings and queens are more to your style."

"You'll have to excuse Jared. He's a bit of a gambler. I don't really think Allison wants to play cards," Ruth said looking at the slightly pale girl on the sofa across from them. Jared looked at his wife then back at Allison. Sighing he frowned, "I guess pianoforte, it is."

"Don't sound so put out. Ruth is very good on the piano," Royce stated grinning. Miles entered at that moment telling them dinner was served and the four moved off into the dining room. Royce wrapped her arm around his, slowing his pace so Jared and Ruth moved on ahead. "The dinning room isn't set up where we sit miles apart from one another so things should go smoothly for you. The servants walk behind and offer the food over your left shoulder, just nod your head and they will place the food on your plate."

Allison smiled. "It's the same at my house."

"Good. The place setting is probably similar as well."

"The glass is on the right and our napkin is always on the plate."

Royce nodded then remembered she couldn't see him do that. "Yes. Ours is the same." He felt nervous for her. Though if she did do something wrong Jared and Ruth would never say a thing.

Allison was grateful for Royce's effort but the unknown was making her stomach flutter. "I probably won't eat much," she blurted letting him know ahead of time.

Royce smiled. "Don't worry. You'll be fine. Just do whatever makes you comfortable. Jared will be to your right, Ruth across from you and I will be on your left. The chairs are three feet apart. I hate the formal tables where you're almost alone at each end while the people in the middle get to do all the talking."

Allison smiled. "Did you have a special table made?"

"No. It came in sections and Miles places in as many as needed for the number of quests. It's quite handy," he said seating her at the table. Allison immediately picked up her napkin and dropped it in her lap. So far so good.

"Jared, I almost forgot to tell you. The Delaney's have purchased two more ships," Royce said smiling.

"That old sea dog. He said he was going someplace else for his ships."

"He fussed over the price but in the end I think he was quite satisfied with the deal," Royce said nodding as the servant placed a bowl of soup in front of him. Allison smiled as the smell of broccoli and mushrooms reached her nose. This was one of her favorite soups. The presence beside her let her know the servant was next to her and she leaned slightly to her right. The bowl clattered on the plate and Allison heard spoons hitting the dishes as the others ate. Picking up her spoon she moved her hand out until she felt the bowl then dipped the spoon in and brought it to her mouth. It was delicious. She'd taken three mouthfuls when she heard Jared ask, "bread?" She froze. Was he speaking to her? Shaking her head she heard the basket hit the table. Good. Relaxing, she finished off her soup and wiped her mouth on her napkin. Melissa had worked with her for almost six months on how to eat soup without making a trail between the bowl and your mouth. She casually reached her hand out to see if she'd made a mess. The tablecloth was dry and she smiled, her attention returning to the conversation.

"Jared, you promised, no business," Ruth said giving him a glare, "Allison, how many children are in your family?"

Allison smiled. "I have four brothers and two sisters."

Royce raised his brows. "I thought you only had three brothers."

"No. Christopher is the oldest then Jonathan, Stephan, and Nathan."

"Jonathan. He's the one I haven't met."

"That's because he doesn't deal with anything related to the sea," she said smiling. "He rears horses."

"Horses," Jared said in surprise.

"Yes, in fact he races them."

"Jonathan Hayworth! He's your brother? Why his horses are the best in the area."

Allison smiled. Jonathan had an excellent line of horses and everyone wanted one. They were good for just about anything. "He's worked hard to get them that way."

"I'd say. The finest race horses indeed."

"How exactly do you know this?" Ruth asked and Allison clearly heard disapproval in her voice.

"Rumor," Jared quickly supplied. Allison grinned at the lie. Ruth knowing it to be so, added fuel to the fire, "you'd better not be at the tracks again."

"Me. Not a chance."

"I'm glad you're keeping tabs on him, Ruth. I don't like having to bail him out all the time," Royce stated leaning back as the next course arrived. Allison smelled fish and onions but couldn't tell what other foods there were. This course was going to be hard. She decided to take a little of everything when the presence was behind her. Jared raised his brows as she was served a scoop of horseradishes. No one ate them but him.

"You like horseradishes?" he remarked then frowned when Allison blushed clean to her roots. Royce scowled at him and shook his head. Jared blushed slightly and let it drop. But as the meal progressed he noticed she didn't eat much and stayed completely away from the horseradishes.

As the main course drew to a close, a commotion from the foyer drew their attention.

Allison stiffened, as the voice shouting for the butler to get his scurvy little ass out of his way, could only be Christopher. Panicking she reached to lay her fork on the table and felt her glass of wine tip and spill across the table, grabbing for it she knocked over a flower vase she hadn't known was even there. Christopher came bursting into the room when she was ready to wilt under the table from embarrassment. Jared and Ruth both jumped to their feet to avoid the liquid coming across the table and Ruth scooted over to Jared's side as Nathan skidded to a halt behind his brother. Royce looked ready to kill.

"Allison, you are coming home with us right now. Get your cloak," Christopher shouted taking two steps closer. Allison, on the verge of tears, overturned her chair when Christopher burst into the room. She had no idea where it was, and furthermore the wine and water she'd spilled was probably all over Jared and Ruth's laps. The tears started down her face before she could even say a word. Taking a step her foot caught on the overturned chair. She tried to catch herself and slipped on the water she'd spilt. She put her arms out to stop her fall only to hit the table with her elbow, tipping her sideways where she hit her head on the chair. Jared instinctively tried to catch the falling woman but missed altogether and wound up staring and doing not much of anything. All five people froze in place as Allison tried to right herself. A sob escaped her lips which sent the men into action.

"You son of a bitch! I'll kill you!" Christopher shouted, lunging for Royce. Royce dodged Christopher's charge, punching him in the stomach as he passed. It didn't faze Christopher, he straightened and swung. His punch landed with sickening force to Royce's jaw. Grabbing Christopher's arm, Nathan took a punch to the jaw from Royce dropping to the floor. Shaking his head he barely scooted to the side before Royce skidded across the floor in front of him. Christopher grabbed Royce's shirtfront, swinging again. Royce kicked out and caught Christopher in the groin sending him to the floor with a groan.

Jared winced as Royce hit Christopher again. It was apparent the fight was far from over. Too enraged to let a little pain stop them, both men went at one another again.

Stooping, Jared picked Allison up, trying to lead her from the room as the fighting continued behind them. She jerked away from him to go back to break up the fight.

"We have to stop them," she said, crying uncontrollably now. Jared quickly led her out of the room with Ruth scrambling along behind him. "Stop! We can't just leave them in there. They'll kill each other."

"Never mind. Nathan's in there. I'm sure he'll stop them before that happens," he said not mentioning the fact that Nathan wasn't doing much of anything curled in a corner dogging furniture. Leading her down the hall he took her into the library, "Ruth get her some water and a handkerchief, will you please?"

Seating her on the sofa he could see she was trying to get herself under control but was failing miserably.

"I should never have come," she said drinking from the glass Ruth pressed into her hand, "I've made a mess of everything."

"Nonsense. How's your head?" Jared asked looking at the bump forming just above her right eye. Allison reached up and touched it, wincing.

"It doesn't really hurt," she said jumping as a large crash came from the other room. Trying to stand she felt hands restrain her.

"They obviously haven't finished yet. Do you want to tell us about it?"

Tears started falling down her face again. "I should have said something from the beginning but...I didn't want to be treated special."

"What should you have said?"

Allison sniffled. "About my blindness," she said sniffling. Hearing them gasp, she frowned. They hadn't known. After her little spectacle how could they not.

Jared stared at the woman in front of him, before raising a hand to wave it in front of her eyes. When she didn't react he glanced at Ruth. Her eyes were like saucers. Ruth shook her head and paled.

"I would have never guessed," Jared said getting himself back under control, "you handle yourself very well."

Allison took a deep breath. "I was afraid to say anything to you. I didn't want to be treated like a child. I just wanted to fit in." Another crash of glass sounded from down the hall followed by shouting. But the words were muffled.

"We understand. Now that we know, we will try to treat you like anyone else."

Allison took another deep breath trying to control the urge to cry. "Don't you think we should go back and see what's going on?"

"Do you feel up to it?"

Allison nodded. Wiping her eyes she felt Jared take her arm to lead her back to the dining room. Once there Jared arched his brows. The room resembled a pub after a fight. The occupants didn't look much better.

"I warned you about my sister. I forbad you from seeing her. You're a monstrosity of a man," Christopher shouted. Allison stopped in her tracks. Monstrosity! She felt Jared stiffen and knew something was going to happen. Pulling away from Jared she walked a few steps and screamed. Everyone turned to stare.

"Christopher Anthony Hayworth, what the hell do you think you're doing?" The three men flushed. "You have ruined a perfectly good evening by barging in here and I've got a lump the size of an egg on my head. I'm sure you've ruined this room."

Christopher frowned. She had hit her head on the table but it didn't look bad from where he was. "I told you, you weren't to see this man. Now get your cloak," he snapped taking two steps toward her.

Allison held up her hand. "Not another step. I will not take orders from you. Father, ordered us to marry. I'm sure the usual proceedings are to get to know the man first. Now, go home."

"I hate to tell you this, Missy, but Father gave me guardianship over you and your sisters. I get to say who and what you date. Now, get your cloak before I really loose my temper," he roared, closing the distance between them. At the pale look on her face he tried to gain control. "Get your cloak!" he repeated, watching her back stiffen and her chin lift. Two seconds later he was doubled over from a well-landed punch to his middle.

"How dare you?" she breathed. "All this time you've known that Father gave you control over us and you didn't tell us. You rotten...cur." she shouted for lack of a better word.

Nathan stepped forward and grabbed her arm, knowing she was unaware of the dark rage of Christopher's face.

"I think you have over done it," he whispered. Allison paled and leaned into him.

Royce stared at the scene in front of him. The father gave the son guardianship over the daughters? For what reason? The man was very much alive. Did he not wish to be troubled with the burden of marriage?

Christopher, after several gasping breaths, got his body under control. Allison had caught him completely off guard and landed a punch that knocked the breath out of him. "Nathan get her out of here," he stated.

"Hold it," Royce said moving closer, "exactly what's going on here?"

"It's none of your business, you freak."

Royce's face darkened. "I warned you never to call me that."

"If the shoe fit's..." Christopher never finished as Royce knocked him unconscious in a single blow. Allison jumped as she heard the body hit the floor.

"What happened? What's going on?" she asked frantically. No one answered. Royce turned and looked in Allison's direction before walking from the room. "Nathan what's going on?" Allison asked.

"Nothing, love. Royce knocked Christopher out," Nathan said. Allison slumped slightly as the tears started again.

"Royce?" she called knowing he wasn't there and probably wouldn't have anything to do with her ever again.

Nathan looked at Jared and his wife then frowned. "He's gone, Al."

Allison sagged at the news then fled the house in tears.

Chapter 18

"MASTER NATHAN," Hobkins stated seeing Nathan carrying Christopher over his shoulder. "What happened?"

"The old man got sorely trounced. Could you help Allison for me?" he murmured struggling up the stairs to the rooms above. Hobkins quickly scurried down the steps to help Allison out of the coach.

"Hobkins, take me directly to Christopher's room," she said sounding quite frantic. "I think Lord Royce hurt him good. He didn't regain consciousness the whole ride home."

The pair hurried up the stairs and found Nathan pouring brandy into a glass. "I think this will revive him."

"My lord, how do you expect him to drink that?" Hobkins observed. Nathan scowled.

"Just throw it in his face," Allison said waiting to hear someone move. Nathan looked at his sister then back at Christopher. His face was swollen and bruised. The poor fellow was in sorry shape. Brandy was always a quick cure. One last look at Hobkins and he threw the entire glass in Christopher's face. Nothing happened.

"Is he moving?" Allison asked when she heard the liquid hit the floor.

"No. Got any better ideas?" Nathan asked looking at the sprawled figure.

"Smelling salts. Hurry Hobkins, Melissa has some," Allison said moving to the bed and running her hands over Christopher's body. "Well, at least he has no broken bones. Even his hands are all right. But his face sure feels a mess." Lowering her head she asked, "did his lordship look like this?"

"Not so bad in the face. His eye will be black and a split lip maybe," Nathan said grabbing Christopher's left leg and throwing it up on the bed.

"Why did you bring him there tonight? I thought Nero made it clear that I didn't want you there?"

"I'll get you for that. I didn't have a choice in the matter. Christopher was half way out the door, before I realized his intentions. You know how stubborn he can be. I didn't think he would react the way he did. Christopher's held a grudge for a long time."

"What grudge?"

Nathan frowned. He hadn't meant to say anything about that. Christopher should handle his own problems. The anxious look on Allison's face changed his mind. "Do you remember Helen Montgomery?"

"She was one of Christopher's ladies. The one we didn't like."

"Yes. Christopher liked her though. In fact, he asked her to marry him." At Allison's gasp, he continued, "she refused, stating he wasn't rich enough. She had excepted Royce instead."

"He's married?" Allison stated, clearly appalled.

Nathan pursed his lips. She obviously liked Royce or she wouldn't be this concerned. "No, he's not married though he would have been, if the accident hadn't happened."

Allison frowned. "I didn't hear anything about Helen dying in an accident."

"That's because she is very much alive and has some children with a very rich, very young, Earl. The accident I'm referring to is the one that happened to Royce."

"Royce was in an accident? Did he get hurt?"

"Allison," he said taking her hand, "he did. He was burned, terribly, and is scarred very badly." Allison paled and snatched her hand away from Nathan's. "I'm serious. His face is burned on the whole left side. Helen didn't want to marry him because of the scars. She's very vain."

Allison pursed her lips. "Is that why Christopher doesn't want me to see him? Because he's ...scarred?"

"I doubt it. He doesn't want you to see him because of Helen."

"But that was years ago."

"Only seven years and to someone in love, that's like yesterday."

"That's ridiculous. I can't believe Christopher would be that silly. The woman was a greedy self-centered bitch with one thing in mind. A rich husband! We all knew it. How can he still even think about her? He didn't even love her."

Nathan shook his head. "I don't know. All I know is that he is still affected by her and I'm sure deep down inside he knows she's a lousy woman but won't admit it."

Hobkins entered the room with Melissa trailing behind him. "What happened?" she exclaimed, holding the salts under Christopher's nose. Christopher bolted upright and knocked the offending smell to the floor. Allison fell along with it. She scrambled to her feet and backed away from the bed.

"What the hell was that?" he shouted wincing as his lips cracked

"I was reviving you with salts," Melissa said smugly.

Christopher frowned at her, then rubbed his jaw, "I think that oaf cracked my jaw."

"Whoever it was, gave you a beautiful black eye too." Melissa said moving back for a better view. Turning her head from side to side she smiled. "Your cheek is blackening and your lips look twice their size," she added with a chuckle.

"Get her out of here, Hobkins, and bring me some ice. Where did all this brandy come from?" he asked pulling his shirt out to look at it.

"I threw it in your face to revive you. It didn't work," Nathan said sitting in the chair by the wall as Hobkins dragged Melissa from the room.

Christopher scowled at him. Moving gingerly to the edge of the bed he settled to assess the damages. His jaw and head hurt like hell. His stomach didn't feel much better and he felt like he'd run ten miles through sand. Glancing to his left his jaw hardened.

"You really shouldn't look at her that way. You're the one fighting like a teenager," Nathan said.

Christopher gave him a withering look before returning his attention to Allison. She was stiff with anger.

"I thought I told you not to see the Earl."

"Earl!" Allison exclaimed shocked at the title.

"Yes, the Earl."

Recovering from the news, she set her features. "In case you forgot, I need to be married in three months. That means I will need a groom. In short, I must visit with men to find a suitable man."

Christopher stood up at her sarcasm. Sometimes she was so like Jessica he felt like smacking her.

"I don't want you seeing that man again. I say who dates who and I expect you to follow my decisions."

Allison tightened her fists. Hearing the rage in Christopher's voice only made her angrier. "I will not let you pick the man I will spend the rest of my life with just because you have problems with a possible husband of mine." she stated trying to keep her voice from coming out in a shriek.

Christopher whirled on Nathan. "You told her," he shouted. Nathan jumped to his feet and backed up a step.

"She asked and I thought it might help. She needed to understand about the accident." Christopher's eyes darkened and Nathan threw his hands in the air. "Well, I guess I was wrong. See if I ever help out again," he said scooting out the door. Christopher clenched his jaw.

"I don't want to fight with you, Christopher. In fact, we probably shouldn't even be having this discussion since the Earl probably won't come within ten feet of me after what you've done," she said turning away from him. "I should have let Father pick my husband from the beginning.

It's too hard for me. I'm at a real disadvantage."

Christopher scowled. He hadn't really thought about her position. All he thought about was revenge against the Earl for stealing Helen. He had the power to withhold Allison from Royce and he had taken advantage of that power. What a fool! She was right. His personal problems shouldn't have interfered with her life. "I think I may have over reacted," he said in a quiet voice. Allison turned slowly around.

"What?"

"I'm saying, I will try to be more reasonable in the future. I will try not to interfere, unless the man's a complete degenerate. Will that be all right with you?"

Allison bowed her head. "Did Father give you the final decision about who we marry?"

"Yes."

"Then I want you to pick someone out for me. I don't care who he is as long as he's kind, gentle, frie..." her voice broke and she swallowed trying to keep from crying.

Christopher reached out for her but she quickly moved back as she felt contact. "I will trust your decision," she finished fleeing the room.

Christopher's head dropped in defeat. He had worried she would react negatively to his interference and now she was completely giving up. What a mess! A quick knock at the door produced Hobkins with a bucket of ice in one hand and a bottle of brandy in the other. Christopher tried to smile but the movement caused his lip to crack. Frowning, he sat back on the bed. What a mess he'd made of things and in less than three hours. Father would be proud.

Chapter 19

JESSICA FROWNED on her way to her room. What was she to do now? Go back to London? Sell her ship? Or worse, have to give it to the Baron?. Scowling she threw her gloves on her bed and pulled the scarf from around her neck. She was still wearing her breeches and shirt. She planned on wearing such attire until she returned to London. The sound of voices coming from the study made her pause. Normally, not one to snoop, she would have went straight upstairs but the voices were raised in anger. Curiosity got the better of her.

Looking around she cautiously walked toward the study. She placed her ear against the door, instantly recognizing Jonathan's voice.

"I don't exactly know what to say. After a discussion with several crew members, it was found that someone was indeed involved with the tampering of your wine."

Jonathan paused to gauge Morgan's reaction.

"Tell me something I don't already know," Morgan growled out.

Jonathan clenched his teeth. Being on the wrong side was a new experience and one he didn't like. "I have discussed this with Stephan and we have decided on a solution to the problem." Morgan's stare didn't waver. Jonathan cleared his throat. He was nervous. He remembered time and again being called into this exact room to hear a confession involving a member of his family. Father would rant and rave at them and finally hand out just punishment. Frowning, Jonathan wondered why his father hadn't kept his nose out of it and made them deal with their own problems.

"Stephan and I thought we would pay you for the lost shipments and explain the situation to Jacque." Morgan didn't move. Jonathan swallowed. "We also plan to give you the ship that was involved as part of the payment. Plus pay you the remaining monies made on the last voyages."

A long silence followed. Jessica felt her stomach knot wondering if the Baron would accept the offer. His few words at the beginning of the conversation sounded so bloody arrogant she wanted to hit Jonathan for sucking up to the man.

Jonathan took his seat letting Morgan know he was finished talking. Morgan sat forward in his chair and looked Jonathan in the eyes.

"We have been friends for a long time, I can't believe I heard that drivel come out of your mouth."

Jonathan flushed. He felt about the size of an ant. He knew he was trying to buy his way out of this mess but he didn't have much of a choice in the matter. Jessica's reputation was at risk.

"First off, I want to know who the captain of the ship was and why they wanted to attack my business. Second, I want to have Stephan here to discuss this situation with him."

Jonathan frowned. The first issue was the one he was trying to avoid. The second issue had already been planned. "Of course, Stephan is on his way here as we speak. I told him eight o'clock."

Morgan nodded. "And the other?"

Jonathan stood and looked out the only window in the study. It was completely dark outside. The moon was starting a new cycle and was hidden from view. "I don't know what to say. The captain has been dealt with and the ship is payment for the wrong doing."

"Not in my book," Morgan exploded coming to his feet. "I want to deal with the bastard personally."

Jonathan flinched. Jessica wouldn't survive one punch. Morgan would strap her to a pole and whip strips of flesh off her back, if he had his way. "I'm sorry that's not possible."

"Is the fellow dead then?"

"No."

"Gravely ill?"

"No."

Jonathan had turned around before answering the last question to show Morgan he wasn't backing down on this issue.

"I can't believe you won't allow me restitution from this man's hide."

Jessica had heard enough. The man was a complete madman. She should have never have messed with his business in the first place. By the tone of Morgan's voice, she could tell Jonathan was beginning to lose face with him. Taking a deep breath Jessica opened the door and stepped into the room.

"I'm the captain you're looking for," she blurted out, closing the door behind her. She placed her feet shoulder width apart and put her hands behind her back. Fixing her eyes on a portrait of a dog hunting with a man for geese, she waited for the men's reply.

"What the hell are you doing?" Jonathan shouted coming around the desk. Morgan stared from Jonathan to the beautiful girl in front of him then back to Jonathan. She was the captain he was looking for? What the hell was going on?

"It's time I took care of my own problems, Jonathan" she said still staring at the dog portrait.

Morgan frowned. She was serious. A woman! Clenching his teeth he took several deep breaths. A woman! Turning he looked at Jonathan and saw the man was ready to throttle the wench. Some of his anger dissipated, but a woman had got the better of him. That hurt his pride. She'd actually gotten into his storehouse. She had successfully removed good wine and replaced it with watered down stuff. Not one of his guards had seen anything.

"I'm sorry for this interruption, Morgan. If you will excuse me, I won't be a moment." Jonathan grabbed Jessica's arm and started to lead her from the room.

"I won't leave until he takes the offer," she stated grabbing onto a chair as Jonathan tried to pull her out the door.

"Let go. You're making a fool of us. Go back to your room," he shouted pulling her away from the chair. She let go only to wrap herself around the legs of the bar table. "You're acting like a child," he said grabbing her by the hair and pulling. Jessica felt the tears rush to her eyes and in that instant decided two could play this game. Surging to her feet she punched Jonathan in the stomach with her hand as he doubled over from the unexpected punch. Then she brought her hand down on his back sending him to the floor. Morgan, stunned by the act, didn't have time to do anything as Jonathan grabbed her legs and pulled them out from under her.

"Bloody hell," she screeched sprawling to the floor. Scrambling to her feet she tried to stop Jonathan as he ducked in to grab her around the waist. Raining punches down on his back, she began kicking her legs, hitting close to his manhood. Jonathan dropped her as she scrambled to her feet crouching ready to strike.

"You're only making it worse for yourself, " Jonathan whispered. Jessica felt the hair rise on the back of her neck. Jonathan meant business when his voice took on the deathly calm it had right now.

"I only wanted the Baron to know who I was instead of laying the blame at the wrong door." she said moving to get the desk between them.

Jonathan smiled a deadly smile at her attempt. "That won't stop me," he said jumping over it sending the papers flying to the floor. Grabbing her arms he hauled her up against him. "You should have gone to your room." She tried to bite his hand. Gritting his teeth, he bent her arm up behind her back. She instantly stopped struggling and stood on her tiptoes to lessen the pain. Morgan watched the pair through unbelieving eyes. A woman who fought that dirty made his hurt pride feel a little bit better. Morgan coughed and cleared his throat.

"I will gladly take her off your hands, Jonathan. A woman with that much fire would be a hell of a treat to a man like me," he said grinning. Jonathan glared at him. He hadn't found that statement the least bit funny.

"She's my sister."

Morgan's grin vanished as a blush crept up his neck. "I apologize. I would have never guessed."

Jonathan nodded but Jessica wouldn't let it go. "I told you he was an arrogant bastard."

Jonathan shook her and pulled her arm higher. "That's enough out of you. You're supposed to be a lady. Mother's probably rolling over in her grave."

Jessica stopped struggling as she tried to lessen the pain in her arm. Her mane of hair was hanging nearly to the floor in waves of black silk. He hadn't really gotten a good look at her eyes but her fiery temper was enough to get a man's blood boiling.

"What are you going to do with her?" Morgan asked watching Jonathan struggle with the problem himself.

"What the hell is going on?" Stephan stated from the door. Everyone looked at him.

"Jessica acted instead of thinking again."

"What does that mean and why are you breaking her arm?" Jonathan lessened his hold, blushing. "She nearly took a chunk out of my arm with her teeth."

Stephan laughed. "My lesson this afternoon wasn't enough for you, aye?"

"What lesson?"

"Shut up, Stephan. I was trying to be honorable like you said." Jonathan frowned again and lessened his hold even more.

"What lesson?" Jonathan growled.

"She tried to relocate, so I convinced her to stay. Or her bottom did anyway." Jessica snarled a curse, getting frowns from both Morgan and Jonathan.

"If you will promise to keep your hands to yourself, I will let you go."

Jessica gritted her teeth. Not only were they making a fool of her in front of the man that was getting her ship, she was afraid if Jonathan let go she would gouge Jonathan's eyes out. "If you value your eyes, I don't think that's a good idea."

Stephan grinned as Morgan lifted his eyebrows. She was definitely one of a kind.

"I'll take my chances," Jonathan said jumping back after he released her. Jessica stood and winced as the blood rushed back down to her fingers. Scowling, she shook her arm to get the pain to go away.

"You did that to yourself," Jonathan said picking up papers off the floor and putting the chair back in place before sitting. "Jessica, we will let you know what happens when we finish with our discussion."

Jessica stared at her brother as if his ears had fallen off. "Excuse me? I'm not going anywhere," she snapped crossing her arms.

"On the contrary. You're going to your room."

"Forget it. I'll smack that smile off your face Stephan if you don't let me stay."

Stephan shook his head. "You're just making things worse on yourself."

"I'm staying," she said, looking for the first time at the Baron. Most of the heat went out of her sails at the sight of him. The man was positively gorgeous. He had blond shoulder length hair, blue eyes, and muscles from head to toe. Letting out the breath she'd been holding, she schooled her features and said, "that's if the Baron can handle my presence."

Jonathan frowned. She was going to cause more problems with that sharp tongue of hers. "Fine. Sit down and don't say a word. If a peep so much as crosses those lips, I will personally carry you to your room and beat that backside of yours until you can't sit down for a week."

Jessica frowned but slowly sat down. Glancing at Stephan she narrowed her eyes as he grinned. Clenching her teeth she returned her gaze to the dog portrait.

Stephan and Morgan resumed their seats. "What I have said earlier still stands," Jonathan said looking at Morgan.

Morgan stared at Jessica for several seconds before he exhaled. "I suppose ripping the humiliation I suffered out of the captain's back is out of the question?" Jessica stiffened at that. "How many runs do you have left?" Morgan asked Stephan.

"Six."

"I'll take those six runs plus the ship," he added his eyes watching Jessica's eyes flinch slightly at the news.

Stephan lifted his brows. "What about your reputation?"

"I'll take care of that. Jacque knows I have good wine. I'll set him straight."

Stephan smiled at the man with respect. "I have to say you handled this situation a lot better than I would have. Thank you."

Morgan nodded and returned his gaze to Jessica. It was obvious she was trying to put up a brave front but the loss of a ship was hard on any Captain.

"'I'm glad that's settled. Dinner should be about ready. I hope in the future you will have no further problems with us. I don't like having you on the opposite side," Jonathan said shaking Morgan's hand. Morgan smiled at Jonathan but he was still watching Jessica.

"It was difficult, wasn't it?" Morgan said.

All three men paused as Jessica stood and left the study without a word to anyone.

"I think she took that a little hard," Morgan said turning to Jonathan.

"Yes. She only had the one ship and I know she won't take one from Stephan unless she pays for it. Besides she has to marry soon and her sailing days will change."

"Marry?" Morgan stated wondering who the lucky groom would be.

Jonathan nodded. "Marry," he stated, "I realize that's hard to believe but Father has a heart condition and ordered the three girls to marry. It's rather a long story, but I doubt her husband will let her go off sailing. I know if I had a wife I sure as hell wouldn't."

Morgan nodded his agreement but his brows drew down in thought.

Chapter 20

MELISSA LEANED BACK on the sofa and popped a chocolate into her mouth. It was early afternoon on a beautiful day and she was looking forward to going to the ball that evening. Nathan had been informed he was to escort her to the affair. She smiled at the look on Nathan's face when she told him. Nathan had thought he would only have to suffer through one of those affairs and that the men would just swarm around the three until they all found suitable husbands. Unfortunately, the gents were a bit shy and Melissa was still in need of Nathan's escort. Things were progressing at a much slower rate than she had expected. It really was ridiculous. The women dressed in beautiful clothes; the men dressed like royalty; both coming together to study the other, hoping to catch the biggest fish. Melissa smiled. Wasn't it grand?

Standing, she moved to the window and opened the drapes to look out over the busy city streets. People milled around and carriages moved up and down the streets carrying eager men and women to unknown destinations. Suddenly the urge to be among the crowd over powered her. She returned to her room and put on a gown she had especially made for shopping. It wasn't cumbersome and covered everything modestly. It was a pale red with white shot through it. Pulling the bell rope she summoned her maid Besty.

In mere minutes the huffing maid burst into the room. Betsy was a heavy set girl with plain brown hair and brown eyes to match. Since her arrival in London, Melissa had come to know Betsy real well and liked the girl. She was shy but very obedient and that was the one thing Melissa liked most.

"I'm going out. I will need the carriage brought around and your company. I want to leave in ten minutes."

"But, my lady. Your Aunt says you were not to go out since..."

"I don't care what Aunt says. I need fresh ribbons for tonight and I want to go get them. Perhaps a few other things as well. Now don't fret about Aunt Ginger. I'll take care of her. Just hurry and get ready. You only have eight minutes left."

With a flustered look and a quick deduction that her mistress wasn't changing her mind, Betsy flew down the stairs and headed straight to the kitchens to inform the footman about the coach. After that she hurried to her own room and grabbed a cloak and gloves and headed directly to the foyer were Melissa was patiently waiting.

"Are we ready?"

"Almost. The carriage should be around directly." No sooner had the words left her mouth, the carriage rumbled to a stop in front of the stoop. Betsy beamed a big smile to her lady.

"That was excellent work, Betsy. I don't think we've ever left so quickly."

Betsy's smile widened as they both were assisted into the carriage. Melissa liked things to go smoothly. Watching the shops and boutiques pass by, Melissa began to relax. It was expensive to be among the social elite but it was worth it. Father would have a heart attack if he just saw one of the many bills Melissa had acquired. Christopher was bad enough with all his blustering about ladies needing too many things. But Melissa figured, since Jessica wasn't spending anything, she would just spend her share too.

"Thank you, Simon. Come back and get us in an hour. We'll be waiting here in front of Miss Debouir's dress shop," she said. Simon gave her a nod, scrambled back up on the carriage, and drove out of sight.

"Isn't this going to be wonderful? Betsy, did you bring any money of your own?"

"No, Miss. I've spent what I had saved."

At the sad look on Betsy's face Melissa instantly felt sorry for her. "That's all right. If you see some ribbons you like I'll be happy to buy you some."

Betsy's brows shot up at that, sending Melissa into peels of laughter. "Come on, you ninny. Let's get shopping. We only have an hour before Simon returns."

Betsy nodded. Her mistress was a fanatic when it came to shopping.

"THAT'S THE ONE!" Caleb Cabot said ducking back behind the wall as the tinkle of the girls laughter reached his ears.

"But that one looks like a damn snob," Keegan Cabot snapped.

"I know. Father will never believe I would choose anything but that. A soft-spoken girl will give us away. This one even has red hair! That means a temper!"

"Her hairs blond. Has your sight failed you as well as your brain? She looks on the small side, too. Are you sure that's the one?"

"I see an unescorted woman with no ring on her finger. She'll do. I'm running out of time. Father is closing in."

"Unbelievable! But remember, you'll be saddled with the shrew for the rest of your life. Don't you even want to talk to her?" Keegan asked shaking his head.

"No. She laughs, and if that body is any indication, looks real good to the eye."

Keegan rolled his eyes. "I think you're daft myself, but if she's the one, let's get on with it. My participation better not get me into trouble later."

"Stop worrying." Caleb said looking around. "Where the hell is Niles?"

"He had an errand to run. He should be here shortly." As the two stood there waiting, Niles strolled up behind them.

"It's about time," Caleb snapped, "the ladies are just now coming out. Remember the plan and please be convincing. This might be my only chance." Niles and Keegan exchanged looks then grinned. "If you ruin this, I'll never let you forget it," Caleb said with a dark look.

Both continued to smile. "Which one is it, the plumb one?"

"Knock it off," Caleb said, "the red head is the one." Standing, he draped his arm over Keegan's shoulder and put his entire weight on him.

"Maybe we should wait until you lose some weight," Keegan said grunting to hold him up.

Caleb ignored Keegan's struggles and raised his brows to Niles. "You're going to have to look more ill. She looks to be bright," Niles said. Caleb frowned as the thought of being married to Angela, who had probably bedded every man in London. Caleb's face seemed to pale on it's own.

"That's better."

"At least you didn't stick your finger down your throat," Keegan drawled starting off toward the store struggling and weaving under Caleb's added weight.

Caleb gave him a dark look before closing his eyes half way. They were almost upon the two women and he was starting to feel nervous.

"Mistress?" Betsy gasped as the three tried to pass them on the walk and bumped Betsy out of the way.

"Excuse us, my lady. Sick man coming through," Niles said trying to brush past them. But Caleb grabbed her arm and the gentlemen holding him up, lost his grip. The patient slumped toward the sidewalk. Melissa crouched to catch him and found herself sitting on the ground with the man's head cradled in her lap.

"Sorry, my lady. Let me pull him back up. He's a lot weaker than he wants to admit," Keegan stated trying to get a hold of Caleb.

Caleb moaned. "This is the one. Please." Caleb whispered. Melissa bent her head to catch the softly spoken words.

"What one? What's the matter with him?" She blurted absently running her hand down the dark hair on the man's head while looking at Keegan.

"He's dying, my lady. Has less than a day." Niles put in.

Melissa paled and lifted her hands away from him. She noticed the dark circles under his eyes and the thin looks. The man was very handsome. His features were rough looking but in this condition he looked soft and in a great deal of pain. Melissa instantly felt sorry for him. "Are you sure there's nothing you can do for him? He seems so young?" she said stroking his hair again.

"He is. Just twenty-six, but it's a rare disease eating away at his body," Niles said sounding like an actor in a bad play. He wanted to throttle Niles. If things got ruined now he would end up with that whore, Angela, as a wife. Groaning he turned slightly toward Melissa.

"Name?" he mumbled grabbing her arm.

"What?" she asked leaning closer. "My name?" At his nod, she straightened. "It's Melissa," she said leaning down to hear his next words.

"You're beautiful." Melissa blushed and looked up at the two men hovering around her. Betsy was wringing her hands in the folds of her cloak with a look of pure fright on her face.

"Thank you." Glancing back to the man in her lap she asked, "Do you need a lift anywhere?"

"He wanted to walk out in the open since it would be his last time. I tried to tell him he was too weak but he insisted," Keegan said dropping into a crouch next to them. The crowd was quickly being shooed away by Niles and Betsy. They were starting to cause a scene.

"Marry me?" Melissa's eyes shot back to the head in her lap. She knew she hadn't heard what she thought she had.

"I'm sorry. What did you say?"

"Marry me?" he repeated, then went into a torrent of coughs. Niles rolled his eyes at Keegan and continued to tell people to leave them alone. Melissa sat there stunned.

"I'm sorry, my lord, but..."

"My lady," Keegan said drawing her attention to him. She was quite shocked by Caleb's question. "He is a very wealthy man and doesn't have an heir. Being only twenty-six he never thought he would need one this soon." Melissa frowned as she looked down at Caleb. He was lying peacefully in her lap. "His father died two years ago and he doesn't have any relatives to inherit. If you would marry him, he would know his money went to someone with his name."

Melissa's frown deepened. "You can't be serious! He doesn't even know me. Why doesn't he just give it to you and him?" she said pointing to Niles.

Caleb coughed and groaned. Keegan took that as a sign to hurry up and blurted out the rest of it. "He hasn't known us that long. This is his physician and I'm just a friend of only a few months. He wants his name to carry on. A wife will manage that. It was something he always wanted. Couldn't you find it in your heart to marry him? You'll be a widow in just one day," he added in a whisper as if Caleb couldn't hear him. Melissa paled at the last words. A widow! A virgin widow, no less. But that would satisfy her father's wishes. She would then be able to take her time in finding a new husband. Keegan watched the woman's mind work. She was really thinking it over.

Caleb reached up a shaky hand and laid it against her cheek. "Please. Such a beautiful wife you'd be. I would be happy and rest peacefully in my grave." Melissa felt tears come to her eyes. Such a young man faced with a disease that brought death. Looking up she saw the hopeful look on the blond man in front of her and quickly made her decision.

"All right. If it will make your last day special," she whispered stroking her hand through his hair again. Caleb felt like jumping up and doing a jig. His plan had worked perfectly. Now for the wedding!

"I think you made the right decision, my lady," Keegan said grabbing Caleb by the arms and hefting him to his feet. Swinging Caleb's arm over his shoulder he jostled Caleb around to get a good grip. Melissa was helped to her feet by a grinning Niles.

"Thank you, my lady. It's nice to see people with a compassionate heart now and then." Caleb coughed trying not to laugh at the irony of the situation.

Melissa smiled at the brown haired man and then saw Betsy staring at her in disbelief. Melissa flushed scarlet. "Betsy, I think you better go back to Miss Debouir and wait for Simon. Then return to the house and don't tell a soul about what happened here. I'll tell them later tonight." Betsy just stood there. Melissa grabbed her arm and moved away from the gentlemen. "I know I seem a bit foolish but I can't just let the man die without his last dream."

"I'm sure they could find someone else. Your brother is going to kill me if I come back without you. In fact, he's going to kill you anyway. I don't know why I'm worried," she finished throwing her hands up.

"Let me take care of that. Just stay in my room until I come home and I'll deal with the family then." When Betsy gave her a scowl, Melissa started to feel foolish. Turning back to the men she suddenly felt the need to back out. A soft moan escaped from the handsome man's lips and Melissa felt compelled to uphold her word. "Not another word, Betsy. Please just go and do as I ask."

Betsy turned and left without looking back. Taking a deep breath, Melissa walked back to the gentlemen. "I think if I'm going to marry this man I should know more about him," she said falling into step beside them. The blond man was practically carrying the sick one and the doctor was walking with a serious look on his face. Melissa trailed along behind.

"There will be time for that when we reach the chapel."

"Chapel!" she exclaimed stopping. "You mean right now?" she blurted out.

Keegan stopped dragging Caleb around to look at her. "Yes, now. We are running out of time."

"I don't have a dress or shoes or anything for my hair."

"There's no time for that," Keegan said turning around and starting off. Melissa watched them walk away then hurried to catch up.

"There's always time. If you will just tell me which chapel I'll hurry back to the dress shop and buy something already made. My size is pretty normal and I'm sure she has something for me that will be more suitable for a wedding."

Caleb grabbed Keegan's arm and he quickly stopped. Caleb with a great show of effort turned and touched Melissa face. "There isn't time. I feel my life slipping away. I want to marry before that happens. Please?" he said as he slumped against Keegan. Niles silently clapped his hands together behind Melissa's back and Keegan nearly burst out laughing. Caleb was putting on one hell of a show and the lady was soaking up every word.

"Very well, lets get on with it then." Niles grabbed her arm and the four of them hurried along to the little chapel at the edge of town. It had a beautiful yard with benches and trees neatly planted around the yard. A wooden fence surrounded the yard and roses were planted to climb up it. The church and yard were quite lovely.

"This is a lovely church," she said as they walked up the three steps and through the double doors. The inside was solid wood with beautiful carvings of angels and murals on the walls and pews. Melissa smiled.

"Yes, a very lovely church," Keegan said looking at her then proceeding down the isle to the front of the church. Setting Caleb in the first pew he turned to Melissa.

"I need to go find the Priest. This is the only time you'll have to talk with him before the wedding ceremony." Smiling, he gave her hand a brief squeeze, then headed off through a door at the back of the church. Melissa sat down next to her future husband and felt a moment of panic. This was a man she didn't even know. One she couldn't even put a name to, yet she was going to marry him. Caleb moaned and Melissa looked around for the doctor. But he was standing politely at the back of the church looking at the carvings. Turning back to Caleb she reached out and pushed a lock of black hair out of his eyes. Caleb moved slightly toward her but didn't open his eyes.

"I...." she faltered. She didn't know how to ask him the things she needed to know. Taking a deep breath she blurted out her first question. "I would like to know your name, please?"

Caleb opened his eyes and looked at her with sadness. "My name is Caleb. Caleb Cabot," he said coughing. She sure was a beauty. Too bad he hadn't had a chance to meet her and get to know her properly. At least she was a decent woman, though she was thinking she was getting a fortune as soon as he died. Women were all alike. Very greedy.

Melissa smiled. "Caleb Cabot. That's a nice name. What do you do for a living?" she asked, already knowing he didn't have any family and was twenty-six years old.

"I deal in horses."

Melissa smiled. "I have a brother who raises horses. Are your horses race horses?"

Caleb shook his head and coughed. A brother! Hopefully he wasn't the killing type. Frowning, Caleb suddenly needed to know more about the woman he was going to marry.

"What is your name, beautiful?" Melissa blushed but didn't turn away from him.

"Melissa Hayworth."

Caleb nearly sat up straight in his seat. He was sure his eyes had widened so he coughed to collect himself. A Hayworth! Good Lord! They were one of the richest families in all of London. She had said her brother dealt in horses. Ha! The man had the best line of racehorses in all of England. The King even requested several for his own stables.

"Are you all right? Do you need me to call the doctor?" Melissa said anxiously.

Caleb shook his head. That's all he needed was Niles or Keegan poking fun at him. Of all the bloody luck. Frowning, Caleb debated about backing out, then a clear image of Angela came to mind and he knew he would have to follow through with this. His father had the wedding set for tomorrow and he was dead set on messing up those plans. His father wanted him to be a seaman. But he only had to step foot on a ship and his stomach rolled. Besides the fact that he had no interest in the sea, Andrew could marry the whore. He loved the sea and wouldn't be home enough to care what his wife was doing. Caleb would even pass the title down to him. He had money of his own. Looking more clearly at the woman next to him he saw that her eyes were green, and she did indeed have blond hair. What would she think of his deception? Would she murder him in his sleep? Would she let her family kill him instead?

Those questions went unanswered as Keegan returned, followed by a man in robes.

"I understand there is to be a wedding?"

Melissa nodded, standing to meet the priest.

"Excellent. I'm Father John. I was faced with an uneventful day and now it's beginning to look up. Lord Keegan has given me the required papers and I will need the two of you to stand at the front of the church."

Melissa frowned. Caleb couldn't possibly stand for the entire ceremony. "Would it be possible to perform the service with us seated? Perhaps with that small bench over there?" The priest looked shocked at her request but Melissa stumbled on. "My future husband is very ill and doesn't have the strength to stand for the entire ceremony. I was hoping to make him more comfortable."

The priest looked at Caleb and he immediately started coughing. The coughs racked his whole body. The priest's eyes softened. "Of course child. It's unusual but I'm sure the Lord won't mind."

Smiling, Melissa pushed Keegan toward the bench. He gave her an odd look but went to fetch the bench. Caleb smiled, his wife to be, was quite an actress. She had really sounded as if she was concerned for him.

"Would it be a problem to shorten the ceremony, Father?" Melissa said.

Caleb nearly burst out laughing at the look on the priest's face. "I'm sorry my child. There are some things you can't shorten."

Melissa blushed as she helped Caleb to the bench. Niles grabbed Caleb's other side and hauled him toward the bench. "For a doctor, you are rough with your patients," Melissa snapped at the flash of pain that crossed Caleb's face. Niles frowned as a blush crept up his cheeks. It had been years since he'd sported a blush. He felt even more foolish when he saw the laughter in Keegan's eyes. Scowling he placed Caleb on the bench and moved away.

"I'll need both of you to witness this blessed event. If you would stand on either side of them I will begin the ceremony." Both men moved into position and gave each other a look that conveyed they thought the whole plan was beginning to get out of hand.

The ceremony was like every other wedding Melissa had ever sat through. But this time she was repeating the vows to love and honor thy husband while a stranger repeated them back to her. She felt like an observer at her own wedding. Caleb placed a beautiful gold ring on the third finger of her left hand. The sapphires and diamonds sparkled in the light. She placed a ring on Caleb's hand that Keegan handed her. She didn't have a chance to look at it as Caleb leaned over to give her the kiss of peace. The kiss was much stronger than she would have thought he could manage in his weakened condition. Still startled from the whole marriage ceremony she vaguely remembered signing her name to the register along with Caleb, Niles, and Keegan. She didn't even know the doctor's name until she'd seen it on the paper.

Five minutes later they were ushered out of the church by Keegan and thrown into a carriage with a lion crest on the side. She found herself sitting next to a sleeping Caleb hanging onto him as the carriage sped off to god knew where. Melissa Cabot, she repeated over in her head. It sounded odd to her. Suddenly the impact of her impulsive marriage sank in and she felt panic like she'd never experienced in her life. Her family was going to kill her!

Caleb felt his new bride stiffen beside him and wondered what she was thinking. He had to play out this charade until he could consummate the marriage otherwise she could have it annulled. If that happened he could still end up married to Angela. Caleb shuttered at the thought. What was he to do now?

KEEGAN WATCHED THE CARRIAGE DRIVE AWAY before turning to judge Niles's reaction to the whole affair.

Niles looked at him. "The poor sod. He's going to be in for one hell of a fight."

"Why do you say that? Caleb is a good man. The ladies say he's quite apt in the bedroom. She'll get over this bit of treachery."

"I assume by your stupidity that you didn't read her last name on the certificate?"

Keegan scowled at Niles. "No, I didn't read her name."

"If you had, you would understand to what I'm referring."

"Just tell me, you idiot. Quit beating around the bush."

Niles smiled at Keegan. He was such an easy man to rile. "Her last name was Hayworth. Does that ring a bell?"

"My God," Keegan said paling, "she can't be one of those. It's just a coincidence."

"I don't think so, my friend. I happen to know there are a couple of girls in that family and Caleb just married one."

Keegan looked back down the road after the carriage. "My poor brother, indeed. Those brothers of hers will kill him if her father doesn't."

Chapter 21

ALLISON MOVED TO THE WINDOW of her room and felt the familiar coat of her tiger slide beneath her hand. She absently stroked his fur as the tears fell down her face. Of all the things to happen. Her first time out of the house without a family member and total disaster struck. Stifling a sob, she lowered herself into a chair and gave herself up to her grief.

A soft knock at the door had her frantically wiping her tears and blowing her nose. Smoothing her hand down her dress she turned her head to the window. "Come in," she called knowing her voice sounded unsteady.

"Allison? Are you in here?" Nathan asked moving into the room. "Where is your lamp?" he asked, leaving the door open to have light from the hall.

"It's by the bed."

Nathan lit the lamp then went back and shut the door. Looking at Allison, he frowned. She'd been crying. "Are you all right?"

Allison's face crumbled as she covered it with her hands. "It's awful, Nathan. Everything is ruined. Everyone will know what happened. I want to go home."

Nathan moved to the bed and hugged her. "You're a beautiful woman, Allison. Someone is going to appreciate that," he said while she sobbed on his shoulder.

"What am I going to do now? Christopher will end up giving me to some old man." she sobbed.

Nathan stiffened. "He won't do that. Besides, I'm here to help you," he said not knowing how but for once feeling the need to do something right.

Allison lifted her head. "You are? How?" she asked wiping her eyes.

Nathan frowned. "I don't know but trust me. I'll come up with something."

Allison made an attempt to laugh then moved out of his arms. "I think I should just leave the decision up to Christopher."

"You don't trust me? Well, don't make any rash decisions. At least give me a chance."

Allison frowned and blew her nose. "All right," she said, wringing the handkerchief, "would you do me a favor?"

Nathan arched his brows. "What?"

"Would you go to the Earl's and see how he is?"

Nathan frowned. "I don't think..."

"If you don't want to do it then I'll go myself," she said effectively cutting him off.

Nathan scowled. "You sure know how to get what you want, don't you?"

Allison lowered her head. "Obviously not. I need a husband but haven't the slightest idea how to get one. And from the looks of my first attempt, it's not going very well."

Nathan frowned at her sarcasm. "I'll go see the man this afternoon. If I get trounced, you'll have to live with that."

Allison smacked his arm. "Quit kidding. This is serious."

"All right, all right. I'll go see him and talk with you sometime tomorrow. Try to get some rest, okay?"

Allison nodded then waited for the door to close before pulling the bell for Netty. Her maid would calm her enough to sleep, she thought. Waiting was going to kill her.

Chapter 22

MELISSA AND CALEB arrived at his house and were greeted by a stern looking giant. He was bald and looked remarkably like a pirate.

"How was your evening, my lord?" The man asked making Melissa jump at his booming voice.

"Very well. This is my wife, Melissa." Caleb whispered struggling to sit up. The giant paused in his movements to look Melissa over. She felt like a horse at action.

"Very lovely, my lord."

"Bragg, help her down then carry me into the house." Caleb watched the giant's unreadable face for any sign of wonder. As usual there was nothing there. Bragg grabbed Melissa by the waist and practically threw her out of the carriage. She let out a slight squeal before feeling her feet hit the ground as the large hands left her body. She stood stunned as Bragg lifted Caleb off the seat, like he was a rag doll. She watched him carry Caleb past her into the house. Standing there, feeling like an idiot, she trailed after them.

Caleb gave Bragg a look and ordered to be taken to his room. Bragg stomped up the steps and deposited him quite roughly into his bed. Caleb saw his wife purse her lips at the rough treatment then almost laughed at the sight of her struggling not to correct the giant.

"Thank you," he murmured sinking down into the covers trying to look sick.

"Is there anything else?"

"Not at this time," he said, as the giant went to leave. "Please do not disturb us," he added. Bragg nodded, neither turning around nor stopping. Caleb glanced at his wife who was standing stiffly at the window. How was he to accomplish his husbandly rights with a woman who would probably kill him once he told her the situation? "Melissa?" he called. His wife immediately turned and headed to the bed.

"Is there something you need?"

Caleb shook his head. It was almost completely dark outside and he knew it would be too early to sleep. "How about dinner?"

Melissa smiled. "I think that would be lovely. Anything you want in particular?"

Caleb tilted his head. "I'll leave it up to you," he said folding his hands across his stomach. Melissa nodded and headed for the door.

Melissa went in search of the kitchen. It turned out the house was much larger than Aunt Ginger's but laid out similarly. She located the kitchen rather quickly and hurried into the room only to jump out of her skin when the giant stepped in front of her.

"Good Heavens!"

"Sorry, my lady. I didn't mean to scare you. Is there something you need?"

The giant had no facial expression at all. Melissa wanted to hit him in the nose to see if his eyes would water. "I wished to tell the cook to prepare something for Caleb, I mean, my husband. And for me, of course."

"I'll take her the message."

"I wanted to choose the dishes myself."

"Tell me and I will tell her."

Pursing her lips Melissa silently vowed not to throw a fit. She was only going to be here a short time. Clenching her teeth, she rattled off one of her brothers favorite dinners then returned to Caleb's room.

She opened the door and quietly closed it behind her. She didn't want to wake Caleb, but as she turned around, she found her husband awake and sitting up in bed. Her eyebrows shot up in surprise.

"Feeling better?" she asked. He nodded then patted the bed beside him. She drew her brows down wondering at his complexion. He didn't look ready to pass away anytime soon and where was the doctor? He said he would be over to check on him early in the morning.

"I feel better. I have a new wave of energy."

Smiling, she moved to the edge of the bed. "Well, don't use it all up. I've ordered a dinner fit for a king."

Caleb smiled. Melissa sucked in her breath. The man was gorgeous. His dark hair hung nearly to his shoulders. His eyes were a soft brown, reminding Melissa of a rabbit she once had. His smile made the hard lines of his face softer. "I would like to ask you something," he said taking her hand and holding it in his lap. At her slow nod he continued. "Would you mind if I tried to consummate our marriage?"

The question hung in the air like a stale odor. Melissa flushed scarlet and Caleb found himself holding his breath. She had lowered her head but Caleb took heart since she hadn't removed her hand from his.

Melissa felt trapped. If she said no, the man would die never knowing the pleasure of his wife's company, but on the other hand she was sure he'd had other women. But what if he died while in the act. Melissa paled. Caleb saw her complexion and wondered what thoughts were making her pale.

"I don't know. I...I don't know the ways between a man and a woman, so if you...if you had trouble, I couldn't help you."

Caleb nearly burst out laughing. Trouble with sex? The thought was even funnier in his mind. "I feel stronger since we wed. I think I will be able to manage well enough."

Melissa raised her eyes to his, looking for something in his eyes but all she read was the need to have her understanding. She lowered her eyes.

"I know it's a lot to ask, but there is a chance my seed will take root, and leave a child to remember me by." The lie slipped easily from his lips. He was already so far down in the muck a few more feet wouldn't hurt anything. Melissa stood and walked back to look out the window. Would it be a sin to say no? Would God forgive her for denying a dying man? Gathering up strength she didn't know she had, she turned and returned to the bed. Sitting down she picked his hand back up and held it in her lap.

"If you feel strong enough then..." she didn't finish she just lowered her head. Caleb couldn't believe she agreed. The guilt at deceiving her was so strong at that moment he almost confessed everything. The arrival of Niles stopped him. Melissa got to her feet and fled the room murmuring something about getting dinner.

Niles watched her hasty departure then turned to Caleb, "Proud of yourself?"

"Don't start in on me, Niles. I am already feeling enough quilt to toss in the towel."

"Then maybe you should. The girl seems like a descent sort."

"I know," he said feeling a new wave of quilt pass through him.

"Keegan wouldn't even come over with me. He's afraid one of her brothers will get wind of the scam and find a new arrangement for his face."

Caleb's frowned deepened, "So you saw her last name?"

"Yes. And I think you're crazy for going through with the plan. She's going to cause a lot of trouble. Not to mention the fact that her brothers are large men."

"Thank you for that information. If you had any idea how much I hate the sea, you would understand my position," Caleb said clearly upset.

"I do understand your position since I happen to be your physician in this scheme. You do realize that I don't know the first thing about treating a patient?"

Caleb grinned despite his guilty feelings. Niles was a friend of his from school. He was also the Earl of March and had spent his time, up until the past two days, running an estate twice the size of Caleb's. Niles had made both of them into very wealthy men. But he was right. He wasn't even close to being a doctor.

"Furthermore, I hope that you will get your wife," he drawled the word making a new wave of quilt flare in Caleb's heart, "to forgive me and Keegan. We don't wish to tangle with that family over some idiotic plan of yours."

"Quit worrying. I'll probably be dead in the morning from Melissa bashing my head in. You won't have to worry about a thing."

Niles grinned, "That would be something to see."

Melissa entered the room and smiled to see them laughing. Caleb immediately started coughing to make it look like he was still sick. "Your color is improving" Melissa said, "isn't it doctor?" Niles glanced at Caleb and remarked that it was.

"I do think a good meal will improve your coloring even more," Niles added heading for the door. "I'll return sometime tomorrow. Take care," he added and when Melissa bowed her head he shot Caleb a wink and a grin then let himself out.

"I did bring a terrific meal," she said bringing the trays over to the bed. Putting one on Caleb's lap she quickly pulled off the lids on all the covered dishes. "What would you like?" Caleb looked at the food and felt his stomach grumble.

"I think a bit of everything."

Melissa smiled her approval and scooped some from each dish onto his plate. Then did the same for herself. Taking the main tray away and setting it on the table to their left, she returned and picked up her tray and settled it on her lap. They ate in silence. Caleb watched the dainty woman across from him eat with grace and charm. He felt a moment of guilt and regret at having this lovely creature for a wife.

"Is the food upsetting your stomach?" she asked, her brows drawn down in concern.

Caleb smiled. "No. The meal is delicious."

Melissa blushed slightly at the compliment as she removed the trays. "Is there anything else you'd like?"

Caleb shook his head, as Bragg opened the door without knocking. Giving the giant a frown Caleb's eyebrows shot up as soon as his wife spoke. "Thank you, Bragg. If you would take these things away and bring us some port...err...and brandy, that will be all for the evening."

Bragg looked down at the woman, took the tray she shoved into his hands, and scowled. Looking at the bed, Caleb gave him a grin and a nod. Bragg turned and left the room.

Melissa frowned at the closed door. "You have a very strange man there. Almost as odd as your doctor."

Caleb laughed at that. "What's wrong with Niles?"

Melissa reddened. "Well, for a dying man no one seems very interested in the state of your health. The doctor didn't even stay in the house. What if you have problems?"

Caleb frowned at that. He hadn't thought about that. "Bragg can locate Niles in seconds. Niles always leaves his direction."

Melissa nodded, "Of course." Suddenly, she began to get very nervous. "Is there something else you need?"

"No." Caleb said shifting on the bed. "Well actually. I should probably get into a nightshirt."

Melissa turned scarlet. Was he thinking she would help him with that? "When Bragg returns..."

Caleb held up his hand. "He doesn't do that sort of work." At her angry protest, he continued, "even for a dying man. It would hurt his pride."

Melissa pursed her lips. She would deal with the servant at a later date after...Caleb...after he... She paled as that thought popped into her head. Her husband was going to die. Turning away, she quickly moved to the window. You could see the square and all the carriages moving around below. Her family would be worried. The ball was about to start and she was nowhere to be found.

Bragg entered, again without knocking. He set the port and brandy down with a smack, two mugs followed then the door slammed, shaking a picture nearly off the wall. Caleb gritted his teeth at the obvious temper his friend was showing but didn't comment.

"Well, really! That servant needs a good tongue lashing," she said standing by the window with her hands on her hips. Caleb took a deep breath. She was a lovely woman. Her eyes were deep green set in a heart shaped face. Feeling a wave of guilt, he sat up in bed and swallowed. He would have to tell her. He couldn't ruin her without her knowing the facts. Hoping she would choose to stay, he nearly jumped off the bed when Melissa touched his shoulder.

"What is it? Are you feeling worse?" she asked, concern lacing her voice. Caleb swallowed and leaned back on the pillows.

"No, I think I should get into that nightshirt," he said not wanting to lie but unable to tell her the truth.

Melissa pursed her lips. "Here then? I'll help you. Can you sit up?"

Caleb sat up and pretended at straining as she quickly unbuttoned his shirt pulling the ends out of his breeches. Having trouble, she sat on the bed and tried to help him sit up and remove the shirt at the same time. He felt a jolt of desire that had her blushing at the whole misguided plan. Leaning slightly toward her, he could feel her breath on his shoulder and knew he wasn't going to say a word about the plan. This woman was his no matter the circumstances. And he wanted her.

Melissa threw the shirt toward a chair as her hands touched bare flesh. Suddenly the room seemed to be unbearably hot. Swallowing, she made her first error by looking into Caleb's eyes. He had beautiful eyes that were deep pools of amber liquid.

Caleb looked first at her eyes then slowly moved his eyes to her lips watching her mouth open slightly at the intake of air. Lifting a hand he ran his finger along her cheek and over her lips. Hearing her small gasp he smiled. "You're so beautiful," he whispered, leaning forward to capture her lips in a gentle kiss.

Melissa felt trapped as desire flowed through her body. She didn't understand the feeling, but knew the feelings were the most wonderful thing she had ever experienced. Giving herself up to the moment she tipped her head slightly and felt the kiss strengthen. As Caleb's hands moved up her back she gave a silent prayer to heaven 'Please don't let him die on me' then lost all conscious thought. As she shifted, she felt his hands moving on her but didn't really pay attention to what he was doing. His kisses were nearly making her faint.

In no time at all she was in the bed without any clothes on and Caleb was kissing her like something out of a fairy tale. She felt wonderful and began running her fingers through his hair. Caleb groaned as she repeated the process. He kissed her throat and shoulders then heard her gasp as his mouth closed over her left nipple. He began pulling and teasing it into a hard peak. She squirmed against him. The heat of his body along the length of her own was causing her to moan as his mouth tortured her right breast in the same manner as it had the left. Her body was on fire and she couldn't seem to help herself. Her hands were all over his body. Rubbing along his back and down his sides as he kissed and licked her neck and breasts. Her breathing came in small pants and she felt a wetness between her legs that wanted something she didn't know how to ask for. Rubbing her body against his, she heard him growl as she moved her hands into his hair. Running them deep through his hair she felt his lips return to hers and the kiss changed. She felt his body against hers, all muscle and hard flesh.

Caleb felt ready to explode. The woman beneath him was a mass of heated flesh and the soft purring sounds she kept making were driving him over the edge. He moved between her thighs knowing it was her first time. When she moved her legs apart and ran her feet down the length of his legs then back up again he nearly came undone. Moving forward he felt the tip of his manhood come up against her swollen flesh.

"Oh God, you're so sweet," he murmured pushing further into her flesh. She was tight but ready and kissing him with a passion that left them both gasping for breath.

"Caleb..." she gasped and he knew she was almost there. Easing against the barrier he steadied himself as she moved her legs along his again and he couldn't take it anymore. Driving himself home, he heard her gasp. He tried to wait but she was still moving and making soft purring noises. He couldn't wait and stopping was out of the question.

"Sorry, love," he whispered taking her mouth and kissing her deep. His tongue delved deep as their bodies merged together. She was frantic beneath him and he began to thrust into her, watching the passion on her face. Seeing that made his own desire rage beyond his control. He drove into her with hard fast thrusts. Melissa cried out as the waves of pleasure engulfed her. Her release brought his forth.

Caleb collapsed on her, holding himself off her just enough not to crush her. Melissa took several deep breaths trying to get her body back to normal. That was the most outstanding experience she'd ever been a part of. Running her hands over his back she tensed. Caleb wasn't moving! Good Lord, he died. Panic seized her. Pushing on him she sighed in relief as he lifted himself above her.

"What's wrong? Did I hurt you?"

Melissa turned scarlet and lowered her eyes. "When you didn't move...well, I thought..."

Caleb flushed as the deception he'd played returned. His face lost some of it's color as her words sank in. She thought he had died on her. Moving slightly off her, he pulled her into the crook of his arm and stared at the ceiling. Melissa shifted and snuggled up to him. What the hell was he going to do now?

Melissa felt shy and uncertain. Had she done anything wrong? Was he disappointed? Not knowing if his last memories would be good or bad she remained silent. Her eyelids began to droop as the steady beat of his heart lulled her to sleep.

Caleb felt her drift off and gave her a small squeeze. This moment of complete contentment wouldn't last. She was going to kill him, he was sure.

Chapter 23

JESSICA CURSED as the carriage came to a halt. Looking out the window she stared at Aunt Ginger's town house. She was again on auction for the gents of London. Scowling, she cursed and was feeling sorry for herself. She was made of sterner stuff than that. Stepping down from the carriage, she thanked the footman and started up the steps to the door. It opened immediately.

"Who is it, Jenkins?" Aunt Ginger asked, stepping into the foyer. "Jessica? Are you back then, Dear? Of course, you are? Let's get you into a suitable gown. We have a ball in less than half an hour."

"I don't plan on attending any damn ball," she snapped moving past her Aunt to start up the stairs.

"Hold it right there, young lady," Aunt Ginger's voice rang with authority. "Your father has asked for my help and I believe if I marched down the hall to the study and put your statement to Christopher, it would change your tune immediately."

Jessica gave her Aunt a level stare. "I'm not going to the ball," she said enunciating each word. Turning she left a speechless Ginger behind. Ginger watched her climb the stairs, and debated whether or not to report her to Christopher. Pursing her lips, she decided to inform Brand. He needed to know that she didn't appreciate him foisting his children off on her. They were entirely too much work!

Jessica scowled when she heard her Aunt's angry footsteps march across the foyer floor. Christopher was going to have a fit if her Aunt truly ratted her out. Continuing up the stairs, she entered her room and flung herself onto the bed. "What the hell am I doing? I should have jumped aboard the nearest ship and high tailed it to some god forsaken place and never returned."

"That wouldn't go over very well. We'd miss you."

Jessica sat and looked around until she located her sister. "Allison, what are you doing in here?"

Allison turned scarlet. "Is this your room, then?"

Jessica sat there a moment then burst into laughter. "Yes it is. How long have you been in here?"

"All afternoon, I'd say. I did wonder about Nero, though. I should go and let him out. He's been cooped up by himself all day."

Jessica chuckled. "I don't mind him in here. Do you want me to fetch him?"

Allison nodded. Jessica left and returned a few minutes later with Nero in tow. Nero spotted Allison and let out a low mew then stuck his big head in her lap. "I guess he missed me." Hearing Jessica reseat herself on the bed, Allison turned toward her. "Now what's all this about going to another country?"

"Never mind. Stephan would only track me down and haul me home anyway," Jessica said miserably. Allison immediately heard the pain in her voice.

"What happened?"

Jessica felt her eyes water and frowned. "I lost my ship."

Allison paled. "Your ship? You mean Stephan sank it? Is he all right?"

Jessica made an exasperated sound. "No, he didn't sink it. I did this all by myself," she said flopping back on the bed. "I'm so stupid. Jonathan has to give my ship away."

"He's giving it away? But why?" After a brief pause and no answer she scowled. "What exactly did you do?"

"I'd rather not say." Jessica heard Allison's foot tapping and snorted. "Oh, very well. A few months ago Stephan and I were having trouble with our business. Stephan said not to worry about it, but things weren't picking up and expenses were piling up," Jessica stated getting up to pace. "You know how I am. I can't stand it when things aren't running smoothly and...well...I did something really stupid."

"What?" Allison whispered afraid of what Jessica was going to say.

"I crawled into the Baron of Essex's cellar and changed several kegs of wine by adding water."

"You did what?" Allison said hardly breathing.

"I took four satchels full of water down there and added it to his kegs. He sold it to a client who promptly dropped him as a supplier. Stephan and I picked up the client. Things were getting back on track until the Baron spoiled it all. Now Jonathan is making me give my ship to the Baron for his loss in clients and Stephan has to pay him a few shipments. I just can't believe I did something that stupid," she finished flopping back on the bed.

Allison pursed her lips. "As usual you get yourself in so much trouble only a saint could save you," Allison said sternly. "Did the Baron agree to this plan?" At Jessica's reluctant 'yes' Allison sighed. "What happens now?

Do you go to trial for stealing?"

Jessica lifted her head and stared at her sister. "No. The Baron didn't mention that. In fact, he agreed to keep my name hidden. I think Jonathan and Stephan convinced him to use a phony Captain for the scapegoat."

"That's good anyway. You can always sail one of Stephan's ships. I don't know why you're so upset?"

"I can't sail his ships! I've always done for myself. I refuse to put Stephan out. Besides he probably won't want to work with me anymore. I almost ruined his name as well as my own," she said dropping her head back on the bed.

"I think you're being stubborn. Stephan will let you sail one of his ships and I'm sure he has already forgiven you for your lapse in judgment."

Jessica again lifted her head. "You just don't get it, do you, Al? I can't ask Stephan to let me sail. It would be like asking Christopher to find me a husband. It's not their burden to look out for me. I can take care of myself." Jessica frowned as Allison turned toward the window and a look of pain crossing her face. Moving to her sister's side she nudged Nero aside and knelt by her legs. "What's the matter? You look like you want to retch?"

Allison swallowed several times to keep the tears from falling. "You're not the only one that has done something stupid," she said still keeping her head turned toward the window. "I too made a fool of myself. I'm surprised Melissa hasn't come storming in here telling me how I've ruined everything for her."

"It can't be that bad. She would have done exactly that if it was really awful. Let's hear it."

Allison lowered her head. "I made a total fool of myself," she whispered. "I went to Lord McMaster's home for dinner and I spilled wine all over his brother and sister-in-law. To top it off, Christopher and Nathan arrived and got in a fight with the Earl."

Jessica's brows shot up. "Christopher and Nathan trounced him?"

"I didn't actually see it," she said with sarcasm, "but Christopher was brought home, out cold."

"All this happened while I was gone. I can't believe it," she said moving back to the bed. "Is Nathan trounced, too?"

Allison frowned at the excited note in her voice. "It really isn't a laughing matter, Jess. I think I just lost all hope of a suitable husband. I will be forced to marry one Christopher picks out." Lowering her head she added, "I told him to choose, just this afternoon."

"You what? Now, that's what I call stupid. Allison, look, I'll help you find a husband. I'm sure the Earl didn't say a word about getting his face smashed in. Men don't like that sort of thing spread to the ton. Believe me. No one will be the wiser."

Allison looked up hopeful. "Are you sure? Christopher, according to

Melissa, has a black eye, cracked lip, and swollen jaw. I'm sure the Earl looks much the same. Won't people ask about that?"

"Sure. They'll even speculate, but you can bet the real reason doesn't come out. Now, the first thing you have to do is go see Christopher and tell him you want to pick your own husband. He can have his opportunity if you haven't found someone in three months."

"We only have two and a half months left."

Jessica scowled. "Don't remind me. Just remember, you pick your own future. Now let's go find Christopher. I should tell him I'm back anyway, though I'm sure Aunt Ginger already has."

"You saw her? Then you know about the ball tonight. Are you going?"

"Hell no! I mean...of course not. I just arrived home. I'll go to the next one." Giving Allison's gown a look, she frowned, "you're going, aren't you?"

Allison shook her head. "I don't want to see anyone."

Jessica snorted. "And you plan to find husband, say, under the bed? Come on. We have to catch Christopher before he leaves. I assume Nathan is taking Melissa."

"I don't know I haven't seen anyone since this morning."

Jessica stopped to stare at her sister. "Since morning? You've been in this room all day."

Allison turned scarlet. "I did wonder where my things were. But Netty just tended me in here and didn't say a word. In fact, she kept Nero with her. I'm not sure if I should holler at her for letting me stay in your room or thank her."

"I think you should just let it go. I wasn't here to complain so whose going to know unless you make a stink about it."

Allison grinned. "You're always so refreshing to have around, Jess. I don't know why everyone has a hard time in your company."

"Who has a hard time in my company? I'm a right lovable gal."

Allison laughed at that outrageous statement and Jessica joined in.

"There you are. Have either of you seen Melissa?" Nathan grumbled looking all decked out in his fine clothes.

Allison frowned. "I haven't. She was going for ribbons earlier, if that helps."

"Did anyone go with her?" he asked looking at Jessica.

"Don't ask me. I just strolled in ten minutes ago." Grinning at his fine togs. Shaking her hand, she whistled. Nathan ignored her.

"Allison?"

"I think she took Betsy."

"I'm going to kill her. She gets me all dressed up then leaves me waiting like a fool," he snapped turning toward the stairs. "Wait until I get my hands on her!"

"Come on, Al. I don't want to miss any of this," Jessica said grabbing Allison's arm and pulling her along the hall. Allison grabbed the rail to steady herself as they descended the stairs at a fast pace. Reaching the study they were just in time to hear Christopher explode. "Damn. We missed it," Jessica snapped pulling Allison into the room.

"Hello, Christopher. What's going on?" Jessica asked.

"Where the hell is your sister? She wanted to go to this damn ball," he shouted, wincing as his lip cracked more.

"Nice face," she said, grinning.

Christopher growled at her. "Don't mess with me, Jess. I'll tan your backside for the least little reason."

Jessica narrowed her eyes thinking he knew about Stephan's little lesson, then laughed realizing he couldn't possibly know. "I'm worried," she said, wiggling her fingers at him.

"What's keeping that girl? I sent for her five minutes ago." Christopher shouted giving Jessica a warning look to keep her mouth shut. Betsy knocked, then entered the study. She looked terrified.

"Relax, Christopher. You'll never get anything out of her by shouting," Allison said taking a seat on the sofa.

Christopher took a deep breath and managed to sit down. "All right, Betsy. Where is Melissa?"

Betsy swallowed. "She was going to look at a church. I didn't want to leave her but she ordered me to."

"You left her alone?" Christopher shouted surging to his feet.

"Alone in the city?" Nathan asked moving closer to Betsy. Betsy promptly burst into tears. Jessica cursed and began pacing.

"Everyone, please, calm down," Allison said getting to her feet and moving to sit beside Betsy. "Shouting isn't going to help any, is it, Betsy?" Handing her a handkerchief she waited while the girl wiped her eyes and blew her nose. "Please tell us everything. Start from the beginning."

Betsy took a hold of Allison's hand and looked at her. Allison was the least frightening of the family. "We were going to get some ribbons for the ball tonight. Lady Melissa wanted to get some for you, too. She even said I could have some."

"I'm sure she did. Melissa can be nice when the mood strikes her."

Betsy smiled hesitantly. "We reached the dress shop and told Simon to meet us back there in an hour but we ended up moving down the lane a bit to several different shops before she found the ribbons she liked. I didn't get any for myself but she did find you a pair."

"That's nice. What happened next?"

"As soon as we stepped out of the shop with the pretty ribbons, these three men came along. One was real sick like and the other two were carrying him. They said he was dying and that his last wish was to go see some church down the way. I told her that she shouldn't go but Lady Melissa wouldn't listen. She told me she would be fine and to go with Simon. She said she would be along shortly."

"You left her?" Nathan snapped moving close.

"I certainly did not!" Betsy stated, stiffening. "Simon and I followed the four of them to the little church in the Square. You know the one with all the statues and angels?"

"Yes, St. Vincent's."

"Yes, that's the one. We watched them enter and we stayed for almost two hours. When she still hadn't come out we went in looking for her. The Father said she had left out the back," she finished, crying again.

"For heavens sakes," Jessica snapped.

"Why didn't you come and tell me right away," Christopher shouted.

"I...I tried. You ordered me to go away."

Christopher reddened. He vaguely remembered yelling at the maid. "If it's important, you should insist," he finished, exasperated.

"See! All you do is rant at everybody. You're going to end up like Father," Jessica said. "How long ago did she go to the church?" she asked Betsy.

Betsy sniffed. "We left here at two o'clock. I would say three or so."

"My God. That's five hours. She could be anywhere." Nathan snapped running his fingers through his hair.

Allison frowned in Nathan's direction. "Relax, Nathan. That isn't helping. I think the first thing we should do is go to the church. The Father probably can tell us something. We'll have to start there."

Jessica grinned. "Yes, she's right. I'll go change and we'll head straight there." No one commented, but both brothers waited for her before leaving.

Chapter 24

MELISSA AWOKE snuggled up to the warm flesh beside her. She instantly stiffened as the situation became clear. My God. I'm married! Shifting a little, she looked up at her husband and sighed. He was a handsome devil, wasn't he? His soft black hair was mussed around his face. She sighed, remembering the brown eyes that had stared at her with such passion. Blushing, she lowered her head back to his chest and sighed again. It certainly wasn't the wedding of her dreams, but so far things had gone with unexpected pleasantness.

Caleb listened to his wife sigh as she snuggled up to him. Looking again at the ceiling he frowned. Now was the time to tell her. She needed to know. "Melissa?"

She shifted again so she leaned over him and smiled. "How do you feel?"

Caleb smiled back. She looked like an angel. Her blond hair was all tussled around her head. Her eyes sparkled with knowledge of a night spent with a man.

"I'm fine, thank you," he said pulling her against him. She smiled shyly and didn't protest when he pulled her head down for a kiss. Melissa felt the now familiar flutter in her stomach and gave herself up to the feelings.

Caleb silently cursed himself for kissing her. He wanted her again and now wasn't the time for that.

Both occupants of the bed sat up as the door to their room flew open. A pile of men followed it into the room. Silence followed as her brothers stumbled into the room only to stop and stare at the bed.

"My God!" Melissa screeched jumping beneath the covers and scooting behind her husband. Caleb looked first at her then at the angry men in his room.

"I'm going to kill you, Cabot!" Christopher gritted out moving toward the bed.

Caleb swallowed and shifted his gaze to his brother's as he came into the room. Keegan shrugged. "You, Sir, are intruding on me and my wife. Now get out?"

"That's it. The man gets his throat slit," Jessica said striding for the bed. Niles grabbed her from behind. "I'd remove my hands, if I valued my manhood," she said firmly.

Niles paled as he felt the length of a knife along the inside of his right leg. Swallowing he removed his hands. The woman had a knife to his private parts. Caleb was on his own as far as he was concerned.

"Wise move," she hissed, pushing him out of the way as she continued for the bed. Nathan and Christopher started throwing punches as Keegan tried to keep them away from Caleb.

"That's enough!" Melissa screeched standing up in the center of the bed a sheet hanging down the front of her. "Get out of this room, this instant! We will talk with you in the library. Keegan please show them where that is," she snapped, her voice ringing with authority.

Nathan and Christopher stared at her. "I'm not going anywhere, until I take a chunk out of that man's hide," Nathan growled moving toward the bed. Keegan again moved to intercede but Melissa held up a hand.

"Get out! I will talk to you in ten minutes," she shouted, staring at each of her family members in turn. Jessica gave her a perplexed look.

"You actually married the man? Willingly?"

Melissa turned scarlet. "Yes I did! Now get out!" she snapped pulling the sheet higher.

Niles and Keegan looked at one another then at Caleb. He was staring at his wife like she'd grown two heads. Instantly, he noted the sheet was awful flimsy.

"Get down here," he snapped pulling her back down into the bed. "Everyone else out. I'll speak with you in fifteen minutes," he stated firmly, not leaving any room for discussion.

Christopher and Nathan hesitated but left the room. Jessica gave another look to the bed. "He didn't force you?"

"Get out or I'll have my servant throw you out?" Caleb snapped.

Jessica's face hardened but she left just the same. Caleb ran his hand through his hair. He hadn't expected them to show up this early. They were supposed to come in the morning. He felt Melissa's hands on his back and glanced over his shoulder at her.

"I'm sorry. They can be a trial I know, but they were only concerned for my welfare," she said biting her lip.

Caleb felt quilt and turned away. "Melissa, I have to tell you something. Before we go down and speak to your family."

"Are you ill? Do you need the doctor?"

Caleb snorted at that statement. "No, I don't need a doctor. In fact, that's what I need to tell you. I don't need a doctor at all. I'm not dying." Melissa's hands stilled on his back then moved away all together. She was pale, uncertain. Caleb felt like a heel. "I was going to tell..."

"You lied to me?" she asked moving away from him further. "You lied?" she said again clutching the sheet to her neck. Caleb watched as the range of emotions crossed her face. Disbelieve, betrayal, and finally anger. "Oh, my God!" she snapped sliding from the bed dragging the sheet with her. Caleb grabbed a robe and slipped into it.

"It's not like you think," he said getting a glare from her. "Well, at least I don't think it is. I did lie to you, but I meant to tell you earlier. Before...but..."

Melissa felt the tears sting her eyes. She wanted to scream. The beautiful night of lovemaking settled like a ball in her stomach. "I am so naive. To think a man like yourself would marry some girl off the street, just because he was dying, no less," she said laughing pitifully as a sob escaped from behind her hand. "What was it? My money? My name?"

"What?" he said, stunned at her deduction. "I never intended to hurt you. I was going to tell you everything and let you decide for yourself if you wanted to stay married to me," he said moving toward her only to stop short as she lifted a hand to stop his advance.

"I want to know everything," she snapped, tapping her foot, waiting.

Caleb ran a hand through his hair. She was listening at least. "My father wanted me to marry a girl to unite our shipping firms. I refused but he set the alliance up anyway."

"You're already married?" she exclaimed coming out of the chair.

"Of course not. I wasn't going to marry until tomo...row," he finished his voice trailing off at the devastation on her face.

"Tomorrow!" She screeched. "You were going to get married tomorrow?" she shouted, shaking with anger. Suddenly her shoulders sagged. "My God," she whispered anguish making tears fill her eyes. "What have I done now?"

"It wasn't my idea," Caleb insisted, his guts twisting at the look on her face. "My father was forcing me. I can't even step foot on a ship without losing my stomach contents," he said moving toward her but stopping as she backed against the wall. "I decided yesterday that I was taking matters into my own hands and finding myself my own wife. I have two other brothers that can marry..."

"You have two brothers? And a father?" Melissa snapped anger making color flood her face. "What else did you lie about?"

Caleb flushed "I have three brothers and a father. My mother is alive as well." Melissa felt panicked. Seeing her struggle and begin to cry, Caleb moved again in her direction.

"Don't!" she said holding out her arm. "I don't want you near me." Tears were streaming down her face now too quickly to check.

Caleb stopped and took a deep breath. "I'm sorry, Melissa. I have no excuse for what I've done and you have every right to hate me." Bowing his head, he moved toward the closet. "I'll leave you to yourself," he added closing the door behind him.

Melissa dropped into the chair and just stared into the empty room. He lied to her. She was married to a man she knew nothing about and who wasn't going to die anytime soon. Looking at the bed she saw the blotch of red on the sheets and paled. She was truly married to the liar and there was nowhere for her to turn. Christopher! She thought remembering her family. She would go to him. She might be married but she wouldn't have to be for long. Scrambling out of the chair she winced at the soreness between her legs. Determined now, she decided then and there to make her husband pay for his deceit.

CHRISTOPHER PACED THE SMALL LIBRARY, "I can't believe she would be so stupid. The man must have forced her."

Jessica, who was cleaning her nails with the tip of her knife, snorted. "She said she wasn't forced. Knowing Melissa he's probably rich. She married him for his money."

Keegan lifted his brows at that. At least the raven-haired girl knew her sister. The money had lured her into matrimony. Though the fact that the groom would be dead tomorrow wasn't exactly ignored.

"I don't like it. Melissa is naive all right but she can't be stupid enough to marry a man she doesn't even know and especially without asking permission."

"She was in his bed. If she isn't married to him I'm going to rip his..."

"I think I like my body parts where they are," Caleb said cutting Christopher's tirade short. "If you would all please sit down," he said, looking at the woman sitting on his desk, "on the sofa, I will be glad to answer your questions."

Jessica paused to look at Caleb. "I don't think you should start by ordering us around. We want to hear all our answers from Melissa."

Caleb's face hardened, "The lady is my wife and if you want any answers they will have to come from me."

Jessica put her knife away. "I see," she said getting to her feet to move and lean against the window frame. "That certainly is a good way to deal with my brothers. Have at him Christopher," She said waving her arm at Caleb.

Caleb scowled at the woman before returning his gaze to the brothers. "I don't see what difference it makes whether my wife is here or not."

"It makes a big difference, Cabot. It lets us know whether you're lying or not. Melissa hardly knows the meaning of the word."

The black haired man had snarled that remark making Caleb swallow. What would Melissa say to their questions? Hell, what was he supposed to say?

"I'm here, Nathan. Exactly what is it you want to know?" Melissa said calmly walking into the room before moving around to stand by the desk. Caleb stared at her but she wouldn't even look at him.

Nathan shifted his feet. "Tell us what made you make such an asinine decision?"

Melissa reddened. "I don't think that was called for," she snapped, already irritated at her own stupid behavior. Tossing her hair over her shoulder she lifted her chin. "What exactly do you want to know, Nathan? Did the man force me? He did not. Did he ruin me then marry me to correct his mistake? He did not. Did he threaten me? He did not. What do you want to know?" she fairly screeched.

Nathan threw both hands in the air. "I want to know why the hell you married him without consent?"

"It's obvious to me," Melissa said snobbishly, "the man's a handsome devil. Father wanted us to marry. So marry I did." Everyone stared at her as if she were insane. Caleb included.

"You married him for his looks?" Jessica said, stunned.

"Don't be an ass. I married him because we both wanted too. We agreed on several points. Isn't that right, Caleb?"

Caleb cleared his face of all emotion as his wife of just hours looked at him for the first time since he told her what he'd done. She almost dared him not to lie. "Melissa is right. We agreed to marry," Caleb said firmly. Keegan's brows shot into the air. This was getting interesting.

Christopher looked from one to the other. "Why didn't you come to me about this?"

"Couldn't wait," Melissa said turning red. Jessica laughed at that.

"A bit lusty, aren't you, Melissa?" she added getting a savage look from both Nathan and Christopher.

"Shut up, Jessica. You're talking stupid."

"She's the one that said it," she added coming away from the window. "I think I heard all I need to know. She's married and that's what Father wanted. I'm going home. Allison will want to know what's going on. I'll send Arty to inform Jonathan and Stephan," she said leaving the study before anyone could say anything.

Nathan stared after her. "I think I better go with her. She might kill someone on the way home." Looking back at Melissa, he frowned. "I don't understand what's happened here, Melissa, but if you need anything remember you have a number of family members from which to choose." Pulling her into his arms, he kissed her head giving Caleb a narrowed look over her shoulder. Caleb stiffened at that and wondered why Melissa wasn't blurting out the whole charade. He'd planned on looking like her older brother did, black eyes and cracked lips.

"All you have to do is ask," he added squeezing her shoulders before releasing her and leaving the study to catch up to Jessica.

Melissa blinked several times waiting to see what Christopher was going to say. Swallowing, Christopher moved to stand before her. "I'll have Betsy pack up your trunks and send them over," he said, towering over her as he stared at Caleb.

"Thank you, Christopher," she whispered, moving to get a hug from him and finding she didn't really want to let him go. She wanted him to make everything all right.

Christopher frowned down at the top of her head bringing his arms around her to hold her. He glared at Caleb, "I think the two of us should talk in private."

Caleb nodded his consent. "Keegan, take Melissa back up to my room. Christopher and I need to talk.

Keegan waited for Melissa to leave Christopher's side. Christopher's temper exploded, as he peeled Melissa's arms from around his waist. For an accepting bride she wasn't acting like one. When the pair left, Christopher whirled on Caleb. "I don't know exactly what happened here but I can sure as hell tell she isn't happy."

Caleb stiffened, "She's just upset at the intrusion."

"That's a bloody lie!" he growled. Both men stood staring at each other, neither saying a word. "I don't know what you did to get her to marry you. Banes weren't read or the proper procedure followed. You need to rectify those issues. We will not stand by and let you ruin her reputation. I will not have her humiliated."

Caleb flushed at the set down, "I'll see to it."

Christopher scowled. "I'll send the contract over for you to review. Though my father has left the decision up to me, I still need his consent. He will also need to be informed of the situation. Care to enlighten me?"

Caleb set his jaw. He wasn't about to tell the brother anything until he had a chance to talk with Melissa, "I think you know enough."

Christopher's face darkened. "If I hear a word that you're not treating her right, you'll have to answer to me!" he snapped slamming out of the room. Caleb sank slowly into the chair behind his desk and leaned his head against the back of the chair.

"Still think it was a good plan?" Keegan asked, coming into the room.

"Shut up, Keegan. It's bad enough I have to deal with her family unprepared, I don't need you yammering at me."

"I told you it was a bad idea. What do you think Father is going to say? Or Angela, for that matter? The woman is planning on marring you tomorrow. Or have you forgotten that little gem of information?"

Caleb groaned. "How could such a simple plan go so wrong?"

"I don't know, but I'm leaving for several weeks with Niles."

Caleb's head snapped up, "Leaving where?"

"I'd rather not say. But I don't plan on marrying the whore because Father is in a snit."

Caleb frowned. "Better take Andrew and Donavan with you. Father will just marry one of them off to her."

"You're right. I hadn't thought of that. Perhaps a nice brotherly jaunt will do us some good," he said turning to leave but stopping at the sight of Caleb's wife standing there with a stricken look on her face.

"You're one of his brothers?" she questioned. Keegan flushed.

Keegan nodded. "Keegan Cabot, at your service."

Melissa felt like crying. "You were to marry Angela?" she said, waiting for her husband to answer.

Caleb nodded. "Her father owns the shipping fleet in Penbrooke."

Melissa frowned. She really didn't know much about shipping. That was Jessica's specialty. Silence descended on the library and Keegan began to sweat.

"If you two will excuse me, I have to pack and catch the stage." Moving toward the door, he hesitated. He leaned forward and kissed Melissa's cheek. "I'm sorry." he said and left. Melissa smoothed her gown and sank down on the sofa.

"Tell me about Angela?"

Caleb frowned. Melissa was a stunning woman but she looked like she hadn't slept in a week. "Maybe we should talk in the morning."

Melissa frowned at him. "Before or after your father attacks me?"

Caleb reddened. "All right. I guess I owe you that much," he said. "Angela Fleming is..."

"Angela Fleming?" Melissa screeched, coming to her feet. "She's the one you were to marry?" Angela Fleming is an heiress. She is the only child to the Fleming fortune and worth a great deal of money. From what Melissa had heard, she was also quite beautiful.

"You know her?" Caleb asked brows drawn together.

"Not exactly," Melissa said chewing her nail as she sank back onto the sofa. "She is quite popular at the balls."

Caleb could hardly keep his mouth shut about just how popular the girl was. She spread her legs for just about anyone with the male anatomy. "Yes, well, I didn't want to marry her. She is shallow and vain. Two qualities I don't care for."

Melissa scowled. "How do you know I don't possess those qualities?"

Caleb frowned back. "I guess I don't," he said remembering her comment on the lack of gown and ribbons. She could be vain. But she wasn't shallow or she wouldn't have married him without knowing anything about him. His frown deepened. The fact that she thought she was going to be rich upon his death began to nag at him. "You aren't, are you?"

Melissa snorted, her back stiffening. "I wouldn't tell you either way."

Caleb grinned. "No, I guess you wouldn't, would you?"

"Is Niles your brother, too?"

Caleb frowned. "Niles? No, he isn't. He's the Earl of March."

Melissa flushed remembering the scolding she'd given him about the poor treatment he was giving Caleb. "A doctor?"

Caleb shook his head. Feeling small, he tried to apologize. "I'm sorry. I didn't quite think my plan far enough through. I never meant to..."

"Whether you meant to or not, I'm married to you and haven't the slightest idea what to do about it." Caleb lowered his head. "Now, if you would please tell me exactly what you were planning, I would be better prepared for your father. Then I am going to bed."

Caleb frowned. "I didn't plan any farther than what you already know. My father is somewhat unreasonable. He will be angry and won't hesitate to rail at me."

Melissa frowned. "Every Father rants from time to time," Melissa stated waving a hand at that. "My father has a heart condition and he ordered me and my sisters to marry. We only had three months or he was going to choose a man for us. Your clever plan of avoiding your own situation took away my hope of not being forced to marry a stranger!"

Caleb reddened. "I think if we work past this rocky start you'll find that I'm not such a bad man. You have more freedom as a married woman."

Melissa scowled. Yes, she would have freedom but she would still have to answer to a man she didn't know. "If you'll excuse me I'm going to bed."

"But we haven't discussed what to say to my father," Caleb said rising to his feet.

"We didn't discuss what we were going to say to my brothers either but we managed. Now good night," she snapped as she left the room and headed up the stairs. Caleb frowned at her retreating back and wondered if Keegan was right. He was very foolish to think that a woman who looked like Melissa would just accept the situation and live happily ever after. Snorting at the thought, he filled a glass with brandy and decided to spend the rest of the night going over what he was going to tell his father. No matter how he looked at it, he was a dead man. If his father didn't kill him Melissa would.

Chapter 25

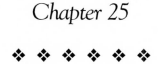

JESSICA ENTERED THE HOUSE and frowned. The silence yawned before her making her instantly alert. "Allison? Aunt Ginger?" she yelled listening for a response.

"Can I help you, mum?" Jenkins asked coming out of nowhere.

Jessica jumped then glared at him. "For one, you can stop sneaking up on people.

"Yes, my lady."

"Could you tell me where my sister is?"

"The Lady Allison went with your Aunt in search of Lady Melissa."

"They left the house at this late hour? Wherever would they be going?"

Jenkins cleared his throat. "Lady Ginger stated something about going to the Wetherton's ball."

"Of course," Jessica said smiling, "she would think that's what Melissa would do with herself. Thank you, Jenkins. Could you tell my brothers that I too am going to the ball?"

Jenkins again cleared his throat. "If my lady would allow my advice, I think a gown is regular ballroom attire."

Jessica grinned. "Of course it is Jenkins, but I don't plan on going into the ball. Tell Nathan or Christopher where I went, please."

Jenkins stood stunned as the oldest female strolled out of the house dressed in black breeches, a white billowy shirt, and a cap slightly askew atop perfectly braided black hair. The girl was a walking catastrophe. He began to close the door, but nearly broke his arm as it was shoved open in his face.

"What the...oh sorry, Jenkins. Have you seen Jessica?"

Jenkins straightened his shirtfront. "As it happens, Master Nathan, your sister just left here to join your Aunt and Lady Allison at the Wetherton's ball."

Nathan scowled. "Damn, I had hoped to get out of going to that wretched affair." Taking a deep breath he headed for the door. "Inform Christopher that I'm heading to the ball also. Someone needs to chaperone those ladies," he added turning to grab his hat and gloves. Jenkins shut the door. Moving off toward his room, he smiled. It was a rare occasion since the Hayworth clan had invaded his home, that he found himself with time of his own. Closing his door, he prayed they stayed away for a good long time. He needed the rest.

JESSICA HURRIED ALONG THE SHADOWS of the familiar streets of London. She was getting quite familiar with the area having traveled through the streets in the dark. Reaching the square, where she knew several of the richer families in society lived, she spotted the one giving the evening's entertainment and smiled. It was on the end of the block with the park at the back of the house. That would make it easy to get word to Allison. She crossed the street and quickly tucked herself into the hedge bordering the house then followed it around to the back of the house where she entered the garden. The lord who owned the house probably had no idea it was this easy to enter his home. Adjusting her position she waited to watch. She needed to get word to Allison without getting caught. Moving slightly she spotted Aunt Ginger and frowned. Allison was no where in the vicinity. Cursing, she hoped her Aunt had enough sense not to have abandoned Allison. Creeping closer to the house she found a perfect bush to hide in that allowed her a clear view of the entire ballroom. Settling herself she spotted Allison standing with her back to the wall talking to the young couple she had met at the first ball.

Jessica bit her nail wondering how she was supposed to get her sister's attention when Allison couldn't see a blasted thing. Cursing, she nearly squealed as a maid stopped to take a break by the bush she was in. Reaching out a hand, she touched the maids shoulder, "Excuse me?"

The maid sucked in her breath to scream but Jessica wiped her hand over her mouth nearly losing her place into the bush. "Don't scream, you ninny. I was just going to ask you to do me a favor?"

The maid relaxed seeing that the culprit in the bush was a woman. "You scared the livin' daylights out of me, mum." As if realizing what she was doing her face turned stern. "Now you get yourself out of here. His lordship wouldn't like knowing some street urchins were crawling around in his garden."

Jessica grinned. "You can rest assured, I'm not a street urchin. But I need you to do me a favor. See that nice looking lady over there with the silver blond hair?"

The maid followed her direction and nodded, "Right pretty girl."

Jessica nodded. "Yes, she is. She's my sister and I'm not supposed to be at this ball. My father forbade it. Could you possible go and tell her that I need to talk with her? But you have to keep it quiet or my father will find out."

The maid looked skeptical. "You're her sister? But you don't look a thing like her."

"I'm her sister, trust me. If you do like I ask, I'll give you this," she said holding up two coins.

The maid snorted. "I don't need your money. I don't think I should as you ask, either. What proof do I have that you will do the lady no harm?"

"She's my sister. What could I possibly do to her? Especially here? You can even stand by and watch us."

The maid finally consented, grumbling the whole way into the hall as she moved toward Allison. Shaking her head she gave Jessica a stern look before turning to speak with Allison. Up close the girl was absolutely stunning. "Pardon, my lady."

Allison practically jumped out of her skin, at the presence beside. "I'm sorry," she said, trying to look casual.

"If you would pardon my intrusion, mum, I have a message for you."

Allison frowned but turned her head toward Jared and Ruth. "Excuse me a moment. I'll be right back," she stated feeling extremely nervous about being left to her own devices.

"We'll wait right here for you," Jared said as if reading her mind.

Allison smiled her gratitude. "Thank you, I won't be long."

Moving off several steps, she paused. "What is this message?"

"Sorry to intrude, my lady, but there is this lady in the gardens who insists that you come speak with her. I don't believe she belongs here, but I thought I would check with you before I turn her in. She looks like a street urchin."

Allison frowned. Would Jessica dare come to a ball looking like that? Nodding her head she knew she would. "Did this lady give you her name?"

"Yes, my lady. She said it was Jess but that really..."

"I know her. Can you tell me exactly where she is?"

The maid paused to stare at Allison. "You know her then?"

"Yes. She's my sister, now where exactly is she?"

"I was supposed to take you there. She..." The maid hesitated. "She said you would want me to talk to you the entire way across the room. I don't know..."

"She's right. I do want you to talk with me. Now show me the way and start telling me about yourself." Allison smiled at Jessica's quick thinking and followed the maids droning voice until they reached the garden doors.

"She's just out there, to the right. I can't stay any longer away from my post. If you will excuse me."

"Thank you. I am happy to have made your acquaintance."

The maid gave her an odd look but dismissed it. If the sister was running around like a common urchin, this one's slight oddities didn't seem to mean much. Allison heard the maid leave and reached out a hand to touch the doorframe. She smiled and stepped through and waited for some sort of sign from Jessica.

"I'm in the bush next to you. Move three steps forward and turn to your left." As Allison moved she smiled. "Good. Now go five steps straight ahead. There's a bench there." Allison did like she said and smiled when she found the bench.

"Okay, Jessica. What's happened?"

"It's Melissa. You'll never guess what happened?"

Allison felt her heart skip a beat. "Is she okay?"

"Of course. She got herself married."

"Married!" she stated then lowered her head to look like she was looking at her hands. "But she didn't see anyone more than twice. It isn't that boring Earl, is it?"

"No. Thank the Lord. That man could kill the dead. No, she married a complete stranger. His name is Caleb Cabot."

Allison frowned. "Why would she do that? She still has two and a half months left."

"I don't know. I didn't hang around to find out. I knew you would be worrying about her, so I came straight here."

"Thank you. Aunt Ginger is in a real panic. I think I better go back and tell her what happened. She was ready to denounce us all." Reaching next to her for her reticule she frowned. "Jessica do you see my reticule?"

"No, you didn't have one with you." Jessica said as Allison paled. Moving to leave the bush she halted knowing she couldn't be seen like this. "Allison, what's the matter?" she whispered.

"Oh, Jessica, I'm in terrible trouble."

Seeing her sister panic, she cursed. "What the hell is the matter?" She felt trapped in that bush. She probably should have changed like Jenkins suggested.

"I lost my reticule in a room upstairs."

"You what?"

"I was going to powder my nose and I asked directions from a lady standing next to me. She said it was up the stairs, to the right, and down the hall two doors." Allison said ringing her hands. "I followed her directions but somehow I ended up in some room. It smelled like smoke and brandy so I turned and left immediately but I must have left my reticule in there."

Jessica cursed. If it were a man's room she would be ruined. "Allison, don't get upset. I'll think of something." Looking back into the ball she nearly shouted for joy at seeing Nathan scanning the room. He must have followed her there. "Allison, get to your feet and move back to the doors. Nathan is in there. I'll go and get your purse."

"But..."

"You're wasting time," she snapped. "He's just inside the doors," she said moving off. She had to find that purse before someone else did. Seeing Allison move back into the room, she knew Nathan would find her. She quickly moved along the bushes until she was along the short side of the house and grinned when she saw a trellis. Looking over the garden she prayed this side of the house was deserted. Moving forward she began to scale the trellis. It took little effort to make it to the narrow ledge just outside a window. Peeking inside she could see a long narrow hall. The stairs came up to the right. She moved along the ledge plastered firmly against the wall. When she happened upon the second window she looked in and couldn't see a thing. The room had the drapes pulled. Cursing she moved to the next window and grinned. The powder room. The next window proved to be a bedroom. Scanning the room she cursed. With just a fire in the hearth, she couldn't see much. Checking below her, she saw no one and quickly tested the window. It opened with ease making her grin. Sticking her head into the room her nose was assailed with the masculine smells of brandy and cigars. Crawling into the room she quickly scanned the floor for the purse. Where the hell was it? This had to be the right room. Frowning, she moved back to the window and looked out again. She could see two windows to the right and two back the way she had come. Suppose it was the one next to this. Cursing, she moved back into the room and looked one more time. A grin split her face when she spotted the reticule peeking out from under a chair. Grabbing the stupid thing she slipped the strap over her head and headed for the window. Lifting a foot, she jumped when a light flooded the room. Turning, she nearly fainted at the sight of the man before her.

"You!" The Baron of Essex growled, seeing her standing by his window. "Stealing from me again?" he asked striding toward her. Jessica scrambled to get out the window but a hand manacled her leg. She screamed and was pulled back into the room. Jessica panicked for the first time in her life. She was trapped in a room with a man that hated her!

"I can explain! I wasn't stealing from you. I swear," she said holding up her hands and backing away.

"Oh? What exactly were you doing?" he asked moving toward her. Jessica moved behind the table and pulled out her knife.

"I think you better just let me go."

His jaw clenched at seeing her threatening him. "Put that knife away. What the hell are you doing in my room?" Jessica paled. She couldn't tell him about Allison. Allison didn't need a scandal on top of her blindness. Trying to think of a reason she stiffened seeing that the Baron knew exactly what she was doing. "Thinking of lying? What was it you were going to steal?"

Jessica's swallowed as her own temper began to boil. "I wasn't stealing anything. I am not a thief."

"That's not what I've been told."

Jessica turned scarlet. She was in fact a thief. She had slipped into his home unnoticed and taken his wine. "I meant to say, I wasn't here to steal from you tonight," she gritted out.

Morgan's smile was cold and dangerous. "Then perhaps you were here to slit my throat."

Jessica stiffened. "If I had thought of that, I might have done it." Seeing that didn't affect him in the least, she sagged. "Just let me go. I made a mistake," she said, knowing there was nothing she could say that would explain why she was in this room. Especially, after the wine incident. He wasn't going to believe her anyway and Allison had to be protected.

"Oh, I think not. In fact, I plan to take my anger out on your backside."

Jessica drew herself up. "You most certainly will not. I'll cut your eyes out first," she snarled her face scarlet at the thought.

Morgan's blue eyes were nearly black and his body was taunt. Grabbing the table he pushed it aside, with little effort, and lunged for Jessica. She dove under the table pulling the chair behind her then made a dash for the window. She was nearly all the way out the window when she was grabbed by the legs and hauled back in. Jessica cursed as her knife was bashed out of her hand. Turning she rammed her head into the Baron's midsection. They toppled over the table, a loud crash followed as the Baron tried to pin her to the floor. Growling with rage she slammed her elbow into his stomach. He grunted but didn't release her. Kicking him in the shin got a yelp out of him and she was momentarily free. Scrambling to her feet she dashed again toward the window only to be pulled up over his shoulder and dumped out flat on the bed. He quickly straddled her and pinned both hands to the sides of her head. Jessica bucked and struggled growling her rage but the Baron held fast.

"I swore to your brother I wasn't going to hurt you but this little adventure has seriously changed my mind," he said as his door slammed open and several men from the ball below poured into his room. His butler leading the group.

The men stopped at the sight before them. Slow smiles spread across their faces as they took in the scene. "I say, Sinclair. Your man, here, had us thinking you were getting mugged or something."

"If you wanted a piece of action, why cause all the racket." A tall thin man asked as a grin covered his face. He stared right at Jessica. "Well, now isn't she a beauty."

Jessica was mortified. To be caught in a man's room was one thing, but to be found with said man straddling you half naked, was another. The color drained from her face.

Morgan looked back to his captive and cursed. Her shirt was open nearly to the waist exposing a great deal of her lovely breasts and her hair had worked several longs strands loose from her braid. Easing his hold on her he moved to sit on the side of the bed. "Gentlemen, if you would excuse..."

"I say isn't that the Hayworth girl." A young blade asked trying to look around Morgan and get a better look at Jessica. Morgan stiffened and his face turned black.

"I think you better leave gentlemen. I will be down shortly."

Several of the men gave him encouraging remarks on what to do with the gal before Morgan slammed the door in their faces. Running his fingers through his hair he cursed, then kicked a chair out of the way. Hopping on one foot, he cursed again.

Jessica hadn't moved from her position on the bed. Tears of frustration stung her eyes as she stared up at the ceiling. "Why couldn't you have just let me go?" she snapped coming up off the bed. Grabbing her hat and slamming it back on her head, she yanked her shirt closed and began buttoning it with angry jerking motions.

Morgan watched her and frowned. Of all the rotten luck. It would be all over London by morning that he bedded the girl, whether those men knew it to be true or not. Cursing, he glared at her. "What the hell were you doing in my room in the first place?"

Jessica set her jaw. She wasn't telling him anything. Allison was more important to her than her reputation. Suddenly she stopped; a small ray of hope began to form. "Do you think those men will say anything?"

Morgan snorted. "Do cats meow? Of course, they're going to say something. They're probably down there right now telling my guests exactly what it is their host is doing up here."

"This is your house?"

"Well, whose house did you think it was?"

"I was told the Wetherton's were having this ball."

"So they are. The Wetherton's are my Aunt and Uncle."

Jessica groaned. Of all the luck. "Well, it doesn't matter now. My reputation is ruined," she said looking at him with excitement.

Morgan's eyes narrowed. "What are you thinking?"

"Nothing and everything." She said moving to climb out the window again.

"Where are you going? You're not leaving until I have my answers."

Jessica frowned at him. "Want to bet." She said ducking her head to climb out the window, only to be pulled back in. Morgan twisted her arm up behind her back. "Here now. Just let me go," she said, trying to get free.

"You'll tell me exactly what I want to know or I'll beat it out of your backside."

Jessica cursed and started struggling. Morgan wrenched on her arm both of them jumping as the door flew open.

"Get out. This isn't a peepshow," Morgan bellowed pulling Jessica up against his chest.

Nathan took in the scene of Jessica struggling in the arms of a man he didn't know and Nathan reacted to it. Morgan saw the intent on the black haired man's face and pushed Jessica onto the bed barely ducking as Nathan threw his first punch. Righting himself, he landed a punch to the Nathan's middle before getting punched in the jaw himself.

Jessica, fighting tears from the pain in her arm, barely managed to pull her legs out of the way before both men landed in a mauling mound at her feet. Each was punching and kicking the other. Jessica would have laughed but now was not th time. Struggling to her feet she tried to leave through the window only to have her feet fly out from under her as Morgan knocked her to the ground.

"Bloody hell," she cursed landing on a man.

"God damn it, Jess. Get out of the way."

"Nathan? What the hell are you doing?" she cursed realizing for the first time who the intruder was.

"I'm defending you," he said coming to his feet ready to charge into Morgan again. Jessica smacked him in the side of the head "What the hell was that for?" he cursed turning to look at her as he put the other hand to his head.

"You're ruining everything," she yelled, moving toward him.

"Now hold on here. What's going on?" Nathan asked holding his hands in front of him as Jessica stomped toward him. He knew her tantrums and this one wasn't going to be good.

"You've ruined everything," she bellowed taking a swing at him. Nathan ducked.

"Ruined everything? You call shacking up with a man good judgment?" he bellowed standing his ground.

Jessica reddened but didn't stop her assault. "No, you dim-witted buffoon, but until you came charging in here I could have prevented it from being confirmed," she shouted taking another swing at him which he effectively ducked. Morgan stood in silence watching the pair circle one another. Who the hell was this man?

"Wait till Christopher finds out about this one. He'll definitely have heart failure."

Jessica stiffened then paled. She hadn't thought of that. Melissa had just went off and got married. Here she was not an hour later, ruining her reputation. Gritting her teeth she turned her gaze on Morgan. His brows shot up at that.

"If you would have just let me go like I asked," she said in a low tone moving now in his direction. He didn't back down.

"If you hadn't come here to steal from me, I wouldn't have taken exception to your intrusion."

Jessica snarled a curse at the man and struck a blow for his head. Morgan ducked and tackled her onto the bed while she spat curses at him and struggled to get away. Nathan while watching the scene, suddenly became aware that someone was standing next to him. Looking down at the petite old lady who was primly dressed, he frowned. The old lady looked sternly at the couple struggling on the bed then to Nathan.

"Aren't you going to do something?" she asked, but didn't give him a chance to answer. "Morgan Anthony Sinclair, whatever are you doing?" Her voice cracked through the air like a whip. Both people on the bed stopped and stared at her. Morgan had the grace to blush.

"Aunt Athea. How good to see you?" he said trying to hold Jessica down long enough to get his limbs and other such parts out of harms way.

Aunt Athea wasn't amused. "Of all the things I've witnessed in my life I never thought to see grown men fighting on a bed. If you hadn't noticed, there is a ball going on!"

Morgan blinked at his Aunt, stunned that she didn't know Jessica was a woman. Jessica bucked once before scrambling free. Nathan's brows shot up at the pale look that came over the formidable Aunt's face. Then nearly laughed at the sheepish look crossing Morgan's face.

"Well, I never," the Aunt said looking at the pair with disapproval. "Of all the places to be carrying on with common trash. This ball is not the place Morgan."

Jessica gasped at the slur but didn't have a chance to correct her as Nathan stepped in. "Here now. That's a lady you're talking about."

"Who the hell are you?" Morgan growled at Nathan.

"I'm her brother."

"Her brother!" Morgan exclaimed looking back and forth between the pair. He scowled at Nathan, "The gambler, I presume."

"I'd keep my mouth shut if I were you. You're already in it deep without insulting me."

Morgan snorted but moved away from the bed. Aunt Athea looked ready to faint. "Morgan do put a shirt on. You've caused enough scandal for one evening," she snapped moving to sit in a chair by the hearth. "Whatever would your father think?"

Morgan's face darkened. His father had never cared what Morgan was doing as long as he didn't bring shame to the family name. Tonight, I guess, he messed that up, too.

"If you will excuse us. We'll just be going," Jessica stated moving to the window to lift her leg up over the sill.

"What are you doing?" Nathan snapped.

"I'm going to meet you in the garden. I can't very well go down to the ball like this," Jessica said ducking her head out the window. Morgan grabbed her and pulled her back into the room.

"I already told you, you're not going anywhere until you answer my question."

"Let go of me, you retch, before I knock you to Bermuda. You've done enough already."

"My word, Morgan. Let her go."

Morgan gave his Aunt an irritated look but didn't release Jessica. "I think it would benefit you to stay here and explain yourself. Otherwise, I'm not going to be responsible for my behavior."

Aunt Athea gasped, "Morgan!"

Morgan sighed in exasperation. "I wasn't referring to anything improper. I was referring to the fact that I would take her over my knee and tan her backside," he finished in a near shout. "I want answers and I want them now."

Nathan glared at the pair. "I suggest you let her go and we discuss this all in the morning."

Morgan stared at the brother a moment then cursed. It wasn't like he could force her to stay with the brother standing right there. The brother had more control than he did. "I think that's an excellent idea. I'll be around at seven."

"Seven!" Nathan exclaimed then frowned. These things were handled at such early hours he was sure. "Seven it is," he agreed taking Jessica's arm. "Let's go home before anything else happens. Christopher is already going to kill you."

"I can't go down there," she snapped pulling her arm free. "Aunt Ginger would parish from disgrace."

"You should have thought of that before you came sneaking through my window," Morgan stated doing up the last buttons of his shirt. Jessica gave him a good glare before moving again toward the window.

"I'm going down the way I came," she said waving him toward the door. "Now get going."

"You're not going out there, are you?" Athea exclaimed seeing the girl poised on the windowsill.

Jessica grinned. "Afraid so," she said disappearing from sight. Nathan frowned at his sister's departure.

"I'll see you at seven," Nathan stated his face grime. Morgan nodded as the man left the room.

"Would you care to explain yourself?"

"No, but I don't think that was a question." At his Aunt's pointed look, he frowned. Running a hand through his hair he sighed. "It wasn't like I brought the girl up here for a tryst. She climbed through my window when I happen to be dressing. After I recognized her we...well, let's just say our tempers got the better of us and we had a bit of a fight."

Athea pursed her lips. "Who is she Morgan?"

Morgan frowned. "I don't suppose you would just let her go as street trash."

"With that handsome buck as a brother? I don't think so."

Morgan frowned, "She's one of the Hayworth girls."

"A Hayworth! You don't mean the Earl of Brentwood." At Morgan's reluctant nod Athea started waving her fan fiercely in front of her face as she sagged into a chair. "Good heavens, Morgan. You are in it deep now. Whatever are we going to do?"

Morgan's head snapped up at that. "What do you mean? The girl was wrong and I plan to get some answers out of her tomorrow. That's the end of it."

Athea laughed near hysterics. "You can't be serious. The Earl of Brentwood will have your hide. You've ruined his daughter's reputation and that is something a father doesn't take lightly."

Morgan drew his brows together. "What are you getting at?"

"You'll have to marry the girl, of course."

Morgan laughed at that statement. "You can't be serious. We'd kill each other in less than a day."

Athea frowned. "It doesn't matter. The father will kill you otherwise. As a Sinclair you must straighten out this matter. Offer for the girl, if they refuse then you at least come out in the right."

Morgan scowled. Things were getting way out of hand here. "I think, dear Aunt, that I need to attend to my guests below. If you will excuse me," he said not waiting for her to finish as he disappeared into the room off the bedroom to finish his grooming.

"All right, Morgan. I'll go, but you better be prepared for tomorrow."

Morgan gritted his teeth at his Aunt's comment. Married! And to that hellcat! No thank you. Snatching up his waistcoat he slipped into it feeling less and less like entertaining. What the hell was he going to do?

Chapter 26

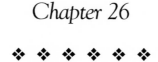

ALLISON TRIED VALIANTLY to keep her face from crumbling and making a bigger fool of herself in public. Jared McMaster had just informed her that Royce had returned to his home in the country and wasn't likely to come back this season. Lifting her chin she blinked her eyes to keep from crying. He obviously didn't want anything to do with her after what happened the other night. Feeling her nerves on end she just wanted to go home. Nathan had left her at least half an hour ago and she was starting to get worried. Jessica hadn't returned, either. What about her purse? Moving slightly she jumped when Aunt Ginger asked her a question.

"Would you like to go home, dear? It's been a long evening."

Allison schooled her features trying not to appear too eager to escape the ball. "I would be happy to leave. I am very interested in what Melissa has done."

Aunt Ginger scowled. "The stupid girl has ruined everything. She did things completely unconventional. When word gets out, the rest of us will have to contend with her rashness."

Allison smiled tightly. "I think we should at least hear who it was that she married before we jump to the conclusion that she ruined our lives. Besides, Melissa is the one who worries about reputations. I'm sure she didn't do anything to jeopardize the rest of us."

Aunt Ginger pursed her lips. "I hope so, dear. Your sister is a bit vain and does tend to think in terms of me, me, me."

Allison smiled. "That she does, but I'm sure she wouldn't risk being exiled from society." Aunt Ginger humphed and took her arm. As they said their farewells and descended the steps to their coach, Allison felt Ginger stiffen. "What's the matter?"

"It's Jessica. Your brother has her in the coach and the pair of them are yelling at each other like common trash." Allison turned her head enough to hear the pair cursing at each other.

"We better hurry," Allison said picking up her pace, "Jessica has a mouth like a sailor."

Aunt Ginger's lips thinned. "I'm going to kill your father. I hadn't planned on any of this scandalous behavior at my age," she stated reaching the coach in time to hear Jessica call Nathan a conceded swine. "That's enough!" she snapped waving a hand at the pair. Giving the footman a strained smile she accepted his help into the coach and waited just long enough for Allison to be tossed in before she lit into the pair. "The two of you are acting like spoiled children and I will not have it. When we are in public, I want the pair of you to act with the utmost care. Melissa has already ruined our name enough to give pause to good families wanting their sons associated with us. We don't need the pair of you ranting at one another," she finished in a huff.

Nathan was looking out the window his jaw stiff and his body taught. Jessica was near tears. Swallowing, she leaned toward Allison and placed her reticule in her lap.

"I forgot to give this back to you," she said seeing Allison visibly relax and give her a brilliant smile. Jessica was immediately guilty. Would her wretched behavior ruin Allison's chances?

"That's all right. I'm glad it was of use to you," Allison said making Jessica frown. Turning her attention to looking out the window she wondered what Aunt Ginger was going to say about tonight's events. As the carriage pulled up to the house all four members were shocked at the activity at their house.

"Oh dear. Whoever could be calling at this late hour?" Ginger asked stepping down from the coach.

Nathan jumped out next turning to help Allison alight. He then held a hand out for Jessica, who gave him a quelling look. "I think we should just quit speculating and go in and see," Jessica snapped moving past the three up the steps and into the house. Ginger for the first time finally noticed her breeches.

Turning to Nathan she practically nailed him to the coach with her words. "Tell me you didn't allow her in the ball dressed like that?"

Nathan lifted his chin. "No, she didn't go to the ball like that."

Ginger practically wilted. "Thank heavens," she said, guiding Allison up the steps and into the house.

Voices were coming from the study and Nathan saw Jessica disappear into the room. "Let's get a move on. Something big is going on."

Allison felt her nerves on end. What could possibly happen next? Nathan guided her into the room and she was instantly assailed with smells associated with horses and the sea. "Stephan, Jonathan. What happened?" She asked, nodding her thanks to Nathan as he guided her into a chair by the hearth.

Jonathan took her hand instantly and kissed it. "Nothing happened. It's nice to see you, Allison. Stephan and I just arrived about five minutes ago. We were heading here to talk with Christopher," he finished giving Jessica's back a look. Nathan followed his gaze and frowned.

"What's going on?"

"It's none of your..."

"Yes, it is," Jessica said getting complete silence in the room. "You see Nathan is having a meeting with the Baron tomorrow and should be aware of all the circumstances surrounding my connections with the man."

Stephan scowled at her. "What happened now?" he growled.

"I think someone should start from the beginning before every statement thrown out is swamped with questions. Jessica?" Christopher said folding his fingers while stretching his legs out in front of him. "By all means, tell us everything."

Jessica stiffened. She hadn't wanted the whole family to know of her thieving. But after what happened tonight she guessed it was unavoidable. "A few months back the shipping firm was having trouble and I was too proud to admit what was happening. At the time, I wanted to show Father and Stephan that I was capable of running the shipping end of his estates. Stephan wasn't aware of the decline in business because I deliberately kept it from him hoping I could take care of it myself." Swallowing she didn't dare look at her family. She knew she would burst into tears. "I guess I thought if we got a really big client, things would change for the better and we would be back on our feet. It would have worked, too."

Silence followed. "And?" Christopher asked, dreading the rest.

Shifting her feet she lowered her head and stared at her hands. "I attacked the Baron of Essex and his business, causing both Stephan and I shame," she said, then told them about her dealings with the wine. How she had crawled through the tunnels dragging the satchels into his cellar and traded the good wine for the bad. "Jonathan and Stephan were only trying to help me when they agreed to give him my ship and the remaining runs as payment for the damage to his reputation. The Baron was more than willing to call it even but after tonight I doubt he will agree."

"Tonight? What happened now?" Stephan said getting to his feet. Christopher waved him to be seated. Scowling he sank back into his chair.

"Finish it?" Christopher snapped.

Jessica frowned at her reflection in the window glass. "I got caught sneaking into the Baron's room. By the Baron himself. He thinks I was there to steal from him, but that wasn't the reason at all. He took exception to my presence in his room, which resulted in my losing my temper. We started fighting and several of the guests from the ball barged in on us." Ginger sank to the floor in a faint. Jessica continued unaware. Jonathan pulled her up into a chair never taking his eyes off Jessica. "The whole situation just kept getting worse. I was recognized by one of the gentlemen, then Nathan barged in swinging. Lady Wetherton came, too. She gave us a good stern lecture." Turning to face the room, she stopped her eyes on Allison, "though I'm not sorry for what I did, I am sorry for ruining your chances, Allison."

Allison was stiff and pale. "Oh Jessica, was this because of my purse?"

Jessica frowned. "That was the reason I was in his room, but that wasn't the reason things got so out of hand."

Allison looked ready to cry. "I'm such an idiot. I'm sorry," she sobbed getting pulled onto Jonathan's shoulder as her tears fell.

"I don't understand. You snuck into the Baron's room for Allison's purse? How did your purse get in his room in the first place?" Jonathan asked stoking her hair.

Jessica answered before she could "You know how she is, Jonathan. If someone gives Allison directions she follows them to the letter. One of the ladies at the ball told her the powder room was the third door from the stairs, when in fact it was the second. She entered the third room and knew she'd made a mistake dropping her purse in the process. All innocent, but a total ruination in the eyes of society."

Jonathan pursed his lips. "That is a fact."

Stephan cursed, then got to his feet to pace. "Instead of one ruined sister, we have two." Turning to Nathan he scowled. "Exactly what is the Baron coming here for?"

"To talk about the wedding, of course."

"Wedding!" Jessica snapped. "You can't be serious."

"You couldn't possibly think anything different was going to happen, Jessica."

"Yes, I do. I'm going to go on sailing my ships. No one will marry me with a ruined reputation. Father will understand. No one will want a ruined wife!" Jessica stated, desperately.

Christopher smacked his hands on the desk and stood. "Are you serious? You actually think we'd let you go off ruined? Father's heart would give out at that news. You're going to marry the Baron and that's that."

Jessica felt rage brewing. "I will not marry that man. We'd kill each other in less than a week."

"Better a widow than a ruined woman," Nathan said getting her glare turned on him.

"Has anyone considered the Baron might not ask for her?" Jonathan said letting go of Allison as she wiped her eyes and blew her nose.

"He'll agree. The Aunt was witness to the whole situation and the man wasn't wearing much," Nathan said looking at Jessica. "Jessica wasn't exactly dressed like a princess, either."

Jessica turned scarlet as her brothers looked at her. "It wasn't like he made it sound. The Baron was evidently changing to go to the ball and I crawled into his room through the window."

"Through the window! What the hell were you doing crawling through his window?" Stephan snapped, staring.

"I wasn't exactly dressed for the ball, Stephan. Allison told me her purse was left in a man's room and I did what I thought best. I figured if I could crawl in the window, get the purse and crawl out, no one would see me."

"You were crawling around on the roof of that house?" Aunt Ginger said looking very tired and pale. "You could have fallen."

Jessica frowned. "I wasn't worried about falling. I was trying to prevent a catastrophe from happening to Allison."

"It's a good thing Father isn't here for this. You girls have been in London for two and a half weeks and already caused enough problems to kill him," Jonathan said, flopping back on the sofa.

"I don't care what you say." Jessica said ignoring Jonathan, "I refuse to marry that man." She stated crossing her arms over her chest.

"You'll do as you're told. I want you dressed in the best gown you have and down here by six-thirty to greet that man or by God I'll drag you down here myself. Do you understand?" Christopher shouted, looking at her like their Father always did. Jessica hesitated then turned and left the room.

The others watched her go. "I guess it doesn't help matters that Melissa married without the proper amount of time set," Jonathan said placing Allison's hand on Ginger's arm as the pair left the room as well.

"No, it doesn't." Christopher said sinking into his chair. "Did you know her husband is going to be the Earl of Canton?"

"Canton? That's one of the richest estates in the area," Stephan said scowling. "Does he sail?"

"No, he sells horses."

Jonathan's head snapped around at that. "Cabot! He's the one she married? The man's a giant."

Nathan frowned at Jonathan. "It would have been nice if you would have been here to tell us that. We had to get the information out of a priest."

Stephan gave Nathan a questioning look only to get a shake of his head.

"I think it best we all get some sleep. We have several situations to deal with tomorrow and I think I'll need every one of you to help me."

All three brothers nodded their consent and filed out of the study. Christopher leaned back with a sigh. "Well Father. Look how proud I've made you," he said to the empty room.

BRAND SMILED as he leaned back in the chair with a nice cup of tea. He was starting to enjoy the stuff, though he still missed brandy. "Where are we off to today, Colan? I haven't had this much fun in years."

Colan grinned. "That, my dear brother, is what having children is for. You turn over work to them and enjoy the money they earn. Justin has been fully running my estates for almost a year and a half now. I get monthly progress reports and lists of investments without the hassles or strain. It's wonderful. Justin seems to enjoy himself, too."

"Christopher's doing fine. He has Jonathan and Stephan helping him. I feel such relief giving things to Christopher. It's like dropping twenty years. I can hardly sit still."

"The doctor said you still have to take it easy. We shouldn't over do."

"Oh posh. I want to die a happy man. I'm not going to lay around in some bed drinking tea and worrying about whether my heart will burst before I make it to the pot or not," Brand said, grinning.

Colan pursed his lips. "I don't think that will be a problem. I think today should be a day of relaxation. I'm worn out myself. The tracks yesterday were enough to wear me out. All that worry and I still managed to break even."

"I like the tracks. Jonathan breeds some fine animals and I can spot them like a flea can a dog."

Colan scowled, "So that's your trick."

"Of course. It wouldn't be as much fun if we both knew the animals that were going to win."

Colan grinned. "I see your point. We could bring in a third party?"

Brand's face took on a look of pure pleasure. "Say now. That is a sporting idea. I think we should test it out immediately."

Colan held up his hands. "Sorry. I'm staying put today and so are you. We'll give the tracks another go tomorrow."

Brand frowned then leaned back in his chair. "I suppose a day of rest wouldn't hurt. Has the paper come?"

Colan looked at his butler. "Rolston, fetch the Earl the paper."

Rolston, a stiff proper butler ran the house in strick routine. The paper was most likely in his vest pocket. Brand kept a straight face as the butler presented the paper in seconds.

"Thank you, Rolston," he murmured taking the thing and ruffling through it. As soon as the butler was clear of hearing he turned to Colan. "That man needs a vacation. He's going to turn to stone."

Colan frowned looking at the door the butler disappeared through, "I never noticed."

Brand rolled his eyes. "How could you not? The man walks around like a living board. Never moving without precise thought as to what his movements will do."

Colan grunted. "I don't have a replacement at this time."

"You better be prepared. One day you'll come down and Rolston will have mysteriously disappeared and you'll swear you see his features in one of your walls."

Colan laughed. "I'll consider it."

Brand nodded opening the paper. The usual boring London life popped out at him. The markets were doing well. The stocks were boring when you weren't worrying over whether yours were doing good or not. Turning to the latest scandals he nearly fell out of his chair. "Bloody hell!"

"What is it? Do you need the doctor?" Colan asked coming out of his chair to stand at Brand's side.

Brand waved an impatient hand at him. "I can't believe it. Melissa got married."

"Melissa! Your Melissa? Your youngest?"

"Yes, yes. But she's only been in London for three weeks." Brand said, still staring at the words. "They didn't even invite me to the ceremony," he said indignantly.

"Who did she marry?" Colan asked impatient with his brother.

"It says she was married yesterday to the Earl of Canton's heir. Who is he?" Brand asked looking at Colan.

Colan leaned back on his heels and whistled. "That's a big fish. The Earl's been trying to marry the lad off now for almost three years. I'd heard the lad was to marry the Fleming child, though. Things must have run amuck. Your girl did good for herself," Colan finished moving back to his chair and resuming his seat.

"So he's rich, then? How old is he?"

"I don't recall. Seems like he was in his late twenties. The boys a real looker. The father's a bit bent, but, all in all, a good match."

Brand scowled at his brother. "Why wasn't I informed?"

Colan smiled. "Now Brand. Christopher was given full power over those girls. I'm sure he's going to be around shortly."

"I'm not leaving England until after the six months is up."

Colan sat up at that remark "But..."

"No. It would take at least six months for news to reach me. I need to be included. I just can't believe one of my children married and I wasn't present. Elizabeth is probably rolling over in her grave."

"Now don't get all worked up. The girl probably couldn't wait and knowing the Earl he pushed the son full tilt, as soon as a wedding was mentioned."

Brand marched to the window. "I think we should pay a visit to my son. I need to know what the hell is going on or it's going to drive me crazy."

Colan's lips thinned. "That isn't a good idea. You're going to start poking around in your son's affairs and end up in the grave."

"You're starting to sound like a wife," Brand snapped waving a hand at his brother. After a moment, Brand turned to look at Colan. "I'll tell you what, if I don't hear something from one of my children in the next three days, I'm heading home."

Colan frowned. "All right, Brand. It's your heart. I'll give you three days?"

Brand nodded and resumed his set and began drinking his tea. "It's not like I shouldn't have been told."

"Of course, Brand."

"For heavens sake. She's my youngest child."

Colan nodded, still not looking up from his book. Brand pursed his lips. Fine! If that was the way things were going to be, he'd sit around idle for the three days like he promised. But let one minute go past that time and he was going home.

Chapter 27

NATHAN MOVED STEADILY along the street, cursing his sisters for being so reckless. They ruined his chances of coming out ahead from the previous nights gambling. He'd planned on visiting a few of his clubs to collect his funds back. Scowling he looked both directions then promptly crossed the street. But instead, he was running errands for his brother like some common serf.

With his temper steadily rising, he didn't see the rider bearing down on him until it was too late to avoid. Suddenly out of nowhere a body slammed into his chest and sent him out of harms way, just in the nick of time. With the breath knocked out of him he could do little more than gasp for air and try to get to his feet.

"You all right, Mister?" came a feminine voice next to his face. Turning his head, he found himself looking into a pair of lovely dark brown eyes. Still gasping he could do little more than nod his head. "Great," she said looking about at the gathering crowd. Pulling the tight wool cap farther down over her ears, she gave him another quick look and was gone.

Nathan struggled to his feet but the crowd had moved in and he couldn't see where the chit had run off to.

"Here now. Let the man up," a tall gentlemen said, as he wove his way to Nathan's side. "Nathan, what the hell are you doing laying around in the streets?" Thomas asked, hauling him to his feet. Thomas Bently was in the same shoes Nathan was. He came from a large family and was one of the younger sons. H also had to make his own way in the world. At the moment, the pair were trying their luck with the cards. Thomas was six foot two, blond haired with blue eyes. A ladies man, if ever there was one.

Nathan scowled at Thomas. "I thought it would put hair on my chest."

Thomas grinned. "I think you better come up with another plan. Are you hurt?"

"No. Who was that?"

"Donavan Cabot. News is, his father isn't happy with the older son and the younger ones are hightailing it out of the city."

Nathan's head snapped up from dusting off his breeches. "Cabot?"

"Yes. Do you know him?"

"We recently met." Nathan said frowning. He wasn't interested in the man who had almost run him down. He wanted to know who the girl was who bowled him out of the horses way.

"Where were you headed? I'll give you a lift."

"I was headed to the post. I need the paper."

"One wasn't dropped by your home."

"Evidently Jessica snatched the thing up and no one's seen hide nor hair of it or the girl."

Thomas grinned. "She's a wild one."

Nathan scowled. "She's my sister, remember."

Thomas flushed. "I keep forgetting. I'll walk with you."

The pair moved down the walk to the post. The crowd was thick with men smoking cigars and drinking whiskey. Moving to the counter Nathan frowned. "I need six papers and I want them as fast as you can."

"Yes, my lord," the short man stated disappearing into the back.

"Six?"

"I am not planning on coming back here because one of my other family members decides to do something stupid with the paper I bring back."

Thomas grinned. "You sure do have a funny family.

A tall gentleman from the walk stopped and looked into the post. Nathan felt the hair rise on the back of his neck. Saul Sheridan, heir to the Baron of Saulton, was a notorious rat. "Hayworth, Bently. I hear congratulations are in order."

Nathan felt Thomas stiffen but to the man's credit he didn't show a reaction. Nathan just nodded his head. Giving a look over his shoulder, he frowned when the little postman wasn't there with his papers.

"Which sister was it?"

Nathan's face darkened, "My youngest."

"Here you are, my lord. Sorry for the wait?"

Nathan gave the man a brief smile and paid him for the papers. "If you'll excuse us Sheridan, I have places to be," he said not waiting for an answer. Brushing past Sheridan he quickened his pace on the walk. "God, that man makes me want to break some bones."

Thomas frowned. "What did your sister do now?"

"She got married."

Thomas stopped walking. "What? The little blond one?"

Nathan still walking just nodded his head. Thomas hurried to catch up. "Whose the lucky man?"

"Cabot."

Thomas stopped again. "Donavan?"

"Don't be ridiculous. The older one, Caleb."

Thomas whistled resuming his walking. "No wonder you nearly got run over. Your mind must be spinning from that one."

"If you don't mind Thomas, I'd rather not talk about it. The house is like a tomb. I'm afraid to say anything, since I might send one of the females into tears or have one of my brothers breathing down my neck. If you're not busy later I'll meet you at White's."

"Sounds good. Are you sure you'll make it?"

"I'll be there, even if I have to crawl out my window."

Thomas grinned as he departed Nathan's company. Nathan scowled at the thought of Saul. The man was one of the lowest, in society, as far as refinement went and Nathan normally liked to goad the man into a game of cards but seeing him today and him knowing about Melissa...

Nathan stopped in his tracks and pulled one of the papers out and scanned the columns. Finally locating the article about his sister, he quickly read the news. Once finished he frowned. At least Caleb had the grace to write something with little hope of people taking it the wrong way. Folding the paper he tucked it with the rest and quickened his pace. The war was about to start with Jessica and Morgan and he didn't want to be late.

Chapter 28

MELISSA FROWNED AT HER REFLECTION. Her hair looked nice pulled to one side, cascading nicely down the side of her head, but everything else was wrong. Her gown was green, a color she preferred not to wear, but the only gown she could get pressed quick enough to wear. Christopher must have packed the trunk himself. Everything arrived all stuffed together. It was all wrinkled and a mess.

Her eyes looked tired and there was darkness under them. Her husband hadn't come to bed and she still didn't know what they were going to say to Caleb's father. Frowning, she rubbed a hand over her eyes then moved to the window to look out. Her window overlooked the park and she watched a little boy throw bread into a pond for the swans. Leaning her head against the frame she sighed. She supposed things could be worse. She was married to a very handsome man. A rich handsome man, according to his brother. Yet, what did she really know about Caleb? Cursing she moved back to give her person a final look in the mirror, then left the room. Walking along the hall she frowned at the unfamiliar passage. She would hate to get lost and end up showing up late for the meeting.

Descending the stairs into the hall below she frowned. Which way would the study be?

"Can I help you, Miss?"

Melissa nearly jumped out of her skin. "Please don't do that, Bragg. I must have aged ten years."

Bragg didn't smile or even acknowledge that he'd heard her. "Would you care to break your fast?"

Melissa pursed her lips. "No. I was looking for my husband. Is he in his study?"

"No, Miss, he's breaking his fast?"

Melissa reddened. "Oh. Then I'll join him." Bragg hesitated then turned and started up the stairs. Melissa frowned at the servant. "Aren't you going to take me to him?"

"I was, Miss. He's in his room?"

Melissa reddened further. "For heavens sake. Just take me to the study. I'll wait for my husband there."

Bragg frowned at her but led the way. "It's in there," he said, moving past the room to disappear down the hall. Melissa frowned after him. He was the rudest servant she had ever met. Opening the door she wrinkled her nose. The study smelled like cigars and brandy. Moving to the window she opened it as wide as it would go. Then surveyed the room. Piles of papers sat on the desk along with several books. The desk was large and had two smaller chairs in front of it. There were three tables in the room, one sporting a decanter and glasses. The ashtray on the table between the chairs by the hearth was brimming over with ask. Picking up the tray, she threw the contents into the hearth.

"Good grief," she snapped seeing that her hand was now black. Moving to the desk she searched for a hanky.

"Looking for something?" Caleb asked from the door. Melissa flushed and snapped erect. Stiffening she stared at her husband. He was dressed in black breeches, a white shirt, and a cream vest. He looked splendid. Caleb gave her a lopsided grin as he caught her looking over his person.

"I was trying to find a handkerchief. My hands are dirty from emptying your ashtray."

Caleb nodded and took the towel hanging by the decanter and handed it to her. She stiffened at his close proximity. She jumped and moved closer to Caleb as loud noises came from the hall.

He smiled at her actions and motioned for her to seat herself by the hearth. "They're here."

"Who?" she asked seating herself in the chair he indicated. As he moved back to his chair, the study door opened emitting a tall lean man with graying black hair and the same brown eyes as Caleb's.

"What the hell is the meaning of this?" he bellowed throwing the newspaper on the desk in front of Caleb. A short woman of middle years followed in his wake. She had brown hair and brown eyes. Melissa knew instantly she was Caleb's mother. Her features were exactly like his.

"Yes, Caleb. You better be joking."

"Nice to see the pair of you, too. And no. It isn't a joke."

His father's face turned to one of rage. "How could you marry this girl? Is she with child?"

"No."

"Did you compromise her?"

Caleb set his jaw. "No. We just agreed out of mutual consent."

Melissa frowned at his choice of words but decided that was easier to explain away than some ridiculous love thing.

"Mutual consent?" His father raged. "What the hell is that?"

"Now, Michael, calm down. What about Angela? You were supposed to marry her today. What are you going to tell her?"

"Same thing I'm telling you."

Melissa looked at her husband. His eyes briefly strayed to hers but they didn't linger.

"Of all the stupid things I've had to put up with from you. The one thing I asked was that you marry the Fleming girl. Yet, you snubbed your nose at me again," he yelled standing stiffly in front of Caleb's desk.

"Please, sit down so I can explain. There..."

"There's nothing to explain. You've always done what you damn well please and to hell with what my wishes might be," he raged.

"That isn't exactly true. The sea...."

"Bah," his father said cutting him off, "you're just weak stomached. A few weeks at sea and you would get your sea legs. Now you've ruined everything."

Caleb went to open his mouth but his words were cut off as Melissa spoke. "Now just one minute. It's bad enough that you come in here ranting at Caleb when he is supposed to be on his honeymoon, but to stand there and tell him he made a bad choice is unforgivable."

At the sound of her voice both parents turned to stare at her. "And who might you be?" His mother asked.

"I'm 'the girl' he married," she said snidely. Moving closer to Caleb she even put her hand on his shoulder.

Caleb hesitated. Was she supporting him or was she planning to tell his parents of his deceit? "Father. Mother. May I introduce you to my wife, Melissa Cabot. Melissa, my parents. Michael and Rachel Cabot, Earl and Countess of Canton."

The father had the grace to flush but the mother studied her with the usual society eyes. Finally, the Earl cleared his throat. "I didn't say he made a bad choice, it's just that he already had a bride."

Melissa reddened herself but forced a smile. "It is awkward, I'll admit. But isn't it most important that your son is happy?"

The Earl frowned, as did Rachel. "As heir to the estates, the boy should do as his father wants," his mother said giving Melissa a measuring look.

Caleb who had stood during the introductions smiled. "Father never has my interests in mind when he suggests the things he does."

The Earl's face showed his anger again, "you purposely ruined the marriage with Angela."

"Not exactly. It was a dilemma. Either marry a woman I didn't love and one that has been with every man in the city or marry a woman I can have a future with. My choice was simple?"

Rachel gasped and turned scarlet. "Caleb, that was uncalled for."

"Uncalled for, but true," he said moving to pour himself a brandy. "Brandy? Port?" he asked to the room. Melissa frowned at him.

"I'll order some tea," she said knowing the mother would never drink this early in the morning. Rachel gave her a good glare as she moved past her, out the door.

The Earl waited just seconds after the door shut to voice his thoughts. "Who is she?"

"What do you mean, Father. You haven't checked her background yet?"

The Earl flushed. "I didn't have time."

"She's from a very rich family. One you would approve of Mother. She's one of the Hayworth children."

"Hayworth? But that man's a recluse. How could you have possibly met his daughter?"

"I don't know much about the father being a recluse but he sent his daughter here for a season and I had the privilege of winning her hand."

The Earl was livid. "I don't care who she is. I want this farce of a marriage annulled."

"Sorry, Father. She could be carrying my heir."

Rachel reddened at such talk, "Really Caleb."

"Sorry, Mother, but the fact is still there. We can't annul the marriage, it's been consummated."

"You've planned this from the start. You never had any intention of marrying Angela. You just went along with the plans like you were going to follow through. I should disown you, by God. I should leave you without title or money."

Rachel paled, "Now Michael, I think it's best if we leave for the time being. What's done is done."

Michael gritted his teeth but finally turned about and left the study. Rachel looked like she was going to say something but in the end she too left without a word. Caleb sighed and ran his fingers through his hair. Things hadn't gone as bad as he thought they would. He was still heir to Canton, though neither of his parents were talking to him and probably wouldn't for a long time.

Melissa entered the room carrying a tray of tea and cakes, then frowned. "Did they leave already?"

Caleb nodded sudden guilt swamping him. Melissa was a nice young lady. She didn't deserve to be burdened with his problems. "They didn't take the news very well I'm afraid."

Melissa pursed her lips. "I think it would have gone better if you had told Angela you weren't interested. I'm sure you could have found a suitable bride."

Caleb laughed. "That, my dear girl, is something I tried on several occasions. My father wanted the connection. He assured the trollop I would marry her and set the date for today."

Melissa paused in pouring herself some tea. "Why would he do that? You're a man."

Caleb laughed. "I'm afraid in this case male or female didn't matter. Father wanted his shipping business joined with Angela's father's firm."

"Why?"

"Father's firm isn't doing well and he felt if his firm was associated with a firm in great standing then it would boost his business."

"But that's ridiculous. In the shipping business, your firm is rated by the service you give not whose name the place bares."

Caleb's brows shot up at that. "Where did you get such a grasp on shipping?"

Melissa flushed. "I happen to come from a sailing family. My father, as well as a brother and sister, all sail."

Caleb's brows drew together. "Hayworth line?"

Melissa frowned. "No. The ships sail under my mother's maiden name."

"Which is?"

"Matherson lines."

"Matherson lines!" he said sitting up straight. "But that firm is one of the best run lines next to the Sinclair bunch."

Melissa shrugged. "I wouldn't really know. My brother and sister run the line. I haven't the slightest interest in ships."

Caleb leaned his head back on the chair. Not only had he married a girl with several large brothers but also he was now connected to one of the best shipping lines in the area. His father was going to have a field day. Melissa studied her husband's face and frowned.

"Did I say something wrong?"

Caleb took a deep breath and let it out slowly. "I think I've made a terrible mistake."

Melissa lips thinned. "Well it's to late to do anything about it now. Believe me, I'd have been packed and back where I belong last night."

Caleb scowled at her. "I didn't mean that choosing you as a bride was wrong I was referring to the fact that I waited so long to choose a bride, then just snatched one off the street." Seeing Melissa getting angry again he hurried to continue. "I should have at least talked with you before committing you to a marriage."

Melissa stiffened. "What exactly are you getting at?"

Caleb leaned forward in his chair. "I already told you about my father wanting to be connected with a well connected firm?" At her nod he added. "I'm afraid once he gets wind of your connection with Matherson lines he'll bring out the big guns. He'll expect to be excepted in that group."

Melissa frowned. "You mean he wants to be connected with my family."

"Exactly. Now all that work I did to make the article in the paper sound like we were a love match, will be for naught. Society is going to see it as a money move no matter what I do."

Melissa frowned. "You mean people will think you married me for my ships?" Caleb nodded. Melissa took a sip of tea. Caleb watched her and could see the wheels turning in her head. "Exactly what did you write in the paper?"

"I have a copy of it here somewhere," he said shuffling through the papers on his desk. Taking up a rather wrinkled sheet he handed it to her. Melissa frowned at the thing but smoothed it out before reading it.

"Lord Caleb Cabot, son to the Earl of Canton, announces his marriage to the Lady Melissa Hayworth, daughter to the Earl of Brentwood. They were wed today the sixth day of September in St. Vincent's church. Lord Keegan Cabot and Lord Niles Deshante, the Earl of March stood as witness." Melissa finished frowning at the script.

"It doesn't say anything about a love match."

"Well, I didn't say I wrote it in print. I dropped a few choice phrases among friends and trust me, the news will spread like wildflowers," he said, his hand running through his hair.

Melissa frowned. "And you say you proclaimed us as a love match?"

Caleb scowled. "You make it sound like that would be impossible."

"Under the circumstances a marriage would be impossible. You lied to me and worked on my feelings of compassion to get what you wanted without regard for my feelings in the matter."

Caleb flushed. "I know and I'm truly sorry for..."

"Forget that drivel. I won't believe it. You were thinking of saving yourself from a marriage with the Fleming girl. What we have to do is establish that it really is a love match. We have to be seen together like real lovers would be."

Caleb's mouth dropped open. "You have to be joking! You expect me to fawn all over you in public?"

Melissa grit her teeth. "I realize you haven't the slightest ounce of feelings in that direction but to preserve our good names and to blot out the stain of standing Angela up at the alter, we must at least try to convey those sentiments to the ton," she said pouring more tea into her cup. "Besides, you did such a splendid job on convincing me you were sick, I'm sure a little fawning will be quite simple for you."

Caleb felt ready to explode. "Men don't fawn and I don't plan on doing any of it."

Melissa calmly set her cup down and got to her feet. "As I figured. Not only do you trick me into a marriage with lies and deceit but you don't have the decency to save my honor or my family's name. I'm going home." So saying, she picked up her skirts and quit the room.

Caleb frowned at the closed door. Was she right? Would they be able to save face by pretending to be madly in love? Caleb snorted at the absurd idea and refilled his glass. Things were going down hill no matter what they did, he thought draining the glass in one swallow. Down hill at a dead run.

Chapter 29

JONATHAN MOVED TO LOOK OUT the window for the fourth time in the last ten minutes. Seeing the street was still empty he frowned. "What time is it now, Stephan?"

"About three minutes later than the last time you asked. Where the hell is your watch anyway?"

Jonathan turned and smiled. "I forgot to pack it in our hasty departure."

"The man's late. I think we should get our cloaks and hats and hunt him down."

Jonathan gave Nathan a tolerant stare. "He'll be here I'm sure. He probably couldn't find the house."

Nathan snorted at that flimsy excuse. Christopher looked up from his stack of papers. "All right, it's finished. Which one of you plan to take this to Father?"

All three men looked at him but all remained silent. "Well, I can't go. I have twenty-five things I have to see to here. Jonathan?" Christopher said still holding up the papers.

"I can't. I have several sales. I set them aside until this week. I have to be on my way home in a little over four hours."

Christopher frowned. "Stephan?"

"Don't look at me. I have three runs to make if I plan on paying the Earl the money I owe him."

"That should be settled as soon as he gets here."

Stephan frowned. "I plan on paying him anyway."

Christopher rolled his eyes. "I swear your honor is too much sometimes. Nathan?"

"Oh no, you don't. I'm not taking the letter to the dragon. He'll string me up by my toes. You're the one in charge, you should do it."

All three men looked at Nathan and he felt the trap closing in. "I think, dear brother, you should ready yourself to leave as soon as Sinclair does."

Nathan felt his temper rise. "I'm not some servant you can boss around, Christopher. Send one of them with the letter."

"It's already after the fact for Melissa and by the time you get to Colan's, Jessica will most likely be a happy bride as well."

"Why does it always end up on me? This is why I never come home. You always send me off on some ridiculous errand."

Stephan grinned. "Comes with being the youngest."

Nathan moved to punch Stephan in the nose but was interrupted by the clearing of a throat. "I hope I'm not interrupting something. I would hate to deprive anyone of getting a fair piece of me."

All four brothers looked at Morgan and scowled. "Sinclair," Jonathan said motioning for him to take a seat.

"I'll stand, thanks. A drink looks good, though."

Stephan narrowed his eyes at Morgan but brought him a brandy anyway. "What do you have to say in your defense, Morgan?" Jonathan asked as Stephan moved back by the window.

Morgan shrugged "Does it really matter?"

Jonathan flushed. "I guess not. Then you plan to do what's right?"

Morgan's jaw drew taught. "I think the lady should be present for this conversation."

"I am present," Jessica said stepping into the room. Ginger had ordered her to dress like a lady and she had complied. She was wearing a deep blue gown with silver shot through it. Her hair was piled on top of her head with small tendrils of hair falling down around her shoulders. Stephan arched a brow at her, she looked like a real lady. "Exactly what am I present for?" she asked moving to stand on the side of the room near the bookcase.

Christopher cleared his throat. At least his sister had seen clear to wear a dress. "If you will all be seated, we could get things underway."

"Cut the crap, Christopher. You're throwing me to the wolf and you expect me to sit and chat like we're at a tea party. Forget it," she snapped giving Nathan a glare as well as Morgan.

Morgan tightened his jaw. "Since the lady doesn't wish to chat, lets get this settled."

"Fine. Then you agree to do what's right?" Jonathan asked again.

Morgan gave him a measuring look then turned his gaze on Jessica. She stiffened and met his stare. Lifting a brow he asked, "Something to say?"

"I don't want to marry you."

"I didn't ask," he answered getting a blush out of her. "Though, I have little choice in the matter."

"Right you are, you bastard." Nathan cursed still smarting from the upcoming trip to see his father. "You'll marry her and fix her honor."

"I'm afraid I'm getting a bit tired of covering for the ladies honor," Morgan said still keeping his gaze pinned to Jessica's. She reddened further.

"Perhaps you can keep her out of trouble since she'll be carrying your name instead."

Morgan didn't like the idea. "I thought perhaps a month or two before the blessed event..."

"Sorry, old chap. A week from Saturday. Christopher obtained a special license. The pair of you will wed Saturday next," Jonathan said interrupting him.

Jessica turned to give Jonathan a glare. "I refuse to marry him. We'll kill each other within a week."

Morgan smiled a smile that didn't reach his eyes, "I predicted a day."

Jessica snorted. "Better to overestimate then to be cut short."

Christopher frowned at the pair. "I think, young lady, that you have nothing to quibble about. If you hadn't been crawling around the man's home and poking your nose in business you had no right to be in, you wouldn't find yourself in this mess."

"Thanks Christopher. You cleared that up rather nicely. For a minute there I was getting fuzzy with the details."

Christopher flushed at her sharp tongue. Jonathan scowled. "If we're through here I'd like a word with Morgan alone."

Jessica turned toward the door. "Gladly. I'm going to the docks," she stated pulling the door open, leaving the men staring after her. Christopher handed Nathan a parcel of letters and things for their father.

"Have a nice trip and don't get lost," he added giving Nathan a firm look that said if he had to come looking for him there would be hell to pay. Nathan cursed as he snatched the parcel from Christopher's hands.

"I'll remember this, don't think I won't," he snapped putting his cloak and hat on. Snatching his gloves out of Jenkin's hands he slammed out of the house. Stephan grinned as he left the room.

"Not a very happy family are you?" Morgan asked sarcastically.

"It just happens we've had trouble with the female members?"

"Oh?"

"I know that doesn't come as a surprise to you but normally we aren't involved in situations like this. Our father handled all this. I'm getting tired of wanting to break some one's bones."

Morgan arched a brow. "I guess it was just a matter of time before we ended up on opposite sides again."

Jonathan scowled. "It wasn't exactly what I would have wished. Especially knowing you like I do."

Morgan hooted. "You're just now worrying about my reputation? Tsk, tsk. You were so determined to see us wed, you didn't consider my past."

"Oh, I considered it. I also know my sister. She isn't exactly a saint."

Morgan stiffened as his face lost all humor. "Are you telling me she's tainted?"

"I should wipe the floor with your face for suggesting such a thing. Jessica is as pure as the day she was born. I was referring to her wild nature and habit of getting into the worst situations possible."

Morgan moved to one of the chairs and seated himself. "I'd rather not know anymore if you don't mind. Just get to the point. Why did you wish to see me?"

Jonathan swallowed and moved to hearth. "It has nothing to do with Jessica. I was wondering what you could tell me about Cabot lines."

"The Earl of Canton?"

"Yes."

"Why do you want to know?"

Jonathan looked over his shoulder at the man seated in the chair. They had been friends now for a while and he trusted him enough to keep things quiet. With the present situation he wasn't sure if Morgan still felt the same way. "It's not common knowledge."

Morgan frowned. "It will remain so," he stated angered by Jonathan's hesitation.

"My youngest sister married the older brother yesterday."

Morgan's face showed his surprise. "But the son was marrying the Fleming girl."

"Exactly. I don't know what happened to cause my sister to marry Cabot but it looks like he saw a bigger fish and jumped at it."

Morgan ran a hand through his hair. "You're sure that's why he married her? For the ships?"

"No. It's just a possibility. Our firm is under my mother's name and not many people are aware that we are involved with the sea."

Morgan frowned, "I never noticed that."

"Because you know me. Is Cabot the sort to resort to that kind of tactic?"

Morgan scowled. "The Earl is. He'd sell a son for the right price but I don't know about the son." Jonathan frown deepened. "I could find out."

Jonathan's head snapped up. "How?"

"Easy enough. I'll send some of my crew to gather information from some of his."

Jonathan grinned. "I hadn't thought of that."

"Of course not." Morgan said with a grin. "You have your mind on horses."

Jonathan nodded. "You're right about that. I have to leave and finalize a few deals. Could you contact me at home?"

"Yours or your father's?"

"Mine. I have several clients coming to pick up animals."

Morgan nodded. "I'll see what I can do." Both men got to their feet and headed for the door. Jonathan frowned as he opened it.

"I hope things work out for the best. Jessica can be a handful."
Morgan gave him a lopsided grin, "I don't doubt it."

Chapter 30

ALLISON SIGHED as she leaned against the tree in the back of Ginger's house, near the roses she had been tending since she arrived. Nero was stretched out at her side and she absently stroked his fur. "I don't suppose you have the slightest urge to cause trouble. Perhaps steal all Cook's sweets." Nero rolled further on his side giving a low mew. Allison smiled. "I didn't think so. It just seems that the mischief makers are the ones getting married, while I sit here getting closer to my deadline." Nero moved his paw to her lap. She felt him squeeze slightly letting her know she was getting lax in her petting. Allison chuckled. "Always a baby, aren't you?"

"Excuse me, Miss. Your brother wishes to see you?"

Allison frowned. "Which one, Jenkins?"

"Lord Christopher. It seems the other three aren't in residence anymore."

Allison sat up at that. "Aren't here! But where did they go?"

"I think you should ask your brother, Miss."

Allison frowned. Jenkins never gave her any information. "All right, Jenkins. Is he in the study?"

"Yes, Miss. Would you care for an escort?"

"No, thank you. Nero knows the way."

"Right, Miss," he said bowing.

"All right, Nero. Find Christopher."

Five minutes later she stood in the study listening to her brother furiously writing in a journal. "You wanted to see me?"

"Yes. Come in please," he said getting to his feet and taking her arm. He moved her into a chair in front of his desk. "I thought you might like to know what happened this morning at the meeting," At her nod, he smiled, "it seems Jessica is getting married. A week from Saturday."

Allison frowned. She had already known that but now it was official. "That's wonderful."

Christopher frowned at her lack of enthusiasm. "Stephan has returned to Brentwood to finish his scheduled trips but he'll be back by the end of next week for the wedding." At her nod he added, "and Jonathan also left. He had a few clients coming to Meadow Acres to buy some horses. He, too, will be back next week." At her continued silence he frowned. "I'm sure they would have said goodbye but they were in a hurry."

"It's all right, Christopher. They have important matters to deal with and I completely understand."

"Nathan is visiting Father. I sent word of Melissa's marriage and Jessica's pending one."

Allison stiffened. She, as usual, was still a burden to her family. They were always forced to care for her and felt guilty about that. "If you have things you have to do, Christopher, do them. You need not worry about me. Ginger is planning things for me."

"Then you've decided to..." his voice trailed off.

"Yes. I see no reason to let what happened the other night ruin my chances of choosing a man I've at least met more than once. And you needn't worry about me seeing the Earl again. It seems the man returned to his country estates," she said rising to move around the room. Nero obediently moved to lie by the door. Christopher frowned. "I was hoping you hadn't had time to look into finding me a husband."

Christopher scowled. "I haven't. With your sisters causing such scandal, I didn't even have a chance to deal with Father's schedule."

Allison smiled. "I'm glad that's settled then. I'll leave you to your work." Moving to the door she turned slightly, "Don't worry about me, Christopher. Aunt Ginger has enough things planned to keep six women busy." Turning, she grabbed Nero's collar and started out the door. Christopher scowled at her retreating back. Out of all of his sisters, Allison was the one with the most heart. She cared for a person unconditionally. Shaking his head he returned to the journal he had been working on and frowned. How his father managed to get things accomplished was beyond him. He had work piled up from weeks ago and still the stack kept growing.

Allison headed straight to her room. Little did her family know she didn't plan to sit around and wait for some perfect man to come crawling out of the woodwork. She was taking matters into her own hands. And she was starting with Jessica's wedding.

"Nero, I think I better marry soon," she said rubbing his fur. Slowly smiling for the first time since she made a fool of herself at the Earl of Salisbury's home, Allison had a plan.

Chapter 31

NATHAN CURSED FOR THE SECOND TIME. He was losing badly at cards and wasn't in a mood to get himself out of it. Picking up his brandy he stood and moved off toward a window. Thomas seeing his friend struggling followed him. "Planning to lose every shilling you own?"

Nathan gave him a sideways glance. "No. I had planned on gaining a fair amount of some other sap's funds."

"I'd try another evening. What's eating at you this time?"

Nathan scowled. "I've been given the honor of telling my father of his most recent son-in-law."

Thomas's eyebrows shot up. "Why not?"

"Exactly. But it seems my brothers all have important matters to see to and my life, as useless as they see it, has opportunity."

Thomas pursed his lips at Nathan's self-pity. "I think, my friend, you should get yourself crocked. It's always better to deal with such a predicament that way."

Nathan gave him a lopsided grin. "I was thinking the same thing. It takes just over four hours to reach Uncle Colan's. The way I see it, if I stop in every pub between here and there I should be feeling right peachy."

Thomas grinned. "I think I might accompany you for a spell, if you don't mind." Nathan studied his friend and laughed. The man was already far into his cups.

"I don't think so. I need to travel fast and I would hate to give my father any reason to rail at me when he's already going to be livid. A foxed guest is not a good idea."

"Now who you calling foxed? I have had a few I admit, but I can still function quite well," he stated swaying from side to side.

"The answer is still no. I'll see you in a couple of days."

Thomas frowned as he watched Nathan walk from the room. As usual Nathan carried himself with grace and dignity. Shaking his head, Thomas frowned. It wasn't like he couldn't have helped Nathan out if he'd got himself into trouble. Shrugging his shoulders he drained his glass. It wasn't Thomas's responsibility to baby-sit the man.

Nathan exited Whites and waved a hand to his coach. Sanders, had been with the family now for almost twelve years and was the best coachman ever.

"I guess it's time, Sanders. I'll want to stop at several of the pubs along the way. Steer clear of the lowest looking ones, huh?"

"Very good, my lord," Sanders said taking up the reins as soon as the door closed.

Nathan leaned back against the cushioned seats and frowned at the package on the opposite seat. What the hell was in the thing? Hopefully Christopher had seen fit to clean up the events a bit. Pleasant occurrences went over better than the irritating events they had been through. Snorting at the thing in disgust he nearly missed the scene taking place in the woods. Lifting his cane he tapped on the roof calling a halt to the coach. Staring hard he frowned. It appeared that three highwaymen were holding up a fancy looking coach. Sanders leaned over the edge and looked at his occupant.

"You're not thinking of interfering are you, my lord? We're slightly outnumbered."

Nathan frowned. He considered moving on, then scowled as two finely dressed ladies emerged from the coach.

"Damn. I think the decision has been taken out of our hands. Get the pistol from under your seat," he stated. Nathan lifted the box near the front of the coach and took out the pistols stored there. Checking each one, he stuffed them into his belt and left the coach.

"If I'm lucky, Sanders, those men won't be looking at me but at the women."

Sanders frowned but checked his pistol. If Nathan ran into any trouble Sanders wasn't about to stand by idle while the man got himself shot. The Earl would have his hide.

Nathan walked steadily toward the coach and noted it had been taken off the main road down a two-track lane for the robbery. The two men were shouting orders to the ladies who quickly removed their jewelry, while a third man searched the coach for valuables. Cursing, Nathan quickly scanned the woods for their mounts. Seeing the animals tied behind them he cursed again. So much for getting rid of their horses. Moving closer he kept behind the trees until he was nearly on the scene. The man in the coach moved to stand by the others.

"That's it," he said stuffing two purses in his jacket and a pistol, "they don't seem to have much."

The tallest in the group frowned. "That's the Baron's coach. I recognize the seal."

Nathan glanced at the emblem on the coach and frowned. It belonged to the Baron of Linwood. The man was a menace to society but richer than tea with cream. These thieves knew what they were doing. The shorter one waved a hand at the ladies.

"Tie them up and make it fast," he snapped making his men scramble to do his bidding. "Of all the times to travel light, my ladies, tonight wasn't one of them. Are you sure that's all the valuables you have."

One woman nodded vigorously, while the other hesitated a moment before doing the same. The short man smiled. "Now it's a sin to lie. Do I need to have my man here search you?" Nathan frowned at the thief. His voice had a peculiar accent to it and Nathan could have sworn he had heard it before. Watching the tall man move like he meant business, Nathan cursed as the young woman reached into the top of her gown and threw a very expensive looking necklace at the man.

"That's it. I haven't anymore," she screeched, "but you're going to be sorry. My brother will kill you for this," she finished giving the sniveling maid a fuming look.

Nathan cursed again. The Baron's sister. This wasn't good. The Baron had a temper like a volcano. It erupted at the least little offense. Pulling out two pistols he stood straight making sure his body was behind the tree.

"I think you better drop your weapons and step back from the ladies," Nathan stated his voice sounding deadly.

The bandit's turned their gazes in his direction but he could see they didn't know where he was.

The short one surged forward grabbing the sister by the hair and pulling her up against his front. The other two followed suit. All three women were screaming until the short one ordered them to shut up. Looking again in Nathan's direction the thief waited, considering his next move.

"What do you want, Mister?"

"I already stated that. Let the ladies be on their way."

The man shifted his feet. "I don't think so. You'll put holes in us the minute they are clear."

"I could have already shot you," Nathan stated watching the man pale, "Now let the ladies go."

The man licked his lips. "Who are you, Mister?"

"Irrelevant. Now release the ladies."

"I don't think so," the man stated making Nathan curse. Nathan was hoping the thieves would do as he asked. Frowning he watched as the little one moved back toward the horses, pulling the girl along with him. As they reached their mounts, the three shoved the women forward and scrambled up onto their backs. Nathan stepped from his place and fired, knocking the tall one from his horse. Taking up the other pistol, he aimed and shot, knocking the one who had searched the coach from his horse. Using Sander's pistol, he aimed and cursed as the thing backfired, burning his hand. Scowling he hurried toward the women, making sure they were all right.

Seeing that he was a gentleman, the women surged around him. Nathan quickly hurried them into their coach. Seeing that the coachman was unconscious he whistled, bringing Sanders hurrying into the clearing. "Return these women to the Baron and explain what happened. Take those with you," he stated holding his burned hand to his side.

"But my lord, what about you?"

"I'll be fine, Sanders. I'll take one of the horses. I'll ride the rest of the way to the inn."

"The next one is just up the road," the Baron's sister said.

Nathan looked at her and frowned. She had blond hair and sapphire eyes. What a beauty. "Next time, tell the Baron not to be so remiss in his duties. You could have been killed."

"Oh, don't worry on that account. I plan to give him an earful." Nathan nodded his head and moved off to put the bodies up on one of the horses that were standing patiently off to the side. Tying them to the horse, he secured it to the back of the coach.

"Once they are safely back to the Baron, return for me at the inn." Sanders nodded, as he scrambled up on the coach. Nathan frowned as they disappeared from sight then looked at his coach. He didn't want to leave it there. Moving back to it, he reached into the box under the seat and quickly reloaded his pistols. He put them on the seat next to him. And tried to think of the best thing to do. Thieves would take the coach in minutes if he left it. Frowning he picked up the reins and studied the setup. There were four straps running to horses. He didn't have the slightest idea how to drive the coach but it was better than leaving it there. Giving the reins a shake he nearly lost his seat as the coach jerked forward. Cursing he pulled back on the reins to keep the horses walking. Cursing again, he sent a quick prayer, to whoever was listening, to get him to the inn without breaking his neck.

Chapter 32

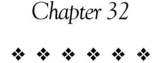

CHRISTOPHER FROWNED at the sight before him. "What the hell is that?" he snapped looking from Stephan to a sack squirming at his feet.

Stephan grinned. "I have just had the honor of repaying our sister for a bit of foolery she dealt me a couple of weeks ago." When Christopher still frowned, his grin widened. "As you know, I've been loading my ships for the trips they're going on. Well, I was loading the Gallant and what should I happen across but a nice nest of clothes all tucked nicely in a keg. I wouldn't have noticed except the thing was lighter than a feather and..."

"Stephan, if you don't mind, I have still several weeks of work to do in four days. Father is due to arrive in two days and I haven't the time to hear your shipping tales. Is there a point you're trying to make?"

Stephan scowled. "Fine, your mightiness, I was getting to the fact that no one owns anything that looks like what I found so I knew I had a stowaway." At Christopher's indulgent scowl, he bent down untied the sack and dumped the contents out on the floor.

"My God!" Christopher said coming to his feet to stare horrified at the dirty figure of his sister tied with arms wrapped around her bent legs unable to move more than an inch.

"She was stowaway on my ship for Northumberland. A good two week trip."

Christopher's face darkened as he moved around his desk. "You were going to run away?" he shouted, glaring at the ball at his feet.

Jessica, tired and dirty after being tied up for almost a day, gave Christopher her a defiant stare. Stephan had caught her right away on his ship but she had been there for almost two days. Her body was dirty and stiff from hiding in the stinking hull. She wasn't feeling generous toward anyone.

"What do you think would have happened once you were discovered missing?" he ranted at her. "I'll tell you. Father would be six feet under, that's what. He would have worried needlessly about where you were. Not to mention the scandal and humiliation the family would have suffered. Don't you ever think of anyone else but yourself?" he shouted turning away from her.

Jessica swallowed as she felt the tears sting her eyes. She was being shallow and inconsiderate like Melissa was. The thought sent her over the edge. Huge tears streamed from her eyes and she began to gulp air around the gag Stephan had shoved in her mouth.

Both brothers turned to stare at her. Stephan was instantly guilty. Going to her, he quickly untied her and pulled her into his arms.

"You witless fool," he stated letting her sob like a baby.

Christopher frowned, but remained silent. Why he was still able to function, he didn't know. His sisters were driving him insane.

"I'm sorry," she said around a hiccup. "You're right. I wasn't thinking of anyone but myself," she sniffed, getting to her feet, giving Stephan a slight shove. Wiping a dirty sleeve across her face, she added. "It won't happen again. I won't disgrace you again," she said trying to leave the room. Pausing she added, "at least not while I carry our name."

Christopher frowned at her retreating back. "She was going to leave him standing at the altar."

Stephan poured two drinks and handed one to Christopher. "I know. What I don't understand is why no one missed her?"

Christopher flushed. "I didn't think it was necessary to watch her. She wasn't required to attend anything, and Sinclair hasn't been around to see her. I don't know, damn it. I didn't think of it," he finished draining his glass.

"Well, I think from now on we need someone here to look after her."

"And just who do you have in mind?"

"I brought Hobkins back with me."

Christopher paused in mid-drink. "What good will he be?"

Stephan grinned. "I'm afraid I can't take all the credit of finding Jessica. It was Hobkins that saw her slinking around the market one afternoon and alerted me to the problem."

Christopher stared at him, then burst out laughing. "No wonder Father seemed to know everything that happened before we barely got out of trouble."

Stephan laughed, too. "If he had to deal with what has happened over the last month, it's a wonder he's as well as he is."

Christopher nodded. "And sane, too."

Stephan hooted harder. "Getting under your skin, brother. You're just lucky Nathan has been good."

Christopher scowled. "He should have been back by now. I told him if I had to come looking for him, he'd be sorry."

Stephan dropped onto the sofa swinging his legs over the arm at the opposite end. "I bet he shows up the same time as Father does. He's not stupid."

Christopher frowned. "He doesn't exactly get along with Father."

"Now who's being stupid? I didn't say he would be with Father, I said he would show up at the same time. He doesn't want to be available for any more of your errands."

Christopher scowled. "I thought you had ships to sail."

"I did. Each one is at this very moment on their present course to various locations."

"You're not sailing any?"

"I'm waiting until after the wedding. I can't say how long a trip will take me."

Christopher nodded then slowly smiled at his brother. "In that case, how about a jaunt to Andrew's"

Stephan stiffened and slowly sat up. "I stepped right into that one, didn't I?"

Christopher grinned. "This makes things easier for me. I can at least trust you to get to the locations I send you without running into twenty-five gamblers or fifteen females."

Stephan scowled. "Is that a challenge?"

Christopher held up his hands. "Good God, I hope not. I have enough trouble without you trying to take over Nathan's role."

Stephan grinned and resumed his reclined position. "Then hurry up and get things ready. I don't want to spend my whole day down there. Andrew is a nice enough fellow but I tell you, solicitors aren't exactly the sort you can chat and have a drink with."

"Andrew isn't so bad. In fact, the man has a damn good sense of humor."

"How so?"

"You'll see when you reach his office."

Stephan, curious, sipped his drink. Being at home without worries, was going to be a nice change. He had almost six days of leave time before he sailed. It was like a regular holiday he thought grinning.

Chapter 33

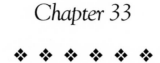

NATHAN PUSHED THE GIRL into a chair just inside his father's foyer giving her a glare cold enough to freeze the Thames. "Just sit here and don't make a sound. If anyone talks to you, act like you're a mute," he snarled thrusting his gloves and hat at a very stiff Rolston. "Watch her," he snapped snatching up the package for his father. Moving along the hall he pushed into the room without knocking.

Brand, who spent several hours each day in his study reading looked up at his son with surprise and relief. "Well, Nathan I must say this is a bit of a surprise."

Nathan, looking like a cat in a cage, gave his father a brief nod then walked over plopping the package in his lap. "Christopher sends this with his warmest regards," he finished holding out his hand for a tip.

Brand scowled. "That isn't funny, Nathan. I don't think visiting your father should be such a chore," he finished making Nathan feel small. Running his hand through his hair Nathan frowned..

"I'm sorry. I'm not exactly myself."

Brand smiled with those words. "Whom should I thank?" Getting an even blacker scowl he chuckled "Lets see what your brother has to say shall we?"

"Oh, please do," he replied with mock joviality.

Brand gave Nathan a disgusted look but opened the package scanning the contents quickly. "I see. So Melissa is actually married to the Cabot man then?"

"Didn't Christopher write that?"

Brand scowled at his clipped remark. "Nathan, I figure Christopher sent you here for a reason and my guess is that you are to answer my questions. If you don't mind, I would rather get them from my son instead of the prickly porcupine I have before me. Perhaps you would care to refresh yourself before I continue."

Nathan ran a hand through his hair again moving around the room with movements of a very troubled man. "I think you should finish your letters before I leave you."

Brand frowned. "I have finished the letter."

"No, I mean all of them."

Brand drew his brows together before opening the next letter. It was just like Christopher to write a separate letter for each topic he wanted to discuss. Brand set that letter aside for later since it referred to his business. Opening the next he quickly scanned the letter finishing on his feet. "Good lord, she didn't do that did she?"

Nathan snorted. "Do you really doubt it? Jessica hasn't a sensible bone in her body."

Brand's head snapped up at that statement. This coming from a man who was in more trouble than a fox in a hen house. "I believe what I read, it's just that I can't believe she's actually fallen in love and getting married."

Nathan choked on his drink but recovered quickly. Feeling like a fool for not reading what Christopher wrote to his father he just shrugged.. "We all agreed to it."

"Exactly what happened?"

Nathan quickly skimmed the details of both his sisters fall from graces altering Jessica's to make it sound like love had made her do the crazy things she had done. "So you see everything is working out, so you have nothing to worry about."

Brand pursed his lips resuming his seat. "I think the trouble is only beginning. There's more to what you just told me, but I'll find out first hand since I plan to attend the wedding."

Nathan looked at his father startled. "But father I don't think that's wise. Your heart and all."

"My heart's fine. Besides I'll bring Colan with me. He can diffuse my temper in seconds."

Nathan frowned. "I wish I would have known that when I was younger."

Brand snorted. "It wouldn't have helped in your case." Nathan clenched his teeth moving off to the window. Brand narrowed his eyes. "What's eating at you boy?"

Nathan punched his fist into the wall, making Brand draw his brows together in concern. "It seems my sisters aren't the only ones getting themselves linked into marital bliss."

"No?" Brand asked excitedly. "Is Christopher getting married perhaps?'

Nathan laughed at that statement. "I'm afraid he's becoming more and more of a lost cause, unless Rolston here has a sister. Christopher is stiffer than wood and I don't mean in the lower regions."

Brand chuckled. "Then to whom are you referring?"

Nathan lost all trace of humor. "It seems, my dear father, that I have fallen for one of the oldest tricks in the books."

"You!" Brand asked his eyes nearly popping out of his head. "I'll be damned," he said speechless.

"On the contrary, father, I think that's my role."

"Well, Nathan, explain yourself."

"It's simple enough. My lovely bride set the trap and I fell in head first."

Brand frowned at his youngest son. "Now, Nathan, you're not talking very clear."

Nathan looked around the room for a drink and frowned. "Where's the damn brandy?"

Brand also scowled. "Colan, took it away. It seems I might have the urge to indulge and the man wants to take away the risk."

Nathan scowled. "Is the whole house empty."

Brand shrugged. "Rolston!" he bellowed bringing the stiff fellow instantly. "Bring some Brandy for my son." Rolston nodded leaving with hardly moving a muscle. "I swear that man's going to break apart one of these days." Nathan just stared at his father. He'd actually made a joke. "Well don't look at me like I have two heads. Start talking."

Nathan flopped into a chair putting his head in one hand. "It all started after Christopher sent me here as his little errand boy. I was being the gallant fellow by rescuing a damsel in distress from thieves in the woods and happened to kill a couple of them in the end. But the lady's coachman was killed so I told Sanders to take them home then return for me at the inn."

"Didn't Sanders do like you said?"

Nathan gave him an exasperated look. "If you want to hear what I have to say then kindly listen and refrain from guessing. If you haven't noticed I'm not the happy groom."

Brand pursed his lips. "By all means continue."

Nathan scowled at his father. "As the scene unfolded again in my mind I realized I'd dealt with the little thief that had gotten away once before. She'd actually saved my life."

"Saved your life? She?"

"Yes, she. The chit pushed me out of the way from getting run over by a horse. Little did I know, she probably picked my pocket at the same time." Shaking his head he returned to the scene in the woods. "Anyway, since I hadn't driven a team of four I really didn't have the slightest idea what the hell I was doing and was an easy target for the thieves to attack. As it happens that group was killed but I was knocked from my perch, hitting my head." he said indicating a slight bump on the side of his head Brand wouldn't even have noticed if he hadn't pointed it out. "I was senseless and that is when the little conniving woman from the first robbery, stepped in. She took me to the inn and then on to a little church. I didn't know it, of course, but somehow the priest married us and I ended up sprawled next to her the next morning when Sanders walked into the room."

Brand was staring at him with his mouth open and quickly snapped it shut. "You married a girl and didn't know it?"

Nathan's face turned savage. "She asked me if I wanted a drink?" he shouted "A drink?"

"What?"

"She asked if I wanted a drink? When I said 'I do' the priest said you're married, kiss the bride," he finished almost at a sneer. "The little witch," he snarled moving around the room in a rage.

Brand shook his head. "Sometimes I think your head is in the sand." At the glare from his son he continued, "Have you ever heard of an annulment?"

Nathan laughed bitterly. "Oh, I've heard of it but the little slut had that covered. She told the priest I was sick and could die leaving her and the baby she carried without a proper name."

Brands mouth fell open again. "I can't believe it."

"Neither can I. Married! Me at twenty-five years of age," he raged throwing a glass of what could only be tea at the wall. "Where the hell is that brandy?"

"Now, Nathan, I think you should go straight upstairs and get yourself changed. Obviously this is a bit of a problem but with..."

"A bit of a problem? You make it sound like I have a whole in my shoe. I'm married Father! I can't just go to sleep and make it all go away."

Brand frowned at his sarcasm. "I understand your situation, but I think you should calm down and use what brains you do possess, and come up with some logical solution."

Nathan snorted, "And pigs fly." Stalking from the room, he grabbed the brandy off the tray Rolston had as he was entering the study. Brand shook his head at the look on the stiff mans face, then leaned his head back on the chair. A slow smile crossed his face. He'd remained calm through that whole tirade. Not one flash of pain. His face broke into a grin; rest must have been exactly what he needed.

Chapter 34

MELISSA TRUDGED into Aunt Ginger's house trying valiantly not to cry. Christopher saw her coming and raised a brow at her. "And to what do we owe the pleasure?"

Melissa's lip quivered and she promptly burst into tears, running past him up the stairs. Christopher's mouth dropped open as he took a step to stop her.

"Nice going. If you're not sending them off in a temper, they're running away in tears," Stephan said from behind him.

Christopher turned to give him a glare. "Get going. Andrew will be biting his nails over what's in there." Christopher returned to the stairs.

"I wouldn't even consider going up there. You're not exactly Prince Charming at the moment."

"Go!" Christopher snarled returning to his study to slam the door. Hearing Stephan's chuckle made him snarl a curse. Stephan was positively the most irritating man alive, next to Nathan, of course. Taking a seat he started on the second pile of papers he had ready. It referred to the shipping portion of the estates, which he couldn't work through without the report from Stephan, which meant he would have to wait for the oaf to return before diving into it. Scooting it to the side, he drew in Jonathan's stack. A slow smile crossed his face. Jonathan had a head for business. He kept immaculate records and if asked a question could answer without looking up the information. Leafing through several papers he frowned, Jonathan's final report wasn't here. Drawing his brows down in concern, Christopher reached for his brandy. Jonathan's report was always early. Thinking back, he produced the proper date and realized Jonathan's report was a week late. That wasn't like Jonathan.

"Jenkins!" he bellowed getting the servant in seconds. "Has Jonathan sent anything recently?"

Jenkins frowned. "Not today, my lord. Anything earlier, would already be in here."

Christopher frowned. "Send one of the lads to Meadow Acres and have Jonathan come home earlier than Friday. I need to see him before the wedding."

"Yes, my lord," Christopher frowned at the closed door. What could possibly be keeping him with that report?

Chapter 35

BRAND LIFTED HIS GAZE from the letter in his hand in stunned disbelief. Married! Leaning his head back against the chair he took several deep breaths. He had been gone from home now for thirty-six days and already four of his children were married. Four! Two were sons who didn't have to marry. Rubbing his eyes he rescanned the paper to make sure he was reading it right, then bellowed for Rolston.

"Get my son down here!" he stated trying to keep calm. Five minutes later Nathan strolled in looking like he'd been carrying a cement block around for weeks. "God lord Nathan, you look like hell."

Nathan smiled a lopsided smile and took a seat. "So nice of you to notice. I was thinking of dancing a jig later but now I might reconsider.

"Cut the sarcasm. Didn't you sleep well last night?"

Nathan's face darkened. "No, I did not! Thanks to that wooden man you call a butler."

"Rolston? What happened now?"

"He put my wife in the same room with me."

Brands brows shot up. "She's here?" At the black scowl sent his way, Brand nearly smacked the boy. "Why didn't you say something? She must think I'm the devil for not talking to her," he stated getting to his feet.

Nathan merely shrugged. "I would like a different room."

Brand pursed his lips. "We'll discuss this later. I have an errand for you to run."

Nathan came out of his chair. "Forget it. Send the wall board."

Brand frowned. "Here I think this will lighten your mood," he said handing him the letter he'd been reading earlier. Watching his son's face go from stunned disbelief to hilarity made him smile, too.

"I can't believe it. He fell for a more gullible ploy than I did," he finished with a laugh.

"So it seems," Brand said sitting. "As it happens, though, I have something for each of you."

Nathan still delighting in his brother's recent marriage looked at his father in confusion. "What could that possibly be?"

"Your mother, God rest her soul, left each of her children a small dowry."

"A dowry! That's ridiculous, half of us are males."

"I know and I told her that was a stupid thing to do but she wouldn't hear of it. She set up several funds for each of you and, upon your marriage, it was to be given to you as a gift."

Nathan sat shocked. "And this gift is?"

Brand bellowed for Rolston again. "Get the packages from my room with the boys names on it, please." Five minutes later he returned laying them on the desk in stiff precise movements. Nathan felt like pushing the man to see if he'd fall over like a tree. "Here we are," he said handing the one with Nathan's name on it to him. "Read that.

"Do you know what's in here?"

"Haven't the slightest idea. Your mother wouldn't let me get involved. She said it would alter my ideas for you boys when you grew up and she knew it would never have remained a secret."

Nathan frowned and opened the envelope. His mind was reeling by the time he was finished reading. He was now the Earl of Alnwick near the border of Scotland with enough land to cover an area the size of London. Stunned, he nearly dropped the draft for the money she had left him. "My god, she left this to me?" he asked in shock.

Brand frowned. "I haven't the slightest idea what you're talking about," he said reaching over the desk for the papers. Quickly scanning the contents, he grinned. "That sly lady. She had several uncles and cousins throughout England that loved her very much. Most didn't have heirs and she came into a great number of titles that aren't part of my estates to Christopher. Now I know what happened to them."

"Do we all get this?"

"I would expect something of the sort, but she was specific about the secret. Once you know you are not to tell the others. They must marry to find out."

"Then I guess Jonathan is also a rich man."

"That is a likely guess but we won't know until you visit him."

"Me!"

Brand nodded. "I thought you would feel delighted to take the news to him."

Nathan slowly smiled. "I think I would at that." Gradually his smile faded. "What about Rae?"

"Who?"

"My wife. Her name is Rae?"

Brand waved a hand at him. "I'll take her with me."

Nathan scowled. He didn't want his father anywhere near the girl. She was a liar and a thief. "Never mind. I'll take her with me." he said getting to his feet. "If you don't mind I'll plan on leaving within the hour."

"But the wedding isn't until Saturday?"

"I know but I need time to figure out what to do with my wife," he stated leaving the room. Brand watched him go then frowned.

"What has him all in a snit?" Colan asked taking a seat in one of the chairs in front of his desk.

"I was just told his wife is here with him."

"She's here?" Colan stated moving forward on his chair. "But he didn't even bring her down for dinner last night. She's probably starving."

Brand frowned. "I think she has it coming to her. If we step in now, things will only get worse. One thing I have learned about Nathan is that he doesn't like to be pushed."

"Well, who is she?"

"He isn't exactly in the talking mood but he did say that her name was Rae. That's all I know about her."

Colan scowled. "That isn't very much."

"I know. I think we should pay their room a visit and meet the girl for ourselves."

Colan grinned. "Good idea, though I'm sure he won't appreciate it."

"Even better reason to go to their room. At least some good will come out of us going up there. She'll know that his family isn't completely lacking in manners."

Colan nodded. "I'm beginning to see why your children behave the way they do," he stated getting a grin from Brand.

NATHAN OPENED HIS DOOR and stopped in his tracks. His wife of one day, was pulling her tunic over her head. Rae gave Nathan a glare, but continued with her dressing. Pulling on some stockings, she slipped her feet into her boots, before moving to sit in a chair where she pulled her black hair back and began braiding it. Rae gave Nathan another glare.

"Did you want something?" she asked knowing full well Nathan hated her and was planning to dump her off somewhere. Swallowing she knew today she would have to tell him about the boys. Sean at five and Ian at three were a handful but they were hers. Well she was all they had left. Her sister had been their mother but Rae was now. And nothing was going to make her give them up.

"No!" he snapped shutting the door with a bang. Moving to his bag he quickly started shoving the few belongings he had back into the bag. "We're leaving for my father's estates in fifteen minutes. Get ready," he added grabbing the bag and moving toward the door.

Rae, panicked that he wouldn't listen to her later about the boys, blurted out that she had them. "We have to stop and get the boys."

Nathan stopped in his tracks and slowly turned to stare at Rae. His eyes narrowed. She was looking at him with eyes of pure green steel. Nathan arched his brows with his next question. "Which boys would that be?"

Rae flushed. "I have two sons."

Nathan's mouth fell open despite his effort to control his emotions. "Two sons?" he squeaked out. "Two sons!" he bellowed, dropping his bag. Nathan clenched and unclenched his hands before moving to the window to keep himself from choking the life out of her. "Two sons," he said, again.

Rae clasped her hands together. Rather than go into the details of their being orphaned and risk having him send them away, she nodded her head. "Sean is five and Ian is three."

Nathan clamped his mouth shut grinding his teeth. Giving a laugh of disbelief, he shook his head. "Should have figured as much. Do you carry a babe as well?"

Rae frowned then flushed remembering her lie to the priest. "No."

"Do they have the same fathers?" he said sarcastically.

Rae turned scarlet. He had just called her a whore. Taking a deep breath she calmed herself. She couldn't explain the situation herself or the boys would have to be explained and he'd have a reason to send them away. "Yes."

"Then, where is he?"

Rae frowned. It wouldn't hurt to tell the truth on that one. "He died of sickness back home."

Nathan frowned. "And where is home?"

"The colonies."

Nathan turned to look at her. "A damn yank." Shaking his head he scooped up his bag. "Ten minutes," he snapped slamming the door as he left.

Rae sighed in relief then drew her brows down in concern. Did that mean he was going to get the boys or not? Scurrying around to right the room she began to panic.

Nathan moved along the hall and nearly collided with his father and Colan. "Come to gloat or look over the addition to the family?"

Brand frowned. "We thought to welcome your wife to the family. You seem so tight lipped about the whole thing we wanted to assess her for ourselves."

Nathan, barely controlling the rage inside him, glared at the pair. "She's a lying thief from the colonies. What more is there to know?" he snarled moving past them.

Brand watched him go and frowned. "He can't be serious."

The door opened at the end of the hall and they watched as a small woman move along the hall with the agility of a deer. She paused as she spotted them, then moved to pass by.

"Now, hold on there, my dear. You must be Rae."

Rae paused, her eyes showing her wariness. "I could be."

Brand chuckled. "Scared you that much has he."

Rae stiffened. "I'm not afraid of him."

Brand smiled. "That's good, child. He has a vile temper but he's a good lad."

Her eyes narrowed taking in Colan with a glance. "Just who might you be?"

"I'm Brand Hayworth, the lad's father."

Rae turned scarlet. "Excuse me. I didn't mean to...it's just that...well, he wants to leave in ten minutes and I'm slightly worried he will go without me."

Colan laughed. "Not bloody likely," he said, then reddened. "Excuse the language."

Brand glared at his brother. "This is my brother, Colan. He's a bit of an ill-mannered rogue."

Rae smiled nervously. "Nice to meet you both but I really must go," she stated moving past them to disappear from sight.

"Well, I don't believe it. He has her hopping about like a dog."

Colan laughed. "If you remember, the girl tricked her way into his life. I'm sure he's making her pay for that privilege."

Brand sighed. "You're right. Nathan can be as stubborn as a mule."

"The girl tricked him. She even lied to a priest."

Brand scowled. "I'd forgotten about that. Do you suppose she is with child?"

"Who's to say? Nathan seems mad enough for it to be true. Of course, he'd have left her at some remote estate, if it were. But you'd be a grandfather."

Brand puffed up with indignation. "My sons would never lay a hand on their wives. As to the grandfather part, I want nothing more than to have a few children call me that. You on the other hand would be a great Uncle," he added happily knowing his brother hated the aging process.

Colan met his look. "I hope you're right," he said, ignoring the age part. "That girl is from the colonies. They're a whole different breed over there. Believe me."

Brand scowled again. "Well, he married her and we'll just have to make the best of it."

Colan laughed. "You sure have mellowed in your old age."

Brand snorted and moved along the hall out of sight.

Chapter 36

"WHATEVER IS THE MATTER?" Allison asked coming to her feet as a sobbing Melissa flew into the room and threw herself on the bed.

"It's just awful," she wailed sobbing harder. Allison frowned. Melissa could have anything, from a hangnail to a broken leg.

"Want to tell me about it?" she asked, resuming her seat at the window.

Melissa sniffed a few more minutes then turned to look at her sister. "It's awful. I'm married to the meanest man in London."

"What did Lord Cabot do now? You've only been married for two days."

Melissa burst into tears at that and Allison had to wait almost five minutes for her to get herself back under control. "He lied to me, Allison."

Her brows drew together. "Lied to you? About what?"

"He told me he was dying and that I would be a widow and rich."

"What?" Allison said confused.

"When I met him on the street, he had two men with him. His brother and a doctor. He didn't turn out to be a doctor at all but the Earl of March. Anyway, they told me Caleb was dying and wouldn't live another day. It was his last dying wish to be married so he had someone to pass his fortune onto. They told me his family were all dead."

Allison bit her lip. Melissa was stupid sometimes but she must have been out of her mind to believe such a story. "So why didn't he give it to his brother?"

"At the time, they told me Keegan was just a friend."

"So you married him for his money?"

Melissa frowned. "No, I married him because I felt sorry for him. He's only twenty-six without any family. He was dying," she said trying to make herself feel better.

Allison couldn't help herself, she laughed. Melissa burst into tears again. "I'm sorry," Allison said, chuckling. "It's just so naive of you to believe such a thing." Melissa just cried harder, making Allison frown. "Exactly what was he dying from?"

Melissa sniffed. "A body eating disease." Allison started laughing again, finally getting Melissa to do the same. "It's so humiliating. I actually believed him," she said getting angry.

"So, what are you doing here?"

"I was coming to you for advice. You always see a situation so clear. I wanted your opinion."

Allison frowned. "Jonathan thinks Caleb's after your shipping connections."

"Oh, no. He's not after them. He didn't even know that I was connected to the sea." Frowning, she added, "but he does now. He's afraid his father will find out and want to get in with Stephan."

Allison whistled. "That isn't going to look good since he was supposed to marry the Fleming girl for her ships."

"She was after his fortune."

"But you're not."

"Absolutely not. I plan to stay here and return to Brentwood. I don't ever want to see my husband again."

Allison laughed. "You're being naive again. Your husband isn't about to let you stay with us. He'll come and drag you home."

"No, he won't. I already told him I was coming here. Caleb didn't care in the least."

"You're not using your head," Allison said, getting to her feet. "Let's go downstairs and get a bite to eat. I missed breakfast and lunch sounds wonderful."

"All right, though, I'm not particularly hungry," she said taking Allison's arm. "I have to tell you, I wasn't exactly stable when I came in and I sort of made a cake of myself in front of Christopher. He probably feels responsible for my tears."

Allison grinned. "I'm sure you're going to rub it in."

Melissa smiled. "Of course. Christopher needs a little excitement in his life."

"I think you and Jessica have taken care of that area."

"Oh? What has Jessica done now?"

Allison stopped in her tracks. "Didn't anyone send you a note?"

"No. What happened?" At her silence, Melissa lost patience "What happened, Allison. I'm dying here?" she said steering her back to the chairs.

"She's getting married this Saturday."

"Married!" she exclaimed. "Good heavens, to whom?"

"His name is Morgan Sinclair and..."

"Morgan Sinclair! Why he's the Baron of Essex. His Uncle is the Duke of Rochester."

Allison shrugged. "That doesn't seem to matter to Jessica."

"Why not? The man is a great catch. She'll be set for life."

"I don't think she's concerned about that. The fact is, she doesn't even like him."

"Then why is she marrying him?"

"It's a long story. I'll skim the details, so don't interrupt. The Baron caught her in his room looking for my purse. They got in a fight, causing members from the ball going on at his home to find them. She was compromised and Nathan and his Aunt forced them to marry."

Melissa was stunned. "You mean, she was actually found in a man's room. Alone?"

"Yes."

"By Nathan and his Aunt, the Duchess," Melissa said excited.

Allison frowned. "I'm not sure if it was the Duchess but his Aunt was there."

"I can't believe it. She actually ruined herself." Laughing, she added, "I'm surprised it took her this long. She doesn't know a thing about society."

"I think you better keep those opinions to yourself. She isn't exactly pleasant to be around." Allison said, worried.

"She's here, right? I think I'm ready for lunch now."

"What are you up to?" At the silence and rush they were in, Allison had her suspicions. "Just be nice. I don't think Christopher can take anymore. He's practically at his wit's end."

"Don't worry," Melissa said, starting down the stairs. Allison held the rail as they descended, sending a quick prayer to heaven for divine intervention.

STEPHAN WALKED ALONG THE STREET looking neither left nor right. He was headed for Andrew's. Christopher had given him a package full of information and knowing Christopher, there was bound to be some sort of reply required. Reaching the small building where Andrew's office was, he paused outside the door.

"Please let this be quick." Opening the door, he stepped into the room and stiffened in surprise. The room was completely out of style for a business.

The walls were covered with various things from long wooden faces to animal heads. Moving farther into the room, he gapped at the line of human skulls along the top of a table.

"You're brother didn't warn you, did he?"

Stephan turned to the little man and grinned. Andrew was out of place among the African and Indian artifacts. "As a matter of fact, he didn't. But

I'm not surprised. As you well know, we delight at putting each other on the spot."

Andrew smiled. "If you'll be seated, I'll have a look at what Christopher sent over."

"Sure thing," Stephan said handing over the package smiling as the man nearly dropped it. "Where did you get such interesting things?" he said, moving to look at the head of a Caribou mounted near the door.

"Like in your case, I have a brother with a sense of humor. He has been stationed in India now for almost thirteen years and delights in sending me the most peculiar things."

"Why do you put them up if you don't like them?" he asked, picking up a shriveled thing looking remarkably like a human head.

"I would hide them away in an attic if I could get away with it, but my brother has covered that avenue by sending my sister here every so often to ask after the things she picked out for me. He has me at a disadvantage."

"Just bring them out when she's going to arrive."

"He never tells me exactly when that is and she ends up staying for two or three months. It's safer to just leave them here at the office. My wife never visit's here. She hates the stuff."

Stephan grinned. "I can see why," he said, holding up a necklace of human teeth. "A bit warped, isn't he?"

"Actually, that came from my sister."

Stephan laughed, replacing the ornament on its hook. The room had spears, arrows, rocks, pictures, statues and jars of god knew what. Stephan busied himself looking around, as Andrew shuffled threw the papers.

"I only have a small bit to send back. If you can wait fifteen minutes, I'll have it ready."

Stephan smiled. "I'll run over to do some shopping. I need to get Jessica and Melissa something for their weddings. I'll stop by on the way home."

"Very good." Stephan nodded and left. He was thankful his brothers didn't put him in a position like Andrew was in: Not wanting to offend anyone and having to display such a crazy bunch of goods. Laughing to himself he hurried to do his shopping.

Chapter 37

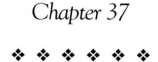

JONATHAN STARED AT THE GIRL riding comfortably in the open carriage his coachman, Miles, was driving. Jonathan chose to ride one of his prize animals, instead of being in the same vicinity as his wife. He was married now and had been for nearly two days. He still couldn't stand to look at her. It brought back the humiliation at falling for such a stupid trap. Most men fresh out of Eton fell for this one, not a man of his years. Moving his horse farther ahead he paused outside his home and waited for the stable lad to come out.

"Take Paladin into the barn then come back and get Mint from the carriage," he said handing over the reins. Moving up the steps to the door, he called for his housekeeper. Matty appeared in seconds as a footman was told to fetch his wife into the house. He then gave complete instructions for his wife to be placed in the opposite side of the house. Matty didn't ask any questions, just did as she was told. Jonathan moved off to his own room to take a bath and change his clothes. Heading back down into the hall, he frowned as the butler gave him a cold glare. Ignoring the man, since he was kin to Hobkins and wasn't likely to tell him what was the problem, he headed into the library for some brandy. Seating himself at his desk, he started in on his ledgers. For the first time in three years, he was sending his reports to his father, late. Only this time, Christopher was getting them. Frowning he nearly snapped his pencil in half thinking of his predicament.

A soft knock at the door made Jonathan frown. "Come in," he said looking up briefly to see that it was Matty. "What is it?"

"I was wondering if you brought any of the ladies clothes?"

Jonathan's face darkened. "She packed a valise. Her trunks were to be sent around by the end of the week."

Matty pursed her lips. "Well, her valise isn't here."

Jonathan cursing the whole stupid event, headed out to his carriage to check for himself. Cursing, he realized he would have to go to Brentwood for something of his sisters. "Saddle Sable for me will you, Billy?" he said heading back into the house. Grabbing up his cloak, he bellowed for Matty. "Obviously, the bag was forgotten. I'll have to go to Brentwood. I'll be back shortly." Turning, he cursed. It was only fifteen minutes to his Father's home, but still a damn inconvenience he wouldn't have to put up with if he hadn't been stupid enough to drink himself into oblivion with a man he didn't know. Cursing again, he mounted his horse and headed off into the night.

Fifteen minutes later he was sitting outside his father's home frowning. It was lit up like a palace. His frowned deepened as he realized no one should be in residence. Climbing the steps to the house, he frowned further at being greeted by an empty foyer. Where the hell was Hobkins?

Walking into the drawing room his face darkened seeing Nathan there. Great! Just what he needed, to be harassed and humiliated by the youngest male in the family. "Hiding from Father?" Jonathan asked, deciding to take the initiative.

Nathan spun around at his voice, then grinned, "On the contrary. I am actually here on Father's behalf. I was waiting until tomorrow to come see you."

Jonathan cursed. "He told you, didn't he?"

"He let me read the letter," he said laughing. "Was it brandy or port?" he hooted falling onto the sofa.

Jonathan clenched his teeth, as he moved to the decanter to pour himself a drink. "If you value those teeth I'd refrain from mentioning the whole incident," he said swallowing the drink in one gulp and pouring himself another.

Nathan sobered knowing his own situation would be treated with the same behavior he was dishing out. "If it makes you feel any better, I have a package here from Father."

Turning he looked at his brother with narrowed eyes. "A package?"

"Yes, but you have to give a promise of secrecy before I can give it to you."

"Why?"

"Because mother left it to you and you can only get it once you're married. Until that happens, you aren't supposed to know about it," he said giving himself away. "Do you agree?"

Jonathan snorted. "Why not?" he stated taking a chair by the hearth, barely catching the envelope Nathan threw at him. Giving Nathan an annoyed look, he opened the letter and read. It was from his mother and it stated he was now the proud owner of Meadowacres and the earldom of Hertford. Lowering the paper to his lap, he frowned at Nathan. "Is this a joke?"

Nathan grinned. "Though it would be a great one, it isn't. You're a rich man, I presume?"

Jonathan frowned. "According to this, I'm a bloody Earl," he stated plopping the entire envelope and contents on the table next to his chair. Nathan reached for it waiting for a nod from Jonathan. Quickly scanning the contents, he grinned.

"Just like I thought. She left you a title from some Uncle of hers. Father said she had several that never married and died without heirs," Nathan said still reading the papers.

Jonathan frowned as a thought formed in his mind. "If I'm supposed to keep this a secret, how come you know about it?" he asked draining his glass.

"Didn't I mention I was also an Earl? The Earl of Alnwick to be exact," he said completely absorbed in the papers sent from their mother. Jonathan sat forward in his chair and snatched the papers from his hands finally getting his attention.

"Then it is a joke?" he asked ready to kill Nathan.

"Marriage has turned your brain to mush. Normally you're quicker than this," he said, getting to his feet for another drink. Jonathan stared at him trying to sort out what Nathan was saying.

"If it's not a joke then how can you be..." his voice trailed off as comprehension came and his eyes widen. "Married!" he exclaimed coming to his feet. "You're married!" Nathan turned around, holding out his hand where a shiny ring sat. Silently toasting his glass to his brother's slow wits. Jonathan snarled at him. "Now I know this is a joke. Are Christopher and Stephan in on this one?" he asked planning to get revenge.

Nathan shook his head, frowning. "It's not a joke and Stephan and Christopher are to remain oblivious to our new titles for as long as possible. Mother didn't want them to know about it until they wed. Once Stephan and Christopher marry, then the truth will dawn on them," he stated returning to his chair. Jonathan watched him, in shock. Could he be telling the truth? Nathan looked at him again. "Still don't believe me?"

Jonathan laughed. "Well, it's a little far fetched. I mean you're not exactly the marrying type."

Nathan scowled. "Believe me, I didn't plan this. I happen to have been caught in a similar predicament as yourself." At Jonathan's still unbelieving look, he frowned. "If you still don't believe me then I'll show you." They left the library and headed up the stairs and down the hall where Nathan stopped before one of the guest rooms. Knocking softly they waited, hearing shuffling feet on the other side. Jonathan frowned as Nathan stiffened. Turning his gaze on the door as it opened, his brows arched in surprise as a small black haired woman opened the door to stare at them.

"Yes?" she asked her voice coming out strained.

"Tell him who you are?" Nathan snapped hardly sounding civil.

"Exactly, how do you want me to put it?" she stated folding her arms across her chest. "I'm what you call a bad dream. Unwanted, but forced on you."

Nathan frowned at her, barely holding onto his temper. "Tell him straight out," he said, gritting his teeth.

Rae looked at him, then shrugged her shoulders. "I'm his wife. Who are you?"

Jonathan stood there letting a slow smile cross his face. She was even worse than his. "I'm his brother, Jonathan."

"Nice to meet you," she said the tone belying the words.

"Likewise, I'm sure," he said feeling his mood lighten. Nathan moved into the room making her step back.

"Go to sleep," he snapped pulling the door closed behind him. Turning to Jonathan, he frowned. "Satisfied."

"She's delightful. However did you find such a sweet one?"

"Shut up. I already told you I was caught in a similar situation as yourself. I wouldn't gloat, if I were you."

Jonathan laughed. "Who is she?"

"I haven't the slightest idea."

Jonathan stopped walking as Nathan reached the bottom of the stairs and moved off toward the drawing room. "You don't know? But that's impossible."

"No, it's not. The girl saved me from some thieves but knocked me senseless in the process. She then dragged me off to a church. We were married before I knew it."

Jonathan burst out laughing. "That's rich. Did she tell the priest you were mute and couldn't speak?"

Nathan scowled. "No."

Jonathan stopped laughing "Then she nodded your head for you?"

"No," he snapped filling a glass.

"But you have to answer the..."

Nathan slammed the glass down on the table and looked at his brother. "She asked me if I wanted a drink. When I answered I do, the priest said you're married. Kiss the bride," he snapped turning away in disgust as Jonathan fell out of his chair in hysterics. Gritting his teeth as his brother's laughter rang through the house, Nathan drained his glass then threw it into the hearth.

Jonathan sobered some and tried to get back up in the chair. "A drink?" he said chuckling. "I can't wait for Christopher and Stephan to hear that one."

Nathan grabbed Jonathan's shirt and pulled his face up close to his. "They're not going to find that out unless I tell them, right?"

Jonathan stared into his brother's eyes then nodded. "All right. They'll hear it from you," he said smoothing his shirt after Nathan released him. "She's a pretty thing."

Nathan scowled. "She has two children," he said turning away.

"What?" he asked, all humor gone.

"She said she married me because of them."

"My god," Jonathan said running a hand through his hair. "I'm sorry, Nathan. That must be hard to deal with."

Nathan shrugged. He didn't really know what to think anymore. The two boys were scrawny little things and he could see the pair would never have made it another month on the streets. They were thin as rails. "What brings you here?'

Jonathan cursed forgetting the reason for his visit. "I was fetching clothes for ...my wife," he finished "I think Allison left some clothes behind that will fit her."

Nathan turned. "What's she like?"

"I don't know. I can hardly be near her, without wanting to beat her. She lied and tricked her way into my life. I haven't really had the time for pleasantries."

"Your letter said you slept with her. You must have liked her some."

Jonathan snorted. "I was drugged."

"Drugged?" Nathan asked brows raised.

"The father drugged me, I think. All I know is later that night, I woke up to a woman screaming and her parents burst into the room. She was standing by the wall, while I was in the bed wearing little more than under drawers, and the sheets were stained with blood."

"Did you..."

"I did no such thing. She was dressed from head to toe in a white gown. She looked like a nun, for God's sake. I never touched her."

"You could have had that checked, right?"

"I could have but every gentlemen in the area would think ill of me and I didn't want Father to suffer for a mistake I shouldn't have made."

Nathan frowned. "Lord, are we stupid?"

Jonathan cursed and slowly sank into a chair. "I feel so humiliated I can hardly think straight."

Nathan nodded his head in agreement. "It's a wonder either of us didn't kill them."

"I thought about it."

Nathan grinned. "Still might."

Jonathan chuckled. "I think I better collect those clothes and return home. I need the next two days to plan a good story before facing Stephan and Jessica. They're going to have a field day with us."

Nathan scowled. "I just hope Jessica's preoccupied with her own situation enough not to take much notice of mine."

"You bringing the family?"

Nathan narrowed his eyes. "No. Are you?"

Jonathan grinned in return. "No." Getting to his feet, he headed for the stairs. He returned ten minutes later with a bag stuffed with things sticking out the sides. "See you Friday at Ginger's."

Nathan nodded his head looking grim. "Friday."

Chapter 38

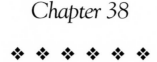

JESSICA **FROWNED** at the seamstress for the fifth time. "I don't plan on putting that thing on, so you can just fit me the way I am."

Melissa snorted in disgust. "You're going to be the laughing stock of all of London. Women do not go around without wearing corsets."

"At least for the wedding, Jess." Allison put in from her position on the sofa. Nero was lying at her feet.

"It's a wedding I don't want. I could care less what people think. No corset."

Melissa gave her a stern look but threw her hands up in the air. "Fine. Just get the damn dress made."

"Melissa! What a mouth." Allison said with a grin.

"Never thought to see the day you'd swear like a sailor," Jessica said laughing.

"I do a lot of things now I normally wouldn't do," Melissa said moving to the window.

Allison frowned. "Has he sent word?"

Melissa lifted her chin. "No. I didn't expect him to." Allison pursed her lips. Melissa's voice betrayed her.

"I suppose, then, you're attending the wedding alone?"

Melissa stiffened. "I guess so."

Jessica watched Melissa with anger growing. Her own situation was going to be similar, only she would more than likely end up killing her husband. Getting a pin stuck in her side made her yelp. "Now, look here. I will personally give you two jabs for each one you give me," she stated glaring at the seamstress. The seamstress stepped back unsure whether to actually do the dress or give up now.

"Having trouble?" A male voice asked from the door. Melissa whirled around to see a very tall blond man standing with one shoulder leaning against the doorjamb, while the other hand held a rose.

Jessica turned scarlet. "What are you doing here?"

Morgan moved forward looking wounded. "Here I thought my lovely bride would honor me with a quick jaunt in the park. What no breeches?" he said handing her the rose as he circled her.

Jessica lifted her chin and started to speak only to be cut off by Allison. "Then you must be the Baron. I'm Allison and this is Melissa," she said getting to her feet and taking Nero's collar. "It's a pleasure to meet you," she said moving toward Morgan.

Morgan watched the lovely girl come toward him and had to make himself stay without bolting for the door. The tiger was looking at him with hunger in his eyes. Jessica grinned.

"Aren't you going to kiss her hand?" she asked trying to keep the humor out of her voice. Morgan shot Jessica a glare but took the hand offered. Melissa moved up next to him and smiled.

"You have to forgive her. She's gotten this silly notion in her head to put everyone on the spot," Melissa said holding her hand out for the kiss. Morgan complied. "Allison really. Nero is drooling all over the Baron's shoes."

Allison laughed. "He doesn't drool. But I'll go back to the sofa. Nero," she said giving his collar a tug. Morgan drew his brows together and gave Jessica a questioning look.

"Is there a problem?" she asked anger in her voice.

Morgan flushed. "I..."

"Jessica, I realize you have a sore spot with the Baron but don't use me to get back at him." Turning her head in his direction Allison added. "I'm blind and Nero is my eyes. He's harmless," she added picking up the tapestry she was working on.

"Don't let her fool you. She can manage quite well without the cat but she knows he irritates the rest of us so forces him on us," Melissa said getting ready to leave the room. "It was nice meeting you," she called heading out of sight.

Morgan turned back to Jessica "Well?"

Jessica frowned. She hadn't wanted to see the man before tomorrow but thinking back on what her brothers had said about her not thinking of other people she lowered her head.

"That would be fine," she said, giving the seamstress a grin. "If it gets me out of standing here getting poked to death." The seamstress reddened but started collecting up her things. "I need at least ten minutes. Allison can entertain you."

Allison lifted her head. "Won't you have a seat, Baron?" she asked setting her work aside while she quickly moved to get him a drink. "Brandy?"

"Yes, thank you," he said taking a seat near the sofa. He felt a little out of place especially with the cat staring at him. "Nice cat."

Allison laughed. "He is overwhelming, isn't he? But I have to tell you, I can hardly function without him. He's wonderful." As if knowing she was talking about him, Nero let out a low mew. "He's also a bit of a baby. Here you are?" she said holding the glass out waiting for him to take it before she released it.

Morgan wondered at her. Jonathan never said a word about having a blind sister. At a loss for what to say, he sipped his drink. Allison, well aware of the kind of tension she drew, picked back up her tapestry.

"Do you plan to let Jess sail?"

Morgan nearly choked on his brandy. Quickly wiping his chin with his handkerchief, he cleared his throat. "I beg your pardon?"

Allison looked in his direction. "I was wondering if you were planning to let Jessica sail. She loves it you know?"

"I'm well aware of her passion for the sea."

"Then you will sail with her?"

"Perhaps," he said, unsure at the sister's motives. "Tell me, are you married?"

Allison frowned. "No. No, I'm not."

"Then the red head was the one to marry the Cabot son?"

Allison smiled. "Yes. She married him last week."

"That's nice. Has your brother arrived?"

"Which one?"

"Jonathan."

"No. We expect him, though. He should be here sometime this morning. Stephan and Christopher are here, though. I'm not sure about Nathan."

Morgan frowned "A real family gathering," he said draining his glass.

"Would you like more brandy?" Allison asked.

Morgan's eyes snapped to hers. His eyes narrowed. "How did you know my drink was empty?"

Allison smiled. "You don't have to be able to see to hear the last of a drink leave the glass."

Morgan was still pondering that remark, when Jessica returned. She looked lovely, though he wasn't about to tell her that. Her hair was pulled up and secured falling in one straight mass down her back. She wore a simple gown of blue with a light shawl over her arm. "Ready?" she said.

Morgan got to his feet. "It's been a pleasure, my lady," he said taking Allison's hand and kissing it. "Have a pleasant afternoon."

"Thanks, Al. I owe you one," she said as they left the room.

Nero growled before jumping up on the sofa to stretch out and lay his head in her lap. "I think you're a little big to be doing this. Besides, Hobkins will have heart failure if he sees you up here." Nero mewed then rolled slightly on his side. "I see you don't care," she added with a giggle.

Chapter 39

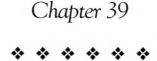

STEPHAN WALKED BACK into Andrew's office, shaking his head at the relics around the room. Moving to the shelf above the fire place, he picked up a strange little statue in the shape of an animal he'd never seen. The thing was huge with long spears coming out of its mouth and a long skinny nose reaching to the ground.

"Looks like the real thing, doesn't it?"

Stephan whirled around at the feminine voice nearly dropping the little figure. "I'm sorry. I didn't know he had someone here," he said putting the statue back.

"That's because he doesn't normally expect me," the petite raven-haired woman said.

"I see you two have met," Andrew said grinning.

"Not formally."

"Then allow me," Andrew said coming farther into the room, "Cari this is Lord Stephan Hayworth. And this is my sister, Lady St. Paul."

"Your sister!" Stephan said smiling. "Well, I'm delighted," he said kissing her hand as he turned slightly to Andrew. "Is this the one with the teeth?"

At Cari's perplexed look, Andrew laughed. "The same."

Stephan grinned at her discomfort and finally pointed to the human teeth hanging on a string from a hook near Andrew's desk. Cari turned scarlet. "Those belong to a friend of mine," she said trying to explain.

"I was hoping they weren't yours," Stephan said laughing as her blush deepened. Andrew hid his smile thankful Stephan happened along. His sister was a trial to a man's patience and seeing her on the defensive was a nice change. "Are the papers ready?" Stephan asked. "I finished wasting my time."

Andrew chuckled. "No luck, then."

"I think a kiss on the cheek will have to do."

"I think your sisters will make you regret it if that's the only wedding gift you give them."

Cari grinned. "I could help you come up with something?" she said picking up one of the funny looking little heads. Stephan grinned in return.

"I think I can manage on my own. But thank you. I have until tomorrow."

"Tomorrow?" she said loosing her grin. "Aren't you worried?"

"No. Melissa, my youngest sister is already married and Jessica, well, she won't expect anything right away. She'll be to busy fretting over having to wear a gown."

Cari's brows drew together and she looked to Andrew for help. Shaking his head he laughed. "I wouldn't even try to figure that one out. The Hayworth family is a bit..." he paused realizing they were his clients and he really shouldn't talk about them in a bad light. "Well, let's just say they're unique."

Stephan laughed. "Not all of us, my man. Not all of us." Turning to Cari, he smiled. "Mainly the females," he said getting a snort from Andrew. Cari smiled at the casual byplay of words between her very ordinary brother and this fascinating man before her. Tall, dark, and handsome, she thought with a grin.

"Well, that's it," Andrew said handing over the rather small envelope. Stephan looked at it and smiled.

"Hopefully, this is the last time he sends me off like an errand boy. Nathan should be home to resume the roll." Andrew smiled at the joke. Turning to Cari, Stephan kissed her hand. "It was a pleasure meeting you, Lady St. Paul. You are bringing her tomorrow, right?" he asked Andrew, who hesitated before nodding. "Great. Then I'll leave you to your afternoon." As he opened the door one of the wooden heads tipped as if it was nodding farewell. Stephan pointed at it and laughed, on his way out.

Cari watched him go. "Rather happy man, isn't he?"

Andrew nodded taking a seat. "He's the jovial one in the family."

Cari seated herself and began straightening the heads along his desk. "So, what am I attending tomorrow?"

Andrew scowled. "I'm not sure we'll attend. The oldest daughter is getting married tomorrow."

Cari smiled. "That sounds lovely. I haven't been to a wedding in years. At least not in England."

"Well, you might not be going now," he said getting back to work. "I'll be home at six for dinner," he said giving her the hint to move along.

Getting to her feet Cari sighed. "You really ought to be a little more social. I've traveled nearly half the world to spend time with you."

Andrew rolled his eyes. "You, my dear sister, are here for a reason. Has Reid something up his sleeve?"

"As a matter of fact, he does. But I think you should ask him yourself." she said scooting out the door leaving him hanging. She was half way down the lane before the door burst open.

"Reid's here?"

Cari giggled. "Yes, he is."

"Well, good lord. Why didn't you say so? Wait right there and I'll be with you in five minutes." Cari laughed as her brother hurried to get himself around.

CHRISTOPHER GOT TO HIS FEET to refill his father's glass with cider while he poured more brandy in his own. "As you can see, things are going fine with the estates."

"I knew they would be. You've a fine head for business."

Christopher smiled as he resumed his seat. A knock at the door brought Jonathan into the room looking haggard and worn. "Well, Jonathan, how goes the married life?" he asked leaning back in the chair.

Jonathan smiled. "You'll be finding out in just over four months, isn't it?"

Christopher lost his smile, getting a chuckle out of Brand. "I'm sure Christopher will have no problems finding himself a suitable wife."

Jonathan frowned at his father. "If he can dish it out, I think he should have to take it. How are you, Father?"

"Fine, Jonathan. I've never felt better."

"Where is your better half?" Christopher asked his smile back in place. "I did hope to meet the woman who married the richest horse man in all of England.

Jonathan scowled at his brother. "She's at Meadowacres."

Christopher's brows went up at that. "Left her behind, huh? What a pity. Now I'll just have to find a reason to visit you at home."

Brand gave Christopher a shake of the head seeing that Jonathan wasn't the least bit amused by his brothers jabs. "How are the horses, son?"

Jonathan took a couple of swallows of his brandy before turning to look at his father. "They're doing well. Two more mares are due in the spring."

"Excellent. I had some luck betting on a few of your breed. Colan hasn't the eye for your horseflesh."

Both sons laughed. "Swindling your own brother," Christopher stated arching his brows.

"It's just a spot of fun," Brand said with a satisfied smile. "Next time we plan to bring in a third party."

"Colan catch on to you?"

As Brand's color heightened, Christopher laughed, "More like the man confessed."

Brand chuckled. "Exactly. I was feeling guilty."

Jonathan nodded. "How's your heart?"

Brand grinned. "I haven't felt this good in years. In fact, I didn't even feel a twinge at all the news you unloaded on me in the last month."

Christopher scowled. "No? I think I'm getting the pains now, but they aren't occurring in my chest."

Brand chuckled. "Better a young man than one my age."

"I'm aging by the minute."

"It's starting to show," Nathan stated from his position by the door. "Is this a private party?"

"Of course not. Come in, come in." Brand motioned getting Nathan a drink. "Where's the family?"

Nathan's lips thinned. "I left them at Brentwood and I would appreciate it if none of you mentioned them until after I leave," he snapped taking the glass from his father.

The room went silent. "I never thought to see the day?"

Nathan glared at Christopher. "Your day isn't far off, I understand."

Christopher scowled. "You two aren't very agreeable."

Jonathan looked at Nathan and scowled. "He just doesn't know the meaning of the words 'let it go', does he?"

"Like having to draw him a picture," Nathan said draining his glass only to refill it.

Christopher flushed but dropped the subject. Brand frowned getting to his feet. "What happened to the girls? I thought they would be down by now," he asked as Colan and Ginger entered.

"I haven't a clue. Those hoydens you call daughters are every bit as stubborn as you are. I've washed my hands of them. They've done nothing but embarrass me at every turn," Ginger said seating herself on the sofa. "You'd think they were raised by barbarians, running off and getting married like common trash. Being in a man's room without any kind of chaperone and half dressed at that. I'm washing my hands of the whole affair, I am."

Colan beamed behind her getting a glare from Brand. "Now Ginger. I'm sure Allison has behaved wonderfully?"

Ginger snorted. "The girl has become just as stubborn as the others. She refuses to go to the balls and teas with me. She sneaks out behind Christopher's back to go to a gentleman's home. No, I'm afraid you'll have to find yourself another to suffer her presence as well."

Brand frowned. "Really Ginger. You act like a paragon or something? They made simple mistakes and were called to the quick about it. It doesn't seem to me like anyone has taken offense to their behavior, if the stack of invitations on the desk is any indication."

Ginger frowned. "What invitations?"

"The ones I was saving for Nathan. He's supposed to arrange the social calendar for the girls."

Nathan frowned. "It doesn't look like I'm going to be available for that sort of thing anymore" he said smiling slowly. "It will just have to be up to you, old boy. I think you need the social interaction anyway. You know the wife hunting."

Christopher stood up at that remark. "You're going to end up with a broken nose if you keep harping on my marital status," he said trying to remain calm. "By the by, how is it being a father?"

That was it. Both brothers ended up wrestling around on the floor. Tables crashed over and Ginger grabbed three vases and ran to the side of the room. Brand moved to the side with Colan close at hand. His frown turned to a scowl as Jonathan cheered the brothers on. Getting a fuming look from Ginger, he clenched his jaw. "All right, boys, that's enough. I didn't come here to see if Nathan could still beat the tar out of my oldest son," he said getting a slow reaction.

"Barbarians. The lot of them," Ginger stated marching out of the room.

Brand pursed his lips. "From now on, I want the three of you to behave yourselves. I need your Aunt Ginger's help in getting Allison married," he said shouting.

"Now, what did I miss?" Stephan asked holding a squirming bundle over his shoulder.

"Again? How did she get out?" Christopher asked wondering where Jessica had Hobkins tied up.

"Oh, no. This time I found a real piece. She was having a devil of a time looking in the windows. She's a little on the short side but she sure is a looker," he finished putting the girl down on her feet.

"Does he do this often?" Nathan asked putting his hands in his pockets.

"He brought Jessica home earlier this week. The chit was trying to set sail for regions unknown."

"Sounds to me like she really wants to get married," Brand commented getting sheepish looks from his sons.

Stephan grinned. "It isn't becoming a habit. The girl is all fire and charm."

"Well, take her outside. I don't think your Aunt Ginger could put up with anymore excitement. Common trollops brought into her home would have us sent packing."

"But Father, this is your house. Besides, this one claims to be family," he said trying to get the cloak off her head. "I just thought Nathan would like to see who his wife is?"

Stephan missed the pale angry look that crossed Nathan's face as he finally managed to unwind his cloak from the girl and wipe it off her. She definitely was a sight to see. Her hair was shooting in all directions from the static, she had Stephen's cravat tied around her mouth and her hands were tied behind her back with what looked like a sailor's scarf. "She kept cussing so I had to gag her," he said grinning at his father.

"Tsk, tsk, Nathan. You could at least dress your wife better? She looks like a beggar," Jonathan said rocking back on his heels.

Nathan growled deep in his throat. Stephan frowned.

"She really is your wife?" he said looking at Brand for confirmation. At Brand's nod his face blanked. "Well, good lord. I wish someone would have told me," he said frantically trying to untie her hands. "This is all your fault, Nathan. I would never have tied her up, if I'd known." Returning to his task, he finally got her untied and tried to smooth her hair down. "Sorry, ah, what was your name again?" he asked scratching his head. A punch landed in his stomach sending him over double, as Rae began to glare at her husband. Lifting her chin she marched from the room. Nathan growled a curse before setting his glass down and going after her.

"Well, I'll say, she sure is a fiery little baggage, isn't she?" Christopher said giving Stephan a grin. The younger man, finally able to breath, moved to sit in a chair.

"How come no one felt the need to tell me that the sod was married? The girl practically begged me to let her be on her way. She said she was married to Nathan. Nathan of all people! I might have believed her if she'd have said Christopher." At the darkening look on his face Stephan grinned. "Well, you are supposed to be getting married."

Brand frowned. "You have the worst habit of tying people up. It's only getting you into trouble. Maybe you should think before doing it next time."

Stephan grinned. "I would have loved to have known about this before I walked in. What a scene I could have made." Jonathan and Christopher exchanged grins, showing they regretted the missed opportunity as well.

"Well, shouldn't we go and cheer the happy couple up?" Stephan asked moving toward the door. When both brothers moved to follow, Brand stepped in their path.

"Don't even think about it. The lad has it hard enough as is. If they are going to make a go of it, they don't need you interfering."

Nathan walked into the room causing all four men to stare at him. He calmly walked to the decanter and poured himself a brandy. Draining the glass he refilled it before moving to stand by the hearth.

Unable to restrain himself, Stephan sighed. "What did you do with her?"

Nathan took a drink. "Aunt Ginger hauled her upstairs before I had a chance to do much of anything," he said his anger evident.

Stephan looked at Christopher as both of them burst out laughing.

Nathan stiffened. Brand pursed his lips. "What did I just tell you? Now cease. We can't afford to ruin Allison's chance at a proper marriage by alienating ourselves from Ginger." When Stephan still chuckled behind his hand, Brand glared. "I can always send you on one of my nasty errands." Stephan's face lost all trace of humor.

"You sure know how to ruin a bit of fun. Nathan knows I'm joking."

"But his wife doesn't and most importantly Ginger doesn't. You are ruining things for Allison."

The doorknocker sounded and moments later Hobkins appeared, "Lord Cabot to see you."

Brand grinned. "Send him in Hobkins."

All four brothers exchanged looks, trying to figure out who invited Caleb. He was dressed in dark trousers with matching coat. His black hair was slightly ruffled from the wind and he looked irritated to be present. Seeing the room full of men he paused at the door his guard up.

Brand smiled. "Come in, my boy. I'm sure you've met my sons. I'm Brand Hayworth"

Caleb frowned but came forward to shake Brand's hand. Caleb was sure Melissa had told her father of his deceit. "I'm here per your request," he said sarcastically. The truth was the note had stated he would find himself in dire straights if he failed to present himself promptly at eight. Brand glanced at the clock seeing the boy was early by ten minutes.

"We're glad to have you. The ladies will be with us shortly," Brand said pouring Caleb a drink.

Caleb took the drink still unsure of the situation. Looking skeptical at the men around him, he frowned. "Exactly why have I been...err...ordered here?" he asked casually.

Christopher shrugged, "Your wife is present. We thought you should be here, also."

Caleb flushed, what the hell did Melissa tell them? "I see."

Brand frowned at Christopher. "Never mind my son. I would like to get to know the young man that swept my daughter off her feet. She hasn't had a chance to talk with me herself but the boys here have told me a little about the situation."

Caleb glanced in their direction getting a shrug from Christopher, a scowl from Nathan, and disinterest from Jonathan and Stephan. Looking at the silent man in the corner, his frown deepened. "Yes, well, I think it would be best to hear the story from Melissa."

Brand pursed his lips. "If I didn't know better I would say you all are hiding something from me. Not one of my sons would tell me much of anything. Now speak out boy. I want to know."

"Know what, Brand? You act like it's a crime to marry your daughter," Colan said from his corner. Looking at the young man, Colan smiled. "I'm

Colan Hayworth, Viscount of Harding." At the hand shake and nod from the lad, his smile widened. "What is it you do for a living, boy?"

Caleb felt a sense of calming from the tall man. "I deal in horses."

Jonathan's interest perked up. "Horses? Like racers or stock?"

"Mainly stock. I haven't the talent to breed like you have."

Jonathan grinned. "Father started that line. I just improved on it."

Caleb nodded looking at Brand. "Fine work, my lord."

Brand waved his hand at that. "You can call me Brand, son. I haven't been my lorded by family in quite sometime."

Nathan scowled at his father. He was welcoming the man into their mitts without even knowing what the hell had happened. They all were still in the dark on that account.

Stephan frowned. "I thought you were into ships?"

Caleb flushed. Was that what he had been ordered here for? To account for his father's interests in expanding into their shipping firm. "Actually, I don't like the sea at all. My stomach doesn't take kindly to the motion of the sea so my interests turned to the horses. My brother, Andrew, is a captain. My father, as well."

Jonathan's brows went up at that. So that was the reason for giving up the Fleming chit and moving to the bigger fish. Frowning, Jonathan asked, "So your father must be pretty happy to be associated with Stephan's line?"

Caleb gave him a measuring look then blanked his face. "Actually, my father doesn't have the slightest clue Melissa is connected in anyway with the Matherson line."

Stephan hooted. "I should have known that would come in handy someday."

Nathan gave him a disgusted look. "You're such an idiot. The slightest thing seems to make your day."

Stephan grinned. "Perhaps being single accounts for a lot of that."

Christopher laughed at the dark look crossing Nathan's face. "Sure doesn't seem happy, does he?" Christopher said talking to Stephan but still looking in Nathan's direction. Stephan still grinning, turned to Caleb.

"You might wish to congratulate our brother here. He is now a happy groom as well."

Nathan glared at Stephan. "I think perhaps a moment outside with you might change your insufferable humor."

"Now boys, we have a guest," Brand said getting a stiff nod from Nathan. Looking at Stephan, Brand shook his head. Stephan held up his hands but the grin said he wasn't about to let promising moments slip by. Brand sighed. It wasn't like he didn't expect their behavior to be like it was but he at least thought they would rally together and work their bazaar sense of humor on the new member to the family. The evening could prove to be long. Looking at Colan, he sighed. Rolling his eyes, Brand wondered what was going to happen when Jessica's intended showed up. Hopefully Nathan's mood would improve.

RAE TRIED TO SLOW HER STEPS as the perfectly dressed woman beside her hustled her down the hall to stop before a room. "Now...err...Rae, was it?" At her nod, Ginger pursed her lips. "I'm going to have Melissa help you get dressed. It isn't proper for a woman of you're standing to be going around dressed...well, like a common," she said knocking on the door and pushing her into the room before hearing an answer. Melissa sat crying on her bed while Allison stood by the window. Nero was beside her with both paws on the sill, his massive head moving back and forth as things moved below on the street. Melissa sat up at the intrusion her face tear stained.

"Jessica?"

"No, dear, it's me. I have here Rae Hayworth. She's Nathan's wife and I would like the pair of you to help her find something suitable to wear," Ginger said, pulling Rae into the room. "She seems to have come without any baggage."

Rae scowled at Ginger but felt self conscious in front of the two beautiful women. Melissa just sat there on the bed staring at her making Rae feel even more uncomfortable. Allison moved forward. "Of course, we'll help her choose a gown. What time do you want us down?"

Ginger nodded her approval. "Your brother has arrived finally and we shall be eating in about an hour. Is that sufficient time?"

Melissa, coming to her senses, smiled. "Plenty. Rae looks like a lovely girl. A quick bath will put her to rights." Coming forward, Melissa took Rae's hand and led her further into the room. "I'm Nathan's sister, Melissa. This is Allison, his other sister. I'm glad to meet you, though, Nathan hasn't had much of a chance to tell us about you. He did say you were staying home with..." she trailed off realizing she was probably imposing on the girl's privacy.

Rae stiffened. "Yes, I was staying home with Sean and Ian but I decided I wasn't going to be left behind again," she reddened, but lifted her chin. "I think he was going to leave me there."

Allison frowned. Jonathan had told her neither Nathan nor Jonathan had wanted to marry and that the ladies had trapped them into it. "Would you care to tell us about your situation?" Allison said, still standing half way between the window and the door. "I think women are a little more level headed than men and personally I wish to draw my own conclusions instead of listening to the drivel I heard earlier."

Rae turned scarlet. "Exactly what did he say?"

Melissa laughed. "Nathan didn't say a word. In fact, the man is so tight lipped I would think his lips have been sewn together," she said steering Rae in front of the mirror. Moving to the wardrobe she flung the doors open. "Jonathan is the one that told us. What color do you like?" she asked opening them to their fullest.

Rae looked at the rows of crinolines in disbelief. She watched in amazement as Melissa moved to a side room and pulled the door open showing a long row of gowns running along the wall. "My god, I haven't seen so many gowns in all my life." Rae said, before she could stop herself.

"Trust me. Melissa is crazy when it comes to clothing. Most people have only half that many," Allison said, taking a seat on the bed. "Now tell us what happened. Did you want a bath?"

Rae did, in fact want one, but she wasn't about to say so. "No, thank you," she said still looking in the room of gowns. No sooner than that statement came out of her mouth Netty came bustling into the room directing the kitchen lads where to put the tub and the process of bringing bucket after bucket of water began. As the last lad left, Netty turned to them with an armload of towels. "Come on, young lady. Let's get you cleaned up. We only have half an hour or so. Men hate to be kept waiting."

Rae frowned at the woman, "I don't want a bath."

"Oh, pooh. If you traveled here on horseback you're needing a bath more than ever. Now get into the water." Netty said collecting the toiletries needed for a bath.

Allison laughed picturing Rae's mouth hanging open at a servant commanding her like that. "You might as well give in, Rae. Netty can be quite persuasive."

Netty smiled. "Let's hurry," she said, moving to help Rae out of her clothes. Rae stepped away from her.

"I don't need your help," she said, looking at them with unease.

Melissa frowned then sighed. "This must be a bit overwhelming. Why don't you tell us all about what happened while you bathe? I think green would look the best on you. Your eyes are such a stunning shade of it. I think I have the perfect thing," she called disappearing into the room.

Allison stood and moved to Rae's side. "If it makes you feel better, I could send Netty and Melissa away and you could bathe while we chat?"

Rae looked at her like she was crazy. "I don't like to bathe in front of strangers."

Allison laughed. "I guessed as much. But you don't have to worry about me. I can't see much of anything. I've been blind since I was twelve.

Rae's mouth dropped open at that, getting a winning smile from Netty. "She doesn't let on now, does she? Lady Allison moves around like the rest of us and that lazy cat does have his purpose. Nero can lead her anywhere and she doesn't so much as harm a single hair on her head."

Rae looked at the tiger and sucked in her breath. She hadn't seen him when she came into the room. The animal was on his feet moving slowly in her direction.

"Nero, go back over there. She isn't used to you." The big cat looked at Allison then his gaze slid back to Rae. Giving a complaining mew Nero turned and jumped up on the bed.

"Get down, you beast! Allison, that thing will have my bed full of fleas," Melissa stated, coming back into the room carrying one of the most exquisite looking gowns Rae had ever seen. It was pale green shot through with streaks of silver. The gown shimmered like moonlight. "This is perfect," Melissa said giving Rae a smile. Rae wanted to turn and flee the room. These beautiful ladies were being so nice to her and they didn't know a thing about her. Well, nothing nice anyway. Lowering her head, she frowned.

"I don't understand why you're doing this for me?"

Allison frowned. Moving closer she held out her hand until she made contact with Rae's shoulder. "Rae, most people go by gossip and base their image of a person on what they hear, but if you're willing to tell us, we want to draw our own conclusions from the truth."

Rae looked at Allison and felt a sting of tears sting her eyes. It had been so long since she had someone to talk to. "Can I just talk to you?"

Melissa heard and pursed her lips. "Come on, Netty. I need your help getting some things for her hair out of Jessica's room. I think it might take us a week just to find them."

Rae watched them go and frowned, "She isn't angry, is she?"

"With Melissa you never know. She easily angers but a few well-placed words and she's back to normal. Now let's get you in that bath before they come looking for us."

Rae undressed and stepped into the tub. The warm water was very relaxing. Scrubbing her hair she hurried through her bath not wanting the other two ladies to come back. Stepping out of the tub she dried herself off and waited.

"Help yourself to the under things in the wardrobe. I don't exactly know where Melissa keeps hers."

Rae flushed. She didn't know what half the things were. She was raised in a rich enough home in South Carolina but she hadn't worn anything that belonged to a woman in quite sometime. "It's been...I mean..." She grew silent. "I haven't dressed in anything like this in a long time."

Allison smiled. "I'll tell you what you need. You take it out and put it on."

Ten minutes later Rae stood dressed in the latest under things complete with corset and pantaloons. Feeling for the first time in years like a lady,

Rae smiled. "It's been so long."

Allison smiled. "Where are you from? Your accent is one I haven't heard before."

Rae paused. "I'm from the colonies."

"A colonist," she said her face lighting up. "Why that's wonderful. My father is planning to go there."

Rae felt her pulse quicken. "How long before he goes?"

"He said a couple of months from now but I think it will be more like five or six months." Rae frowned. That was too long to wait. "Have you any family?"

"I had a sister but she drowned almost a year ago when we were coming here to live with our Aunt."

"I'm sorry," Allison said, "that must have been hard. Do you live with your Aunt, then?"

Rae frowned. "No. When we left home after my parents died we didn't have much and Emily, that's my sister, had just lost her husband. When we arrived in England, we were notified immediately that our Aunt had died and her things were given to a distant Nephew who didn't want anything to do with us." Rae paused studying Allison for a moment. Deciding the truth was the way to go, Rae lowered her gaze. "Instead of living in a country we knew nothing about we booked passage back to America. The ship sank just out of the harbor and Emily drowned, leaving me with her children."

"The children are hers?" Allison asked in shock.

Rae nodded. Then frowned realizing Allison couldn't see that. "Yes. Her husband had died of sickness and she came back to live with us and just shortly after that Mama and Papa died from the same thing. I don't know why we didn't get the sickness. Since Emily died, I've looked after the boys. Some sailors brought us back to shore when the ship went down."

"That's awful. Did you go back to the Nephew?"

"No, and all my money was lost when the ship went down."

Allison felt anger rising at her brother's atrocious behavior. "Then that's why you married my brother?"

Rae's head snapped up. "Not at first. I hadn't even thought of marriage," Rae said looking out the window. "In fact, I haven't been much of a lady lately."

Allison felt her heart break. "Did you…?"

"No." Rae said before Allison could ask her if she had been a whore. She had never lowered herself to that state and would have died first. "No, but I didn't behave very ladylike, either."

Allison felt relief at knowing she wasn't a soiled woman. Her brothers would never understand that. "What exactly did you do?"

Rae felt tears sliding down her face as she remembered the months she spent robbing people on the street. She stole food for her and the boys and worst off, she had held up the well-to-do and taken everything they had. "I robbed the rich," she whispered crying. Allison moved forward and put her arm around the girl's shoulders.

"Shh, now. I'm sure it was the best you could do with the boys to consider. Now stop that crying or your eyes will be all puffy. You don't want to look dreadful on your first night with our family, do you?"

Rae sniffed a couple of times before wiping her eyes. "I'm so ashamed of the things I've done," she said sniffing. "Especially to your brother. I don't think he'll ever forgive me," she said crying again.

Allison chuckled. "Nathan may seem like an ogre but I'll tell you a secret. He has the biggest heart in the world. If you tell him the truth, I'm sure he'll..."

"Oh no. You don't understand. I tricked him into marrying me. I actually took advantage of him when he was senseless from a blow to the head. I knocked him off that carriage to prevent those men from shooting him and he hit his head. I realized he was half out of it and my first thought was to take his money and run. But my conscience wouldn't let me and I took him to the next inn instead. The proprietor there recognized him right away calling him my lord and everything, then the idea of marrying him took hold of me. It was just a matter of getting him to the church and telling the priest the story I'd thought up." Rae finished near tears. "I actually told the priest I was with child," she said, crying.

Allison just listened to her story not understanding all of it but getting enough to know she had used Nathan's delirious state to haul him off to get married. "I'm sure God will understand that you did it for the children."

Rae couldn't believe what she'd just heard from the woman beside her. "Didn't you hear me? I lied to your brother," she said, getting to her feet, "I trapped him into marriage and now he's stuck with us. I even told him about the boy's father."

Allison sat straight. "I heard exactly what you said and I still believe you wouldn't have done it if it wasn't for your sister's boys."

Rae's brows drew together. "Are you for real?"

Allison got to her feet and held out her hand. "I already told you from the beginning that I was going to judge you from what you told me and I have. I think you were in a desperate situation and acted like any human would. You found a solution for survival. Now don't get me wrong, I don't like the fact that Nathan was deceived but I can understand why you did it."

Rae cried again feeling even more ashamed in front of this extremely unique woman. "I don't know what to say."

Allison laughed. "I think first thing you should do, is finish dressing. I'll get Netty in here to help. I would be happy to do your hair but it would only come out lopsided." Moving toward the door, she paused. "Don't worry. Things have a way of working themselves out and you'll find that most of my siblings are understanding people. If you keep to the truth from now on, they'll see what I have," she said leaving the room. Rae stared at the door for a few minutes feeling guilt at the lies she had told the man to which she was now married. Sitting back on the bed she wondered if Allison had been right. Would Nathan understand if she explained what had happened? If she told him about living in the cave for nearly five months barely able to feed herself and the boys, would he understand? How she had worked beside a man of lesser character for food and clothing?

A big furry paw landed in her lap sending her for cover on the opposite side of the room. Nero was watching her with his golden gaze his tongue coming out to lick each side of his mouth. Rae took several deep breaths trying to stay calm and to keep the scream lodged in her throat from coming out.

"Good Lord, Allison. I think Nero bit her hand," Melissa said as she and Allison returned.

Allison frowned. "Rae?"

Rae still watching the cat swallowed slowly removing her hand from her mouth. "He..."

Nero let out a slight roar and moved to Allison's side for petting. "You bad kitty," she said, swatting at the head rubbing her leg. "Rae, I'm sorry. He really is harmless though he can be a little rough. Did he bite your hand?"

Rae flushed. "He put his paw in my lap?" she said feeling her face redden further.

Allison laughed. "He has a tendency to do that. Why don't you come and pet him? He really is friendly."

Melissa snorted. Putting her hand on Rae's arm. "He scares the hell out of me. She's had him for eight years now."

"Melissa!" Netty said clucking her tongue, "Such language.

Melissa gave her a wink as she scooped up the dress from its perch on the chair. "It was a necessary bit of vocabulary. Now let's get you into this. Netty can do wonders with your hair. It's just the right length, isn't it?" Melissa said bringing the gown over and stuffing Rae's head through the center. Pulling it place she spun Rae around and did the buttons up her back. "I knew this would do wonders for your hair and skin. You look wonderful!" she finished. Netty smiled at Rae's reflection, getting a hesitant smile in return.

"Sit here, love." Netty said patting the back of the chair.

"Well?" Melissa whispered, as Rae took the seat indicated.

Allison pursed her lips. "You'll have to ask Rae?"

"You're not going to tell me?" she said looking at Rae to see if she noticed Melissa's raised voice. "Please. Just let me know if what Jonathan said was true."

Allison rolled her eyes. "Did you think it was?" At the silence, Allison knew that Melissa had thought that. "No it's not true. They haven't the slightest idea of what Rae has been through."

Melissa smiled. "Good. I was starting to like her, but if she was as bad as Jonathan said then things would have to be different. "You look lovely, Rae," Melissa added moving to look over Netty's shoulder. Melissa's brows scrunched up, "How old are you?"

Rae arched her brows at the red head, "How old are you?"

Netty grinned but kept silent. Melissa tossed her head and smiled at Rae. "I'm eighteen."

Rae smiled back. "I'm twenty-one."

Melissa's mouth fell open. "You have a son that's five!"

"Melissa!" Allison said moving in their direction.

Rae frowned. "It's all right Allison. She will know everything eventually. The children aren't really mine. They were my sisters but she died six months ago. I've been taking care of them ever since."

Melissa snapped her mouth shut. "I don't understand. Why did you tell Nathan they were yours?"

Rae lowered her head. "I had already lied to him about everything else. I figured he would send the boys away, so I lied. When Thomas brought the boys to meet your brother I could see he wasn't going to send them away, but the lie was already told," she finished quietly.

Melissa watched her, then sighed. "Well you're going to tell him..."

"Melissa. I think Rae will do whatever she feels is right and you are going to remain silent. Let them work it out."

Melissa scowled at Allison. "But he should know. I mean..."

"It isn't for us to decide. Rae and Nathan will have to work that out themselves."

Melissa was about to protest again when the door opened admitting Jessica with a blond haired girl of about twenty clinging to her for dear life. "Where have you been?" Melissa blurted forgetting Rae for the moment.

"I've been to Meadowacres," she said moving into the room and closing the door. "Ashley, I'd like you to meet my sisters, Melissa and Allison."

Both ladies nodded their heads getting a scowl from Jessica. "Ashley is Jonathan's wife," she said, getting a gasp out of Melissa. "Allison, you're not going to believe this, but Ashley has a great deal in common with you."

At the expectant look on the four women's faces she paused as her eyes narrowed on Rae. "Who is she?"

Melissa frowned. "This is Nathan's wife, Rae."

Jessica's brows shot up. "His wife but I thought...never mind. Nice to meet you. I'm Nathan's sister, Jessica," she said, getting a confused look from Rae. Ignoring her, Jessica returned her attention to the terrified girl beside her. "Ashley, here, is blind."

"Blind?" Melissa blurted still unable to keep control of her emotions. "I don't believe it," she said moving forward.

Ashley shrank closer to Jessica. "I didn't either when I first arrived. Our nitwit of a brother had the girl stuffed in the farthest reaches of Meadowacres with no contact except Musa."

"Musa? But she's a mute!" Melissa snapped.

"Exactly. Now you know how things were going. She's been there for four days by herself with little or no help from Jonathan."

Allison felt her anger boil. "I can't believe he would do that. He treats me like a baby half the time."

Ashley spoke at this point. "He doesn't know."

Melissa felt herself straining to hear. "He doesn't know what?"

"That I can't see."

This time it was Jessica's turn to gap, "You didn't tell me that."

"You never asked."

"Well, neither did they."

Ashley clamped her mouth shut and didn't plan to speak again.

Allison moved to her side and reached out, feeling the other girl flinch. "Then I think we should let him know right away."

"Oh no. I don't want to see him. He is very angry with me. He was cheated and forced into a marriage he doesn't want with a woman that is useless," she said, crying.

Allison lifted her chin. "He will get over his anger and you will refrain from calling yourself useless. I have been blind for twelve years and I function well enough."

Ashley pursed her lips. "You're a burden to your family, just like I am. Now I'm a burden to your brother," she said, sniffling.

Allison stiffened. "I am not a burden to anyone."

"I don't believe you," Ashley said unable to believe a blind person could be anything but.

Jessica held up a hand, cutting Melissa off as she waited to see what Allison was going to do. "Jessica, is she dressed for dinner?"

"She is."

"She is not!" Melissa put in. "She has on a day gown," she snapped getting a glare from Jessica.

Allison frowned. "Get her a gown so we can go downstairs. I am personally going to take her there myself."

Ashley paled. "I don't want to see anyone. I'm staying here."

Jessica sighed. "I had to kidnap her."

Melissa returned with a blue gown with white roses and bows on it.

"Did you make her ride a horse, too?" she asked glaring at Jessica.

Jessica scowled back. "No. She rode in a carriage."

Melissa snorted and moved to work on the buttons down the back of Ashley's gown. The girl whirled. "Leave me alone. I'm not going anywhere else."

Jessica gave Melissa a smug look. Melissa pursed her lips. "Look here. You're married to my brother whether you like it or not. Our father is here and he wants to see his family happy and together. Now if you don't get yourself in this gown in ten minutes I'm going downstairs and bringing Jonathan up here."

Ashley paled. "Why are you doing this? He doesn't want me."

Allison felt her heart twist. "Ashley? I don't know what happened to get you two together but..."

"I'll tell you what happened. My family foisted me off on your brother using my sister to lure him to our home. Your brother happened to be in the wrong place at the wrong time and fell prey to my father's final attempt to rid himself of me," she said, an angry flush marking her lovely features. Silence filled the room. Each person was unsure of what to say. "I just want to go home," Ashley whispered "please," she said breaking down into tears. Allison moved forward to put her arm around the girl.

"Now you listen to me. Jonathan, once he understands, will come around." The girl's silent tears turned to sobs. "In fact, you couldn't be married to a better man. He fairly dotes on me."

Ashley was still crying when Jessica finally snapped. "I can't take it anymore. She practically cried the entire way here. Get some backbone!" Jessica said moving to stand by the window.

"Jessica!" Netty said giving her a firm look.

"Well, she's such a weakling. Even in the beginning, Allison was never this pitiful."

"Jessica you're not helping," Allison said, "I happen to remember a time when I didn't leave my room for nearly six months." At Ashley's slight fight for control she continued. "If it hadn't been for Jonathan coming faithfully everyday, I might still be in there."

Ashley stopped crying some as Melissa stuffed a handkerchief into her hand. "He..."she sniffed. "He did that."

"Yes, though my other three brothers came, as well," Allison said hearing the uncertainty in Ashley's voice. "I do understand your situation and I think maybe bringing you here tonight wasn't such a good idea, but now you're here. Why don't you try to come out of that protective wall you've built around yourself and join the rest of us in the real world?"

Ashley swallowed several times, "I don't want to see him."

Allison frowned. "Well I think you have your wish. You won't see him at all." When no one seemed to get the joke she sighed. "I'm afraid it's impossible for you to avoid Jonathan now that you're here. If it makes you feel any better, we won't let you fend for yourself."

Ashley's brows drew together and her eyes widened with fright, "I can't do it."

"I'll stay with you the whole time."

"But you can't..."

"I have Nero. He's more than capable of seeing that we make it from one room to another."

"But..."

"No more buts. Melissa put that gown on her so we can go downstairs." Melissa sent Jessica, Rae, and Netty an impressed look. All three grinned in return. Fifteen minutes later, dinner was about to be served.

"I DON'T LIKE IT. They've had her up there for almost an hour," Nathan snapped picking up his drink only to set it back down on another table.

"I'm sure they're not secreting her off somewhere so you can't get a hold of her," Stephan said swinging a leg back and forth while he lounged in one of the high backed chairs.

"That isn't what I'm worried about," he snapped. "The stupid chit was supposed to stay put."

Jonathan grinned. "Did you tell her that or assume she would know that was what she was supposed to do?"

Nathan scowled at him just as the knocker sounded. Brand grinned at the arrival of his last guest, "that should be Lord Sinclair."

"Lord Sinclair? Why Father, you've been busy," Jonathan stated guessing Cabot was ordered there by their father.

Brand smiled. "I wanted to meet the men my daughters married. I would hate to have one of my friends ask me a question about one of my new son-in-laws and draw a total blank."

Jonathan grinned. "You'd at least give the gossips something to talk about at their teas."

Ginger scowled. "Trust me, you despicable bunch of barbarians have given them enough to gossip about for years," she snapped, sticking her nose in the air.

Christopher frowned. "It's been the women folk in the family. They are ill..."

"Watch it. One of those happens to be my wife and I'd hate to have to defend the lady in her own home," Caleb said leaning a shoulder against the mantle, his comment drawing seven pairs of eyes in his direction. Lifting his brows, he waited for someone to comment. The only approving look he received was from Aunt Ginger and Brand.

"Lord Sinclair, my lord," Hobkins announced bringing the gentleman into the room.

Morgan didn't appreciate the means for which he was summoned to the home, and by the looks of it, he was in trouble.

Brand intercepted Morgan before he had a chance to say a word to the others. "I see you received my note," he stated getting a disbelieving look that turned to bewilderment.

"You ordered me here? And who are you?"

Brand stiffened at the man's tone. "I happen to be Jessica's father."

Morgan flushed, looking at the brothers for support. He received grins and shrugs and knew he was on his own. "Forgive me. I wasn't expecting you to be here, my lord. Your sons told me you were ill."

Brand scowled. "Well, I am, but not to the point where I can't see my own daughters get married," he stated giving Caleb a glare.

Morgan looked at the young man and frowned. "What, my I ask, is the reason for this visit?"

"Now relax, young man. I just wanted to meet the man who captured Jessica's heart." Nathan spewed brandy all over the floor. That outrageous statement got a few snorts from the others in the room. Morgan was livid at the situation. Brand gave Nathan a questioning look. "Isn't that what you all told me, son. Jessica and this young man have a bit of a love match going."

Nathan's face was completely innocent. "Oh definitely. She has lost her head over the man," he finished grinning as soon as Brand turned his back.

Stephan punched his shoulder in approval. Morgan narrowed his gaze at the pair. Seeing Brand was waiting for an explanation of sorts, he swallowed. "Well, we have the sea in common."

Brand frowned. "I think you all are..."

"Why, Father, you look absolutely wonderful. The rest has done you good." Melissa said coming into the room and giving her father a kiss and hug. Brand beamed at the attention.

"Thank you, my dear," he said his face turning stern. "What is this I here you got married without waiting for your own father?"

Melissa turned scarlet. "Well...it was...I didn't have time to really think about it," she finished looking around the room where her eyes collided with her husbands. "Caleb?" she said paling.

Caleb smiled, coming to stand by her side. "I'm sorry it took so long to finish with my work," he said hoping she hadn't said anything to anyone else about his deception. She forced a smile feeling her stomach knot.

"Why my dear girl, you look lovely," Brand said moving forward to pull Rae into the room. She smiled hesitantly, her gaze going to Nathan's. He looked surprised but quickly returned his face to the mask of disinterest. Snapping her gaze back to Brand's, she nodded.

"Thank you," she said, disappointed. Brand quickly introduced her to everyone.

"Well who the hell invited you?" Jessica snapped, drawing everyone's attention as she stared at Morgan.

Morgan grit his teeth and pasted a smile on his face, moving to her side he kissed her cheek keeping her firmly in place when she would have pulled back. "Your father thinks we're in love," he whispered pulling back still smiling. Jessica wanted to smack the smile off his face but his words sank in drawing her gaze to her father. Turning scarlet from her outburst, she smiled.

"I was kidding."

"I see that." Brand said knowing something was going on that his children were keeping to themselves but if Jessica was playing along he would wait to see what it was.

"You're looking good, Father," she said moving to kiss her father's cheek.

Silence filled the room as Allison and Ashley appeared in the doorway. Allison was holding Nero's collar and a petite blond was clinging to her side looking as white as a sheet. "What's the matter, are we wearing our gowns backwards?" Allison said feeling the girl beside her stiffen. When no one answered, Allison frowned. "Jonathan, your wife needs to be introduced, come get her. We'll have to look into getting her some sort of pet like Nero."

Finally, the married fact sank in for Stephan. "You're married too?" Stephan asked stunned. "Well, why doesn't anyone tell me anything?" he said moving forward to kiss Allison's cheek. "You look lovely my dear." Turning to the blond beside her he smiled. "And such a lovely lady you are to have married that rogue brother of mine," he said wrapping her arm around his own, knowing she was blind right away. "Of course. It was his looks, wasn't it?"

The blond was stiff as a board. "I...I can't see him."

Stephan frowned at the girl. She wasn't as comfortable with her sight as Allison was. "I know that," he said softly. "I'm sorry for making a joke of it. I guess it comes from teasing Allison."

Ashley swallowed, trying to smile and relax the grip on his arm.

Jessica stared at Jonathan. He was as pale as snow and looking like he wanted to cry. She knew the guilt was eating him alive and that he really hadn't known she was blind. "Jonathan, your wife is lovely," she said getting his attention. She saw him swallow before moving in Ashley's direction.

"She is, isn't she?" he answered as Stephan looked first at Jonathan then at Ashley before extracting his arm from her grip and turning her over to Jonathan. As Stephan moved off, Jonathan cursed. How could he have not known? Remembering back as she cowered against the wall, not really looking at anything, he realized then that he had been a fool. Feeling her try to remove her hand from his arm he clasped his hand over hers. "As Allison said this lovely lady is my wife," he said frowning for a moment trying to remember her name. "Ashley, I'd like you to meet my family." As each person came up, he introduced them, while they kissed her hand. As the room erupted into conversations, Brand smiled.

Colan moved to stand by his side. "Proud of yourself?"

Brand arched a brow. "I only brought the men. The lady's presence here is somebody else's doing."

Colan frowned. "Most likely Nathan's wife came on her own but Jonathan's wife was definitely dragged here."

Brand frowned. "I don't think he knew."

"Obviously. More than likely one of those sons of yours hauled her here."

"No, you dolt. I don't think he knew she was blind."

Colan's face blanked. "That's impossible."

"No, it isn't. The man is stubborn as a mule and if he was tricked into marriage like he claims, you can bet he locked her away somewhere in his house and didn't want anything to do with her."

Colan looked again at the couple talking by the window away from the others. Jonathan seemed to be doing all the talking while the girl looked ready to cry. "Perhaps you're right."

"I'd bet on it. The poor thing. She must have been living in terror for the past few days."

Colan frowned. "She couldn't have married a better man. Jonathan will be good for her."

Brand smiled with pride. "I'm sure of that."

Colan grinned. "I think Allison's idea of a pet is my department."

Brand's face lost all trace of happiness. "Good lord, I'd forgotten about that bit of drivel."

Colan smiled. "I know a man who has all sorts of animals he has trained. I'm sure he'd have something fitting for her."

Brand groaned. "Remember, Jonathan works with horses and those large cats send those animals into fits."

Colan frowned. "You're right." Getting thoughtful for a second he smiled. "Perhaps a wolf or a monkey would do better."

Brand gave him a disgusted look. "I think you should ask them before you go off and get them a pet," he said moving off to interfere in a conversation between Jessica and Morgan that looked more like a war than the love match they claimed.

ALLISON FELT THE STRAIN around the table but was ignoring it. Her entire concentration was on the girl next to her. Ashley was seated to her left and wasn't eating or drinking a thing. Stephan was on her right and she casually leaned over his way.

"Carry on the conversation no matter what I do, all right?"

"What?"

"No matter what I'm doing, keep talking to me."

"Fine," he said giving her a puzzled look.

"Stephan, how is your shipping business doing? I know Jessica was worried," she said reaching next to her and taking Ashley's hand and moving it toward the glass.

Stephan, realizing she was trying to help the girl, grinned, "It's going great. I have several ships going up and down the coast," he said still talking as Allison guided Ashley's hands to the glass then the utensils beside the plate. Stopping on each one and running the girls hands over the things to show her what each item was. Ashley resisted at first but very much wanted not to be a burden to her new husband.

Jonathan watched in amazement as his sister guided his wife's hand around the place setting. He was almost to the point where he was going to feed his wife himself. When Jessica joined in the conversation asking questions about her end of the line, Allison stood up and moved behind Ashley, leaning over her back to help her guide her hand better.

Morgan looked around the table his gaze locking with Caleb's a moment before both men turned to watch in fascination as this very different family worked together to put the girl at ease. Ashley started to feel like a fool having Allison showing her how to eat when she herself couldn't see. Her family had always fed her. She had never done anything for herself. Jonathan seeing the change in his wife touched Allison's shoulder. She stopped and immediately sat down. Ashley shook her head slightly sending her hair bouncing over her shoulders. Reaching hesitantly forward she tried to remember where the glass was located. Opening her hand wide she moved slowly toward the object, unaware that everyone was watching her while Allison and Stephan carried on a conversation about goods shipped to various locations. When her hand touched the glass and she managed to drink from it and return it to its place without spilling it, she smiled.

Rae watched in fascination as Allison ate and talked like a normal person. Her movements were sure and precise, "Amazing isn't it?" Christopher said when she looked at him.

Rae flushed at being caught staring, "she doesn't look like she can't see."

Nathan scowled at Christopher who just grinned, completely ignoring Nathan's glare. "She wasn't always like that." Looking again at Nathan he decided to voice his next thought. "Nathan here has worked with her for months on dancing."

Rae turned to look at her handsome husband. He was glaring at the man next to her. "Dancing, huh? I didn't think you'd be able to manage that?"

Nathan stared at her unsure what to say to that as Christopher chuckled. "I'm sure there are a great many things about me that you don't know." Nathan's tone clearly saying she never would. Rae reddened in anger. The man had every right to be angry but he'd ordered her around all week. She was truly getting tired of it.

"I'm sure there are," she said smiling.

Christopher grinned. This girl had spunk at least and Nathan needed someone with a head on her shoulders to keep him out of trouble. "So how is married life?" he asked knowing neither person wanted to talk about that.

Rae frowned at Christopher. He was handsome, with his blond hair and green eyes, but he was trying to cause trouble and she knew it. Taking up her drink she decided to give him back some of his own medicine. "It's hard to say this early, but I'm sure a man of your years has been married for a while and has forgotten how being newly wed is?"

Nathan looked at his wife with wide eyes, then seeing the stunned look on Christopher's face, grinned. "Yes, Christopher, what does someone of your years think of marriage?"

Christopher scowled at the pair. The little minx had turned the tables on him. "I wouldn't know. I haven't found the right female, yet," he said stressing the fact that he was picking out his own mate instead of falling into some sort of trap. Nathan scowled. Rae, oblivious to the jab, sighed.

"It must be making you nervous that the right female hasn't shown up yet," She said implying he was seventy instead of thirty. Nathan grinned.

"Just how old do you think I am?" he asked getting angry at being called old.

Rae laughed. "I was only teasing you for putting us on the spot," she said not looking at her husband. Christopher let a slow smile cross his lips.

"Touché" he said holding up his glass, "you are very astute."

Rae grinned. "Have to be in this day and age."

Nathan scowled at that comment knowing she was referring to stealing.

Jessica hid her smile at the words going on across the table knowing if Christopher focused on her, her own situation would be drawn out for mulling over.

"Why the smile?" Morgan asked.

Jessica clenched her jaw. "I was thinking of something that happened earlier," she lied.

Morgan ground his teeth. She was more than a sane man deserved. Their little trip to the park had proved to be nothing but a complete test of his will. She attacked him both verbally and mentally. "Care to share it?"

"I don't think it would interest you."

Ginger scowled at Jessica's behavior. The girl was getting one of the best catches in London and she was treating him like a leper. "Jessica, did you tell Lord Sinclair that you have almost your complete trousseau already?"

Morgan smiled pleasantly at the older lady. "No, she didn't tell me that. Is it in gowns or breeches?"

Jessica shot him a murderous glare before laughing. "It's gowns, of course," she said looking to see if anyone was watching them. She blushed when nearly everyone was looking at her with various degrees of hilarity.

Brand frowned at the table at large. Melissa hadn't said two words the entire dinner. Her husband, either, for that matter. Christopher and Nathan were busy trying to send the other into a rage, using the young girl as a target. Though Rae was holding her own. Morgan and Jessica were definitely not in love with one another and if his guess was right the chit had forced the man's hand on accident but someone of importance had interfered making the gentleman come up to snuff. Jonathan didn't even know his wife and looked pained trying to keep her seated at the table without looking like he was forcing her. Stephan was acting like a wolf in a sheep pen uncertain at which sheep to jump first. Out of all his children Allison was the only one going on about her business. Asking questions here and there to start conversation. Sighing he caught sight of his brother who grinned at him. Having enough of the whole evening he slowly got to his feet.

"I would like to propose a toast to my three married children. May your lives be filled with happiness and love," he said raising his glass to take a sip. "I would also like to congratulate Jessica and Lord Sinclair on their happy union tomorrow. May you enjoy a long and happy life together as well."

Cheers went up as Jessica silently glared. Brand placed his glass on the table. "Now if you would all excuse me, I will retire."

Silence filled the room. "Father, are you ill?" Allison asked getting to her feet.

"No, no. Just tired. I have a long day tomorrow and I need the rest."

Allison pursed her lips. "I'll walk up with you." Moving around the table with Nero's help, Brand waited for her smiling. "Good night, then."

As they climbed the stairs Allison sighed. "I suppose you have questions for me."

Brand smiled. She always was very astute. "Well, since you brought it up"

Allison held up a hand "No need to ask. Jessica and Morgan, as you guessed, are not a love match. They were caught in the same room together. I personally think they are good for one another. It will just take time.

Nathan you know more about than I do. Rae is very lovely. I think Nathan is wrong but he'll have to find that out for himself."

"I suppose you won't tell me what that is?"

"No. Mother told me you can't keep a secret and I know this one is too big for you to remain silent."

Brand scowled. "She would have to tell you kids that."

"Ashley on the other hand, is going to need my help. I hope Jonathan will allow it."

"You know he was the one to teach you. I'm sure he can handle his wife on his own."

Allison frowned. "I know but he doesn't understand how it feels to be unable to see anything."

"You turned out rather well. I'm sure his wife will, also. Besides, they need to be together to get over the rocky start they had."

Allison tipped her head as they reached her room. "You're right on that point, but if I think they are floundering too much I'm stepping in."

Brand didn't argue with her. "Has Christopher tried to find a wife?"

"No. He'll research the position completely and handle it like an interview."

Brand scowled. "That's no way to go about marriage."

Allison frowned. "I don't exactly have high prospects myself. I'll have to settle for what I can get."

Brand frowned. "I'm sorry for the situation, Allison. I would like to relent and let you have more time but..." His voice trailed off.

"Father," she said moving to his side. "It isn't your fault and I completely understand. Now, don't worry. I'll be fine."

Brand uncomfortable with that situation asked about Melissa instead.

"She's deeply in love with her husband but doesn't know it."

Brand's mouth fell open. "But she didn't say two words to the man."

Allison moved to her window seat and sat down. "I know. They're being silly but I guarantee, in a few months, they'll be looking at each other in that disgusting way lovers always do."

Brand flushed. "How would you know about that?" he asked.

"I heard Christopher and Stephan talking about it."

Brand snorted. "That pair wouldn't know the meaning of the word love let alone what love looks like."

Allison laughed. "I hope someday they will and I can tease them about it."

Brand smiled. "You're such a kind soul, Allison. Just like your mother," he said touching her cheek. "Now, I'll leave you to retire. We have guests converging on us early tomorrow. Your Aunt Ginger had the other part of the house opened up and I can see swarms of people milling around the house."

Allison smiled until he left, then frowned. More people meant more things out of place and the risk of making a fool of herself. Undressing and crawling into bed she pulled the covers up to her chin feeling the bed sag as Nero climbed up on the end of the bed. Frowning she wondered what the next day was going to bring.

MELISSA HURRIED TO HER ROOM, slipping away from the room full of men. The ladies had retired before her, except Jessica who was more like a man anyway. Opening the door she closed it and leaned against it. Who had invited Caleb? She hadn't wanted to see him ever again. Cursing, she paced. That was a lie. She had wanted to see him and hating was impossible. She found that deep inside she was glad he had came tonight. It would make tomorrow exciting as well. All of society would see them together like a married couple. Sighing, she undressed and slipped into her night gown. It felt good to snuggle in her bed, she thought, as she pulled the covers up. Rolling over on her side she quickly drifted off to sleep.

Caleb hesitated outside the door to the room Netty had showed him. He wondered if his wife was in there. Turning the knob, he moved inside and closed the door waiting for his eyes to adjust to the darkness. When he looked around the room, he could see he was indeed in a ladies room. The gown Melissa had worn earlier was draped over the back of a chair and her shoes were in a pile by its hem. Cursing softly he wondered whether to desert the room or risk being near a wife he couldn't forget. The wedding night spent together had played itself over in his mind every night since then, making it harder to sleep. It had killed him to remain in his home wondering if his wife was forgetting she had a husband. Seeing her tonight had brought the dream back, so vividly that he didn't trust himself to stay with her. Turning to leave he heard the bed creak and stopped in mid-turn.

"Netty, is that you?"

Caleb frowned into the darkness. What to do now? Turning back to face the bed he sighed. "No, it's me."

The bed creaked with the jerking motions of a person startled about. "What are you doing in here?"

"Your Netty brought me here," he answered not adding that he could leave and would. "I think she thought as your husband I would want to be in here with you."

Melissa reddened though he couldn't see that. "Fine. Then find someplace to sleep and be done with it. I don't want my family to think anything is wrong between us."

Caleb frowned into the darkness. "Is there?"

Melissa pursed her lips. "Our marriage has started out on nothing but lies and I can't help but feel you don't really want to be married. After all you left me here for almost three days."

Caleb's mouth fell open. "I left you here? You're the one that ran away.

"But you didn't come after me," she said, lowering her voice.

Caleb frowned. "I wasn't sure if you wanted me to."

Melissa lowered her lashes. She had and it had hurt to know he didn't want her bad enough to come after her and explain why he'd done what he had. "So what are you doing here?"

Caleb snorted, "I was ordered here by your father, I think. The message said I would be in dire straights if I didn't show myself by 8:00 sharp."

Melissa frowned. "That could have been anyone of my brothers but you're probably right about it being Father. He wanted to see what kind of person I married."

Caleb hesitated before moving closer to the bed. "What exactly did you tell them?"

Melissa wanted to lie but instead she looked away from his shadowed outline. "I didn't tell anyone anything. I said I was coming here to help with the wedding," she said then added. "Except Allison. I did tell her the truth."

"About my deceiving you?" he asked.

"Yes, but she won't say anything to the others."

"Melissa," he said moving to sit on the edge of the bed. "I really didn't think far enough ahead when I formed that plan of mine and I'm sorry about the way things went. It was a stupid thing to do."

Melissa whole-heartedly agreed but she didn't exactly mind all together. She would have never have met this handsome man and when she did, he would have already been married to Miss Angela Fleming. "I think we both acted out of hand," she said.

"Are you sorry you aren't a rich widow?'

Melissa slapped his arm. "Don't even talk that way. I didn't marry you for the money."

Caleb's brows went up. "Then why did you marry me?"

Melissa turned scarlet. "I felt sorry for you."

"You married me because you felt sorry for me?" he asked not believing that for a minute.

"Yes, I did!" She said knowing he didn't believe it. "I felt bad that you were so young and had no one to care for you in your last days."

Caleb frowned at that. She probably did feel like that. He had said he was an orphan. "I'm sorry for all the lies."

Melissa frowned. What to do now? Lifting her chin she hesitated. "Perhaps, we could start over. A whole new beginning."

Caleb felt a shock run through his body. "You'd be willing to do that?" At her nod, he sighed. "I'd be willing to do that in a minute. Are you sure?"

Melissa nodded, never more sure in her life. "I'm sure." Caleb felt a surge of joy. She was giving him and their marriage a chance. Getting to his feet he headed for the door. She would need time to think things over.

Melissa panicked. "Where..." She cleared her throat. "Where are you going?"

"You want me to stay?"

Melissa frowned. Isn't that what she just said? "If you'd like."

Caleb smiled at her answer. She didn't want to admit that she wanted him there. "All right. Should I sleep in the chair or by the hearth?"

Melissa frown deepened. "I don't see any reason why we can't share the bed. It's large enough for the both of us."

Caleb grinned as he seated himself to remove his shoes. "All right. I know my back will thank you in the morning."

Melissa nodded her head not trusting herself to speak. She was unable to see him undress but she remembered very clearly what his body looked like which started a funny feeling in her stomach. Scooting down under the covers, she pulled them up to her chin and waited in silence. The bed sagged as Caleb climbed in and stretched out fully on his back. Giving a sigh, he grew still. Melissa, also lying on her back, frowned. She didn't exactly know what she expected but to have him just crawl into bed, with her, without so much as a good night kiss made her temper ignite. Leaning up on one elbow she punched the pillow then flopped back on the bed to stare at the ceiling. Almost ready to voice her anger she nearly screamed when a face appeared over hers.

"Thank you again for sharing your bed," he said looking into her shadowed face before slowly lowering his head to brush a kiss on her lips. Just inches away he paused as if he was going to change his mind. "Good night then," he said starting to pull away. Melissa fueled by anger and irritation, reached up and grabbed his head brought his lips to meet hers. Caleb wanted to grin but the kiss was turning serious and he didn't want her to be angry come morning. Pulling away some he looked at her in the dark. He tried to think of something to say that expressed how he felt, but finally gave up and lowered his head to hers again. Hearing the soft moan come from her throat, he was lost.

JESSICA, seeing Melissa sneak from the room, decided to follow suit. Getting to her feet, she moved like she was refilling her glass but instead left the room. Hurrying to the stairs she nearly jumped out of her skin as a hand clamped on her arm.

"Leaving so soon?"

Jessica spun around surprised. "I was going to retire. I have a long day tomorrow thanks to you."

Morgan smiled. "I, too, have a long day tomorrow. It's only the beginning and will go on for years and years. Thanks to you."

Jessica flushed with anger. "If you would have just let me go that night, we wouldn't be in this situation."

Morgan gripped her arm and led her out the back door into the garden. "Since you brought it up, I think it's the least you can do to explain to me what you were doing in my room that night." Jessica lifted her chin to tell him exactly what she thought of that idea, when he clamped his hand over her mouth and pulled her up against his chest. "Remember, before you speak, that in little over fifteen hours you will be my wife and that gives me leave to beat you."

Jessica paled, before pulling out of his grasp. "You lay one finger on me and I'll cut it off," she snapped moving away from him. Morgan glared at her. To be forced to marry was one thing but to be marrying this shrew before him was entirely too much to ask.

"Then you were out to kill me that night?"

Jessica turned to stare at the man like he'd grown two heads. "I was doing nothing of the sort."

"It must have been stealing then?"

Jessica pursed her lips. "If you must know I was looking for a purse."

Morgan's brows drew together then his eyes narrowed. "A purse? Whose purse?" "Allison's."

"Allison's?"

"Do you have a hearing problem?" she asked since he repeated her words again. "She was sent up to the powder room and miss calculated the number of doors and ended up in your room. She dropped her purse when she realized her mistake and I was going up there to get it," she snapped turning her back on him.

Morgan frowned at her. "Then why were you climbing about my house like a regular street urchin?"

Jessica gritted her teeth turning to face him once again. "I happen to have just come from a meeting with my family. Allison didn't know what had happened to Melissa at that point, so I was going to the ball to tell her so she and Aunt Ginger could relax."

Morgan snorted. "You weren't even wearing a gown?"

Jessica's hands balled into fists. "Exactly. Why do you think I was climbing around on the outside of your house? I didn't want anyone to see me but at the same time, I couldn't let Allison's purse be found in a man's room," she finished letting him conclude the rest.

Morgan's face turned harsh. "Then why didn't you just say that?"

"And have Allison's name spread all over the city as being some kind of ...of whore. I don't think so."

Morgan reddened. That was true. Society would have had a field day with the incident even if nothing had happened. "So you're telling me you were trying to prevent Allison's name from being ruined?"

Jessica lifted her chin. "Yes."

"What of your own? Someone else could have been in that room."

Jessica, anger making her rash, snapped out. "It would have been better if it had been someone else. At least then I might be marrying a gentleman."

Morgan growled deep in his throat, grabbing her by the arms and hauling her up against his front. "Since I have earned such a low opinion in your mind, then you won't mind this," he gritted bringing his lips down on hers. The jolt of desire that shot through him made him even angrier. The little shrew didn't deserve to be treated nicely.

Jessica stood there stunned as Morgan kissed her like she had never been kissed before. She could feel his masculine power holding her close, at the same time the smell of brandy and leather mingled with his musky cologne made her head light. She was thrust away so fast she staggered to catch herself before she fell. Feeling embarrassed for not having fought the man, she clenched her hand into a fist and swung. Missing his head by an inch she over threw her punch, sprawling to the ground in the folds of her balky dress. Morgan, however, was madder than she had guessed. Pinning her body to the ground he held her there with his own body.

Jessica watched the muscles move along his jaw and his lips were pressed into a tight line. Lips that moments ago were kissing her with anger and passion so fierce it left her wondering what else went with it.

Morgan watched her face trying to keep his head straight and refrain from kissing the chit again. Looking at her lovely mouth he cursed. Then lowered his head to claim her mouth again.

This kiss was different. A natural kiss, minus the anger. Jessica felt her breath coming in short gasps and realized a moment later that her hands had some how worked there way up around his neck. He kissed her mouth running his tongue along her lips, until they parted and his tongue delved in bringing a soft moan from deep in her throat.

Stephan paused at the edge of the garden and gave Christopher a nudge. "I think they are more agreeable to each other than they let on."

Christopher looked where he was pointing and his mouth dropped open. Giving Stephan a disgusted look he started in their direction. "I think it's very late for you to be up, young lady."

Jessica and Morgan snapped their heads apart, and they both stared at Christopher. Both looked like they were unable to comprehend his simple words. Jessica collecting her thoughts, snarled deep in her throat and bucked her body to get Morgan off.

"Get off me, you cretin."

Morgan, confused at his own behavior, slid to the side while she scrambled to her feet. Turning she marched from the garden without saying a word to her brothers. Morgan's brows arched as he slowly got to his feet.

Stephan burst out laughing. "Muddles the mind, doesn't it?" he said clapping Morgan on the back."

"Stephan, that happens to be your sister you're talking about?" Christopher managed still glaring at Morgan.

"I know that. I didn't say anything bad about her. Morgan here is going to marry her tomorrow anyway."

Morgan scowled at the thought. The whole incident had gotten out of hand. Giving both gentlemen a nod, he left the garden.

"Well, I say. That was rather rude of him. He hasn't a clue what to do now."

"What are you yammering about? The man was trying to seduce Jessica the night before her wedding."

"From what I heard, he already had the opportunity to do worse if he had wanted to."

Christopher smacked his arm. "You're such an idiot. They were out of line here."

Stephan snorted. "You're a stiff neck. Can't you for once let go and see that those two people like one another and kissing is a good thing?"

"You would think so. You kiss just about any female that crosses your path."

Stephan grinned. "Lucky I didn't do the same to Nathan's little wife."

Christopher finally grinned. "That would have been something to see."

"Which one, me kissing his wife or Nathan laying me low?"

Christopher shrugged. "Either one but Nathan laying you low would have gotten money out of me."

Stephan laughed. "I sure do wonder about you sometimes. How is such a stiff necked chap ever going to find himself a lady?"

Christopher scowled. "You're getting off the subject here," Christopher said heading back toward the house. "I'm going to bed."

Stephan grinned at his retreating back. "Now don't get all sore. I was only kidding."

When Christopher didn't come back he sighed. Well, at least he was being consistent with the rest of the family. All of them were thick headed but thin skinned, he thought walking toward the house.

JONATHAN MOVED ASHLEY along the hall toward their room. He felt like a complete idiot for not having known she was blind. Cursing, he looked at her scared face and regretted his whole behavior. He hadn't said two words to her since their marriage. He had just dropped her off at his home sending her to the farthest reaches of the house, so he wouldn't have to see or deal with her. Frowning he opened the door and swallowed.

"We're here," he said, his voice filled with regret.

Ashley moved several steps into the room then stopped. "Is there someone here to help me?"

Jonathan frowned. There could be but he would rather help her himself. "With the festivities tomorrow it's rather difficult to find someone free," at her scared look he quickly added, "But I'm here."

Ashley stiffened. "I don't want your pity. You made it clear how things were going to be between us."

Jonathan frowned. She was right, of course. He shouldn't have expected her to just accept his help now. "You're right. I was wrong about that, though, and I would like to make amends."

"Why? Poor little blind girl needs your help?" she sneered, tears stinging her eyes. "I don't want that."

Jonathan set his jaw. "Whether you want it or not I'm your husband and you're going to take my help."

Ashley felt the tears flowing now and buried her face in her hands. "I didn't want to have a husband. I wanted to join the sisters. They treated me like a person," she whispered her face still hidden.

Jonathan felt a small tug of regret at those words. Her family had done her a great disservice if that is truly what she had wanted. "I'm sorry but that path has been closed to you."

Ashley lifted her face. "You could get our marriage annulled?"

Jonathan shook his head. "I can't. You've been at my home too long now. Even if it were proven that you were still a virgin, your reputation and mine would go through the ringer. As a gentleman, I can't allow that."

Ashley's face crumpled and she drew in a great shuddering breath. She sobbed silently into her hands. Jonathan hesitated then moved and took her in his arms. She stiffened some but in her grief she cried on his shoulder. Jonathan held her head against his shoulder and whispered words to her. Later he wouldn't be able to recall but soon she quieted and moved away from him.

"I don't want to be a burden to you or anyone else. I tried to tell your sister that but Jessica refused to listen. She kept saying she would straighten things out and that everything would be fine. I am still blind and you are still married to me against your will. What kind of a life is that for you?" she finished tears again on her cheeks.

Jonathan frowned at her, knowing he was going to kill Jessica next time he saw her. "I was not exactly forced to marry you. I could have said no. Many men do, you know?"

Ashley frowned. "Then why didn't you?"

Jonathan snorted. "I am a gentleman, I guess. But I think Jessica was right in a way. I think we will work things out."

Ashley sniffed. "Work what out?"

Jonathan moved to take her hand. She jumped from the contact. Pursing his lips he led her to the chairs by the hearth. When she was seated he moved to squat in front of her. "I want to help you." Holding his hand against her lips he stopped her protest. "It isn't out of pity, either. I want your family to see beyond the fact that you're blind. I want them to see the young lady you are."

Ashley frowned. "I don't understand."

"I think you do. When I made a deal with your father to sell him those horses he mentioned dining with his family. He mentioned his daughter but her name had been Christine. He made no mention of you."

Ashley frowned, "That doesn't mean anything."

"Then why weren't you present for dinner?" When she lowered her head, he added. "They kept you hidden away, didn't they?" Though he had suspected it was because she was a tainted woman. When she didn't answer, he added. "Allison wanted to stay in her room for a long time after her sight was taken away. She's happy we didn't let that happen, I am sure."

Ashley shook her head. "I don't understand what this has to do with anything we were talking about?"

"I am trying to tell you that you can choose a life of seclusion or you can work with me and become a person."

Ashley felt her heart constrict. To actually move about in society and function like a normal person would be something she never had. Without her sight, though, that was nothing but a dream. "I will never be anything but a burden. Just send me away."

Jonathan frowned at the lady before him. She was a pitiful sight. Yet, he knew she could function like anyone else. Taking her chin he drew her face up so he could see her eyes. "Contrary to what you just said, I happen to know that just because you are blind doesn't make you a burden to anyone. Including yourself." Letting go of her chin he moved to pour himself a drink. "Whether you wish to wallow in this self-pity or step up to the challenge, is your decision. But either way, you are still my wife. I am going down to the library and will be back in exactly twenty minutes. If you are still dressed and sitting in that chair, I will personally undress you and put you in the bed. The choice is yours." Staring at her for a full minute he shook his head and left the room.

Ashley listened for movement when none came she felt panic. She didn't have the slightest idea where anything was. Feeling fresh tears again run down her cheeks she cried. "How much more am I suppose to take?" she sobbed burying her face in her hands.

Jonathan heard the soft crying and frowned. It had always worked with

Allison to make things into a challenge. Cursing he placed his hand on the knob to go back in and help her but the faint sound of her moving within the room made a smile form on his lips. At least she was determined to undress her. Turning he softly moved away from the room and headed for the library. Hopefully no one was still awake.

Chapter 40

RAE CLUTCHED HER COVERS for several minutes as the grip of fear still held her. She had the dream again and was suffering the after affects of it. Usually, she had the boys to cuddle up against but since they weren't with her she was struggling to keep from crying.

The dream was always the same. Her sister was with her and they were in the water. She was struggling to keep the boys afloat, while her sister disappeared from sight. Feeling the overpowering sense of loss, she threw back the covers and walked to the door connecting her room with Nathan's. Pausing long enough to listen for movement on the other side, she slowly opened the door knowing she needed to be with someone and Nathan was the only one she could think of. Peeking into the room she could make out the bed in the moonlight. Frowning, she bit her lip to keep from letting a sob escape as tears coursed down her cheeks. She quickly closed the door and made her way to the bed. She could see Nathan was lying on his back with his head turned away from her. Watching the gentle rise and fall of his chest, she pulled the covers back and slide into the bed. Tucking the blankets under her chin, she held her breathe to see if Nathan awoke. When he didn't move she expelled the breath she had been holding in a soft sob. Turning she silently cried her grief into the pillow.

Nathan let his body relax at the muffled sounds coming from next to him. He had been ready to knock her senseless if she had come in there to kill him. Listening to her cry and feel the bed shake with her tremors made him frown. What was she crying over? Was she upset that he didn't want anything to do with her? What did she expect? Frowning at himself he discarded that fact. If she were angry with him she wouldn't have come to his room. Something else was bothering her.

He lay there for nearly ten minutes trying to decide whether he should hold her or just leave her be. Her sobs eventually calmed and the shaking almost completely ceased. Soon after that her breathing turned to deep even breaths and he knew she was asleep. Turning his head he looked at the slight form next to his and frowned. What would send her crying into his room? Frowning he turned on his side and tried to go back to sleep. Sleep eluded him as the fact that he didn't know his wife occupied his mind. Rolling over on his back he stared up at the ceiling. He would have to talk with her tomorrow. He had to know who the hell she was?

Chapter 41

JONATHAN MOVED INTO THE LIBRARY and frowned. "What are you doing up?"

Stephan grinned at him from his reclined position on the sofa. "I happen to have a cold lonely bed to go to unlike someone else in this room?"

Jonathan frowned. "My actions aren't run by the thing in my pants," he stated pouring himself a drink. "She doesn't even know me."

Stephan frowned. "I gathered as much when Allison walked in with her."

Jonathan ran his hands through his hair. "I was set up for one of the oldest tricks in the book and didn't stop to think that maybe Ashley had been too."

Stephan shrugged as he moved into a sitting position. "I'm sure she will come around. You just need time together."

"I know." Looking into his glass, he frowned. "I feel like such a cad. I treated her terribly."

Stephan lowered his head. "You didn't know. Besides it isn't like it was months or something. The girl seems like a nice sort. She'll come around. Personally I think she ended up with a good husband. You did wonders for Allison."

"Yes, but Allison had a stubborn streak and wanted to prove to herself that she was capable of living like a normal person. I don't think Ashley has that."

Stephan looked at his hands. "I think it's too soon to say that. You've only talked with her a short while."

Jonathan frowned. "I guess. But I still worry that I'm climbing a hill that doesn't have another side."

Stephan smiled crookedly. "Perhaps a bit of sport will keep your mind occupied."

Jonathan narrowed his eyes, as he studied his brother's face. At twenty-seven Stephan looked like a pirate. His black hair hung to his shoulders and his blue eyes could wage war or glimmer with charm. The man was trouble, though Nathan tended to get in deeper, leaving Stephen's behavior to go almost unnoticed. "Exactly what do you have in mind and who is the victim?"

Stephan grinned scooting forward in his chair. "I have spent the last five days with Christopher and have decided the man will more than likely interview for a wife." Pausing he waited for Jonathan to snort and nod in agreement. "That's the reason I think we should find a woman for him."

Jonathan's mouth fell open. "You're crazy. Christopher will skin you alive."

Stephan chuckled. "I hardly think so. Besides we'll just have a bit of fun with him."

Jonathan waited several seconds before laughing. "You're serious," he said getting a satisfied grin out of Stephan. "I can't believe you," he said getting to his feet to refill his glass. "I suppose you plan on letting the rest of the gang in on this one?" Stephen's brows drew together considering the suggestion. "God lord, I was only kidding."

"But that's not a bad idea. Melissa has style and fashion, Jessica has grace and...let's just say she's outspoken, and Allison has the biggest heart in the whole of London. Together with each of their input we should be able to come up with a right suitable gal."

Jonathan held up a hand. "You can stop right there with the 'we' thing. I don't plan on stepping one foot into this mess you're concocting and I know for a fact Allison won't either."

Stephan got to his feet. "A challenge!" he said, rubbing his hands together. "If I can get the girls to comply, will you lend a hand?"

Jonathan looked at Stephan, than ran his hand along his jaw. "If you can get all three girls to help search, I'll do my part." Holding up his hand as Stephan was about to whoop, he added. "But I want to be told exactly what's to happen before you do anything once the girl is found."

Stephan grinned. "You got it. Nathan will probably find her tomorrow."

Jonathan held up a hand. "Nathan? You didn't say you were bringing him into this. He'll get us shot!"

Stephan smacked Jonathan's arm. "Now that's not nice. Nathan, if you'll remember, is in the state of wedded bliss and probably won't have much time for us. After all, he is a father."

Jonathan grinned. "I'm surprised you didn't say something to him about that."

"If I would have known that earlier I would definitely have said something. Christopher told me in the garden, when we caught the wedding couple in a compromising position."

Jonathan arched his brows. "Compromising?"

Stephan grinned. "I'd say the pair like each other a bit more than they let on. Their lips were locked tighter than a barrel of pickles."

Jonathan grinned. "Christopher probably thrashed Morgan a good one."

"Morgan was handling that part all on his own."

Jonathan's grin widened. "Couldn't help himself, huh?"

"Tomorrow is going to be a great day. Ten pounds, Jessica will never get through the day, without losing her temper."

"That would be a stupid bet on my part. The girl can't go through a single day without doing that, let alone her wedding day."

"Then ten pounds she swears in front of someone important."

Jonathan considered that a moment. "Just during the celebration?"

Stephan grinned. "Deal."

The brothers shook hands. "I think I should head back to bed. I'll see you tomorrow."

Stephan nodded moving back to his sofa. Lying back he frowned as his father moved into the room from the door connecting the library to the study. "Been there long?"

"Long enough to know the pair of you are up to no good."

Stephan smiled. "Sorry to disappoint you but we were just placing a few bets on tomorrow."

Brand scowled. "I hope you didn't bet something ridiculous. I can just see the pair of you going out of your way to get the bet to go in your favor."

Stephan grinned. "Now there's an idea."

"Stephan, I do hope you plan to behave yourself. The family has suffered several embarrassments since I left and I don't think it can take much more."

Stephan frowned. "It isn't making you sick, is it?"

Brand snorted. "I feel better than I have in years," he said moving to look out the window. "I just was trying to prevent something scandalous from happening tomorrow. The papers are glued to our every move."

Stephan tucked his hands behind his head. "I could provide them with some sort of entertainment in someone else's home."

Brand turned to look at his son. "You're a bigger scoundrel than I thought."

Stephan looked over his shoulder at his father. "Now you know I was bluffing."

Brand smiled. "Of course." Turning back to the window he cleared his throat. "A bit of a shock wasn't it?"

Stephan laid his head back. "Which shock would that be?"

"My two sons getting married."

"More like loss of brain cells to me."

"You think you would have avoided their predicaments?"

Stephan sat up and turned to look at his father. "I would be a fool to say that. I was just saying they both put themselves in available positions for that sort of thing to happen."

Brand looked at his hands. "That is true." Looking again out the window he pursed his lips. "Do you suppose they will get around to grandchildren sometime in the near future?"

Stephan frowned at his father's back. The man wanted grandchildren, he knew, but these probing questions made it seem like he barely had any time left before he died. "Nathan has a pair already."

Brand turned and glared at Stephan. "That isn't funny. Those two boys are probably fine lads but I want grandchildren of my own blood. With the seven of you, I should be able to manage a few, don't you think?"

Stephan laughed getting to his feet. "Not any from me in the near future but I think Melissa and Caleb will be your best bet."

Brand frowned. Smacking his hands on the table causing the decanter and glasses to rattle. "It's just my luck that my offspring can't seem to go about finding themselves suitable mates in the normal fashion. Whatever happened to going to a few balls, finding a young lady, and courting her?"

Stephan grinned. "Now, Father, you have raised yourself a bunch of special people. You really didn't expect them to catch their fish the same way other people do." At his father's deepened frown he laughed, "Christopher might, if that helps you out any."

Brand's mouthed moved into a flat line. "That boy will end up putting an ad in the Post, if I'm not careful."

Stephan's brows arched. "Not a bad idea."

Brand's gaze swung to his son's "Don't you even think of it."

Stephan grinned. "Lighten up. I was only joking. Maybe the Gazette but not the Post."

Brand let a slow smile cross his lips as Stephan left the room. That boy was walking trouble.

Chapter 42

THE NEXT DAY started out like any other until the guests started to arrive. Droves of people showed up for the ceremony at the church, putting the bride in a foul mood.

"Who the hell invited the whole of London?"

Melissa pursed her lips. "Aunt Ginger was just trying to make your initiation into society right. You messed up the beginning part and she's only trying to finish things the right way."

Jessica cursed. "I don't plan on parading about on the Baron's arm with that bunch of two-faced jackals," she said sitting patiently, while Betsy, fixed her hair for the fifth time.

Melissa sighed. "I give up Allison. She's impossible."

Allison frowned. "You're just teasing her because you got out of all this hassle."

Melissa frowned. "I would have loved to have married Caleb with thousands of on lookers."

Allison lifted her head in Melissa's direction. "You've made up with the man?"

Jessica saw Melissa's face flame and snorted. "She hopped in bed first chance she got."

Allison blushed. "Jessica, I hope you don't plan to talk like that in front of anyone that isn't family."

Jessica rolled her eyes. "I don't see why I should hide the way I am."

"You will have a husband in less that two hours. Maybe he will care." Melissa put in holding up the fancy thing that was to sit on Jessica's head.

"What's that for?"

"It goes on your head," she said holding up the long gauzy material covered with small flowers and what looked like doves stitched into the material.

"I'll look like an idiot."

"It's what every bride wears," she finished draping the thing over a chair.

"Well, I don't like it."

Melissa gave her a look of disgust. "You're a fool. That Baron of yours has already saved your name not once but twice yet you continue to try to ruin his good name by shaming him."

Allison nodded her head. "It wouldn't hurt you to try and behave like a lady today. If for no one else's sake, for Daddy."

Jessica cursed. "You two are ruining a perfectly nasty mood."

A soft knock sounded on the door and Nero growled. "Does that cat have to be in here?" Melissa asked as Rae opened the door and moved into the room.

"I was wondering if I might help?" she asked quietly.

Allison smiled. "Wonderful. You can help me. I'm putting a few more flowers in the back of her gown."

Rae flushed. "I'm not very good at sewing."

Melissa shifted her feet. "Then just do what you feel comfortable doing," she said pulling out several pairs of shoes. "I think these white ones with the lace are perfect." Holding up the pair out for inspection, she smiled.

Jessica turned her head then stuck her finger in her mouth and pretended to be choking. "They're fairy shoes! I'm wearing the plain ones I wore to that damn ball you dragged me to."

"You can't wear those."

Rae stared at the woman before the mirror with brows arched. Jessica was talking like a sailor.

"I bloody well can or I'll put on my boots," Jessica snapped, getting a frustrated frown from Betsy.

"My lady, if you don't hold still I'll have to start all over."

"Betsy," Jessica stated looking her in the eye. "If you don't finish with this mess you call a hair style, I'll do it myself."

Betsy paled but pursed her lips getting a grin out of Rae. Melissa looked at her again. "How about these? They're fancier than those plain ones of Jess's but they're not as fancy as the flowered ones."

Rae looked at the white shoes and frowned. They were ten times fancier than anything she'd seen in her life. In fact, the whole room was filled with more things than she'd seen even in the stores in which she shopped. "I think they are lovely but shouldn't Lady Jessica choose her own shoes."

Jessica looked at her through the mirror and grinned. "Yes she should." Looking sideways to Melissa she grinned. "Now, did you hear that? Rae thinks I should choose my own shoes. Listen to the girl, you could learn something."

Allison lifted her head from her work. "Rae, you don't have to keep putting Lady before our names. You're one of us." Moving her head in

Melissa's direction she added. "Don't start something. Rae successfully made the grouchy bride smile. Let's leave it at that."

Melissa grinned in Jessica's direction getting a blush from Rae when Jessica's green eyes locked with hers in the mirror. "Is that what you were doing?

"Jessica, she doesn't know you're kidding," Allison said knowing Jessica was looking at Rae with that 'don't disobey me' look. "Rae are the boys coming up?"

Rae frowned. "No. In fact I was thinking of leaving myself."

Melissa's head snapped up at that. "But you can't leave. Nathan will be furious."

Rae snorted then blushed knowing that wasn't lady like. "I think he would be much happier if I wasn't here."

Allison still stitching frowned. "He's a stubborn one but not anything like Jonathan. Be thankful you aren't married to him."

Rae frowned. "I thought he was the mild tempered one."

Allison laughed. "Oh he is, but when his mind is set on something it's very hard to turn him from it. Nathan at least can be reasoned with. Stephan is the easiest one of the lot."

Rae frowned. "He's the blue eyed man that tied me up?"

Melissa frowned. "He tied you up?"

Rae turned scarlet. She hadn't wanted to say that. "He sort of caught me peeking in the windows."

Jessica frowned. "He tied you up in that gown?" she asked looking over Allison's gown that Rae was wearing.

"Not exactly," she said, knowing wearing breeches was probably something these fine looking ladies never thought to wear. "I was kind of in disguise."

Jessica grinned. "Perhaps looking like a boy?"

Rae's eyes snapped to hers. "How did you know?"

"I prefer that attire myself. I thought you were like me when I first met you."

Rae smiled hesitantly. "You wear breeches?"

"Of course, can't Captain a ship in a damn dress."

Melissa snorted at the look of astonishment on Rae's face. "Don't let her get you all worked up to hero worship now. She's a good Captain, but she is a lady too. She should dress as such."

Jessica stuck her tongue out a Melissa getting a disproving look from Betsy who dropped her hands with a sigh, "that's it."

Jessica grinned. "Thank God. All right, where are all the clothes you plan to stick me in? I have how long until the wedding?"

Melissa pursed her lips. "You have exactly one hour."

"An hour. Well hell, what am I suppose to do until then?"

Melissa sighed. "You're supposed to be getting dressed."

"That will take ten minutes."

"Not with the stuff Melissa has picked out," Allison said still stitching.

Jessica scowled at her. "What exactly are you putting on this gown?"

"I'm adding some more flowers. Melissa said they're spaced too far apart."

Turning to give Melissa a glare, Jessica received a wide grin in return. "If you keep fussing, I'll get Aunt Ginger in here."

Jessica stiffened. That meant even more poking and fussing than she was already getting. "Fine, but remember I'm not wearing a corset."

Melissa opened her mouth to speak then clamped it shut. "Fine. It's your husband you're humiliating." Jessica moved to the sofa and flopped out on her back. "Watch your hair." Melissa snapped, seeing the gorgeous concoction shift.

"If it can't last ten minutes then I'll have to do it over."

Betsy pursed her lips to keep from saying something she shouldn't. Rae watched them with unbelieving interest. It was obvious they all cared for one another, but they teased each other mercilessly. Moving to look out the window she frowned. Her own sister had been the same with her. They had spent hours during the night talking to one another about their dreams and hopes. When Emily had met her husband, Aden things had changed, but not drastically. Emily had bought a home close to where their parents lived and Rae had visited regularly. Lowering her head to look at her hands she felt tears in her eyes. She missed Emily terribly.

"Rae, did you bring any kind of luggage with you?" Melissa asked still sorting through the shoes, every so often holding up a pair for Jessica to look at.

Rae stiffened then turned slightly. "I don't have anything with me."

Melissa grinned. "Wonderful. You're welcome to come to my room. I have several gowns that would be perfect on you," she said getting to her feet and dropping two different shoes on Jessica's chest. "You're on your own for a while." Taking Rae's arm she led her from the room.

Allison smiled, "She seems nice enough."

Jessica snorted throwing the shoes on the floor. "Where the hell did Melissa get so many shoes? I feel sorry for Caleb. She'll make him poor with all this garbage."

Allison grinned biting the thread on the last flower on the dress. "She just loves fashion. I'm finished," she added, getting to her feet and shaking the dress out for Jessica to see. "How does it look?"

Jessica stared at the beautiful gown and frowned. "Like it should be on one of those empty-headed girls out for rich husbands."

Allison frowned. "You don't like it?"

"I didn't say that. I just don't think it's me."

Allison frowned. “You have more grace in your little finger than any one of those ladies.”

Jessica sighed. “How would you know that?”

“I can tell by the way you walk. Light on your feet and the grace of a deer.”

Jessica looked at Allison then grinned. “I guess it doesn’t really matter. I’m stuck wearing the thing, aren’t I?” she said standing to hold the gown up in front of her. “What do you think?”

Allison made a great show of turning her head left and then right. “I think you’re too fat.”

“Fat!” she said sucking in her breath. Allison laughed at Jessica’s tone until Jessica started too.

“This is one of those moments I wish I could really see,” she said resuming her seat. Jessica frowned at her sister then took a seat beside her.

“Me too, but I think you’re perfect the way you are,” she said getting a smile from Allison “Besides if you could see, as well as look beautiful, everyone would probably hate you. You’d be a paragon.” Allison burst into laughter at that crack getting a slow mew from Nero.

“A paragon, huh? I’ll have to remember that as I’m looking for a husband in the next two months.”

Jessica lost her smile “I still plan to help you.”

Allison nodded her head. “I know. I didn’t plan on letting you off the hook just because you snagged yourself a handsome man.”

Jessica snorted. “A blind person would think so.”

Allison giggled. “Looks like a boar then?”

Jessica drew her brows down. “Actually no. He is rather handsome. As far as black haired blue, eyed devils go.”

“What about Lord Cabot?”

“He’s handsome too. Black haired and blue eyed as well though he’s taller than Morgan.”

“And Rae?”

“She’s black haired, too, but her eyes are green. They look like grass in the early morning light.”

Allison smiled. “And Ashley?”

“She’s blond haired and brown eyed. Both girls are quite pretty, if you ask me.”

Allison smiled. “I am asking you.” Frowning, she swallowed. “Can I ask you something?”

“Sure,” she said, throwing the gown over a chair. “It seems like you aren’t holding back so let’s hear them.”

Allison hesitated. “Do you remember the Lord of Salisbury?”

Jessica frowned. He was the man with all those terrible burn marks down the side of his face. “I remember him. Why?”

"Would you tell me what he looks like?"

Jessica's brows shot up at that. "You want to know what he looks like? Why?"

"Just tell me."

Jessica pursed her lips "He's tall, about six foot four. He has brown hair and dark eyes, I think. Brown probably."

Allison frowned. "Are...is he handsome?"

Jessica started to get irritated. "Why do you want to know?"

Allison got to her feet. "I like him."

Jessica's mouth fell open. "You like the Earl of Salisbury?"

Allison frowned at her tone. "Yes. Is that a sin?"

"No. But...it's just that..." she trailed off not wanting to say that his burns were distracting because that sounded shallow. "I thought Christopher had a problem with him?"

"He does, but that shouldn't matter. I haven't a lot of choices in the area of suitors. At least with the Earl I already know him some what."

"Are you serious?" Seeing Allison's lips set in a determination, she sighed. "I can see that you are. So what are you planning?"

"I don't know. He's left London to return to his estates in the country. I'm probably just wishful thinking. Have you met anyone else of interest to me?"

Jessica frowned. "I haven't exactly had the time to look but I promise to help you after I'm done committing myself to hell."

Allison frowned. "You shouldn't talk that way. Your man seems like a nice enough sort. He's been very polite to me."

Jessica snorted. "An act, you can be sure."

Melissa swept into the room with Rae right behind her. Both were dressed to the hilt. Melissa was in yellow and Rae wore red. The color made her skin look even tanner than it was. She was beautiful. "Doesn't she look great?"

"She looks lovely. Nathan will be proud."

Rae flushed. "I don't think so."

Allison moved to look out the window getting a frown from Jessica. "Well, how long do I have now?"

Melissa checked the clock and sucked in her breath. "Less than half an hour!" she blurted running to the closet to pull out a pair of white shoes with just a touch of lace on the toe. "Let's get you into that gown. It still may need a little bit of adjusting."

Jessica slowly got to her feet. "I really could care less," she said but her voice was laced with anxiety. Reaching for the gown she pulled it over her head and tugged it into place. "It's itchy," she said reaching up to tug at the lace around her neck.

"Hush now. We spent hours making this gown. The least you could do is pretend to like it," Melissa stated doing up the many buttons on the back of the gown. "Get the veil, please, Rae?"

Rae started at her name but moved to the chair where the veil hung over the back. Picking it up she noted how soft the material felt as she handed it to Melissa. Rae smiled watching Melissa place the veil on Jessica's head.

Jessica stood stiff as a rod until Melissa had stuffed several pins in her hair to hold the veil in place. "Are you finished?"

Melissa lost her smile instantly. "Yes," Melissa snapped moving to the door to put her own shoes on. Her gown was also trimmed with lace, fitting tight in the bust and hanging loosely over the crinolines underneath. Melissa was beautiful.

Jessica snorted at herself in the mirror. "I can't wear this. I look like a sail mast draped in mosquito netting," she snapped reaching up to pull the thing off her head.

"Hold it right there," Ginger snapped coming into the room. "You're wearing it and that's final. Your father is in enough of a panic that you won't go through with the wedding that coming down half naked would send him into convulsions. The veil stays!" Ginger finished with authority. Moving to Jessica's side she fluffed the veil to fall around her gown. She looked absolutely stunning. "Lord Sinclair won't even recognize you."

Jessica pursed her lips. "Let's hope not. Maybe I'll end up married to someone else."

Ginger pursed her lips as Melissa dropped the shoes she was about to help her put on.

"You're despicable," she snapped leaving the room.

Rae watched the whole affair in silence. Jessica was indeed stunning and why she didn't want to marry the handsome Baron, Rae couldn't even guess. He was like a Fairy Prince. Turning to see what Allison was doing, her brows shot up when she saw that she was gone. "If you'll excuse me I'm going to help Allison get dressed."

Ginger nodded her head with a smile as she fussed over a fuming Jessica. Moving along the hall she paused at Allison's door. Hearing nothing within she knocked.

"Allison?" A soft mew came from within making Rae swallow. "Can I come in?"

Allison opened the door as she moved back to her gown. "I was just getting dressed. Melissa said we have only ten minutes." Allison slipped the light blue gown over her head and pulled it into place. Rae sucked in her breath. Allison looked like an Angel. Allison smiled hearing her gasp. "Is it caught up in back?" she asked fidgeting with it to get it right."

"Oh no. It looks perfect!" she said moving forward to help her with the back of the gown. "Who did your hair?" she asked admiring the blue ribbons holding the mass of dark hair to the side in soft ringlets.

"Betsy. She's a marvel."

"You look lovely."

"Thank you, Rae. What color gown did Melissa put you in?"

"Red. She said it made skin glow," she answered, flushing. "Personally, I think I look better than I have in a long time. You, on the other hand, are definitely glowing."

"Me?" she said laughing. "I haven't glowed in years. We better go down. Nathan and Stephan will be charging up here in a minute to drag us down there. We're supposed to be at the church by 3:00," she said taking Rae's arm.

Rae glanced at the mantel then frowned when she didn't see a clock. "I'm sure they wouldn't drag us anywhere."

"Ha! You don't know my brothers. They love causing a scene," she said closing the door behind her as Nero mewed. "Sorry Nero, not today," she called taking Rae's arm again.

"WHERE THE HELL ARE THEY? Jonathan left with Ashley over fifteen minutes ago." Nathan snapped lifting his glass to drink only to change his mind. Setting the glass on the table by the hearth he leaned against it the mantel.

Stephan grinned. "Quit fretting. How many ladies have you known that are on time? They spend hours in front of a mirror."

"Why, Stephan, what a thing to say?" Allison answered grinning. "I think a few more minutes might be necessary," she said her face looking concerned as she lifted her hands to adjust her ribbons. Stephan laughed and moved to her side.

"I was just trying to get Nathan to relax," he said kissing her cheek. "You look like an Angel," he said. Turning to Rae, he smiled. "An Angel and a rose. What more could a man want?" he said giving her a kiss on the cheek as well. Rae turned scarlet as Allison swatted his arm.

"You've still got that suave tongue, I see?"

Stephen's grin widened. "Ah, my dear. You wound me. I meant every word," he stated, taking her arm to leave.

Rae watched them go with a smile on her lips. Turning she lost her smile as Nathan looked at her like she should be on fire. Drawing her brows down in a frown she swallowed.

"Is there something wrong?" she asked lifting her chin.

Nathan's face darkened even more. His wife was beautiful and women like that didn't just fall into a person's lap. She was up to something though he hadn't as yet figured it out. He had been a poor man up until he married which she couldn't know anything about. What did she hope to gain by marrying him? Moving to her side he frowned.

Rae feeling his anger, gave him a glare of her own. "What?"

Nathan growled deep in his throat. "You should have stayed at Brentwood." Was all he said before taking her arm and practically hauling her out of the room.

Chapter 43

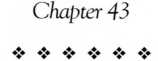

JESSICA STOOD IN THE FOYER her nerves on edge. Had she known it would feel this wrong to get married she would have worked harder to get out of it. Her father was taking his sweet time about getting her to the church too.

"Where the hell is he? We were supposed to be there by now," she snapped lifting her skirt to march into the drawing room. Seeing it empty, she cursed. "Hobkins?" she bellowed heading back to the door. A nervous Betsy followed her. Hobkins arrived looking frazzled.

"Yes, Miss. What is it?"

"Where is Father?"

"He was getting together some papers. He should..."

"I'm here Hobkins. That bellow could have woke the dead. Anxious Jessica?" he asked getting a deep blush on Jessica. "The carriage ready?" He asked Hobkins. "Shall we go then?"

The ten-minute ride to the church was spent in silence. Jessica fidgeted with a length of rope. She worked a knot into it then took it out only to rework the knot again. Brand smiled. "You can't be nervous?" he asked seeing the rope disappear along the side of her leg.

"I'm not nervous. I was just practicing," she snapped looking out the window. "How much longer?"

Brand grinned as the carriage pulled up to the church. The lines of carriages made Jessica pale. Frowning he took her hand. "Relax, Jessica. It's a simple ceremony."

Jessica snorted then frowned. "It doesn't feel right?" she whispered looking at the people file into the little church.

Brand frowned. "Every person that has gotten married experiences the same thing. Trust me, it will all work out in the end."

Jessica scowled and lowered her eyes. "I ended up with an arrogant peacock anyway, didn't I?"

Brand smiled. "He's a bit arrogant but a peacock, I don't think so? I think Lord Sinclair is a fine gentleman and the two of you, once over your differences, will be happy together."

Jessica swallowed near tears. "I don't know if I can stand to see him sail away and leave me behind."

Brand scowled. "I'm sure he won't do that."

Jessica snorted wiping a tear off her cheek. "The arrogant bastard better not," she snapped throwing the door open. Brand hesitated wanting to say more but changed his mind. They would have to work it out between themselves. Stepping out he helped Jessica out as several couples smiled and nodded in their direction.

"At least smile and do your family name proud. Your mother would have wanted that. And for god sakes quit swearing."

Jessica stiffened but pasted on a smile. Knowing she was marrying a man who wanted to kill her was slowly making this the worst day of her life. Taking a deep breath, she relaxed her hold on her father's arm.

MORGAN WATCHED the veiled figure walk gracefully toward him and scowled. She was stunning. She walked with such grace and poise that Morgan wondered if it was a different woman. But seeing the midnight hair fall in soft curls under the veil, he knew it was Jessica. Shifting slightly he waited until they were just about to him then held out his hand. Brand smiled as Jessica hesitated before taking Morgan's hand. Brand nodded to him then moved back amongst his family.

Jessica's legs were shaking worse than they ever had, even in the storms at sea. Looking at the man beside her, she scowled. He had every hair in place; no sweat trickled down the side of his face and his hand was even dry. Swallowing she listened to the priest talk not really catching what he was saying. Soon Morgan was saying his vows to her and she was vowing her love to him. Then the priest announced them man and wife and in set reality. She had actually married a stranger. A stranger that didn't like her.

Morgan lifted the veil over her head and stared into her eyes. Jessica's eyes widened at the look he gave her, then all thought left her as he lowered for the kiss of peace. He gave her a brief smile before turning toward the group of clapping and cheering well wishers. Jessica drew her brows together as she was pulled along beside her husband into the crowd.

She was hugged and kissed by dozens of people before finding herself inside a carriage moving at a steady pace to an unknown destination.

Morgan studied the woman across from him. She was beautiful, he'd give her that. That dark hair was like waves of obsidian. Her eyes, a deep green like the color of grass after a rain, sparkled with every emotion she felt from anger to pain. It was like having a mirror to her soul. Seeing her brows draw together slightly, his lips thinned. What was she thinking now? How to sneak off and never see him again?

"Drink?" he asked holding up a bottle of wine.

Jessica's eyes snapped to his, and then lowered skimming the wine. Shaking her head she returned to look at the things passing by as the carriage moved along at a slow clip.

Morgan frowned then returned the bottle to the basket someone had stuck inside the carriage. "It's been almost twenty minutes."

Jessica frowned. "Twenty minutes?" she asked shaking her head slightly having know idea what he was referring to.

"Well," he said holding his hands out to either side. "Since we've been wed." At her scowl and still confused look, he grinned. "Both of us are still alive."

Jessica paled then scowled. "I did estimate a week, my lord."

Morgan sighed. "My lord, is it? Do you actually know my name?"

Jessica snorted. "Arrogant pissant?" she asked, her eyes wide saucers full of innocence.

Morgan's mouthed thinned. "You know that's wrong."

"Should I try again?" she asked her face turning thoughtful. "I believe someone mentioned it to me but..." she said tapping a gloved finger to her nicely shaped lips.

Morgan's eyes narrowed. He was actually enjoying her game.

"I have it, it's Milton," she stated, beaming with her triumph. Morgan scowled "Wrong again? I know it starts with an M. Martin?" A thinning of his lips and she shook her head like a simpleton. "No, wait a minute." Drumming her fingers on the seat for good measure she nearly burst out laughing at the look on his face. "I have it!" she exclaimed straightening in her seat. "It's Myron," she stated giggling like a tart. Seeing his blue eyes turn black she added another giggle. "That's it, isn't it?"

Morgan growled before pulling the girl from her perch where she ended up between his legs. Jessica gasped at the unexpected move but felt the stirring of what she'd felt in the garden yesterday in the pit of her stomach.

"Myron, is it," he said loosing his anger. Quickly the look of shock on her face slowly turn to confusion and then fear. Moving his eyes to her lips then back to her eyes he kept them there as he lowered his head to brush his lips across hers. He felt her stiffen against his legs then sag against them as he deepened the kiss. Soon swamped with a rush of desire he slid his tongue into her mouth and rubbed it against her tongue sending waves of desire coursing through his blood.

Jessica caught up in the storm of emotions, nearly fell off the seat when her husband of thirty minutes placed her back on her seat and exited the carriage. She stared after him, then felt the heat rise up her face like a torch. Seeing his hand thrust inside the carriage, she hesitated. Several deep breaths and a quick pat to her head, she placed her hand in his and left the carriage.

Morgan, his face unreadable, smiled at the butler to his home. Placing his hat, cloak and gloves in the man's hand, he nodded. Turning to Jessica he removed her cloak as well. "Thank you, Davis," he said. Jessica still a little on edge from what happened in the carriage frowned at the butler, before moving into the foyer. The noise was deafening as people milled around the great house. Having crawled around on the outside of the Baron's home, she scanned the rooms, as she was lead along. The house was magnificent.

Morgan was trying hard to figure out what his body was doing betraying him at this point. He had dissected the incident in the garden and had come to the conclusion that it wasn't going to happen again. He had intended to marry the girl and leave her in Essex and head for Amsterdam. Sailing her ship, no less. The chit had forced her way into his life but he would be damned if he was going to let her change it. Cursing, he finally conceded his body was fighting him as well, which meant coming up with a better plan.

"Lord Sinclair and Lady Sinclair. The bride and groom," the footman announced, as they stood at the top of the stairs overlooking the ballroom. A cheer went up as they descended into the throng.

Chapter 44

MELISSA FELT HER BODY IGNITE everywhere Caleb's body touched her. She swallowed again knowing he was just as aware of her and frowned. "I think, my dear husband, that a spot of fresh air is in order."

Caleb let a slow smile cross his lips. "Fresh air? Are you sure?"

Melissa's eyes snapped to his. Seeing the mischief there, she returned her gaze to the dance floor. Stumbling, she rubbed her hip against his body getting an intake of breath from him. "Excuse me," she said sniffing.

Caleb growled softly. "Fresh air does indeed sound good."

"I've changed my mind," she said smiling at a handsome man near her father.

Caleb picked up the pace and twirled them right out the doors. "As your husband, you have to obey me," he said grabbing her hand and walking steadily toward what looked like a small maze.

Melissa covered her mouth, giggling as they disappeared into the hedge.

Stephan smiled as the pair disappeared out the doors. "I believe Father will have a grandchild sooner than we all expected."

Allison frowned, "Grandchild?"

"Melissa and Caleb. They are about making me sick. The look in Caleb's eyes when he looks at her is close to worship."

Allison laughed then slowly frowned. Leaning slightly into Stephan's side she drew her brows together in thought. They had only been there for four hours but already she was feeling tipsy. Stephan glanced in her direction then grinned. "Is there a problem?"

"I think I'm foxed," she said then giggled. Covering her mouth she gasped. "Now I know I'm foxed. I never giggle," she said, feeling them in her stomach aching to escape between her fingers.

Stephan laughed then quickly looked around to make sure no one was staring at them. Setting his glass on a table he snatched her empty one and put it next to his before leading her onto the dance floor. "They say activity will get rid of it," he said as he twirled her around the floor. Allison giggled again then cursed.

"Well, good lord. A little bit of celebrating and look what happens to me. I'm starting to sound like Melissa and Jessica rolled into one," she snapped but soon let another giggle escape. Stephan was grinning from ear to ear. As they twirled by the beautiful cake Aunt Ginger had worked hours to perfect, Stephan nearly knocked them both flat.

"Ouch, damn it. Those are my feet," Allison said, then laughed.

Smiling to the guest that had heard her, he hurried to move her back around to the cake.

"You are losing your finesse, Stephan. I suggest you refrain from embedding deeply in your cups when you plan on courting yourself a lady. We do tend to like our feet to remain in one piece," Allison paused a moment then covered her mouth. "My god, that sounded remarkably like Christopher."

Stephan grinned before leaning close to her ear. "I don't believe I said anything about being foxed and yes that drivel sounded just like our dear brother but never mind that." Licking his lips, he leaned even closer. "Don't panic, love, but we have a problem."

"A problem?" she blurted.

"Shhhh." he snapped looking around and smiling to the guests that looked at them. "I'm afraid we have a guest that will undoubtedly send the people fleeing in terror."

Allison's brows dropped in confusion then she paled, "Nero?"

"The very same."

"Where is he?"

"I'm afraid that's another problem. It seems your beloved pet has worked his way into the ferns behind the master piece of Aunt Gingers."

"The cake. My god. He'll never stay put. Is he sitting or crouching?"

Stephan wove back and forth until he saw the cat again. Just his head was showing but his feet were placed next to one another. "He's just sitting."

"Hurry then. Get me over there."

"My lord, nice to see you again," Came a feminine voice he recognized. Stephan cursed to himself then glanced at the female. Clearing his throat he smiled.

"Yes, it is. I'm glad you chose to attend," he said kissing her hand. "Lady St. Paul, may I present my sister, Lady Hayworth." As the women exchanged pleasantries, he glanced at Nero and nearly raced in his direction. The cat was perched on one foot, the other lifted in what looked like a position to pounce. Looking back at the Lady St. Paul his mouth fell open. "What the hell is that?" he said turning red the minute the words left his mouth.

Cari laughed. “This is Ranki and he’s my monkey. I brought him back with me from India.”

Andrew who had been her dancing partner scowled at his sister. “She wasn’t supposed to bring it here.” Looking a little concerned he cleared his throat. “It is all right, isn’t it?”

Stephan grinned. “Of course. I’m sure it’s harmless.” The monkey at that moment reached out and pulled Stephan’s hair aside as if looking for fleas. One leg balanced on Stephan’s shoulder while the other foot and the tail were wrapped around Cari’s head.

“Ranki, stop that. You’ll get us kicked out for sure,” she snapped as the monkey returned completely to her shoulder.

Stephan fluffed his hair back in place but gave the monkey a stern look. Spotting Nero in the background moving back and forth on each of his front feet, Stephan grabbed Allison. “Well, by all means, keep the monkey here,” he said absently. “If you’ll excuse us.”

Cari watched them go and frowned. “He didn’t seem to happy today. In fact, he was almost rude.”

Andrew snorted. “If you just had a monkey look through your hair for bugs, what would you do?” he said leaving the dance floor. Cari frowned a moment then smiled.

“You do have a point,” she called hurrying her step to keep up.

JONATHAN STOOD WITH ONE HAND on his wife’s stiff shoulder, as she sat on a chair next to him. Christopher sat right beside them. Since they had arrived neither of the three had danced. “I believe Stephan is getting himself in trouble over there.”

Jonathan looked in the direction Christopher indicated. Both brows went into his hair. “What is that on that girl’s shoulder? Looks like a cat.”

Christopher laughed. “Who knows? Knowing Andrew’s brother it’s probably something very brazen.”

“Why do you say that?”

“Have you been to his office?” At the negative shake, Christopher grinned. “His brother sends him little things. Usually skulls and teeth. The poor sod has to display them somewhere because the brother sends the sister to check. His wife put her foot down on him having them in their house.”

Jonathan frowned. “You’re saying his office is full of skulls and teeth?”

Christopher chuckled. “Exactly. No doubt that bit of fluff, on his arm with the cat perched on her shoulder, is one of those rare gifts.”

“He has a wife?”

“Indeed. But the brother is here to check on his gifts himself this time. He has a devilish sense of humor.”

Jonathan grinned. "Poor sod."

"What has the pair of you smiling?" Nathan asked coming up next to them.

Christopher made exaggerating moves to look for his wife. "Where is your better half?"

Nathan scowled. "I left her with Aunt Ginger."

Jonathan grinned. "Looks like she was pleased with that position," he said nodding toward the dance floor. Nathan turned to look and nearly bit a hole in his tongue. There amongst the throng was his wife looking like a beautiful rose but she was dancing with a thorn.

"Looks like Sheridan knows your wife?" Christopher said seeing the couple talking and Sheridan throwing his dark head back in laughter. Nathan's grip tightened on his glass enough to make the stem snap, sending liquid all over the floor.

"Bloody hell," he snapped, handing the top end to his brother. Moving steadily in her direction Christopher scowled at Nathan's back.

"Of all the stupid things to do," Christopher stated moving out of the way as a footman cleaned up the mess.

"Not so stupid. His wife looks pleased."

"Sheridan doesn't. The man's dangerous."

"Oh, quit worrying. Nathan knows what he's doing."

TAPPING SHERIDAN'S ARM, Nathan removed his wife from the dance. "If you'll excuse us my wife has yet to see the gardens," he said, moving straight out the garden doors. Leading a squirming Rae behind him he dragged her into the maze and pushed her onto the bench. Still not trusting himself to speak he paced back and forth in front of her.

Rae watched her angry husband work the grass into mush. "Is something wrong?" she asked, lifting her chin.

Nathan whirled. Grabbing her chin he pulled her up straight then lowered his head to within inches of hers. "I realize your type can't help themselves but as my wife you will refrain from collecting men. I will not be made a fool of."

Rae felt those words like a knife in the chest. The last few nights she had thought her husband wasn't so bad. Rae had several dreams about her sister drowning, but last night she had dreamed that her sister was alive. The dream had been so vivid. Emily had been gagged, with her hands tied in front of her, while several men bet over who was going to have their turn with her and in what order. It was terrifying and she could feel Emily's fear. She had awakened shaking and drenched in sweat. Turning again to her husband she moved to his room and crawled in bed with him. She had stayed far into the morning hours, before returning to her own bed. But to be called a whore, for dancing with a man, hurt worse than anything else he could have said.

"Your life is now as my wife whether I want it that way or not," he raged moving back to pacing. Seeing her chin lift and the anger forming in her eyes he scowled. "If you can't do as I ask, then you leave me no choice. I will take those brats of yours and send them away." Hurt flashed through her eyes as she paled. "I see you understand. If I catch you again setting your hooks for a tryst, I will send the boys on their way," he finished, letting her chin go and marching from the clearing. Rae sat stunned for a few moments then felt her own anger growing. With a snarl she heaved herself off the bench and took off to tell her husband just where he could go.

Chapter 45

"MY GOD," Stephan said, as Nero pulled his front end up on the table and proceeded to eat the miniature bride and groom. "We're too late. He's eating the cake."

Allison groaned as they reached the cake table. She could hear globs of cake hitting the floor as the crowd screamed and hurried to get away from the area. "Nero, get down!" Allison said.

"He can't hear you," Stephan said, pulling her closer. Allison struggled to the table feeling the edge with her hand. Her slippered feet slipped on icing sending her nearly to her knees. Stephan tried to catch her, only to slip on the slippery stuff pulling both of them to their backsides.

"Bloody hell!" he snapped feeling the pain shoot up his arm from his wrist. "Nero, I'm going to..."

His voice trailed off as the cat in question grabbed his pant leg and began to pull him across the floor. The entire cake toppled from the table to land with a splat, moments before Nero dragged Stephan through it. "Nero!" he bellowed trying to swat the beast. Stephan sucked in a breath as he was pulled under a table and out the other side. His arm hit a leg jarring the hand that was no doubt broke.

Rounding the corner, Stephan shouted for Nero to stop as people pulled their ladies out of the way just in time for the cat to pull him past. Globs of cake smeared the beautiful marble floor.

"Good lord. What's he doing here?" Jonathan snapped grabbing Christopher's arm and hurrying toward the confusion. "He's supposed to be locked up at home."

"Who the hell cares? Let's get him before he completely ruins Jess's party."

Rae moved to Ashley's side just as they departed. "Jonathan?"

"It's all right, Ashley. I'm here. It's Rae, Nathan's wife," she said sitting down as Stephan went scooting by with Jonathan and Christopher chasing behind. Both were slipping and sliding through the icing trail Stephan was leaving behind.

"What's going on? Why is everyone screaming?"

"Allison's cat is here. He's dragging Stephan around by his pant leg," she finished with a giggle as the Lady Wetherton jumped up on a chair just in time to avoid getting bowled over by the passing cat and man. Christopher stopped momentarily to steady her chair before hurrying on his way.

"Help him, Mason," Jessica snapped, at her gapping husband. Morgan glared at her as she grinned giving him a push in Nero's direction. Morgan confused by the feelings her actions caused, followed the crazy procession.

Stephan struggled to get his leg free. It was impossible to keep his hand from harms way when he was being pulled all over the room. Seeing the cake table with Allison clinging to it he shouted for her to help him. She screamed in Nero's direction but the big cat ignored her caught up in the fun. "Nero, you damn thing. Stop this in..." his voice trailed off as a small furry thing landed on his chest jarring the hand. The monkey screeched in his face before placing both small hands over his eyes. "Bloody hell," he roared getting a small hand quickly moved to cover his mouth. Seeing the room through one eye he began to laugh. This was absurd. The ton was going to have a field day with this. Man pulled around his sister's wedding celebration by large tiger while a monkey sat on his chest playing 'no see, no talk' with him.

Nathan poised behind a plant, counted to ten then jumped, landing on the back of Nero as the cat tried to pull Stephan by him. Nero came to a sudden halt dropping Stephen's leg with a clump. "Thank the lord," Stephan said, before the monkey covered his mouth again.

Nero in the mean time not liking that his game had ended, pulled Nathan beneath him and began licking the icing off his face.

The room slowly quieted as the bride and groom worked their way toward the pile of icing covered people. Jonathan and Christopher had skidded to a halt seconds later. Both ending up on their backsides as their feet slipped on the icing. Stephan started laughing sending Christopher into laughter. Soon all four brother's were laughing as the rest of the room went silent.

"Will someone get this animal off..." Stephan's voice was muffled again as the monkey placed both hands over his mouth.

Cari, completely scarlet with embarrassment, moved forward to snatch Ranki off Stephan's chest. "I'm so sorry, my lord. He normally doesn't do that. It looked like such fun, I'm sure he couldn't help himself," she stated getting four pairs of male eyes turned in her direction before all burst into laughter again. Cari hesitantly giggled before laughing with them. Ranki covered her eyes.

Stephan and Jonathan laughed harder as each slowly got to their feet. "I think I broke my bloody hand," Stephan said as Brand, Colan, and Aunt Ginger moved into their circle.

"How many times do I have to tell you, Stephan, this kind of activity is for outside?" Brand said grinning from ear to ear. Stephan laughed.

"I think you should help Nathan there before Nero decides to take him for the same ride I just had."

Brand glanced at the cat and frowned. "Well, good lord, Nero get off him," he said moving to push the cat off Nathan. Nero reluctantly slide off his body rolling to his side, knowing he was in trouble.

Jessica looked at her family still laughing and began to laugh too. Morgan scowled but finally broke into laughter too. Each person was laughing harder as the entire scene played over in their minds. It didn't take long for everyone to join in. Soon the entire room was laughing.

Allison moved toward the sound of their voices nearly tripping over Nero, who sat up so she wouldn't. "Nero, you bad kitty," she stated, still foxed. Nero rolled on his back all four feet in the air.

"He needs a good lesson this time," Stephan said getting those yellow eyes centered on him. "Don't even think about it," he said getting in a few more chuckles. Jessica moved forward to look at his hand. It was beginning to turn purple.

"You need a doctor," she said, not laughing anymore.

"I know. This has been lovely but due to the entertainment I must retire," he said bowing over her hand with a gallant kiss. When he straightened his face was ashen.

"You fool," she snapped taking his arm to lead him to a chair.

"You are newly wed. I will take myself off with Christopher and Allison's help, if you don't mind. The three of us are now inappropriately dressed," Stephan added, shutting his eyes.

Jessica pursed her lips. "I think the whole evening will be cut short," she said as people filed out the front entrance.

Lady Wetherton, with the Duke right beside her, made her way to their side. "Well, introduce us," she snapped at Jessica.

Jessica flushed at the woman's directness. She quickly made the introductions and was pleased to note that her family was supporting her without snubbing the Duchess. They waited for Jessica's cue. The room was now almost completely empty.

"Now you," she stated, looking at Stephan. "You get yourself to a doctor. You look ready to faint." Stephan arched his brows. She sounded vaguely like his mother. "Whose beast is this?"

Allison, who at this point had been trying to slip away unnoticed, stopped in her tracks and straightened. "He belongs to me."

"Why ever would you bring a thing like that to a wedding?" she said her voice echoing off the ceiling.

Allison stiffened. "I didn't bring him with me. He followed us. But as it happens, I can leave your company now that he is here," Allison stated tugging Nero's collar and walking slowly toward the door.

Aunt Athea gapped at the girl. "Well, really!"

Jessica snapped her mouth shut. Allison's rudeness was new but the Duchess was working herself into a snit. "My lady," Jessica said taking the Duchess's hand, "you must understand about Allison," she hesitated looking at her father. Brand nodded as Jessica continued. "Allison is blind. Nero is her companion. He helps her from place to place. He's like her eyes."

Athea's mouth fell open as her head snapped back to the girl gracefully climbing the stairs out of the ballroom. The cat did indeed seem to be steering her clear of obstacles. "Incredible," she said in awe. Morgan moved forward then. "I think, Aunt, that we should leave things as they are for now and retire. It's been entertaining," he said giving the group a glance. Brand chuckled as he helped Nathan to his feet. Melissa and Caleb charged into the room then, both looking rumpled.

"What happened?" Melissa asked skidding to a halt next to Jessica. When Jessica didn't answer, Melissa scowled at her. Seeing Jessica scan her person and raise a brow, Melissa blushed clean to the roots of her hair. "We were lost in the damn maze," she said as if that explained her stained gown and tousled hair. Caleb looked sheepish, giving the staring family a weak smile.

"We heard the carriages leaving and thought maybe someone died."

Jessica snorted. "Not yet," she said under her breath looking at Morgan, who scowled. "You missed some damn good entertainment."

Melissa slowly turned back to her normal color, "What entertainment?"

"Nero arrived and demolished the place," Jonathan said grinning in Stephan's direction. "Then proceeded to drag Stephan around by his breeches."

Everyone tried to hold it in but at Stephan's disgruntled look everyone burst back into laughter. "Fine. By this time tomorrow it will be all over London anyway," he snapped marching from the hall. Jonathan took his wife's arm and nodded his farewells to the family before dashing after his fuming brother. Ashley was barely able to keep up.

Melissa frowned, "Are you joking?"

Jessica chuckled. "No. Nero really pulled Stephan all over the ballroom. People scattered in every direction until Nathan finally jumped on Nero and forced him to stop."

Melissa looked at Nathan who grinned. "For once I did something good."

Brand snorted. "It's a wonder you aren't in worse shape. That cat has always been trouble," he said giving Colan a glare.

Colan held up his hands "I only gave him to her as a gift. I can't be held responsible for the baby she turned him into."

The Duchess followed the conversation in stunned disbelief. "That's all you have to say about the ruination of my nephews wedding celebration."

"Aunt..."

"It wasn't like it ruined anyone's reputation. Allison is the only one who will suffer for what happened tonight."

Brand frowned at Christopher's words. That was true. Tomorrow by noon everyone will know she is blind and worse, that she has a tiger for a pet. "Damn," he stated running a hand through his hair, "I'm too old for this."

"Exactly. That's why I'm the one shouldering these problems," Christopher stated moving to give the ladies a peck on the cheek. "I'm off to prepare," he stated bowing to the Duchess, he turned in a graceful move to mount the stairs and disappear from sight.

Brand nodded his agreement. "I'm sorry, Jessica. It's a shame things went as they did but it's pointless to stay. We'll have to have a dinner party and celebrate in private," he said, taking Aunt Ginger's arm to lead her from the ballroom, Colan close on his heels. Nathan took his own wife's hand and followed their lead. Melissa laughed.

"It would have to happen this way. I miss all the exciting things," she said taking her husband's arm.

"The most exciting things, huh?" Caleb said getting a deep blush from her. As they reached the stairs, Jessica distinctly heard giggles.

"That's disgusting, isn't it?" she said quietly to her husband. "Thank god we aren't in that position," she finished watching the door close behind the last of their guests. The Duchess marched into the drawing room. Jessica scowled but followed her. Morgan poured the Duchess some port as Jessica seated herself stiffly at the opposite end of the sofa.

Lady Athea took a sip from the glass then cleared her throat. "As usual Morgan, things could have gone better."

Morgan choked on his brandy wiping the dripping mess off his chin. "Me! She's the one with the atrocious family."

Jessica snapped instantly to her feet. "You leave my family out of this. They are not responsible!"

Morgan smiled coldly. "Your family does own that cat?"

Jessica flushed. "Allison didn't intentionally bring Nero here."

Morgan shrugged. Aunt Athea scowled at the two of them. "It doesn't really matter. What does matter is the fact that by noon tomorrow the whole of London will be whispering about the incident."

Jessica paled then sagged in her seat. "My god, Allison will never leave the house."

Morgan stiffened. "Why ever not? She didn't drag Stephan around by his leg, her tiger did."

Jessica glared at him. "It will take those gossip mongers longer to fix their hair than it will for them to discover Allison is blind. They'll run her through the ringer," she snapped getting to her feet to pace. Morgan watched her admiring her sweet derriere. Cursing he told his body to forget it. She was a spiteful, conceded woman, who forced him into marriage. She wasn't going to get away with that.

"Perhaps your sister can retire to the country," Athea stated getting stunned looks from both people.

"And show the snobs of society that they broke her? No way. Even if I have to drag her around myself, I'm not letting her hide. She'd die from the confinement," Jessica snapped. "Now, if you'll excuse me, I have things to see to before tomorrow," she finished tipping her head politely to the Duchess before exiting.

"I can't believe it. No wonder the other one was just as rude. It runs in the family."

Morgan scowled. For some reason that comment bothered him. "Aunt, if you have nothing nice to say about my wife, then I, too, will retire."

Athea clamped her mouth shut. "Well, they ruined the party. I'll be the laughing stock of the season."

Morgan laughed. "I highly doubt people are going to laugh at the Duchess of Wetherton. You, my dear lady, are a formidable dragon."

Athea puffed up. "You're absolutely right. They will take it out on the girl like your wife suggested."

Morgan scowled. Allison seemed like a pleasant enough sort and probably didn't deserve to be publicly humiliated. "Aunt, you don't plan on humiliating the girl, do you?"

Athea got to her feet. "And bring shame on this family more than you already have, I think not. I will conduct myself as I always do," she finished marching from the room. Morgan shook his head. At least Allison would have one person on her side that ranked high in the ton. Running a hand through his hair, he looked up at the ceiling. The brandy was making him aware that this was his wedding night. Planning to leave the chit a virgin and sail for the far reaches of the sea was one thing, but actually following through with the plan was becoming another matter. Cursing his stupid body, he drained his glass and poured himself another. Looking into the amber liquid, he envisioned his lean muscled wife letting her ebony hair loose as she stepped out of her gown revealing a body meant to be worshiped. Cursing, he set the glass down. He definitely was going to have to come up with a different plan. A plan that didn't include leaving his wife a virgin.

STEPHAN SANK INTO THE COACH SEAT next to Allison, shifting slightly as Ashley and Jonathan slipped into the seat across from them. Nero slunk in onto the floor. Jonathan barked out an order and the coach lurched into motion. Clenching his teeth against the pain Stephan gave Nero a murderous look, "Does he have to ride in here? I've seen enough of him to last me for years."

Allison blushed. "Nathan wouldn't take him."

"That rotten sod," Stephan said getting a soft mew from Nero. "Oh, forget it, you ungrateful beast. It will take a great amount of heel kissing to get back in my good graces."

Nero shook his head then turned to watch passing scenery. Stephan huffed. Seeing Jonathan grinning, Stephan scowled. "As it happens, the evening wasn't a total loss."

Jonathan looked skeptical. "Now, what are you up too?"

"I found her."

"Found who?" Allison asked.

Jonathan grinned. "You haven't told her?"

Stephan scowled. "I was planning on it this evening but Nero changed my plans." The cat shifted feet giving Stephan a look over his shoulder before returning his gaze to look out the window. "But I found the perfect lady."

Allison frowned. "If I was supposed to know something about what you're talking about, would you mind telling me now?"

"By all means, fill her in," Jonathan stated waving a hand in Allison's direction. Ashley sat stiff just listening to the conversation.

"Jonathan and I..."

"I only plan to participate if everyone agrees. That means Melissa and Jessica, also."

"Would you let me tell her?" Stephan snapped. Jonathan just grinned. "We have decided to find Christopher a wife."

"You what?" Allison stated incredulous. "Christopher will kill you. He's going to run an add and except some mousy woman who will kiss his boots in appreciation for allowing her to marry him. What could you possible be thinking?"

Stephan grinned. "That's just it. I want to make sure he has an angel on the outside but someone who can't help but get in trouble. He needs someone to make his life interesting."

Allison bit her lip. "When you put it that way, it doesn't sound so bad."

Jonathan snorted in shock. "You're actually considering him?"

Allison frowned. "Weren't you?"

"No, damn it. I didn't like getting forced to marry anymore than anyone else would but the worst of it was not getting to choose my bride." Once the words were out he could have kicked himself. Forgetting his wife was in the carriage he cursed as she moved away from him. He could clearly see tears glistening in her eyes. "Bloody hell. I didn't mean that the way it..."

"Never mind," she said in a quiet firm voice. He watched her swallow several times but she seemed in control of her tears now. Jonathan gave Stephan a glare.

Allison frowned at the silence. "Well, who is she?"

Stephan scowled. Allison was aware of the tension but was ignoring it. "She's Andrew's sister, Lady Cari St. Paul."

"The monkey lady?" Allison squealed.

Stephan grinned, as Jonathan looked in his direction "You've completely lost your mind."

Stephan just kept grinning. "Just think about it. She's nice to look at, seems educated, and has social manners." At his still skeptical look and Allison's deep scowl, he added, "She smells nice."

Jonathan snorted. "What does that have to do with anything?"

Stephan shrugged. "I'd rather have them smelling like roses than cow dung."

Allison slapped his arm. "You're despicable."

"So you agree."

Allison slowly smiled. "I think it would do Christopher some good to have chaos added to his life."

"You're insane. That young lady is trouble with a capital T."

Ashley sniffed. "Why do you want to get him a wife to begin with? Is he deformed or something?"

All three gaped in her direction. Christopher was stunningly handsome. He was six foot four, blond haired, and green eyed. Thirty years old with a body as hard as nails. "On the contrary, Christopher is something to look at," Stephan said answering her question. "As to finding him a wife, well, let's just say our brother isn't too swift in that department. He will more than likely go about finding himself a wife by interviewing women, like it was a job."

Ashley gasped. Jonathan scowled. "He's joking. Though, Christopher probably has thought about it. In reality, Christopher will attend several of the debuts then systematically select himself the perfect wife."

"Like I said earlier, she'll be some mouse with worship tendencies toward Christopher the God."

Stephan laughed then sucked in his breath as the carriage halted, jarring his hand. "Bloody hell," he said, then flushed at the scowl on Ashley's face. "Pardon the language."

Allison pursed her lips. "Let's get you inside. I'm sure the doctor will be here by now."

"That's if Nathan did like he was told," Jonathan added helping Stephan out, then each lady after that. "I still think you're insane to consider messing in Christopher's business."

Stephan paused stopping Allison in her tracks. "If we go ahead with it, are you in?"

Jonathan grinned. "Of course," he answered sending Stephan up the steps chuckling.

NATHAN SCOWLED INTO THE DARKNESS through his carriage window. The doctor had been easy to locate and was now on his way to Ginger's house to meet up with Stephan. Shifting his leg he accidentally brushed his wife's leg causing her to snap the limb out of reach like he'd scorched her. Gritting his teeth he tried to think of other things but the image of her smiling up at Sheridan's face was enough to send him into a rage. It was just the thing Saul Sheridan would love to do. Cockhold him. They had been friends a long time back but Saul had turned to the darker vices of life and Nathan wanted no part of them. Saul was no gentlemen and Nathan wanted his wife to know from the start, Nathan wasn't going to tolerate infidelity, especially with the likes of Saul Sheridan.

"So tell me, what was the plan for this evening?"

Rae stiffened at Nathan's tone of voice. He was calling her a whore again. "Why do you insist on calling me a whore?"

Nathan's mouth lifted in a satanic smile as he turned his head to stare at her. "Is that not what you are? The boys are results?"

Rae sat stiff, barely able to control herself. "Sean and Ian our legitimate children. Their father was husband and father to us."

Nathan scowled at her. "Then you never sold yourself for survival."

Rae flushed. Once she had almost been desperate enough to do just that and in fact had made the deal only to slip out of the room when the man passed out from too much drink. She had kept the money.

Nathan's eyes narrowed. "I repeat, what was your plan for this evening?"

Rae ground her teeth. "I was forced to attend a ball to which I had no interest in going with a man who despises me, no less. I had no plans for the evening," she sneered.

Nathan's lip curled. "It doesn't feel good to be forced, does it?"

Rae's blush deepened. "I didn't force you."

Nathan snorted in disbelief. "I suppose I was willing to pledge myself to a complete stranger. A thief, no less." At her pale look, he grinned. "Oh, yes, sweetheart. I know exactly who you are. That little scene in the woods nearly got you killed."

Rae lifted her chin. "I repaid you for your help."

Nathan turned fully to face her. "Repaid me! You knocked me senseless then hauled me off to the nearest priest. You call that repayment?"

Rae lowered her gaze. "I hadn't planned to do that."

Nathan took a deep breath. He wanted answers and getting irate wasn't going to get them. "What did you have planned?" he asked calmly.

Rae narrowed her eyes warily watching her husband. He was a dangerous man when angry. She knew that just from the way his body moved beneath his clothes. "I had intended to help you get away. But seeing you senseless, I choose to rob you instead." Nathan growled but Rae hurried on, wanting all of it out. "But when you didn't revive I felt guilty and couldn't just leave you there. Who knows what could have happened to you?" "How kind of you," he said, sneering. "I suppose that was when you decided to suck the poor sap for all he was worth?"

Rae blushed with anger. "It wasn't like that. I had the boys to consider."

Nathan turned his attention to the darkness, completely ignoring her. The boys were pathetic looking. Neither child had color worth mentioning and the youngest one was skinnier than a fence post. At least on that point, he had to acknowledge that she was desperate. But to go as far as forcing marriage, that was unforgivable.

"What do you intend to do with me?"

"Dump you off in some far off hovel and act like you don't exist. What else?"

Rae paled at those words. He had every right to do that and the bitterness in his voice made her believe it. Looking at her lap she felt the urge to cry and steeled herself against it. Her husband was definitely one not to like tears, yet she felt the overwhelming need to shed a few now. Looking at his angry profile, she frowned. He was a handsome man, all dark and mysterious. She frowned, realizing for the first time, that she didn't really know her husband. He was connected to a large family but that was all she knew.

"What are you staring at?" he snapped, glaring at her.

"Nothing," she said, scowling.

"Then look at nothing out the window," he snapped. The carriage moved along the street to Ginger's home, in which he dreaded having to spend another night with his insufferable brothers. But traipsing off to Brentwood at this late hour would probably get them robbed. Snorting to himself, he pictured his wife jumping out of the carriage brandishing a pistol telling the robbers to just try it. Shaking the image away he exited the carriage and entered the house leaving his wife to fend for herself.

MELISSA SNUGGLED UP against her husband's shoulder and felt herself drifting off to sleep. Their stolen moments in the maze had been so exciting she could hardly keep the smile off her face. Caleb felt his wife sigh and snuggle closer and smiled. He was a lucky man. Forcing a woman to marry the way he had and ending up with a person so special it made his heart ache thinking of her. How he had ever lived without her he didn't know. Pulling her close he frowned when they pulled up to his townhouse.

"We're home, love."

Melissa smiled. "Do we have to go in?"

Caleb chuckled. "I think Anges would have a heart attack if we rocked the coach for the next several hours."

Melissa turned scarlet sitting up to slap her husband in the chest. "You're despicable."

Caleb grinned, holding his hands up to protect himself. "I was only stating what I planned for the evening."

Melissa still red, let a slow smile cross her face. "It does have merit."

Caleb's smile flattened some at the flash of passion crossing his wife's face. Leaning forward he captured her lips in a kiss full of promise.

The carriage door opened and both occupants turned to stare at the rude attendant. Melissa flushed scarlet when she saw Keegan standing there. "Excuse the intrusion but it can't wait."

"What's wrong?" Caleb asked, exiting the carriage then helping Melissa out.

Keegan smiled grimly. "I'm afraid I didn't know where else to turn."

Caleb studied his brother then took his wife's arm. "Let's go into the library and talk about whatever is bothering you."

Keegan nodded. "Niles wasn't home.

Caleb frowned at his brother as Wyatt opened the door for them. Handing the man their cloaks and things, he led his brother to the library. "If you'll wait while I take Melissa up, I'll return in..."

"If you don't mind, I would like her to stay."

Melissa arched both brows at that request. She hadn't exactly forgiven Keegan for his hand in the deception. Caleb looked at her but nodded to Keegan.

"All right. Wyatt, bring us some tea and cakes," Melissa said moving to sit in one of the high backed chairs by the fire. Caleb got his brother a drink.

"Let's hear it," Caleb said.

Keegan ran a hand through his hair. "It's Donavan."

Caleb straightened. "What happened?"

Keegan waved a hand. "He's fine. It's Father. He wants him to marry. Caleb cursed. "Angela?"

Keegan looked at him blankly then shook his head "No, Father planned on marrying her off to Andrew but the lad hopped on a ship and can't be found. "Smart man."

Keegan nodded his agreement. "No, it seems Father has been busy lately."

"Who does he have in mind?"

Keegan paused waiting long enough for Wyatt to place the tray before Melissa and depart before continuing. Looking at her, he turned his gaze to the fire. "Melissa's sister, Lady Allison."

Melissa gasped spilling tea all over the table. Setting the pot down she quickly shoved a few napkins on the spill, her mind locked on Keegan's words. "Allison? But why?"

"For her dowry."

Melissa frowned. "I don't understand"

"Correct me if I'm wrong but I believe your sister comes with a sizable money portion but also has land with her?"

Melissa flushed at the way he'd stated that, but nodded her head. "Yes, she has land. The same as Jessica and me."

"Her land is near Blyth?"

"You have land?" Caleb asked, stunned.

Melissa scowled at her husband. "I believe Allison's land is near Blyth, but I still don't understand."

Caleb did. It was a port to the sea. "Blyth has access to the sea."

Melissa paled. "He wants your brother to marry my sister for her land?"

Caleb frowned but Keegan stared into the fire. "He doesn't care that people are involved, all he wants is a northern port." Turning to Caleb he sighed. "He knows about Matherson too." Caleb cursed. "The bastard."

Melissa stood. "You're not going to let him get away with this are you?"

Caleb arched his brows. "Exactly what do you expect me to do about it?"

"I don't know but you can't let him ruin Allison's life."

"Now hold on a minute. Donavan is a fine man. Your sister wouldn't want for anything." Caleb stated.

"She's blind remember. Would your Donavan be able to handle that?"

Caleb flushed. He'd forgot that little fact completely.

Keegan frowned. "Your sister's blind."

Melissa paled. "You must promise not to tell anyone. She would never forgive me."

Keegan nodded. "You have my word."

Melissa narrowed her eyes. "If you fail to keep that promise I'll hire someone to see that you regret that decision."

Keegan stared at her with brows arched then turned to look at Caleb. He was grinning from ear to ear. "A bit vicious isn't she?"

"So, it would seem."

Melissa reddened but lifted her chin. "Trust me. I know where to find men who would do that sort of thing for nothing."

Keegan smiled a lopsided grin. "There won't be a need."

Melissa nodded lifting her cup to take a sip. "So what have you come up with?"

Caleb frowned. "I think more than two minutes is required in this case."

Melissa reddened but didn't look away. She held her husband's gaze. Caleb was struck with a bolt of desire so powerful he felt like throwing his brother out on his ear and taking his wife were she sat. Shifting, he dragged his gaze away from her. "I'll talk with you tomorrow on this." At Keegan's nod he added, "You're welcome to stay here."

Keegan shook his head. "I need to find out exactly what Father intends to do and home is where I'll get that information. Besides, Donavan is still two days ride from home."

"Took off like a shot out of hell, didn't he?"

"Angela isn't exactly what one wants in a wife," Keegan said grimly.

"You don't have to tell me about it. I found a wife that satisfies me," he stated getting a deep blush out of Melissa. Keegan laughed and let himself out. "Well, wife, let's carry on where we left off."

"What about Allison?"

"Let's sleep on it."

Melissa stood and moved to her husband's side. Licking her lips slowly she smiled as his eyes followed her tongue. "Sleep?"

Caleb growled scooping her up in his arms and running up the stairs. Melissa giggled the entire way.

CHRISTOPHER HEARD VOICES in the drawing room and headed in that direction. He frowned, thinking of all the papers on his desk. Things had gone from organized with minimum attention to frantic chaos. He had several deals to finish and at least six men to visit. He was even behind on a report for Andrew. Shaking his head, he walked into the room and arched his brows. "Do you enjoy having that icing all over you?" he asked noting that all three of his siblings were still coated in cake.

Jonathan turned at his voice and grinned. "Unlike you, old man. Some of us have mates to attend to."

Christopher scowled. "How is your arm?"

Stephan frowned. The laudanum the doctor had given him was just starting to work. "It's broke, thank you."

Christopher arched a brow. "Shouldn't he be in bed?"

Allison pursed her lips. "I've been trying to tell him that for the last fifteen minutes but he seems to think he needs to sit and chat."

Stephan smiled, slowly resting his head on the back of the sofa. The rest of him was stretched out in front of the sofa. "I think a nice bath wouldn't be remiss."

Allison frowned. "If you promise to keep that hand dry."

"I promise."

"Come on then," she said, helping him to his feet. "You're such a baby,"

Stephan hissed air as his arm was jarred.

"You're all heart," he whined. "Do you think you could get me something to rest this on while I sleep?"

Allison shook her head. "Like I said, a baby. Come on."

Christopher smiled as they departed the room. "Has she mentioned any suitors calling?"

Jonathan frowned. "I don't think that's going to happen after tonight."

Christopher frowned. "Why not?"

"Everyone will know she's blind and if that doesn't scare them off. Nero will."

Ashley tensed as he spoke. Jonathan had treated her with such care for the last week and she honestly had liked the attention, but she wasn't stupid. She knew he regretted being married to a blind person, especially one like her. She couldn't dress herself without assistance, barely could eat, and needed help getting around. Getting to her feet she moved in the direction of the window. Moving slowly forward she felt a hard surface along the side of her right leg. She desperately wanted to hold her hands out in front of her but was determined not to do that. Feeling the temperature change she knew the window was close. Holding out her hand she touched the glass and smiled. It felt cold and wet. Leaning her forehead against it, she imagined what the street looked like below.

"Ashley?" she jumped as someone touched her arm. Lifting her head she turned it slightly. "Would you like to retire?" Jonathan asked.

Lowering her head, she nodded. Jonathan took her arm and wrapped it around his own. Moving toward the hall he called a good night to his brother as they disappeared out the door.

Christopher frowned watching them go. Ashley was a beautiful woman and Jonathan was going to have himself a fine lady someday. Taking a seat on the sofa he stretched his legs out and casually sipped his brandy. He had just over four months to find his own wife. How the hell was he supposed to find one? His brothers had been lucky. Both had found beautiful women amongst the rabble. He looked into his glass and frowned. Every woman he met at the ball tonight was overly concerned with fashion and gossip: two things he knew little about. Granted, he liked to look good but he trusted his valet to dress him appropriately. He had the man buy his clothes for him so he wouldn't have to bother with it himself. The young ladies and their mothers wanted rich husbands, as well. Scowling, he wondered how he should handle the situation. He had been collecting women's names that he thought possible as a wife. He then slowly gathered information on them. Taking a swallow he leaned his head back on the sofa. Only two women came even close to what he was looking for and both of them were heading for the discard pile fast.

The first candidate was the lady Linwood, Ana Lionard. She was tall and graceful but she was brazen and outspoken. He wanted a meek wife, who would be the proper hostess and know her place. The second candidate, was Mary Stetson the only daughter of the Earl of Bentley. She was shorter with dark hair and eyes that could make an angel weep but the woman was vain. She spent hours talking about herself and Christopher feared a woman like that would drive him to drink.

Running a hand through his hair he swallowed the rest of his drink and stared at the ceiling.

"I see the icing came off," Brand said stepping into the library.

Looking up, Christopher smiled. "I thought you'd retired?"

Brand shrugged. "I thought about it. How's Stephan doing?"

"He broke his hand."

"Broke?"

"Yes. Just above the thumb. Doc says he can't sail."

Brand arched his brows. "The lad must be fuming about that one."

Christopher laughed. "The last I saw him he was acting the silly fop from the laudanum the doctor gave him."

Brand nodded. "How are things with you?"

Christopher frowned. "Your estates are a mess. I have twenty different things going at once." Seeing his father's concerned look he quickly added, "But now that the wedding is over and things are back to normal, I think I'll have things back in order by the end of the week."

Brand smiled. "Of course," he said, knowing Christopher exaggerated the word mess. He probably had a report late to Andrew.

Christopher studied his father then frowned. "Why are you really here?"

Brand smiled again. "You do know me well, don't you? The fact is, I'm concerned about Allison."

Christopher scowled. He was too, but he wasn't telling his father that. "Well, don't be. By the end of the week I'll have things in order and devote my time to taking Allison to the things a young lady attends when coming out for her first season. She'll be a hit."

Brands frown deepened. "They'll know she's blind now."

Christopher lowered his head back to the sofa. "I know," he stated, looking at the ceiling full of Angels. "But we all knew it was bound to come out."

"I think your sister is going to hide away in her room after tonight."

Christopher sat up. "Why do you say that?"

"She looked deflated when she walked out of that ball. Society can be so damn cruel. That's the reason I quit going."

Christopher frowned. "She's made of sterner stuff than that."

"I don't know," Brand said, shaking his head.

Christopher got to his feet. "I'll help her. Don't worry."

Brand looked at his oldest son and frowned in concern. Christopher handled everything like a business. Allison had a heart to consider. "I think you should enlist Aunt Ginger's help."

Christopher turned to stare at his father. "What do you mean, again?"

"She's leaving tomorrow with Colan and myself."

"She can't do that! I don't know the first thing about sending a girl off into the ton. They'll eat us alive."

Brand arched a brow at his son. "You sound like you're scared?"

Christopher humphed. "I'm not scared I just don't want to ruin Allison's already fragile chance."

Brand nodded his agreement. "I suggest you put 'winning Aunt Ginger over' first on your list."

"What happened?"

"After tonight, she says she'll never be able to hold her head up properly in society."

Christopher frowned, "She's deserting us?"

"In a matter of speaking, yes. She claims to be too old for such scandal."

Christopher resumed his seat. "I'll talk with her tomorrow."

"Colan said we were leaving by three o'clock."

Christopher nodded.

Brand hesitated, wanting to tell his son that everything would work out but he hadn't the slightest idea how. "Good night, then."

"Night," Christopher said watching the Angels above frolicking in the clouds. Life sure was full of surprises.

Chapter 46

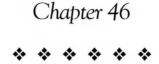

JESSICA MOVED around her room preparing for bed. She had dismissed the maid after letting the girl unbutton all the small buttons down her back. Pulling the gown off she threw all the female trappings that went with it in a heap by the wardrobe then tossed the shoes on top. If she could help it, she wasn't about to wear those blasted clothes again. Sinking into one of the high backed chairs she poured herself a brandy. Sipping the amber liquid a slow smile crossed her face at the picture of Stephan being dragged around her wedding by his pants. She chuckled sipping more of the fluid. Thanks to Stephan, she didn't have to dance with all those men wanting to salute the bride. She had actually made out rather well. She slowly lost her smile at the thought of her groom. The man was a puzzle. Not only had he been exceptionally polite to her but that smile during the ceremony had been so unexpected she had actually felt a stirring in her belly. Snorting at the thought she finished her brandy and bent to remove her stockings. Bringing one foot up on the chest under the window she nearly jumped out of her skin when Morgan spoke.

"You sure hide that well."

Jessica snapped up straight, paling some. "What are you doing in here?"

"Now is that any way to greet your husband?" he asked, moving into the room and closing the door. "I would have thought something more along the lines of 'what took you so long' would be better."

Jessica snorted and resumed pulling off her stockings. "Forget it, Melvin. We both know ours is not a proper marriage."

Morgan's face hardened at her words. How dare she turn the tables on him. He was the one that was going to leave her alone on her wedding night not vice versa. "Melvin?"

Jessica smiled. A very simple, very pleasant smile making Morgan's blood heat. Cursing, he glared at her, "Am I wrong, again?"

Morgan relaxed his stance. Two could play this game. "My name will come to you in time, I'm sure."

Jessica, dressed in a filmy shift, snatched the robe off the end of the bed and slipped it on. "Exactly what are you in here for?"

Morgan arched a brow. "No one told you about what happens between a man and a woman?"

Jessica stiffened and slowly turned to face him. "You don't expect..."

Her voice trailed off and Morgan nearly crowed his success. The woman was so easy to bait. "Of course. You didn't think I married you…" he hesitated. "What? In name only?" Seeing her pale, he laughed. "I'm afraid that's not possible. I'm to sire an heir, after all."

Jessica turned scarlet. "I see," she said swallowing as the fact that she was in way over her head sank in. "I think we should postpone that sort of thing, until we have a chance to...to like one another."

Morgan scowled. "You don't like me?" he asked sarcastically moving toward her slowly.

Jessica moved to put the table and chairs between them. Her mind was whirling from the brandy she'd drunk and the sight of her husband removing his clothes piece by slow piece. "I think you're well aware of what we feel for each other."

Morgan nodded, "Lust."

Jessica reddened further. "I don't lust after you," she snapped picking up her glass from the desk to refill it.

Morgan watched with eyebrows raised. "You drink that?" he asked watching her nearly drain the glass and pour more.

Jessica grinned never letting her eyes leave him for a moment. His jacket and cravat were laying in a pile on the floor, his boots beside them. His shirt was unbuttoned nearly to his middle and he was presently working his belt loose. "Of course you would. Most women such as yourself do."

Jessica's gaze narrowed. "And what kind of women are those?"

"Women who want to be men, of course."

Jessica gasped at that absurd remark. "Men!" she snapped her temper doubling. "If I had wanted to be an arrogant domineering pissant, I'm sure I would have been born male."

Morgan stiffened at that remark. She had already called him that earlier. "I think, dear wife," he said, stressing that word, "that you have a need to have your mouth cleaned."

Jessica reddened but her anger was running hot. "I think, you popinjay, that you should leave if my mouth offends you."

Morgan glared at her no longer liking the names she was calling him. He wasn't arrogant and a popinjay? Ha. Moving toward her, dropping his shirt as he went, Morgan smiled. It was a smile he used with his crew. "Enough pleasantries, I think. Jessica ducked away from him but he snagged her robe. Slipping her arms from the stupid thing she grabbed up the first weapon she came across. The candlestick from her desk but the stick was heavier than she thought and she ended up with a foot long candle instead. Holding the ridiculous weapon in front of her to defend herself she ground her teeth at his amused look. Jabbing the thing at his face, she watched him duck and noticed, with her own look of triumph, that his amusement was gone.

"It will go easier for you if you move quietly to the bed and let me have what I want."

Jessica paled. "I think not."

Morgan leaped for her getting the candle jabbed in his middle. Feeling the thing crumble in her hand, Jessica squealed as Morgan pulled her to the bed and straddled her. "You choose..." he didn't finish his sentence as she bucked and knocked him off. Morgan grabbed at the nightstand to keep from falling all the way to the floor but the thing tipped sending the vase of flowers and the other small contents flying to the floor. Jessica covered her mouth as silence descended in the room. Her husband's hand was all she could see and it wasn't moving. Cursing, she felt a moment of panic. What if she'd killed him? What if he'd hit his head and broke his neck? Swallowing, she tried to see her husband's face but nothing came into view.

Licking her lips, she swallowed. "Maynard?" she called, hoping to make him rise in furry rather than lay there dead. When his hand didn't so much as twitch, she frowned. "Bloody hell," she snapped, moving to the edge of the bed. Looking down at the mess on the floor she screamed when Morgan pulled her into a heap on top of his chest.

"Maynard?" he stated, pulling her beneath him to kiss her firmly on the lips. She stiffened as he expected but he turned on the charm. All that arguing with her wearing that transparent gown had ruined his last hope for leaving her a virgin while he sailed off in her ship. He deepened his kiss until he felt her respond. He slipped his tongue into play getting a passionate response that surprised him. Her tongue played a war of its own. Morgan moved his hands along her back and down to grab her buttocks. Noting the entire way how firm and lean her body was. She responded, unknowingly he was sure, by rubbing against him causing his nether regions to rise in stiff attendance.

As their barrier of clothes was removed and they lay together skin to skin, Morgan felt guilt rise. She didn't warrant his guilt but every form of his being demanded he let her decide. Pulling his mouth away, he looked into her face waiting for her an answer.

Jessica, still thoroughly excited, didn't know what to do. All she knew was she liked what they were doing and didn't want it to stop. Not being one to back down she slowly got to her feet.

Morgan pursed his lips at her approaching denial. He watched her stand over him, his mouth dropping open in surprise as she held out a hand to him. Unsure of her actions he got to his feet taking her hand once there. Jessica licked her lips slowly watching his eyes follow her tongue. He was magnificent.

His body was all lean and muscled. He didn't have an ounce of fat anywhere.

Morgan couldn't believe his eyes. His wife, of six hours, was standing before him wearing nothing but a ribbon in her hair as she boldly searched his body with her eyes. Feeling his desire increase, he grabbed her by the arms and lifted her to the bed. She smiled slightly accepting his kiss as they once again were caught up in their new passion.

Jessica felt a desire for the unknown burn deep in her belly and knew she would rather die than go without it. Moving her body along his she arched into his hands as they roamed along her body all the while his mouth was steadily keeping hers busy.

Morgan couldn't control his desire any longer and knew he was taking her quicker than he normally would but her freely given response was so unexpected that it fueled his passion to new heights. Moving between her legs he steadied himself easing into her slowly, kissing her lips, his tongue delved deep in her mouth.

Jessica felt the pressure between her legs and welcomed it. She opened her legs wider to accommodate him, surprising him further. He felt the barrier in a woman far to passionate to still have that in tact and steeled himself to break through. Kissing a trail to her breasts he kissed and suckled each globe until they were hard with passion. Plunging into her in one clean stroke he felt her stiffen a moment then heard her moan as he continued to suckle her breasts. Returning to her mouth with his own he began to move within her and her response was overwhelming. She bucked and made keening noises deep in her throat driving him mad with desire. Feeling her tighten around him and her nails sink into his back he gave himself up to his own release. Pumping into her with long hard strokes until he stiffened with a groan of release. Collapsing on her to catch his breath he noted she was sweaty and breathing as hard as he was. Moving to his side he pulled her with him.

As his breathing slowed, he leaned over her a moment and stared at her in surprise. She had been more passionate than any woman he had ever bedded, and that wasn't a small number.

Jessica felt self conscious, at his close scrutiny, and began to feel like she had done something wrong. No one had told her what it was like and she had never asked. She had just let her feelings and her body do what it wanted. As he just stared at her, not moving or saying anything, she felt her anger coming back.

Morgan saw her eyes darken to jade and knew she was getting angry but to tell the truth he didn't know what to say to her. Smiling slightly he pushed her to her side and pulled her back up against his front. "We need to rest," he said.

Jessica felt her anger leave and she smiled slightly as his arms began to relax. He must have expected her to fight him she drew her brows together, in wonder, confused at what they had just shared. For someone she hated, she sure felt pretty good inside.

Chapter 47

NATHAN AWOKE WITH A START, hearing the door to his wife's room open and the soft patter of footsteps come toward his bed. He lay still and concentrated on breathing like a person asleep as his wife looked into his face. Letting out the breath he had been holding, he watched her through slits as she moved to the other side of the bed and crawled in. He had purposely left the blankets, so she could pull them over herself. He waited for her to settle before relaxing. She had been coming to his room every night since they had been away from the boys and he wondered at it. She came crying and shaking and he knew she was having bad dreams. Feeling the bed shake with her silent sobs he cursed himself for feeling something for her. She was a thief and a liar and she had ruined his life but something about her silent sobs caused tender feelings to surface. Rolling over in his sleep he casually pulled her into his arms and up against his body, snoring to make it seem like he was sleeping.

Rae stiffened feeling Nathan's arms come around her and then panicked. She didn't want him to know she was there. So far she had managed to stay away from him but it was cold in his room and tonight with the covers available she had slipped under them, a mistake she now knew.

Nathan felt her slowly relax and frowned in confusion at the way this felt. Oh, he had been with several women before but never overnight and never to just lie in bed and hold them. Hearing her breathing change to that of sleep he frowned into the night. She was having bad dreams. What about? He had again yelled at her this evening. Was she having dreams because of his foul temper? Shaking his head he relaxed, enjoying the feel of her in his arms.

"Let her go!!!" she screeched sitting up in bed sweat soaking her. Slowly the realization of where she was and the bad dream became to much and she covered her face with her hands and cried. Feeling a hand touch her shoulder, she bolted out of the bed, dragging the blanket with her to pull it up in front of her staring at her husband's open mouth. "I..." she began still crying but more afraid of what her husband was going to do than the men in her dream.

Nathan stared at her. Her hair was tangled and loose about her face. She was wearing a sleeping gown he could practically see through. Frowning, he watched another tear run down her face. "What's wrong?"

Rae shook her head and moved back toward her room. She took small steps backwards as she kept her face on Nathan.

"Rae, why are you crying? What were you dreaming about?"

Rae flushed then paled realizing he knew she had been coming into his room. Feeling panic and grief she began to sob and started backing toward her door.

Nathan frowned and slipped out of bed. He had been going to bed in night pants knowing she was coming into his room at night. Moving around the bed in her direction, he stopped before her, then wrapped his arms around her. Rae crumpled against him sobbing uncontrollably. Nathan surprising himself, spoke to her in a calm relaxed voice. Leading her back to the bed he sat down still holding her in his arms. As she quieted he frowned at her. "Would you care to tell me about it?"

Rae shook her head. "It's nothing. I'll be fine," she said starting to rise.

Nathan scowled at her then slipped back into bed pulling her in with him. Rae stiffened instantly. "You'll stay here tonight."

Rae paled. "I'll be fine in my own room," she said trying to rise.

Nathan's arms tightened. "You'll stay," he said holding her in place with his arms.

Rae swallowed. "Why? You don't even like me?"

Nathan scowled. "You're staying here and that's that."

"But..."

"You're staying," he said.

Rae frowned into the darkness as images of the dream she had just seen went trough her mind. Nathan felt her tremble and frowned. What was she dreaming about? Was it him? Cursing under his breath, he scowled.

"Can I ask you something?"

Nathan stiffened not sure if he wanted to talk with her. She was a thief and a had married him for his money. "Hum?" he said hoping she would think he was more asleep than awake.

"Can a person survive a shipwreck?"

Nathan frowned in confusion. "What kind of shipwreck? Did the ship explode? Did it get attacked by pirates, what?"

"The ship went down just out of port and only five others made it," she paused then added, "it wasn't far from shore."

Nathan frowned, "You were in a shipwreck?"

Rae hesitated. Did she want to tell him anything? He hated her and knowing too much would turn him further against her. Images, of her sister struggling to stay afloat then disappearing under the water, sent her to trembling again. "Yes."

Nathan tightened his hold on her. She was shaking worse than when she had first come to his room. "You survived," he said answering her question.

"Yes, but I was in the lifeboat."

Now he understood. Someone had not been in the boats with her and she wondered if they'd survived. "Who didn't get in the boat?"

Rae frowned. "Never mind."

Nathan felt his temper returning. It had to have been a man. Why else would she be so upset? "Fine. Go to sleep."

"I think I'll go back to my own..."

"Go to sleep," he snapped leaving no room for argument.

Rae tried to relax but soon the image of her sister fighting off several men, came back again and she wondered if maybe she had survived the wreck. It had seemed so real. Exhausted mentally she drifted off to sleep, comforted by the strong arms that held her.

Chapter 48

ALLISON TOSSED IN HER BED, getting a complaining mew from Nero. Sitting up she lightly kicked him with her foot. "It's all your fault, you know. I'll never find a man now. No one will want a blind woman let alone one with a disobedient tiger like yourself."

Nero grumbled deep in his chest before moving off the bed to the window seat overlooking the street. Allison heard him go and frowned. "What am I supposed to do now?" It was chilly in her room so she got up and added wood to the fire. When she felt the heat warming her face she moved into one of the high backed chairs pulling her feet up beneath her. "It's not like I can waltz into a ball and pretend your little escapade never happened." Nero didn't make a sound. "I suppose I could attend the balls with you at my side." Nero let out a small roar making Allison laugh. "Shh, you're going to wake up the whole house. I'm sure it's not morning yet. She moved to touch the glass in the window and felt the cool glass. Definitely still night time. Dropping her hand, she ran it over Nero's fur feeling the deep rumble of him purring. "I don't think the ton would be happy if I attended the balls with you." Nero kept purring, while Allison stood at her window deep in thought. Perhaps letting her father choose wasn't such a bad idea. At this point, how bad could he do? Moving to her wardrobe she pulled out a gown and quickly dressed. Nero protested, but Allison needed to speak with her Uncle Colan and Nero was the only way she could get there. Moving along the hall she counted seven doors then knocked. No answer. Knocking again she heard movement inside.

Colan sat up in bed straining to make sure he had actually heard someone knocking at his door. When the knock came again he cursed before climbing from the warm cocoon and slipping into his robe and slippers.

"I'm coming," he called when the knock came once again. Pulling the door open his brows shot up in surprise. "Allison? Is something wrong?"

"No," she said frowning. "Is it too early."

Colan looked at the clock and frowned. It was five to six, early for most of the world but obviously not to Allison. "Not too bad."

Allison reddened. "I'm sorry. I'll come back," she said turning to leave.

"Hold on there, lass. I didn't say I wouldn't see you. Now, come on in. I'll ring for a servant." Colan moved aside as Nero headed straight for the bed. Colan scowled as the cat jumped up and snuggled into the covers.

"Perhaps it's too early for the servants?"

Colan turned his gaze on her. "If I'm up, they should be," he said, pulling the rope. "Now, what's on your mind?" he asked putting several logs on the fire to heat the room.

Allison took one of the high backed chairs before the fire and sighed. "It's obvious I'm not going to be welcome into many parlors and ballrooms in the near future."

Colan raised his brows. "I think you're overreacting some. It will all die down. You'll see."

Allison nodded her head. "I really don't have a choice in the matter. Father has asked us to marry or he'll choose one for us." Pausing she clasped her hands in her lap. "I'm sure Father will have a hard time finding me a husband now that Nero has made my blindness known." Colan moved to the other chair and frowned in concern.

"You don't plan on hiding away again do you?"

Allison laughed. "As if that would help. No, I don't plan on hiding but I don't plan on going to any balls either. I'm not ready for the taunts and whispers I'll end up hearing."

Colan frowned in confusion. "Then why are you here?"

Allison smiled. "I want to find a pet for Ashley."

Colan's brow shot up. "A pet?"

"Yes. I figure it will take me at least three weeks to get up the nerve to accept any invitations and in that time I can work with the animal enough for it to understand how to lead a blind person around."

Colan sighed, running a hand through his graying hair. "I don't know. Why didn't you go to your father?"

Allison's smile faded. "He'd more than likely demand to take me to the balls to insure that no one said a word. He can't afford to have the stress and I can't afford to be helped like that. I know people will talk, especially, in the ton. I'm prepared for that, but I want to go back in my own time."

Colan stared at her in amazement. The girl was very perceptive. "I'll need time to come up with the proper pet."

Allison's face fell. "You don't have anything in mind?"

Colan leaned back in his chair. "Well, I really haven't thought about it. Perhaps you should ask Ashley about it?"

"Oh, I did somewhat. She's afraid of most animals but her family always had dogs. I was thinking something along that line. At least, Jonathan's horses would get used to that a lot quicker than a cat."

Colan grinned, knowing none of his horses had ever gotten used to Nero. "A dog, aye?"

Allison smiled. "A large one. I don't want her bumping into things."

Colan laughed. "I don't think they come in Nero size."

Allison giggled. "Then you know someone?"

"As a matter of fact, I do," he said scowling. "It's just that I haven't the time to go out there and get the animal for you."

"That's all right. Stephan has a broken hand and I'm sure he will be happy to go with me."

Colan smiled. "That would work out fine. I don't remember the lord's name but I do have a location. I know they breed exceptional hounds there."

Allison smiled. "Then it's settled. I'll head out there tomorrow with Stephan."

"Now hold on. I think I should write to the lord."

"I don't have time."

Colan reddened frowning at her. "Allison, your father would never force you to marry."

Allison smiled sadly. "He already told me he wasn't backing down. I have to do this. I can't face the ton yet and this is the perfect excuse not to."

Colan didn't like the idea of her hiding behind something but he didn't say anymore. "All right. I'll hunt up the exact location and give it to Stephan."

Allison jumped to her feet. "Thank you, Uncle. I'll owe you one."

Colan smiled hugging her. "I'm glad to be of service," he said moving to the door. He frowned as she left. It was the strangest thing but he felt like he had just been manipulated into something but he didn't have the slightest idea what.

STEPHAN CAME AWAKE CURSING, as the throbbing in his hand increased. Someone was in his room. "Who the hell is in here?"

Allison smiled. "It's me."

Stephan scowled. "It's to early to be up. Go back to bed," he said rolling over.

"I know it's early. I need to talk with you," Allison insisted.

Stephan groaned. "If you haven't noticed, I'm trying to recoup from the damage your cat did." Nero grumbled at this point, getting a startled reaction from Stephan. "You brought him with you!" he stated squinting at the cat in the dark. "Well, keep him over there. One busted limb is enough for me." Allison pursed her lips. "He's not going anywhere," she said moving to sit on the edge of the bed. Stephan scowled.

"It's still early."

"Well, I wouldn't think it would change in just seconds."

"You're awfully damn lippy for someone who is barging in on a sleeping invalid."

Allison grinned, "I need a favor."

Stephan groaned rolling on his side. "I don't hand out favors until after ten."

Allison's swatted at him. "I'm serious."

Sighing, he flopped on his back. It was still dark out and Allison was just a shadow of a person. "What do you have in mind?"

"I'll help you with your scheme for Christopher if you will come with me to get a dog for Ashley."

Stephan lifted his head, "A dog?"

"Yes. A hound."

"A hound? How come I have a feeling this isn't just a dog?"

"It is, believe me. Remember the animal has to like horses. How wild can it be?"

Stephan dropped his head back on the bed. "How wild indeed." Running a hand through his hair he pulled the pillow back under his head. "I guess it wouldn't hurt to go with you."

"I'm leaving tomorrow."

"Tomorrow! I can't go tomorrow. I have ships to sail. Cargo to load."

"The doctor says you can't sail for six weeks."

Stephan scowled. He'd forgotten that. "Bloody hell. I'll lose my business."

Allison frowned. "If you go with me tomorrow, I'll help you persuade Jessica to help you with the shipping."

Stephan lifted his head to squint at her in the dark. "Why do you want to do this?"

Allison frowned. "I can't stand the thought of walking into a ball with Aunt Ginger and having everyone whispering and talking about me."

Stephan closed his eyes. He had figured it was something along those lines. "All right, Al, if..." he said pulling himself into a sitting position. "If you can get Jessica to help me and if you can get real chummy with Cari St. Paul, I'll take you tomorrow for the dog. It won't take more than a day, will it?"

Allison frowned she didn't have the slightest idea. "No, it will only take a day."

Stephan frowned. "Let's shake on it then," he said as Allison held out her hand. Taking it he pumped it twice. "Now, go away I need my rest," he said flopping back on his pillow with a sigh.

Allison grinned. "Thank you Stephan. I owe you for this."

Stephan lifted his head at those words and watched her walk out of his room into the darkness. What the hell had he been thinking? He had a business to run. He couldn't go traipsing off to god knows where to get some stupid dog. He cursed when he felt his hand throb. It was just his luck to have something like this happen. A broken hand! How the hell was he supposed to sail a ship like this?

"Bloody hell," he snapped swinging his legs out of the bed to dress. He had a lot to get organized or his business was going to sink fast.

Chapter 49

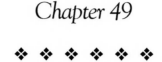

JESSICA AWOKE to the feel of a warm body next to hers and froze remembering everything they had done the night before. Her heart started to beat wildly and she felt a bit suffocated. She'd slept with a man that hated her and one she hated back. Easing onto her back she turned to see if she'd awakened him and froze at the piercing blue eyes staring back at her. Shutting her eyes she turned her head and scowled up at the ceiling.

Morgan watched her a moment, laughing at the thoughts that must be running through her head. "Sure are wanton, aren't you?"

Jessica turned scarlet as she struggled to a sitting position. "You bastard. You couldn't wait to say something."

Morgan laughed trying to pull her back down on the bed. He couldn't deny she was a calculating bit of baggage but he wasn't about to deny the fact that she was wild and natural in bed. That was something very hard to find. Jessica slapped at his hands managing to escape his grasp and pulled the blankets with her to the safety of the hearth. Morgan leaned his head on one hand, while laying the other casually near the red spots on the bed sheet. Jessica flushed at the sign of her weakness to him. "I suppose a repeat of last night is out of the question?"

Jessica snorted heading for the table to pour herself some water. Morgan smiled. He was in for one hell of a fight. Getting to his feet he walked across the room, not bothering to cover himself. Jessica stared at his body in shock but was unable to look away. Morgan cursed his body's reaction to her stare but slipped into a pair of breeches and shirt anyway. Jessica frowned in confusion as he began to pack a bag.

"Where are you going?"

Morgan paused, in his labor, to look at her. "I do run a shipping business."

Jessica paled. He was leaving her. He was going to sail away and leave her on land. Swallowing she tried not to panic. "Are you planning to sail?"

Morgan watched her face and saw the fear there. Cursing, he looked away. "That is what I do."

Jessica slipped into a chair. "Where..." she swallowed. "How long will you be gone?"

Morgan scowled at his own weakness. Why should he feel sorry for the chit? She's the one that forced his hand. She's the one that practically ruined his business. Yet he was the one feeling guilty, "I have a day run."

Jessica looked at him. She wasn't about to ask if she could come but she knew it was written all over her face.

Morgan crammed several shirts in the bag and closed it. "I have to go."

Jessica jumped to her feet and ran to block his path. "Why...that is packed for a long trip."

Morgan glared at her, then shocked the hell out of himself by saying, "I have a long trip on Friday. I will be gone for almost two weeks, stopping in several ports along the way." At her stricken look, he cursed. "If..." he said closing the distance and taking her chin in his hand. "If you can restrain yourself from making a fool of my name by wearing breeches or causing trouble, I will take you with me. Otherwise, I sail without you," he snapped pushing her aside and stalking from the room. Jessica, stunned for a moment, darted out of the room after him, the blanket barely covering her.

"On Friday?"

Morgan paused on the steps to look up at his wife. She was so breathtakingly beautiful at that moment that the thought of being at sea with her for a full two weeks was very appealing. "Friday," he said turning and descending the stairs.

Jessica watched him go a smile creeping onto her face. Three days. She could manage three days as a lady. Smiling she turned to head back in her room oblivious to the opened mouth stare of the butler as he got a complete view of her backside.

STEPHAN CURSED HIS STUPID MOUTH. How could he possibly leave his business for another day in the care of the man that was running it now? He needed to go to both ports. Fourwinds, his fastest ship was docked in the south port and it needed his personal attention. Cursing his promise to go with Allison he mounted the steps to Jessica's new home and knocked.

A short middle-aged man, dressed immaculately, answered the door. "Can I help you, my lord?"

Stephan grinned. "I am here to see my sister, Lady Jessica. Is she home?"

Davis smiled and nodded his head. "If you'll just wait in the parlor, I'll tell her you're here."

Stephan grinned. "Thank you," he said moving into the well-lit room. It had several sofas and chairs in it. All of them looked rather stiff and boring, but were what many of the ladies had in their homes. Looking around the room he settled himself in a chair in front of a window. It was the only one solid enough to hold his weight.

"Stephan!" Jessica said crossing the room to kiss his cheek. "What brings you here so early?"

Stephan smiled. "I need a favor," he said noticing for the first time she was wearing a gown. "My god! You're in a dress."

Jessica's smile wavered. "It's either wear a dress or get left behind when my husband sails."

Stephen's smile widened into a grin. "Clever man."

Jessica shrugged. "What's your favor?" she said, scowling to let him know the subject was getting to her.

Stephen's face turned serious. "I'm in a bit of a fix. I need you to come down to the office and help me get things in order today. I have three ships in port."

Jessica arched a brow. She normally handled all the ships docking in Canvey. "How many are in Thurrock?"

"One, but it's the Fourwinds."

Jessica frowned. "I'm not supposed to wear breeches."

Stephan frowned. "That's a stupid thing to restrict you from," he said, changing his earlier opinion.

"I think he figures I'll stay out of trouble tangled in all this material."

Stephan smiled. "He's probably right." Moving to pace, he frowned. "Could you send for Dane or Arty to come with you?"

Jessica arched a brow. "They have decided to stay with me here. Both work in the house."

Stephan looked surprised. "Dane?"

Jessica grinned. "The staff is terrified of him but he's an excellent butler."

"He didn't answer the door."

"I know he starts tomorrow."

"Great then he could come with you to the office today."

Jessica frowned. "I don't know."

"Did he tell you not to go near the docks?"

"No."

"Did he tell you not to work for me?"

"No."

Stephan arched a brow at her in question.

"Bloody hell! But if I get left behind, I'm going to hunt your sorry butt down and rearrange your face."

Stephan grinned. "Thank you, Jess. I owe you."

"You owe me big."

"I'll meet you in Canvey in an hour."

"An hour?"

"I'm in a hurry."

"Fine," she said watching him head for the door. "How is the hand, by the way?"

"A pain in the ass."

Jessica grinned. "That's what you get for trying to show off."

Stephan scowled at her. "An hour."

Jessica nodded her head still smiling. Davis looked at his mistress with an odd expression but Jessica ignored him. She needed to find Dane and Arty. Both men were going to have to come with her.

Chapter 50

"PLEASE, AUNT GINGER. The rough edged members are safely married, you should have no problem with Allison and me," Christopher said sitting on the sofa facing his Aunt while the pair sipped tea and ate cakes.

Aunt Ginger pursed her lips. "You know I have been humiliated almost beyond repair."

Christopher nodded. "I'm sure the ton understands with Jessica and after seeing what happened at the celebration, I'm sure they understand about Melissa, also."

Ginger smiled grimly. "She'll do exactly what I say? No lip or sass?"

Christopher grinned. "She'll behave like an angel."

"What about that beast?"

"I'll put extra locks on the windows. He'll stay locked in her room."

Ginger sat straight. "You'll attend the balls with us?"

Christopher scowled. "I'll attend most of them but when I can't, Stephan will."

Ginger narrowed her eyes. "I want complete control of the girl's social calendar. No men interfering."

Christopher frowned. "All right but remember she's blind."

Ginger waved a hand at that. "She's beautiful and compassionate. Her blindness will not hinder her."

Christopher arched a brow at that. "Then you agree?"

Ginger nodded. "I agree, but the first sign of humiliation and I'm going to Colan's."

Christopher grinned, taking her hand and kissing it. "That won't be necessary. Thank you, Aunt Ginger. Allison will be happy to hear it."

Ginger humphed at that watching her nephew leave the room. She was probably crazy to take on the last of these barbarians but how much harm could the girl possibly be?

Christopher left the parlor grinning. One thing at least was under control. He just needed to get Andrew over here and finish getting the things in order. Moving into the library he arched a brow at his sister. "What brings you here?"

Melissa got to her feet tipping her head as Christopher placed a kiss on her cheek. "I have a problem."

Christopher scowled. "Is this a lovers spat?"

Melissa blushed. It was one thing to have a husband but it was entirely different to discuss such intimate things with her brother. "No, it's not. It concerns Allison."

Christopher held up his hand. "Not to worry. Aunt Ginger has personally said she will see to the rest of her season. I plan to escort Allison myself. Stephan will help, of course."

Melissa, who was still standing, moved to sit in the chair across from Christopher's desk. "It's not about her social calendar. Caleb's father knows about the Matherson lines and wants his other son to marry Allison."

Christopher's brows shot up. "What other son?"

"Donavan. He's the third son. I think he's twenty-four or so dark haired with blue eyes."

"What does he do for a living?"

"He sails just like the youngest one."

"How many sons are there?"

"Four. The second one is an investor."

Christopher frowned. "Is Donavan interested in that idea?"

"I don't think he knows yet. He's to return home tomorrow and the father was going to send him courting then."

"How do you know all this?"

"Keegan, that's the second son, he came to see us last night. He told us everything. Caleb's father wants a northern port and connections with Matherson Lines."

"That bastard," Christopher said, then flushed. "I'm sorry."

Melissa frowned. "Don't be. I agree whole-heartedly. So what are you going to do?"

"Is the son respectable?"

"I don't know. Caleb says Allison would be happy to have a man like Donavan but when I reminded Caleb that Allison is blind, he didn't say much. "Well that's a vital fact."

"Are you going to let Donavan court her?"

"What choice do I have? Allison has the right to choose her own husband. Who are we to say this Donavan isn't the one?"

Melissa bit her lip. "You're right. I suppose when I meet him I can judge if he's respectable or not. If he isn't, I'm telling Allison what Caleb's father plans."

Christopher nodded his head. "That sounds like a plan. It seems you made a good choice in a man."

"Since it's only been a week, I think I did, too."

Christopher smiled. "I'm sure it won't be wedded bliss forever Melissa, but at least you look happier than you did when I first found you married."

Melissa reddened at the intimate talk. "Yes, well, things are good so far."

Christopher grinned. "Are you ever going to tell us what happened?"

"Not on your life," she said getting to her feet and leaving the room. Christopher heard the front door close. Getting to his feet, he moved to the window and watched her carriage drive away. His father was leaving in an hour to return to Colan's. Frowning, he wondered if Nathan was staying. Jonathan had left earlier that morning. He had several horses that needed his attention. Moving back to his desk Christopher ran a hand through his hair. The desk was still piled with neat stacks of papers but at least he knew exactly where everything was headed.

Nathan watched his brother from the door for several minutes watching the thoughts cross his face as he ran whatever was on his mind through his orderly life. Nathan smiled a lopsided grin. Christopher's life was so damned organized that Stephan was right about finding him a woman, with a bit of life to her. Clearing his throat Nathan brought Christopher's eyes to his.

"Nathan? What brings you here?"

"I thought I might inform you of our plans."

"Which are?"

"I've sent for the boys."

Christopher arched his brows. "What for?"

Nathan moved into the room shutting the door behind him. "I need to get them clothes, a governess and a few other things."

Christopher sat there stunned. "You're going to be staying here?

"My wife is."

"Where are you going?" Christopher asked, scowling.

"I'm not sure yet."

Christopher narrowed his eyes. "Then why are you leaving?

"I didn't say I was. Yet," he added taking a seat.

Christopher shook his head. "She doesn't seem that bad, Nathan."

Nathan scowled at his brother. "The woman is a thief."

Christopher's brows shot up. "A thief?"

"Yes. I caught her robbing the Baron of Linwood's sister." Guessing Christopher's next question he held up his hand. "She robbed many of the ton."

Christopher's mouth dropped open. "She did what?"

Nathan smiled bitterly. "I just happened to be the lucky sap she swindled into marriage."

"I'm sure she didn't intentionally..."

"Oh, she meant to marry me, though I think she thought I was a lot richer than I am."

"She married you for your money?

"And a provider for her children."

Christopher leaned back in his chair. "What a pill to swallow?

Nathan scowled. "I didn't come here for sympathy. I wanted to know if you might be able to persuade Aunt Ginger to help Rae find a governess."

"Me? But I have a thousand other things to do."

"I'll help you."

Christopher's mouth fell open. "You'll help me?"

Nathan's face darkened. "I refuse to be an errand boy but I'll gladly help you with whatever else needs doing. That is if you can get Aunt Ginger's help."

Christopher frowned. "Why don't you ask her?

"The woman spent a full week telling me exactly how to behave in all aspects of my life. Obviously, I failed to measure up to her standards and now find myself with a wife and two children. She has to be asked by you."

Christopher couldn't help himself, he laughed. "I'm sorry. It's just hard to believe you're a father."

Nathan got to his feet. "Will you help or not?

"Of course. I couldn't say no to such a plea for help. I'll ask Ginger today."

Nathan ground his teeth at his brother's grin. "Thank you," Nathan said leaving the study. He was going to be happy to help with Christopher's 'fall into hell.' The girl at the party last night with the monkey was exactly the type of chaos his brother needed and Nathan was going to be the first in line to push Christopher's buttons.

Chapter 51

STEPHAN MOVED ALONG THE WATERFRONT, paying little attention to his surroundings. He had several things he needed to see to before he spent the day away with Allison. Ducking out of the way of a swinging net full of tuna, he moved in the direction of his office. Suddenly off to his right a woman caught his eye. Stopping near some crates he watched with his mouth hanging open as the girl walked along the waterfront snatching items here and there from people walking by. How he knew it was a woman, he wasn't sure, but seeing her face he knew for certain that Nathan's wife had no business picking pockets along the waterfront. Setting his lips in a firm line, he started in her direction appalled by her actions. She had on a pair of old tattered breeches with a white shirt just long enough to cover her backside. Stephan frowned but had to admit her backside looked real desirable. Scowling, at his thoughts toward his brother's wife, he picked up his pace. She wasn't even wearing shoes, he cursed, knowing she was going to catch her death walking around like that.

As if sensing his presence, her head snapped up and her green eyes collided with his. She paled then turned and took off toward the buildings along the waterfront. Stephan cursed and started after her. Seeing her round a corner heading for one of the worst sections of town he shouted her name. As he turned the corner he cursed. She was no where to be seen. "Bloody hell!" he muttered, feeling his hand throb from running. "Stupid girl," he cursed, turning to head back to his office. Nathan was going to have to be told, he thought grimly.

The girl watched him move back in the direction he had come. Drawing her brows down in confusion she wondered how he had caught her stealing. She would have remembered picking his pocket. The man was gorgeous compared to most of the men on the docks. His height alone would have deterred her. Frowning she watched as he disappeared amongst the other dock lot before venturing out from her hiding spot. That was one fellow she was going to have to keep an eye out for. The man looked like he would have killed her if he had gotten a hold of her. Deciding she had enough for one day, she made her way back toward Pemberton Avenue. She had a small apartment there that she shared with four other women. Glancing over her shoulder she had the funny feeling she was going to see that man again.

JESSICA STEPPED FROM THE CARRIAGE, while Arty held the door for her. "Are ya sure ya want to be doin this? Yer husband doesn't seem to like his wife traipsin around the docks."

Jessica glared at Arty. "It's my decision. He never said I couldn't come down here."

Dane moved to her side, as several people stared. Jessica lifted her chin. She knew it was foolish to be on the docks dressed like she was but her stupid husband had forbid her from wearing breeches. Now, here she stood risking her neck plus Arty's and Dane's. "Lets get in the office."

"Yes, captain."

"Don't call me that!" she hissed, moving as fast as she could to the nice two-story building her brother had built for their office. Going inside, she scanned the room to make sure no one was inside then turned to Arty.

"Stay out here and keep an eye on things," she said looking at the large mass of sailors that were watching her. "Stupid pissant!" she said under her breath knowing she wouldn't have attracted half as much attention dressed in breeches. "If anything goes a muck knock on the door twice. I'll be ready."

Arty eyed her closely, and then nodded. She was a tough young lady and he didn't doubt she had a plan if things got out of hand.

"Remember, Stephan should be here any minute. Let him in. No one else."

Arty nodded again. With a final look around the dock, she stepped into the building and closed the door. It smelled like the sea and she felt tears form in her eyes. What was she supposed to do now that she was married? This is where her life was. Lifting her chin she moved to the desk and sat down. Rummaging through several of the shipping orders she separated them into piles according to ship.

"Arty?" she bellowed getting his head poked in. "Get some boy to send for the captains of the Gypsy, Galiath, and the Neptune. I need to see what they sold and brought back."

Arty nodded his head and ducked out only to pop back in. "Yer brother's here."

"Thank god," she said getting to her feet. "Where have you been?" she asked seconds after he came into the room.

Stephan cursed. "I just saw Nathan's wife."

"His wife? Down here?"

"She was picking pockets along the waif."

Jessica stared at him then started laughing. "You have to be joking. The girl wouldn't last a second in this area."

Stephan didn't laugh. "I tell you it was her. She was wearing breeches and a shirt so tattered that most people would mistake her for a male. I happen to have seen her dressed in that fashion the night before your wedding. Besides she recognized me if her pale complexion was any indication."

Jessica frowned. "Why would she be picking pockets?"

"How the hell should I know?"

"Are you going to tell Nathan?"

"Well, of course. He has to know she was down here. She could get killed or something."

Jessica nodded in agreement. "Maybe you should wait and see if she does it again. She did see you, maybe that will deter her from coming again."

"But whose to say she won't go someplace else."

Jessica nodded grimly. "You're right," she said resuming her seat behind the desk. "I was going through the papers and I'm shocked. Didn't you do anything while I was gone?"

Stephan reddened. "I loaded the ships and sent them on their way. That's work."

Jessica nodded. "Yes, it is work but you didn't fill out anything. That's how people get robbed."

Stephan frowned taking a seat on a wooden chair with no cushion. "Fine. Can you catch us up?"

"I'll have to take this stuff home with me. I can't stay here dressed like this. It will be pushing my luck."

Stephan smiled. "Excellent idea. I'll get the captains..." he said rising.

"Never mind. I sent someone to bring them here. Who are they?"

"Henderson, Michaels, and Sawyer. O'Brien is sailing my ship," he said resuming his seat.

Jessica frowned. "Are you sure Michaels is trust worthy?"

Stephan grinned. "He is now. I threatened to cut off sections of his body. I told him he could live without those parts but he would suffer an eternity without them. He quickly handed over the funds he stole and the crew that was in on it." At her skeptical look, he added, "I also have several of my own crew on that ship. He knows it."

Jessica bit her lip then nodded. "Fine. If you feel he's reformed I'll go along with it but I suggest you only send him on runs that need no bartering. He'll pocket the profit."

Stephan grinned. "I knew you were handy to have around. I didn't think of that. Can you arrange it?"

"How soon before they sail?"

"The ships need to leave tomorrow."

"Are you going to be here?"

"That's another favor I need from you."

"Where the hell are you going?"

"I have to go with Allison to get some dog for Ashley."

Jessica instantly lost her anger. "She's hiding behind that."

"So it seems, but at least she's staying in London."

Jessica nodded. "All right. I'll get the invoices checked and the ships loaded for sailing in Canvey. You have to keep the Fourwinds records straight and load that one yourself."

Stephan grinned. "No problem."

"You've told me that before. Look what a mess you've made since I've been in London. "Thanks Jess," he said getting to his feet. "I have to go. I need to be in Thurrock and back home by tomorrow." Pausing with his hand on the door, he frowned "Are you going to be all right?"

"I'll be fine. I don't plan on staying more than a couple of hours. That's probably as risky as I get in these clothes."

Stephan grinned, and left with a wave. Jessica sighed at the mess before her. It would take her all week to get things back in order. Cursing Stephan for being so unorganized, she rummaged through the papers waiting for the captains to arrive. She was sailing with her husband on Friday no matter what.

Christopher smiled, as Aunt Ginger entered the library. "Thank you for coming. You look lovely this afternoon," he said, kissing her hand with a smile. "I appreciate you taking the time to talk with me, again."

Aunt Ginger snorted getting a raised brow from Christopher. "That's one of the better lines I've been given. What is it you want this time?" she asked settling herself on the sofa.

Christopher flushed. "You're right. I do want something but I still appreciate you taking the time to come down here and listen. Of course, you look nice too."

Ginger straightened, further pleased with his praise. "I have only a short while before I need to get ready for the Atherton's ball tonight."

Christopher nodded. "Fine, I won't keep you. I was hoping you would see fit to find a governess for Sean and Ian."

"Who?"

Christopher smiled slightly. "Sean and Ian. Nathan's new children."

Ginger looked at him like he'd grown two heads. "They have children?"

Christopher chuckled. "I'm afraid so. Sean is five, I believe, and Ian is four. No. I think he's three. Anyhow they shall be arriving sometime tomorrow."

Ginger was pale and looked like she was going to faint. "Your father never tells me a thing. Does anyone else have children?"

"No, but I'm sure their working on it." Ginger scowled at him making him redden a bit for his slander. "I meant nothing by that," he said, holding up his hands.

"Yes, well...what about his wife? Shouldn't she be the one to take care of this sort of thing?"

Christopher smiled. "Of course, but she's an American and doesn't know London very well. It would help Nathan to have you guide her in finding the governess. The boys should be educated."

Ginger perked up at that. "Of course they should. We wouldn't want any more barbarians in the family. I'll speak with the girl tomorrow. I'm sure I can find a suitable governess by the end of the week."

Christopher grinned. "Thank you very much. Nathan will be relieved."

Ginger pursed her lips. "What is he doing in the mean time?"

"He's working for me."

Ginger nodded and Christopher could see she was hard pressed not to ask what he would be doing? "All right. I will help her as much as I can."

"Thank you. That's all I ask."

Ginger got to her feet. "You'll have to clothe the boys."

"Of course."

Ginger nodded her approval and left the room. Christopher grinned at the closed door. At least that went smoothly. Returning to his papers, he actually smiled. With Melissa and Jessica settled, things should move along at a more normal pace.

Chapter 52

RAE PAUSED outside Allison's door biting her finger in hesitation. Would it seem strange to come and talk with Allison? Would she want to listen?

The decision was taken away from her as the door opened and Allison stood there. "Who's there?"

"It's me, Rae."

Allison smiled. "Come in. How have you been? You must miss your boys terribly," she said closing the door.

Rae moved into the room hesitantly. "I miss the boys tremendously," she said not sure where to go or sit.

"Nero get in the window," she said knowing the cat was ready to scare the life out of Rae. "He's really harmless," she said, steering Rae to the sofa.

Rae watched the large orange and black tiger move to the window seat. It jumped up with such ease she swallowed. Those large paws could mangle a person in seconds. "I don't think he likes me," she said as the large yellow eyes stared at her.

Allison laughed. "Is he licking his chops?"

Rae stared at her in surprise. "Yes. Yes he is."

"He does that to scare you. It's like a game."

Rae didn't smile and she didn't think it was funny.

"Trust me he's harmless. Now what brings you here?"

"Your Aunt Ginger. She wants to take me to the ball tonight."

Allison arched a brow. "That usually happens after you marry. Don't you want to go?"

"But Nathan isn't going?"

"He'll show up later, trust me."

Rae lowered her eyes. "You don't understand. Your brother and I…well, we…that is, he's very angry about the way I married him."

Allison frowned. "To be honest with you, I haven't spoke to Nathan much in the last week. Really I can't say how he feels about things, but I will say this. My brother runs when he doesn't like something and since he's still here, I would think he's not as against what happened, as he lets on."

Rae looked up at her. "He runs?"

"Yes. In fact, Nathan is known in our family as 'the gambler.'

"He gambles?"

"Oh, here and there but I know he manages his money very well. In fact he lets Stephan and Christopher believe he's in deep water, all the time, when I know he's never taken a loan."

Rae frowned at the picture Allison was painting of Nathan. She was making him sound honorable. "But he acts very irresponsible."

"That's exactly what he wants. People expect less then. Nathan is responsible to a fault. He always keeps his word and if you make a situation sound desperate enough, he'll drop everything to help you."

Rae frowned at that thought. "He'll never forgive me then."

Allison put her hand on Rae's leg. "He'll forgive you. It will just take time. He doesn't like to be cheated."

Rae felt worse. "I did cheat him."

"But you could change his opinion by telling him the truth. I know he'll understand your reasons for doing everything you did."

Rae lowered her head. "I can't tell him. If he sent the boys away I would never forgive myself," she said frowning further. "Besides, the fact that I haven't a drop of society grace in me, grinds on his nerves."

Allison laughed. "That, my dear Rae, is something you're wrong about. Nathan puts on an act where society is concerned. If he had his way, he'd run off and retire somewhere in the country."

Rae frowned. "But he dresses perfect and goes to those clubs all the time."

Allison chuckled. "He has a front to uphold. Being a bachelor, an ex-bachelor, he used that front to send my father and brothers into fits. I know Nathan would like nothing more than to farm."

Rae looked at her in surprise. "Farming?"

Allison laughed. "That's my opinion, mind you, but I think he really would love it."

Rae drew her brows together. Her father had been a farmer. They had farmed wheat, corn, and potatoes. Picturing Nathan digging in the dirt to pull potatoes out of the ground, made her shake her head. "I think you're wrong. Nathan likes the social whirl."

Allison sighed. Until her brother talked with his wife she wasn't going to see him any other way than the way he behaved. Cursing him under her breath she frowned. "I'm sure you didn't come here to talk about Nathan, what else is on your mind?"

Rae flushed. "I wanted to ask you something. Do you think someone could survive a shipwreck? Without getting rescued by a lifeboat?" "Anything is possible. Why?"

"My sister drowned on the ship when we were trying to go home, remember?" Allison nodded. "Well, the lifeboat that picked up the boys and I, didn't save her. There was no other lifeboat that made it to shore, but I've dreamed about her being alive."

Allison frowned, "People usually dream of those we lose. It's normal."

"But you don't understand. Emily and I were twins."

Allison's brows shot up. "Twins? Then, that is different. Maybe she landed somewhere along the coast."

Rae frowned in concentration. "I thought about that last night. If she had, why wouldn't she contact me. After all, I have her boys."

Allison shrugged. "Maybe she didn't know you were rescued."

Rae felt her hopes soar. "How can I go about finding her?"

"Hire a runner."

"A runner?"

"Yes. A bow street runner. Nathan knows lots of them."

Rae arched a brow. "What for?"

"I don't know but I know he's in touch with several of them." Rae frowned "Would you ask him to hire one for me?"

Allison shook her head. "I think you should talk to him about your sister. He needs to know those children aren't yours."

"But they are mine and I don't want them sent away."

"Nathan won't send them away."

"I think he would."

Allison didn't want to argue with her so she shrugged. "It's your decision but Nathan is in touch with a network of people in the city and they could find Emily in no time at all."

Rae bit her lip. What if Allison was right? Emily could be starving somewhere in the city. Rae needed to know if Emily was alive. Getting to her feet, she frowned. "Are you going to the ball tonight?"

"No," from the look on Allison's face, Rae hesitated. After the spectacle the other night Rae didn't blame Allison for not wanting to go to the ball. Dropping the issue, Rae twisted her hands in her lap.

"Do you think I could borrow one of your gowns? I only have the one and your Aunt will expect me..."

Allison got to her feet. "Say no more. You can take whatever you need. I can't believe Nathan hasn't bought you clothes."

Rae panicked shaking her head. "Oh, I can't take more than the one," she said seeing Allison push the gowns along their hangers

Allison pursed her lips. "I really don't mind," she said. "Just pick a few gowns out of my wardrobe. Say five. I don't plan on going out for at least a week."

Rae frowned. This could make Nathan remotely happy if she was dressed better than a common street urchin so she consented. "Thank you."

Allison smiled "Jessica says you have black hair. I think you should choose colors that compliment that. Maybe you should look in Melissa's closet, also. She hasn't taken everything yet."

Rae stared at the gowns lined neatly along the wall and felt a moment of jealousy. These Hayworth girls were lucky. They had gowns to dress differently for at least three months. Taking out several gowns in green, blue, and yellow she smiled. "These are fine. I'm not particular."

"Did you find shoes too?"

Rae frowned, "I'll come back."

Allison nodded returning her attention to the tapestry she had picked up to work on. "That's fine."

Rae puzzled over the gowns as she dragged them into her room and flopped them out on the bed. They were far prettier than anything they had ever worn in North Carolina. Society was different here. The women gossiped over everything and they invented stories to ruin one another. Going back to Allison's room she picked three pair of shoes. "Thank you, again."

"Betsy can do your hair."

Rae frowned. "Thank you. I'll remember that."

"Have fun," she said still absorbed in her sewing. When she heard the door close she threw the tapestry aside. Laying her head on the back of the sofa, she sighed. Being this charming and sweet when you feel rotten inside was horrible. Jessica never seemed to worry about other people's feelings. She just snapped at them and that was that. Remembering her idea at getting a pet for Ashley, Allison calmed some. She needed to work to keep her mind off life and it's unpredictability. Tomorrow couldn't come soon enough.

Chapter 53

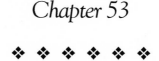

JESSICA JUMPED TO HER FEET when the door to the office slammed open. "Morley! What are you doing here?" she asked. Morgan's face darkened.

"I should be asking you that," he snapped shutting the door with a bang.

Jessica felt her hands fidgeting with the material of the gown and quickly placed them on the desk. "I'm dressed in a gown."

"So I see. This isn't exactly the place for a lady to be spending her day."

Jessica turned red with embarrassment and anger. "I happen to be working. I do own part of Matherson lines, you know."

Morgan placed his hands behind his back as he paced back and forth in front of the desk. "I see. So a newly married woman goes to the docks to work."

Jessica reddened further. "I don't give a fig what society might think. Our business won't just run itself."

Morgan stopped to glare at her. "You, my dear lady, are my wife. I own the business part in Matherson lines and I will keep the business running like it should. You are to remain at home and do what it is ladies do?"

Jessica went rigid with anger. "You can't possible expect me to dress up in frilly clothes and walk around like some...some doll."

"You're wrong, I do expect you to do that."

Jessica's mouth fell open in disbelief. Morgan narrowed his eyes as her. She lifted her chin defiantly. "I won't do it."

Morgan smiled. "You will do it, or you will never find yourself on the sea again."

Jessica paled. "You're going to use that against me forever, aren't you?"

Morgan's smile widened. "Are you forgetting who forced this marriage."

"It sure as hell wasn't me," she bellowed, her hand grabbing an ashtray off the desk.

"I wouldn't throw that if I were you!" he said eyebrows arched stressing the point.

"Well, you aren't me," she snarled, throwing the thing at his head. Morgan ducked to the right his eyes turning dangerous.

"That wasn't a smart move," he growled ducking just seconds before a little statue of a ship sailed past his head. Jessica didn't give him a chance to say anything more as she grabbed everything within reach and hurled it at him. He growled his rage, seconds before scrambling over the desk to get her. Jessica, waiting for just such a move, shot for the door.

Screeching in dismay as she fell to the floor in a heap from her legs getting caught in her skirts, Morgan took advantage of her mishap to clamp his hand on her arm and haul her within inches of his face.

"That was the most childish thing I've ever seen," he snapped, shaking her. "In the future, I would curb that habit right quick. Otherwise, you'll find yourself standing for weeks." Jessica breathing hard with anger and exertion pursed her lips to spit in his face.

"I wouldn't if I were you. I won't hesitate to tan you backside here and now!" he roared.

She swallowed clamping her mouth shut to keep from screaming at him like a shrew.

"I think we better get something straight. From this day forward you are to dress and behave as a proper lady, not some hoyden just in off the sea. I want the proper wife out of you."

Jessica felt the sudden urge to cry. This was the exact reason she hadn't wanted to marry. Men didn't like the idea of her as a Captain and she didn't fit in as a lady. They had too many damn rules. Wrenching free of his grasp she turned away from his gaze. Morgan cursed at the pain in her eyes. He felt unease at what he just told her but he had a business to run and hadn't asked for a wife. Since she wanted that role so bad she could at least be the type of woman he wanted.

"Furthermore, I do not want my wife on the docks unless I am with her. Understand?"

Jessica ground her teeth but nodded. She wasn't mentally prepared to have this argument.

Morgan frowned at her submissive behavior. It was so unlike her he narrowed his eyes wondering what she was going to do next. Straightening his coat he forced the next issue "Explain what you are doing down here?"

Jessica moved back to the desk and began picking up the papers off the floor. Keeping her gaze on the papers in front of her she set them on the desk then crossed her arms across her chest.

Morgan ground his teeth. "Like I said, tanning your backside is starting to appeal to me."

Jessica gave him a fuming look. "I came down here because Stephan needed my help with the business. I don't think it's any of your concern," she snapped out as if he were her crew.

Morgan gave her one of his darker smiles. "As my newly acquired wife, it is my business. Now talk."

Jessica just arched her brows, a look of pure disregard on her face.

Morgan was ready to snap her neck but calmly moved closer to place both hands on the desk in front of her. "I seem to recall that bottom of yours is quite easy to find," he said seeing her face turn scarlet. "I also know my hand fit's perfectly on said region. Do you wish to feel its sting?"

Jessica ground her teeth, looking at him with such hatred he told his conscience to mind it's own business in the future. Seeing his patient look slipping she shook her head then cleared her throat.

"It seems Stephan has three ships in port. Two are here and one is in Thurrock. The one in Thurrock is his largest and carries the most valuable cargos so he asked me to come down and make sure these two were loaded and ready to sail by tomorrow," she said running a hand under her nose. "Since I am familiar with the Captains of the two ships here in port I saw no reason why I shouldn't help him. This is the part of the business I usually handle," she added still defiant.

Morgan listened to her, amazed that she had run the business part of the shipping firm. He kept his amazement to himself. His wife was already trouble, a little praise from him and she'd be a monster. "Why didn't you ask me about this at breakfast?"

"I didn't know about it then. Stephan came to your house shortly after you left."

"From now on, I want to know what's going happening in the business."

Jessica grew angry. "That is not part of my dowry. The business remains mine."

Morgan smiled cruelly. "Afraid not, wife. What you come to the marriage with, belongs to me."

Jessica's gaze flew to his. Was that true? "You already have my dowry. The business is mine."

"I think you'd better ask your brother about that. He'll tell you exactly to what I'm entitled. Jessica snapped her mouth shut. "I came to this marriage with a fair amount of money and a fine piece of land, the least you could do, is let me keep my business."

Morgan arched a brow. He had known about the money but the land was new. He hadn't read her dowry, yet. Feeling like a fool he let more of his anger show.

"I should be generous to a woman who discredited my name, tried to steal from me, and finally forced my hand in marriage. I think not."

Jessica clamped her mouth shut refusing to speak. She needed to see her father or Christopher. She wasn't about to let Morgan get away with this.

Seeing her determined look, he sighed. "I guess that means you don't like what you heard." At her stubborn look, he added. "If you're done with your little display of temper I need to get back to work. I do captain a ship after all," he said, wanting to grin when her face turned to fury. "Hurry now. I sail on Friday and have tons of things to do," he finished just barely keeping his face stern.

Jessica kept herself from looking at him but knew by the tone in his voice he was gloating over the fact that he was leaving her behind on Friday. Snatching up the papers on the desk, she shuffled through them, stuffing the finished ones in the drawer. Quickly picking up all the ammunition she had thrown at Morgan she didn't acknowledge the fact that he was in the room, as she returned to the desk and lifted the few documents she needed to take home. Opening the door she gave both Arty and Dane a glare for not warning her Morgan was coming. Both men stared straight ahead. Snorting as she passed she headed slowly toward the carriage waiting for her.

Morgan frowned at her back. This argument was far from over. Seeing her two accomplices standing there brought back another bit of anger and he gave the pair a glare. They had a job to do and bringing his wife to the docks was not part of it. Looking at the pair he frowned.

"What have you two to say for yourselves?" he snapped.

Jessica snapped around looking. "It wasn't their fault. I was coming here with or without them," she said lifting her chin.

"I didn't ask you," he said looking at her with no emotion. "Get in the carriage," he added, before dismissing her by turning his back. "Well?"

Both Dane and Arty saw the murderous look Jessica gave Morgan before she turned and climbed onto the carriage. Arty swallowed, knowing Dane wasn't going to say a thing. "She was comin alone, my lord. I figured it was best if we were with her. She's a tough lady and has a good head on her shoulders," he said his eyes widening as Jessica pushed the carriage driver to the ground and took up the reins in her hands. "Most of the time," he finished as she snapped the reins, sending the team of horses off with a start.

Morgan whirled around and watched in stunned disbelief as his wife charged down the waterfront nearly tipping the carriage over as she rounded the corner to disappear from sight. "My God, she'll kill herself," he snarled, turning to stare at the pair before him. "Well don't just stand there, get us some horses," he snapped, looking back in the direction his wife had taken. A slow smile started across his face and he felt some of the tension leave his body. His life had been predictable and somewhat boring before he'd taken a wife. He knew for certain things were never going to be the same. Wiping the smile from his face he glared at Dane. "She isn't going to come back, is she?"

Dane looked at the man his Captain had married and shrugged. She had always been impulsive and none of the crew could predict how she was going to behave. Eventually, they just did like she asked and quit guessing. Looking at her husband he felt the urge to laugh. Many times he had felt opposed to what she was doing, but had little control or choice in the matter. Seeing him curse and looking around for a horse, Dane felt relief for Jessica. This man just may prove to be the man she needed to curb her bad habits or she was going to get herself killed.

"Where the hell is Arty?" Morgan cursed all trace of humor gone. His anger was back in full force. "She better have gone home," he snapped seeing Arty coming on a horse pulling another behind him. He was going to have to teach her a lesson. One she wouldn't soon forget.

JESSICA RACED ALONG THE STREET seeing people gap at her and felt her face redden. It wasn't the thing for a young lady to be driving a team at break neck speed through the streets of London. Knowing she had once again reacted before thinking, she immediately regretted leaving like she had. She definitely wasn't going to sail on Friday. Feeling the tears threatening, she pulled on the reins making it look like the animals were out of control.

"Someone help me, please," she yelled, hoping someone would rescue her.

The team slowed as a nice black haired man, with a body to make the gods weep, jumped on the back of one of them and dragged them to a halt. Climbing down from the horses back he faulted up on the carriage beside her. Jessica, momentarily stunned by the handsome man saving her, barely remembered to look scared and worried.

"Oh, thank god," she gushed, wanting to puke with disgust at her behavior. "I thought they would never stop," she sniffed. The man smiled gently taking the seat next to her. "It's all right now. Are you hurt?"

Jessica let the tears she had been holding back come forth managing to shake her head in response. The man was completely at her disposal.

"Shh, now don't cry. It's over now," he said taking her hand and patting it. Jessica wanted to laugh at the gesture, wondering what it was supposed to be accomplishing but she was truly crying now. "What happened? Where's your driver?"

"He...I left him on the waterfront."

The man's face turned hard. "Were you attacked?"

Jessica sniffed a few times trying to think of a good reason for the driver to be missing. "He was checking on something for me and the horses started to get nervous, so I climbed up here thinking I could keep them quiet. Next thing I know I'm barreling down the street out of control," she said covering her face with her hands while taking small peeks to see if he'd believed her or not. Seeing that he had believed her she took the handkerchief he handed her and delicately wiped her face like she had seen Melissa do several times before.

"Would you like me to see you home?"

Jessica lifted her teary eyes to his. "I would be very grateful to you...err...my lord."

"Lord Hampton, at your service."

Jessica gave him a watery smile. "I'm Lady Hay...Sinclair," she said, frowning at his his startled expression. "Is something wrong?"

Recovering from his shock, he smiled. "Of course not. It just happens we're related in a sense. Through marriage."

Jessica drew her brows together in confusion.

"I'm married to your husband's sister, Rachel. "And how is my sister doing?" Morgan stated making Jessica jump and turn to look at him. His face was expressionless but his eyes were so dark she couldn't tell what color they were. Feeling more the fool for acting like a complete nitwit to someone that she would have to see often, she stiffened.

Anthony frowned at the currents running between the pair, "Rachel is just fine."

"And Chad and Michael?"

"Fine. Both boys are growing up so fast." Morgan smiled but Anthony could tell it was strained. "So tell me, when was the blessed event? Rachel is going to be hurt she missed it."

"Saturday. We tried to wait but you know how these things go."

Jessica reddened, wondering what the handsome blue-eyed devil was thinking. Morgan scowled at her admiring look feeling something close to jealousy. Which was ridiculous since he didn't care what the hell she did as long as she didn't drag his name through the mud.

"I'm sure she'll understand."

Morgan nodded climbing up on the carriage to assist his wife off the box. Jessica hesitated knowing he was probably going to beat her. Turning to Anthony she smiled. "Thank you again for stopping the horses."

"My pleasure," he said kissing her hand. Morgan practically snatched her off the seat and pushed her inside the carriage.

"Coming to the house?" Morgan asked.

"Is that an invitation?"

"You know it is," he said his foot on the step. Anthony swung down with ease, still looking immaculate. His hair was barely mussed.

"I'm sure Rachel will be over as soon as I tell her."

Morgan smiled knowing his sister was going to be over in an hour or so. "Can we drop you?"

"No. I have business to take care of before going home," he said, feeling the tension. Smiling with a hint of humor in his eyes, he watched Morgan scowl at him. "It was a pleasure, my lady. Until this evening."

Morgan shut the door in his face tapping on the roof to get the present driver going. Jessica watched her husband's face flex with anger.

"He seems nice," she said, getting his piercing blue eyes turned on her.

"I would advise you to remain silent until we reach the privacy of our rooms."

Jessica snapped her mouth shut. He was going to beat her. She knew it now. Turning her gaze out the window she tried to think of other things but knowing a man was going to beat you was hard to not think about. Suddenly a scraggly looking person turned to look directly at their carriage. Jessica craned her neck for a closer look. It was Rae! She was dressed just like Stephan had said, in an oversized shirt and breeches. Hanging out the window she screamed for the driver to halt. The carriage stopped instantly but Jessica never made it out the door as her husband yanked her back inside.

"What the hell are you doing?" he snapped holding her arm.

Jessica winced at the pressure. Looking back out the window she could see that Rae was nowhere in sight. "Damn, she's gone?"

Morgan took a deep breath, barely controlling himself. "Who's gone?"

"Never mind," she said trying to pull away.

"Who?" he said, shaking her.

Jessica's lips thinned. "I can't tell you," she said feeling vaguely saddened by that thought. If she had a husband she could trust she could confide in him. They would be able to communicate on any topic, share each other's dreams. Frowning, she suddenly felt like crying. She was married to a man that wanted her to behave in a manner so ill-suited for her that she was going to be miserable for the rest of her life. Feeling her spirits dampen she sagged in his hold. "It doesn't matter anyway. She's long gone by now."

"Who, damn it?"

Jessica looked at him. "Can you keep a secret?"

Morgan arched his brows. She didn't trust him! He didn't trust her either but he had good reason. He hadn't done anything to make her not trust him. In fact, he had been damn nice to her. "Who?" he said again making it clear he wanted an answer.

Jessica sighed. "It was Nathan's wife."

Morgan's face turned to confusion. "His wife?"

"Yes. Stephan saw her on the waterfront, and I just saw her back there."

Morgan shook his head to clear it. "Hold on. She was on the waterfront? Doing what?"

Jessica hesitated. She didn't want people to know Rae had been a thief. It would be something society would never tolerate. "I haven't a clue," she said turning to look out the window, refusing to say more.

Morgan ground his teeth. She had just added ten more whacks to her backside. Giving the roof a pound, he leaned back in the seat keeping his gaze well away from his wife. He was going to ring her scrawny neck if they didn't get home soon.

Chapter 54

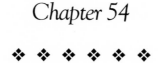

CHRISTOPHER MOVED ALONG THE HALL, intent on cleaning himself up for this evening's ball, when the door opened. Arching his brows at his sister, he said, "running away again?"

Melissa lifted her chin. "No, I'm not running away," she said lowering her gaze from his. "Is Allison upstairs?"

"I haven't a clue."

She turned to mount the stairs then paused suddenly remembering Stephen's proposal to find Christopher a wife. "Any luck on a wife?"

Christopher's look was instantly replaced by one of irritation. "I haven't really had the time." Holding up his hand to stop her from going further, he added. "And I suggest you leave it at that. Now go find Allison."

Melissa grinned. "All right" she said but couldn't miss adding. "If you would like some help, I'm sure any one of us would pitch in and help you look for one."

"Go," he stated turning on his heels and heading into the library. Melissa giggled as she climbed the stairs feeling some of the tension leave her. Knocking on Allison's door, she waited.

"Come in."

Melissa opened the door and frowned. Allison's room was completely dark. "Where is the light?"

"Melissa? What are you doing here?" Allison asked lighting a candle by the bed. "Is that better?"

"Some," she said moving to light a few more. "Aren't you cold?" she asked noticing the fire was out.

"I hadn't really noticed," she said, as Melissa moved to put more wood on the coals.

Melissa pursed her lips. She hated to see Allison pull into herself like this. "I came to ask you to the ball tonight."

Allison smiled. "Thank you, but no. Ginger already asked, as did Rae.

I'm not going."

"But you don't have a lot of time to find a husband. I'll be glad to help you, as I'm sure Caleb will."

Allison frowned. "I don't need your help. I will find someone on my own or Christopher will pick one for me."

Melissa sighed. "I was only trying to help," she said, sitting on the bed.

"I know, but I'm not ready to face the gossips."

Melissa reddened; glad for once that Allison couldn't see. This afternoon she had been visited by several ladies for tea. They had been very polite about it but she could tell they had been probing for information to twist around to harm Allison. "Gossips can be such petty creatures." Allison laughed at that. "What is this? A change of heart?"

Melissa frowned. "I have never liked gossips."

Allison still chuckled. "Melissa, you are a gossip. You know a lot about other people. How do you think you get that information?"

"I happen to be a nice person and people talk about themselves to me," she said indignantly.

Allison straightened her face. "Of course."

Melissa sighed. "I still think you should come tonight. When you fall off a horse you're suppose to get back on or you'll be afraid to ride again."

Allison frowned. "I'm not planning on hiding, if that's what you're getting at. I just need time to prepare myself."

Melissa felt her eyes tear. "I'm so sorry, Allison. I don't know why people work so hard to hurt others."

Allison turned her head toward the fire. She didn't want Melissa to see the hurt on her face. She had always wondered at that herself. "I'll be all right. I need several days to recoup."

Melissa wiped her eyes. "Are you sure?"

"I'm sure."

Getting to her feet, Melissa frowned. "If you need anything, send a note. I'll get here as fast as I can."

"Thank you."

Melissa paused with her hand on the doorknob, she turned back to Allison. "Did Stephan mention to you about Christopher's surprise?"

Allison turned toward Melissa. "He has picked her out already."

Melissa's brows shot up. "Who is it?" she said excitedly coming back into the room.

"I don't know if I can tell you."

Melissa scowled. "I can keep a secret."

Allison sighed. "If this information gets out, I'm telling Stephan you're the one that said something."

Melissa frowned. "Deal. Now talk."

"It's Lady St. Paul."

"Who?"

"Lady St. Paul. She's from India."

"India?"

Allison laughed. "Well, not exactly. She was born here but her parents died and she was sent to live with her brother and his wife in India."

Melissa stood. "How do you know all that?" she asked. "Is she wild?"

Allison's smiled. "Stephan told me as much as he knew. As to being wild, who's to say? If you're asking if she is like most of London's ladies, then yes and no. She behaves with grace and style but underneath all that, she's another Jessica."

Melissa paled. "And Stephan plans to set her up with Christopher?"

Allison laughed. "Yes, isn't it great."

Melissa stared at Allison a moment, then slowly smiled. "I suppose so. I just thought we would pick someone more suitable."

"It's supposed to cause trouble. I really don't expect them to marry."

Melissa frowned. "I'll have to hunt her up tonight at the ball. Lady St. Paul, you say?"

"That's right," she said hearing the door open. "And Melissa," she called before Melissa could leave, "she'll be the one with a monkey on her shoulder."

"A monkey?" she asked remembering the lady at Jessica's celebration. "Her? Stephan's planning on using her?" Melissa stated in disbelief. "He's crazy. It will never work," she said closing the door. Allison could hear Melissa muttering as she moved off down the hall. If it did work out, that would be a miracle. Christopher was too rigid to find a 'normal' person. He was going to get himself some imitation girl who never did anything she wasn't supposed to do. Shaking her head, Allison sighed. At least he had hopes of finding a wife, her chances of getting a husband were pretty slim and the one man she wanted had moved away from her. She thought about Lord Salisbury. The man had been nice and funny. She was relaxed and free in his company. Sighing, she closed her eyes, picturing what the man would look like. Allison felt tears in her eyes at something she knew she wouldn't have. Finally burying her face in Nero's fur, she cried. For the first time in years, she felt completely lost without her sight.

Chapter 55

STEPHAN OPENED THE DOOR almost knocking Hobkins in the head. Pulling up short, he grinned. "Sorry, Hobkins. I didn't know you were lurking back there," he finished closing the door behind him. "Is Nathan in?"

"As a matter of fact, he is."

Stephan looked at Hobkins waiting for him to continue "And where might he be?"

"In the garden."

Stephen's brows shot up. "What, pray tell, is he doing there?"

Hobkins shifted his feet. "I'm not certain. Would you like me to find out?"

Stephan grinned. "You're starting to act like Colan's man, Hobkins. Loosen up," Stephan said smacking him on the back making him stumble a couple of steps.

"Of course, my lord," he said, watching Stephan whistle his way toward the gardens.

Stephan slowly lost his smile as the thoughts of why he was here came back. How was he supposed to tell Nathan about his wife? Moving into the gardens, he frowned at the mess. Dead weeds were everywhere as servants worked frantically to get the beds ready for planting. Seeing they worked by torch light, he frowned further. Spotting Nathan, shovel in hand, he smiled. Nathan was working. Moving in his direction Stephan's smile turned to a grin.

"Well, well, what is this? You're sweating!"

Nathan scowled at his brother, wiping his brow with the back of his arm. Leaning on the shovel, he paused. "What do you want?"

"Such a warm welcome. Why are you digging holes?"

"Like an idiot, I told Christopher I would work for him if he helped me out. He did his part, so here I am digging?"

"In the dark?"

"I have things to do tomorrow."

"You could be an errand boy, you know. It saves on the blisters."

"I refuse to do that," Nathan said, smiling a lopsided grin. "What brings you here?"

Stephan lost his smile. "Ah, it's kind of personal. Can we go somewhere more private?"

Nathan frowned. "Is this about the woman?"

Stephan drew his brows together in puzzlement, then laughed. "No. I'm still working on that one, but Allison is helping," knowing he was talking about Christopher's girl.

Nathan smiled, sticking the shovel in the ground he grabbed a torch before turning to move to the far end of the garden. "How is Allison?"

"Fine, I think. I'm taking her to get some dog for Ashley tomorrow."

"Hiding behind that, huh?"

"I guess. Honestly, I don't think that scene affected her like she's letting on. She was already prepared for her sight to be announced."

Nathan frowned over that. "I guess we'll find out."

Stephan nodded knowing he had put off long enough what he came here to say. Running his hands through his hair, he gave a half laugh. "This is harder than I thought," he said looking at Nathan before pacing.

Nathan scowled at Stephan in concern. Stephan paced when he was in troubled. "What's happened? Is someone hurt?"

Stephan shook his head. "No ones hurt, but they could have been," he said stopping to look at Nathan. "Ah, hell. There's no easy way to say this. I saw your wife on the waterfront this morning. She was dressed like a boy and picking pockets."

Nathan stared at Stephan with his mouth hanging open. Snapping it shut, he frowned. "My wife was on the waterfront?"

Stephan watched his brother's face darken. "She was on the street near my office when I saw her but she ran before I could catch her."

Nathan turned his back on Stephan placing his hands on the rock wall surrounding the garden. His wife was a stranger to him but he knew she was probably down there for more than picking pockets. "Was she alone?"

Stephan frowned at Nathan's calm question. "Yes."

Nathan moved away from the wall. "Thank you for telling me," he said moving in the direction of the house.

Stephan moved after him. "Where are you going?"

"To speak with my wife."

Stephan stopped in his tracks watching his bother slam into the house. Damn. He hadn't wanted to send him to Rae in a rage but the waterfront was dangerous. Taking up the torch he moved to dismiss the servants. Nathan was not going to be returning.

NATHAN TOOK THE STEPS THREE at a time barging into Rae's room, he frowned finding it empty. Where the hell was she? Moving out of her room, he checked his. Seeing his clothes laid out for the evening, he groaned. The ball. He'd forgotten. Damn, he hated the season more and more. "Jefferson," he bellowed.

Jefferson appeared in seconds. "Yes, my lord?"

"Get me a bath and something to eat. Why didn't you remind me about this blasted ball?" he asked pulling off his soiled clothes.

Jefferson didn't answer. Nathan was quite cranky of late. A soft knock at the door brought him around to stare at the intruder. Seeing it was Allison, he relaxed. "What do you want?" he asked not wanting to take his ill temper out on her, but unable to help it.

Allison heard the anger in his voice and frowned. "I heard all that banging around in here and wanted to make sure you were all right."

Nathan snorted. "If I didn't have a wife, I might be," he said before he could stop himself. Seeing her frown, he groaned.

"Nathan, why don't you give her a chance? She really isn't that bad."

Nathan stopped in his undressing to look at his sister. She was an innocent angel, her silver hair was loose around her shoulders. Shaking his head he put his hands on her shoulders.

"You don't understand the things she's done. Frankly neither do I but I do know it's between she and I."

Allison bit her lip. She wanted to tell him about Emily and that the kids weren't Rae's but she knew it wasn't her place. Nodding her head she leaned up and kissed his cheek. "All right. I'll let it go but I want you to remember, I'm willing to listen and a woman's point of view is sometimes helpful."

Nathan let go of her frowning. She was such a kind-hearted person. Scowling, he wondered how he ended up with a lying, selfish, thief for a wife. His anger flared anew as he emptied his pockets on the dresser. Pick pocketing of all things! Cursing, he moved to find out what was taking so long for his bath.

Chapter 56

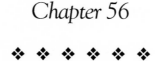

JESSICA WAITED NERVOUSLY in her room. Morgan had dragged her up the stairs and locked her in there, almost two hours ago. She was now sufficiently mad herself, though he was probably staying away to control his anger. That helped her maintain hers.

Hearing footsteps outside her door she felt fear. Hurrying to the soft cushioned chair by the window she sat down pulling her feet up under her gown and picked up a book. She barely managed to get it open before Morgan walked into the room. Glancing up like she hadn't a care in the world she nearly dropped the book at the look on her husband's face. Calmly closing it, she set it on the small table next to her, waiting for him to speak.

Morgan had purposely stayed away hoping his anger would cool but all calming had fled the minute he opened the door and saw her calmly reading a book.

"Has your sister arrived?"

Morgan swallowed. "No. They are coming at nine."

Jessica looked at the clock and frowned. That was an hour away. "Are they the only ones coming?"

"Yes."

Jessica waited for him to continue but he just stood there staring at her. She began to fidget.

Morgan calmly removed his jacket draping it over one of the chairs by the hearth. He unbuttoned two buttons. Jessica puzzled over his movements but purposely kept her face clear. "I suppose you have a good reason for your behavior this afternoon?"

Jessica swallowed. She didn't have excuse. She hadn't expected him to give her a chance to explain herself. Frowning, she bit her lip. "I regret doing it."

Morgan looked at her briefly but returned his attention to pouring himself a brandy. "The reason?"

Jessica clenched her teeth. He was starting to annoy her with his attitude. He wanted a certain answer every time. "I was angry at the callous way you treated me in front of my crew."

Morgan paused in pouring his drink. She had a reason, not a good one, but a reason all the same. Finishing filling his glass, he put the decanter down and replaced the top. "I don't think I was callous."

Jessica lifted her chin. "You ordered me to the carriage like a dog."

Morgan swirled the liquid around in the glass. He had done that, but she had butted in where she didn't belong. "I had planned on beating your backside."

Jessica stiffened. She knew that.

"Of course, I don't think it would do much good," he said seeing her tense. "So, instead, I have decided to deal with you in a different manner."

Jessica slide her feet to the floor. He was going to leave her behind. Feeling a deep emptiness inside, she swallowed trying to look at ease.

"I have decided not to take you on Friday and instead hire a personal guard. You may not leave the house without him." At her dejected look, he added, "the waterfront is, of course, off limits."

Not see the sea! That was worse than a spanking. Turning to look out into the darkness she frowned. It was what she deserved for all the bad things she had done lately. Life attached to a pig-headed dictator was starting to wear thin. "It won't matter, you know? I can't be something I'm not," she said quietly.

Morgan narrowed his gaze at the hearth. She was right about that, but at least he could restrict her from ruining his name. "Just keep yourself out of trouble and act like the lady you've been brought up to be."

Jessica's frown deepened. That was just it. She hadn't been raised to be a lady. Oh, she had been taught her values and basic manners but her father had let them do as they saw fit after their mother died. Jessica had been twelve, at the time. She had played the piano and wore dresses above the knee before then but she hated it. Many a day she would head to the pond and go fishing with Stephan or Nathan wearing breeches. It was just who she was. The ultimate freedom had been being allowed to sail. She had savored her nights at sea many a time staying at the wheel just looking up at the stars. She had several nights on her ship when it was docked. The sea was everything to her. Knowing her mother wouldn't have liked the person she turned out to be she lowered her head, feeling the tears in her eyes.

Morgan watched her face in the reflection of the window. She looked like a lost puppy. Hardening himself against that look, he drained his glass. "I will see you downstairs in an hour," he said leaving the room.

Jessica slumped in her chair. She was up against one of the hardest tests of her life. Morgan wanted a woman like Melissa. Jessica couldn't behave like that. It was stupid behavior. The act she gave Anthony this afternoon had made her sick. Life was so much simpler when all she had to do was sail.

Getting to her feet she moved to the mirror and stared at her refection. Her hair was mussed and her gown was smudged with dirt in several places. She even had a smudge on her cheek. Frowning she seated herself.

"Mama, help me act the proper lady. I want the sea back and I don't think he'll let me have it if I don't," Jessica said, laying her head in her arms and crying. This was something she hadn't done since she was a little girl.

Chapter 57

NATHAN CAME INTO THE HALL and frowned. "Going somewhere?"

"I thought I'd go with you. I have a certain interest there," Stephan said dressed from head to toe for the ball.

Nathan turned from straightening his cravat to look at Stephan. "She'll be there, then?"

"From what I understand."

Nathan finished with his cravat and put his coat on. "You aren't going for any other reason, are you?"

Stephan put on a look of innocence. "None that I know of," he said spreading his hands out to either side. Nathan scowled at him.

"She's my business."

"Right you are."

Nathan pulled on his gloves. He hated balls as much as the rest of them. His thoughts were interrupted as Christopher descended into the hall also dressed immaculately. His slow grin made both brothers arch their brows.

"I thought I might join you this evening."

Nathan's gaze snapped to Stephen's. Stephan just shrugged looking as surprised as he was. Nathan narrowed his eyes.

"You're coming to the ball?"

Christopher stopped on the last step. "Is that a problem?"

Nathan grinned. "No. You have almost four months left. Why the rush?"

Christopher's face darkened. "I'd control that tongue if I were you or tomorrow you'll find yourself at Andrew's"

Nathan's smile faded. "You sure can't take a joke."

Christopher smiled slowly. "I'm a bit sore on that subject. I'm sure you understand?"

Nathan cursed, heading for the door, which Hobkins promptly pulled open. “Good evening, my lords.”

Stephan and Christopher grinned at Nathan’s retreating back. “Now who can’t take a joke?” Christopher said following Stephan out. “Oh, Hobkins. Let anyone know that we’ve gone to Atherton’s ball.”

“Right, my lord,” Hobkins said watching the three handsome men climb into the carriage. Closing the door, he sighed. Lady Allison would have been smart to go with that trio. The gossip he was hearing would have died down some if she had been seen with those handsome bucks. Shaking his head he climbed the steps to see if she needed anything.

The carriage came to a halt in front of the ball. It wasn’t soon enough for Nathan. Whenever Stephan and Christopher got together they were worse than a swarm of bees. They wouldn’t let up until he was good and mad. Pushing open the door he climbed out leaving them grinning at one another.

“In a hurry, Nathan?”

“Shut up, Christopher or I’ll send every available girl and her mama in your direction,” Nathan finished, getting a bark of laughter out of Stephan.

When Christopher glared at Stephan, he pointed to Nathan. “He’ll do it, too.”

Nathan glared at Stephan. “I can send them your way, too.” he said with a smug smile as Stephan’s face darkened. Moving up the steps they were ushered into the ball. It was late and no one was there to announce them. The three stood at the top of the stairs overlooking the immense ballroom. Nathan quickly scanned the crowd looking for his wife. Seeing her dancing with Saul Sheridan his temper went over the edge.

“If you will excuse me,” he snapped, starting down the stairs.

Stephan grabbed his arm and pulled him away from the dance floor. “Nathan, don’t do anything rash,” he said smiling and nodding to people in the crowd. “We wouldn’t want any more scandal, would we?”

Nathan pulled his arm free as they reached a secluded spot on the east side of the ball. Christopher strolled up looking bored. “I’m trying to prevent scandal to my name. Saul Sheridan is lecherous rake.”

Stephan smiled at a couple passing by. “I’m well aware of Sheridan’s past but use your head,” he said taking two glasses from a passing servant and shoved one into Nathan’s hand. “He’s only doing it because it bothers you.”

Nathan gritted his teeth. “That’s just it. I don’t care but it’s the principle of the thing. I may not want my wife but no one else can have her either.”

Stephan stared at him in surprise. Christopher shook his head. “I think we should pay our respects to Aunt Ginger. Rae will more than likely be taken back there.”

Nathan frowned but nodded his consent. Rae was in deep trouble when he got ahold of her.

Chapter 58

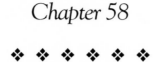

MELISSA WATCHED HER BROTHERS argue in the corner and frowned. They looked like they were calmly discussing an ordinary topic but by their stiff manner, she knew something was up. Wondering at the presence of Stephan and Christopher she nearly missed a step with her current partner. "Sorry," she said, giving Lord Atherton a smile.

"It's quite all right, my dear," he said as the music wound to an end. "You're a lovely dancer," he said taking her to Aunt Ginger's side and kissing her hand. "Ladies," he added before disappearing into the crowd. Melissa looked back at her brothers and frowned.

"I can't believe they're here. I figured Nathan would show up but the other two?" she said getting a smile out of Aunt Ginger.

"Your brothers have improved in manners, I trust."

Melissa gave her an exasperated look then smiled as her brothers walked over. "What brings you out?" she asked excepting a kiss on the cheek from all three.

"Thought I might be needed," Stephan said, scanning the crowd.

Melissa wasn't fooled. He was here to talk with Lady St. Paul. "Christopher, are you wife hunting?" she said, low enough not to be overheard.

Christopher smiled coolly. "No, I was hoping to diffuse some of the gossip."

Melissa lost her smile. "It's been bad," she said looking to see if anyone was within hearing. "Mainly from those women still in need of husbands. They want to make sure Allison is out of the picture."

Christopher's face hardened. "I was afraid of that," he said watching as Rae was ushered toward them by Sheridan, who had taken her for punch. "I'm glad, in a way, that Allison has chosen not to come to these things for a while."

Melissa sighed. "Yes, I tried to get her to come tonight. She said she wasn't ready for the taunts and gossip yet."

Nathan spotted his wife coming toward them and cleared his face of expression. Stephan smiled at Rae. "Nice to see you again, Rae," he said stopping Nathan from making a fool of himself a second time. Rae smiled hesitantly knowing by Nathan's angry eyes that he was furious with her.

Nathan again in control nodded to Sheridan before taking his wife by the waist and kissing her cheek. "How is the ball?" he asked trying to seem casual.

Rae, confused at this nice Nathan, smiled again. "It's all right. Your sister has been very nice," she said smiling at Melissa.

Melissa giggled. "Nathan, Rae is an excellent dancer," she said with a look that said take her out there.

Nathan smiled making Rae catch her breath. "Shall we?" He was so handsome. He was dressed like every other lord here but for some reason she was thoroughly aware of him tonight. His black hair was combed nicely curling slightly by his collar. Returning his smile she nodded then nearly tripped when their eyes met. His blazed with anger letting her know he wasn't pleased. Keeping the smile in place, she felt panic in the pit of her stomach. As he led her out on the floor for a dance, she frantically tried to think of what she had done to earn his anger.

Stephan watched them thankful that Sheridan took himself off to another area. Watching Nathan dance with his wife he sent a silent prayer to whoever was listening to keep Nathan in line at least until they got home.

Caleb moved up then slipping his arm around Melissa's waist. "How about a dance with me?"

Melissa tipped her head to the side. "I don't know. My card is quite full."

Caleb looked hurt but spoiled it with a grin. "I'll rip up that card," he said nodding to her brothers. "Gentlemen, if you don't mind?" At their smiles, Caleb whirled a giggling Melissa into the crowd.

Ginger pursed her lips. "That's almost scandalous," she piped from her seat on the sofa.

Stephan arched his brows. "They seem to like one another."

Ginger frowned. "Exactly, but such behavior should never take place in public."

Stephan grinned. "It could be worse. Jessica could be here with Morgan. Perhaps a fight or two would suit you?"

Ginger, forgetting herself for a moment, turned to glare at Stephan. "Your father didn't take a stick to your behind enough when you were a child. You are an insolent pup."

Stephan laughed. "I'm afraid you could be right," he said getting a stern look from her.

"Your sister refused to come," Ginger said.

Stephan sobered. "She'll come around. Give her a few days."

Ginger nodded "I had planned to, but tonight is a large affair. She could have made a stand tonight."

Stephan frowned. Allison wasn't one to handle matters like that. "I think she needed time to prepare."

Ginger smiled, "Of course."

Stephen's smile widened. "Would you care to dance?" he asked, looking down at her, amused at the gentle woman she just gave him a glimpse of, when most of the time she acted the tyrant.

Ginger looked up startled, a moment then recovered blushing slightly. "I don't think that I would. I haven't danced in years."

Stephan grinned at Christopher. "More the reason to enjoy the dance."

Ginger's blushed deepened at their teasing. Both men grinned. "Maybe later," she conceded knowing she was going to loose against the pair, otherwise.

Stephan shrugged. "This is a perfect song."

Christopher chuckled seeing his prefect Aunt squirm in her chair. She was actually embarrassed. "If it's the partner, I'd be happy to give you a twirl."

Ginger swallowed knowing her face was noticeably red now. "I think it best if I just go and powder my nose," she said getting to her feet and walking gracefully toward the stairs. Christopher watched her climb the stairs.

"That wasn't sporting of us was it?"

Stephan laughed. "She blushed. Did you see that?"

Christopher grinned. "I did. I wonder if she has ever been courted. She did seem to like the attention."

Stephan snorted. "She's fifty-two, for gods sake. She had to have a suitor here and there."

Christopher drew his brows down. "Perhaps we should find someone for her."

Stephan looked at him as if he were mad. "I think she's more than capable of finding herself a man."

Christopher smiled. "But she's always launching young girls in society. Maybe she let time slip away from her."

"I think you're crazy. If you are really set on this endeavor, I think you should speak to Father or Colan. They would know right off if she was still looking."

Christopher shrugged. "Perhaps I will."

Stephan rolled his eyes. "I, on the other hand, have spied a friend who looks like she could use a twirl around the dance floor," he said moving off toward a pretty brunette wearing a green gown. She was something to look at and vaguely familiar. Frowning to remember where he'd seen her, he was approached by Lady Anderson and her daughter. Smiling he nodded and spoke a few polite words to the pair. His eyes collided with Nathan's, who lifted his glass at him. Christopher returned a nod. He'd get even with him later. Christopher watched Nathan lead Rae out into the gardens. Knowing there was going to be trouble out there, he looked again at Lady Atherton's daughter. If this was the type of lady being offered as wife material, he was definitely going to need four months. A sudden urge to see the gardens made him escape their company. Walking quickly toward the gardens he slipped out.

Chapter 59

JESSICA LOOKED AT HER REFLECTION in the mirror and wanted to retch. The woman staring at her was definitely pretty. Her hair was piled on her head with small ringlets hanging down in back. Her face had been slightly powdered giving it an unnatural look. Her gown was deep red, cut modestly and tapered at the waist. For the third time, in her life, she was wearing a corset. The thing was impossible to breath in and she was sure to faint. Lifting her chin she watched the perfect lady mimic the move. She looked like Melissa. Getting to her feet, she slipped her feet into the most uncomfortable shoes she had. She teetered around the room several times before managing to stay upright without holding her arms out for balance. Walking around again she worked on looking demure and proper while keeping a smile on her face. Picking up the glass of brandy on the vanity, she drained it. Ladies weren't supposed to drink, but in this case she had allowed herself the privilege. She was, after all, meeting the man she had made a fool of herself in front of. He wouldn't know that, though. She looked like the crying female he had seen on the run away carriage. Nodding to her image in the mirror, she turned and left her room.

Moving along the hall she stumbled, biting her lip to keep the curse from coming out. Damn shoes. She should have worn her regular flats. She had them specially made due to her height. Cursing Morgan and his stupid ideas of a perfect wife, she managed to descend the stairs without breaking her neck but was gasping for air. The stupid corset was so tight. Janie, the maid who normally straightened the chambers upstairs, had pulled the thing very snug around her middle making her breasts pop out the top. It was a ridiculous piece of clothing. Pausing, she took several shallow breaths and found her breathing returning too normal. She really needed more time to practice before showing her husband what a proper little wife he had.

Moving into the drawing room, she smiled. No one was present. Thank god, she thought, moving into the room. She stopped in her tracks as her husband turned from the window on the far side of the room. They both stared at one another. Jessica blushed as Morgan's eyes traveled her body from head to toe then back up again. Lifting her chin, she moved into the room and looked for the most uncomfortable chair in the room. Ladies sat prim and proper.

Morgan watched her with brows arched. She looked exquisite, yet out of place some how. His brows slowly drew down in a frown, as he watched her move gracefully toward one of the stiff high backed chairs, on either side of the sofa. He knew they were uncomfortable and his brows went up as she sat in one looking stiff and proper. Frowning, he wondered what the hell she was doing now. Moving so he could see her face he was surprised. She was wearing powder. It looked completely out of place on her sun tanned face. Pursing his lips, he decided to let her have her little game. "Can I get you something?"

Jessica smiled. "Yes, thank you."

Morgan gritted his teeth at the artificial reply but moved to the decanter and poured her a brandy. He knew she liked the stuff. Putting the top back on the bottle he took up the glass and handed it to her.

Jessica smiled at him then looked at the glass he offered and looked shocked. "What is that?" she asked before she could stop herself.

Morgan frowned. "It's brandy. Isn't that what you drink?"

Jessica lifted her chin putting her nose in the air. "No, it is not. I happen to like port," she said, sniffing. She hated port.

Morgan pursed his lips, as he swallowed the brandy himself before refilling the glass with port and handing it to her.

"Is your sister older or younger than you?" she asked sipping the nasty liquid while keeping a smile on her face.

"Younger."

"Is she the only other sibling you have?"

"No, I have another sister."

"Is she younger, as well?"

"Yes."

"What is her name?"

"Monica."

"Is she married?"

Morgan frowned at his wife. She was acting like a bit of fluff. She reminded him of the dozens of women fawning over him at the balls. "Yes she's married. To the Earl of Havenston, in fact." Moving to sit in the soft cushioned chair on her left, he placed his elbows on his knees. "I'll need to see the records for the dock work of the ships going in and out of Canvey," he said watching her for anger.

"I had Davis put it in your study," she chirped, taking a sip from the glass. Morgan scowled at her. What the hell was going on? "So, your sister is a countess and the other one is a baroness?"

Morgan wanted to slap her. She was acting like a simpleton and Morgan found himself just nodded his head.

"I suppose I have a title, also," Morgan forced a smile at that comment. "Do you think I'm dressed appropriately? I wouldn't want to be out of style."

Morgan's smile fell like a rock. Where the hell had that drivel come from? "You look fine."

Davis cleared his throat from the door. "The Baron and Baroness of Bolton," he announced, as the couple moved into the room.

Morgan grinned at his sister. He hadn't seen her in almost a year. "Come here, squirt," he said, holding out both arms as Rachel flew across the room, throwing herself into them.

"Oh, Morgan, I can't believe it," she said hugging him fiercely. "You married without waiting for me," she said pulling away from him to look at Jessica, who had risen to her feet.

Jessica smiled noticing instantly that she towered over Rachel. Cursing herself for not wearing her flats, she moved forward still smiling. "You must be Lady Rachel. I'm glad to meet you," she said giving the girl a kiss on both cheeks.

Morgan gapped at her with brows arched, while Rachel smiled back warmly. "I'm glad to meet you, as well. I still can't believe Morgan actually found someone to marry him," she said making Morgan sound like a toad. Jessica nodded her head wanting very much to say 'I can see why you would have your doubts,' but knew that a lady never spoke so frankly.

Anthony moved forward to take Jessica's hand and give it a kiss. "I trust you haven't been swept off by anymore run away carriages."

Jessica reddened and wanted to applaud her body for doing so. "No, I haven't. Thank you again for your help," she said keeping a smile plastered on her face. This was the comment she hadn't wanted Morgan to hear. Peeking at him she could see he was angry but wasn't saying anything in front of the pair.

"Anthony," he said shaking his hand. "How have the two of you been getting on?"

"Wonderful," Rachel said beaming. "You're going to be an Uncle again," she said, getting an answering smile from her husband and a hug.

Morgan grinned. "Well, I'll be damned. That is wonderful," he said hugging his sister. "What do Chad and Michael think of that?"

Rachel beamed with pride. "The boys are delighted. They each have given us several names, in fact."

"Mostly female names. I think they want a little sister," Anthony said laughing.

Jessica smiled at the couple, feeling awkward in the stupid corset. She felt like a stiff doll.

Davis cleared his throat. "Dinner is served," he said disappearing out the door.

Morgan grinned. "Shall we," he said taking Rachel's arm, leading her from the room. Jessica smiled up at Anthony, as he held out his arm.

"Do me the honors?" he asked grinning as she took his arm. "I must tell you, Morgan is a lucky man."

Jessica smiled up at him feeling nervous. She stood eye level with him. Swallowing, she prayed she would make it into the dining room without falling flat on her face. The shoes were starting to hurt her feet. Reaching her chair, smile still in place, she sent the lord a quick "thank you" before sitting down as Anthony pushed in her chair. Nodding her thanks, she picked up her napkin and placed it in her lap. The corset was cutting off her circulation and she knew she wasn't going to get to eat much. She realized at that moment that this was a stupid plan. She wouldn't last more a week having to wear this sort of contraption. Smiling, she mimicked Melissa's every move. She even managed a few giggles here and there, disgusting herself completely. Morgan gave her glare after glare the entire meal.

After dinner they retired to the drawing room. Rachel moved to the pianoforte and began to play and Jessica felt nervous. She couldn't do a single womanly thing. She never had an ear for music, couldn't sew, hated fashion and balls, and never spent a single evening in a salon with the women. She had no idea what ladies did. Realizing she would have to spend sometime with Melissa to copy her, she smiled and clapped when Rachel was done. The men talked of shipping. Jessica was dying to join in but instead chatted with Rachel about her children and her home. She even managed to gossip, something she never did.

As they said their farewells, Jessica felt like she'd run up and down a beach of soft sand. Her back ached from trying to stand perfectly straight, just so she could breath, and her feet were ready to fall off. Morgan shut the door and turned on her, "Just what the hell was that?"

Jessica arched a brow. "Whatever do you mean?" she asked turning her back to walk gracefully toward the stairs.

"I'm talking about your behavior tonight?" When she didn't stop but kept moving he cursed. "For god sakes, you giggled."

Jessica stiffened, biting her tongue. She was well aware of her behavior tonight and wasn't proud of it. She had been exactly like Melissa, a perfect lady. "Most ladies giggle, Milton," she said, before she could stop herself. Mounting the first step, she turned to look at him. "If you don't mind, I'm going to retire."

Morgan stared at her in disbelief. She had behaved like a stranger tonight. Smiling and chatting about the drivel of the ton. She hadn't once had a sip of brandy, which he knew she liked. She had smiled and laughed, no giggled, at several things he hadn't thought were remotely funny. Suddenly, her last statement clicked in his mind. She had called him Milton. Setting his face, he smiled.

Jessica didn't like that smile and tipped her head like a simpleton. "Good night, then" she said climbing the stairs with care. Her feet were killing her. Reaching the top step she turned to head toward her room.

"Milton?" Morgan asked from the bottom of the stairs.

Jessica stiffened glancing at him. Seeing his intent, she bolted for her room, as he pounded up the steps behind her. Reaching her door, at a slide, she cursed as her sight darkened. She was going to faint. "Bloody hell," she said crumpling to the floor, as Morgan reached her.

Morgan stared at her in shock then narrowed his eyes. "Fainting? Another of your games?" he asked, watching her face for any sign of movement. Seeing her pale face lying on the floor, he frowned. "Jessica!" he said, sternly. Nothing. Her face remained the same. Cursing, he bent to scoop her up and felt the corset. "Stupid fool," he said, kicking the door open. Moving to the bed he placed her head on the pillow, then quickly undid the buttons on the back of the gown. Pulling the laces loose he flipped her over on her back and pulled the garment loose in front. He watched, as her breathing got better. Reaching over to the bowl and ewer on the stand by the wall, he poured some in the bowl and wet a cloth. Ringing out the excess he placed the cloth on her head and along the side of her face.

Jessica moaned as her eyes fluttered open. Looking up into Morgan's face she stiffened. "What happened?"

"You fainted."

"I fai..." she let the sentence trail off. That stupid corset! Pursing her lips, she tried to sit up but Morgan placed a hand on her chest, his fingers touching her breasts.

"You're staying here."

Jessica closed her eyes. Fine, she could lay here all night.

"Now, you can explain what you were doing tonight?"

"I don't know what you mean. I was entertaining your sister and her husband."

"That." Morgan said frowning. "That's what I'm talking about."

Jessica's eyes widened. "What?"

"That sweet voice and those false smiles," he mimicked in a high-pitched voice.

Jessica wanted to laugh. "My voice is the same as it always is. I smile when I'm enjoying myself."

Morgan cursed, getting to his feet. "You were acting like a simpleton."

Jessica frowned. Melissa wasn't a simpleton. "Is there something else you wish or may I retire?" she asked changing the subject.

Morgan scowled. "I want an answer, damn it."

Jessica sat up. "I haven't a clue as to what you're talking about," she said clutching her bodice as the gown slipped. "Now, if you will excuse me, I would like to retire."

Morgan stared at her then turned and slammed out of the room.

Jessica cursed, flopping back on the bed. Her charade had worked but for some reason she didn't feel like a winner. Getting to her feet, she pulled off her gown and threw the offending corset in the corner. That garment wasn't going back on her body no matter how unlady like it was. Removing the rest of her clothing, she slipped on one of Morgan's shirts and buttoned it up, then crawled into bed. Victory wasn't as sweet as she remembered she decided but froze as the door to her room opened.

Morgan moved into the room, wearing only a robe. He walked around her garments that were scattered on the floor and arched his brows when she sat up wearing his shirt. Shaking his head, he slipped off his robe and moved toward the bed. With eyes like saucers Jessica swallowed.

"What are you doing?" she squeaked.

"I'm exercising my husbandly rights?" he said getting into the bed and pulling her against him.

Jessica's pulse quickened. "Murry, I think..."

She didn't get to finish as Morgan growled and pulled her close to start kissing her. Jessica thought about fighting him but as he deepened the kiss bringing his tongue into play, she forgot everything.

Their lovemaking was passionate and satisfying and Jessica wondered how they could be compatible in that way but hate each other in every other. As she lay there in his arms, afterwards, she cursed to herself. Ladies were supposed to lie there and let their husbands have their way. Frowning, she sighed. That was one area she didn't think she could ever manage to remain the proper lady. Feeling Morgan squeeze her close, she closed her eyes. Tomorrow would be another day.

Chapter 60

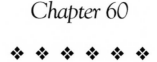

STEPHAN, concerned for Rae's welfare, sighed in relief at seeing Christopher follow the pair into the gardens. Looking down at Lady St. Paul, he couldn't help but smile. Christopher was going to die if the pair ended up together. She was graceful and smart with a sense of humor to rival his own. She'd fit into their scheme perfectly. All they needed now was her cooperation.

Cari smiled back at him, surprised that he was speaking to her after what Ranki did the other night.

"So, how is the little monkey?"

Cari turned scarlet. "He's fine and again, I apologize to you for his behavior. He can't help himself."

Stephan laughed. "Looking back, it is rather funny."

"But you hurt your hand?"

"Just a small break," he said, smiling. "Nothing that won't heal in time."

Cari swallowed, relaxing at his easy manner. "You're an excellent dancer, Lord Stephan. I must confess, I haven't done much of this lately."

"Oh really. Do they not have balls in India?"

"They had quite a number of balls there but I didn't attend very many. My brother wanted me to but I...well, I was off on tour."

Stephan arched his brows. "That sounds interesting. Did you travel the entire country?"

Cari laughed at the statement. She had indeed traveled the country but not like he pictured, she was sure. Her brother had been against it from the start. But she was twenty-two and had money of her own so he didn't have much to say about it. She had packed up her belongings, strapped them to the back of a burrow, and set off with her grandfather on a two month trip. They didn't see any civilization and she had lived like a native. Her grandfather showed her how to live off the land, eating bugs, berries, and rabbit. It was something these stuffy society types wouldn't understand. "I didn't travel every last inch of the country but I saw a large part."

Stephan smiled. "It must have been fascinating."

Cari frowned. Most people thought of India as a large desert. To them it wasn't fascinating at all. "It was quite lovely. So, anymore problems with your family?"

Stephan, who had been scanning the crowd, brought his gaze back to hers in surprise. It was improper to ask such a question but the lady before him, didn't seem to know it. Stephan grinned, Christopher was going to love it. "Ah, not since the wedding celebration."

Cari grinned. "Your family does seem to get itself in trouble."

Stephan chuckled, at her bold statement. "Yes, they do. How is it you know about my family?"

"Why, Andrew, of course. He raves about your family," she said then blushed, realizing she probably shouldn't have told him that.

Stephan grinned. "Christopher is the only one that could use that statement against Andrew."

Cari smiled. "You're very perceptive."

Stephan smiled. "You have to be now a days." Knowing he wasn't likely to get another chance, Stephan pursed his lips. "Since you're being rather frank in your questions, I think it only fair that I be the same."

Cari frowned in puzzlement. "Was I?" she asked letting a smile slowly cross her face.

Stephan laughed. "You're going to be perfect?" he said swallowing when her brows drew together in confusion.

"Perfect for what?" she asked.

"I have a proposition for you. One you'll find amusing. Your brother did say you loved putting people on the spot."

Cari frowned. "He said that?"

Stephan frowned realizing he must have offended her. "Well, not exactly in a bad way. He just told me about the gifts you send him."

Cari laughed, making Stephan grin. "Andrew is on the stiff side. I'm just trying to loosen him up."

Stephan smiled. "That's kind of what we have in mind. I know someone who needs...er...loosening up. The man's wound tighter than rope."

Cari chuckled, her curiosity perked. "You want me to send gifts to a friend of yours?"

Stephan shook his head. "Not exactly. I want you to spend time with him maybe get to know him and disrupt his perfect life, as much as possible."

Cari frowned. "I don't think that would be a good idea."

Stephen's eyes widened. "Why not?"

"I don't deal well with people, especially someone I don't know."

"Oh, you know him. It's my brother, Christopher."

Cari's mouth fell open. "You want me to rile up your brother's life?"

"Not in a bad way. I want him to become aware of life. Know that it's more than just business."

Cari shut her mouth. In the last three days, almost every member of the Hayworth family had found a chance to talk with her. Frowning, she now knew why they had been so friendly. They wanted her to court their brother. Walking with Stephan to the punch table, she accepted the glass he handed her with a thank you. Stephan took her elbow and led her out into the gardens for a stroll to finish their conversation. "Why would you ask me?" she asked.

Stephan smiled. "There are several things that led me to you. First, your brother has mentioned the fact that you are independently stable, making it possible for you to do as you please. Second, you have a passion for life that you keep well hidden but I think under normal circumstances you're swinging from the trees, so to speak."

Cari turned scarlet. He was so close to the truth that she felt like he'd looked inside her. "How do you know that?"

Stephan smiled sheepishly. "Andrew is very friendly."

Cari scowled. "And did my brother tell you everything about me?"

"No. In fact, I had to pry a lot of it out of him."

Cari looked at him with narrowed eyes. "What did you hold over his head?"

Stephan looked up at the stars above their heads. "I told him my plan."

"What plan?"

"The plan I had for Christopher. He loved the idea."

Cari stared at Stephan's handsome profile. Standing in the moonlight, she wondered why it was she hadn't lost her temper and stormed away from him. Frowning, she realized he reminded her of someone. As the answer came to her, she looked away. He reminded her of her brother. Her brother that had loved to sail. His name had been Blake but he had died three years ago, in a bad storm off the coast of Australia.

Stephan watched her face sadden and frowned. "I'm sorry. If you would rather not have anything to do with it, I understand. Jonathan told me it was a stupid idea."

"Jonathan?"

"My brother."

"Your brother knows about this," she asked knowing perfectly well they did.

Stephan smiled again. "They all know about this. As a matter of fact, I had to get their approval before I could approach you."

Cari was stunned at the whole idea. Usually, the man was trying to win the woman and her family over, not the family trying to win the girl for an oblivious man. "You're saying your family picked me for Christopher?"

Stephan nodded. "They each have their own reasons for wanting Christopher's life given a dose of fun. Mainly, it's the fact that in four months he has to have a wife. We don't want him to put an add in the Post."

Cari was nodding her head before he even finished. "I see. So, you all want someone a little wild and free?" Stephan put his hand to his chest in shock, but Cari wasn't fooled. "I understand. I'm not a paragon when it comes to mixing with society."

"Believe me, that's a good thing."

Cari laughed, unable to stay angry. "I have to agree with you. Society in England is very proper."

Stephan smiled "For the most part, it is. You understand what we're up against? We either end up with an artificial lady with nothing but fashion and gossip on her mind or someone like yourself, which I might add, is very hard to find."

Cari laughed at his suave talk. "Now, I know why they chose you to be the negotiator. You have a very glib tongue." When his face looked confused, she laughed harder. "They didn't tell you?" she said holding her sides. "You and your family are very strange," she said between laughs.

Stephan felt himself grinning at her laughter, but still didn't understand what she was laughing about. "What didn't they tell me?"

Cari chuckled. "Each one of your family members has talked with me. Nathan, at Andrew's office; Melissa, at the ball tonight; Jonathan, at the wedding celebration; Jessica, at the post; did I miss anyone?"

"Allison?"

"Oh, yes. The angel. Well, I guess she spoke to me at the wedding."

Stephan grinned. "They are rather persistent once their minds are set."

Cari slowly stopped laughing, her smile fading. "Whose idea was it to use me?"

Stephan didn't like the way that sounded, "We're not using you. Andrew says you have just under a year to find yourself a husband, so I figured you'd be..." his voice trailed off at her furious look. "What?"

"I have to find a husband in less than a year?"

Stephan arched his brows. "It's what he said. Didn't you know that?"

Cari began to pace. "Well, I knew it was getting close. I just thought I had longer than that. I'm going to kill him." "Who?" he asked dying to know exactly why she only had a year.

"My brother, of course. He sent me here with the impression it was just a visit. Now I know why he left the comforts of his home, with a wife expecting, mind you, to accompany me here. He's planned this all along."

"Planned what?"

"That I had to marry. Aren't you listening?" she asked looking at him like he was daft.

Stephan scowled. "Andrew didn't say why, you know?"

"Well, good lord, that is a shock. He told you everything else it seems."

"Not everything."

She gave him an exasperated look then resumed pacing. "I only have a year because that is what Father stipulated when I inherited my grandfather's money."

"He set a time limit?"

"Well, Father wasn't happy about the money. But when Grandfather died and he named me his heir and gave me all that money, Father added that I had to be married by a certain age or loose everything."

Stephan understood now. "So, your father added that as his part in your inheritance. But, I thought your father died?"

"He did. But in the will, Reid, my oldest brother, would become responsible for me if Father died before I wed."

"Then this could work out for the both of you."

Cari frowned. She had only met Christopher twice and after meeting Stephan, Christopher was as boring as they said. "I'll think about it," she said walking back toward the ball. Stephan watched her go, a slow smile crossing his face. She was going to send Christopher on a wild ride if she went along with them.

NATHAN PULLED RAE INTO THE GARDEN, barely hanging onto his temper. Moving to the far bench, he pushed her down and began to pace. Turning to look at her, he frowned. Stephan was right about one thing, she was a real looker. But she was still a lying thief. "Care to tell me what you were doing?"

Rae frowned. Nathan was angry and with him, it could be any number of things. "Exactly, to what are you referring?"

Nathan put his hands in his pockets to keep his temper under control. "I'm referring to your dancing partner. I thought I warned you about making conquests here?"

Rae turned scarlet. "How dare you? I haven't done anything improper since I married you." Getting to her feet she moved closer to him. "In fact, I've had just about enough of you ordering me around. I'm a human being and deserve to be treated as such."

Nathan grabbed her shoulders pushing her up against the brick wall. "What you deserve and what you've earned are two different things. I have every right to order you to do as I wish. I happen to have married you," he said, taking a step back from her to resume pacing. "I don't want to see you anywhere near that man again. He's dangerous."

Rae snapped her mouth shut. He was right, about being able to restrict her from seeing certain people, but she still deserved to be treated with respect. "Fine, may I go?" she asked lifting her chin when his gaze came to hers.

"No, you may not go. I want to know what you were doing on the waterfront today?"

Rae drew her brows down at that statement. "The waterfront? I haven't been anywhere near the sea, since I came here from America."

Nathan ground his teeth. "I happen to know that's a lie and I advise you to cease lying to me or I'll take each lie out on your backside."

Rae reddened but her anger was making her reckless. "I'm telling you, I haven't been to the sea in six months."

Nathan narrowed his eyes. She looked like she was telling the truth but Stephan had seen her there. His brother never lied, so she must be. Taking her arm he started back for the ball.

"Where are you taking me?"

"We're going back to Aunt Ginger's."

"Why?"

"I have to continue this in private," he stated stopping to look at her. "Or would you like me to bare your bottom here and now to meet out your punishment for lying."

Rae turned scarlet. "You still think I'm lying?"

"I know you are," he said pulling her along behind him. Rae snapped her mouth shut. She wasn't about to let him lay a hand on her. Privacy was fine with her. There was no way in hell this arrogant, blind-sighted man was going to spank her like a child for something she didn't do. Moving back into the ball, she envisioned smacking him, as he led her along by her hand toward the stairs acting like nothing was wrong between them. Knowing it was stupid, and something she was sorely going to regret later, she did something she never would have done if things were different between them. As they passed the punch table, she grabbed a pitcher full of punch and poured the entire contents over Nathan's head. Not missing a step, she continued up the stairs and out of the ballroom.

Nathan swallowed several times as the red liquid ran down his face and soaked into his shoes. Several of the ladies around him were crying at how Rae had ruined their gowns, each looking at him as if he were to blame. Feeling like a complete fool, he accepted a towel from the footman that Rae had snatched the pitcher from. Smiling tolerantly, he casually walked up the steps, moping his face as he went.

Christopher watched his brother leave the ball, with as much dignity as one could while leaving large puddles of red liquid on each step.

"Good lord, what happened now?" Stephan said.

"I believe the Hayworth's have just suffered another scandal."

"Aunt Ginger is not going to like this."

Christopher gave Stephan a disgusted look, but looked at Aunt Ginger to gauge her reaction. Seeing her glaring at him, like it was his fault, made him angry. "What the hell is wrong with this family? We never had this kind of problem when Father was in charge."

Stephan grinned. "At least Allison's escapade will diminish some."

Christopher rolled his eyes. "First icing, now punch. What next?"

Stephan shrugged. "I'll leave that up to you. It seems you're the only one that hasn't been touched by scandal."

Christopher looked at him with narrowed eyes. "You better hope nothing comes my way, or by god, I'll take it out of your hide," he snapped moving to calm Aunt Ginger. Stephan looked back toward the stairs with a frown. Nathan was going to kill Rae. Hurrying after the pair, he hoped he would reach home before they did.

NATHAN CLIMBED INTO THE CARRIAGE and was surprised Rae was in there. He had expected her to run off and make an even bigger fool out of him. Sitting in the seat with a squishing sound, he toweled off his head throwing a piece of pineapple out the window, as it came loose from his hair. Removing his jacket, he threw several more pieces out as he removed them from his collar.

"I think that was uncalled for?" he stated, laying the jacket on the seat next to her as the carriage began to move.

Rae swallowed. It had been an entirely impulsive act, one she regretted immensely. Lifting her chin for courage she licked her lips. "Yes, you're right."

Nathan didn't look at her. He didn't trust himself to keep his hands off her. He wanted to beat her, for again causing problems for his family. He didn't care what the people would say about him, but Allison. Damn. "Do you realize what you've done?"

Rae pursed her lips. "I'm sure your precious friends won't look upon you with disfavor."

Nathan frowned. "It isn't me I'm worried about." Rae was taken aback by that remark. Was he concerned for her? "You have just put another wall up between my sister and her chances at finding a suitable husband."

Rae paled. My god, was that true? "But she didn't do anything."

Nathan pulled off his left shoe and held it out the window letting the excess liquid run out. "Society doesn't look only at the female. It looks at the whole family."

Rae paled further, "I didn't know."

Nathan cursed. It was too late now. "Damn it, do you have to act this way? Can't you just follow the rules and behave like you're supposed to? A lady doesn't do the things you're doing. She doesn't dance with another man two balls in a row. She doesn't flirt with men in public, she doesn't pick pockets on the waterfront, and above all she controls herself when in public," he finished, glaring. "I keep labeling you with the title of lady, but perhaps it doesn't apply."

Rae felt her stomach knot. She hadn't known about the dancing thing. This was her first time in England and things in America were different. They weren't as strict with etiquette. Looking at her hands she felt the urge to cry. Half the things he had said weren't even true. She didn't know whom she had flirted with and she had never picked pockets on the waterfront, though she was very good at such a thing. Turning further away from him, she frowned.

"I'm sorry," she said, looking out the window.

Nathan snorted lifting his other shoe to empty its contents. "Like it will matter," he said putting the shoe on as the punch began to dry making his hair stiff. "Allison is the one this is going to hurt the most."

Rae felt the first tears run down her face and shifted so Nathan couldn't see. She knew he would only get angry. As the carriage began to slow she took several breaths trying to stop. Knowing it was a losing battle, she pulled the hood, of her cloak, up over her hair to help hide her face. She would have to go to Allison first thing in the morning and explain everything. Hopefully, Nathan didn't lock her away.

Chapter 61

JESSICA WALKED INTO THE STUDY with a smile pasted on her face. Stephan was there with Morgan and they were discussing Stephan's ships. She had caught the tail end of their conversation.

Stephan smiled at her. "Good morning, Jess," he said giving her a kiss on the cheek. "I'd like to thank you for talking to Morgan for me," he said laughing. "I really was in a bind."

Jessica smiled and nodded. All the while, looking at Morgan with a questioning look and a bit of a blush remembering last night.

Morgan turned away and moved behind his desk. He didn't give her so much as a hello. "Then it's settled, I'll run Canvey with my three ships and you'll take care of Turrock."

Jessica nearly broke her ankle at that statement. Her high shoes, which she had made herself put back on, had turned with her surprise. So that was how he was going to get at her business.

Stephan in his gratitude didn't notice Jessica's silence. "That's fine. You have two ships that come in every other week, right?"

Morgan nodded. "The Reliant will be here in two weeks. I'm taking the Phantom out Friday."

Jessica's head snapped up at the name of her ship. He was leaving her behind on her own ship! Seeing the mocking triumph in his face hurt worse than being left behind and she rose to her feet to look out one of the windows over looking the gardens. Why should she care what he was doing? For some reason, she did. Feeling the hurt from Morgan's look deep in her gut, she suddenly realized she carried some deeper feelings for her husband. Knowing he had gone out of his way to hurt her, made those feelings feel betrayed.

Stephan glanced at Jessica but continued on with the conversation. "Will you have someone to keep an eye on things in Canvey when you're gone?"

"Of course. You have nothing to worry about. Just keep the records straight in Turrock and our business should thrive. The lessened travel time should help out tremendously."

Stephan grinned. "Now, it's just until my hand heals."

Morgan returned his smile. "Of course," he said seeing a lot of Jonathan's qualities in Stephan. "Say hello to your brother for me, then."

Stephan smiled. "He wasn't thrilled about trading with me but knowing I would owe him one, must have been enough." Moving to give Jessica another kiss he whispered his thanks "You look good in a gown," he added frowning slightly at her stiff response. Being in a hurry, he didn't have time to pursue it. "I'll show myself out," he said leaving the study whistling.

Morgan watched his wife stand gracefully at the window and wondered at her thoughts. She now knew he was taking her ship on Friday. Seeing the hurt flash in her eyes, made his revenge less triumphant. "Are you going somewhere?" he asked noticing she was dressed in a pretty rose-colored gown.

Jessica stiffened at his question. Turning to face her husband, she put on the most emotionless face she could manage and gave the lines she had practiced all evening after their argument. "I am to receive callers today. Your Aunt Athea is coming with a couple of her lady friends," she piped.

Morgan smiled. "Very good. Have you broken your fast?"

Jessica nodded. "Can I get you something?"

Morgan drew his brows down at her manner. What the hell was going on now? "No. I've already eaten."

"Very good. If you'll excuse me, I have a few things to get ready."

Nodding his head he waved his hand toward the door. Seeing her tip her head in his direction, he scowled at her retreating form. She was acting just like she had the night before. Cursing, he scowled at the door. What the hell was she up to now? She hadn't said anything about taking her ship. Shaking his head, he stared at the door, confused.

Jessica left the study, pulling the door closed behind her. Leaning her head against it, she closed her eyes and swallowed several times trying to keep the tears from coming. A huge knot was in her throat. He had planned on leaving her behind on her own ship she knew that now. The look of triumph in his eyes had confirmed it. Lifting her head, she moved along the hall knowing her next plan of action to be right. If he wanted a perfect woman, that was what he was going to get.

Chapter 62

"COME ON, ALLISON. I haven't got all day. We have to ride almost two hours in one direction."

Allison pursed her lips. "Jonathan, I planned this day with Stephan. If you made him keep his word, I wouldn't have to put up with this kind of abuse. Stephan never notices the time."

"I happen to have several horses to sell tomorrow and don't want to spend too much time away from Ashley."

Allison smiled. "Fine, I'm ready," she said pinning her cloak in place. "Did you bring her with you?"

"It's about time," he said, giving Hobkins a grin. "No, I didn't. She insisted on staying at Meadowacres to get familiar with the house. She's actually come along way. Tell Christopher where we went," he said to Hobkins.

Hobkins nodded. "Very good, my lord." Seeing Jonathan arch his brows, he smiled slightly. Jonathan grinned.

"Much better, Hobkins. Still a little like the wood man, but definitely better."

"What woodsman?"

"Colan's man. Stephan is worried we'll end up with a wallboard like Uncle Colan has for a butler. I'm told Colan's butler actually blends into the wall."

"Then I'll be sure not to visit there. I'd never be able to find the man." Allison said laughing.

Hobkins felt his face twitch and quickly closed the door, before chuckling. It wasn't a servants place to show emotion to his employer's conversation but that Miss Allison was a regular stitch.

Jonathan helped her into the carriage and they were off. "Did you lock Nero in like I told you to?"

"Yes. Hobkins had Timmy, from the stables, put the bars on my windows."

"Good. I don't plan on being dragged home by my leg."

Allison smiled. "Who is it we're seeing?"

"The Lord of Salisbury? He's suppose to have the best Wolfhounds in the area."

Allison paled at the name. "Who?" she squeaked.

"Colan wrote it down here, just a minute." he said pulling the paper from his pocket. "Yes, it's the Earl of Salisbury. An earl, imagine that," he said putting the paper back.

"Yes, imagine that," she answered absently. Her mind reeling from the thought of being in the same vicinity as Royce. "And Ashley likes the idea?"

"I didn't exactly tell her about this. She's had so many new things lately, that I think we should wait to see if the animal can be trained."

Allison nodded. "All right, but we'll have to tell the earl that we might need to exchange this one if it doesn't work out."

Jonathan frowned. "That's a good idea. I wonder if the man will agree."

"I think we can persuade him."

Jonathan looked at Allison and smiled. "I'm sure you can."

"So, what did Nathan do last night?"

Jonathan arched a brow at her change of topic. "What did you hear he did?"

"Rae came to see me this morning. She was quite upset that she'd ruined my only chance at finding a man and promised she would correct the bad impression she had made at the ball last night." Tipping her head slightly, Allison smiled. "Did she really pour a pitcher full of punch over Nathan?"

"Pineapples and all," Jonathan said laughing, "I would have loved to see that one."

"Me too," she said "But I can picture it pretty well. Can I ask you something?"

"All right, but not too personal. I've only been awake for three hours."

Allison laughed. "I was just going to ask if you think the punch incident would have any effect on my finding a husband?"

"Personally? No. I don't think so."

"The cake incident is the big one, isn't it?"

"Not so much the incident, as the fact that you're blind and own that cat."

Allison smiled her thanks. "That's one of the reasons I like having you for a brother. You're honest with me and answer me direct."

Jonathan chuckled. "I just hope I can manage that with Ashley. She's very fragile," he said his voice going soft.

Allison placed her hand on his leg. "She's not as fragile as you think. If you make her do for herself, she'll be fine. I know if I rely on Netty and Nero to do everything for me, then I become more dependent on them."

Jonathan smiled. "I knew it would do me good to come along today. Actually, Ashley and I have come to a sort of understanding," he said feeling a deep satisfaction.

"An understanding?"

"I've agreed not to wait on her hand and foot and she's agreed to treat me without prejudging my actions."

Allison smiled. "That's wonderful. I knew she was a smart girl."

Jonathan laughed. "Let's just hope things go smoothly from here on out."

"If you can keep Stephan occupied with Christopher, I'm sure it will. By the by, you're still getting that favor out of Stephan, aren't you?"

"You bet," he said with a grin hugging her shoulders.

Chapter 63

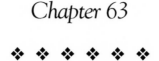

"NOW SEE HERE, LADS. Ye do what they tell ye and everything will be fine. Remember yer ma will be there, too."

Sean being five nodded his head, in understanding. Ian at three, was full of questions. "Do you think they'll like us?"

"Of course, lad. Everyone likes children."

"But Mama Rae isn't the same. She's sad."

Thomas frowned. "Now, Ian, I told ye about that. Yer ma has a new husband. She's not sad, she's just getting used to having someone tell her what to do."

Ian grinned. "Like you do Sean and me?"

Thomas smiled, nodding his head. "Aye, like I do to ye."

Sean looked nervously out the window. "How much farther?"

"We should be there any minute."

"Are you staying?" Ian asked.

"Well, now, I don't know," Thomas said, not wanting to scare the boys further. "It's up to Master Nathan," who hadn't been to thrilled with him the first time they had met. Thomas knew a gambler when he saw one and was sure Nathan had pinned him as a thief, whether reformed or not.

"Well, I'll just tell him you have to stay or I'll cry for days."

Thomas turned his head to the window, hiding his grin from the boys view. Composing his features into a stern mask he turned back to them. "If yer smart, ye'll let yer new da tell ye what's what. Don't go caus'in trouble from the start."

Ian frowned. "But they got to let you stay. You're important."

Thomas wanted to tell the boy that men like him weren't made to grace the halls of society but just pointed his finger at the lad for emphasis. "Ye do like yer ma said and remember to behave yerself." Sean and Ian exchanged looks, then both nodded at him. "Good, cause I think we're here," he said, feeling the carriage slow. "Now, remember to stand tall and act like yer ma's been tellin ye."

Sean and Ian stiffened. "Don't worry. I'll try not to cuss and send grandpa into a tizzy," Ian said moving to look out the window. Thomas rolled his eyes heavenward. Ian was going to get himself sent to an orphanage within the day.

The carriage rumbled to a halt and the footman pulled the door open. "Remember yer lessons," Thomas said.

"You're starting to sound like Mama Rae," Ian said dashing out the door with a hop. The footman looked at him with brows raised.

"Ian, you're going to get us sent to become sewer rats."

Thomas's mouth fell open, at that statement, and then quickly snapped shut. "Yer ma's going to have a vapor attack, if ye keep up with that sort of behavior," Thomas said grabbing up the two little hands and starting up the steps. "Sure is fancy," he added minutes before reaching the door.

HOBKINS HEARD THE BELL SIGNALING the arrival of a carriage and quickly straightened his coat. Lord Nathan's two little mites were arriving today and he wanted to make a good impression. Running a hand through his white hair, he gave his coat a final pat and pulled open the door. Seeing the trio mounting the steps, he barely caught himself from letting his mouth fall open. The children were thin little waifs with brown hair and sunken eyes. Their clothes, though better than most street children's, hung on their bodies. The littlest one had a sole loose on his right shoe and as he climbed the last three steps, he saw it flap against the ground before his foot covered it. Pursing his lips, he stared at the man holding each child's hand. He was five foot eight, with graying hair tied back at the nape, but his clothes were neat. His eyes were light blue and he was smiling, showing that he was missing three of his teeth.

Swallowing, Hobkins remembered his manners and moved to open the door to admit them.

"We'd like to see Mama Rae, please," Ian stated, lifting his chin with authority. Hobkins felt his heart soften at the boy's remark.

"Of course you would, young man. If you will follow me, you can wait in the drawing room."

"Outstanding!" he said, following Hobkins as they moved off down the hall. "Did you hear that Sean? They're going to let us draw while we wait."

Hobkins nearly laughed at the outrageous statement, but managed to keep his face straight. "I'll send Mrs. Lang in with some refreshments."

Ian moved into the room and looked around. It had several chairs, a desk, three tables, and a fireplace. Looking at Sean, he frowned. "There isn't anything to draw with in here," he said, as Hobkins pulled the door shut behind them.

Thomas glanced at the door and then grabbed Ian's shoulder. "Look, lad, the drawing room is just a name they call a place like this. No one draws here."

Ian looked disappointed. "What are we supposed to do then?"

"Yer gonna sit in one of those chairs there and stay out of trouble."

Sean obediently went to one of the chairs and sat. Ian, on the other hand, shook his head. "I think I'll look at that thing on the desk," he said moving to stare at the candleholders with fascination. They were shaped like men in robes, each holding a candle above their heads. "Why are these men wearing their nightclothes?" he asked looking at Thomas.

Thomas dragged his eyes away from the decanters along the far wall and moved to look closer at the figures holding the candles. "Them there are wizards, lad,"

"Wizards?"

Sean got out of his chair and moved to have a look. "Just like Merlin, Ian." he said excitedly.

Ian's eyes brightened. "Do you think they have a wizard here?"

"No, silly. Wizards don't live in the city."

Thomas smiled, at the boys, as they talked about the figures from the stories Rae had told them. Hearing the door open, he turned to see a medium built woman, with brownish gray hair, move into the room holding a tray full of cookies and milk. She smiled with genuine warmth. "Here now, you little mites must be famished."

Ian screwed up his face at that. "What's famished?" he asked Sean.

"I don't know," he whispered back "But she brought cookies for us." Moving forward, he sat on one of the chairs around the tray and waited. Ian, seeing his brother sit with his hands in his lap, followed suit for once. Hoping the cookies would be his prize for good behavior.

"Go ahead, children. Help yourself," Mrs. Lang said placing milk in front of them on the small table. Sean looked at Thomas, who nodded his head, holding up one finger so Mrs. Lang couldn't see. Sean reached forward slipping out of his chair just far enough to take a soft yellow cookie. Ian jumped from his chair and took two.

"Ian!" Sean yelled trying to take the extra cookie away from him but Ian hopped up in his chair holding the prize just out of his brother's reach.

"It's mine," Ian screamed getting a startled look out of Thomas.

"Here now, what's all the racket?" Stephan said from the door. Both boys froze in place, each staring at the man with black hair towering at the door. "Awe, cookies," he said smiling at the boys. "With a pile like that, I don't think you need to fight over that one. I'm sure Mrs. Lang has more in the kitchen," he said moving to kneel on the other side of the table looking at the two boys with a smile.

Sean moved back to his chair. He glared at his brother. "He was only supposed to take one," he said getting a tongue from Ian.

Stephan grinned, reminded instantly of his brothers and himself. "Well, now," he said, handing Sean another cookie. "If you take another one then things will be fair."

Sean looked at the cookie in Stephan's hand, then up at Thomas who nodded. Taking the offering, he smiled. "Thank you," he said scooting up in his chair to eat the cookies. Ian moved forward in his chair to grab his glass. Taking a large drink he set the cup back down spilling a little on the table.

"Are you a pirate?" he asked stuffing a piece of cookie in his mouth.

Stephan grinned. He supposed he looked like one. He was wearing black breeches, a white billowy shirt, a wide black belt around his waist, high black boots on his feet and a red scarf about his neck. "Not exactly, I'm your Uncle Stephan," he said feeling happy at the thought. "I was on my way to my ship."

"Then you are a pirate. Do you sink and pillage ships like captain Hook?" he asked looking excitedly at his wounded hand.

Stephan chuckled. "Nothing so great. Maybe you can come and see my ship sometime. Would you like that?"

Sean grinned eating his cookies quietly from his chair, while Ian jumped up and down in place, sending bit's of cookie off in several directions. "Whoopee, let's go now," he said taking a gulp of milk and another cookie, then moving toward the door.

Stephan grabbed his arm to stop him from bolting from the room. "Hold on there, young man. You have a mother that's wanting to see you. Maybe in a day or two," he added seeing the disappointment. Running back to his former place, Ian leaned toward Sean.

"Did you hear that, Sean? We're going to sail like real pirates.

Sean grinned excitedly but remained in his chair. Stephan got to his feet as Melissa swept into the room dressed from head to toe in a gown of yellow and white.

"Oh my. Aren't they cute," she said smiling at the boys who were staring at her wide-eyed.

Ian recovered quicker than Sean and looked at Stephan with saucer eyes. "Is she a princess?"

Melissa laughed. "Heavens no. I'm your Aunt Melissa and you are?"

"I'm Ian. He's Sean," he said pointing a cookie in his brother's direction.

Melissa smiled at Sean who turned red and looked at his lap. "I see you've been eating Mrs. Lang's pastries. Good aren't they?"

Ian grinned. "I think they're the best thing I've ever ate," he said stuffing the last of his third cookie in his mouth.

Thomas moved to the window hoping not to be noticed. The lovely vision that had just walked in was far more lovely than he imagined the people to be that lived here and he felt completely out of place. Mrs. Lang gave him a smile as she moved to his side. "If you'll come with me, I'll get you settled in and you can unpack."

Thomas nodded his head and began following her. Glancing to see if the boys were going to be all right he frowned. "Don't worry about them. Master Stephan and Lady Melissa are wonderful with children."

Thomas put his fears to rest as they left the room hearing the adults laughing at something Ian had said. Seeing Nathan coming down the hall, Thomas turned his attention to the housekeeper. Evidently, they did plan on letting him stay.

Nathan walked into the drawing room and stopped. Stephan was kneeling on the floor, while Melissa perched on one of the chairs with the boys sitting in the chairs opposite them eating cookies. It was such a homey scene he felt his mood change. These children were his responsibility, whether that came about forced or not, and seeing them looking pale and thin made him angry at his wife's neglect. Moving up to place his hands on the back of Melissa's chair, he smiled at the boys. "I see you've made it here safely. Did it seem to take a long time?"

Ian looked up and smiled. "I was a trial to Thomas," he said proudly.

Sean hit his arm. "That isn't something to say to him. You were being bad."

Ian's face turned angry. "I wasn't bad," he said glaring at Sean.

"Were too. Thomas said you made his backside ache."

Melissa covered her mouth trying not to let the giggles escape but Stephan out right laughed, getting a grin out of Nathan. "Ian, finish your milk," he said nodding to Sean to do the same. "Today, after you meet everyone else who's in residence, your Aunt Melissa and I are taking you shopping."

"Shopping!" Ian screamed. "What are you going to buy me?"

Nathan knelt down in front of the boy as he bounded around Melissa's chair. "Well, for starters some new clothes and shoes."

"We're going to buy you all the things a boy needs to grow up."

Ian wrinkled his face up. "But we can't grow up or Peter Pan won't come to our house."

"Peter Pan!" Melissa exclaimed, looking at Nathan.

Stephan, seeing his brother at a loss, stepped in. He happened to have read that tale and knew exactly what the lad was talking about. "Even Peter Pan had to have clothes."

Ian looked at Stephan then back at Nathan. "All right, but I want a sword and helmet to be like Sir Lancelot."

Nathan smiled. "I think, Uncle Stephan, can manage that."

Stephan gave Nathan a scowl, but smiled the minute Ian looked his way. Sean watched the entire scene, without saying a word.

"Sean needs a horse to fight dragons," Ian said knowing his brother wouldn't ask.

Stephan chuckled at that order. "Swords I can handle but horses will have to come from your Uncle Jonathan."

Ian frowned. "Who?"

Nathan smiled. "You'll meet him tonight at dinner, with the rest of the family. For now, we have to get you upstairs and show you your room."

"Where's Mama Rae?" Ian piped making Nathan loose his smile.

"She's out with Aunt Ginger but I'm sure they'll be back soon. In the mean time, let's go up and see your new room." "Whoopee." Ian hollered grabbing Nathan's hand to pull him toward the door. Nathan came to a halt and waited for Sean.

"Come on, Sean," he said holding out his hand to the boy. Sean looked at Stephan then Melissa before moving away from the chair to take Nathan's hand. Nathan smiled down at him. "Your mom has given you the only room in the house, that has enough space in it for the two of you to each have your own bed."

Sean looked wide-eyed at Ian as they moved out of the room and up the stairs.

Melissa got to her feet and watched Nathan climb the stairs holding a small hand in each of his. "He does make a good father, doesn't he," she said feeling Stephan behind her.

"Who couldn't be with that pair? They remind me of our childhood."

Melissa snorted. "You were never so quiet or self contained. The four of you were always fighting with one another."

"We didn't fight. Sometimes somebody just needed to be straightened out."

Melissa smiled. "It's nice to have children around, isn't it?"

Stephan smiled back. "Father's going to be pleased."

Melissa's smile widened. "I'd forgotten he was coming tomorrow. I have a million things to do, including shop for those children. Nathan has waited too long in dressing them," she said moving to climb the stairs.

Stephan sighed as she disappeared from view. Swords! Where the hell was he supposed to find swords for children? Nathan had said helmets too. It would take him hours. Shaking his head, he left the house.

RAE FROWNED AT NELLY. "What do you mean, Nathan took the boys shopping?"

"That's what they said. Lady Melissa and Lord Nathan took off just over an hour ago and said they were going to get the boys the things they needed."

Rae felt her temper rising, as the hurt settled somewhere in her stomach. It wasn't that she didn't want to get the boys the things they needed, but she would have like to have been included. Her husband hadn't said a word about it. "Did they like their room?"

Nelly smiled. "Oh, my yes. They said it was bigger than their whole house."

Rae reddened. The room was much nicer than anything they had stayed in before. "Thank you, Nelly. I'll just put these things away." Pausing, she turned, "Nelly, did they say when they would be back?"

Nelly frowned. "I expect they would be home in a few hours. Lord Hayworth is returning tomorrow."

"Tomorrow?"

Nelly frowned. "Yes. He's expected at six o'clock."

Rae kept her face straight. How could Nathan not have told her any of this? "Thank you," she said climbing the rest of the way up the stairs. After they arrived home from the ball, Nathan had yelled at her for almost half an hour. He'd finally ending up calling her a whore and storming out of the room. He hadn't returned till dawn. Rae had felt horrible and the dreams about her sister were getting worse. Rae was angry with herself for not asking Nathan to hire a runner, but she figured he wouldn't do it.

Moving into her room, she frowned, realizing her nephews were already here. Why hadn't they waited for her? Wondering, at the feelings of jealousy, she sat down on the bed. It bothered her that Nathan was taking such interest in the boys, when he never once said anything good about them. She wondered what the rest of the family was going to say about the boys. They were the sweetest little things but she knew, well enough, that people thought she was some street urchin and that the boys were products of her way of life. Frowning further, she got to her feet and cursed. It was just her sort of luck to be living a role she had no idea how to act in. She wasn't used to fancy clothes and social talking. After the past few months as a thief, her conversations had been reduced to her famous line 'Stand and deliver.' Moving to the window, she frowned again. Allison had been nice enough to give her seven gowns. Two ball gowns, four day dresses, and one riding habit. Rae much preferred breeches, when riding a horse, but knew she had shocked Nathan's family enough and would have to follow their rules, while in the city.

Her brows furrowed at the last thought. Nathan had mentioned sending her off to some far off plot of land to live. Little did he know that is exactly the type of lifestyle she would love to have. A small house with a barn, fields for a garden, a couple of horses to plow with and a couple to ride, maybe a wagon. It was the sort of place she had planned on getting eventually for her and the boys. Thomas had farmed once, in his life, and she thought they could make a go of it.

Looking at the packages on the bed, she frowned. Aunt Ginger had insisted she purchase stockings and things. She had wanted other things but thought them too frivolous to buy. Nathan was mad enough at her, she didn't need to be buying herself clothing, but Aunt Ginger had forced her to. Moving to the door, she frowned. If they were having company tomorrow, she needed to do a bit of refining on her manners. Taking a deep breath of air, she left her room in search of Aunt Ginger. If anyone could help her, it would be Ginger.

Chapter 64

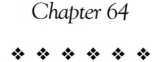

ALLISON FELT HER NERVES ON END, as the trip grew longer and she knew they were getting closer. Swallowing, she shifted.

"Are you all right?" Jonathan asked. "We could stop?"

Allison waved a hand at him. "I don't need to stop. I'm just nervous."

"Nervous? Why?"

"I don't like people staring at me."

Jonathan frowned. "I doubt this man will stare at you. He's an Earl. A recluse Earl, for that matter. He's most likely going to be short with us and get the deal over quickly, so he can get back to doing whatever it is recluses do," Jonathan said, looking out the window. His eyebrows shot up at the sight of the ancient castle that rose up before them. "Good lord, I think the man must be really old."

"Why do you say that?"

"He lives in a castle out of the sixteenth century. It even has a moat," he said looking down as the carriage rumbled across the bridge.

Allison felt butterflies in her stomach. "Do you think he's home?"

Jonathan frowned. "Uncle Colan seemed to think so, but there's only one way to find out," he said as the carriage stopped in front of the castle.

The footman opened the door and Jonathan bounded out. Holding his hands up, Jonathan helped her out of the carriage. "This place is something else," he said walking her toward the front door.

"What do you see?" she snapped, wishing Melissa were there to describe everything to her.

Jonathan laughed. "Sorry. We've driven through a thick rock wall with a massive arch over the drive. The drawbridge spans the moat and seals the castle off when drawn up. It's right out of history," he said excitedly, "we're climbing steps toward two massive doors made of oak."

"Twelve," she said as they reached the top.

"Twelve what?"

"Steps," she said smiling.

Jonathan smiled. "Fine, twelve steps." Reaching out he grabbed the knocker. "He has two lion head knockers on the doors with rings in their mouths. This is fascinating."

Allison reached out a hand to trace the head, smiling at the detail. Abruptly the door moved away from her hand and she moved back a step.

Jonathan smiled at the little man holding the door open. He was five foot two with gray hair tied by a string, at the nape of his neck. He wore tan breeches and an oversized shirt. He even had a patch over his left eye. "What do you want?" his raspy voice asked rudely.

"We've come to see the Earl."

The man narrowed his good eye at them. "What for?"

Jonathan frowned. "We've come to discuss business with the man. Is he in?"

"I don't know," he said slamming the door in their faces.

Jonathan's brows shot up at the man's rudeness. "Does that mean go away?" he asked, turning to Allison.

Allison frowned. "But we can't. I need one of those dogs."

Jonathan looked at her. She was pale and he knew she was relying on this for strength. "All right, Allison. We'll try again." He raised his hand to knock but the little man snatched the door open.

"He said come in and he'd talk with you, but I'm telling you to be brief. The lord doesn't like your kind."

Jonathan arched his brows again. What were their type?

"Were you born in a barn? Shut the door," the man ordered, moving along the hall ahead of them.

Jonathan scowled as he shut the door. "That servant needs training," he said taking Allison's arm to follow the little man. Looking at the walls, he frowned, "this Earl must be rich. He's has paintings and tapestries worth quite a bit of money."

Allison stopped and touched one of the tapestries. She ran her hand over the material and could feel the extraordinary work. "This is magnificent," she said.

Jonathan grabbed her arm. "Come on, you can admire that on the way out. That little man isn't waiting for us," he snapped, seeing the man round a corner. As they hurried to catch up, the hall opened into a grand hall. It had several long wooden tables with benches, two hearths with chairs before them and a raised dais with another table and chairs. It was exactly like he pictured. "I can't believe this," he said pulling Allison along in his haste. "It's exactly like a Great Hall would have been in the old days."

Allison sniffed. "Someone's cooking."

"His Lordship says to sit," he said moving off toward their right to disappear through an opening.

"He's a pleasant sort, isn't he?" Allison said sitting down on one of the benches and running her hand over the wood table. "This isn't the original table," she said.

Jonathan sat across from her looking at the wood. "How can you tell?"

"Back in those days they used knives to eat. The table would be gouged and scratched from eating."

Jonathan smiled. "You're right." Looking up toward the dais, his mouth fell open. "Allison, the Earl's coat of arms is hanging from the ceiling. It's a white tapestry with a black raven in the middle that has two arrows crossing behind it and a sword clenched in its talons. It even has a red rose in its beak."

Allison smiled at the image. "I wish I could see it."

Jonathan didn't answer her as the man standing at the back of the hall started toward them. He was tall, about six four or so. His brown hair was long and loose around his shoulders. His face was stern from this distance and Jonathan felt nervous under his look. He was dressed in black breeches with a white shirt opened at the collar. He wore a black belt with a clasp that looked to be in the shape of a bird's head. Jonathan smiled as the man drew closer. Getting to his feet he moved to help Allison to hers.

"We're sorry to have bothered you without sending ahead."

Royce frowned as the lady turned and faced him. It was Allison. He should have known her just by seeing that silver hair. Looking at the man next to her, he could see the man had seen his scars, though his face registered a little shock, the smile stayed in place. "Why have you come?" he asked directly.

Jonathan smiled further. "It's said you have the best wolfhounds in the area and we've come to purchase one. Are you willing to sell any?"

Royce didn't change his features but looked at Allison again. She was pale. "How have you been, Lady Hayworth?" he asked watching her stiffen, as the man beside her snapped his glance at her in disbelief.

"You know one another?" Jonathan asked.

Allison reddened. "I met him, at one of the balls, with Jessica and Melissa. He builds and sells the ships Father purchases," she said, licking her lips.

Royce watched her, wondering why she hadn't said anything to the man beside her.

Jonathan frowned, wondering if this was all a ruse. "I suppose you have known all along?"

Allison's blush deepened. "No. I only realized who we were going to see, this morning, when you mentioned his name."

Royce frowned at the man glaring at Allison. "Is there a problem?" he asked his voice spitting nails.

Jonathan's head snapped around at the tone. "No. There no problem.

I'm just surprised, is all. We still have come for the dog, right?" he asked taking Allison's arm.

"Of course," she said standing straighter.

Royce glared at Jonathan, was he her suitor? "Since I already know the lady, might I ask who you are?"

Jonathan laughed. "Forgive my manners. I'm Jonathan Hayworth, Allison's brother."

Royce's brows shot up at that remark. Her brother. The one that dealt in horses he presumed. "I'm pleased to meet you. Your father talks of you often," he said politely.

Jonathan grinned. "I'm sure you exaggerate. Father doesn't brag often about any of us males."

Royce smiled, a rare thing Jonathan was sure. "I don't, particularly, have a dog I wish to sell at this time. Is there a specific reason you want one?"

"I have a wife and, well, I was going to..." he stammered, unsure exactly what to say.

Allison gave a sound of disgust and turned more in Royce's direction. "Jonathan's wife, Ashley, is blind. We were hoping to train one of your hounds as a guide dog." At the silence, she added. "Sort of like the pair of eyes she doesn't have."

Royce stared at her. "Like I said, I have a few young hounds but I don't think they are suited for what you have in mind. So, if you'll excuse me," he said, turning to have Ellis show them out.

Allison felt her insides clench, at the pain in his voice. The coldness he tried to deliver masking the real inner pain. She didn't realize, until that moment, how much she had let herself like this man. Remembering his kindness and the easy manner in which they conversed, she suddenly knew she didn't want to let him turn them away. Moving up closer to him, she reached out and snagged his arm. "Please my lord, if you'd only let us see the dogs and judge them for ourselves," she said unaware of the darkening look crossing Royce's face.

Jonathan saw it and took Allison's hand. "I think we've disturbed his lordship, enough for one day. We'll have to find another dog someplace else," he finished trying to pull Allison loose.

Royce glared at Jonathan watching the other man lower his eyes. Clenching his jaw, he moved back a step pulling free of her arm. "Ellis, show them out. Good day." he said striding from the hall. Allison felt her heart clench. Royce obviously didn't feel the same as she did. Allison dropped her head.

"Allison, I think you've placed to much on this training thing. If you need time away from the gossip, you're welcome at Meadowacres," Jonathan said dipping to peer into her face. Jonathan expelled a breath as he saw that she wasn't crying.

"Come on then. I don't have all day sending you on your way. I already told you the lord don't like your kind," the crotchety old man said. Making to follow, Jonathan paused when Allison didn't move.

"Al, what is it?" Allison lifted her face to him and he felt his heart twist at the lovely face looking sad. "Oh, Allison, I'm sure something will come up to make the gossips loose interest. You'll see."

Allison's face crumpled as she began to cry. Jonathan put his arm around her shoulders and led her out of the hall. Jonathan was concerned with her worry over the silly gossip that would probably only last for a week or so. Knowing Jessica's presence in society was like to cause trouble and turn the gossip onto her.

"I'm sure everything will work out," he added picking up his pace. Allison tried valiantly to control her tears wanting very much to tell Jonathan she didn't give a fig what the gossips said. She was upset and crying because, for once in her life, she wanted something far beyond her reach and knew she would never get remotely close. Fresh tears trickled down her face as Jonathan helped her into the carriage. Leaning her head, on his shoulder, her tears turned to sobs.

Royce frowned as the carriage moved away, from his home, disappearing under the arch. Turning slightly away from the window, he frowned. To see Allison again had made his heart race and he had wanted nothing more than to take her around his home describing everything to her, showing her where he worked to design the ships that sailed the sea. But the disgusted look, on the brother's face from his appearance, had been enough for him to stay behind his barrier. He felt the old bitterness seeping slowly back into his soul. His short jaunt to London had sent the recluse, in him, back to the fore. Smashing his fist, on the ledge, he turned away from the window furious. He had overheard their conversation. Something had ruined her in the eyes of society and the gossips were working their awful magic.

Moving to the small room to his left he entered and poured himself a brandy, then moved to look out the window. It overlooked the moat and a lovely view of the forest. Jared would know what had happened. He was informed about everything in London, nearly to the minute. Moving to his desk, he quickly penned his brother a note then rang for Ellis.

"Have one of the grooms, preferably Jonas, take this to my brother." Royce said, as soon as Ellis stuck his head in the door.

Ellis took the letter and nodded. "Anything else?"

"No." he snapped draining his glass.

"It seems to me those hoity toity folks would stop coming around here if you don't like them. Yet, every now and then they fall upon us sending you into a rage. I'm thinking of going to London and spreading the word that the woods are haunted or something. That should keep the rotten curs at bay," Ellis snapped striding from the room.

Royce watched the crotchety man amble out of the room and frowned. Ellis was definitely due for a vacation. Looking deep into his glass he swirled the amber liquid around and frowned. What would things be like if he could have courted Allison like a real man would, unscathed and whole. Feeling the self-pity well up in his chest, he cursed and threw his glass into the hearth. His brother better show early tomorrow, or there was no telling what he'd be like.

Chapter 65

JESSICA HANDED THE LETTER to the footman and nodded. "Take this and have it delivered to my family." At his nod and departure she closed the door and frowned. Her family was having a dinner tomorrow night and she was supposed to attend. Well, it would be her last evening, before Morgan sailed away on her ship. Cursing, she frowned. Morgan hadn't been home all morning and she was glad, in a way. It was almost impossible for her to behave in the manner she had been. Being like Melissa, sickened her. She was giggling and primping all the time. It was so fake. Lifting her brandy she took a swallow then stared at the glass. Ladies didn't drink brandy, either. Moving to look out the window, her eyes watched her husband's carriage pull up in front of the house. She found herself leaning her forehead on the glass as the footman opened the door and Aunt Athea stepped out. Disappointed, at the sight, she moved away from the window to check herself in the mirror to make sure she was dressed properly. She'd changed into her flat shoes knowing her feet weren't going to last an afternoon with Aunt Athea. Leaving the room, she descended the stairs and nodded to Davis. "I'll be in the salon," she said, her face remaining straight. Davis watched her walk stiffly into the room and frowned. The new Baroness was not happy and anyone seeing her a few days ago would know exactly why. She had come to their home dressed like a pirate with a bit of a swagger and smiling readily. She joked with the servants and truly seemed to enjoy life. But now, she was dressed as the master liked. Head to toe, in society fashion and Davis wasn't the only one to notice. Morgan watched, from his library, as his wife grimly walked into the salon to await his Aunt. Cursing under his breath, he moved to greet his Aunt at the door.

"It's nice to see you again, Aunt," he said smiling warmly.

Athea looked at him sternly giving him her cheek. "I'm sure it is," she said as he kissed her cheek. "Where's your lovely bride," she said moving along the hall toward the salon.

"She's waiting for you in there," he said following along behind her.

Athea entered the room and arched her brows at Jessica in surprise, who was likewise looking at her husband. The girl was dressed in a day gown, of green, setting off the stunning color of her eyes. Her midnight hair was pulled back, from her face, to cascade down her back in soft curls. She looked stunning. Moving into the room Athea watched Jessica send a maid off for refreshments then turn and smile at her.

"It's nice to see you, Lady Athea. How was the ride over?" she asked as the woman seated herself on a sofa. Morgan had been home the cur.

"The ride was fine, Dear. Sit down, please."

Morgan smiled at his Aunt giving his wife a glare over Athea's head. "If you'll excuse me ladies, I'll leave you to your chat."

Athea waved a hand at him. "I came to tell you about the scandal," Jessica put on a face of interest, though she could hardly care less. "It seems someone in your family ruined the ball last night. I'm afraid people will gossip."

Jessica frowned wondering what happened last night at the ball but not wanting to ask his Aunt. She'd definitely give a tainted picture. "I'm sure it will blow over."

Athea pursed her lips. "I'm afraid it has only made matters worse concerning your celebration ball. The Ladies of the ton are making the whole thing into a huge mess."

Jessica frowned. So? What the hell was she suppose to do about it. Smiling sweetly she waited for the maid to set the tray down, then scooted forward to pour the tea. "I'm afraid I don't quite understand."

Athea humphed. "Of course not, Dear. Since you are still, technically, newlyweds it will seem a little strange for you to have a ball but that is exactly what I want you to do."

Jessica set her cup down and crossed her hands in her lap. "You want me to have a ball?" she asked shocked.

"Yes. The weekend after next, should do."

Jessica swallowed, smiling the whole time. "Of course, but I think it should be just a bit further away. Say a months time."

Athea scowled. "The weekend after next. I'll help, of course. Lady Atherton, who couldn't make it today, is already helping me spread the word. You must get the invites out immediately. I brought a list with me," she said digging in her reticule for the paper, which she quickly shoved at Jessica. "They must go out by the end of the week."

Jessica took the list still smiling. "Of course," she heard herself reply. Athea beamed at her, then got slowly to her feet.

"I'll leave you then to get started. Remember, invite everyone on the list," she said moving toward the door. Jessica barely got to her feet, before the woman was gone. Sinking back in her seat, she frowned. A ball. She didn't want to host a ball. It was such a stupid affair. Pulling open the list, she scanned the thing noticing well over five hundred names. Most of whom she didn't even know.

Morgan watched his wife, before moving further into the room. She was looking very pale and shocked but her face changed, to that false smile, as she became aware of him. "Where did Aunt go?"

"She left," she said smiling. "It seems, I'm to host a ball weekend after next," she piped, picking up her teacup and sipping. She hated tea, almost as much as port.

Morgan scowled at her. "I won't be here then."

Jessica's head snapped to his. "But you must. We're to host it. Your Aunt says."

Morgan scowled at her. "You knew I was going to be gone for two weeks. I won't be here."

Jessica frowned then quickly changed it to a smile. "Then I'll have to find someone else to help me. Your Aunt insists," she said getting to her feet to leave. Morgan stared at her, surprised at her behavior. "If you'll excuse me," she said brushing past him. Morgan followed her, but stopped as she hurried up the stairs to disappear from sight. Cursing, he moved into the drawing room and poured himself a drink. Hell, he couldn't let her host a ball on her own, no matter what he thought about the whole thing. Society would have a picnic with that tid bit of information. Besides his Aunt would probably die over the fact that newlyweds weren't together. Looking out the window, he sighed. He hadn't planned on going very far in the first place. He could easily change his trip to be back by next weekend. Frowning, he left the study to fix his plans.

Chapter 66

MELISSA SHOOK HER HEAD AGAIN as the man brought another little suit out for the boys. "No. They only need four, a piece. Let's work on the breeches and shirts. They need durable but stylish and a couple of riding coats, she said holding another shirt up to Ian's front. "This one is perfect. We'll need several like this in different shades," she said pulling Sean closer. "The one Sean has on is good as well. Let's have the same amount for him in that style." She finished looking at a pile of cravats. "Did you pick out the ties?" she asked Nathan.

"How about these?" he said knowing she wasn't going to like them.

Melissa pursed her lips and looked at them. "The one on the left is fine, the other one is too flimsy," she stated picking up six more to add to his hands. "These are good. Let's see now. Stockings, too," she said taking up several pair for each boy.

The older man returned carrying the different shirts, holding them up for her inspection. "That will be fine. These jackets are good," she said, throwing the ones she didn't like on the chair near the door. "What do you think?" she asked looking at Nathan.

Nathan smiled. "I think they'll be the best dressed boys in all of London," he said flatly.

Melissa frowned at him. "They need these clothes, Nathan. What do you think boys?" she asked bending over in front of them.

Ian looked at the clothes then back at her. "Are all those for me?"

"The smaller ones are," she said smiling.

"But, I won't be small forever."

Melissa laughed. "You'll need them, you'll see. You have school every day and if your Mother and Nathan hold a party, you'll have to dress for that."

Sean smiled at her. "I like the ones for riding."

Ian frowned. "Do I get some for the horse?"

Melissa nodded. "Of course. You'll need to take riding lessons wearing something."

Ian and Sean looked at each other then back at her. "We don't need lessons. We already know how to ride."

Melissa arched a brow at the boy. "Really? Well, you'll still need something to wear while doing that."

Ian beamed a smile. "Yippee," he said looking at Nathan. "It's all right with you?"

Nathan grinned at him. "It was my idea. Now, let's go get you some shoes and boots."

"Boots?" he asked looking at Nathan's feet. His boots were black and shiny reaching almost to his knees. "Like those?"

Nathan smiled. "Like these." Taking his hand, he nodded to the man helping them. "Put that on my account and have the things delivered tonight," he said watching Melissa take up Sean's hand. Leaving the store, he frowned as Saul Sheridan moved away from his post and walked to their side.

"What have we here?" he asked eyeing the little boys with laughing eyes. Melissa scowled at the man. "My lady," he said tipping his hat to her.

Nathan nodded at him putting the boys into the carriage, one at a time, then helping Melissa in. "If you'll excuse us, Sheridan," he said trying to enter.

"I wouldn't have believed it, if I hadn't seen it with my own two eyes. You make a rather young father."

Nathan met his sister's eyes then smiled at the boys. "Take them to the store. I'll be along in a few minutes," he said, shutting the door behind him and nodding to the coachman to go. As the carriage moved away, he turned to glare at Saul. "If you have something to say, say it."

Saul smiled like the devil. "What's it like to be the father to another man's brats?"

That was enough for him. Nathan smiled harshly pulling back his fist and punching Saul in the nose. The man staggered back hitting the side of the store while holding his face. "Get up," he said wanting to pound the man's face into the ground.

Saul held up a hand. "I was only wondering," he said, wiping his nose with his hand. He pulled a handkerchief from his pocket and held it to his face. "I must hand it to you, Hayworth. You stay consistent. A whore with two brats for a wife. What a bargain."

Nathan snarled, as he leaped on the man. He landed several good punches to Saul's face and stomach before he felt someone pulling him off.

"Nathan, knock it off," Thomas Bentley yelled pulling him off Saul. "What has gotten into you?" he said close to Nathan's face.

Nathan pushed away from him and ran his hand through his hair. Looking at Saul, he frowned. "I'll let the slander go this time. Next time, I'll call you out."

Saul slowly got to his feet. Wiping the blood from his lip and nose, with a handkerchief, he glared at Nathan before turning on his heels and walking away. The crowd slowly dispersed, while Nathan's frown deepened.

"Just what was that all about?" Thomas asked picking up Nathan's hat.

"He made a remark against my wife and I took exception to it."

Thomas pursed his lips. "If I were you, I would handle it in a different way. Your family is causing quite a stir."

Nathan cursed, running his hand through his hair again. "I can't believe I just did that."

Thomas glanced around again. "Let's go have a drink, huh?"

Nathan cursed. "I can't Thomas. I have to meet Melissa. We're buying the boys some boots."

Thomas nodded his head. "All right, maybe later then. Need a lift."

Nathan smiled. "That is probably a good idea."

Thomas chuckled, "Let's go then."

Chapter 67

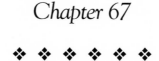

STEPHAN MOVED ALONG THE WATERFRONT, holding the two small swords securely in one hand. It wasn't as hard as he had thought it would be. It had cost quite a bit but it was worth it. The helmets were a different matter. The man said it would take him five or six days to make a pair. Thinking of the faces the two boys would make when he gave them the swords, made Stephan smile.

Movement, to his right, drew his attention and he felt his heart leap in his throat. Five men stood circled around a grubby looking Rae. All five were looking like the cat with a mouse cornered. Cursing, he moved to the edge of the building so he could see into the alley better. Maltose's men were a dirty bunch willing to do just about anything, if the price was right. Gritting his teeth, he frowned at not having a pistol with him. All he had was a knife in his boot and the swords. Looking at the wrapped bundle in his hands, he quickly unwrapped them and tested the edge with his thumb. They were duller than wood. Scowling, he could see they would have to do, as two of the taller men moved toward Rae. Stepping from behind the crate, Stephan walked toward the men.

"I don't suppose you fella's would be moving along anytime soon?"

Emily paled at the sight of the black haired man who had almost caught her yesterday. Funny but she was actually comforted by his presence. She watched as Stephan looked at her, then smiled. "I thought I told you to wait on the ship," her eyes widened as a couple of the men looked at her closely.

"She belongs to you, mate?" a big blond man asked.

"She does," Stephan barked, his face like stone.

"Well, she was picking our pockets. That calls for a little restitution," a man with a patch and no teeth said, grinning. "Being she's female, I know what I want from her."

Stephan's face darkened and the man's smile slowly slid from his face. "I suggest you get that thought right out of your head. Whatever she took, I'll pay for it."

The men looked at one another then back at her before returning their gazes to Stephan. "I'm thinking you are in no position to be tellin us anything. Why don't you just leave the gal here and she'll be along shortly."

Stephan's eyes narrowed. "Maltose isn't going to be pleased with what you have been up to lately."

Two of the men paled, while the third narrowed his eyes. "What are you talking about, mate? Maltose loves a fresh morsel," he said, getting laughs from his companions.

"I'm talking about the skimming you've been doing. I think he'd be more than interested in that bit of news."

"He knows, Frank."

"Shut up, you fool," Frank snapped looking at Stephan with a nod. "Maybe we've overstepped ourselves here with your gal. I'm sure we can come up with some sort of agreement."

Stephan smiled satanically. "I'm sure we can," he said removing a bit of cash he threw it at their feet. "That should more than cover anything she might have picked from your hides."

Frank glanced at the sac and smiled. "That seems about fair," he said, nodding for the toothless man to grab it. As the four men moved along the alley out into the street, Frank lingered. "I'd watch myself, if I was you," he added, before following his men out of sight.

Stephan waited to make sure they didn't come back before grabbing Rae's arm. "I can't believe you actually came back here," he snapped pulling her quickly along the street toward his office.

"Look, mister..."

"Shut up." he barked again dragging her the last block into his office where he slammed the door. "What the hell possessed you to come back here?"

Emily straightened to her full height. "I don't happen to live as well off as some people," she sneered inching her way toward the door.

Stephan glared at her. She looked a mess. Her hair was braided tightly hanging down her back but wisps of it were shooting out, in all directions. Her face was scratched, along her right cheek and she had a tear in her shirt exposing a good portion of her stomach. Gritting his teeth he shook his head. "You're insane."

"I'm determined."

Stephan's head snapped around to meet her steady green gaze. For a minute there he felt a bolt of desire that made him blush. This was his brother's wife. Turning away from her, he scowled. "I don't suppose you plan on telling Nathan?"

Emily frowned. "I'm not telling anyone," she said. Having no idea who

Nathan was. Seeing her only chance of escape was now, she bolted for the door pulling the thing open. She shrieked as Stephan's hand clamped down on her shoulder. Pulling her back into the room, he slammed the door, while she fought and kicked him. Stephan struggled with her, finally, pinning her up against the wall. His thigh shoved between her legs, while he held both her arms behind her back. Their faces were inches apart. Both were breathing heavily and as Stephan watched, her tongue move over her lips. His mouth, with a will of it's own, moved down and kissed her. He felt her stiffen then melt against him. She could feel his heart pounding against her chest and knew hers was doing the same. Feeling the intense feelings building deep in her gut she moaned as he pressed her closer to the wall, lifting her slightly, his thigh came in contact with her sex.

Her groan penetrated his mind and Stephan jerked away, aghast at what he'd done. "My god," he said moving several steps away from her. She stared at him wide eyed wondering why he was so appalled, then comprehension came to her and her face hardened. He didn't like her kind. She wasn't good enough for him. She was appalled at her own behavior, most men would have found themselves sliced for taking such liberties. Yet, this handsome man had sparked some inner core of her being that she had thought was long dead. Shifting feet, she pulled her torn shirt closed keeping her skin well hidden.

"May I go now?"

Stephan turned scarlet. He didn't know what to do. He had just kissed his brothers wife. Running a hand through his hair, he frowned. "No, I'll have to take you home. Those men will have their eyes out for you. Next time you won't get away."

Emily paled. She would have to relocate and work another area. One with a lot less danger. "I can find my way on my own," she said moving toward the door. Stephan was there blocking it.

"I said, I'll see you home," he said, making her back away from him. Pulling open the door he signaled to a scrawny lad, who nodded and headed off in an easterly direction. "I must apologize for my earlier behavior," he said not looking at her.

Emily's mouth dropped open. "You're apologizing for kissing me?" she asked brows up in shock.

Stephan reddened. "Yes, I am. I'm really sorry. I shouldn't have done that," he said feeling even smaller than he had before. What was Nathan going to say?

Emily couldn't help herself, she laughed. "That's a new one," she said getting his eyes turned on her, in confusion. At his look, one corner of her mouth lifted into a smile. "I haven't been apologized to before. Most of the fella's don't get the chance," she said, a knife appearing in her hand. Seeing his eyes widen then narrow, she chuckled. "They get what they deserve.

Now if you'll excuse me, I have to be going," she said flipping the knife from her right hand to her left and back again. "Unless, you want to stop me." At his fuming look, she smiled again. "I'd hate to cut that handsome face of yours," she said moving closer to the door.

Stephan cursed at himself for not checking for that sort of thing. She was a thief after all and most thieves carried some sort of protection. "You're in deep enough already, without adding my wrath to your head. Why don't you put the knife away."

Emily smiled, one of the sweetest smiles Stephan had yet to see. "Oh, your concern is very gallant but I have been taking care of myself for quite sometime now and I don't need a hero looking after me," she said moving her left hand to the door. Stephan watched her for his opportunity. Suddenly, the door opened, making Emily look to see who it was. Stephan kicked the knife out of her hand and had her pinned up against the door in seconds.

"Captain, you okay?" a young voice called through the door.

"I'm fine, Robby. You have the coach?"

"Yes, my lord. It's just at the end of the dock."

"Thank you. I'll be there in a minute. Keep watch, will you?"

"Yes, my lord," the boy stated, silence following.

Stephan again plastered against her body frowned into her angry face. "You sure find trouble easier than a ship lost at sea," he said moving her away from the door and up against the wall again. His thigh rubbed against her again and he heard her gasp bringing his gaze back to hers. Feeling desire again, he lowered his head to hers knowing it was wrong but unable to help himself.

Emily wanted to fight him but somehow those thoughts scattered the minute his lips touched hers. He deepened the kiss bringing his tongue into play. Emily hesitated a minute, then joined hers with his, moaning when he didn't release her hands. Stephan moved his thigh higher against her legs feeling her desire building.

"My god, Stephan. What are you doing?" Christopher said stunned at the sight before him.

Stephan sprang away from her looking at Christopher in horror. "I ...it..."

Emily paled at her behavior. She had acted like a whore. Something she had made sure she didn't rely on for a living. Instead, she had turned to thieving, yet here she was kissing a perfect stranger. A very passionate stranger, that kissed her like she had never been kissed before. Shaking her head, she stared at the blond man that had barged in the office.

Christopher's face darkened. "I wouldn't have believed it if I hadn't seen it with my own two eyes. What were you thinking?"

Stephan let the breath leave his chest, his heart beating fast. "I don't know. It just happened," he said running a hand through his hair. Christopher moved farther into the room shocked at what he'd witnessed.

Emily saw her opportunity and dashed out the door not looking right or left, but running as fast as her feet could carry her. Turning right then left dashing down alleys she knew like the back of her hand. She ran until her sides ached and she was forced to stop. Turning to look if the dark giant was after her, she sighed knowing she had lost him. She needed a new place to live and she needed it fast.

Stephan cursed as the little minx disappeared as if in thin air. "Do you see her?"

Christopher shook his head panting, his hands on his knees while he was bent over. "She's going to get herself killed," he said between breaths.

"This is the second time I've seen her down here and I know for a fact that Nathan told her to stay at home."

Christopher straightened giving Stephan a glare, while he took several deep breaths to control his breathing. "Now, tell me what the hell you were doing back there?"

Stephan turned scarlet before turning his back on Christopher and walking back down the several alleys toward his office. The truth was he knew if he ran into Rae again, he would most likely kiss her again. His body wanted her and it didn't seem to matter that she was Nathan's wife. Cursing at the disgust his brain was making him feel, he nearly punched Christopher in the face when he pulled him around to face him.

"Answer me!" he thundered.

"I already told you. I don't know. One minute I was in a rage at finding her here, the next, I was kissing her."

Christopher cursed. "I should have known. As usual you can't keep you hands off a woman. Even if she belongs to your brother."

Stephan paled. "God," he whispered in sick panic. "What is Nathan going to say?"

Christopher frowned running a hand through his hair. "I don't know if you should tell him. He'll kill you."

"Not tell him? But, I have to. Rae needs to be locked up and kept safe. If my kissing her has to be known, then so be it."

Christopher stared at him, then nodded his head. "You're right. I guarantee it won't go good for you."

"I wouldn't doubt it. I'll tell him tonight."

"Better make it in the morning. The boys are here. Remember? He needs to be with his family."

Stephan felt his stomach clench at those words. A family. He had kissed his brothers wife. God what a mortal sin that was. Moving into his building, he prayed for guidance.

Chapter 68

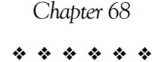

ROYCE SAT BEHIND HIS DESK, staring at his brother, like the fool wasn't really there. "How, pray tell, did you manage to get yourself here in such a short time? I just sent Jonas off for you a little over an hour ago."

Jared grinned. "Miss me, did you? I'm flattered."

Royce scowled at him. "Well?"

"I happened to be on my way here and Jonas nearly ran my horse off the rode in his haste to do your bidding."

Royce sipped his brandy. Jared waited patiently for him to say something but knew he wasn't going to.

"What was the reason for my summons? More currier work?"

Royce scowled again. "As it happens, I wanted to get some information out of you, but since you were all eager to visit, I wish to know what brought you here, first."

Jared grinned, sipping his drink. Royce was hiding something and he knew it. Getting to his feet, he moved to the window. "I have a bit of news I thought you might be interested in."

"Which is?"

"Your silver haired angel has an admirer." Turning to stare at Royce, he noticed Royce was tense at that news. Good, then he had been right, in assuming that his brother still liked the girl. "It seems Sheridan has the idea of calling on the gal tomorrow."

Royce soared to his feet. "Sheridan!" he shouted. Seeing his brother's amused, look he reseated himself. "Her family won't approve, I'm sure."

Jared smiled. "It would seem, it's the oldest ones decision in that matter and Sheridan is a bit of a catch."

"He's a sadistic womanizer. Her family will know that and protect her."

"I thought you might say that, so I also have brought a second bit of news with me."

Royce waited. His temper getting the best of him, he snapped. "Which is?"

Jared turned back toward the window, a grin playing across his features. "It seems the Earl of Sandalwood is also making his interest known."

Royce couldn't help his mouth from falling open. "The man has to be almost seventy."

Jared turned to look at his brother. "That doesn't seem to bother him. He says he still has the basic functions and can still get himself an heir before he dies. He seems to think a young blind bride would be just the thing."

Royce felt his insides clench. "Why are you telling me these things?"

Jared shrugged refilling his glass. "I just thought you might be interested. The lady asks about you from time to time."

Royce frowned. Seeing Allison today he believed his brother. She had seemed upset that he had thrown her out.

"What, dear brother, is the reason for my summons?"

Royce flushed. Jared was going to laugh if he asked the real question he wanted to know. Imagining Allison with Saul made his stomach turn and the thought of Newton touching her positively made him sick. "It seems the lovely lady, was here today."

Jared nearly spit the brandy out, at that bit of news. "She was here?" he said wiping the dribble off his chin.

"She was. Her brother brought her here. It seems the brother married a blind wife and wanted one of my hounds for a companion to the lady."

Jared's brows shot up. "Did you sell them one?"

"No. My hounds aren't exactly the nicest things where other people are concerned."

"You don't have to tell me that. I still have a scar where Thor took exception to my late night arrival."

Royce chuckled remembering all to well, seeing Jared clinging to a tree branch, while Thor yanked to pull him out of the tree. Thor's teeth had given Jared a good gash along his inner calf. "By the way, how did you manage to get in here tonight?"

Jared grinned. "I came prepared."

Royce's face turned stern. "You didn't bring another cat, did you?"

"No, the last one barely got away."

Royce didn't like the sound of that. "Jared, how many times do I have to tell you that all you have to do is let me know ahead of time and I'll lock them up."

"I like the excitement."

"What was it this time?"

"I brought a couple of chunks of meat with me."

Royce scowled. "Now Rufus is going to have a devil of a time getting them to eat the regular fare."

"That's not my problem."

Royce scowled again. "It would be, if I made you take care of them for a week."

Jared paled. "You can't do that. I'm expected back in the city tomorrow."

Royce arched a brow at him. Jared, knowing he wasn't getting anywhere with that line of conversation, suddenly smiled. "So, what was it you wanted to know?"

Royce scowled and lowered his gaze back to his brandy glass. "It has to do with Lady Hayworth. It seems she had trouble at a ball?" he asked letting the question hang as he moved to look out the window.

Jared grinned. Royce did care. "If you're asking what happened, I'll be happy to tell you?"

Royce frowned. "Isn't that what I just did?"

Jared grinned. "Of course. It was at her sister's wedding celebration. All of society was there. A smashing success," he said, regretting his choice of words considering the place was smashed to bits. "Lady Allison arrived with her brother, Lord Stephan. She hadn't been there very long before things broke into utter chaos. It seems she has this tiger that..."

"A tiger?" he asked turning to look at Jared.

"Yes. A tiger. It sort of helps her around like eyes. The way her sister tells it, the thing is actually like a pair of eyes for her."

Royce felt his blood pounding in his veins. He had been such a knave for turning her away. "Go on."

"Well, it seems this tiger turned up at the ball and before anyone could stop the thing, it decided to help itself to the cake."

"It ate the cake?"

Jared laughed. "It not only ate it, it hauled it's huge upper body up on the table. The whole time the ladies were fainting and screaming. It was wonderful."

"Jared!"

"Right," he said shifting. "Well, as this tiger is lapping away at the cake, Lady Allison and Lord Stephan try to stop it. Both of them end up slipping on the icing covering the floor and end up flat on their backsides. Next thing you know, the cat has Lord Stephan by his left leg and proceeds to drag him around the room."

Royce's mouth fell open. "He was dragging him around the room by one leg?"

Jared laughed harder barely able to finish the story. "Yes, yes. He was pulling him under tables, around chairs. People were scattering in all directions, trying to get out of the things way. Practically, every female there, if asked today, would swear the cat was eating Lord Stephan."

Royce gapped at him.

Jared held up his hand stopping his brother from saying anything. "Wait there's more."

"More?"

Jared nodded still laughing. "It seems Lady St. Paul, recently here from India, was also present at this ball."

"Who?"

Jared waved a hand. "It isn't important but what is, is that this eccentric young miss has this monkey."

"A monkey?"

"A monkey. The thing's about the size of a small cat and rides around on the lady's shoulder. It's really rather friendly but in society you know how well it goes over. Anyway," he said, seeing Royce's face completely shocked, "It seems this monkey, seeing the fun going on, decides it's missing out and takes off after the tiger. It catches them and sits itself on Lord Stephan's chest and proceeds to ride around the hall on the gent's chest." He hooted watching Royce's face twitch with mirth. "Wait, wait. Not only does the monkey ride there, it takes it's little hands and covers Lord Stephan's eyes and mouth every time he wants to talk or shout. It was the most comical evening I've spent in years," he finished holding his sides from all the laughter.

Royce began laughing. He was sorry he missed it. Gaining control, he glared at his brother. "You're telling me that those animals actually showed up at a wedding?"

Jared nodded his head. "It seems the tiger escaped it's confinement," he said wiping his eyes. "It was the most amazing thing," he said shaking his head.

Royce shook his head in disbelief. "What happened to Lord Stephan?"

"The cat dragged him around for a good fifteen minutes before his brother, Nathan, jumped on the thing dragging it to the ground. The other two brothers were chasing after the thing and ended up completely covered in icing."

Royce couldn't help himself, he laughed again. It was too funny not to. Three grown men chasing after a tiger, dragging a man around by his leg while a monkey played peek a boo on his chest. It just didn't happen every day. "Did the cat stop after that?"

"Oh, yes. In fact, Allison scolded it a good one. But by then the damage had already been done."

"What damage?" he asked feeling his humor flee.

Jared frowned into his brandy glass. "Lady Allison is the topic, at almost every tea or ball. The ladies are tearing her apart, really. Her sisters are trying valiantly to keep it contained but you know how society is. The poor thing hasn't been seen since."

Royce felt his chest tighten. "Yes, I know how society is."

Jared looked at his brother and frowned, years of gossip had surrounded him. If anyone understood, it was Royce. "Lady Sinclair has decided to host a ball to help lessen the gossip. I just thought maybe you'd like to go."

"When is it?"

"Saturday after next."

Royce frowned. He didn't want to go at all but maybe his presence would help Allison cope with the cruel gossip. Their venom would be directed at him. "I'll be there," he said quietly.

Jared smiled. "Wonderful. Ruth will be pleased. She thinks you're a fool for coming back here and letting the ton win. You'll return with me, then?"

Royce frowned, then slowly smiled. "Of course, why not. It saves me the hassle of finding a coach," he said neutrally. He really didn't care what society thought of him anymore. He wanted a family and London was the place to find a wife. Lady Allison's plight was as good as anything. Lifting his glass he drained the contents, then signaled for his hounds to enter the room. The beasts had sat there for a good ten minutes, while Jared told his tale, now it was their turn to have a bit of sport with Jared. He slipped by them nine times out of ten and they didn't like it.

Chapter 69

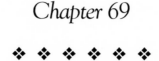

NATHAN PULLED THE CURRICLE to a halt staring over the lake.

"Are we here?" Ian asked, moving to jump out the side of the buggy.

"Hold on there, young man. We need to get a few things straight before we go down to the water," he said, climbing down from the buggy to lean back inside and stare at the pair. "I need you to promise to stay dry and not to go wandering off.

"All right. Let's go," Ian yelled, moving again for the edge.

Nathan grabbed him and helped him down then took Sean under the arms and set him on the ground.

"What kind of fish are there?" Ian asked moving to look in the water like the fish would be right there looking back at him.

Sean scowled at Ian, as Nathan took out the poles and worms. "I think we have all kinds," he said, moving along the shore with both boys right on his heels.

"I want to catch a big one," Ian said running ahead to a log that was laying four feet in the water. Walking up on it he looked back at Nathan. "Is this a good spot?"

"Looks as good as any," he said handing a pole to each boy. Putting a worm on their hooks he seated himself on the ground watching each child settled into place. Ian was perched on the log while Sean seated himself a couple of feet to Nathan's right. Silence descended as each boy worked on getting their hooks in the water. Ian pulled his in several times to make sure there wasn't a fish on yet.

"I'm not catching anything," he complained pulling his line in for the eighth time.

Sean snorted at him. "If you'd leave your hook in the water, maybe you would." he said wiping one of his small hands under his nose.

Nathan hid his smile as Ian looked at him. "Am I doing it wrong?" he asked giving Sean a glare.

"No, you're not doing it wrong but maybe a few more minutes in the water wouldn't hurt anything," he said trying not to hurt the boys feelings.

Ian didn't seem to notice. He quickly threw his line back into the lake and started swinging his legs. "I like fishing. Thomas takes us to the river. We've never been to a lake."

Nathan frowned. "Is that so?"

"Yep. Sean catches the most but I'm getting better. Thomas says I have the jitters. That means I move around a lot. The fish know I'm here," he said frowning at his legs.

Sean scowled at him."He also says you talk too much," he said pulling his line in.

Nathan watched the pair and smiled. They reminded him of when he was little. Their father had taken them fishing, hunting, and trapping.

Ian scratched his head then turned to look at Nathan. "Do you like Mama Rae?" he asked, sneezing.

Nathan's brows shot up at that. Pulling in his line to cover his reaction he quickly dug into the worm box looking for another one. Did he like mama Rae? How was he supposed to answer that? He didn't know what he thought of Rae. The last few days, since she had been coming to his room, he had started to weaken toward her. Her crying and distress over the nightmares she was having were making him feel something for her.

Ian fidgeted on the log. "Our first mama was real nice but she didn't tell us the stories like Mama Rae does?"

Nathan nearly dropped his pole. Sean jerked his pole out of the water. "Ian shut up. You're not supposed to talk about that," he said looking at Nathan like he was ready to bolt. Nathan cleared his features. He wanted to take the boy by the shoulders and shake answers out of him.

"I forgot," Ian said throwing his line out again. "I don't remember her much."

Sean's face turned red with anger. "Ian shut up," he said climbing to his feet.

Nathan looked at Sean, watching his face pale. "It's all right, Sean. I'm sure Ian didn't mean to break a promise," he finished, giving Ian a smile.

Sean cast weary eyes in Nathan's direction. He was unsure of his reaction.

"Besides, I can keep a secret," Nathan added, throwing his line back in.

Ian looked at his brother sheepishly. "See he wasn't mad like mama Rae said he would be. You do like her, don't you?" he asked his trusting eyes turned on Nathan.

"Of course, I like her. I married her, didn't I?"

Sean moved further away before sitting down. "Thomas said you would come around to liking us once you got to know us but that Mama Rae shouldn't have pushed us on you."

Nathan frowned wondering what else Thomas had told them. "I like you. You are well mannered boys," he said feeling awkward with this sort of conversation.

Ian grinned. "I like you, too. You have a real nice house and I like my big room. Some of the clothes are itchy but I like them, too, 'specially my sword. Uncle Stephan gave it to us. Sean has a nice long one. Do you think he kills pirates at sea?" he asked his legs swinging again.

"I'm sure Stephan does rather well at sea but I think he spends more time carrying cargo back and forth to different ports than he does killing pirates."

Ian frowned. "But a good Captain kills pirates," he said, scratching his chin "Maybe he's a pirate and steals treasure," he said smiling again.

Nathan listened to the boy prattle on nodding his head here and there but he desperately wanted to know about this other mama. "I'm sure your mama didn't tell you about those pirates."

"Mama Rae did. She likes to tell stories. She says our mama used to draw the places mama Rae talks about. I think it would be something to see what a real dragon looks like. Right, Sean?"

Sean was frowning as he looked right at Nathan. Nathan smiled at the boy hoping he would say something on the subject. "He wasn't suppose to say anything."

Nathan looked back out over the lake. "Sometimes secrets hurt people more if they're kept hidden," he said turning his gaze on Sean. "I think your Mama would have liked to be remembered, not kept a secret."

Sean bit his lip, his gaze on his lap. "She hated secrets," he said his voice catching a bit.

Nathan frowned. These weren't Rae's children. Whose were they then and why did she say they were hers? Frowning, he nearly cursed at his slow wit. Of course she wouldn't have said they were someone else's for fear he would have sent them away.

"Mama Rae doesn't like secrets, either. She cries a lot," he said looking at Nathan. "Do you make her cry?"

Nathan reddened at the innocent question. Did Rae cry about him? "I don't know."

"She comes to our room to sleep. She thinks we don't know she's crying but she is." Sean said. "I think she misses Mama just as much as I do," he said wiping at a tear running down his face. Ian sniffed from his place on the log.

"Don't cry Sean. I don't like it when you cry," he said sniffing again.

Sean wiped at his face. "I'm not crying," he snapped turning his back. "I'm five now and I don't cry," he said sniffing.

Nathan frowned searching for something to say before he had a couple of bawling kids on his hands. He needed to know who their mother was. "Was your Mama a friend of Mama Rae's?"

Ian wiped his face on his sleeve. "She looked just like Mama Rae only she had pretty eyes."

"Pretty eyes?" he asked wondering what Ian meant by 'looking like Rae'.

Sean scowled at Ian. "He doesn't remember. He was just a baby."

"I was not. I remember her."

"Do not."

"Do so."

"Boys." Nathan said grabbing Ian as he ran down the log and across the shore to reach his brother. "Hold on now. I think you both remember her well enough. Now, Ian, what did you mean by pretty eyes?"

"They were green," he said.

"Mama Rae's eyes are green." he said scowling at himself for knowing that.

"But Mama's eyes were real green like...like..." he said looking around. "Like that line on your carriage."

Nathan craned his neck to see. It indeed had a line of green running several inches below the rim. It was a very light color green. "Just like that, huh?"

"Yep and she had longer hair than Mama Rae."

"She always wore her hair in a braid," Sean said. "I used to measure it for her. It grew just like a weed, she said."

Nathan found himself feeling more and more stunned as the boys spoke. Not only did these children belong to someone else but they had known their mother real well. "Where is your mother now?"

Sean ducked his head. "She died. Mama Rae said she drowned. She could swim real good but Mama Rae said it was too far to get to shore."

Nathan frowned. Their mother had drowned. How awful. "I'm sorry."

Sean sniffed. "She is with the angels."

Nathan reached out a hand and just barely touched his shoulder. "I'm sure she is Sean. She sounds like a real nice lady."

"She liked music. Mama Rae says she plays harps."

Nathan couldn't help but smile. "I'm sure she plays real fine."

"Are you angry she kept the secret," Sean asked looking up at him with tear rimmed eyes. "She said you wouldn't understand."

Nathan scowled but quickly changed his expression. Rae had a great number of questions to answer but it was really between him and her. These boys didn't need to be caught in the middle.

"Well, she's wrong about that. I do understand and I think she did the right thing, taking you in as her own and I'm happy to be able to have you as part of my family," he said slightly vulnerable with that statement.

Ian smiled and threw his arms around his neck. "I'm happy, too. She will be happy when we tell her. Maybe she won't cry anymore."

Nathan pulled his arms down beside him and frowned. "I have a favor to ask the pair of you."

Sean looked up from his hands as Ian bounced up and down. "You want us to hunt up a rabbit?"

Nathan chuckled. "I think Cook has something already planned," he said ruffling Ian's hair. "No. The favor I want to ask is that you don't tell Mama Rae that you told me about your mama."

"But that's a secret. She doesn't like secrets."

"I know but it would hurt her feelings to know you told me and I want to have a chance to talk with her before she hears it from you."

Sean frowned. Ian looked desperate. "Is she gonna be mad? I don't like when she's mad."

Nathan smiled. "I'm sure she won't be mad but just to make sure, I think you should let me talk with her first."

Sean looked at Ian then back to Nathan. "All right, but it will make her cry, won't it?"

Nathan frowned. "I don't know, Sean, but at least there will be no more secrets."

Sean jumped to his feet with a yelp as a fish took his bait and ran with it. Ian started screaming and hollering for him to pull it in.

"Come on, Sean, get him," he hollered running along the shore behind his brother.

Nathan watched the pair with excitement but his mind was already going over the questions he wanted to ask Rae.

Chapter 70

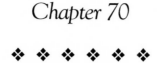

JESSICA PACED HER ROOM like a caged cat. Morgan was supposed to be home half hour ago and still she'd seen no sign of him. Her family was expecting them for her father's dinner later that evening and she was dressed to play the simpleton.

"Damn," she cursed moving again to look out the window at the street below. Seeing nothing she turned and caught her gown on the table sending a vase crashing to the floor. "Damn thing," she snapped grabbing up her glass of brandy. The stuff went down her throat smoothly and she sighed in satisfaction at the rich amber taste. She was getting sick of sipping Porte. Resuming her pacing she looked at the clock again. Normally she wouldn't have bothered dressing in such a priggish fashion but her plan was to let Morgan know she wasn't about to become his piece of fluff. She wasn't cut from that kind of cloth.

Swallowing the remains of her glass she left the room and moved steadily along the hall. She tripped several times the last almost falling on her face. Wearing these stupid shoes, was insane. Pulling the things off her feet she flung them over the banister and smiled in satisfaction as they clumped in the foyer below.

"Captain?" Arty asked his head coming into view.

"Hold on there, Arty," she snapped moving with determination back to her room. Pulling open the wardrobe she scooped up every high heeled shoe she possessed and marched back to the banister. Dumping the lot over the side, she smiled at the racket it made. "Take those and dump them in the sea."

"In the sea, captain?"

"Yes," she said leaning over the rail. "Is Dane about?"

"Yes, captain, but are you sure..."

"Put them in the sea and that's an order. My husband did sail, correct?"

"I don't know, Captain. I don't think so."

"It doesn't matter, the arrogant fool can stuff his gowns and shoes on some other miss. I'm not wearing that drivel." Moving back to her room again she yanked the mass of dresses she'd specifically picked out for their lace and femininity. Smashing them over her arm she pulled the drawer open to her left and pulled out the one and only corset she possessed. Moving back out the door she headed for the stairs.

"My lady, is something wrong?"

Jessica looked over her shoulder giving Amy a dashing smile. "Nothing Amy, just cleaning house. You wouldn't be tending any of this frivolous stuff, would you?" she asked still moving toward the stairs."

"Yes, my lady. I have your gown for the ball ready."

Jessica stared at her then grinned. "Get it, please."

Amy nodded staring at the pile of clothes in Jessica's arms but she moved off to fetch the requested gown.

Jessica took her burden and pitched all of it over the banister. "Arty take those to the sea as well. Have Dane help you."

"But Captain..."

"Just do it. If you can't bring yourself to pitch them in the sea, give them to the poor. I don't want them," she said pointing at the floor.

"My lady," Amy said, waiting for Jessica to look at her. "Here it is." she added holding the gown out to her mistress.

"Excellent," Jessica said, pulling the silver blue gown out of her grasp and pitching it over the rail. Amy gasped and quickly moved to the banister. "That one too, Arty. Hurry now," she said, frowning at the gown she still had on. "Wait a minute," she snapped moving to her room to rip the gown off her body. Pulling the door open she bellowed for Amy. The second she appeared she threw the gown at her. "Give him this one, too."

Amy, wide-eyed, looked at the gown in her hands. "But my lady, I haven't another ready for this evening."

Jessica waved a hand at her then smiled. "I won't be needing one," she said, shutting the door in her face. Amy stared at the closed door for several seconds before frowning. She could hear drawers and doors slam around in the room. Looking in both directions she moved back to the stairs and walked down into the foyer where a confused Arty stood scratching his head.

"I think she bloody well lost her mind." Arty said to Dane. "But an order is an order. Hold out yer arms." He finished scooping up a pile of the frilly gowns and pushed them into Danes unreadable features. Grabbing up the remainder of the lot he stared at Amy. "Give me that one, too. The Capt...I mean, her ladyship, doesn't like to be disobeyed and she said pitch the gowns. So we're pitching the gowns."

"She told you to throw them out? But they're so expensive."

Arty stopped. "I don't care if they were pure gold. She can be a real tyrant if you cross her."

Amy frowned. "The master isn't going to like this."

Arty frowned. He'd forgotten that one. The man seemed as merciless as his captain was. "What are ya gettin at?"

Amy frowned. "I'd suggest some mutiny. Take the things to my chamber and I'll keep them there in case the mistress changes her mind."

Arty looked at Dane and frowned. Dane shrugged, nodding his head toward the girl. "Bloody hell it is, working for this lot. Sometimes I think I lost a few wits myself. Come on then girl. Lead the way. If we're going to disobey, we might as well get to it. Slowness is grounds for lashes when she's got her temper up."

Amy paled knowing the master's wife had been a captain before coming to be the genteel lady they'd known the past few weeks. Yet she sure looked happier this evening than she had in a long time. Frowning, she shook her head. Arty was right, working for this household was definitely a risk to ones health.

Jessica moved along the hall to the banister and looked over the edge and smiled. Not a trace of the frivolous mess, was anywhere in sight. Arty and Dane would be occupied for some time. Scooting up on the banister she slide down to land in the foyer with a laugh. Her breeches gave her so much more freedom. Throwing her braid over her shoulder she turned around to see if she'd been observed, grinning when no one was in sight. Jessica grabbed her gloves and a cloak then scooted out the door. It was time Morgan Sinclair met his real wife.

Chapter 71

STEPHAN SCOWLED, as he left his office with Rae over his shoulder in a sac. The stupid chit had come to the docks again. Stephan frowned further, remembering the shouting that had come from Nathan and Rae's room the night she had poured punch all over him.

Shaking his head he moved along the wharf.

"Ready to go, my lord." Robby asked pulling the door open for him.

Stephan scowled. "I was hoping to return home in a happy mood. This package has soured my evening," he said, smacking her behind.

Robby kept his face straight as the bag squirmed and murmured sounds remotely like curses.

Stephan hefted the bag into the carriage and climbed in behind it. Situating Rae on the seat opposite he leaned his head back on the seat. How stupid could she be? She had come back to his office just hours after almost getting herself killed on the waif. Cursing, he ran a hand through his hair. God what a mess. Not only did he have to tell Nathan that he had kissed his wife but he had to return the chit to Nathan trussed up like a pig.

"Damn, can't you do anything your told," he said to the squirming bag. Hearing her cursing and ranting at him he was thankful he'd stuffed the gag in her mouth. It muffled the worst of it.

Twenty minutes later he found himself staring at his Aunt Ginger's town house from inside the carriage. Feeling like a lad being called to account for his bad behavior, he frowned further. "I don't know why I end up in these situations. Running into you on the waif was one thing but kissing you is another. Nathan isn't going to like either one but I know the kissing is going to send him through the roof. He probably won't speak to me for years." Cursing, he poked the bag with his finger. "You hear me?"

The bag squirmed again and he swore he heard her call him a bastard. Frowning, he took a deep breath before scooping her up and getting out of the carriage. Throwing her over his shoulder, he paused. "Don't suppose you would mind waiting out here for a bit? I think I'll be going someplace shortly," he asked the driver.

The hack driver scowled down at him. "It's yer money."

"Fine. Say twenty minutes. If I'm not back by then go ahead and leave," he said handing him a few extra coins for waiting.

"Sure thing, governor. I'll be here twenty minutes," he said pulling out his bottle and getting comfortable.

Stephan arched his brows at the man nearly dropping Rae when she squirmed to be put down. "Hold still, you idiot," he cursed smacking her back side. "I'll drag you in there, if I have to. Stop squirming," he added, as he mounted the steps to the town house.

Chapter 72

CHRISTOPHER LOOKED UP as Hobkins entered the study then arched a brow, waiting for the man to speak.

"My lord, there's a woman here to see you. It seems she has something to return to you?" Hobkins said red in the face. Christopher frowned at his behavior.

"Did she say who she was?"

"No, my lord."

"Show her into the drawing room. I'll be there in a moment," he snapped waiting just long enough for Hobkins to leave before getting to his feet to pace. A woman? Who the hell could it be? He hadn't kept a woman in years. In fact, he hadn't been with a woman for weeks. Ever since coming to London, in fact. Moving to the window he looked out trying to see the coach that had brought her but the dusk of the approaching night made it impossible to see. Cursing, he wondered who would be calling on him in the evening. Taking up his coat, he slipped it on straightening his cravat and patted his hair. Draining his brandy glass he moved to the door and walked slowly to the drawing room where a smiling Hobkins was standing just outside the door. Giving him a narrowed look he received an answering grin before entering the room. One of his brothers was up to this he was sure. Seeing the lady standing by the window looking out, he frowned. This was one woman he didn't know. She was on the petite side. Guessing to stand about five four with black hair tied and flowed nicely down her back. Her gown was a light rose color and she clutched a reticule in her right hand. Clearing his throat he watched her spin around and face him. Her face was pale and nervous looking. Seeing those blue eyes looking at him in what only could be fright he forced a smile.

"I don't seem to remember inviting such a lovely lady to my home," he stated, arching a brow.

She smiled at that remark. "You didn't."

Christopher nodded for her to take a seat while he moved to the tray and offered her a drink.

"Porte please," she said, nervously sitting on the settee. "Thank you," she said taking the glass from him. Now that she was here she felt like a school girl waiting on her first caller. This was harder than she had thought.

Christopher waited a few minutes watching he struggle with an inner problem before he broke into her thoughts. "What can I do for you?" he asked taking a seat in one of the high backed chairs across from the settee.

Cari St. Paul frowned. "I think it best if I introduce myself. I'm Lady St. Paul, Andrew's sister."

Christopher's brows went up in shock. He remembered the young lady now but he hadn't remembered her looking so beautiful. Getting to his feet, he moved to stand in front of her. "I remember meeting you" he said with a smile, all trace of suspicion gone. "I'm sorry for the unfriendly welcome I was just worried my brothers had played some sort of trick on me," he said bending to kiss her hand before returning to his seat.

"A trick?" she asked nervously. "With a woman?"

Christopher laughed. "It's usually not their sort of thing but lately I wouldn't put it past them. Now what can I do for you?" he asked again sipping from his glass.

"Well," she said turning red. "I have come out of necessity really. Andrew insisted," she added, reaching for her reticule. "I...well...oh, this is much harder than I thought it would be," she said lowering her face so he couldn't see it.

"What's much harder than you thought?" he asked confused at her behavior.

Cari looked at him, dressed so elegant his cravat slightly ruffled. He looked every bit as handsome as she remembered and suddenly the deal she had made with Stephan didn't seem to matter. She wanted this man for her own purposes. Not to satisfy them. Lifting her chin she withdrew a watch, some coins, a ring, looking suspiciously like his and a small stone he knew was his cause he carried the thing around for good luck. Holding the things out to him she placed them on the table between them.

Christopher stood for a moment searching his pockets for the items he knew he wouldn't find. Drawing his brows down in confusion he stared at the now scarlet face. "I don't understand."

Cari jumped at his outburst. This was the most embarrassing thing she ever had to do. "It seems the other night at the ball. You know the one held for your sister?" she said, as he nodded, she lowered her eyes. "Well, it seems that my monkey, Ranki, sort of borrowed those things from your pockets," she finished twisting her fingers in her gown.

Christopher watched her with brows raised. "You're telling me I was pick pocketed by a monkey?"

Cari felt her face redden but nodded. "He has gotten much better about borrowing but occasionally he falls back into his old ways," she said looking at him through her lashes. Seeing that he was slightly amused and less aggravated she lifted her face. "Andrew said you would understand. I'm truly sorry for what Ranki did. I returned them as soon as I found them."

Christopher frowned. He hadn't realized they were missing himself. It had been a few days since the ball. "It's perfectly all right, Miss St. Paul. To tell you the truth, I hadn't missed the items."

Cari smiled. "I knew they were yours right away," she said blushing when she realized how intimate that sounded. "I mean, the ring has your crest on it and the watch has an inscription so I was hoping Andrew would just return them to you for me but he insisted I do it myself."

Christopher smiled at her. She was really quite lovely. Nathan barged into the room at this point looking more the rogue hell than usual. Seeing Cari, he drew up short.

"I'm sorry. I didn't realize you had company," he said turning to leave.

"It's all right, Nathan. You remember Lady St. Paul?"

Nathan smiled preoccupied but gentleman enough to take her hand and kiss it. "It's nice to see you again," he said getting a scowl from Christopher. Nathan ignored him and went for a drink.

"I was just getting ready to invite her to dine with us," Christopher said looking at Cari.

Cari looked at the pair of them and was shocked at the difference in the pair. One had dark hair, hazel eyes, and was handsome as the devil, the other had green eyes blond hair and looked like a god. Smiling, she nodded to Christopher. "I wouldn't want to intrude."

"I wouldn't have asked if you would be. As it happens, my brother here, and his wife just received their children today. We're having a sort of celebration dinner for them."

Cari smiled. "How nice."

Nathan scowled from his position in front of the decanter. He knew the dinner wasn't in their honor but seeing his brother acting so unlike himself with the woman Stephan had played match-maker with was worth the lie he guessed. Stephan sure was right about her being lovely. She even had a beautiful voice. He found himself grinning at her getting presented to Christopher and working a dinner invite out of it so quickly.

"I hope it isn't to formal," she said looking down at her gown.

Christopher smiled. "It's just family. My father is coming home, as well. You're dressed lovely."

Nathan rolled his eyes at Christopher's flattery. "Need another, Christopher?" he asked, holding up the brandy. Christopher scowled at Nathan but smiled when Cari looked at him.

"No, thank you," he said, narrowing his eyes the minute she looked away. Nathan chuckled setting the bottle back on it's stand. Picking up his own glass, he moved to sit on the settee next to Cari.

"So Miss St. Paul, what brings you to our home?" he asked taking a sip.

Christopher sent him a murderous glare but Nathan arched his brows, when Cari ducked her head and turned scarlet. "Really, Nathan. I don't think that is any of your affair." he snapped nodding for him to leave.

Nathan frowned at the absurd attack looking at Cari in confusion "I'm sorry if I offended you," he said feeling even more awkward for that remark. "How's your..er...pet. A monkey, wasn't it?" he said smiling.

Cari turned even redder, as she glanced at Nathan then peeked at the items on the table, before lowering her head from view.

Christopher set his face in a fierce scowl and glared at Nathan. Shaking his head, he hoped Nathan would get it and leave her alone.

Nathan shrugged, letting Christopher know he had no idea what was going on. "I think I'll remove myself until dinner. I seem to be sticking my foot in my mouth," he said getting to his feet. Moving to the door, he swore he heard her giggle.

Christopher watched him go then frowned at Cari. "I'm sorry. He really didn't know."

"It's all right. After talking with Lord Nathan, I really understand. He seems quite blunt in his speech," she said smiling. "Then again, so am I," she said grinning.

Christopher smiled at that, but wondered at a feeling he had in his stomach. If he didn't know any better he would think he was jealous of the way she had just spoken about Nathan. The thought was so ridiculous he chuckled over it. "How about a stroll in the garden?"

Chapter 73

JESSICA SWUNG DOWN from her horse to the gawking groom and grinned. "Rub him down, please, and see that he's comfortable," she said, throwing the reins to the lad. The groom caught the reins effortlessly then gapped at the lady before him as she sauntered toward the house. She was dressed like a man wearing black breeches, black boots, and a white shirt that billowed around her upper body molded only by a simple vest. Shaking his head, he frowned. His master was bringing around the strangest guests. First, his recluse of a brother, now this odd mannered lady.

Jessica chuckled at the look on the groom's face. The seven glasses of brandy were making her feel relaxed and reckless. Moving up to the door, she went to knock only to have the door open before she had the chance.

"Can I help you...er...Miss?" the butler asked, looking her over from top to bottom.

"You sure can, my good man. I'd like to see Jared McMaster, please."

The butler coughed. "Is he expecting you?"

"I should say not, but I'm sure he'll speak with me," she said moving into the foyer.

The butler scowled at her behavior. "And who should I say is calling?" he asked closing the door looking none to pleased.

"Lady Sinclair, please," she said, smiling as the butler's brows arched. He'd heard the Lady Sinclair was a stunning beauty. The chit before him wasn't exactly the model of femininity.

"Wait here, please," he said, hurrying down the hall, stopping a footman to have him keep an eye on the girl while he hurried into the study. Knocking on the door, he waited a second, then moved into the room.

"What is it, Saunders?"

"There's a Lady Sinclair here to see you, my lord. She says you'll wish to speak with her."

Jared arched a brow, giving his brother a quizzical look. Royce shrugged. "All right. Show the lady in."

"But my lord she's ...well she could be an imposter."

Jared's brows moved higher. "Is that so?" he said smiling at Royce. "Well, show her in anyway. I'm sure we can handle her."

Saunders reddened but bowed and went to fetch the girl. Jared watched Saunders leave and grinned. "It seems the Hayworth clan never ceases to provide us with amusement."

Royce sat up at that. "She's a Hayworth?"

"Figured you'd forgotten already. She's the newly married captain."

Royce's face cleared with understanding. "The wedding celebration. I see why you're amused. What business could she have with you?"

"I haven't the slightest idea but I'm dying to find out."

Saunders knocked before admitting Jessica. "Thank you," she said to the disgruntled butler. Grinning at the pair of men in the study she moved to allow the butler to shut the door. "I don't think he likes me," she said smiling at Royce and Jared.

Jared arched a brow at the lady before him. She looked and walked like the Captain she proclaimed to be. Put a patch over her eye and tie a handkerchief about her head and she'd be a pirate. "What can I do for you, Lady Sinclair?"

Jessica smiled as each man tried to decide whether to kiss her hand or not. "I still get my hand kissed when visiting the ton," she said, as Jared grinned and complied. "Actually, I'm glad you're here, my lord. This is the reason for my visit. I wanted to have your brother bring you to my ball on Saturday."

Royce frowned, as Jared grinned at him, "A ball?"

"It's nothing grand. Just five hundred people or so," she said, giggling.

Jared and Royce arched a brow at her. "You're foxed," Jared said moving around his desk grinning.

Royce scowled at his in appropriate words. "Would you care to sit down, my lady."

Jessica smiled at them then moved to pop the top off the decanter near the book shelves. "No. A glass of brandy wouldn't be remiss," she said, pouring herself one. Lifting the glass, she took a sip and sighed. "It's such a heavenly drink. I'm sick to death of tea," she said, looking at them frowning. "Excuse my manners. Would you care for a drink?"

Jared nearly burst out laughing at her behavior. She was offering him a drink from his own stock. Royce nudged him to keep quiet. "No, thank you, my lady. What can we do for you?" he asked, smiling slightly.

Jessica moved to the window to put her rump on the ledge and cross her legs out in front of her. "I must say. Allison is right about you. You are a handsome devil. You have a wonderful sense of humor, too," she said, smiling at Royce.

Royce flushed scarlet his brows arching at the thought of Allison talking about him. "Did she say that?"

"Oh, yes. Those scars are barely noticeable once you get to know you. Being the second time I've seen you, I'd say handsome is appropriate," she said getting to her feet. "Well, enough about you. I suppose that isn't at all proper. Allison will probably have my head. Anyway," she said waving a hand at them, scowling. "I need to buy a ship?"

"Buy a ship?" Royce asked, frowning.

"A ship. Mine...well...mine got misplaced," she said smiling. "Yes. I misplaced it and need a new one. I need a new one by tonight."

Royce and Jared looked at one another then back at her. "You misplaced a ship and want another one by tonight?"

Jessica frowned at Jared. "Are you hard of hearing?"

Royce couldn't help himself and laughed drawing an indignant look from him. "Excuse me. I don't know what came over me," he said still chuckling as Jessica pushed a strand of hair off her forehead. "I haven't any ships available," he said knowing how difficult it was to talk with someone so deep in their cups.

Jessica scowled. "Now see here, if my husband has said something to you about me it's a lie. I can sail if I want to."

Royce frowned, so that was it. The husband didn't want her on the sea. "You'll have to take that up with your husband, my lady. I haven't any ships available. Whether it was you or another standing here, the answer would be the same. I should have one in three weeks, if you're interested."

Jessica scowled, then drained her glass. "This could be a problem," she said, moving to refill her glass.

Royce glared at Jared. Do something, he mouthed only to get a 'what' mouthed back. "Perhaps I can be of service. If you permit me to give you a lift home, I'm sure we can figure something out."

Jessica looked at him and smiled. "All right, but I have my horse."

Royce frowned at his brother. "I'm sure Jared won't mind if you leave your horse here. We can borrow his coach."

"I'd prefer to ride," she said taking a drink from the glass. Giving Jared the half full glass, she patted his shoulder. "Thank you for your help," she said pulling the door open and weaving down the hall.

Royce grabbed Jared's arm and cursed. "Get word to the husband. I don't want my head blown off because the chit decides to do something stupid."

Jared laughed. "I can't believe this. Ruth is going to die."

"You're not going to say a word. This can only hurt the family," he snapped, moving to follow Jessica, hearing the butler having problems. "Just send word to the husband," he finished taking up his cloak and gloves. "If my lady can wait a moment, I'll need a horse."

Jessica grinned. "Of course, it's not like I'd be able to share mine," she said pulling open the door to head for the stables. "My horse, please."

Royce gave his brother a stern look. "The husband."

"She is a polite drunk," Jared said chuckling when Royce paused to glare at him. "Go on. I have a message to send," he said, shutting the door.

Royce scowled at the door, vowing to throttle his brother later. Moving to the stables, he arched a brow, seeing a large gray waiting for him. Jessica was seated on a roan. "Let's get moving. I have to be on that ship tonight."

Royce scowled at her, but swung up into the saddle anyway. At least she wasn't spouting that handsome drivel anymore. He just hoped he didn't get shot for his concern.

Chapter 74

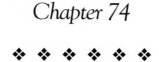

NATHAN SHUT THE DOOR behind himself, cursing Christopher for his stupid behavior. How was he supposed to know Cari had a problem with her monkey? Hell, he barely knew the lady. Moving along the hall, he paused wondering where he should go. He didn't want to see Rae. He needed more than a half an hour to talk with her and that's all he had before his Father arrived.

Looking up, he arched his brows as Hobkins pulled the door open. Stephan stood there carrying a squirming bag. "Don't tell me you've kidnaped Jessica again?"

Stephan turned scarlet. "No, it's not Jessica," he said, moving in as Hobkins shut the door. Cursing, Stephan frowned at meeting Nathan just seconds upon entering the house.

"Well, if it's not Jessica, then who do you have trussed up this time?" he asked putting his hands in his pockets. The bag started squirming and murmuring words remarkably like curse words.

Stephan flushed trying valiantly to hold the bag on his shoulder with his one good arm. Seeing he was losing the battle he moved past Nathan heading for the drawing room.

Nathan, seeing his intent, raised a hand to stop him. "Wait. Stephan, Christopher has..." his voice trailed off as he watched Stephan barge into the room.

"What's going on? Who do you have in there this time?" Christopher shouted, forgetting he had company.

Nathan moved into the room pulling the door closed behind him, as Stephan dumped his package on the barely vacated settee.

"Nice to see you again, Miss St. Paul." he said, taking her hand, "I'm sorry for the intrusion," he said, suddenly nervous.

Christopher stared at Stephan as if he'd sprouted horns. "Stephan, I hate to remind you that Father is at this very moment on his way here.

Who did you bring home wrapped up like a pair of new shoes," he finished, anger clearly written all over his face. "Father is going to expire for sure."

Nathan smiled at Cari as she slowly moved herself away from Stephan and Christopher.

"Christopher, if you haven't noticed, you have a guest. I suggest you take her for a walk around the gardens or something. I seem to recall Nathan doing a superb job in their making."

Christopher reddened as Nathan glared at Stephan. "It was better than running around like an errand boy," he snapped, seeing Stephan flush.

Stephan ran a hand through his hair. He hadn't meant to get Nathan angry, especially with the news he had to tell him. "I'm sorry. I didn't mean to intrude but if you would excuse us, I need to speak with Nathan," he finished giving Christopher a pointed look.

Christopher's eyes snapped to the sac. "You have her in there?" he said before he could stop himself.

Stephan scowled at Christopher as Nathan moved up behind the settee to look down at the bag. "Who do you have in there?"

Stephan swallowed, absently rubbing his arm just above the bindings holding his break. "I think we should be alone...I..."

"Who is it?" Nathan snap, his suspicions turning rapidly to his wife.

Stephan opened his mouth to protest to privacy but seeing Nathan's face slowly darken with anger, he sighed. "Fine," he snapped taking the end of the sac and pull it off of Rae's head.

Nathan glared at Emily, then stiffened with shock as the green eyes staring back at him were the same hue as his coaches stripe. It wasn't Rae.

"I found her on the waif. She probably got lost or something. I'm sure Rae didn't mean..."

The mention of Rae's name drew Emily's head to Stephan with a snap. Nathan watched as the lady on the settee flushed, paled, then slowly sagged in a faint.

"Well, good lord. You both sent her into a swoon with those fierce scowls," Cari snapped, moving to Emily's side. "Lord Stephan, I hate to point this out to you," she said untiing the gag from Emily's head. "But I don't believe this is the proper way to treat a sister by marriage. Fetch some salts, please, Lord Christopher. She doesn't appear to be coming around," she said, gentle patting the ladies cheeks.

Stephan watched in shock as the Cari berated him seconds before ordering Christopher to fetch salts.

"Well, don't just stand there. Hurry up," she finished, glancing at the three of them before pulling Emily against her chest so she could untie her arms.

Christopher left by the side entrance as Stephan bent and knocked her hands away. "I can do that," he said, taking just seconds to loose the knot.

Moving to Emily's feet, he quickly untied them, too. Cari pushed her back on the settee swinging her legs up so Emily was laid out flat.

Nathan turned and pulled the doors to the drawing room open. Walking to the bottom of the stairs, he took them two at a time.

Stephan watched him go, then cursed. "Damn."

"Excuse me," Cari said giving him a stern look. "Do you mind telling me why you had you brothers wife trussed up like a pig?"

Stephan turned scarlet. "I...she was on the docks..." he began only to stop abruptly as Nathan reentered the room dragging Rae behind him. "Good God," he croaked, his mouth hanging open as his eyes snapped back to the settee.

"My word. This is a bit of a mess, isn't it?" Cari said, getting to her feet slowly.

Rae stared at them, completely confused. "Nathan, I don't understand why you..."

Nathan took her by the shoulders and placed her in front of him. Leading her to the settee he stopped as her body came up against it's back. "What are you doing? I'm not even ready..." her voice trailed off as her eyes moved to see the person stretched out on the settee. As the image of her sister's face registered in her brain she felt the floor drop from beneath her.

Nathan caught his wife as she sagged in his arms. "Bloody hell," he cursed, scooping her up to move her to a chair.

"What the hell did you do that for?" Stephan snapped looking back and forth between the twins.

"Sure are a fainting bunch," Cari said, looking at the door Christopher had taken. "Where is Lord Christopher with those salts?" she added.

Nathan knelt before his wife. "I didn't think she would faint," he said patting her face. "Where did you get that one?"

Stephan still stunned at having two Rae's sank slowly into a chair. "I didn't kiss your wife then." he said staring at Emily.

Nathan turned from his crouched position. "You kissed Rae?" he asked, menacingly.

"No. I kissed that one," he said, pointing a finger at Emily.

Nathan turned his attention back to Rae. "What's her name?"

Stephan frowned. "I don't know. I thought she was Rae."

Nathan slowly turned around again. "You kissed her, thinking she was Rae," he asked getting to his feet slowly.

Stephan furrowed his brow. "I...technically, yes. But..."

"You bastard!" Nathan said, moving to swing at his brother. Nathan's punch sent Stephan and his chair over backwards.

Cari shot to her feet, as Nathan scrambled over the chair after his brother. "Gentlemen," she snapped, her voice cracking through the air like a whip. Both men looked up from their locked position. "If you two would kindly look around you, you will notice two women laying here completely senseless. If it wouldn't be too much trouble, I would think the pair of you could deal with whatever problems you have at a later date," she finished, getting blushes out of both of them. Straightening her gown, she turned back to kneel by Emily.

"What's going on in here?" Christopher snapped, seeing Nathan getting to his feet while Stephan remained on the floor holding his hand against his chest. Seeing Rae in the chair, he frowned. "She came around then," he stated then frowned further. "Why is she still unconscious." As he moved around the settee, he stopped in his tracks. "My god. Who is that?" he stated staring at Emily.

"I believe these two ladies could answer your questions better, if you would hand me those salts" Cari said holding out her hand.

"Of course," Christopher said, oblivious to her tone. He was staring at the pair in shock. Seeing Nathan kneeling by his wife, he turned to Stephan. "What's going on?"

"I don't know. All I know is that I didn't kiss Rae," he finished with an attempt at a grin.

Christopher scowled at him then watched Cari stick the salts under Emily's nose. Emily jerked to a sitting position smacking Cari's hand out of the way to rid her nose of the offensive smell. "Good God. What was that?" she snapped, her eyes burning from the effect.

"How are you feeling?" Cari asked.

"Who are you?" she snapped, looking at Christopher then to Stephan. Her face paled at the last. "You know my sister," she said, getting to her feet to move in front of him."Where is she? How do you know her? Take me to her this instant," she said grabbing his shirt front.

Stephan took hold of her arms. "You're Rae's sister?"

"Isn't that what I just said. Now where is she?" she said, getting hysterical.

"I hate to do this to you..."

"Oh, god. She's dead, isn't she?" she said, lowering her head to his chest. "Oh, that is so unfair," she mumbled into his shirt.

Christopher scowled at Stephan who glared in return. Taking her arms firmly, Stephan pulled her away from his chest. "She isn't dead. In fact she's right behind you."

Emily turned around so fast she smacked his bad hand as she pulled away to move to Rae's side. Stephan let out a hiss of air.

Emily pushed everyone out of the way as she knelt in front of Rae. Holding her hands over her mouth to keep from screaming she slowly reached out a hand to touch her cheek oblivious to the tears coursing down her cheeks. As her fingers came in contact with Rae's face an animalistic sound escaped from her throat. Pulling her hand back she wiped at the tears blurring her vision. "What's wrong with her?" she snapped, glaring at Nathan.

"She fainted seeing you," he said studying her face

Emily ignored him. "Where is that awful smelly stuff?"

Cari moved forward handing it to her. "Just hold it under her nose."

Emily glared at Cari but pushed the stuff under Rae's nose.

Rae reacted much the same way Emily did only the vial of smelling salts sailed across the room from her swat. As her eyes focused on Emily's face she let out a screech clutching her in an embrace that sent both girls into Nathan who steadied them while they cried over one another. Several minutes passed as the pair cried and hugged pulling away to look at each others face only to dissolve in another bout of tears and hugs.

"I just can't believe it. I thought you were dead," Rae said pulling Emily again into her arms. "Sean and Ian... my God. The boys. They're here, with me," she finished watching Emily dissolve in another fit of tears, unable to do little more than cry from shock and relief.

Stephan moved forward to pick Emily up and lift her onto the settee. Rae clutched her hand never letting go as she seated herself next to her.

"They're here. We've been so lost without you and to think that you've been alive all this time," she said, dissolving into more tears. Nathan moved to sit behind her rubbing her back as she cried against her sister. Nodding to Christopher he watched as he ushered Cari from the room.

"Rae, what are we going to do about the boys?" he asked as Emily and Rae moved to look at him. Emily crying at the mention of the boys.

Rae sniffed several times hiccups taking over. "Go...get...them." she said between hiccups.

Nathan frowned. "They can't be shocked into this," he said trying to reason with her.

Emily moved away from Rae. "They'll be fine. I want to see them immediately," she said getting to her feet.

Stephan stood as she did. "I don't think that's wise," he said drawing her attention again.

"Who the hell are you?" she said wiping her face and sniffing. "I want to see my children. Now. Immediately," she said moving to leave the room.

Rae seeing the logic in waiting, took Emily's arms. "Emily, Sean and Ian think your dead. We can't just go barging in on them all teary eyed and looking like a couple of waifs. They'll think you're a ghost or something. Their imaginations are extraordinary."

Emily sniffed a couple of times looking at Nathan then over her shoulder at Stephan. "What are you saying then?"

"I think we should go upstairs and bathe. Then we'll see the boys. That way they'll have time to see us looking happy and presentable."

Emily frowned. "I don't want to wait," she snapped. Fresh tears formed as she held up a hand. "But I understand what you're saying. I'll take the bath but I want to see them in fifteen minutes.

Rae grinned, tears in her eyes. "I just can't believe you're here," she said putting her arm around Emily's shoulder and leading her from the room. Nathan and Stephan stood staring after them.

Chapter 75

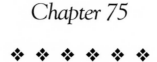

MELISSA LOOKED AT HERSELF in the mirror and smiled. As usual the face looking back at her was practically perfect. Not a hair out of place. Giving her hair a final pat she got to her feet and shook out her gown. It was rather exciting to see the boys so happy with their new things yesterday. Nathan had been a real charmer. Taking them from shop to shop buying them whatever they needed. At last settling on a pair of fishing poles. He promised to take them fishing right after shopping. Laughing, she bent to put her shoe on.

"Now that's a view I don't want to miss very often," Caleb said moving into the room dressed from head to toe.

Melissa straightened looking at him with a practiced eye. "It's one I rarely give, you know."

"I hope not to miss them, then," he said, taking her in his arms to give her a sound kiss.

Keegan stared at the pair, then frowned. It seemed that's all they did anymore. Looking at Niles who stood next to him, Keegan rolled his eyes, getting a grin out of Niles. Clearing his throat Keegan watched the pair snatch their heads apart like school children caught kissing under a tree, "Are we interrupting?"

Caleb scowled at his brother. "Did it look like we wanted to have company?"

Keegan grinned as Niles moved into the room. "We're surprised the two of you are agreeable," he said, getting a cold look from Melissa. "Is that what eligible men are doing now a days? Dying to get a wife?" he asked referring to Caleb's deception. Getting a glare from both of them, he grinned.

Keegan laughed at the teasing Niles was doing, knowing he didn't dare do it himself. "As it happens, I was hoping I would catch you before you left this evening."

Caleb ran a hand through his hair. "What could possibly be that important?"

"Donavan."

Niles flopped into one of the chairs and propped a leg up over the arm. "I've been doing a lot of thinking on that subject," Niles said, looking at the pencil he twirled between his fingers.

Melissa's gaze snapped to Keegan's, "You told him," she snapped, moving away from Caleb. "I warned you about that," she snapped looking for a weapon.

Keegan held up his hands in reflex. "I was only doing what was best," he said quickly. Caleb moved up to his wife and took her shoulders.

"Exactly what's going on here? I seem to be lost," he said squeezing Melissa's shoulder's when she made to protest.

"I spoke to Father about Donavan's situation, in a casual way, mind you. I've found out the lad has fallen head over heels for some Scot."

"He did what?" Caleb asked unbelieving. Their father hated the Scottish people. "So that's the bait he's holding over Donavan's head."

"So it seems," Keegan said nodding.

Niles frowned down at his hand. "As Keegan said earlier, we discussed the issue at some length and I have come to the conclusion that, to save your family from going to war with one another, I should step in and rescue you."

Caleb stared at him, blinking. "What are you babbling about?"

Niles got to his feet slowly throwing the pencil on the table. "I plan to ask the Lady Hayworth to be my wife."

Melissa's mouth fell open at that. "You're going to what?"

Niles smiled lopsidedly at her. "It seems the only solution. I'm a respectable noble among the ton. I haven't got a wife," he said, looking at Keegan "And I am richer than most men ought to be," he finished, smiling.

Caleb stared at him like he'd grown an extra head. "You can't be serious? You don't even know her."

"It doesn't matter. I've seen her at a few of the functions. Besides I'm sure, with a little tutoring from you, I can play dead real well." Caleb gave him a disgusted look while Melissa stood there in shock. Sinking into a chair, she shook her head.

"But she's blind," she said, unsure of what to say.

"I am well aware of the lady's situation and I find it to be a challenge."

Melissa frowned. "A challenge? You make it sound like an experiment or something," she snapped, instantly feeling guilty at ruining a good catch for Allison.

Niles hesitated. "I didn't wish to imply that. I was only stating the fact that the young lady is in need of a husband and since I need a wife sometime in the future it seems rather logical, don't you think?"

Keegan grinned, as Niles finished speaking. "That would solve all our problems. Donavan could marry his Scot, you two could stay happy, and Father gets held up in his plans."

Melissa scowled, wondering where Keegan's wife was. She hadn't even known he was wed. Caleb sighed, running a hand through his hair. "I think it is really up to your sister, Melissa." Melissa scowled. "I know that, but it doesn't mean I have to like it. I think going about marriage this way is appalling."

Niles raised a brow. "You married a man for his money and look how happy you are?"

Melissa turned scarlet. "I did no such thing. I was concerned for him," she said, knowing they didn't believe her. "But I do see your point."

Keegan winked at her grinning, while she scowled back at him. Caleb frowned at his brother. "Then what do you propose to do about it?"

Niles stuck his hands in his pockets. "I'll go see the brother tomorrow."

Melissa, still scowling, studied the man. He was tall with black hair and brown eyes. His features were almost perfect and he lied real well. "I don't like this. I don't even know you."

"You're not marrying me."

Melissa ground her teeth. "Allison isn't like other women. She's special and needs to be handled with care. I don't want to see her hurt," she said, leaning into her husband as he moved to put his arm around her shoulders.

"Believe me, my lady, I don't plan to haul the girl about by her hair or anything."

Melissa reddened. "I still don't like it."

"It solves a great many problems as far as I can see."

"But I still don't understand your motives. Why would you want to marry her when you can have any woman you want?"

Niles shrugged. "I have already seen her and she isn't sore on the eyes. She's tall, which I am. She's gentle and kind. It's what any man would want in a wife."

"I'm well aware of my sisters attributes. I just want to know why you would do this."

Niles frowned. "I need to marry eventually. My father insisted on heirs," he said, leaving it at that.

Melissa scowled. "I don't like it."

Caleb pulled her close. "I really think you should let Allison decide. Niles isn't so bad," he said, grinning at the snort he sent his way. Melissa, still frowning, nodded her head.

Chapter 76

JESSICA REINED IN and dismounted throwing the reins to the waiting groom. "Take his lordships horse, too. Don't unsaddle them right away. We may need them again," she said, grabbing Royce's arm when he was on the ground. Royce gritted his teeth, as she dragged him along beside her. She definitely didn't care if she made a fool of herself. No wonder the family was high on the gossip list.

Moving along at a brisk walk, he pulled his arm free as they reached the foyer. "I'll be leaving now," he said, turning to go.

Jessica whirled on him, steading herself on the stand near the door. "I don't think so. You promised to help me," she said, moving closer.

Arty opened the door and scowled, seeing a gent scowling at Jessica something fierce. "Captain, is everything all right?"

The lord answered instead. "Is the Baron in?"

"No, my lord. He sent a note that he would be detained."

Jessica turned around and glared at Arty. "Detained? Well, we'll just see about that," she said, brushing past Royce so fast he didn't have a chance to stop her. Looking at Arty, he frowned.

"Get word to the Baron that his wife needs attention."

"Where should I send him?"

"How the hell should I know. She's befuddled with drink and could be off to God knows where. Just tell him to hunt us down," Royce snapped, running for his horse seeing that Jessica was already mounted and taking off down the lane. Arty watched them go with his mouth hanging open. Shaking his head, he scowled.

"The master ain't goin to like it none. His wife traipsin all over the country side drunker than a skunk with a gent, I don't know." Turning, he closed the door and wondered if he should just send a note or go in person. Cursing he moved to find his coat. The lord would surely kill him if he just sent a note. Why did he ever come ashore?

"SHE'S WHAT?" Morgan exploded pulling Arty into the cabin and slamming the door.

"It's like I told you, she come home all in a snit and didn't like the fact that you weren't coming home then marched herself off with some gent."

"Which gent?"

Arty fidgeted. "There wasn't time to find out. Yer wife wasn't exactly herself. She was befuddled with drink and could barely stand," he said, ringing his hat in his hands. Please let the sea swallow him up, Arty thought, as Morgan's face darkened.

"Describe him."

"He was tall, like yerself. He had brown hair and green eyes, I think."

"You think?"

"Well, now. I wasn't looking at his looks. The Captain, I mean yer wife, wasn't exactly being a saint. He did have scars on his face. I remember those."

"Scars?" Morgan said, turning from gathering his gloves and cloak.

"Yes, my lord. All along the left side of his cheek.

Morgan frowned, trying to think of someone like that and could only come up with one person. Salisbury was a recluse. Could it be him? "Get back home and send word to me at her family's home. I'll start with the one on Covington."

Arty nodded, barely believing he was getting off so lightly. He jumped out of the way as the Baron stormed past him out of the cabin. Sighing, he leaned against the wall. Life was ten times more simple at sea.

Chapter 77

"I DO BELIEVE, that things are starting to come around, after all," Brand said, sitting in the drawing room nursing a cup of tea. Scowling down at the amber liquid he curled his lip slightly. He was never going to get used to drinking the stuff.

Nathan paced back and forth before the window. He was dying to run upstairs and ask his wife the billions of questions running through his mind. She was in no condition to speak with him. Her sister was only newly arrived and the pair of them had been locked up tighter than a drum with the boys.

Brand frowned, as Nathan's pace quickened. He kept looking toward the stairs as he passed the door. "Did you know, thet're having flying rat races at the tracks now?"

Nathan barely glanced at his father but nodded his head anyway.

Brand laughed. "Nathan, I don't know why you're killing yourself down here. Just go up there and talk with them. You're a big part of their lives."

Nathan ran a hand through his hair before looking at his father. "What's going to happen? Those children aren't Rae's. They belong to the sister. She can't support them."

Brand frowned into his cup. "The way I see it, the sister will have to stay with you, until she can provide a suitable home for the boys. Do you have a problem with that?"

"Of course not," he snapped, returning to the pacing.

"Then what's eating you?"

Nathan moved to stop in front of the window. The fact that he and Rae had never consummated their marriage made him worried sick the twins would hightail it out of there taking the boys with them. Running a hand through his hair, he frowned. He couldn't possibly tell his father that. Brand didn't need the worry. "I just have a few unanswered questions, that's all."

Brand grinned. "She'll get around to you, Nathan. Give her some time."

Nathan scowled at his reflection in the glass. Rae would get around to him sometime but would her decision be him or go back to America with her sister.

"How are you feeling, Father?" Stephan said, as he sauntered into the room. "You're looking well. It must be the tea."

Brand scowled. "I'm so sick of tea that just smelling it makes my stomach roll. Colan's starting to act more like a wife with his nagging and if I so much as smell the stopper on the decanter, he doesn't talk to me for days."

"It's for your own good you know," Colan said from the door. "If you want to be worm food then by all means help yourself to the brandy."

Brand scowled at his brother while Stephan turned and shook his hand. "It's nice to see you Uncle and I might say I'm glad to know someone has the ability to tell this old goat what to do with himself to keep his heart ticking."

Brand rolled his eyes at the pair. "I'm sure my heart is in fine condition. I don't think I need coddling for the rest of my life."

"I'm sure Uncle doesn't wish to be thought of as a coddler."

Brand chuckled at the scowl crossing Colan's face. Stephan lost a little of his humor seeing Nathan standing at the window. Excusing himself from his father and Uncle's company, he moved to Nathan's side. "How's it going?"

Nathan looked at him, then turned back to the window. "How the hell should I know?"

Stephan frowned. "I'm sure if you went upstairs and talked with them you'd know what was going on."

Nathan frowned. "I don't know if I want to know."

Stephan arched a brow at that. "What's that supposed to mean?"

Nathan glanced over his shoulder to make sure his father was occupied, then turned his gaze back to Stephan's "I've never been with Rae."

Stephan's brows shot up. "Never been with her, as in sex."

"Well, of course, sex. Unlike the rest of you walking hormones, I happen to have a problem doing it with just anyone."

Stephan chuckled. "You're joking, right? You've been with several ladies I can name off the top of my head, and I'm not even trying."

Nathan scowled. "If you recall, those women happen to be old acquaintances of someone's. I always knew them before hand. Rae was a stranger to me and since I haven't had much of a chance to talk with her, without wanting to ring her neck, she still is."

Stephan whistled at those remarks. "That's a bit of a problem, isn't it? I'm sure you'll get things straightened out, in time."

"That's just it. What if she wants to go back to America with her sister? She has grounds for an annulment, you know."

Stephan bite his lip, rocking back and forth. "I see your point," he said, watching Christopher and Cari enter. "But I think you're worrying over nothing. Whether you know it or not, I think Rae has stronger feelings for you than you realize."

Nathan's gaze snapped up to his. "How so?"

"Since I didn't know the pair of you weren't...well, you know, I assumed the looks she was giving you were normal but under the circumstances, I'd say your little wife is falling in love with you."

Nathan stared at him a full minute before snorting and turning back to the window. "That's ridiculous. I haven't given her any reason to fall in love with me. We've been at each others throat since she dragged me off to the priest."

Stephan just shrugged. "Whatever you say. I happen to know she's been sleeping in your room."

Nathan's gaze snapped to Stephan's again, narrowing in the process. "How do you know that?"

"Allison told me."

"Why were the pair of you discussing me and my wife?"

"Allison was concerned about Rae and asked if I thought things were going all right." When Nathan just scowled at him, Stephan cursed. "To tell you the truth, she asked me if the pair of you were giving one another those disgusting lover's looks."

Nathan frowned. "She wanted to know that?"

"Apparently. It was then that I started watching both of you. Rae gives those looks to you but I must admit I haven't seen anything like that on your face."

Nathan scowled. He was beginning to like his wife. That was why he was feeling so panicked at the thought of her up and leaving with her sister.

"Allison said you're the blind one in the family," Stephan added, slapping him on the back before making his way toward Christopher.

Nathan watched him go and frowned.

"He's right, you know?"

Nathan turned further around to see Allison standing with Nero casually leaning against her leg. His large yellow eyes staring at Nathan. Scowling, he took a drink. "I didn't realize I was part of your pastime."

Allison laughed. "I normally don't make it a habit but your wife has come to me a few times for advice."

Nathan's brows shot up at that. "She has?"

Allison shrugged. "From my point of view, Nathan, the pair of you are too stubborn for your own good. If you'd just drag her upstairs and make her talk with you, I'm sure things would get straightened out in no time."

Nathan scowled. "I suppose you knew she was a twin."

Allison blushed. "I promised not to tell."

Taking a deep breath, he sighed. "I just hope it isn't too late."

"It's never too late," she said taking his arm and kissing his cheek. "It can be humiliating, though."

Nathan smiled crookedly. "I suppose you're telling me to grovel."

"Just a bit," Allison said, laughing.

MELISSA LOOKED AT NILES one last time before walking up the steps of her father's town house. "I still think he should have waited until tomorrow."

"But tonight is perfect. With so many people here, they'll have a chance to really get to know one another."

"It's just my family, and you can bet the lot of them, will be hanging on Niles every word to Allison. It'll be a mess."

Caleb stared at Niles who seemed to fidget. "You can still back out, you know."

Niles scowled. "I don't plan on backing out. Perhaps your wife's right, though. Maybe tomorrow might be more private."

Melissa beamed at him. "That's wonderful. I'll present the subject tonight and tell her you'll be calling around eleven," she said, taking his arm to pull him back toward the carriage. Caleb nearly laughed at her behavior while Niles stared at her with arched brows. "She'll be more receptive tomorrow I assure you."

Niles frowned at Melissa. She acted like he was a disgrace to her family. Pulling his arm free, he stopped. "I don't wish to intrude but I think tonight would work out well enough. You said your father isn't staying very long. I want him to get to know me," he said, arching his brows meaningfully at her. He was letting her know he wasn't going to let her slander his character.

Melissa's lips thinned. "Fine. If you insist on this nonsense, then let's go in. The sooner I'm free of your company, the better," she snapped, irritated with the whole incident.

"Melissa, Niles is only trying to help."

"I know that but ...well never mind," she finished giving Niles a neutral stare before walking up the steps toward the door. It promptly opened before she reached it. "Hello Hobkins. How are things?"

"Splendid, Miss. Your father is in high spirits with you all present." Melissa smiled, as Caleb took her wrap and handed it to Hobkins along with his own things. Niles handed over his, as well. "Are they in the drawing room?"

"Yes, Miss. Almost everyone's here except Lady Jessica."

Melissa pursed her lips. "Naturally," she said, taking Caleb's arm she looked at Niles before looping her other arm through his. "At least keep the lies to a minimum, will you?"

Niles reddened but smiled as Caleb grinned at him like an idiot. "I'll do my best," he said, giving her a rakish grin. Melissa sighed and tossed her head.

"I suppose that's the best I'm going to get."

Caleb chuckled at that. "I promise to drag him outside and blacken an eye if he steps out of line," he said, squeezing her hand.

Melissa smiled. "I'm sure you will."

Niles just smiled at their remarks.

"WELL, I'LL BE. Isn't that the Earl of March?" Christopher asked staring as Niles entered with Melissa and Caleb.

Stephan shrugged. "I suppose. It's been a while since I've seen him."

Cari craned her neck around Christopher's shoulders to stare at the handsome man standing near the door. He towered over the lady and her husband but had a smile that was devastating to a woman's heart. Christopher frowned, as Cari stared. Stephan drank a sip from his brandy to hid his grin at Christopher's behavior. So the old boy liked her. Great! He thought, watching Brand and Colin move to the door to greet the new arrivals.

"I don't suppose you'd care to introduce me to the Earl. Being so knew to London, I really haven't had much of a chance to meet very many of the ton," she said, smiling at Christopher.

Christopher put a smile on his face, unnerved at his feelings. It was odd, but he could swear he was jealous. Moving toward the door, he nodded to Melissa. "It's nice to see the pair of you still smiling," he said kissing her cheek and shaking Caleb's hand. "This, as you already know, is Lady St. Paul." Turning to the Earl, he added, "Lord Devane," he said shaking his hand. "Lady St. Paul."

Niles smiled at the black haired beauty and kissed her hand, "A pleasure, my lady."

Cari smiled, wanting to giggle for some reason. Worried that she might, she just nodded her head instead of speaking. She didn't want to gush over such a handsome man. Stephan moved forward and shook Niles hand, also.

Christopher watched Cari from the corner of his eye and saw she was watching the Earl with interest, though she looked at Stephan just as much. Cursing himself for his idiotic behavior, he took a long drink from his glass, then spotted Jonathan in the entry way. Nodding to Jonathan he received a grin in return.

Stephan smiled. "His wife sure is something," he said, watching Ashley walking with more confidence next to her husband.

Christopher smiled. "I think that was a good match, whether the couple was agreeable or not," he said, then frowned as Cari looked up at him. "It's a long story."

Cari smiled. "I understand," she said watching the couple move into the room.

More introductions occurred as everyone settled into the room which buzzed with conversation. Niles smiled and nodded at the conversation around him but his attention again strayed to the silver haired angel standing with her brother by the window. She sure was beautiful. Her face was an artists dream while her body moved and flowed with grace. She would make some man a perfect wife. Scowling at his thoughts, he cursed. He really didn't want a wife, especially one he didn't really know. But seeing Allison again, he understood his earlier motives. She was something to look at.

"Do you want an introduction?" Caleb asked, watching Niles look at Allison.

Niles smiled. "Is your wife going to go into vapors?"

Caleb laughed. "She's not that set against it. She's just concerned."

Niles nodded. "Then introduce me."

NATHAN WATCHED CALEB and the Earl make their way in his direction. "To your left about six two, black hair, and blue eyes," he said just as they reached them.

Niles nodded to Nathan then stiffened as the large cat hidden behind the settee moved into view. God the thing was huge. It's massive head shook as the yellow eyes settled on him. No wonder the gossip still flew about strong.

"Lady Allison? I'd like you to meet the Earl of March. He came tonight with Melissa and I."

Allison smiled in the relative direction Nathan had said, then felt her hand lifted and kissed. Niles had smooth strong hands. "It's a pleasure to meet you, my lord."

Niles smiled. "The pleasure's all mine. Hayworth," he said shaking Nathan's hand.

Nathan nodded to Niles, distracted as Nero moved to lay at their feet resting a paw on Niles shoes. Looking at Niles he nearly laughed. The man was the color of snow. "Al, Nero is mussing up his shoes."

Allison blushed. "Nero, go back over there," she said, waving at the cat. Nero grumbled but returned to his place behind the settee. "I'm sorry. He's just trying to make you nervous," she said, accepting the drink Nathan pressed into her hands.

Nathan and Caleb grinned at Niles. "It's working," Niles said, trying to relax. The cat was huge. He could probably eat Niles' leg off in two bites.

Allison felt her nerves on end as the men carried on a conversation. She so wanted to march over to Melissa and wring her neck. The Earl of March was probably her idea. It was obvious the man was there as a prospective husband.

"If you gentleman will excuse me," she said, snapping her fingers for Nero. "I need to speak with Father a moment," she said gripping Nero's collar. "It was nice meeting you, my lord," she said as Nero led her away.

Moving toward her father, she heard people shift to let her pass. "Father?'

"Right here, love." Brand said smiling as he took her arm. "How are things with you?"

"Fine. I was just wondering if Rae has come down, yet?"

"No. I think the pair plan to hide up there all night."

Allison smiled. "I don't think so. I'm going to get them," she said, kissing his cheek. Moving toward the stairs she slowly climbed. Nero right beside her.

Jonathan watched her leave, frowning at Christopher. "What's with her?"

"She's still upset about the ball."

"Has she been out since?"

"No. Rae and Ginger have been trying but she still refuses to go."

Jonathan squeezed his wife's hand. "I'm sure she'll go when she's ready," he said, knowing Ashley was almost at that stage, herself. "Maybe the pair of you could go together?"

Ashley smiled. "I'd be happy to bring her with us. She's helped me so much."

Jonathan smiled. "I'll ask her when you're ready."

Ashley blushed. She was truly married now, and she was so attuned to Jonathan now that she felt the urge to cry just hearing him speak to her in that soft loving tone. The man was her savior and she would be forever grateful to him. Smiling, her blush deepened remembering Christopher still stood with them. "I think your sister's ball is going to be my first ball."

Jonathan grinned. "I was hoping you would go."

Christopher smiled. "So, she's really having that ball? I thought it was a joke."

"Apparently she's trying to please her husband. Stephan says she was wearing a dress the other day. With high heeled shoes, no less."

Christopher arched a brow at that. "Jessica in high heels."

Jonathan laughed. "I know. I thought it was rather funny myself." Ashley pursed her lips.

"I'm sure lady Jessica looks fine in those shoes," she said, making both men just grin.

"It isn't that she looked bad, my sweet. It's that she's already five foot eight. In those shoes, she's nearly six foot."

Ashley frowned. "Oh."

"It's going to be worth the trouble just to see what the chit wears tonight."

"I'm sure she'll dress appropriately. Your father is sick, after all."

Christopher smiled. "If it was anyone else, I would agree with you, but Jessica," he said, shaking his head. "You never know."

NATHAN FROWNED as Rae entered leading Allison along beside her. She was radiant. Her face was happy and swollen from crying. Scanning the room, he noticed the sister wasn't anywhere in sight. As they drew near he put a smile on his face.

"How are things going?" he asked watching her blush.

"I'll leave you two to talk," Allison said moving along the settee toward Christopher and Jonathan. Nero sniffed the tray of pastries, as they passed.

Rae smiled at her retreating form, before looking back at Nathan. Suddenly she was nervous and licked her lips.

Nathan looked briefly toward the doors leading to the gardens, then took his wife's arm, "Care to step out for a moment?"

Rae smiled. "That sounds nice."

Nathan moved her into the gardens, closing the doors behind them as they seated themselves on the bench just off the to the side. "Is she settled in?"

Rae grinned. "She's still with the boys. They could hardly stop jumping around the room in happiness. Sean didn't let go of her hand the whole time."

Nathan stood up and started to walk around the clearing, "And Ian?"

"Well, he was full of questions, as usual. He never stopped and he was chattering about everything that happened to him since she was gone. It took a while to sort through what was real and fictional," she said, looking at her hands.

Nathan glanced in her direction and frowned. "I suppose she needs a place to stay."

Rae swallowed. "I was hoping you would let her stay with us. She won't be any trouble, I assure you."

Nathan turned slightly so she couldn't see his face. She must really think he was an ogre, if she thought he would throw her sister out into the street. "Of course, she can stay. We'll fix her up a room on the other side of the boy's."

"Oh, but she wants to stay with them."

Nathan turned slightly. "The room connects. They can leave the doors open."

Rae hesitated then smiled. "Thank you. She'll be happy to hear that."

Nathan paused then tipped his head back to look up at the moon. Rae sighed at the handsome profile he gave her. His hair was bunched at his collar in soft waves. He was dressed immaculately as usual and standing there with his hands in his pockets. Rae suddenly wanted to cry. He was a stranger to her and knowing that, made her slowly lower her gaze to her lap.

"I know I haven't been a very good husband but I would like a chance to change that," he said turning his gaze on her. "I've been slow at realizing what a fool I've been. I'd like a chance to get to know you."

Rae held her breath. He was saying words she thought she'd never hear. After all the things she'd done to him, she never expected him to actually want to stay with her. Swallowing, she felt her stomach flutter as he slowly walked to her side. Reaching out a hand, he pulled her to her feet.

"I've spent many nights wondering about everything that's happened to us, but mainly about what kind of a life you've led before you came into my life. I've come to the conclusion that it really doesn't matter. What does matter, is that you and I get to know each other, as husband and wife."

Rae felt her breath catch at the words Nathan said and found herself hoping beyond hope that he spoke sincerely. She didn't know if her heart could stand to be walked on. She was already in love with this man and that kind of rejection would be devastating. Always one for the risk, she licked her lips.

"I've spent several nights thinking, also. I've prayed day after day for a way to connect with you without our tempers getting in the way," she said, swallowing. "Is this my chance?"

Nathan smiled slowly, making Rae catch her breath. "As a former highwayman, I would have thought you would have resorted to much harsher measures."

Rae grinned, surprised at his humor. "I did think up a few, but discarded them for worry that you would get hurt."

Nathan returned her grin pulling her close. "I myself have thought of a few things to keep you in line. Imagine, all this time I've thought you've been crawling around the docks, when it's been your sister instead," he said. "I'm sorry."

Rae frowned. "She's a good person. She's just had bad luck, that's all. She never... that is, she stuck with stealing just like I did."

Nathan's smile faded. He was well aware of what she was saying. "Though I'm glad to hear it, it really doesn't matter," he said, lowering his head to gently kiss her lips. Rae felt tears sting her eyes at the ground they'd covered in such a short time and felt for the first time since they were married that they actually had a chance with one another.

"MY LORD, DINNER IS SERVED," Hobkins announced.

Brand grinned. "Wonderful and about time. I thought perhaps you'd decided not to feed us."

Hobkins just nodded his head getting an arched brow from Stephan. Really, Hobkins thought, giving Lord Stephan a scowl, the man probably expected him to do some sort of jig or something.

"Hobkins, you really need to visit Uncle Colan's house and meet his butler. I guarantee you won't think my words of advice are drivel, I promise you," he said, pulling Allison along beside him. Nero came in to lay behind a potted fig near Allison's chair.

Melissa frowned at her brother. The stupid cur. He could have let Niles walk Allison in. How was Allison supposed to get to know Niles if Stephan kept interfering. Caleb stared at Melissa as her gaze bore holes into Stephan's back and chuckled.

"Is he wearing the wrong coat?"

Melissa clenched her jaw. "That isn't funny. I thought he'd at least let Niles walk her in there. She'll never discard him at this rate."

Caleb laughed. "Poor Niles. He really isn't a bad fellow, you know."

Melissa just tossed her head.

Cari frowned at the conversation in front of her. Were they talking about the handsome Earl and Lady Allison. That was definitely a bad match. The Earl was far to outgoing and carefree to take the time to care for a blind wife. Besides, Nero didn't like him. Already the cat went out of his way to make the Earl uncomfortable.

"Is something wrong?" Christopher asked, seeing Cari frown.

"No," she said smiling. "I was just listening to a comment your sister made. She's not a very good matchmaker, is she?"

Christopher frowned. "Matchmaker?"

"Yes. It's obvious she brought the Earl of March here to meet Lady Allison."

Christopher's gaze snapped up at that and he watched as Melissa worked it around so Niles was seated next to Allison. Arching a brow, he shrugged. "What's wrong with the Earl?" he asked with dual purpose. He had seen Cari looking at Niles and wanted to know what she thought.

"Nothing's wrong with him. He's handsome and charming but he's just not your sister's type."

Christopher scowled, at those words. "Not her type?"

"No, she needs someone more solitary. Someone who has time to spend with her and doesn't mind doing that. The Earl would find that it would hamper his normal life style."

Christopher stopped, pulling out the chair for her. Once seated he turned and softly whispered to her. "How do you conclude all that from just these few short hours?"

Cari blushed. How was she supposed to explain this one. "Well, I just know."

Christopher frowned. "Care to elaborate."

"Not at this time," she said, smiling.

Christopher scowled but slowly smiled. "I'll remember to bring it up later," he said watching her closely. She just smiled and nodded.

Shaking his head, he frowned when he saw the chair to Cari's right was empty. Looking around the room, Christopher frowned further. Jessica and her husband weren't there yet. Turning to his left he waited as a flushed Rae was seated by an equally flustered Nathan. Scowling, Christopher leaned behind Rae to tap Nathan on the shoulder when Nathan turned he arched a brow at him.

Nathan narrowed his eyes in warning, Christopher grinned. "I was wondering if you heard anything from Jessica?"

Nathan still on guard, looked around to see that Jessica wasn't there. "Maybe Morgan couldn't get her in a dress."

Christopher rolled his eyes. "So you have no idea where they are?"

"How should I know. She doesn't tell me what she's doing."

Christopher's face stiffened. "If you'd stay out of the gardens, you might have heard," he said, seeing both people blush.

Rae felt like crawling under the table but cleared her throat instead. Turning to look at Christopher, she smiled sweetly. "At least he has someone to go in the garden with," she said picking up her glass.

Nathan laughed at the shocked look on Christopher's face which caused the others to look at them. Holding up his hands, Nathan waved their attention away. Christopher, embarrassed, smiled at Rae. "I'd forgotten how sharp that tongue of yours gets when provoked."

Rae just nodded. "You won't forget again, I'm sure."

Christopher couldn't help himself, he grinned, "She's a live one."

Nathan grinned, finally getting a blush out of Rae.

Dinner progressed with its usual flourish as course after course appeared before them and they slowly satisfied their hunger. Nearly all the way through the meal, there was a clattering at the door when a very disheveled Jessica stumbled into the room.

She was wearing a white shirt tucked into a pair of black breeches belted at the waist. Her hair was braided but quickly working it's way free and she was carrying a bottle of brandy three fourths of the way gone.

"Good evening," she said leaning against the door frame while Hobkins hopped about behind her. "I see I've missed dinner," she said, moving to walk into the room only to grab the frame again while a laugh escaped her lips.

Brand slowly got to his feet. "Jessica, what's going on?" he asked, seeing she was well on her way to being drunk.

"Father, it's so good to see you. You're looking fit. Colan must be a good mother hen."

Colan reddened and scowled. "I've had about enough of being called a mother."

Brand waved a hand at him while Ginger laid a hand on his arm to keep him seated. "Why don't you go into the drawing room with me and we'll have a nice chat," Brand said to Jessica ignoring his brother completely.

Jessica laughed coming away from the wall. But Father you're eating," she said, moving around to Nathan. "Hello Nathan. How's the children?" she said, giggling. "Rae isn't that a pretty gown. Mine seem to have come to a bit of a mishap," she said, full out laughing at that. Pausing at Rae's chair, she took another sip while everyone looked at Brand for guidance.

"Jessica, if you'd just come along ..."

Jessica looked back at her father. "You're eating. Now sit down," she said seeing Christopher next. Steering wide of him, she squinted at the lady beside Christopher. "Aren't you the one with that monkey?" she asked, not stopping for an answer. Kissing Colan on the head she moved around to Ginger and grinned like a fool.

"I think I failed in etiquette tonight," she said, with a snort moving on to Jonathan, who was scowling at her. Spotting Royce in the doorway she smiled. "Lord Royce, do come in and quit lurking around out there. Everyone this is Lord Royce. Here's the rest of my family," she said, waving a hand as she tipped the bottle again.

Seeing Christopher's face darken, Jonathan tried to get to his feet. "Now, Jess. Let's just go..."

Pushing on his shoulders, she kept him in his seat. "Forget it, Jonathan. I don't need your help. Your pretty wife does, though," she said, patting his cheek. Moving again she scowled at Stephan. "You're supposed to be sailing." she said. "Oh, I forgot the hand. Does it hurt?" she asked, sipping again.

Stephan made to rise but she rested the bottle on his head and leaned over him slightly. "I think Al wants you to stay there, Stephan. How are you, Al?" she said, her face turning sad. "I didn't mean to bring your lord. He followed me." she said standing, messing Stephan's hair with a giggle. "Say, now. Whose the handsome buck?" she asked, one hand on Allison's shoulder while she stared at Niles. Moving past him to see Melissa's disgusted face, she laughed. "I really planned on wearing a gown, Melissa, but they got misplaced. All gone," she said, holding the bottle out wide knocking a plant off the stand behind Niles' chair while her hand rested on the back of his. "Oops," she said turning to look at Niles. "Want to clean that up, Handsome?" she asked, giggling as Nero growled from the pot crushed near his feet. Moving past the mess, she patted Caleb on the head before setting the bottle in his lap. "Here. Keep this for me will you?" she said, looking about the table. When she didn't move for a few minutes, Stephan slowly got to his feet.

"All right, Jessica. Let's go have a talk, aye?" Jessica swung her gaze to his then shook her head.

"Can't. I have to go. I came to say goodbye."

Brand had just about enough. Nodding to his son he watched as Stephan and Christopher moved around the table in opposite directions toward her.

Seeing the trap, Jessica laughed. "Now hold on there." When neither stopped their pursuit, she frowned. "I mean it." As they drew closer, she licked her lips, wiping a hand across her mouth. "All right, you asked for it," she said, dropping to the floor to scurry under the table.

Brand's mouth dropped open. "Jessica! Get out of there," he roared seeing his family scoot there chairs back to let her through.

Jessica chuckled from under the table. "Send the bullies away. I'm leaving on a ship."

Nero seeing the opportunity for another romp with the family, crawled under the table between Ginger and Colan.

Brand took a deep breath. "All right, Jessica. Where are you planning to sail?" he said, somewhat calmer.

"I'm sailin' for America," she said, sadly.

Stephan scowled at her. "Sailing away in what?"

"The Gypsy," she said, then cursed. "I mean, a ship. Allison, Nero is slobbering on Handsome's shoes," she said, slurring.

Stephan scowled. "You're not going anywhere," he snapped, moving along looking under the table to see her progress.

Jessica stared at him from her position near Niles' legs. "You'd better let me go. I need to go. I can't do anything else," she said hiccuping. Stephan narrowed his eyes at her, as Nathan and Christopher moved behind her. "All right, Jess. Let's go talk about it."

"Nothin' to say," she said, bumping her head on the table. Christopher chose that moment to duck under the table and grab her leg. Pulling her from under the table, he cursed as her other foot landed on his thigh dangerously close to his manhood. Cursing, he shouted at Nathan.

"Grab her other leg, damn it. Allison the cat."

Nathan made two attempts before securing her leg, while Allison called Nero to her. Jessica shouted at them to let her go, all the while cussing like a sailor. Stephan grabbed some napkins to tie her hands and gag her before she hurt someone. All of them were panting, as Jessica cursed behind her gag.

"Take her to the study," Brand snapped, watching the three of them haul a wiggling Jessica from the room. Running a hand through his hair, he looked at the remaining people in the room. "I don't know what's gotten into her. I'm sorry for the interruption to those of you who don't know the family very well. Please finish your dinner. Excuse me," he said, turning to follow his sons. "Sit down, young man," he said, to Royce as he passed him at the door.

Allison frowned at the tension in the room. "Well, that's one event I'm sorry I couldn't see," she said sending Nero back to his plant. "How about you, Ashley?" Several chuckles sounded around the room as everyone moved the chairs back into place. Allison got to her feet and moved toward the door. "Lord Royce?" she asked, nearing the door. "Since you're here, would you care to join us?" she asked when he touched her hand to let her know where he was.

Smiling at her, he nodded. "I'd be happy to, though I hope you don't have anymore entertainment for me. She practically killed me."

Allison laughed. "Jessica tends to do that to a person," she said, leading him to the table to seat him in Stephan's vacated seat. "Hobkins, bring his lordship a plate and clear away anything in the way. I don't think they'll be back anytime soon." Hobkins smiled at his lady. She was making a bad situation tolerable. Hobkins ordered the footman to clean up the plates and the plant mess, before finally getting the room to rights.

Niles stared at Allison and found himself smiling. She sure had a grip on things, didn't she?

Royce seeing the look, scowled before glancing around the room at the stares he was getting. So much for seeing her in private.

BRAND STALKED DOWN THE HALL his temper ready to explode. It was one thing to have a son embarrass the hell out of you, but to have a daughter come barging into dinner drunk, was entirely different. Pushing open the door, he frowned, seeing his sons standing awkwardly around a very upset Jessica. Closing the door behind himself, he frowned.

"All right, young lady. What is the meaning of that little show?"

Jessica pushed her hair out of her face. The string that had been holding it in it's braid was long gone. "I'm sorry," she said, tears streaming down her face. "I just can't be like Melissa," she said, getting to her feet to get a drink. Stephan stepped in her way grabbing up the decanters as he went. "Bring that back," she sniffed, seeing him head for the door. "Stephan, please," she called, as he pulled open the door.

"Forget it, Jess. You've drunk more than your share," he said, moving out the door only to run into a very furious Morgan. "Sinclair?" he said, stepping aside.

Jessica paled then set her features in an unreadable mask. "Hayworth," Morgan said, stepping past Stephan. Nodding to each of the others his gaze settled on his wife. "Care to explain?" he asked, watching her face as each thought crossed her face.

"No," she said, defiantly.

"I think you'd better come home with me and we'll talk about it, after you've rested," he said quietly.

Jessica's face turned harsh. "I don't need to rest. I'm perfectly fine. Just go off and get your ship going. Or my ship, rather. The sooner you're gone the better," she said, near tears again.

Brand seeing the situation was going to get out of hand, cleared his throat. "Come on boys. Let's leave these two to themselves. We've left a room full of people that need our attention," he said, giving Sinclair a sympathetic look as Nathan and Christopher moved out the door. Giving Jessica a stern look Brand pulled the door closed behind himself.

"Just what the hell are you doing? You could have been killed riding around like that?" Morgan asked, anger evident.

Morgan stared at his wife, waiting for her answer.

"I can't do it," she said, lifting her chin. She moved to the desk and plopped her boots up on the edge.

Morgan narrowed his eyes, "Can't do what?"

"I refuse to play your sweet genteel lady, when I'm hardly close to either word," she said, pulling her legs off the desk to check the drawers for brandy.

Morgan watched her, his temper rising. "I'm sorry, Jessica. You're not making much sense. You've got about ten seconds to get something to sink into my brain before I take you over my knee and tan your backside," he finished with a shout.

Jessica stared at him then slowly got to her feet. "You want me to draw pictures," she snapped. "I can't be like you want. The dresses are uncomfortable and I haven't knocked so many things over in my life. They are ugly and the shoes make my feet ache. It's hard walking around in those stupid things," she said, pacing in a wavy line. "It takes me hours to get ready and the make up makes my face itch. I've got headaches all the time from the pins holding my hair in place and I've lost several reticules in the past week. I'm just not cut out to walk around dressed like some china doll. It just isn't me," she said, going over to the refreshment stand looking for brandy. "Where the hell is the brandy?" she asked, pulling open the door under the stand.

Morgan frowned at her. So he had been right, when he'd accused her of acting the simpleton but why had she done it. He never said he wanted a paragon of femininity he just didn't want her walking around as she was this evening. "Jessica," he said frowning further when she ignored him and moved to look through the desk again. "Jessica," he said more sternly. When she stopped and looked at him, he scowled. "I don't recall telling you to dress in clothes that make you uncomfortable. I just forbid you to wear breeches."

Jessica's face hardened. "Well, I like wearing breeches. I can move around with more grace than I ever have in a gown and these boots," she said plopping one up on the desk, "my feet could walk around in them for days," she finished, barely getting her foot under her before she fell over. Lifting both hands she pushed her hair out of her face.

Morgan felt a jolt of desire but quickly squelched it. The woman was never going to understand he was the one in charge if all he did was bed her every time they had an argument. "I think we should go back home. It's more private there," he said.

Jessica smiled, crookedly. "Murphy, I don't plan on returning home until you let me be myself." Morgan's face darkened at the purposeful misuse of his name. Moving toward her, he watched her eyes widen.

"You're coming home with me if I have to tie you up and carry you there," he said, barely finishing as she made a dash for the door. Morgan made a grab for her only to come up empty handed. "Jessica!" he bellowed, as she shot out the door knocking a vase off the table near the door.

BRAND ENTERED THE DINING ROOM and everyone quieted. "Well, Father, did you kill her?" Jonathan asked, grinning.

Brand scowled at his son. "As it happens, her husband showed up and he's taking care of things."

Jonathan's brows shot up at that. "Is he now? Things should get interesting from here," he said, getting a grin from Stephan who quickly handed the brandy to Hobkins.

"Hide this. She's liable to club Morgan over the head and come looking for it."

Christopher cleared his throat. "If everyone is done, perhaps if we retired to the drawing room, Melissa could play something for us on the pianoforte."

Melissa flushed. "I haven't played in quite sometime," she said, when Caleb grinned at her.

"I'm sure you'll be fine," he said helping her to her feet.

Christopher moved around and took Cari's arm. Jonathan helped Ashley to her feet and followed Nathan and Rae into the drawing room. Allison slowly got to her feet.

"If the two of you don't mind, I won't" she said, holding both arms out to her sides.

Royce locked gazes with Niles' briefly, then took her arm. "Not at all," he said watching Niles wrap her other arm around his.

"You're both far too handsome to share just one lady," she said, getting a chuckle out of Royce while Niles stared at the lady in shock. Royce was far from good looking. Frowning, he realized that these two knew one another better than he had thought. He was definitely in the way. As they reached the drawing room, Niles moved away from the pair and nudged Caleb in the shoulder.

"It doesn't look like I'll be necessary," he said, giving Melissa a grin.

Melissa scowled at the man. "What are you talking about now?"

"Your sister already has someone. She isn't going to need me stepping in," he said looking relieved.

Melissa frowned. "So you were sacrificing yourself. I knew it. That's why I didn't want you here in the first place."

Caleb chuckled, as he squeezed Melissa around the shoulder. "Shhh, love. The whole room doesn't need to know."

Melissa reddened, as Christopher motioned for her to play. "I'll have to talk with you later, my lord," she said glaring at Niles.

Niles grinned back. "She's not prone to murder, is she?" he asked.

"Not that I'm aware of, and she has had ample reason to kill me."

Niles looked at him. "You're right. My little stunt shouldn't rate as high on her murder list."

Caleb grinned in return. "You forget, my man, that I can make it up to her in other ways, while you can only use your charm."

Niles slowly lost his grin. "I suppose a brief absence might be called for."

Caleb laughed, slapping him on the back. "She isn't that fierce. In fact, she'll forgive you in no time once she sees that you've quit lying all the time."

Niles scowled at him but slowly smiled. "I have been doing that more than a body should, haven't I?"

Caleb grinned. "Almost enough to give up bachelorhood."

CHRISTOPHER SCOWLED AT ROYCE who was still standing with Allison's arm around his.

Cari watched Christopher's face with confusion. The lord standing by his sister was perfect for her yet Christopher stood there looking like he was ready to kill the man. "Does your sister have food on her chin?" she asked, peeking up at him with a small smile.

Christopher brought his attention back to the beauty at his side and smiled. "No. She hasn't done anything like that in years," he said frowning. "Except at the ball, of course."

Cari laughed. "That was out of the ordinary, wasn't it?"

Christopher returned her smile. "I'd say. Stephan would probably have a few choice words for the evening."

Cari smiled at that.

Christopher grinned at her. "Would you care for a walk," he asked watching Melissa play the piano beautifully.

Cari felt nervous, but nodded.

Stephan grinned from his position near the window, as Christopher led Cari out the doors into the gardens. Things were working out splendidly, though he guessed it was more to the fact that she liked him than with the deal they had struck. Frowning, he shook his head.

"A penny for your thoughts?" Jonathan asked, his hand resting on Ashley's shoulder as she sat listening to Melissa play.

"I was just thinking about our bet. I don't think it was much of a bet at all."

"What do you mean? I think she's doing an excellent job."

"That's just it. She likes him too much for it to be just a bet."

Jonathan frowned. "Do you think so?"

"Yes," he said, taking a drink.

"I think the two of you should keep your noses out of other peoples business. If they come together on their own that's wonderful but this playing with a person's emotions is just plain stupid," Ashley said, shifting in her chair. "Now, shhh. I can't hear."

Stephan arched a brow at Jonathan who grinned and shrugged. Ashley had never said much of anything to him and here she was making him feel like a school boy caught talking out of turn. Shaking his head, he resumed his position and decided to enjoy the show.

JESSICA SCRAMBLED ALONG THE HALL Following the sound of the music, recognizing it instantly as Melissa. She could hear Morgan's hot pursuit and sped up. "Jessica" he hissed from behind her. Scooting into the room, she ran past Allison, bumping Royce's arm only to end up pulling Niles and Caleb in front of her for protection.

"Here now," Niles said, his drink falling from his hand as he righted himself to stare at a very furious Morgan halting in front of him. Caleb glanced behind him and straightened his face to keep from laughing.

Morgan stared at the men as Melissa quit playing. "Jessica get out of there," he said trying to remain calm but extremely embarrassed.

"No. I already told you, I'm not going anywhere with you, Milton, until you can take me as I am."

Caleb arched a brow at the misuse of his name. Niles just stared at Morgan before mouthing "Milton" at him.

Morgan gritted his teeth. "If I have to drag you home, it will only go worse for you," he said.

"See here, Jessica. You've ruined a perfect rendition of Bach," Melissa said, turning fully around on the seat. "Just go with him. You're drunk anyway," she said, tossing her head.

Jessica narrowed her eyes at but didn't take her eyes off Morgan. "You play worse than a beggar," she snapped. Morgan slowly moved forward and she took a firm grip on her bodyguards and pulled them back with her.

"Jessica," he said calmly.

Brand frowned at his daughter. She was getting completely out of hand. Moving to stand behind her, he waited until she walked into him.

"Sorry, Father. Could you move?" she said feeling a little sick from the brandy.

"No. I will not. Now get yourself over there and go home. You're messing up the entire evening. I'm sure by now, these gentlemen are sorry they associated themselves with us," he finished, taking her arm and marching her toward her husband. Niles and Caleb stepped out of the way. Handing her over to Morgan, he frowned. "I suggest you tie her up if she doesn't go quietly," he said, returning to his seat.

Jessica stared after him then glared at her husband.

Morgan arched a brow. "Don't blame me. You're the one making an ass of yourself."

Jessica reddened then paled. "Oh no," she said, then made a dash for the doors.

Morgan, seeing that she was going to be sick, let her go. As he reached the door and heard her retching he turned and nodded to the group. "Sorry for the interruption. It won't happen again," he said, pulling the doors closed.

Brand cleared his throat. "All right, Melissa. Continue."

"No, thank you, Father. After her snide remark, I lost my ability," she said, moving away from the seat. Brand frowned at her.

"Melissa," he said, ready to plead with her.

"Ashley can play," Jonathan said, trying to get his wife to her feet.

Ashley paled. "Oh no. I don't want to," she said, sitting back down.

"Come on, sweet. It isn't fair that only I get to hear you play," he said, pulling her to her feet.

Ashley turned scarlet as he led her to the seat and helped her get situated. Ashley sat there until Jonathan sat beside her. Slowly she began to play.

The group listened as she played song after song, with ease and perfection, making the pianoforte sound like an orchestra.

Allison smiled like a simpleton.

Royce smiled at Allison's happiness. Feeling guilty over the incident with the dogs, he bent close to her ear. "Would you care for a stroll in the garden?"

Allison felt herself blush but nodded, trying not to seem so anxious. She'd wanted to be with him more than anything and was happy he had come tonight.

Royce smiled and led her to the doors, as they moved into the gardens, he immediately moved her in the opposite direction of the hollering Jessica was doing.

Allison giggled, nervously. "She is getting it good, isn't she?"

Royce chuckled. "I'm not surprised. I felt like throttling her myself and I was only with her for an hour."

Allison laughed at that. "She does seem to bring that feeling out in everyone."

"I wanted to apologize for my behavior the other day when you came to my home," he said, seating her on a bench. "I was still unsure of the circumstances surrounding our association," he added, frowning. "Your brother doesn't like me very much."

Allison frowned, then made a decision. "But I do," she said quietly.

Royce turned to stare at her. "You don't even know me?"

Allison licked her lips. "I've been to several balls already and can tell people aren't as receptive to others as one would think. They act a though I can't function on my own. But with you, from the very beginning, I felt comfortable and relaxed."

Royce frowned. He'd felt the same way about society and could see by her blush she was embarrassed by what she'd said. "I've never been much of a social person. Balls and things tend to be more Jared's style."

Allison smiled. "I don't care for them, either. I would much rather spend my time in the country."

Royce arched a brow. "In the country?"

Allison laughed. "Yes. Like I told you before, I've only come to London to get married. My father is ill and it's his wish for us females to be wed."

Royce's frown deepened. That was a bit cold of the father but under the circumstances he could see why it was necessary for the other two sisters but Allison was so quiet and genteel. "Are you betrothed?" he heard himself ask and tensed. What prompted that question?

Allison blushed. "No. I was hoping to be though," she said getting to her feet to move to the honeysuckle bush to her left.

Royce frowned. "Is that why the Earl of March is here?"

Allison chuckled. "I'm sure it is, through no doing of mine, I can assure you. I think Melissa was hoping to arrange that one."

"And has she?"

Allison turned toward his voice. "If you want to know the truth, Jessica brought the right man with her, not Melissa," she said, turning away, fearing she'd said too much.

Royce felt the shock of her statement warm his blood. She wanted him. Him! A scared deformity of a man. "You're young yet, you don't know what you want."

Allison chuckled. "I'm considered old for a season," she said, running her hands along the branch smelling the sweet fragrance of the flowers.

Royce frowned. "Allison," he said taking her hands and turning her to face him. "I'm almost a complete stranger to you."

Allison held his hands in return feeling her blood sing. "You're the only man I've talked with so easily and I do know that I like you more than just on a whim."

Royce frowned down at her. She was so beautiful. Her hair sparkled in the moon light and her eyes were like emeralds. "You're far too lovely to waste away in the country with me. You should be draped around some man's arm, enjoying London's finest."

Allison felt her heart sink. "I don't care one whit about London. I hate the city. To much going on for a blind person to possibly function within. The country is exactly what I want," she said squeezing his hands.

Royce hesitated a moment before taking her chin in his hand and drawing her into a kiss. Allison melted into it, feeling all the excitement and hope she had carried around with her since they'd first met. Nero choose that moment to make his presence known by dropping down from the tree overhead. Royce pulled away from Allison and gapped as the large cat jumped up on him pushing the pair apart his front legs resting on Royce's chest.

Royce stared into the yellow eyes and frowned.

"Nero, get down," Allison said, grabbing his collar but Nero just continued to stare at Royce.

"I don't think he likes me much," Royce said scowling.

"Oh, he likes you. I'm afraid he doesn't understand why...well what you and I were doing."

Royce let a smile slowly cross his face. He was used to animals behaving out of jealousy. Though he was unsure of the cat, his dogs were fiercely protective. Lifting his hands, he slowly took a hold of both paws. "I think, my large feline friend, that you'd better get those feelings of yours under control. I plan on continuing with mine, you see," he said, stepping out from under the large paws while Nero dropped gracefully to the ground, his eyes on Royce. Nero gave a growl then moved off to flop his big body along the bench near the honeysuckle, getting a grin out of Royce. "Good choice," he said taking Allison's hands.

"He's a bit of a baby," she said, blushing.

Royce pulled her closer "I'm sure Nero and I will be the best of friends, in no time," he said, kissing her as she leaned into him. Pulling back some, he frowned. "You're sure you can put up with me?"

Allison broke into a smile. "I can put up with you for as long as you'll let me," she said, giggling.

Royce smiled then slowly frowned. "Allison, your family doesn't like me, remember? Your brother will never let us be together."

Allison, still in shock at the turn of events and the heavenly kiss, sighed. "Then we'll elope. Greta green."

Royce scowled. "We'll do no such thing."

"Well, I refuse to let my brother ruin my chance at happiness," she said, scowling.

Royce slowly smiled at her conviction to him. "I'll think of something," he said, lifting her chin to claim another kiss.

Chapter 78

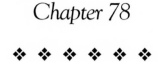

JESSICA AWOKE THE NEXT DAY with a splitting headache and instantly groaned.

"That's what you get for consuming more alcohol than most men."

Jessica opened one eye to stare at her husband who was leaning over her. "How did I get home?" she asked, wincing at the effort to talk.

"I carried you screaming and kicking the entire way," he said smiling.

Jessica closed her eyes. "I must have missed hitting that handsome face of yours. You're still smiling."

"Not at all. You just treated me real nice once we got home," he said, slapping her on the rump as she rolled to get away from him. Getting to his feet, he pulled on breeches and stockings.

"I was delirious, for sure." she said frowning. "You're not angry?"

"We settled that last night."

Jessica stuffed a pillow under her head and stared at Morgan. "What did we settle?"

Morgan grinned. "You agreed to wear gowns and I agreed to let you choose the style," he said, getting to his feet to pull on a shirt.

Jessica frowned again. He had taken advantage of her situation. Cursing her stupidity for getting drunk, she watched him dress. He was magnificent. Seeing him scoop up a bag, she arched a brow. "Going somewhere?"

"I leave today remember?"

Jessica frowned. "No. I don't," she said, rolling on her stomach, the pounding in her head killing her. Morgan grinned, then moved to leave the room. Little did she know, he didn't plan on sailing anywhere this trip. His ship sailed hours ago. He was just going to make her sweat a bit. "By the by, you didn't go anywhere else last night other than your Aunts did you?"

Jessica stiffened then groaned. "I made such an ass out of myself," she said wanting to cry but the pain was not worth the effort.

"Where did you go?" he asked concerned now.

"McMaster near Covington square," she murmured.

Morgan frowned by now his Aunt would have gotten wind of the events and would be paying Jessica a visit. "Then I suggest you get up. Aunt should be here any moment to lecture you."

Jessica tensed hearing the door shut. His Aunt. Lord what had she gotten herself into now.

Chapter 79

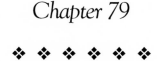

CHRISTOPHER FROWNED at the man before him. "You plan to what?"

"I plan to marry Lady Allison, if she'll have me," he said smiling.

Christopher drew his brows together, studying the man. He was tall, black haired and blue eyed. It was obvious he didn't mean what he said. "Why would that be?" he asked, trying to find the truth from this farce knowing full well this man's father was behind it.

Donavan Cabot shrugged. "She's beautiful, or so I've heard. She's smart and graceful and comes with land to the north. All things I need in a wife."

"She's also blind. Did you take that into account when you arrived here?"

Donavan got to his feet and moved to the window. He knew she was blind but Donavan didn't have much choice. Hopefully Christopher would reject him. "I realize her handicap. I don't think it will come between us."

Christopher scowled at the man's back. This was definitely not what this man wanted. It wasn't his place to choose for Allison, though. She had a month in which to find herself a husband. "Well, I can't make that decision alone. We'll have to include my sister. I give you permission to court her," he said getting to his feet.

Donavan frowned. His father wasn't going to like that he only accomplished permission for courting. Turning to face Christopher he smiled. "Thank you, my lord. I'd like to go for a ride in the park with her this morning, if that's permissible."

Christopher nodded. "I'll send for her. Help yourself to a drink and make yourself comfortable," he said leaving the study to climb the stairs.

Allison frowned, as Nero growled at her door. "Who's there?" she called before hearing the knock.

Christopher smiled."It's me."

"Come in," she called brushing Nero's fur.

Christopher entered and smiled."I see that cat is back in your good graces."

Allison laughed. "He didn't stay out very long. I'm too soft, I know."

Christopher smiled, hesitating a moment. "Allison, there's a gentlemen downstairs that wishes to take you for a ride in the park. I'd like you to go."

Allison frowned. " Who is it?" Knowing it wasn't Royce because Christopher hated him.

"It's Caleb's brother, Donavan."

"His brother?" she said shocked. First the Earl of March now the brother. "They sure have been busy?"

"Who?"

"Melissa and Caleb, who else? They sent the Earl last night and today the brother."

Christopher smiled. "I'd forgotten that. Will you go then?"

"Of course," she said, getting to her feet as she threw the blanket on the window seat. "I don't have a lot of hair on me, do I?"

Christopher scanned her gown and smiled. "Not a speck."

"Wonderful then I'm ready," she said, taking Nero's collar."

Christopher frowned. "What are you doing with him?"

"Taking him with me."

"Whatever for?" he asked scowling.

"First, to see if Nero likes him and second, to see if the man likes Nero," she said remembering Nero's reaction to Royce and vice versa.

Christopher scowled at her. "I think he should stay."

Allison frowned. "He goes or I don't."

"Fine," he said, glad in a way that the man wouldn't be around long. The situation was too suspicious anyway.

Allison smiled, tugging on Nero to get him going. "Lets go," she said taking Christopher's arm.

Chapter 80

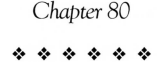

STEPHAN SMILED AT HIS REFLECTION in the mirror. He'd finally managed to tie his cravat and it came out looking halfway decent. Scowling at his broken hand, he cursed. It would be two more weeks before he could sail. Two more weeks of feeling useless before things would be back to normal and he could quit worrying about being cheated. Moving into the hall, he struck up a whistle.

Shaking his head, he arched a brow as the door down the hall opened and a woman dressed in a blue gown stepped out into the hall. Glancing in his direction, she paused then smiled and moved in his direction. Stephan felt uneasy. Which one was she? Looking around he tried to find someplace to go. He just wasn't ready to face Emily. He found he wanted to kiss her senseless more than talk with her. Something neither of them needed at the moment.

Emily drew her brows down at the skittish look crossing Stephan's handsome face, but her smiled remained in place. Moving to stand in front of him, she grinned. "I'm glad I ran into you. I wanted to thank you for giving me back my family."

Stephan smiled at her, feeling the earlier unease leave him as her husky voice ignited the male in him. It was Emily. "You're welcome. Glad to be of service. I apologize for my behavior in bringing you here. That wasn't very gentlemanly of me," he said, grinning.

Emily cocked her head to the side. "It's a great deal more gentlemanly than I've been witness to in the past few months."

"I would imagine."

Emily suddenly felt shy, as her body flushed and she began to fidget. "Well," she said, swallowing, "thank you, again."

Stephan frowned. "So what have you decided to do?" he asked, knowing it was none of his business but needing to know the answer anyway. Something about this woman made him feel fiercely protective.

Emily arched a brow. "Well, I don't know. I haven't had time to think about it."

Stephan cursed, for asking such a thing. She obviously didn't have any money. She'd been stealing just yesterday. "Well, you're welcome to stay here," he said, knowing his father would never throw her out.

Emily smiled, her brow creasing in wonder. "I...well...thank you. Rae has already said as much. I don't like to owe anyone and I'm sure I can find a place for us relatively soon."

Stephan frowned. If she couldn't find a place while she had been stealing, how was she supposed to find one with two young boys to support. "Well, just remember, you only have to ask and I'm sure any one of us will help you."

Emily smiled lowering her head at the warm feeling those words inspired. "Thank you. That is very kind," she said, turning toward the stairs. Stephan watched her go, wondering at his behavior. He acted like a brother to her though he knew his feelings were far from brotherly. Those few kisses had fired his blood enough to tell him to steer clear of her or he'd cause her more trouble than she already had. Shaking his head, he went out the back, not wanting to run into her again.

Chapter 81

BRAND GAVE COLAN a pathetic look. "You are serious, aren't you?"

"Well, of course. What other choice do we have? Your children are beyond troublesome, they're renegades. I don't think I've ever witnessed so many catastrophes in two months. It's almost too many to be believable," Colan said, sipping his tea.

Brand scowled down at his own cup, then set it aside. "Well, I think they've handled the situations with remarkably good judgment. No one seems to be the worse for wear."

Colan looked at him with brows arched. "Poor Sinclair is probably aging as we speak."

Brand scowled at Colan. "I admit Jessica is a bit on the rough side but the lad will come around. She will eventually settle in."

"He'll die of depletion within the month."

Brand couldn't help himself, he laughed. "I can't believe she came to the dinner crocked."

Colan shook his head. "She was always more like Elizabeth's side."

Brand sobered at that. "You leave Elizabeth out of this. She was the sweetest person that you've had the opportunity to meet. Allison reminds me of her in so many ways. Such a kind-hearted soul."

Colan frowned. "You're worried about her, aren't you?"

Brand sighed, leaning back in the chair. "She's so innocent that I can't possibly hold myself to the decision I made two months ago. I don't have the heart to just give her to some young buck. She'll get her heart crushed."

Colan grinned, making Brand narrow his eyes."You know something," he said, leaning forward. "Tell me, old man."

Colan arched a brow. "Old man, am I? Then why are you closer to the grave than me?"

Brand chuckled at that."Let's hear it. Has Allison found someone?"

"It's just a suspicion I have, of course, but the man that came last night with Jessica was not pleased that the Earl of March was next to your lovely daughter."

Brand scowled in thought. McMasters seemed like a decent sort. "And you think they like one another?"

"He likes her, I would wager, but as for, Allison. Who can say? She doesn't often announce to the world what's going on in that head of hers."

Brand nodded. "Of course. A little chat with the lad might help things along."

Colan scowled. "Don't be stupid. That would send your heart to bursting in seconds." he said, pouring some more tea. "But a couple of competitors wouldn't harm anything."

Brand drew his brows down in confusion. "You think if we send a few gentlemen Allison's way, McMaster's would come around?"

Colan shrugged. "It's worth a try, don't you think?"

"I don't know. What if she likes someone already and I complicate things."

"It was only a suggestion," he said, pushing his tea away. "Now enough with your seditious family. Let's have a nice game of chess."

Brand arched his brows. "I don't know why I even get myself thinking about these things. Christopher will handle this. Hobkins!" he bellowed.

Hobkins walked into the room and smiled. "Yes, my lord?"

"Bring us the chess table. We're too old to go in the other room."

"Very good, my lord," he said, turning about. They weren't too old. Ha! Lazy was more like it.

Chapter 82

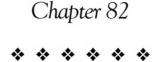

"WELL, YOU CAN'T LEAVE NOW," Melissa said, stomping her foot. "Allison still needs to find a husband. Don't you feel the least bit guilty for not helping?"

Jonathan arched a brow. "Then the Earl of March was here for her?"

Melissa reddened. "No, but Caleb insisted I let Allison decide. I don't like the man."

Jonathan laughed, "I didn't know you were that well acquainted with him."

"I know enough to know the man doesn't care one wit about a woman or her feelings. Allison needs someone more sensitive. She needs special care."

Ashley giggled at that causing Melissa to redden further.

"I didn't mean to imply that..."

Ashley held up a hand. "That's all right, I understand. Allison needs someone like Jonathan."

Jonathan turned and looked at his wife. She was so beautiful and special. Her family never knew what they had. "Do you have someone in mind?"

Ashley frowned. "No. It's hard to admit, but I am not high on society's social list."

Jonathan grinned, "Aren't we lucky."

Ashley laughed, getting a smile out of Melissa. "Well, I still think you should stay and help her."

Jonathan frowned. "I'll tell you what. I have several horse deals in London and I'll keep my eyes open for any gentlemen that might...er...treat her special."

Melissa pursed her lips. "You can joke all you want but Allison is stuck up there in her room and doesn't wish to go out. Frankly, I'm concerned."

Ashley smiled. "I'm sure things will work out. I have a hunch Allison already has someone in mind."

Melissa stiffened at that remark remembering Niles comment about the same thing. "Who? Who do you think she has in mind?"

Ashley held a finger to her lip. Getting a grin out of Jonathan. "Sorry, Melissa, it isn't gentlemanly to force a mother-to-be to spill the news." At her startled look Jonathan took Ashley's arm and the pair left chuckling.

Melissa watched them go, waving as they entered the coach. Turning to Hobkins, she scowled. "I hate when he does that. He knows damn well, I'm going to die wondering who Allison has in mind."

"Yes, my lady."

"It isn't like she's been out much. Who do you think it is?"

"I haven't the slightest idea, my lady," he said, trying hard not to laugh. She still hated being left out of the loop.

"Well, at least someone else is having a child," she said, grinning as Hobkin's mouth opened a fraction then closed. She could surprise people just as well as the next person.

Chapter 83

CARI FROWNED AT HERSELF in the mirror. She was in deeper than she wanted to admit. Christopher Hayworth was a man sent from heaven. His blond hair and green eyes made her heart race just thinking about him. Shifting in her chair, she frowned. Her eyes even looked starry. She was definitely in love. Damn. That was unfair. The man would throw her out on her ear the minute he found out she was conspiring with his brothers to make his life miserable. Laying her head on her arms, she groaned. Ranki chattered next to her as he quickly moved to run his hands through her hair looking for bugs.

"What do you do now, you fool?"

"I'm sorry, Miss. I can come back later when I'm not so clumsy," Jenny, her maid, said turning pale.

Cari laughed, lifting her head. "I wasn't talking to you, Jenny. I was calling myself a fool. I've got myself in a real pickle this time." Tipping her head as Ranki pushed it over to get a better view of behind her ear, she scowled.

"Can Master Reid help you, my lady?"

Cari arched a brow. "If he could, I'd become a nun. No. This is all my own doing and as usual I've ruined a perfectly good situation with my insane behavior," she finished, dropping her head back in her arms. Ranki climbed on her back to search beneath the mass of ebony curls.

Jenny frowned at her mistress, not understanding a bit of what she said. "Perhaps you'd like to send a gift?" she asked, knowing that always lifted her spirits.

Cari's head snapped up at that. Jenny paled as a slow smile crossed Cari's face. "Of course. A gift," she said, getting to her feet to move about the room looking at the various things she'd acquired from India. A love charm! She thought with a laugh, holding up one of the little shrunken heads. Jenny's face crinkled in distaste getting a laugh out of Cari.

"Not a good choice. How about one of those stones?"

Jenny's face brightened. "Now you're talking, my lady. I'll fetch a right pretty one. Is this for a lady, then?"

Cari laughed. "No. He's quite masculine," she said, as Ranki jumped from her shoulder to the bed.

Jenny paused at the door. "You're sending a man a rock?"

Cari pursed her lips. "They're not rocks, they're stones. Rare exotic stones, said to bring instant love to the giver."

Jenny arched a brow in disbelief. "You sent one of those to your brother?"

Cari reddened at Jenny's look. "He was very angry about the dead eel."

Jenny pursed her lips. "Are you sure you're not making another mistake?"

Cari lifted her chin. "No. Go get the stone, please."

Jenny smiled and went for the stone.

Giving Ranki a thoughtful look, she smiled. "I wonder if his lordship will come crashing down my door once he receives that stone. He's quite large, you know?" Ranki just stared at her turning his head from side to side while chattering at her. Moving to the bed, she scooped him up. "Come on then. I'll get you something to eat," she said as he moved up to settle on her shoulder, his tail going around her neck for support.

Chapter 84

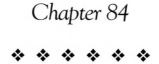

ALLISON MOVED INTO THE ROOM on Christopher's arm and paused hearing someone gasp loud enough to wake the dead.

Christopher cleared his throat. "Allison, may I present Lord Donavan Cabot. Donavan, Lady Allison Hayworth, my sister."

Allison smiled and held out her hand. "It's nice to meet you and thank you for the opportunity to ride in the park."

Donavan stared at the tiger beside her and barely managed to kiss her hand and utter the proper words. The animal was actually licking it's jaw. Scowling at the brother, Donavan frowned.

"I'm honored you have accepted," he said, ready to kill his father. This was an insane idea and something he hadn't wished to do in the first place. His lovely Heather was the woman he wanted and the faster this chit turned him down the quicker he could high tail it back to the highlands. "Shall we go?" Allison smiled. "Of course," she said removing her hand from Christopher's to wait for Donavan to take it. Donavan hesitated, as Nero shifted his feet and yawned, showing a mouthful of large teeth.

Allison coughed into her hand to hide the laugh knowing Nero was putting on his usual show. "He's really not so bad, you know. You'll get used to him while we ride in the coach."

"Coach?"

Allison paused. "When I came to London I didn't bring my horse so I must ride in a curricle or carriage," she said waiting for him to back out.

"Oh, of course. Forgive my foolishness. Of course, a curricle would be fine. I should have thought of that myself," he said feeling every bit the fool. As they moved to the door Hobkins handed her things to Donavan who quickly helped her into them. Handing her gloves to her, he smiled. "Hopefully I'll manage to keep you from thinking I'm a complete imbecile by the end of the afternoon."

Allison slowly smiled getting an arched brow from Donavan. She sure was a beauty. "I'm sure we'll get along fine. Especially if you're anything like your brother. I just might have a story to tell, if you're interested?"

"Always," he said, his interest perked.

NATHAN ARCHED A BROW seeing Allison ride into the park with a handsome man who looked more out of place than the cat beside her. "Well I say, whose the gent?"

Stephan lifted his head from the papers in his hand and frowned. "I don't know. Never seen him before," he said watching as they moved along talking. "Sure seems on the pale side." Nathan laughed. "Nero probably has him ready to bolt."

Stephan grinned. "He does have that effect on people, doesn't he?"

Nathan still chuckling, nodded to the papers. "Well?"

"I don't know. I guess everything is in order."

"You guess? What's that mean? Yes, go ahead and take them to Turrock or no, I'll deal with it myself. I hate being your errand boy."

Stephan grinned at him. "I know but I have to go to the Gypsy to make sure Jessica doesn't slip on board. You never know if Sinclair can keep her at home or not." Nathan arched a brow, still waiting for Stephan's answer. "Yes, these will do fine. Tell Sinclair I have two shipments coming in on Friday and two more next week."

Nathan frowned. "Just write it down."

"Is that too many things to remember?"

Nathan's face turned angry. "Watch what you say or I'll just leave the matter to you. You're lucky I'm helping you at all."

Stephan smiled slowly. "I appreciate it. I know you have other more intimate thoughts on your mind."

Nathan flushed at that. "Just give me the damn papers."

Stephan laughed at his reaction. "What Jonathan and Christopher wouldn't do to know our baby brother is almost as bad as a virgin about his woman."

Nathan was fast losing his patience. "Like I told you before, I've had my share of women but I feel more inclined toward one woman, instead of walking about like a rutting boar."

Stephan arched a brow. "A rutting boar?"

Nathan snatched the papers out of his hand. "I'm warning you Stephan, you know I'll get even."

Stephan laughed, his gaze going to Allison as Nathan rode out of sight. I wonder who that is and what he's up to? Mounting his horse, he headed for the open land by the lake. A nice brisk ride would clear his head of any thoughts concerning one black haired beauty with a startling pair of green eyes.

"HE IS TOO!" Ian said, his little face flushed red. "He's the best pirate on the seas."

Sean smiled. "Why is his hand broken then."

Ian frowned, then grinned. "He was in a bad storm and the wheel jerked and he was forced to steer the ship with one hand. He's a hero. He saved his whole crew," he finished lifting his chin.

Sean frowned. "Well, he's still not our Uncle."

Ian frowned. "But I want him to be. I like the new family we have."

"But their not ours, stupid. Mama isn't married to anyone and I heard her say she was going to find some cousin of hers to work for."

"But I don't want to go. Uncle Jonathan promised to get me a horse."

"He's not your Uncle, either."

"But he promised."

Sean moved to sit on a rock and began throwing pebbles into the pond. "It doesn't matter. We are just children. Why should they give us anything?"

"What's this I hear?" Stephan said walking his horse to the water's edge to drink. Sean turned scarlet dropping his head from Stephan's view. Ian, being younger and not so shy, pipped up.

"Sean says you're not our Uncle anymore. Uncle Jonathan isn't, either."

Stephan frowned at the boys then hunkered down to scoop up a handful of rocks to cast into the pond. "Whether we're related or not I still want to be your Uncle."

Ian's face turned instantly into a mask of happiness. "See, Sean. They want us. We're not orphans again."

Sean gave his brother a pathetic look. "Don't be so stupid, Ian. Mama isn't going to stay here. We won't see them anymore, no matter what they say," he finished, giving Stephan a sad look before turning away.

Stephan frowned, feeling butterfly's in the pit of his stomach at the mention of Emily leaving. "Your mother is leaving?"

"She wants to govern somewhere," Ian pipped out.

Sean frowned. "She's going to be a governess," he said, shaking his head at Ian.

Stephan frowned. "Does she already have that post?"

"No. She said she would have no trouble getting it," Sean said.

Stephan turned his head, knowing Emily wasn't getting a post anywhere with two children in tow. "Perhaps she'll decide to stay with your Aunt Rae and Uncle Nathan."

Sean looked at his feet. "She says they are two hooked on one another, to need us hanging around."

Stephan frowned. "I'm sure things will work out Sean. You'll see," he said, getting to his feet. "How about a ride back to the house? Galiath here is a fine mount."

Ian jumped up and down stating his answer plain as day. Sean, though his eyes said he wanted too, shook his head.

Stephan moved to stand by the boy. “Come on, Sean. Whether I’m your Uncle or not, let’s decide that when your mama gets a post, huh.”

Sean hesitated before getting to his feet. Stephan grinned tossing each lad up on the horse. “Now hang on,” he called leading Galiath in a slow trot toward the house.

Chapter 85

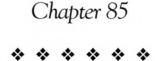

"...AND THE MAN settled for a lump of granite barely etched with gold. He gave up his chance of ever finding the real nuggets."

Donavan stared at Allison as she finished the tale with both brows arched. Clearing his throat, he frowned. "I have a feeling you don't want to be my nugget."

Allison laughed. "I haven't exactly had it said to me in that way but I already am a nugget to someone else."

Donavan's face brightened. "I see."

Allison smiled shyly. "I'm being quite frank with you because I can tell from our outing that you aren't really interested in me. Did Melissa put you up to this?"

"Who?"

"Melissa. My sister?" When he still didn't answer, she frowned, "Caleb's wife?"

Donavan's brows arched."Caleb's wife is your sister?" he asked straightening in his seat.

"They didn't tell you?"

"Bloody hell!" he snapped, then blushed. "Forgive my language. My father is the recipient of my wrath, not you."

Allison nodded. "Am I to understand then, that your father wanted you to marry me for the ships?"

Donavan arched a brow. "Your ships?"

Allison chuckled. "It's all right. That's was one of the reasons my brothers were upset when Melissa married your brother so quickly."

"This is getting way out of hand? I didn't even know Caleb was married to your sister until seconds ago. My father didn't mention ships, other than to be able to unload them in the north on the land you provide." Allison frowned. "He's after my land?"

Donavan frowned. "I shouldn't have said that." "It doesn't really matter.

I'm not available to you."

Donavan grinned. "I am relieved," he said, then paled. "I mean. I have a lass already. I mean, a nugget. She's a bonny lass from the highlands. She has hair like midnight and eyes like purple velvet."

Allison smiled at the heartfelt words. "Then why come for me?"

Donavan lost his smile. "My father doesn't like the Scots."

"I see," she said stroking Nero's coat. "Sometimes we do things for our own reasons and to hell with everyone else's," she said smiling. "Forgive the language."

Donavan slowly, grinned. "I find myself at a complete loss. You're a rare gem indeed. Your man will feel lucky to call you his own."

Allison sighed. "I do hope he thinks the same way you do?"

"I'm sure he does."

Allison smiled shyly. "Well at least one good thing has come out of this outing. I've made myself a friend?"

Donavan grinned. "I would be honored to fill that role. I find myself wanting to say thank you."

Allison smiled in return, as he kissed her hand. "Just keep your nugget happy."

Donavan laughed slapping the reins to pick up the pace.

Royce frowned at the pair on the curricle and had the urge to chase the cart down and beat the man to a bloody pulp. Was Allison like every other female? Fickle and unfaithful? Did she just tell him those things last night or had she meant them? Frowning, he moved his horse onto the path and followed discreetly behind them.

Chapter 86

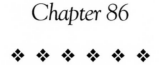

"JESSICA, what on earth are you doing here?" Melissa said, coming into the salon.

Jessica turned from her position by the window and frowned. "I have to dress myself in gowns but I refuse to wear corsets. I need a compromise."

Melissa arched a brow at her. "You want to compromise what?"

"I need to dress more like a lady of society yet I don't want to give up my easy movements. I can't walk around in the fluff you wear and the shoes kill my feet. Do you think you could help me find some sort of middle ground here?"

Melissa slowly grinned. "You're actually asking my advice?" she said with a laugh

Jessica sent her a murderous glare. "I still know where to find my crew and I wouldn't hesitate to send one after you for a short two day trip up the coast."

Melissa frowned. "You're always so nasty," she said moving to the settee as Mary brought in some tea. "Would you care for some tea?" she asked, knowing she wouldn't accept.

"I hate tea," she said, moving to flop into one of the chairs across from the settee. "Pour me some, though. I'll have to get used to it."

Melissa pursed her lips. "You don't have to drink it, you know. You can just give it to your guests and pretend you're drinking it. It's really simple," she said, pouring herself a cup and mimicking the act of drinking though she didn't take a drop.

Jessica rolled her eyes. "That would be what those simpletons would do."

Melissa sighed. "All right. What exactly do you have in mind?" she asked, looking at Jessica's breeches and boots with disgust.

"I'm not giving up all my breeches, so get that look off your face. I am willing to dress in gowns, however, when I'm in society."

Melissa arched a brow. "That still doesn't explain what you plan on wearing."

"I want simple gowns, like I wore before. Just plain tight waisted gowns without all those fluffy things. And no corset."

Melissa frowned. "That isn't dressing right for society, you know?"

"I don't care. I'm compromising here. Can you help me or not?" she said, making to stand.

"I'll help you but I don't want to hear a complaint out of you."

Jessica hesitated, but relaxed back in the chair swinging one leg over the arm. "He's not sailing," she said smiling.

Melissa frowned,"Stephan?"

"No, silly. Morgan."

"Oh, he's not?" she asked, having no idea he was supposed to be sailing anywhere.

"No. He just went to his office on the docks in Thurrock."

"And?"

"I had Dane follow him and fill me in. The man's staying in port." At Melissa's still confused look, she rolled her eyes. "That means he's not leaving me behind, which means he's trying to be nice."

Melissa stared at her a moment. "He's being nice by not sailing?"

"Yes. He was going to sail on my ship, now he's not going at all. That's why I'm dressing in dresses."

Melissa held up her hands. "I don't care," she said, thoroughly confused. "Just let me help you with the dresses and you go back to whatever it is you are doing with that man of yours. Frankly, I'd have beat you black and blue for your behavior at Father's dinner. I'm surprised Father's still breathing."

Jessica reddened. "I was a bit in my cups, I admit..."

Melissa snorted then quickly covered her mouth. " 'A bit in your cups' doesn't half explain the drunken mess I saw retching her guts out in the garden."

Jessica slowly smiled. "It was a rare sight, you can be sure."

Melissa curled her lip. "You're disgusting," she said, sipping her tea. "By the way, is Rae bringing Emily to your ball?"

Jessica shrugged. "I don't think so. Stephan says Emily is trying to find a post somewhere. I don't know if I'm even having the ball."

"A post? Whatever for?"

"I would assume money. You forget the woman doesn't have a shilling to her name. She's a widow with two children and needs some means to support them." "But surly Nathan isn't planning on throwing her out. Is he?" she asked, scowling.

"Of course not. But if it was me, I wouldn't want to live as a poor relation."

Melissa pursed her lips. "I'm sure she isn't a poor relation." Jessica just arched her brows. Melissa's face broke into a huge smile as Caleb and Niles strolled into the room. Coming to her feet, she moved to greet Caleb. "Good morning, my lord."

Jessica turned in her chair then reddened as the handsome Earl arched a brow at her.

Caleb grinned. "I see you're not any the worse for wear after your performance last night."

Jessica smiled, crookedly at him, as she got to her feet. "I was always able to hold my liquor. Nice to see you again, Handsome."

Melissa pursed her lips. "Jessica, really. You don't even know the Earl."

Niles smiled. "It's all right. I believe the lady is just being blunt."

Jessica laughed. "A wee bit. Well if you'll excuse me I'll be on my way. Melissa two o'clock at Ginger's?" At Melissa's nod, Jessica smiled. "Excellent. See you then. Good day, Gentlemen," she said, bowing before she strode from the room.

Niles watched her go with arched brows. "I'm surprised Sinclair is sane. She's quite the handful."

Melissa frowned at him, as Caleb laughed. "Too bad she's already wed. You could sacrifice yourself to her." When Nile's gaze came to rest on Melissa's, she added. "But since you want to be a martyr, perhaps I could interest you in a widow. She comes with children."

Niles arched his brows at her in tolerant mirth.

"Melissa," Caleb warned in a stern voice laced with laughter.

"No, a widow won't do you? She's family. Obviously a good breeder," when his face looked completely filled with shock, she shook her head sadly. "Well, think about it," she said, patting his arm as she walked from the room.

Niles turned to Caleb and frowned. "I think perhaps that week or two away from your wife, is in order. I'm getting a prickly neck here."

Caleb laughed, slapping him on the back. "You're still a lying sod in her eyes," he said, laughing harder. "Come on. Let's get some brandy," he added moving toward his study.

Chapter 87

NATHAN MOVED HIS HORSE into the stables and threw the reins to Timmy. "Thank you, Tim. Make sure you treat him real nice. It was a long trip to Turrock." At the boy's huge smile, Nathan nodded and left the barn. It was nice to be away from the sea. He'd never particularly liked the sea though he could sail, just as well as Stephan. The sea just never held his interest. Pulling off his gloves he swatted them across his thigh watching the dust rise. Frowning, he headed toward the house and a bath. Rae would be home and after the last few nights, she would be just as eager to see him as he was to see her. Picking up his pace, he slipped into the house giving Hobkins a brief nod, before heading straight to his room. Pausing outside the door he could hear movement inside. Smiling he eased the door open seeing Rae laying out a gown on the bed. Smiling, at her shapely backside he moved forward silently. Getting closer, he could hear her humming a soft melody sounding faintly like a Scottish tune. Grabbing her about the waist he pulled her around for a kiss.

"I've missed you," he said, pulling her close. His lips stopped any protest she might have made.

Emily stood there in shock as Rae's husband kissed her with a passion of a man in love. Pulling away, she tried to protest only to have his tongue invade her mouth. Squirming to get free, she panicked.

Nathan frowned wondering why Rae was acting so stiff when suddenly it dawned on him. Snatching his head back his eyes met mint green ones and he jumped back so fast she teetered to the side. Grabbing, her to steady her, he snatched his hands back to his side and stepped back two more steps. "Good lord, I'm sorry. It's just that...well...Bloody hell!" he finished in a shout.

Emily arched a brow at him then smiled embarrassed by the whole thing. "It's quite all right. It was a mistake."

"A mistake? You're damn right, it was. Hell, you two are going to have to wear name tags or something."

Emily giggled at the thought then outright laughed as his face reddened.

"I mean it. I can't go around kissing you."

"You did what?" Rae asked from the door, a gown hanging from her hand.

Nathan turned to her and instantly looked like a child caught with his hand in the cookie jar. "I...she...I came in here looking for you and ended up kissing her," he said, pointing at Emily.

Rae pursed her lips trying not to laugh. "Well, couldn't you tell the difference?" she asked laughing as his face turned scarlet.

"I didn't see her face until it was too late. She was bending over..." he said, his voice halting at the thought of describing Emily's backside. "Just wear the damn tags. And stay out of our room," he added to Emily before storming out the door.

Rae waited two seconds for the door to slam before bursting into laughter. Emily immediately followed suit. "I can't believe it. Are we still that much alike?"

Emily smiled. "From the back view, I guess so," she said, holding her sides from laughing so hard.

Rae straightened from where she leaned against the wall. "Don't get any ideas. Nathan is a gentleman and he belongs to me. One kiss is all I'm going to allow," she said sobering at the thought of what actually happened.

Emily took the two gowns in her arms. "It was a right hearty kiss, too!" she said, pulling the door closed behind her. Rae threw something that hit it with a thud. Smiling, she moved off toward her room, her mind wandering to the searing kiss Stephan had given her. He kissed much better than Nathan. Feeling her heart beat faster she hurried to her room. Those kind of thoughts weren't going to get her anywhere.

Chapter 88

ROYCE WATCHED the dark haired man return Allison to her home then frowned as he didn't reappear for almost thirty minutes. Cursing, he had to restrain himself from stalking across the street and hauling the man away himself. Feeling his anger riding him good, he decided to follow the man as he appeared and mounted up. A little threat could do wonders for ones temper.

He trailed the man for nearly fifteen minutes, until the man finally stopped in front of a shop. Bringing his horse up along side the man's, Royce dismounted and tied his mount.

"Stay away from her," Royce said quietly, as the man turned and arched his brows at him. Royce cursed at Donavan's handsome face. His face was flawless.

"I beg your pardon," Donavan asked, thinking he must have misheard the man.

Royce stiffened at the man's stance. "I said stay away from Lady Hayworth."

Donavan's brows moved up another notch. Could this be Allison's nugget? "Is the lady an acquaintance of yours?"

Royce growled at the man's nonchalance. "She's my fiance and I don't particularly like you hanging around her," he said, finally turning so the man could see his face.

Donavan couldn't help his surprise at the scars on the man's face, though he'd seen far worse. Clearing his throat as Royce's face darkened, he sighed. "Forgive me, Lord..."

"McMasters. The Earl of Salisbury," hoping to intimidate the man.

"Yes, well, Lord McMaster. I was just informed along those lines by the lady herself. I hope I haven't caused a problem?"

Royce, surprised by the statement was at a loss for words. "Is that so? Then I won't see you hanging around the lady's home in the future," he snapped, feeling foolish for acting so jealously. Jared would be on the ground laughing at this point.

Donavan grinned. "As to that, I'm not quite certain," he said, then quickly added as Royce's face darkened. "It seems the lady has a sister wed to my brother."

Royce arched a brow. "Your brother?" he asked, wondering which one that could be.

"Yes. Caleb Cabot is my brother. I'm Donavan," he said extending his hand.

Royce, at a loss for the warm welcome he was getting from this man, frowned down at the hand before shaking it. "It seems I was a bit hasty in my warning."

Donavan grinned. "It's understandable, considering what a lovely lady your fiance is," he said, getting a semi smile from Royce.

"She's something all right," he said moving back toward his horse. "If you'll forgive my intrusion, I'll just be on my way."

Donavan nodded watching the giant mount up and move off to disappear among the streets. Shaking his head, he couldn't help but smile. Lady Hayworth definitely was that man's nugget and Royce was one lucky man.

Chapter 89

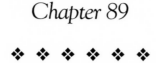

"I CAN'T STAND IT. One more of those things stuck in my side and I'm going to club you over the head," Jessica snapped, glaring at the seamstress.

Madame Larorange pursed her lips. "If my lady would wear the corset this would not happen."

Melissa turned around to hide her smile. Madame Larorange was handling Jessica the way Melissa only dreamed of. Every vile word uttered by Jessica was completely cut off by Madame's stern look or rap of her pencil.

"I'm not wearing that confining contraption and I won't stand here and get poked to death, either," she snapped, lifting her arm as Madame pushed it in the air.

"I just need this one gown. I can make the rest from this. Now hold still," she fussed, sticking pins here and there."

"Madame Larorange, I have chosen several colors for Lady Sinclair and with such a simple style," she said, giving Jessica an irritated look, "How long before you have several of them made?"

"Wee, Lady Cabot. I can have several made up in just a week."

"A week! That's too long. She can't very well walk around in the gowns she has."

"I don't have any," Jessica said, grinning as Melissa turned a fuming look on her.

Madame glanced at Jessica then back at Melissa. "No, gowns?"

"They were...er...ruined." Jessica said, shrugging her shoulders as Madame looked away to Melissa for help.

"Her trunks were lost in the sea," Melissa said, blushing at the lie. "Now we need several gowns in three days. One ball gown, for sure."

Madame pursed her lips, tapping her pencil against them before smiling. "It will be expensive but I can have them in three days."

Melissa smiled, a very fetching smile. "Thank you. I'm sure Lord Sinclair will not object," she said moving around the shop selecting things to hold up for Jessica's perusal.

Jessica was ready to kick the little french woman in the ribs and clobber Melissa over the head by the time they managed to get the gowns settled and all the things that went with them.

"You'll look fine once you get used to wearing these things," Melissa said, not completely pleased with Jessica's under things.

Jessica tossed her braid over her shoulder as they moved along the street. "Personally, I think half these things are a waste of money."

Melissa pursed her lips. "You have no sense of fashion," she said, suddenly smiling. "Why lady St. Paul. How have you been?" she asked, pausing as the woman turned to look at her.

Cari smiled and nodded. "Lady Sinclair, Lady Cabot. I'm fine, thank you. How about yourselves?"

"We're fine," Melissa said.

"How's the romance with Christopher going?" Jessica asked, getting a poke from Melissa.

"Jessica, you don't just blurt something out like that."

"Why not? You were thinking it and I want to know the answer," she said, her brows furrowed as she looked back at Cari. "Well?"

Cari smiled stunned by her question. "I haven't really been doing much about that lately."

Melissa smiled. "You've seen Christopher several times," she said, giggling.

Jessica rolled her eyes. "I'm going to be sick. Quit giggling."

Melissa's face turned angry. "I've had it. You're impossible. I'm going home," she said moving past Cari. "Good day, Lady St. Paul."

"Good day," she said, watching Melissa stride off in a huff.

Jessica took Cari's arm and moved her toward the door. Perhaps a bit of lunch will loosen that tongue of yours. Christopher is becoming a recluse. He barely leaves his study."

"Well, I really shouldn't. I have these packages to send," Cari said, trying to get away from the questions.

Jessica stopped and looked at the boxes.

"Maybe some other time," Jessica said, as Cari pulled her arm free and moved away. Jessica watched her hurry toward the post and frowned. What was that all about? Cari scowled on her way to the post. How could she have made such a mistake? Christopher was going to throw her aside once word of her game got out. Whatever possessed her to agree to such a stupid plan? Shaking her head, she frowned down at the package addressed to Christopher. Hopefully the stone charm would help.

Chapter 90

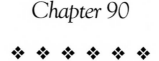

BRAND FROWNED AT COLAN. "You mean he actually threatened the man?"

Hobkins nodded,"I was standing right there, my lord."

Brand slowly smiled. "Well then. It seems, I don't have to send in Lord...er..."

"Cantonberg,"Colan supplied.

"Right. The man was so boring I could of fallen asleep just looking at him. See to it Cantonberg isn't on any of our lists, all right, Hobkins?"

"Of course, my lord. Anything else?"

"No, just that," Brand said as Hobkins left. "I think I worry for nothing."

Colan frowned tapping his fingers on his lips. "I do have a problem that I can't keep from you any longer."

Brand scowled. "Which child did what?"

Colan arched a brow. "It's not so much as doing anything wrong. It's doing nothing at all. Lady Emily is going off to some cousin in Scotland."

Brand slowly stiffened, "She's what?"

"Now calm yourself, Brand, or I'm not telling you a thing," Colan said, picking up his tea.

Brand wanted to smack the tea out of Colan's hand but leaned back in his chair and sighed. "Fine. I'm calm."

Colan looked at him then nodded. "It seems Emily doesn't wish to be a burden to Nathan and his wife. She wants to earn her own way."

"Then I'll give her a job."

"She's already refused Stephan. He offered to let her run the shipping firm since Jessica is tied up with whatever mess she's into this week."

Brand scowled at that. "Stephan's office is hardly suitable for a young lady."

Colan arched a brow. "You let Jessica go down there."

"Exactly. Emily would be eaten alive with that brawny bunch."

"Well, from what I understand, Emily plans to leave in just over a week. The part I haven't told you about is that Ginger thinks the cousin doesn't plan to give her a job but plans to marry her off to bind his clan or some such thing."

Brand cursed and got to his feet. "Well that simply can't happen. Has Ginger told Emily this?"

"It seems the girl thinks she can take care of herself, but you know how uncivilized those Scots can be. She'll be forced to wed, not to mention what could happen to the boys."

Brands face hardened. "I won't have it. Christopher will have to marry her. He has to marry anyway."

Colan's mouthed dropped open. "You gave him a chance to choose."

Brand waved a hand at that. "He'll do like I ask. He always does."

Colan frowned. "Do you think that's wise?"

"I don't care. I will not stand by while that girl is married off to some barbarian. Those boys are more important than that. Christopher will marry her."

"Should I send for Hobkins?"

"No. I'll get Nathan here, right away. He can take Christopher the message along with the package from Elizabeth."

Colan smiled. "You handled that surprisingly well. Any pain?"

Brand arched his brows. "Not a twinge," he finished, smiling.

CARI STARED AT HER REFLECTION in the mirror and sighed. Tonight was the night. She was taking matters into her own hands. It had been over a week since the dinner with Christopher's father and Cari knew she was deeply in love with Christopher. Frowning at herself, she sighed. She just didn't know how he felt. He'd only kissed her once and that had been last night. A small brush of his lips to hers on the stoop of her home. In two days, they were to go to the Ashton's ball.

Groaning, she got to her feet and began pacing. Things were going too slow for her. She wanted him. She wanted to press herself against his hard lithe body and kiss him until she couldn't do it any more. But the blockhead was so proper and stiff it would take her years at this rate. Moving to her wardrobe, she pulled the thing open. "Jenny!" she bellowed, not bothering with the rope. She wanted the perfect gown for tonight.

"Yes, my lady?"

"I need your help. I need a gown for tonight that's going to make me look like a queen."

Jenny arched a brow. "A queen?"

"Don't get sassy on me. I'm not in the mood," Cari said, pulling out a deep red gown with black lace and bows. "I think this will do," she said, smiling at her reflection in the mirror.

"It was your mama's. I'm sure it won't fit."

"Then we'll make it. I want to wear this one."

Jenny frowned. "Didn't the stone work, my lady?"

Cari scowled. "No. That's why I'm wearing this gown."

Jenny pursed her lips. "All right. It seems to me you're going to a lot of trouble in an area you're not wanted," she said, taking the gown and helping Cari slip into it. Jenny ignored the scowl her mistress sent her as she worked on making alterations to the gown.

Chapter 91

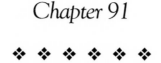

ALLISON MOVED INTO THE GARDEN along the well memorized path to sit on the bench in the far corner. Nero growled low in his throat. "Quiet. I don't want anyone to know I'm out here," she said, shifting on the bench to wait. Smiling slowly, she let her mind wander as Nero curled up at her feet to chew on a piece of wood he'd found in the bushes.

Ever since the night Jessica had so rudely blundered into their father's dinner party, Royce had been meeting her in secret. Her smile widened as she remembered their last meeting. Lifting a hand to her lips, she sighed. The feel of his strong lips upon hers was bringing forth a yearning she couldn't possibly understand but one she wanted to find out more about.

Royce watched Allison's face flush slightly in the moonlight and smiled. "Do I detect a blush on that lovely face of yours?" he asked, moving to stand before her.

Allison smiled and slowly got to her feet. "I was just thinking of this," she said, sliding her hands along his chest and up around his neck then into his brown hair to gently pull his head down for a kiss.

Royce growled at her boldness. "Such a wanton I have here," he said deepening the kiss further as his hands moved down her back to cup her buttocks. Allison groaned, against his mouth getting a chuckle from Royce. "And impatient as well."

Allison pulled back. "Is it set?"

"All is ready."

"When?" she asked leaning against him.

"Two days."

"Two days!" she said, her face showing her disappointment. "But why so long?"

Royce chuckled again. "It's not so long, besides I plan to make it seem like just hours from now," he said, pulling her again into his embrace. His mouth ravaged hers as his hands moved along her body. Allison felt the familiar stirring deep in her belly and groaned as their tongues touched in heated battle.

Royce pulled back, setting her quickly from him. At her whimpered protest, he chucked her under the chin. "Sorry, love. Someone comes," he said moving into the shadows. "Sit down you look like someone's been ravishing you," he said, as Allison reddened but sat down.

Stephan rounded the bend in the garden and drew up short as Nero growled a warning. "Allison? What are you doing out here?" he asked moving cautiously toward the bench, giving Nero a stern look.

"I...I needed some fresh air," she said, straightening her skirt. "And you?"

Stephan smiled, placing his foot on the bench beside her. "Needed a little time to think is all."

Allison frowned, at the tone of his words. "What's wrong?"

Stephan looked at her and smiled. "Can't hide a thing from you, can I?"

Allison grinned. "Not when you're moping."

Stephan scowled. "I'm not moping. I just don't know what to do with myself. This stupid hand of mine," he said again looking at Nero with a scowl.

"Nero didn't mean it. I'm glad to hear it's healing well."

"Doc says another week."

"If you'd have listened to him in the first place, you wouldn't be in this predicament."

Stephan smiled. "I know."

"That isn't what's bothering you, though," she said smiling. "Come on, out with it."

Stephan frowned and looked into the brush. "It doesn't concern you," he said.

"No, but I can bet it concerns a lovely brunette that looks remarkably like Rae."

Startled, Stephan stared at her. "You're crazy," he said, moving to pace.

Allison laughed. "I think you should just ask her straight out and get it over with."

Stephan gapped at her. "Exactly what am I suppose to ask her?"

"To marry you, of course. It's so obvious that you want the girl."

Stephan arched a brow at her. "To whom?"

"Rae, Melissa, Nelly, and me. Jessica would have noticed if she wasn't so deep in her own misery."

Stephan frowned. "You're all discussing my business?"

Allison held up a hand. "No. It's just that those people I mentioned, have found time to speak to me on the matter and I am not about to keep my opinion to myself. I think you're making a big mistake by letting her go to the Scots. Those children need a father and they are already so attached to us it would kill them to have to adjust again. Not to mention what this will do to Father."

Stephan scowled at that but frowned at the news of a Scot. "What Scot?"

"She says there's a cousin living in Scotland that has already stated he would accept them in his home but she didn't seem too thrilled at the prospect," Allison said, hesitating. "Rae says she was hoping for something else, but married to a Scotsman is better than stealing."

Stephan frowned. "What?"

"If you're that dense then let her go to her cousin. I'm sure he'll marry her off for a nice profit. Those boys will get on well enough. Course Father will be stressed at losing them but I'm sure he'll manage," she said getting to her feet.

Stephan frowned. "You like doing that, don't you?"

"What?" she asked, a look of innocence on her face.

"Butting into a person's business at a crucial moment. It sends them careening off in a different direction than they were going."

Allison smiled. "Is that what I did?"

Stephan growled, before grabbing her and pulling her into a hug. "You know it is."

Allison giggled as he released her. "I just hope you do the right thing."

Stephan frowned. "So do I."

Chapter 92

"YOU LOOK LOVELY." Christopher said, kissing Cari's hand. "Just like a princess.

Jenny rolled her eyes behind his back as she placed the tray of tea and cakes on the table. "She was hoping for a queen," she mumbled standing to await Cari's command.

Cari turned scarlet at that crack narrowing her gaze at Jenny the minute Christopher looked at her. "That will be all, Jenny."

"Whatever you say, my lady," she said walking out like a queen.

Christopher returned his gaze to Cari and smiled. "A queen, was it." Taking her hand, he spun her around then slowly shook his head. "I still see just a princess. Queens are stern and boring. Princesses are lovely beyond imagination."

Cari blushed in pleasure at his words then tipped her head in gratitude. "You, then are my bold and gallant prince," she said, smiling, "where are we off to tonight, Sir Gallahaid?

Christopher smiled. "Henderson's are having a ball and I thought maybe a jaunt to Veux Hall would be in order afterwards."

Cari beamed a bright smile. "That sounds lovely. Shall we go?"

"By all means," Christopher said, offering his arm.

"By the by, did you like my gift?" she asked, feeling nervous about the whole thing.

Christopher arched a brow. "You sent me that?"

Cari's face blanked and she felt her stomach knot. Did he have someone else who would send him gifts? "I...I thought you would like it," she said lowering her eyes.

Christopher frowned then took her hand. "I thought it was a joke," he said, sorry he'd hurt her feelings. "I forgot you like to send those sort of things."

Cari drew her brows down in a frown. "Those sort of things? What exactly did you receive?"

It was Christopher's turn to be surprised. "You don't know?"

Cari wanted to stomp her foot in frustration. "I know what I meant to send you. I can't see where that would make you act like I'd sent you one of those shrunken heads."

Christopher reddened, then laughed. "Why don't you tell me what you sent me?"

Cari scowled then blushed. How was she supposed to say "I sent you a love charm in the shape of a rock." Clearing her throat, she licked her lips. "I sent you a very valuable stone from India."

Christopher arched a brow. "Well then somehow your packages got mixed up."

"Mixed up?" she asked with dread.

"Yes. My package had a rather funny looking little man in it with the foulest smelling odor coming from it."

Cari paled. "Oh no," she said, slipping into a chair. "That means Reid got your stone." she said, thankful she hadn't sent the charm to someone that would cause a problem if the charm actually worked.

"Reid?"

"My brother. He was supposed to get the Pigamin."

"The what?"

"The little man. He's to let the person know that receives it that you're angry with them. My grandfather showed me them."

"And you're mad at Reid?"

"Yes. Sort of," she said, turning red, "he left here telling Andrew that...er...that I was his responsibility," she said, searching for a reason other than that she had to marry by age twenty-five.

"I see."

Cari got to her feet as Christopher rose with her. "I'm sorry. I'll get you another stone," she said, moving to do that.

Christopher grabbed her arm and hauled her to a stop. "That's all right. You can do that another time," he said, still holding her hand.

Cari felt her pulse quicken at the look on his face. He was going to kiss her.

"I think we should go," he said, clearing his throat before looping her hand around his arm.

Cari wanted to kick him for not following his feelings. She would have bet money that Christopher's face was flushed with desire. Turning they left the room only to be brought up short by Andrew.

"Off again, my dear?"

"Yes. Lord Hayworth and I are off to the Henderson's ball then on to Veux Hall."

Andrew smiled at her before turning to Christopher. "Have a good time," he said, a little awkward that his client was dating his sister.

Christopher grinned, smacking him on the back. "Sure thing, Andrew. We won't be late."

Andrew frowned at the show of affection from Christopher. The man barely displayed any emotion in public. Maybe Cari was changing him some. Lifting his brandy to his lips Andrew swallowed toasting to the possibilities.

Chapter 93

JESSICA STARED AT HER REFLECTION in the mirror and slowly smiled. Morgan was going to be happy tonight, she thought running her hand down the deep blue velvet of her gown. It was a simple cut, fitted to the waist then flaring out to fall in gentle folds to the floor.

Smiling she turned seeing not one ounce of lace or fluff anywhere. It was perfect. Slipping on her shoes, she grinned. Flat shoes done over in the blue velvet. No heels, no corset. This was going to work out fine. Grabbing up the handbag she stuck her wrist through the loop and held her arm out to her side. The bag hung down but left her hands free to do whatever they needed. Smiling, she left the room. Now all she needed was her date. Moving down the stairs into the foyer her smile widened as both Arty and Dane whistled their appreciation.

"Captain, you are looking finer than land after a long voyage."

Jessica laughed. "Thank you, Arty. Is he coming home?" she asked, Dane. He had been following Morgan around for the last week. Dane had reported back telling her whatever she needed to know.

Dane nodded, then held up one finger.

"An hour," she said, frowning. "We'll be late but I guess that can't be helped. Melissa is going to have a fit."

Arty grinned. "That one needs a few fit's. She's strung tighter than rope."

Jessica smiled, crookedly "Don't I know it. I'll be in the drawing room. Send him in, when he gets home."

Dane nodded while Arty chirped his usual 'aye, aye, Captain.' Moving into the room, Jessica absorbed herself in a book about ships. It always helped to stay current on the latest ships.

Morgan stared at his wife with his mouth gaping. She looked so refined and elegant dressed in that deep blue. Thankful for once that her first mate had insisted that he change, he now felt equal to her. Moving into the room, he slowly closed the doors behind him. She looked so genteel reading that book that he realized as he watched her that during the week and a half he'd been gone, he'd missed her. She weaseled her way into his life and now he knew he couldn't live without her. Stunned at the realization he sighed, drawing her attention.

Jessica gave him a dazzling smile as she slowly got to her feet dropping the book in the chair as she walked toward him. "You're home," she said, stopping a couple of feet in front of him.

Morgan nodded, amazed at the gown she wore. It wasn't the least bit gaudy or frivolous. She'd done like he'd asked and compromised into wearing a fashionable dress suitable to them both.

"You look radiant," he said taking her hands and holding them out to the sides as he studied her. Jessica blushed, one of the few times she found herself truly doing that.

"Thank you, Malcolm," she said, slowly smiling as his gaze snapped to hers.

Morgan growled deep in his chest as he pulled her into a hug, tipping her face up to meld his lips with hers. Jessica felt her insides warm as Morgan kissed her. She didn't know how it happened but somewhere between wanting to smash his head in and sending his soul to the devil, she'd fallen in love with him. Sliding her hands up his chest she wrapped her arms around his neck, her hands going into his hair.

Morgan moved his hand to her buttocks pulling her up against his body. They clung to one another pausing only to catch their breath.

Pulling away slightly Morgan held her loosely. "Are you planning on going somewhere?" he asked, as he watched her fight to gain control of her passion.

Jessica felt like stripping off her carefully donned gown and begging him to take her right here and now but instead slowly licked her lips. "I was supposed to attend the Ashton's ball. Your Aunt insists."

Morgan frowned. "You were going alone?"

Jessica slowly smiled. "No." At Morgan's scowl, she laughed. "I was waiting for you," she said, losing her smile as he pulled her against him.

"You little vixen," he growled pulling her tighter as he kissed her further.

Jessica faintly acknowledged the fact that they weren't going to make the ball. They were too caught up in the magic Morgan worked on her before the hearth in the drawing room.

Chapter 94

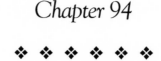

"WHAT IS SO DIRELY IMPORTANT that you send me such a message?" Nathan snapped seeing his father sitting there calmly sipping tea. He looked perfectly fine. "I thought you were dying."

"Everyone dies sometime, Nathan. My time isn't up yet."

Nathan's face darkened and he whirled on his feet and quit the study.

Brand glanced at Colan for a second then frowned when Nathan didn't return.

"Well, what did you expect? You did tell the boy you were near death. That it was with worry, didn't seem important to you. I'm surprised the lad didn't clobber you over the head."

Brand scowled. "I only wanted him to hurry. You know how slow he can be."

Nathan reentered the study followed by Hobkins who was aiming a gun at Nathan's belly.

Brand jumped to his feet. "Hobkins put that away."

"My lord?"

"I told you to keep him here, not put holes in him."

"Yes, my lord, but as he's bigger than I. I figured this would be the only thing that would work."

Nathan was scowling at the pair. "You realize the grave offense you are committing, Hobkins. I am an Earl, after all," he stated, resting the haughtiest glare he could muster on the man.

Hobkins swallowed, then calmly set the gun on the tray. "Only following orders, my lord."

Nathan turned to his father and shook his head. "Look what you made Hobkins do? He threatened a pier of the realm, for God's sake. Your little dramas have to cease," he finished in a shout. A brief look around the room proved not a drop of brandy in sight. "I'll consider forgiving your offense if you fetch me some brandy, Hobkins." Hobkins lifted his chin then slowly walked out of the room. "What happened to your man, Uncle? Did he finally turn into the wall?"

Colan scowled. "I sent him on vacation for causing stress to your father. Not a day went by that Brand didn't try to make the man crack. It was enough to make me daft."

Brand grinned, as Nathan lifted a brow at him. "All in a good fun. Hobkins is only here temporarily."

"And what, pray tell, am I here for?"

"You, my dear Earl, are here to deliver another package from your mother."

Nathan arched both brows at that. "Did Christopher finally wed then?"

"No, but he will."

"Shouldn't I wait until after he's married. At his rate, he'll wait until the last minute before he weds."

"That is another matter I wish you to handle. I'm ordering Christopher to wed now. Within the week."

Nathan scowled. "And I'm to deliver this news? And who might I say he's to wed?" he drawled accepting the brandy from a straight faced Hobkins. Moving to the window, he leaned against the edge, looking over Colan's gardens.

When no answer came, Nathan slowly turned around "Who?"

Brand lifted his chin. "Emily."

Nathan nearly dropped his drink. "Emily?" he said, turning fully to face his father. "Emily! You're insane. Christopher will never agree. She's too wild and impossible for his taste. And the boys they're...well...they're a couple of devils. There's no way Christopher will accept that."

Brand scowled. "I expected a different reaction from you, especially about those boys. I think they're fine young lads and with the right education and proper tootaliage they should grow into respectable men."

Nathan ran a hand through his hair. "I didn't mean to imply that the boys were rotten but they are special boys and Christopher will ruin them. You can't possible be thinking that is a good match."

Brand lifted his chin. "I want those boys to remain here with us. If they aren't to be yours, then I plan to keep them and that means Christopher has to marry their mother. She seems a fine lady."

Nathan frowned, realizing his father was attached to the boys and was grasping at straws to keep them. "Then you've already heard that she was planning to go live with a cousin in Scotland."

"I heard. The cousin will no doubt marry her off to one of those barbarians and those boys will be ruined."

Nathan scowled, having thought of the same thing himself. "I don't think Christopher is the answer. Perhaps we could locate some other suitable husband for her. That will keep the three of them safely in England

and we'll be able to visit anytime."

Brand set his jaw. "Christopher will marry her and that's the end of it," he said turning away.

Nathan saw the stern shake of Colan's head and sighed. Once the mother hen got his feathers up, there was no arguing with his father. Colan would only halt the conversation leaving them in the same situation they were before. "Fine. I'll head back in a day or so."

"You'll leave first thing in the morning." Brand said glaring at him.

"Now, see here. I'm an Earl. I won't be ordered around like some errand boy. If you want the news there any sooner then send Hobkins. Lord knows the man can handle the order. A pistol to Christopher's head is probably to what I'll have to resort."

Brand slowly got to his feet and moved to stand in front of Nathan. "You are first and foremost my son and I'm asking you to take this message to your brother. I can't do it myself. I don't want to hear another word about it," he finished shouting.

Nathan frowned at his father's back and then bowed his head. "Very well, but this is the last time. I don't want to do this errand boy thing anymore."

Brand slowly turned to look at Nathan a small smile playing around his lips. "Stephan is still unwed, I cann't make any promises."

Nathan slowly smiled in answer. "Actually," he said sipping his brandy. "This could prove to be quite entertaining if I play my cards right. I do love to make Christopher squirm now and again."

Brand smiled. "This is why I asked for you."

Nathan frowned. "Why not have Jonathan handle this. He's more apt at this kind of thing. Especially where Christopher is concerned. I think you'd get better results."

Brand waved a hand at him. "You'll do fine. Besides, Jonathan is too preoccupied with becoming a father. He's hovering over his wife like she were made of glass."

Nathan's glass stopped half way to his lips. "A father?"

Brand turned and looked at him. "You didn't know?"

"Bloody hell. No one tells me a damn thing," he cursed, moving to fling himself into a chair. "So Ashley is pregnant?"

"Melissa, too."

"Melissa too!" he whined, looking like Brand had kicked him in the stomach. "I hate this family. I'm good enough to send off as a common lackey but when it comes to good news, let's not tell the errand boy," he finished, tipping the brandy to drain the glass.

Colan laughed at the sarcastic tone. "Well, just think. You get to know first, that Christopher is going to wed."

Nathan scowled. "Whoppie. I'll get my head shot off for delivering that information."

Brand and Colan laughed, both knowing full well Nathan would handle the situation just fine.

"ONE MORE DAY. Is everything ready?" she asked laying her head on his chest. His strong arms holding her tight.

"Everything is fine. I'll be around to get you at two." Royce said, kissing her hair.

Allison frowned. "No, I'll meet you here. I don't want to risk Christopher seeing you."

Royce scowled into the darkness. "I don't care if he sees me. We're going to be man and wife, for gods sake. I'll have to see him sometime."

Allison pulled her head away. "I know that, but once we're wed there's nothing he can do. Please. It's such a silly thing. I'll wait right here for you and you can take me out the way you come in." Royce frowned. "I climb over the wall."

Allison blushed. "Oh. Well, I'm sure I'll manage."

Royce shook his head. "Absolutely not. I won't have you break your neck just to avoid your brother."

"I shouldn't think I'd break my neck. You're there to help me. Two o'clock will be fine," she said, trying to change the subject.

Royce frowned but as her hands moved up to wiggle through his hair, he felt himself weakening. Like she said, with him there to help her, what could go wrong? Taking her chin in his hand, he brought her lips to his and kissed her, thankful he didn't have to wait much longer to make her his.

Chapter 95

AS THE CARRIAGE ROLLED ALONG at a slow clip, one of it's occupants sat nervously within. Cari peeked at Christopher who was deep in thought watching whatever was passing by the window. Just do it, you idiot, she thought, shifting on the seat. Just move next to him and kiss him. It's as simple as that. What's the worst he could do? Drop you at your door and never see you again.

Scowling, she took a deep breath and slowly let it out. Tonight she hadn't worn her corset knowing she wanted the least amount of clothes between them as possible. As the carriage hit a nasty rut in the road she took advantage of it and threw herself into Christopher.

"Ho! Steady there. Are you all right?" he asked, looking down into Cari's upturned face as she knelt between his legs. Her upper body was resting on his thighs while her arms clutched his chest.

Blushing, she stared up at him thinking of the things she dreamed about at night and wondered how she was ever going to get those thoughts into action.

Christopher stared at her for several seconds feeling desire so strong he couldn't resist lowering his head and kissing her. It was gentle at first but at her eager response, he found himself pulling her up for a deeper kiss. The motion of the carriage was soon forgotten as the pair lost themselves in the kiss. Feeling his lips ravaging her mouth, Cari gave herself up to her feelings and moved further against his body. Feeling him pulling away she panicked, shoving her hands inside his coat. She ran her hands slowly up his ribs while she allowed a small whimper to escape her lips.

Christopher felt desire so strong his sanity fled. He wanted this girl more than anything he'd ever wanted and he was willing to throw his principles out the window. Pulling away from her he quickly set her on the seat opposite him, while he pulled his coat back into place.

Cari frowned at the man across from her. As she watched him button his shirt where she'd undone them. She left her gown where it was. It had slipped showing her breasts almost to the dark circles. Shifting, she pulled the hem of her gown up to straighten her stockings.

"What are you doing?" Christopher said, wanting to turn his head from the sight of her lovely legs but failing miserably.

Cari saw the desire and pulled the gown to the middle of her thighs. "I have a stocking that's slipped," she said, placing her foot on the opposite seat. Her gown fell in enticing folds around her leg, making Cari smile..

Christopher, realizing his mouth was hanging open, snapped it shut before reaching over to yank the gown back into place. Grabbing his walking stick, he pounded twice on the ceiling and abruptly the carriage picked up speed.

Cari clenched her teeth at the whole evening. Every attempt she had made on his person was interrupted or ruined by one catastrophe after another. She was riding with the most honorable gentleman in London. Christopher had shown her the most response yet in that last kiss but even then, he wasn't about to be dishonorable. Feeling deflated Cari adjusted her clothes back into place. At least she was thankful for the absent corset. The feel of Christopher's chest had felt heavenly.

Christopher watched Cari from his shadowed position and cursed their slow progress. His curse quickly changed into a prayer that Cari wouldn't try to entice him again with those silky white legs of hers. He was a man after all and his will was crumbling fast. Wiping a hand across his brow he licked his lips. The kiss kept repeating over and over in his mind.

Cari arched a brow in his direction when he shifted on the seat for the third time. He was as affected as she was, she thought smiling. Humming, she began to formulate a plan. Her plan dissolved instantly as the coach drew to a halt in front of her brother's home. Cursing the world in general, she sighed. She should have known his will was going to be as strong as stone.

Christopher bolted out of the carriage, taking a couple of deep breaths before turning to help her out. Cari narrowed her eyes slightly then purposely leaned against him. Her chest rubbed along his arm producing a hiss of indrawn air from Christopher. He felt like he was being scorched alive every time she touched him. Hurrying her up the steps, he meant to give her a small kiss and depart but she didn't stop as the door opened, but marched into the house and on into the drawing room.

Hesitating, he eyed the butler. Seeing no help there, he pursed his lips and marched after her. He couldn't just leave without saying anything. Entering the drawing room, he frowned at what appeared to be an empty room. Moving further into the room, he circled the settee and looked at a puddle of silk that could only be Cari's gown. Whirling to escape the trap, he halted as the girl in question stood with her back to the now closed doors dressed in little more than stockings, crinolines, and camisole. Her glorious hair moved about her waist in waves of ebony curls. She was by far the most stunning woman he'd ever seen.

Swallowing, he backed up a step. Cari moved away from the door, casually dropping the key into a vase as she walked toward where he stood. Christopher felt suffocated and quickly loosened his cravat only to blush at her arched brow and slow smile. Backing up again, she still moved forward. Christopher frowned. This was getting out of hand.

"Cari, this isn't funny," he said, sounding very much like a frightened boy. Blushing further, he frowned as she moved toward him. Her hips swayed and she had a look of longing on her face. His pulse quickened. He backed up bumping into a chair where he sank into the soft cushion only to spring back to his feet as she quickened her pace. Moving around the settee he gave the vase a quick look before returning his attention to Cari. If she touched him, he was lost.

"Miss St. Paul. This is improper. I must insist that you put your gown back on."

Cari just smiled steadily moving closer. Christopher froze at the sight of her dropping a mass of crinolines on the floor. His mouth fell open at the sight of her thighs encased in stockings held to her waist by blue silk ribbons.

Cari, knowing exactly what she was doing, took advantage of his shocked composure to move to stand before him. Lifting her hands, she placed them on his chest and made quick work of his coat to place her hands against his ribs and run them along his chest.

His hands of their own violation, moved to slide up her arms. He intended to push her away but his body had a mind of it's own and he found himself kissing this desirable young lady like there was no tomorrow.

Cari wanted to cheer her triumph but at the moment she was so caught up in the feelings they were creating she quickly lost all thought on gloating. She quickly undid the buttons on his shirt and soon reveled in the feel of his chest as her fingers roamed the entire expanse.

Christopher pulled back to stare down at her passion aroused face and hoped anger would stop him from going any further. Dropping his head, claiming another kiss, he scooped her up in his arms and carried her before the hearth. Dropping her legs he let her slowly slide down his body as he deepened the kiss bringing his tongue into play.

Several things ran through his mind, the first being, she was no virgin and the second, being he didn't have to marry the chit in the morning. As her soft little hands pushed his shirt off his shoulders and found their way to his waist his final thought fled in an instant. If she didn't care that they were in her brother's home then neither would he.

Cari smiled as Christopher kissed her neck and shoulders. Her crow of delight turned into a groan of pleasure as he untied her camisole to take one breast in his hand while the other was thoroughly kissed and suckled. Christopher, now fully aroused made short work of their remaining clothing and quickly lowered her to the soft Persian rug. Pulling her beneath him, he suckled her breasts further before pulling away to stare at the perfect body lying before him.

Cari blushed at his perusal but quickly lost any trace of shyness as she felt his hands along her body were no man had touched her before. Feeling things she'd only heard others speak of, she moaned as his mouth began his magic taking each breast to lavish with such care that she was weak with need. Pulling back he smiled down at her, further melting her heart.

"You're perfect," he said, before claiming her mouth again. "I am sorry I took so long to comply with your wishes," he murmured, raining kisses along her jaw and neck.

Cari didn't want to talk, she wanted whatever came next. Her body was on fire and felt as though she was stuck at the top of a hill and couldn't figure out how to get to the bottom.

Christopher, sensing her need had risen, felt his own desire heighten and found himself acting the young fool. Pulling her fully beneath him he nudged her legs apart as she arched her chest against his. Lifting his body, he kissed her mouth with all the passion he was holding back as his body slowly entered her. Feeling the tight passage expand and encase him was something he couldn't describe. His body was on fire for fulfillment but he knew she needed to be satisfied first. Pushing into her with one quick thrust he stiffened feeling the barrier he'd ripped through causing him to rear up in shock.

"My god! You're a virgin!" he said, seeing her flush with anger and pain and still unsated passion.

"Is this it?" she asked, looking disappointed.

Christopher frowned at her, then paled, as she moved causing him to slide deeper. Sweat broke out on his forehead as he told his body to pull out and get the hell out of there, but feeling her flesh tighten around his shaft he knew he wasn't going anywhere. Slowly smiling down at her, he shook his head. "This is far from it," he said pulling out and slowly sliding back in. Seeing her eyes widen and a flush cover her face he lowered his head to kiss her while starting up a rhythm she naturally followed.

Christopher felt even more desire at her natural response barely holding out long enough for her body to constrict with her release before pumping into her and satisfying his own.

Chapter 96

STEPHAN MADE HIS WAY DRUNKENLY toward his room, trying hard to remain quiet but the hall was to narrow and he couldn't seem to keep from pumping into the walls. Chuckling to himself he paused to look back at the stairs and tried to count the doors. Suddenly, the door behind him opened, and Emily or Rae stepped out as he turned. Leaning his left hand against the wall, he teetered a bit narrowing his eyes at her.

"I thought Nathan put tags on you two?" he asked wiping his hair out of his eyes.

Emily giggled, pulling the door closed behind herself so Stephan wouldn't wake the boys.

"Nathan can order Rae to do what he likes, but I'm not his wife."

Stephan grinned. "Thank god for that," he said, then scowled at having said that. "If you would be so kind as to point out which door is mine, I'll just be on my way," he said, still holding himself up with his left hand.

Emily smiled. "I should think you'd know that better than I."

Stephan smiled lopsidedly, causing Emily to suck in her breath at the striking figure he made. His hair was mussed but his body was dressed casually. Blushing some at the long vee of chest she could see where his shirt opened, Emily moved to pass him. "This one's yours," she said, stopping by his door.

Stephan pushed away from the wall then crept slowly toward her and his door. "Thank you," he said, pulling her to him for a kiss that curled her toes. How long it lasted she couldn't say but the feel of his arms around her waist sent shivers of passion coursing through her body.

Pulling away, Stephan smiled at her. "You're so beautiful," he said, slurring those words before opening his door and closing it in her face.

Arching her brows at the whole scene, she turned to check both directions before her hand lightly touched her mouth. A kiss like that made her feel like a virgin again. Shaking her head, she slipped into her room frowning at finding the door open slightly. Dismissing it as not having closed it fully she knew her mind wasn't going to be on sleeping, but on those feelings the handsome man down the hall had started.

Chapter 97

NATHAN TROMPED INTO THE HOUSE, clutching the package for Christopher under his arm. He shoved his things into Carson's hands and moved toward the study. "Is my brother in?"

Carson shook his head. "He left early this morning. He didn't say when he'd return."

Nathan arched a brow. Christopher never left without telling someone exactly what he was doing. Shaking his head, he climbed the stairs instead. Rae would be happy to see him, anyway. He needed a few hours of rest and wifely administrations before he faced his brother, anyway. Climbing the steps he paused, watching his wife or her sister coming his way. He wiped his face clean of all emotion.

Emily burst out laughing as Nathan practically pushed himself into the wall to avoid her. "It's all right, my lord. I was just heading down to break my fast. Rae is still in bed, I believe."

Nathan gave her a stunning smile reminding her remarkably of Stephan's, "Thank you. I shall try not to wake her," he said moving past her.

Emily smiled feeling herself blush, knowing he wasn't going to let Rae sleep at all. A night away from a spouse was tough especially in the beginning of a marriage. "That is very thoughtful of you," she added disappearing down the steps.

Nathan watched her go, marveling at how similar the two of them were. In body they were exact copies but everything else was like night and day. Rae had a light musical voice while Emily's was deep and husky. Rae was strong and competent while Emily was sturdy and efficient. The two were rather scary to watch, like looking in a mirror. Shaking his head he slowly turned the knob on his door peeking into the room to find that his wife was indeed in bed. Slipping into the room he inched his way toward the bed dropping articles of clothing along the way. One whole day was way too long to be away from her luscious body and he was more than willing to make it up to her. Crawling into bed he did just that.

Chapter 98

"ROYCE?" Allison called, wondering where he was. She had been standing out in the garden for fifteen minutes.

Nero growled his complaint at her nervous pacing wanting her to settle down so he could nibble his wood.

"Do you see him, Nero?" she asked, hating not being able to see at times like this.

Royce smiled at the cat who wasn't saying a word but was staring at him with those big yellow eyes. Moving closer to his future bride, he blew in her ear making sure he didn't touch her.

Allison reached a hand in the direction of the wind then frowned when she didn't encounter anything. "I don't really want to marry him, anyway," she said sinking down on the bench. "You know, Nero. There are several men who want me for wife. I know for a fact that they would be on time." Royce arched a brow at her. "They'd be early I'm sure and bring me a nice gift before my wedding. Like a bouquet of flowers or diamond earrings," she said, running a hand through her hair absently. "And I'm sure they'd have nice muscular bodies, making my lord Royce's look puny and saggy."

Royce scowled at that remark, getting a soft rumble from Nero who was now contentedly chewing his log. Moving to stand behind her he moved the rose under her nose then quickly jerked it away when she moved her hand to catch it.

"I'm sure they wouldn't stand around teasing their future bride, either," she said smiling, when she heard him behind her. "Course they wouldn't be as handsome and as funny as my lord Royce."

Royce smiled at her "I see they were smart enough to stay away from you. I, on the other hand, am standing here risking my neck to marry you."

Allison got to her feet with a grin. "And loving every minute. What took you so long?"

Royce arched a brow. "I'm sorry, love. I think your little clock is off. It's not even two yet."

Allison giggled. "I know. I'm anxious. Let's get going."

Royce smiled taking her in his arms. "You're sure you want to do this? There's still time to back out."

"No. I'm sure. I want to marry you more than anything else in the world. I love you with all my heart and soul."

Royce smiled tenderly, never imagining himself receiving either one. "I love you, too."

Allison smiled, reaching up to kiss him. "Then let's go. I want to announce to the world that you are mine."

Royce, who was shocked she loved him, grinned. "All right. We shouldn't wait another minute."

Moving to the gate, he pulled her through it to emerge just south of his carriage.

"I thought you said you climbed the wall?" she asked, knowing they were no longer in the garden.

Royce just chuckled as he pulled her along the street. "To the church, Emerson. Make it quick," he added knowing his driver liked to dawdle. Lifting Allison into the waiting carriage he climbed in after her.

"It smells like roses in here," she said, sniffing.

Royce smiled. "That might be because I've brought along a few," he said handing her a bouquet of twenty deep red roses tied in the center with a blue ribbon.

Allison smiled as her fingers touched the soft stems and petals. "Thank you, Royce. They're lovely," she said, lifting them to her nose to smell.

Royce stared at her, feeling truly lucky to have found a woman such as she. How long they sat, her holding the flowers, him holding her hand, he didn't know but soon they came to a halt in front of the church. "We're here," he said taking her chin and kissing her.

Allison smiled, as he pulled away. "Thank god. It seemed to take forever," she said excitement making her giddy.

Royce climbed out and helped her down. "Wait here, Emerson. We'll be back shortly," he said, tucking Allison's arm around his as she clutched the roses in her other arm. "I hope you like the church."

"Which one are we at?" she asked, knowing there were only three in the area.

"St. Augustines."

"Oh, Royce. This is were my father and mother got married," she said excited he had chosen the oldest one out of the lot. "Are the gardens still surrounding it?"

Royce smiled. "That's the reason I choose this one," he said watching her with pleasure. "I take it you are familiar with it then?"

"Oh yes. Melissa and I used to come here every now and then when we were small with Aunt Ginger but I haven't been here in almost ten years," she said. "I'm so glad you choose this church," she whispered. "It makes me feel my mother is here watching."

Royce smiled down at her tenderly. "I'm happy too," he said lifting his head as the priest came toward them. "Father Holmes?"

"Yes, child. I see you've brought the lovely bride with you. Shall we begin."

"By all means," Royce said, pulling Allison along with him as Nero padded down the outer isle of the church. Frowning, he wondered how the cat had come to be there. "Allison, Nero is here."

"I know," she said smiling. "Is that going to be a problem?"

"Not for me but I think Father Holmes may have something to say about it."

Father Holmes was staring at the beast stiff with fear.

Allison frowned. "Nero, sit down," she snapped, knowing the cat was probably enjoying Father Holmes's fear. Nero swung his large head in her direction then climbed up on the pew and stretched out to his fullest. "It's all right, Father. He won't hurt anything," she said, yanking Royce's arm to get him to take charge.

"Come on, then. Let's get on with the wedding," he said, taking the priest's arm to lead him to the front of the church. Father Holmes, after a quick look over his shoulder, cleared his throat.

"Yes, well. Have you the license, son?"

"Of course," Royce said, handing the documents to the man. Father Holmes looked them over before moving to climb the two steps onto the dais. He moved to a small pulpit where he picked up a bible. Turning back to them he began the ceremony.

"IT'S SETTLED and you have no further say in the matter except the required 'I do'" Christopher said as the carriage rumbled along toward the little church.

Cari smiled slightly. "You're making an honest woman of me then?"

Christopher pursed his lips. "The least you could do is seem a bit ashamed of yourself. You acted the perfect little wanton."

Cari smiled crookedly as she ran a hand along his arm her breast touching it by the elbow. Christopher felt his desire heighten though he was well aware of every part of her. "I think you better behave yourself for the next few hours until we are man and wife," he said putting her hands in her lap and crossing his own over his chest.

Cari frowned at him a moment. Was he really this serious all the time?

Christopher peeked at her briefly smug with her reaction to his set down. The truth was the woman was all fire and passion making him walk around in an aroused state since he'd taken her several times before the hearth. Shifting on the seat he frowned feeling her gaze snap to rest on him.

"This coach is no place for trysting so get that thought out of your mind," he snapped looking out the window to keep from laughing. If he so much as gave her a hint of the desire he was feeling she would be crawling all over him.

Cari narrowed her eyes at him. Was he serious? Seeing him shift again she slowly smiled. He was as aroused as she was, she was sure. Shifting slightly she moved her thigh next to his brushing it against his. His leg snapped away from hers as if it'd been burnt. Smiling slightly she turned further toward the window so he couldn't see her face. As the carriage moved along the road she moved against him every opportunity she got muttering a 'sorry' each time.

Christopher was ready to toss her skirts up any second now. His heart was pounding, sweat broke out on his brow, he even had casually moved his hand between his legs to shift the stiff occupant to relieve the pressure. He couldn't believe his reaction to the fiery little chit next to him. He wasn't even a tad bit angry with her for forcing him to take her in her brother's home. He'd just gotten up early and headed straight to obtain a special license then hurried to collect his bride. Now he sat, stiff as a poker, barely able to keep from disgracing himself while the little wanton next to him kept playing with fire.

The carriage finally rolled to a halt getting a sigh from Christopher. Cari, taking full advantage of his discomfort, waited until he disembarked before moving to the door, tipping forward just enough to expose her chest. Hearing his breath hiss between his teeth she purposely fell out the door her body sliding along his.

Christopher scowled at her. "You have no shame," he snapped pulling her along behind him up the steps and into the little church.

"...TO HONOR OBEY TILL DEATH DO YOU PART?" Father Holmes asked, pausing as a commotion at the back of the church drew his attention.

"I do," Allison said, ignoring the noise behind her.

Christopher stared at the couple in the front of the church for two seconds before realizing who they were. "Oh, my god. Allison Marie Hayworth, just what the hell are you doing?" he bellowed, stalking down the isle toward her.

Allison stiffened, hearing Christopher's voice and clutched Royce's arm as he tried to turn to confront him. "Nero, get him," she said, over her shoulder. Returning her attention to the priest, she smiled. "Please, continue, I do," she said again.

Father Holmes stared at the beautiful lady before him and then frowned as the large tiger climbed into the isle before Lord Christopher. Christopher seeing Nero, paused to push Cari into a pew.

"Allison!" he said frowning, as Nero crouched as if he meant to pounce. Moving backwards, he scooted around the back pew and headed up the outer isle while Nero moved down Cari's row brushing her legs as he went. "Call him off, damn it."

"My lord, I must ask you to control you tongue while in God's house. It is most unseemly," Father Holmes said forgetting he was in the middle of a ceremony.

Clutching Royce's arm to keep him beside her, Allison practically shouted for the Father to continue. "He's just angry we didn't invite him to the wedding. Now, please continue."

Father Holmes looked at the lord who was climbing over the pews to get away from the large Tiger that was stalking him. "I think maybe..."

"Do like the lady asks. Finish the ceremony, please," Royce said, pulling Allison closer.

Christopher, having reached the second row from the front, dropped to the floor. He crawled into the isle, and hurried forward only to have Nero pounce on his back with a whoosh of air.

Cari, having been stifling her laughter at the antics of the cat, saw that the man she loved was lying flat on his stomach while a three hundred pound cat sat on his back. "Lady Allison? I believe Nero is killing your brother," she shouted to be heard over the growling Nero was doing.

Allison turned toward the feminine voice behind her. "Lady St. Paul?"

Cari walked to the front of the church pausing beside Christopher as Nero swung his head to block her from passing. "Yes, it's me."

"What are you doing here?"

"Christopher and I are doing the same thing you are doing."

"You're getting married?" she said, shocked. "But I didn't even know you were seeing one another. Especially on such a serious note."

Father Holmes, always attentive to people's affairs, frowned at the scene before him. "Should I continue this ceremony?"

"No, she isn't marrying that bastard," came Christopher's muffled voice.

"Christopher, Father Holmes asked you not to swear," Allison said, toward the floor. "Nero move and let him breath," she said, returning her attention to Cari. "I'm sorry to say it but I'm shocked."

"I'm sure most people will be but it's best that we marry, I could be carrying his child."

Allison sucked in her breath, hearing Christopher curse from the floor. Royce for once was laughing. "Really Royce. That isn't a laughing matter."

"Why not? He plans to marry her." Royce said, still laughing.

"He shouldn't have taken liberties with her before they were wed. Really Christopher. I'm shocked."

Christopher, shocked at Cari blurting out their private business, cursed. "Just get this cat off me," he snapped.

"Nero, back on the bench," she said, hearing Christopher groan as Nero crawled off him and up on the pew. "Well?"

Christopher slowly got to his feet, giving Cari a glare that silenced anything she might have been about to say. "What is important here, young lady, is that you were told not to see this man. But here you are marrying him. Care to explain?"

"I'm a grown woman, Christopher. I don't answer to you. Besides, we're practically married already. It's too late."

Christopher looked at Father Holmes for confirmation.

"She has consented but I haven't, as yet, asked his lordship."

Royce arched a brow at Christopher. "Well?" Christopher demanded.

"I love her and have every intention of marrying her."

Christopher's face flushed with anger. "I forbid this marriage," he snapped, seeing Father Holmes shift.

Cari frowned at the scene Christopher was causing. "Then I refuse to marry someone so selfish," Cari snapped spinning on her heels.

Christopher grabbed her arm before she'd taken more than two steps. "You will stand here until I'm finished with Allison, then we'll marry."

"No."

"No?" he bellowed. "You will marry me and that's the end of it. The child you so casually mentioned, could be a real possibility. Father Holmes won't let you walk out of here without matrimony."

Cari, aware of the devastated look on Allison's face, straightened to her full height. "Christopher? Have you ever thought that maybe your sister might find herself in the same position I do."

Christopher flushed at that then glared at Royce. "Does she?"

Allison having had enough, stepped forward and punched Christopher in the stomach. As the breath whooshed from his lungs, she stomped her foot. "I can't believe you, Christopher. I had to sneak out of Aunt Ginger's to marry the man I love. Father is again going to miss seeing one of his daughters get married and you stand here accusing us of behaving improperly when you yourself have done just that. Royce and I love each other and I want to get married. If you can give me a good reason why we shouldn't marry, then I won't," she said crossing her arms.

Christopher, slowly getting his breath back, stared at his sister in amazement. She had actually stood up for herself. Straightening his coat and cravat he glanced at Royce before looking at his sister again. "I'll give you a reason. The man you're trying to marry is a woman snatcher."

Allison arched her brows. Turning to Royce she frowned. "Do you have women hid in your dungeon?"

Royce grinned, "Not a one."

Christopher turned scarlet as Allison turned back to him. "Sorry, Christopher. I believe him."

Christopher was furious. "You can't marry him."

"The reason?"

Christopher frowned. He really didn't have a reason other than what had happened all those years ago. "I've had bad dealings with him."

Allison frowned. "Such as?"

"He was to marry the woman that I was."

Allison again turned to Royce. "Did you marry someone else?"

"No, she married someone else. He was younger and richer and whole," Royce said faintly.

Allison's face softened at the last statement. Reaching a hand out to touch his scarred face she smiled, "She was a fool."

Royce, overcome with emotion, took her hands in his. "I will never understand how an angel like yourself could settle for someone such as me."

Allison smiled. "I'm the one that's lucky," she said, dropping her hands and turning back to Christopher. "Care to try again?"

Christopher stared at the couple before him and all the reason's of the past seemed not to matter. What he witnessed between them was love. Feeling Cari rub against his arm he understood love perfectly. "No," he said taking her hands. "Forgive me. I've acted like a fool," he said looking at Royce. "You're right."

Allison arched a brow. "I'm right? Exactly what about? Do you plan to let me marry Royce?"

Christopher stared at Royce then looked back at Allison. "It isn't up to me. I won't interfere again. Father," he said, stepping back pulling Cari with him.

Royce looked at Christopher then took Allison's hands. "Do you wish to continue?"

Allison confused at Christopher's complete turn about, nodded, "More than anything."

Royce slowly grinned. "Then Father, please continue."

Father Holmes smiled, and clearing his throat, he proceeded to marry the two happy couples.

STEPHAN WALKED into the drawing room pausing long enough to pour himself a drink. His head was pounding from the drink the night before and he prayed the brandy would soothe his hangover. Clutching the drink in his hand he moved toward the hearth only to draw up short seeing Cari standing there.

"Oh, I'm sorry. I didn't realize anyone was in here," he said looking around for one of his family members. "Can I get you something to drink?"

Cari smiled sensually at Stephan. "I think a drink isn't exactly what I'm looking for," she said, sauntering toward him.

Stephan felt the hairs on his neck prickle. Swallowing he looked toward the door. "Perhaps I should get a servant in here. You..."

Cari pulled the ribbon from her hair, shaking the mass of ebony curls loose to swing around her waist. "I think a big handsome man like yourself can find something to make me happy."

Stephan arched a brow at her, feeling his nerves flutter. "Ah. I thought you were here to see Christopher?"

"I am, but he's not half as handsome as you are and those broad shoulders," she said, reaching out to run a hand along his arm.

Stephan jumped back as if he'd been burned. "I...er...I will go get Christopher for you. I'm sure he'll be happy to see you."

Cari smiled wantonly, backing Stephan up against the table holding the brandy.

Christopher, having seen enough, burst into the room. "What the hell is going on?" he snapped, seeing Cari leaning toward Stephan. Barely able to contain his laughter, Christopher watched Stephan try to get away from his wife without touching her. Cari was doing a fine job, to good a job, he thought scowling.

Stephan, seeing Christopher, felt relief. "Christopher, I'm glad to see you. Miss St. Paul here..."

"Hayworth. Cari is my wife." Christopher snapped, seeing Stephan's mouth drop open. "Were you kissing my wife? Wasn't Nathan's wife enough?"

Stephan mouth moved open and shut several times before he finally spoke. "Your wife?" he said, staring at her in shock. She had been trying to seduce him while she was married to Christopher.

Christopher barely controlling his laughter went for the kill. Marching to the hearth he reached above the mantel and pulled one of the swords free of it's holdings. Turning to face Stephan, he made his face as fierce as possible. "I'll kill you for this. I will not tolerate you messing with my wife," he said, swinging the sword back and forth a few times.

Stephan stared at Christopher as if he'd gone insane. "I didn't kiss her, I swear. She was...was..." Clamping his mouth shut, he refused to say she was throwing herself at him.

"She was what? Throwing herself at you?" Christopher laughed nastily. "You don't expect me to believe that. When you have kissed Nathan's wife with me as witness. Get that sword or I'll slit you in half without it.

Stephan didn't even glance at the sword, he turned his gaze to Cari. "Tell him," he said.

Cari sniffed, wiping at a fake tear. "He tried to seduce me. He...he loosed my hair then tried to kiss me," she finished sniffing as she covered her face with her hands.

Stephan's mouth dropped open at that nonsense, barely managing to push a chair between himself and Christopher. "She's lying," he shouted, ducking as the sword swung over his head.

Cari, peeking through her fingers, watched her husband's superb body move as he swung the sword.

"She threw herself at me, I swear," Stephan said, dodging to his left as Christopher sliced a pillow sending feathers into the room. Cari sniffed again to keep herself from laughing.

"Cari is innocent. She wouldn't know the first thing about seduction," Christopher said, swinging his sword to keep from laughing at that outrageous statement. Cari was far to naturally wanton to be innocent.

Cari seeing Stephan's face pale as he again dodged Christopher's sword couldn't contain her laughter any further. She laughed so hard she slowly sank into the chair next to her. Her laughter filling the room.

Stephan glanced at her a second, though his concentration was on Christopher as he crouched before him ready to dodge Christopher's next blow.

Christopher hearing Cari laugh, slowly began to smile.

Stephan stared at the pair as if they'd grown two heads. When Christopher started laughing, that deep belly laugh, Stephan knew he'd been had. Lifting his chin, he walked around Christopher's laughing form and left the room with as much dignity as he could muster.

Christopher laughed even harder seeing him go.

Cari, getting her laughter under control, stood and moved to Christopher's side. "He'll probably never forgive us," she said, sinking down against his chest.

Christopher sobered some, feeling her luscious form against his own. "He deserves it. I can't believe he formulated a plan to have you ruin my life."

Cari smiled. "You should have thanked him instead of teasing him this way," she said running her hand along his jaw.

Christopher paused in thought. "Ah, perhaps you're right. Stephan did open my eyes to something I probably never would have noticed."

Cari fast losing herself to desire, got to her feet. "Maybe we should apologize to Stephan."

Christopher also climbed to his feet, lifting her against his body. "So you like his body better than mine, huh?"

Cari slowly smiled. "I would have to see yours again to be sure," she said huskily.

Christopher growled letting the sword drop to the floor before he pulled her close for a kiss.

Stephan marched back in on this scene. "Just what the hell was that little drama for?" he bellowed. His hangover making his temper soar.

Christopher slowly lifted his head from Cari's lips to glare at Stephan. "Next time, I'd think twice before messing in my life."

Stephan understood then. Cari had told him about their plan. Turning on his heels he decided he'd gotten off light. Christopher could have done worse.

NATHAN HEARING THE SHOUTING moved toward the study only to run smack into Stephan. "What's going on?"

"Nothing," Stephan snapped, marching around him and out the front door. Slamming it in his wake.

Nathan arched a brow. Someone had gotten under his skin. Still staring at the door he arched a brow as Jessica marched in with Sean in tow.

Seeing Nathan standing there, she marched to stand before him. "I need your help."

Nathan arched a brow. "You need my help?"

"Yes. Sean, tell Nathan what you saw," Sean not liking the tone of Jessica's voice, hid his face in her gown.

Nathan frowned at her. "Do you have to yell at him. I'm standing right here," he said, looking again at Sean. "Come on, Sean. Maybe a little food will help.

Jessica bit her lip to keep from shaking the child but seeing that Sean was willing to go with Nathan for the food, she released his hand and followed along.

As they sat there, each with a plate piled high with food Nathan finally got back to the subject. "All right, Sean. Let's here it."

Sean, knowing he was in trouble for snooping set his fork down.

"Come on. Out with it."

Sean lowered his head. "Last night, I saw Uncle Stephan kiss Mama."

Nathan felt his insides knot then relaxed knowing it was Emily he'd kissed not Rae. Emily! Well, good lord. That was a problem. She was supposed to marry Christopher. "He kissed her on the forehead?" he asked, hoping that was right.

"No, you idiot. On the lips and she went to his room," Jessica said, stuffing another mouthful of ham in her mouth.

Nathan paled. "This isn't good."

Sean began to fidget.

Seeing the boy was nervous, Nathan nodded to Menson. "Come, Sean. Go with Menson here and finish your food in the kitchen, huh."

Thankful to get away so easily, he smiled grabbing up his plate. Menson quickly took it from the boy as the pair left the room.

"So you see the problem. Stephan is messing with Rae's sister. Father is going to die when he hears about this."

Nathan arched a brow. "That isn't the half of it. Father sent me here to make sure Christopher married Emily."

"Christopher and Emily?" she said in shock. "My god. This is going to cause definite problems."

Nathan scowled at the possibility, then frowned. "Hell, what a mess. How come I am always involved in these things?"

Jessica got to her feet. Her gown moving about her gracefully. "I think I'm leaving this one to somebody else. Where's Allison?"

Nathan, ready to tell Jessica she was doing no such thing, was interrupted as Christopher and Cari entered the room. Seeing them smiling and happy, made him scowl.

Christopher, seeing the fierce look, laughed. "What's the scowl for Nathan?"

Nathan flushed. "I can see myself sinking into a hole and haven't the slightest idea how to get out," he muttered, dropping his head in his hands.

Jessica scowled as well. Cari was snuggled up close to Christopher's side.

"I thought you and Morgan were sailing today?"

Jessica's scowl darkened. "He saw to it that I wouldn't be setting foot on any ship for a while," she snapped, snatching a piece of bread off her plate.

"Oh, and how did he manage that?"

"By getting me pregnant, that's how. I can't even step foot on a ship without heaving my guts out," she snapped, eating the bread.

Christopher stared at her in shock, while Nathan slowly lifted his head. "You're going to be a mother?" At her narrowed look, he burst out laughing. "Unbelievable. That makes three of you," he said, still laughing.

"Three of us?" she snapped. When he didn't answer, she threw the remaining chunk of bread at his head. "Who else?"

"Melissa and Ashley," he said tossing the bread on the table. "Father told me," he said, losing his smile as Christopher seated Cari at the table and whispered something in her ear that made her turn scarlet.

Jessica, surprised at hearing about the other women being pregnant, curled her lip at Christopher. "Why is she blushing?" she snapped, grabbing up some cheese.

"Didn't I mention it?" he said, setting a plate of food before Cari. "I married Cari yesterday."

Jessica's mouth fell open as Nathan threw his hands in the air. "Doesn't anyone in this family tell anybody anything," he snapped, leaning his head back on the chair. "Now what the hell am I supposed to do?"

Regaining her composure, Jessica smiled. "I must say, I'm surprised Christopher. You still have nearly four months left."

Christopher reddened as Cari turned on him. "Yes, well. I couldn't see waiting."

Cari snorted at that, drawing both Nathan and Jessica's attention. "That's putting it mildly."

"Cari!" he said warning her.

"What? You don't want them to know that you made love to me before marrying me?" she said, sweetly.

Nathan and Jessica's brows shot up at that. "You ruined her?" Jessica said laughing in his face. "Well, that's rich. My honorable brother has become a scoundrel," she said laughing as he turned red.

"It wasn't like that," he said, giving Cari a dark look.

"Then how was it, Christopher. Did she seduce you?" Nathan said then laughed harder as Christopher turned redder. Jessica was holding her sides in hilarity.

"I can't wait to tell Stephan," she said still laughing.

Christopher's head snapped up. "Stephan? Why should he want to know?" he asked knowing full well the reason.

Jessica still laughing didn't see the warning sign. "He set the pair of you up," she said still laughing.

Christopher slowly got to his feet. "The way I hear, it's the six of you who were involved."

Jessica, her warning signal finally working, stiffened. "Ah...well...now, Christopher. I don't think it really matters now especially..."

"Oh, it matters," he said, moving toward her.

"Watch it now I'm going to be a mother. You wouldn't want to hurt the baby," she said, backing toward the door.

"Oh, a little wallop on your backside won't do a thing to the baby," he said seriously.

Jessica snatched up her skirts and headed for the door. "Maybe later," she shouted, slamming the doors behind her.

Nathan left by the side entrance not taking any chances with Christopher.

Christopher turned and smiled at Cari. "This is going to be fun," he said, laughing as Cari winked outrageously.

NATHAN MOVED ALONG THE HALL nearly getting run over by Jessica. "Slow down. He isn't following you," he snapped, keeping her from falling down.

"Well, I know what it's like to get spanked. Believe me, it's not a pleasant experience."

Nathan slowly smiled. "Is that how Morgan does it?"

Jessica's face darkened. "No. Morgan wouldn't even think of spanking me."

"It's nice to see, you know my name," Morgan said, from behind her.

Jessica whirled around and frowned.

"What are you doing here?"

"Hunting you down."

"I don't wish to see you."

Nathan arched a brow as Morgan nodded in his direction. "I could spank you."

Jessica's eyes narrowed. "You wouldn't dare."

It was Morgan's turn to arch a brow. "Oh no?" he said coming toward her.

Jessica turned livid. "If you so much as touch me, I'll scream," she shouted, pushing Nathan in front of her.

"Here, now. Leave me out of this," he yelped, as she pinched his arm.

"Jessica, I don't understand. I don't recall doing anything the least bit offensive." Morgan said, wondering at her behavior all day. She'd refused to say two words to him. She'd departed the ship without a word.

Jessica felt tears spring to her eyes. She hated weakness. "You ruined everything. Well, I won't stand here and let you gloat," she snapped, pushing Nathan toward Morgan. "I don't want to see you until May," she said, her voice catching as she slammed out of the house. Nathan pushed away from Morgan, smiling nervously at the awkward position.

Morgan glared at him. "You know something?"

Nathan's first impulse was to say no and get the hell out of there but being left out of the loop himself he decided to fill Morgan in. "Your wife is having a baby and she gets sick on the ship."

Morgan's brows shot up at that. A baby! A slow smile slowly lifted his lips. "A baby," he said, getting used to the idea. So his hellion of a wife was pregnant.

"Don't look so smug. She thinks you did it on purpose so she couldn't sail with you."

Morgan's face slowly lost it's smile. "Well, that's ridiculous," he said, then scowled as Nathan just shrugged.

"Women are ridiculous most of the time. Hell, everyone knows I can't figure them out," he said, turning to leave Morgan standing there.

Morgan frowned. "Bloody hell," he snapped, following his wife. Things never went along smoothly where Jessica was concerned.

STEPHAN STARED INTO THE BOTTOM of his glass and frowned. Everyone in his family was married and having children. God what a mess.

"Care to talk about it?" Morgan asked, taking a seat opposite Stephan.

Stephan smiled crookedly. "As you know, everything with my family is difficult."

Morgan nodded. "They do seem to cause scandal wherever they go."

Stephan frowned. "What brings you here? Has Jessica sent you packing?"

Morgan snorted "Not likely. Your little sister is about to be a mother and that temper of hers doesn't allow me within inches of her."

Stephan sat up. "Jessica is pregnant?"

Morgan nodded. "You'd think she'd be delighted but she blames me for making her pregnant to prevent her from sailing," he finished, draining his glass.

Stephan chuckled at that. "She just needs time to think it through."

Nathan, shook his head at the pair before him, then raised his eyes to heaven in prayer. Please let Stephan take this well.

Morgan nodded hello while Stephan scowled at Nathan. "Christopher knows."

"I know. Jessica has a big mouth."

"Jessica told him?" Stephan asked, getting a nod out of Nathan. "I was sure it was Cari."

Nathan shrugged. "It doesn't really matter. He knows and I'd watch my back if I were you."

Morgan scowled at the pair. "Christopher knows what?"

"That Stephan set Cari...er...Miss St. Paul to ruin Christopher's perfect life when Christopher took such delight in our plights."

Morgan arched his brows. "I have to hand it to the bunch of you. There is never a dull moment."

Stephan smiled. "Stick around, I'm sure it will only get worse."

Nathan swallowed and decided this was a perfect opportunity. Taking a deep breath, he sighed. "It gets worse for some of us," he said, giving Stephan a pointed look.

Stephan felt the hair rise on his neck. "What happened now?"

"It seems Father has ordered you to marry Emily," he said, filling his glass with brandy to cover up his lie. Father had said Christopher was to marry Emily but since he was already wed, that left Stephan. Sean said they were kissing anyway.

Stephan gapped at his brother. "Excuse me?"

"You heard me. Father has ordered you to marry Emily. He wants it done before the cousin comes for her."

"And when, pray tell, is that?"

"Saturday."

Stephan leaned back in his chair, shaking his head. "The man's lost his senses. I can't support a wife and two children. My business has suffered since Nero broke my hand," he snapped.

Nathan frowned. If his guess was right, Stephan was a very wealthy man thanks to their mother. Money wasn't a concern. "Trust me. That part will be taken care of. Do you at least like her?"

Stephan laughed at that. "She's a woman, for gods sake."

Nathan frowned. "But?"

"I already told you. I haven't the funds to take on a wife, let alone one with children."

Morgan frowned at them. "Your business isn't doing that bad."

"It is, if I'm not sailing those ships. I've lost hundreds of pounds since the captains are unfamiliar with the sea. They are slower than me."

Morgan frowned, he couldn't argue with that. A man knew his own finances.

Nathan scowled. "I already told you. You're probably very wealthy right now."

"How Nathan? A fairy bringing me a couple bags of gold?"

Morgan laughed at that, getting a smile out of Nathan. "No, but mother did."

"Mother?"

He nodded. "She left each of us a gift."

"What sort of gift?"

"I'm not at liberty to say but when you get married, you'll know."

Stephan narrowed his eyes. "Sounds like a trap to me."

"It's not. I just promised not to tell. Besides Father ordered you to marry."

Stephan slowly got to his feet. "No. I will not be ordered," he said, walking away.

Nathan watched him go with a scowl. Morgan laughed.

"You're always getting into trouble."

"I'd keep my mouth shut if I were you. A few words of encouragement from me and Jessica will keep your life a living hell."

Morgan smiled nastily. "Jonathan is missing quite the fun."

Chapter 99

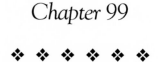

BRAND WALKED into Aunt Ginger's house and frowned. "The place is deserted."

"Yes, my lord. It does look that way."

"Well, go find someone, Hobkins. Preferably Christopher."

"Ah, it's late, my lord. Perhaps you'd care to wait for morning, before..."

"If I'd have wanted to wait until morning, I'd have stayed at Colan's another night. Now, fetch the boy. I'll be in the study." he said, marching off in that direction.

Hobkins, thoroughly hated this part of his job.

Brand moved into the study and instantly smelled brandy. "God, what a heavenly scent," he said moving to the decanter to pull the stopper off and smell it. "Heavenly."

Christopher came running into the room, his pants undone and his shirt unbuttoned. "What's wrong? Are you ill?"

Brand stared at his son, then frowned. "Nothing's wrong. I just wanted to make sure everything went as planned."

Christopher stared at his father a good two minutes before moving to pour himself a brandy. "You pull me from my room, where I might add I was spending a comfortable night with my wife, to ask me your plans?"

Brand grinned. "You married her then?"

Christopher paused with his glass almost to his lips. "You're involved in this, too?" he asked frowning.

"Of course. I ordered Nathan to tell you."

Nathan! he thought, wondering why Cari had said Stephan was the one responsible. "I don't understand."

"I wanted those children taken care of, Emily and those children would be in Scotland."

Christopher's mouth fell open. "You ordered me to marry Emily?"

Brand's grin widened. "I'm glad you didn't argue over it. I knew you would do the right thing."

Christopher scowled at his father. "I hate to disappoint you but I didn't marry Emily."

"You didn't...but you just said you were spending a comfortable night with your wife."

"Oh, I have a wife but Emily isn't her. I married Lady St. Paul."

"What?" Brand said, shocked that Nathan had messed things up. "Who?"

"Yes. I married her yesterday when Allison married the Earl."

"What? Allison married who? The Earl of March?"

"No. Salisbury."

Brand ran a hand through his hair before slowly sinking into a chair. "I can't believe it. That takes care of everyone doesn't it."

"Stephan isn't wed."

Brand sat up and slowly smiled. "He isn't, is he? Then he shall marry Emily."

"What's so important about her?"

"Nothing is important about her. I just don't want to see her turned over to some Scot and have those boys ruined."

Christopher smiled crookedly. "You just want to keep the boys."

Brand reddened. "I like the girl, too."

"But you want the boys."

"They're fine young lads," he said in his defense. "Besides, they like Stephan."

"Oh, I'm sure they do," he said feeling the need to laugh. Stephan was being forced to wed!

Brand frowned at his son. "You seem to be gloating."

"Let's just say, I owe Stephan a bit of revenge. Seeing him married, will be payment enough."

Brand waved a hand at his son. "I don't want to hear anymore. What goes on between you children is your business. Where is Stephan?"

"In bed, I assume. Everyone else is, as well."

"Such as."

"Jessica, Nathan, Rae, Emily, the lads, my wife."

"Jessica's here."

Christopher grinned. "Seems Sinclair got her pregnant so she couldn't sail and she's letting him know he shouldn't have done that."

Brand arched a brow. "Is that what she thinks?"

"I don't know. Nathan told me that."

"That makes three of them now. I should have a healthy brood of grandchildren in no time at all.

Christopher smiled tenderly at his father. "It does seem likely."

"YOU EXPECT ME TO MARRY HER TODAY?" Stephan asked staring at his father in disbelief.

"Yes. The sooner the better. The cousin is supposed to be here this afternoon."

"But I haven't even courted her or anything. She'll think I'm some sort of lecher."

Brand scowled at his son. "She won't think any such thing. Rae assured us, she liked you. She'd said you were handsome."

"Figure that out," Nathan said, rolling his eyes.

Stephan gave Nathan a glare. "I don't like this."

"It doesn't matter," Brand said, handing him the package from his mother. "Now open this. Maybe this will help you get comfortable with the decision."

Stephan opened the package and quickly scanned the letter. It stated he was now the Earl of Queensborough and it told the worth of the estate. Looking up at his father he gapped at him. "This is a joke, right?"

"No. Your mother left each of you boys a nice title fully entailed. What did she give you?"

"Queensborough."

"Oh, oh. That's a big one." Brand said smiling. "The Earl of Queensborough. That makes three of you."

"Three of us?"

"Yes, Nathan is the Earl of Alnwich and Jonathan is the Earl of Hertford. You make three."

"What about Christopher?"

"He's the Viscount of Rochdale along with my heir."

Stephan stared at his father before he cleared his throat. "Did mother leave the girls anything?"

"Of course. They each received a small chest full of jewels. Your mother had hundreds of heirlooms. The passing of so many lords without heirs, left a sizable fortune. All three girls are quite well off."

Stephan stared at his father for several seconds. "And we weren't to receive these things until we wed?"

"Yes. Your mother made certain of that. She knew I couldn't keep a secret therefore, she never told me what was in them."

Stephan frowned. "I still can't ask for Emily's hand."

"Why not?"

"It just doesn't feel right. I haven't so much as taken her to a ball."

"So?"

"I feel like I'm buying a horse not taking a wife."

"There isn't time for all this nonsense. Marry the girl then court her. But do it before the cousin gets here."

Stephan scowled as his father stalked out of the room.

"You're trying to kill him, aren't you?" Nathan said crossly.

Stephan glared at him. "Shut up, Nathan," he said following his father from the room.

"Touchy," he said, drinking his brandy with a smile.

STEPHAN TOOK THE STEPS two at a time, stopping in front of Emily's door. Running a hand through his hair, he paced. The cousin would be there in a few hours and he needed to ask her immediately. The fewer people hearing her rejection the better. Taking a deep breath, he knocked. A second later Emily opened the door.

"Lord Stephan? Can I do something for you?"

Stephan felt his tongue swell and found he couldn't say a word. He'd known it was useless to ask her. He wasn't one to deal with serious matters. Giving up, he turned to leave only to have Emily place a hand on his arm.

"Is something wrong?"

Stephan frowned down at her. She was so beautiful. Those eyes of green velvet and that silky black hair. "Ah, hell. You'd never agree."

Emily tightened her hold on his arm, keeping him from turning away. "Agree to what?"

Sean and Ian peeked around the door at this point. "Hello, Uncle Stephan."

"He's not your Uncle," Sean corrected quietly, eyeing Stephan. "You shouldn't have kissed Mama. Lady Sinclair said so," Sean added, turning red but looking like a man protecting his lady.

Stephan stared at the boy as an idea formed in his head. "You're right. I should never have kissed your mother but since I did, I've come to ask for her hand."

"What do you want her hand for? Isn't yours healed yet?" Ian asked staring at his bandage.

Stephan turned scarlet, clearing his throat as Emily turned her head to keep from laughing. They weren't making it easy on him, she thought, stunned that he was asking her to marry him. Rae had said he was going to.

"I, ah, don't want her hand. I want to marry her." Ian's mouth formed an oh while Sean stared at him wide-eyed. "If it's all right with your mother and it's all right with you, I'd like to become part of your family?"

Ian looked up at his mother and smiled. "Can he Mama? He's a real nice Uncle."

Sean frowned at Ian. "He'd be your father, stupid."

"Sean, that isn't polite. Now apologize."

Sean frowned further. "Sorry." Then stuck out his tongue, when Emily looked away.

"Well can he?" Ian asked ignoring Sean completely.

"I don't know," Emily said, looking at Stephan. "Do you know what you're getting yourself into? These two can be a handful."

Stephan felt his body relax, seeing the answer written in her eyes. She was saying yes. Moving into the room, he waited for her to close the door before answering. "I admit, two boys like this pair can be a trial to a body, but I'm sure my crew can take care of them if I have any trouble."

Ian moved to grab his mother's leg while Sean stared at Stephan. "Does that mean you're going to take Mama's hand then."

Stephan laughed. "Yes. I'm going to marry your mother as soon as possible," he said, looking at Emily. "Right?"

Emily smiled slowly. "I think that's the best idea I've heard in quite sometime."

"Whoopie," Ian whooped. Jumping up and down. "Did you hear that Sean? We have a pirate for a father," he said running around the room finally looking at Stephan. "Does that mean we have Uncles and Aunts again?" When Stephan nodded, he bounded off to whoop some more.

Stephan moved to Emily's side and smiled down at her. "Are you sure you want to marry into such a strange family?"

Emily reached up and touched his cheek. "They're not so bad. Besides, I have the most handsome one in the bunch."

Stephan grinned at her compliment. "That you do," he said, wanting to kiss her soundly but settling for a peck on the lips instead, "That you do."

Epilogue

"ROYCE, they'll be here any minute. Hurry up." Allison said, nursing two month old Megan while Royce dressed squirming four year old Ben.

"Ben, please, hold still." Royce said, giving Tiffany a quick look to make sure she wasn't in the hearth again. "What happened to Nelly? She was supposed to do this," he complained as Ben pulled his arm out of his coat.

Allison smiled. "She took Tearle down to the great hall to wait for everyone to arrive. She's worried everything will fall apart."

"Here? You have nearly thirty servants at your beck and call."

Allison reached over and grabbed a pillow tossed it in his direction. "I'd watch what I say or you'll find yourself doing some errands as well."

Ben laughed at his mother's game. Picking up the pillow, Ben threw it back at her making his father drop the small cravat he was trying to tie.

Royce scowled at his son. "Ben, hold still or I'll leave you in the tower," he said sternly.

Ben stiffened poker straight making Royce almost burst out laughing. His home, a castle remake from the sixteenth century, was a marvel among the ton. It had nearly one hundred bedrooms, a great hall, trestle tables, and the halls were lined with knights in armor. It was a virtual masterpiece.

"Did you put all the weapons in the vault?" Allison asked, righting her clothing as she laid baby Megan in the bassinet.

Royce paled. "Damn."

"You forgot?"

"Well, Thor and Apollo got into a tussle with Nero, sending cook into a fit. I had to calm them all down, then Nelly sent me off to find a place to lock up the dogs while Tearle kept setting them free. For a six year old he can open just about any lock."

Allison pursed her lips. "Well, if Stephan or Jessica's children get into trouble with those swords, I'll skin you alive."

"Can I go down now?" Ben asked pulling at his cravat.

Allison walked to stand before him reaching out to run her hands over his body. Feeling everything in place, she patted his head. "Yes. But please stay out of trouble."

"Okay," he yelled running from the room. Royce watched him go before turning and grabbing Allison in a hug.

"Have I told you how luscious you look today?" he whispered, pulling her close.

"I can't recall," she said, rubbing her cheek against his.

"Let me refresh your memory," he said lifting her chin to kiss her lips tenderly. Tiffany seeing the nice plant by the window tried to pull herself up into it. Plants made good places to stick your fingers. Zeus, lifted his head from his paws, seeing her where she shouldn't be, whined.

Royce hearing the dog pulled his head up. "God lord, Tiffany. Get out of there," he said moving away to fetch her.

Allison, dazed from his kiss moved her hand to her head. "It's all coming back to me now," she said, getting a growl from Royce. Tilting her head to the side, she smiled. "Here comes a carriage," she said, picking up Megan. "Hurry, Royce. I want to be downstairs when they arrive."

"All right, all right," he said brushing off Tiffany's little hands. "Come on, Zeus. I'll need you now more than ever," he said taking Allison's arm and leading her to the hall.

The wolfhounds had become a big part of the family in the last six years. Allison and Royce had worked with the animals getting them to understand what was expected of them. Now each of their four children had a dog that kept a close eye on what they were doing. Nero still lead Allison around but each child was like a kitten to him. He watched them more than the dogs.

"Who is it?" Allison asked, hearing the footman climb down from the box.

"Looks like Nathan," he said, pulling Ben back as he tried to run over and help with the horses.

"How do they look?" she asked trying to hear everything. "Tearle go help them," she said knowing the six year old was dying to get closer. Nathan had a son the same age and Tearle and he were best of friends.

"He looks the same to me. Rae looks to be pregnant again."

"She is? Oh, that's wonderful."

"Little Lauren is getting big. That black hair of hers is starting to curl up just like her mother's."

"What about the youngest one? Alden, no Aden."

"I don't know, he hasn't come out yet. David is off and running with Tearle. Stay away from the moat," he yelled, making Megan jump in Allison's arms.

"Shhh, Royce. She just went to sleep."

Royce looked at his daughter and frowned. "You should have left her in the bed. Hera would have watched her. She's worse than a nanny."

"I know the dog is good but I wanted to show her off," she said, as Nathan approached.

"How's it going, old man?" Nathan asked shaking Royce's hand. Turning to Allison he leaned forward and hugged her mindful of the baby. "And how's my favorite sister?"

"I'm fine, though I know you're only calling me your favorite because the other two aren't here," she said grinning. "Rae, how is everything? How's the children?"

"Wonderful. Oh, Allison she's beautiful," she said peeking at the bundle in her arms. "I can't wait for mine."

"Royce said you were carrying. How long?"

"Two more months," she said happily. Another carriage rumbled to a halt and instantly all four people knew Jessica had arrived.

"Evenlyn wait for the footman," Jessica hollered as a young girl of six bounded out of the carriage, her black hair coming loose from it's braid.

Morgan climbed out next, pausing to wave at Allison's group, seconds before Eric jumped out the door into his arms. "Ho, now. Take it easy," he said setting the five year old to the ground. "Stay away from the moat," he called as the boy ran after his sister to disappear from sight. Swinging the two year old Leland into his arms he reached up to help his wife alight.

"Looks like Jessica is ready to have that child any day now," Nathan said grinning.

Allison smiled. "That will make four for her."

"Seems like you're having a contest with one another," Royce said getting a swat from Allison.

Morgan set his son on the ground and took his hand as his other arm went around Jessica. "How's everything?" he asked, shaking hands with Royce and Nathan.

"You're looking good, Jessica." Nathan said, kissing her. Royce did the same. "How much longer?"

"Two weeks."

"Two weeks! You shouldn't be traveling," Allison said concerned.

Morgan pursed his lips. "It's about time someone took my side. She refused to miss this. Said this will be the first time everyone has been together in nearly seven years."

Allison frowned. "Has it been that long?"

"Yes. Someone is always having a baby, since our men can't keep to themselves," Jessica said as they moved to a canopy where chairs had been set out in which to sit. "Your home is lovely, as always," she said looking around at the neatly tended gardens.

Leland, Aden, and Tiffany giggled as Nero stretched out on his side and let them climb all over him.

Christopher arrived then, followed closely by Jonathan. Both alighted pausing long enough to shake hands before pulling their families from the carriages. Ashley held her youngest son Perry in her arms while Jonathan carried the three year old Rachel on his shoulders. Nolan, being six, was off and running. Christopher's oldest, Jordan, was close on his heels. Christopher carried two-year-old Bethany in one arm and six-month-old Alex in the other while Cari held four-year-old Bryan in her arms as Ranki, her monkey rode wrapped about her shoulders. The four adults laughed and conversed the entire way to the group where more happy greetings occurred.

"You're looking good, Ashley. How's the little one?" Rae smiled.

"He's doing better, now. The doctor says he should be fine. The lungs are clear and not a trace of pnemonia remains."

"Thank heavens. I was praying for him," Allison said, knowing every mother's worst fear was to loose a child.

Cari set her children down with the others and slowly sank into a chair. "I always hate those carriage rides. It seems to take forever to get here," she said, accepting the glass of lemonade Nelly handed her.

Melissa strolled up then holding her two youngest while Caleb watched his sons Philip and Rhys dash off to disappear over the bridge. Moving closer to the group he frowned. "When are you going to fill that moat with dirt?"

Royce grinned. "It wouldn't be a moat, now would it."

Melissa sank down on her knees, releasing three-year-old Katrine while one year old Markus clung to her arm for support. "Oh, Allison. She's so beautiful. What did you name her?"

"Megan," she said, tipping her slightly so Melissa could see better.

"That's lovely."

Stephan arrived in a great bout of commotion, his family of six pouring out of the carriage. Ian and Sean now eleven and nine hurried across the lawn with Karen and Kate on their heels. Stephan laughed as they disappeared from sight, then helped Emily climb from the carriage, one-year-old Sara in her arms. Stephan pulled three-year-old Jeremy from the carriage and quickly swung him up on his shoulders before marching toward the clearing.

As the family welcomed its last member they laughed and told what had happened to them over the past year. Time slipped by while the mass of children played around them.

Brand watched his grandchildren playing at his children's feet and grinned. "See Colan, I told you I'd live to see my grandchildren."

Colan snorted. "More like a horde of dwarves," he said watching Morgan grab Leland by the pants and lift him off the buried Nero while Stephan hauled a squirming Aden and Sarah out of the bunch.

"Fine, grandchildren they've given me. Elizabeth would have been proud," he said tears coming to his eyes.

Colan grinned watching the group of older children making their way to the adults. "Fine grandchildren indeed," he said laughing at the sight of David wearing little more than a burlap sac while the rest of them were dressed to look remarkably like a mass of pirates.

"Well, good lord, son. What happened to your clothes?" Nathan asked, getting to his feet while he handed Markus back to Melissa.

David turned scarlet. "I lost them," he said.

Ian snorted. "Evenlyn took them," he said grinning as David shot him a murderous look.

"Evenlyn?" Morgan asked seeing the one in question sauntering toward them dressed in David's pants and shirt. Her hair was covered with a red bandana while a belt and sword hung at her waist.

Jessica tried to get to her feet then gave up. "Young lady, what is the meaning of this? Where is your gown?" she asked.

Evenlyn lifted her chin "I captured their ship, Mother. His clothes were my booty," she said, getting a nod out of the other girls surrounding her.

"She cheated. Sean was helping them."

Sean shrugged his shoulders when the adults looked at him. "It was just in fun."

"The dress?" Jessica repeated.

"Nolan, why are you all wet?" Jonathan asked his son.

Nolan frowned. "I fell overboard," he said scratching his head.

Stephan started to laugh. Royce's dogs came running completely soaked from their swim in the moat. Venus was wearing what looked like Evenlyn's dress. The others burst out laughing as the dogs ran amongst them sending children squealing off in every direction.

Brand grinned at his family at large. "Elizabeth would be proud. This is beyond our dreams."

THE END